Hidden

Turning to Karen, Grant wondered whether she'd join in the debauchery without the need for him to send out inducing thoughts. Her blue eyes widening as she placed the bottle of wine and glasses on the table, she watched Julie slip the blouse over her shoulders . . . Gazing at Julie's firm breasts, her young milk budlettes, as the girl slipped her bra off, Karen dropped to her knees and tugged her young friend's miniskirt down. Gazing at his victims bulging red panties, Grant sensed his penis twitch and stiffen. This was going to be a night to remember!

'Lie on the table and rest your head on the cushion, Julie,' he ordered softly . . .

Also by Ray Gordon in New English Library bind-ups

Naked Lies and Red Hot
Hot Sheets and Sextortion

And in Single volume paperback

The Uninhibitied
Submission!
Depravicus
The Degenerates
Sex Practice
Addicted
Sex Thief
Doctor Sex

Girl School and Sextro

Ray Gordon

NEW ENGLISH LIBRARY
Hodder & Stoughton

Girl School copyright © 1997 by Ray Gordon

Sextro copyright © 1997 by Ray Gordon

This collected volume first published in Great Britain in 2000
by Hodder and Stoughton

The right of Ray Gordon to be identified as the Author of the Work
has been asserted by him in accordance with the Copyright, Designs
and Patents Acts 1988.

A New English Library paperback

10 9 8 7 6 5 4 3 2 1

All rights reserved. No part of this publication may be reproduced,
stored in a retrieval system, or transmitted, in any form or by any
means without the prior written permission of the publisher, nor be
otherwise circulated in any form of binding or cover other than that in
which it is published and without a similar condition being imposed
on the subsequent purchaser.

All characters in this publication are fictitious and any resemblance to
real persons, living or dead, is purely coincidental.

ISBN 0 340 79335 X

Printed and bound in Great Britain by
Omnia Books Limited, Glasgow

Hodder and Stoughton
A division of Hodder Headline
338 Euston Road
London NW1 3BH

I

Girl School

Chapter One

Sitting at her desk, the headmistress of Bellend Independent Boarding School for Girls looked up, gazing at a slim woman wearing a grey woollen skirt and cardigan as she entered the study. 'Ah, Miss Frigidus!' she greeted the Latin mistress. 'I trust you enjoyed the Easter break?'

'Yes, thank you, Miss Gussetpiece,' the nervous woman replied, wringing her hands as she stood before the antique mahogany desk. 'Headmistress, I'll be taking this year's sixth-formers for their last term of Latin, and I'm rather anxious because . . .'

'Anxious?' Miss Gussetpiece echoed, patting down her blue-rinsed curly grey hair. 'Why are you anxious? Does anxiety run in your family?'

'I think it must, Headmistress. You see . . .'

'Fear not, Miss Frigidus! I'm sure you'll cope admirably with the girls who have risen through the ranks to the final term of the sixth form.'

'But . . . but I'll be teaching Maxine Mayhem and her friends – those horrifying girls, the Bellend Rebels! Now that Maxine's nearing the end of the sixth . . .'

Miss Gussetpiece sighed, holding her head in her hands at the mention of Maxine's name. The girl had wreaked havoc during her five years at Bellend, driving two teachers to a mental home and another to attempting to fling herself off Beachy Head. The headmistress knew only too well that no one could cope with Maxine Mayhem – least of all Miss *timidus* Frigidus! Rising and moving to the leaded light window, she swung round on her heels to face the distraught teacher.

'God moves in mysterious ways, Miss Frigidus. Look upon Maxine as a test, sent by God to try you.'

'Sent by Satan, don't you mean?'

'Satan? Goodness me! I thought you'd had a decent Catholic upbringing?'

'Oh, I have, Headmistress!'

'In that case, don't mention Satan – you'll be struck down! Cast into the internal fires of hell!'

'Eternal, Headmistress.'

'Internal, eternal – you'll be struck down, all the same!'

'Oh, dear!'

'Look, I realize that Maxine can be difficult at times, but she . . .'

'But Miss Gussetpiece, I can't face it! Please, I'm in no fit mental state to cope with Maxine Mayhem any more! Look at my hair! It used to be a lovely chestnut colour, and now it's turning grey!' Sobbing uncontrollably, the woman pulled a handkerchief from her cardigan sleeve. 'Because of that dreadful girl, I've become addicted to Valium! I'm *non compos mentis*!'

'Take control of yourself, woman! Maxine does tend to drive people to drink and drugs, I agree. But you must calm yourself, Miss Frigidus! Have a triple vodka, it'll steady your nerves,' the Head recommended, opening a cabinet and pouring a liberal drink.

'But it's eight o'clock in the morning, Headmistress! I can't drink vodka at eight o'clock *ante meridiem*!'

Girl School

'Have a large gin, then. A nice drop of mother's . . .'

'I *never* drink alcohol, no matter what the time of day!'

The portly principal took a swig from the vodka bottle. 'Over the years, I've discovered that downing a few stiff drinks is the best way to begin the day!' she retorted. 'Here, get this down you and you'll be able to cope with anything. Well, almost anything!'

Knocking the neat vodka back, Miss Frigidus gasped. 'Oh, my goodness! It's like drinking petrol!'

'It'll do you good!' Miss Gussetpiece assured the frail woman.

'It's burning my stomach!'

'Take a grip on yourself, Miss Frigidus!'

'But I already have terrible womb ache, my ovaries are playing up again, my Fallopian tubes are inflamed, my nipples are cracked and dry – and it's all down to that awful girl! I'm falling to pieces, Headmistress!'

'It's psychosomatic! Pop a couple of Valium and have another drink and you'll be as right as rain within half an hour. Ah, here comes the first wave of girls!' Miss Gussetpiece declared, snatching another swig from the bottle as several cars pulled up outside the study window. 'Go, Miss Frigidus!' she ordered, gulping from the bottle again. 'Man your post! Or, I should say, woman your post – there's work to be done!'

Placing her neatly folded netball skirt and hockey kit in her locker, Hilda Hillock jumped as Maxine Mayhem crept up behind her and jabbed her sides with her rigid fingers. 'If it's not little Miss Hilda Hillock!' Maxine sneered, staring into the terrified girl's blue eyes. 'And what's Miss fucking *Pill*ock doing all alone in the locker room wearing nothing but her knickers and bra? Checking to see whether your pussy's sprouted any pubes yet, were you?'

'Jolly well leave me alone!' Hilda cried, desperately trying to turn away as Maxine grabbed her shoulders and swung her round. 'I'll report you to Miss . . .'

'Report me?' Maxine laughed, yanking the girl's bra up and exposing her firm young breasts. 'Oh, look at your little titties!' she giggled, pinching her nipples. 'I'll bet you've never had your teats sucked!'

'Get off me, you hateful beast!' Hilda protested, struggling to pull away as Maxine squeezed her nipples harder.

'So, what did you get up to during the Easter hols? I suppose you spent all your time swotting? Well, I'll tell you what I did, Miss *Pill*ock! *I* starred in a blue movie!'

'What's going on in here?' Braying like a rampant donkey, Jo Blob, the geography mistress, strode across the locker room in her long tweed skirt and ballooning blouse. Eyeing Hilda's pert breasts, her erect brown milk buds, she frowned. 'What *are* you doing, girl?' she demanded.

'Hilda was trying to make me touch her, Miss Blob!' Maxine sobbed, rubbing her eyes woefully with her fists, her curtain of long black hair concealing her wicked grin as she hung her head. 'It was absolutely awful!'

'Is that true, Hilda?' the butch woman asked angrily as the girl slipped her rounded breasts into her tight bra. 'I've never known such wicked behaviour! You were in line to be Head Girl this year, but when Miss Gussetpiece hears about this, no doubt she'll have second thoughts! Put your uniform on, girl! You'll report to my study immediately after assembly!'

Girl School

Giggling as Miss Blob left the locker room, Maxine yanked the front of Hilda's navy-blue knickers down. 'Oh, look at your little pussy-slit! Been frigging your clitty, have you?' she taunted. 'And your knickers are stained with cunt juice! Been having naughty thoughts about sucking boys' knobs, have you?'

'Leave me alone!' Hilda cried, pulling her knickers up and concealing her tightly-closed vaginal crack. 'You're a horrid girl!'

'Well, not a very good start to the term, is it? You're in trouble already! You know the rules, don't you? No fiddling with each other! No masturbating! No screwing the boys from the Uni! What an awful beginning to a new term! Show me your cunt!'

'No! Go away, you unbearable creature!'

'Show me your cunt or I'll set fire to the contents of your locker!' Maxine threatened, taking a lighter from her breast pocket.

'Maxine, please, I . . . I don't want to show you my mini!'

'Your *mini*? Is that what you call it? Mini!'

'Yes, what's wrong with that?'

'Is that what your mummy calls it?'

'When I was a child, she did, yes.'

'Well, you'll show me your mini, pillock, or I'll set fire to your things!'

Tentatively slipping her knickers down, Hilda knew that she had no choice. Maxine was an infamous pyromaniac, and Hilda knew she'd have no hesitation in torching Hilda's precious books and sports kit. 'Come on, pillock – pull them down further!' Maxine taunted. Her sparse blonde pubes barely concealing her tightly closed pinken girl-slit, Hilda's face flushed as her tormentor dropped to her knees. 'Open your cunt with your fingers and show me your clitty!' she ordered.

'Maxine, I . . .'

'Do it!' Maxine bellowed, igniting her lighter.

Peeling her young vaginal lips apart, Hilda exposed her moist inner flesh, her clitoris, to Maxine's wide eyes.

'I like your cunt!' Maxine giggled. 'Do you frig yourself off?'

'No, never!' Hilda sobbed.

'I'll bet you do! I'll bet you finger your cunt and frig your clitty! Would you like me to push my finger up your bum?'

'Miss Blob knows all about you, Maxine Mayhem! She knows what you get up to!' Hilda retorted as she tugged her knickers up and grabbed her gymslip.

'Does she, now?' Maxine hissed through gritted teeth as the blonde girl pulled her gymslip over her head, tugging the garment down to conceal her shapely young body. 'In that case, you must have fucking well told her!' she growled as she rose to her feet. 'Well, I'll tell you something, Hilda Pillock – you're going to suffer for your sins! This term, you and your Jolly Hockey Sticks Club are going to go through sheer hell! My Bellend Rebels will ensure that you and your pack of fucking little goodie-girlies are expelled!'

'I'll see to it that *you*'re jolly well expelled, Maxine Mayhem!' Hilda snorted.

'Will you now? Well, may the best girl win! And that'll be me!'

Wiping a tear from her eye as Maxine flounced out of the room, Hilda closed her locker and grabbed her school bag. Maxine had meant every word she'd said, she reflected as she hooked her bag over her shoulder and walked down the corridor. The girl had been the bane of her life at Bellend School for almost six years, the passing of time only exacerbating her mutinous behaviour.

'Hi, Hilly!' another pretty blonde trilled.

'Hi, Candida!' Hilda smiled, pushing the degrading act she'd been forced to commit from her mind as she turned to face her friend. 'How were the hols?'

'Jolly good fun! Good old daddy took me to Paris and bought me a complete new wardrobe! And a new stereo!'

'I say, Candida, you are an awfully lucky thing!' Hilda sighed as they entered their classroom.

'What did you do during the hols, Hilly?'

'I spent my time brushing up on my Latin, Greek and German. By the way, that horrid Maxine Mayhem's started her tricks. She forced me to . . .'

'Forced you to what? Gosh, she didn't make you do something terribly rude, did she?'

'She made me . . . Never mind. Anyway, we'll have to sort her out this term!'

'She *is* a jolly nuisance!' the other girl complained. 'But there's nothing we can do, Hilly!'

'Hi, you two!' Breezing into the classroom, a petite girl with flowing auburn tresses greeted her friends excitedly, her white blouse straining to contain her ample breasts as she bounced onto her desk.

'Hi, Patsy! Did you print the Jolly Hockey Sticks Club membership cards and rule books?' Candida asked excitedly.

'Yes, daddy bought me a spiffing new computer and a laser colour printer. I've designed and printed a club ensign: the name of the club encircling two hockey sticks and a ball. I'll show you later.'

'Gosh, that sounds cracking! You are a clever old thing, Patsy!' Candida cried as the classroom filled with chattering sixth-formers. Taking their seats as their form mistress entered the room, the twittering evaporated.

'Good morning, girls,' the middle-aged woman greeted the class as she stood behind her desk, her beady eyes peering over the top of her bifocals.

'Good morning, Miss Shaftgrinder!' the girls responded in a monotone.

'Unfortunately, there'll be no assembly this morning. I've received word that Miss Gussetpiece has been taken ill, so . . .'

'She's probably pissed again!' Maxine giggled under her breath.

'Who said that?' Miss Shaftgrinder asked angrily.

'It was Hilda Hillock, Miss Shaftgrinder,' Maxine lied.

'Hilda, you'll see me immediately after registration! Miss Blob has already spoken to me about your lewd behaviour in the locker room this morning. As there's no assembly, you'll report to her directly after seeing me!'

Cursing Maxine under her breath, Hilda bit her lip as Miss Shaftgrinder took registration. Seething with anger, she swore to put an end to the little fiend's perpetual trouble-making. Stealing a glance at Maxine from the corner of her eye, she nudged Candida. Turning her head to follow Hilda's gaze, the girl placed her hand over her mouth and gasped. Her gymslip pulled up, her hand down the front of her knickers, Maxine was vigorously rubbing herself, her dark eyes rolling, her face flushing as her ecstasy rose and shook her young body.

'Crikey! One of these days that vile girl will be jolly well expelled!' Candida whispered angrily.

'Yes, and the sooner the better!' Hilda declared, staring in disgust as Maxine slipped her hand from her knickers and sucked her sticky fingers. 'Gosh, she's insufferable, she really is!'

'Now, girls, you'll find the last term of the sixth form a very different kettle of fish,' Miss Shaftgrinder began, leaning on her desk, her beady eyes darting between her impossibly fresh-faced pupils. 'For one thing, you'll have more freedom. But I'm warning you – do not abuse that freedom! You'll study at every opportunity. You'll cram your pretty little heads with knowledge during every waking moment. I want one success story after another this term! I want to see every one of you working hard and fulfilling your true potential! Now, as there's no assembly, you've a free half-hour before your first lesson. You may go to your dormitories and organize your belongings. And, please, go quietly!'

Remaining behind as the girls filtered out of the classroom, Hilda gingerly approached the teacher. 'Please, Miss Shaftgrinder, it wasn't me,' she pleaded sheepishly.

'I'm surprised at you, Hilda Hillock! From what Miss Blob told me, your behaviour in the locker room this morning was downright decadent! *You*, of all people, behaving like that!'

'But, Miss . . .'

'If this is the way you intend to behave this term, you'll find yourself in trouble, my girl! Perhaps it wasn't you who made the lewd remark in class, but what you did in the locker room was . . . You'd better report to Miss Blob. And if there's one more incident, you'll be up before Miss Gussetpiece!'

Wandering down the corridor, Hilda knocked on Miss

Blob's door, determined to prove her innocence as the woman bid her enter. Closing the huge oak door behind her, Hilda walked tentatively across the parquet flooring, brushing her long blonde hair away from her delicate face as she stood trembling before the manly mistress's desk.

'Now then, Hilda – what, exactly, were you doing in the locker room this morning?' the grey-haired, crop-headed woman asked sternly.

'Changing, Miss Blob – that was all.'

'Your brassiere was pulled up, exposing your lovely . . . What I mean is . . . Tell me the truth, Hilda – what were you up to?'

'Nothing, Miss Blob! That beastly Maxine Mayhem was trying to get me into trouble, as usual.'

'As Maxine Mayhem was involved, I'll give you the benefit of the doubt on this occasion, but next time . . . Hilda, sit down, I want to talk to you.'

A lecture, Hilda mused as she sat in a leather upholstered chair opposite Miss Blob. Gazing at the stubble on the woman's chin, she wondered whether the rumours about her being a man in drag were true. Her voice *was* rather low, she reflected, and her large, rough hands far from feminine.

'Now then, Hilda,' the teacher began pensively. 'You're at that difficult time in a girl's life, a time when you might have certain problems. I want you to look upon me as someone you can confide in, someone you can come to with your problems – whatever they might be. You're eighteen now. You're no longer a child, but a young woman. You've led a somewhat sheltered life, I believe?'

'Yes, Miss Blob, I have. We live in the country and . . .'

'Do you have any brothers, Hilda?'
'No, Miss Blob.'
'What experience have you of boys?'
'None at all!' Hilda gasped surprisedly.
'You have no leanings towards your own sex?'
'Leanings, Miss Blob?'
'Tendencies, Hilda. Do you find the female form sexually attractive?'
'I find that some girls are prettier than others, Miss Blob – if that's what you mean.'
'Blimey, so do . . . Er . . . What I mean is, Hilda – are you sexually attracted to other girls?'
'Gosh! Certainly not, Miss Blob!'
'I see. Several sixth-form girls come to me with their problems, Hilda. My rooms are always open to you, remember that. Many girls find it difficult to cope as their hormones stir and their lovely bodies begin to develop and their beautiful breasts swell and their . . . er . . . Yes, well . . . As I said, if there's anything you wish to talk about, please don't hesitate to come and see me. You don't touch yourself, do you Hilda?'
'Touch myself, Miss Blob?'
'Yes, you know – *down there.*'
'Never!' Hilda cried.
'All right, don't distress yourself, girl! If you ever feel the urge to touch yourself, Hilda, the need to explore between your legs, your beautiful, warm . . . If you ever feel the urge, then come and tell me and I'll . . . Well, just come and see me. A little light caning does wonders for some girls, you know.'
'Caning, Miss Blob?'
'Yes, a little whipping can . . . You'd better go to your first lesson. What is it, by the way?'

'Latin, Miss Blob.'

'Ah, with Miss Frigidus! Work hard and enjoy your lesson, Hilda. And do steer clear of Maxine Mayhem.'

'Yes, Miss Blob.'

'Remember, you may come to my rooms during the evenings and we'll talk things over – discuss things and . . . Anyway, off you go!'

Leaving Miss Blob's study, Hilda sighed. She'd been looking forward to returning to school but had guessed Maxine would spoil things. *There's always one jolly rotten apple!* she thought dolefully as she climbed the stairs to the dormitories. Entering a six-bedded room to discover Maxine placing her things in a cupboard, she gasped.

'What are you doing in here?' Hilda demanded.

'I don't like it any more than you do, Hilda Pillock!' Maxine hissed as her rival moved to her usual bed by the window. 'And you can leave that bed, it's mine! There's only one left, over there in the corner!'

'Ah, it's Hillock!' a befreckled girl breathed in the doorway. 'She's not sharing with us, is she, Max?'

'Yes, I'm afraid she is, Ginger!'

'Well, we'd better initiate her then!' the redhead grinned, grabbing Hilda's arm and pulling her down onto a bed.

'Leave me alone!' Hilda protested as Maxine tugged at her navy-blue knickers. 'I'll tell Miss Gussetpiece if you dare to touch me!'

Her knickers forcefully dragged down her legs and over her ankles, Hilda could do nothing to defend herself as her assailants spread her thighs, exposing her young pussy-crack to their wide eyes. 'Let's finger her fanny!' Maxine cried, parting Hilda's fleshy vaginal lips. 'Oh, she's very tight!' she squealed, pushing a finger deep into the struggling young girl's vaginal sheath. 'You have a nice wet cunt! Do you like the word, *cunt*, little Miss Pillock? Have you heard the words *prick* and *wank* and *spunk* and *fuck* and *arse* and *shag* and . . .'

'You're a dreadfully vile creature! You just wait until Miss Gussetpiece hears about this!' Hilda warned as she struggled to free herself.

'You tell anyone anything, and you'll be sorry!' Maxine threatened, driving a second finger into her captive's tight pussy-hole. 'Hold her still, Ginger! I want to taste her cunny juice!'

Pinned to the bed, her legs held wide open, Hilda grimaced as Maxine knelt between her feet and swept her tongue up her glistening sex-groove. 'Mmm, she tastes delicious!' the dark girl murmured, pulling Hilda's golden-fleeced pussy lips wide apart and licking her wet inner flesh. 'Nice and fishy! Shall I make you come, Miss Pillock?' she taunted, exposing the girl's pinken clitoris. 'Shall I lick your clitty and finger-fuck your cunt and make you come in my mouth?'

Hearing movement outside the dormitory, the aggressors leaped to their feet and dived onto their beds, leaving their captive to pull her knickers on and adjust her gymslip. 'I'm not sharing a dorm with you beasts!' Hilda shrieked. 'I'll go and see Miss . . .'

'That won't do you any good!' Maxine giggled. 'Several girls have asked to change rooms, and they're not allowed to! I'll be able to have some fun with you at night, won't I? I'll teach you how to frig me off, pillock! You can be my personal lesbian sex slave. You'll lick my clitty and finger my cunt and bring me off every night: how does that sound?'

'You disgust me, Maxine Mayhem!' Hilda spat as she fled the room in tears.

'You disgust me, Maxine Mayhem!' Maxine mocked as the door slammed shut.

Staggering to the study window, Miss Gussetpiece gazed out across the grounds. 'Thirty years!' she slurred, downing a glass of neat gin. 'Do you know, Madame Fissure, I've been principal of this school for thirty years? Here, have a drink,' she offered, passing the olive-skinned woman a gin.

'Thank you, Headmistress. Yes, time does fly!' Madame Fissure agreed, sipping her drink. 'I've been teaching French here for ten years.'

'Ten years? Goodness me, I remember the day you arrived from Frankfurt as if it were yesterday!'

'From *France*, Headmistress. I arrived here from France as if it were yesterday – Brest.'

'Madame Fissure, please!'

'What's the matter?'

'Talking about breasts when there might be innocent young girls lurking outside my study door! What's the matter with your breast, anyway?'

'I was born and bred in Brest.'

'Fed on the breast? What *are* you talking about? Are you feeling mentally ill, Madame Fissure?'

'No, I meant . . . Oh, never mind.'

'You're not mentally unstable, are you?'

'Of course I'm not, Headmistress!'

'Are you sure that mental instability doesn't run in your family?'

'There's no record at all of mental illness in my family.'

'I'm pleased to hear it! I detest people who suffer from

mental problems. Anyway, Frankfurt, France, it's all the same now this bloody government's gone and cocked . . . What I mean is . . . Pour me another large gin, there's a dear.'

'Don't you think you've had rather too much to drink, Headmistress?' Madame Fissure ventured, brushing her lank raven bob behind her ears. 'I mean, you were unable to take assembly today because of your heavy drinking.'

'Good grief! Of course I haven't had too much to drink! Are you suggesting that I'm starting the first day of term by going on a bender?'

'No, Headmistress, I'm not!'

'Actually, that's not a bad idea! Er . . . Yes, well. I've a lot to do today. What did you want to see me about? This is the first day of term and, by its very nature, it will be a busy day.'

'*You* wanted to see *me*, Headmistress.'

'Did I? That's odd! I wonder why? Ah, yes, that was it! There's a new girl starting at Bellend today. She's German – I mean, she's French. I don't know, whatever she is, her chaperone doesn't speak English. When they arrive, I'd like you to be present.'

'Yes, of course, Headmistress. There's your gin.'

'Ah, thank you. Now, they'll be here at noon so . . .'

'I'll be here to meet them. I have to take my class now so . . .'

'I'd rather you left your glass here, it's one of a set!'

'No, Headmistress, my French class.'

'I thought you taught German?'

'No, Fräulein Vulvahausen teaches German.'

'Ah, yes, yes – so she does.' Rubbing her chin thoughtfully, the headmistress frowned. 'Who teaches French, then?'

'I do, Headmistress!'

'Oh, yes. Right, well, I'll expect you at noon.'

As Madame Fissure left the room, Miss Gussetpiece checked her watch. 'Ah, they'll all be having their lessons now,' she drooled, leaving her study and making her way to the locker room. Taking the skeleton key from her deep cleavage, she opened the first locker. 'Aha, two hundred cigarettes! I'll have to confiscate those!' she giggled in her drunken stupor. Opening the second locker, the befuddled Head removed two bottles of gin. The third containing three bottles of vodka, she gleefully continued her pillage, piling the illicit goods on the floor. Calling the maintenance man into the room as he passed by, she instructed him to take the contraband to her study.

'Say nothing about this!' she warned the good-looking young man as he took a laundry basket from the corridor and wheeled it into the locker room.

'Don't worry, Headmistress,' he replied, filling the basket with the booty. 'I won't remember anything about this.'

'Won't you? I find that rather odd! Do you suffer from amnesia?'

'No, Headmistress. What I meant was, I know nothing about the drink and cigarettes.'

'I find that incredibly strange, seeing as you're actually loading that basket with the drink and cigarettes! You must have an inconceiv— . . . an incon— . . . an unbelievable short-term memory! Anyway, your mental problems are no business of mine. I'll not have my girls drinking and smoking!' Miss Gussetpiece slurred, staggering behind the handyman as he wheeled the loaded laundry basket to her study. 'It's not good to drink and smoke at their age! It's ungodly!'

'Indeed it is, Headmistress!' the young man agreed, concealing a grin as he parked the basket by her desk.

'Right, I'll take it from here, Jones!' she garbled.

'Johnson, Headmistress.'

'What?'

'Johnson.'

'Who's he when he's at home?'

'Me, Headmistress. I'm Johnson.'

'Well, whoever you are, take a bottle of Scotch and two hundred cigarettes for your trouble. And say nothing about this! Don't even mention it to your psychiatrist!'

'Psychiatrist, Headmistress?'

'One would assume that you're seeing a psychiatrist, what with your mental state.'

'I've never seen a psychiatrist in my life!'

'Well, you should! You don't even know who you are! I'll ask Miss Frigidus to give you the name of hers.'

'Yes, Headmistress. I'll come back for the basket later.'

Collapsing in her chair, Miss Gussetpiece rubbed her bloodshot eyes and downed another glass of neat gin. 'It's the little darlings' money I want!' she drooled. 'Little rich kids! Huh! It's their money I want!' she slurred as she slumped over her desk in an alcoholic haze and passed out.

'Does *cum* mean orgasm, Miss Frigidus?' Maxine asked the flustered Latin mistress.

'No, Maxine, you know very well that "cum" does not mean . . . I am not going to begin the lesson until the girl who drew this . . . this thing on the blackboard, owns up!'

'What is it, Miss Frigidus?' Maxine asked innocently.

'You can *see* what it is!'

'I can't quite make it out. What are those big, round hairy things and . . . Oh, yes, I know what it is – it's an erect penis with something spurting out of the end!' the girl giggled wickedly, causing the class to erupt with shrieks of laughter.

Popping another Valium, Miss Frigidus wiped the board, her head spinning at the prospect of teaching, or trying to teach, Maxine Mayhem. 'May I be excused please, Miss Frigidus?' Hilda asked, holding her hand up.

'If it's really necessary, Hilda!' Miss Frigidus replied irritably.

'May I be excused too, Miss Frigidus?' Maxine called as Hilda left the classroom. 'I'm desperate for the bog!'

'Maxine, will you please curb your disgusting language!' Miss Frigidus admonished the girl. 'You'll stay where you are! You'll have to wait until the lesson is over!'

'Sorry, Miss Frigidus, but I'm bursting for a piss!'

'Maxine! Oh dear, I really can't . . . You'll have to wait!'

'I'll wet my knickers. I can feel it coming! I'm going to piss myself!'

'Oh, very well! Go to the lavatory – and then report to Miss Gussetpiece and tell her of your vile language! No doubt she'll think of a fitting punishment!'

Leaving the room, Maxine nipped into the toilets as Miss Blob strode down the corridor. Lighting a cigarette and blowing smoke high into the air as she leaned against the tiled wall, she planned her next wicked move. Hearing Hilda shuffling around in a cubicle, she grinned and tossed her cigarette under the cubicle door.

Girl School

'Miss Blob!' Maxine called as she dashed out into the corridor. 'Miss Blob, someone's smoking in the toilets!'

'Smoking? Do you know who it is?'

'No, Miss Blob, but they're still in there.'

'Right, thank you, Maxine!' Miss Blob bellowed as she flung the door open and stormed into the toilets.

Emerging from the cubicle with the burning cigarette between her fingers, Hilda froze. 'Miss Blob!' she gasped. 'I . . .'

'Hilda Hillock! Your behaviour leaves me speechless!'

'But, Miss Blob!'

'You'll come to my rooms this evening at eight o'clock! I'll have decided your punishment by then. A light caning will suffice, I think! Yes, I'll enjoy that. What I mean is . . . Put that filthy thing out and return to your class immediately!'

'Yes, Miss Blob,' Hilda sighed despondently, tossing the cigarette down the toilet.

Creeping into the headmistress's study, Maxine grinned. 'The old bag's out cold!' she giggled. 'Fuck me, what's this!' she gasped, eyeing the laundry basket. 'This is a stroke of luck!' Wheeling the basket out of the room, she ran down the corridor, the fifty-odd bottles rattling loudly as she rounded the corner and crashed through the swing doors leading to the back yard. Dashing across the yard, her firm breasts bouncing, her short gymslip riding up over her shapely buttocks, she made for the gardener's potting shed.

'What you doin' in 'ere, Miss?' the ageing gardener demanded as she burst into the shed. 'No girls ain't allowed in 'ere!'

'Shut up, you old fool!' Maxine hissed, dragging the basket through the door.

'What you got in there, then?' the old man enquired as he rose to his feet.

'What the fuck's it look like?'

'Looks like ciggies and booze to me. Where'd you get all that from, then?'

'I nicked it, all right? Now, listen, you stupid old bugger! You're going to look after this stuff for me, do you understand?'

'Can't do that, Miss! It ain't allowed!'

'Fuck what *ain't allowed*, you daft old tosser! Help me to push it under that bench over there.'

'Well, I don't know. I mean, gettin' meself involved with stolen goods ain't right! How much you payin' me to store the stuff, then?'

'Pay you?' Maxine shrieked as the gardener helped her to push the basket beneath the bench. 'You'll look after it, and tell no one – or I'll tell the headmistress that you tried to rape me! I'll tell her that you stuffed your hand down my knickers and fingered my cunt!'

'That the way they learns you to talk 'ere, then?'

'Listen, you old wanker! You'll keep your fucking mouth shut or I'll tell the headmistress that you flashed your cock at me, do you understand?'

'Well, in that case, I don't see that I 'as a choice. I don't want it 'ere too long, mind! You'll get me into trouble, you will!'

'Just shut up and get on with whatever you're supposed to be doing! Is there a spare key to this place?'

'There is, up there on that 'ook. But you ain't 'avin' it!'

'Listen, you daft old fart! I'm taking the key, all right?

Now, you just keep your fucking mouth shut!' Maxine spat as she left the shed and dashed across the yard.

Returning to the Latin lesson, the girl took her seat and grinned as Miss Frigidus enquired whether she'd reported to the headmistress. 'I'll find out if you haven't been to see her!' the tremulous woman snapped.

'I did go to see her, Miss Frigidus. But she's out of her tiny mind!' Maxine smirked as the frail teacher neared her desk.

'Out of her mind? What do you mean, girl?'

'The headmistress – she's pissed out of her head.'

'Maxine, your language is . . . Miss Gussetpiece doesn't drink!'

'Doesn't she?'

'Well, she . . . Just settle down, Maxine! You've missed so much of the lesson that I don't suppose you'll be able to catch up! I don't suppose you *want* to catch up!'

Returning to the front of the class, Miss Frigidus sat at her desk, her hands trembling as she watched Maxine take her books out. 'Right, girls!' she spluttered as authoritatively as she could. 'Conjugations of Latin verbs!'

'Fucking boring!' Maxine sighed, slipping her hand down the front of her knickers to appease her insatiable clitoris.

'Headmistress! Headmistress, wake up!' Madame Fissure called, shaking the woman's shoulder.

'What? What's . . . Where am I? God, my head!'

'It's five to twelve, Headmistress! The new girl and her chaperone will be here any minute!'

'New girl? Oh, yes! Goodness me, I feel dreadful! Pour me a large gin, will you?' Miss Gussetpiece asked as she staggered to her feet. 'Now then, is she French or German?' she mumbled, sifting through a pile of papers on her desk.

'She's French, Headmistress. Here's your drink.'

'The chaperone's French?'

'Yes.'

'What's a German girl doing with a French chaperone? That's a terrible blunder on someone's part!'

'No, the girl's French.'

'Then, what's a French girl doing with a German chaperone?'

'They're both French, Headmistress!' Madame Fissure replied patiently, raising her eyes to the ceiling in despair.

'Really? What a coincidence! Oh no, that must be them!' Miss Gussetpiece gasped as someone knocked on the door. 'Er . . . Entrail!'

'Headmistress, you mean, *entrez*.'

'Oh, yes, of course – entrez!'

Followed by a petite brunette in her late teens, the chaperone walked across the study to Miss Gussetpiece. Extending her hand, the headmistress smiled. 'Bumjour!' she greeted the Frenchwoman.

'I think you mean *bonjour*,' Madame Fissure corrected the confused Head.

'Oh, how silly of me! Yes, bonjour!'

'Bonjour, Madame Gussetpiss. Je m'appelle Célestine. Permettez-moi de vous présenter Véronique,' the visitor smiled.

'Er . . . Yes, well – I think you'd better translate, Madame Fissure.'

'Don't you speak French, Headmistress?'

'Yes, yes, of course I do! Fluently, I'll have you know!

Well, not exactly fluently. I seem to have forgotten most of it.'

'I would have thought that, being head of a school such as this, you'd . . .'

'It's a long story. I . . . I lied to get the job, all right?'

'Oh, I see! Well, this is Célestine, and she was introducing you to Véronique.'

'Ah, welcome to Bellend School, Véronique,' Miss Gussetpiece gushed, shaking the young girl's hand.

Leaving Madame Fissure to do the talking, the headmistress poured herself another large gin. 'What's she saying?' she asked as Célestine rambled on.

'She wants to know how many girls are at the school.'

'What difference does that make? Now what's she on about?'

'She wants to know whether Véronique can have her own private room rather than share a dormitory.'

'Tell her she can't. We have no private rooms. Good grief, this isn't a hotel! Bloody foreigners! Tell her that I don't like her bourgeois attitude!'

'I'm going to show them around the school, Headmistress. We'll come back later.'

'Right, I'll be here. Bonjour, Célestine. Bonjour, Véronique,' Miss Gussetpiece slurred as they left the study.

Suddenly realizing that the laundry basket had gone, the headmistress grabbed the phone and rang the maintenance man. 'Is that Jones?' she asked impatiently.

'No, it's not.'

'Do you know where he is?'

'I don't know anyone called Jones.'

'Who are you, then? What are you doing in maintenance? Are you a robber?'

'A robber?'
'Why did you answer the phone?'
'Because it rang.'
'Come on, tell me who you are, or I'll call a police officer! You're not one of these sexual perverts you read about in the Sunday papers who hang around girls' schools, are you?'
'No! My name's Johnson – I'm the maintenance man!'
'Oh, yes, of course! How silly of me! It's Miss Gussetpiece here – did you take the laundry basket from my study?'
'No, I haven't had time, Headmistress.'
'Well, it's gone!'
'I'm sorry, Headmistress, but I can assure you that I've not moved it!'
'Damn and blast!' Miss Gussetpiece cursed as she banged the receiver down. 'Who on earth would have been in here and . . . Maxine Mayhem!'

Gathered in a clearing amongst the trees edging the school playing field after the final school bell, Maxine and the Bellend Rebels settled down with a bottle of vodka, discussing their plans to wreak havoc.

'OK!' Maxine yelled to quieten the half-dozen girls as she stood in command on a fallen tree, her short gymslip barely covering her bulging navy-blue knickers. Lighting a cigarette, she gazed at the group of young Jezebels. 'I've nabbed a load of fags and booze from Knickergusset's study – more than enough to last us for the term,' she enlightened her gang.

'Where's the stuff now?' a reckless redhead asked excitedly, sitting cross-legged to expose her damp, swelling knickers.

'In the gardener's potting shed.'

'Won't he report . . .'

'No, I've threatened the old git! Later, we'll stash the stuff in the woods somewhere. Now, the first thing we'll do this term is set fire to something. Any suggestions?'

'The kitchens!' one of the gymslip rebels proposed, swigging vodka and passing the bottle on.

'No, we've got to eat, Kelly!'

'The library!' an exquisite Japanese girl suggested.

'Yes, Fukui, the library – that sounds good!' Maxine grinned, her dark eyes reflecting her devilry.

'We'll do it this evening, after . . .' Kelly began.

'Shush!' Maxine breathed, leaping off the tree at the sound of twigs cracking underfoot. 'Someone's coming!'

Blissfully unaware that they were nearing the enemy camp, Hilda and Candida trod their way through the wood. 'There are plenty of squirrels around,' Hilda observed. 'Do you remember we had a cuckoo nesting here last year?'

'Yes, I do. They're awful creatures, laying their eggs in other birds' nests! Gosh, Hilly!' Candida exclaimed as they drew ever nearer to Maxine and her cronies. 'Don't you just love being close to nature?'

'Oh, I do! As you know, I live in the country. Daddy constructed a smashing hide in the woods at the end of our garden. I spend many glorious hours bird watching.'

'Gosh, I wish I lived in the country! The sun filtering through the trees, the scented air, the wildlife, the . . .'

'Well, if it's not a couple of Jolly Hockey Stick girls!' Maxine shrieked as Hilda and Candida wandered into the clearing.

Trembling, rooted to the spot, the girls gazed in terror at Maxine's gang. Until now, the Bellend Rebels had met in the boiler room, leaving the wood a safe haven for Hilda and her friends. But, Hilda realized as two of the gang leaped to their feet, there was no escaping Maxine and her rebels this term.

'What shall we do with them, Max?' Kelly asked, her voice husky, her green eyes sparkling mischievously as she stood before Hilda and squeezed the girl's pert breast.

'Let's get them to strip off!' someone giggled.

'Yes, good idea!' Maxine replied. 'Go on, take your clothes off!' she ordered her prisoners. 'Hurry up, quick strip!'

Gazing forlornly at each other, the terrorized girls pulled their gymslips over their heads. They had no choice, they knew – either they did as Maxine said or their clothes would be torn from their curvaceous, young bodies. Unbuttoning their blouses and kicking their shoes off, they tossed the garments to the ground, standing before their audience in their bras, knickers and white ankle socks.

'Come on!' Maxine hissed impatiently. 'Show us your cunts and titties!'

'Maxine, please!' Hilda sobbed as she reached behind her back.

'Do it, pillock! Unless, that is, you want us to do it for you!' Maxine grinned treacherously, prodding the girl's smooth stomach.

Unclipping their bras, the girls peeled the cups away from their firm young breasts to the accompaniment of shrieks of laughter. Tugging their navy-blue knickers down their shapely legs, they stepped from their armour, their sparse pubes, their pink vaginal cracks, blatantly displayed to their delighted tormentors.

Girl School

'Well now!' Maxine giggled. 'What pretty little things you are! Both turn round and bend over. Stand with your feet wide apart and touch your toes.' Complying, the girls exhibited their taut buttocks, their full vaginal lips nestling below their tight bottom-holes. 'I think we'll give them a good spanking!' Maxine chortled, standing behind Hilda. 'Come on, Ginger, you can spank the other one!'

Grimacing as her tensed buttocks received the first hard slap, Hilda had never felt so humiliated in her life. The stinging pain causing her to whimper, she swore to get even with Maxine, no matter what it took. Candida's sobs filling the wood as her virginal orbs received their thrashing, the naked girls' faces flushed with shame.

'I want to finger-fuck her!' Fukui squealed as she knelt behind Hilda.

'Someone finger Miss sweet, sticky Candyfloss!' Maxine ordered, slapping Hilda's buttocks again, turning the girl's twitching flesh crimson. Fingers delving into their tight vaginas as the spanking continued, to their surprise the girls sensed their stinging punishment radiate into a deliciously warm pleasure zone of sexual arousal. Their clitorises massaged by female fingers, they began to tremble as their orgasms stirred deep within their virginal wombs.

'She's going to come!' Fukui cried, sensing Hilda's pussy-hole tighten and her clitoris stiffen. Reaching their shuddering climaxes together, Hilda's and Candida's orgasmic wailings resounded through the wood as their burning buttocks tensed with every slap, their sex-buttons pulsating visibly between their rubicund labia.

'If only the boys from the Uni were here!' Maxine cried as she spanked Hilda's taut bottom-orbs. 'They could give them both a bloody good fucking! *And* shag their arse holes!'

'It could be arranged!' Ginger laughed, slapping Candida's bottom as hard as she could.

'It *will* be arranged!' Maxine decreed as her prisoners collapsed to the ground, their naked bodies writhing in the aftermath of their sensory explosions.

Pinning their victims down, the Bellend Rebels took turns to lick their captives' sticky vaginal cracks. Each lapping up the flowing come, driving their tongues into the girls' tight pussy sheaths, they became lost in their frenzy of lesbian lust. Moving their attention to each other, frenziedly tugging and ripping at knickers and bras, the gang finally ignored their prisoners. Taking their chance as the girls mouthed and sucked each other's pussies, Hilda and Candida grabbed their clothes and fled into the bushes.

'Leave them!' Maxine ordered Fukui as the girl was about to give chase. 'They can't exactly go far, can they?'

'No, I suppose not,' the exquisite doll replied, reclining on the short grass as another girl settled between her splayed thighs. 'Ah, yes, I like that!' she gasped as a female tongue swept up her opening sex-fissure. 'Mmm, that's good. Mmm, yes, lick my cunt! Lick my clitty!'

The other girls joining in, they ran their tongues over Fukui's curvaceous body, licking her navel, her smooth stomach, sucking her dark nipples into their hot mouths. Her pretty face contorting, her jet-black hair dishevelled as fingers entered her tight vagina, she shuddered. 'God, I need to come!' she cried as a finger slipped between her buttocks and drove deep into her hot rectal sheath. 'God, I'm nearly there already!' she sang.

Girl School

Writhing as tongues lapped between her rubicund pussy lips, Fukui reached her mind-blowing climax, her lithe oriental body trembling, her beautiful almond eyes rolling as her friends attended her every crevice, her every feminine curve. Settling her open vaginal crack over Fukui's face, Maxine lowered her body, pressing her wet sex-folds over the girl's gasping mouth. 'Lick my cunt out!' she ordered as Fukui's tongue entered her drenched vaginal sheath. 'Ah, yes, drink my come!'

Hiding in the bushes, Hilda and Candida slipped into their clothes, gawping at the lesbian orgy. 'Gosh, Hilly!' Candida gasped as she gazed at Maxine rocking her naked body, grinding her open cunt into the Japanese girl's hungry mouth. 'They're jolly rude!'

'They are! I've never seen anything so disgusting! What mummy would say, I really don't know!'

'Hilly, did you have a . . . you know, when they rubbed our minis and did those terribly rude things to us, did you have a goodie?' Candida asked tentatively.

'Well, yes, I suppose I did,' Hilda replied, her face flushing.

'It was frightfully naughty of us, wasn't it?'

'It wasn't our fault!' Hilda replied as Maxine's orgasmic cries reverberated through the trees. 'I mean, we were *forced* to have goodies, weren't we?'

'Yes, we were. But we must never have them again, Hilly. It's not right to do that!'

'I agree! We'll never allow ourselves to have goodies again. We'll make it a Jolly Hockey Sticks Club rule. It'll be Rule Fifteen – no mini-rubbing and having naughty goodies. Come on, let's go to supper – I'm famished!'

'Gosh, I'm jolly well starving, too! And talking of goodies – I could eat a horse!'

Chapter Two

Reporting to Miss Blob's rooms after supper, Hilda tentatively knocked on the door. 'Ah, come in, Hilda!' the geography mistress invited with a strange glint in her brown eyes. 'Come and sit in the lounge,' she continued huskily, leading the girl through a dimly-lit oak-panelled passageway. 'We need to have a long talk, Hilda.'

'Yes, Miss Blob,' the girl sighed, sitting on a leather Chesterfield and gazing at the hundreds of books lining the walls.

Wearing a short red skirt, fishnet stockings, red stilettoes and a tight blouse, Miss Blob's contours were somewhat bizarre, Hilda mused. Lacking any hint of feminine curves, she thought the woman's legs might well be those of a man. Her bust was ample – rather too ample, considering that she appeared to have no cleavage at all! *Do women grow chest hair with age?* the girl wondered, gazing between the woman's partially open blouse at several sprouting grey hairs.

'Smoking isn't allowed in school, Hilda,' Miss Blob began as she joined the girl on the sofa. 'I know that it's tempting to . . .'

'But I wasn't smoking, Miss Blob!' Hilda protested. 'I was in the toilet cubicle, and someone threw the lighted cigarette under the door!'

'Really? Do you know who it was?'

'No, Miss Blob, I don't.'

'I think I have an idea who it was! Anyway, we'll forget the incident,' Miss Blob smiled, rolling a cigarette. 'So, how are you getting on at Bellend?'

'Very well. I enjoy school very much. I didn't realize that you smoked, Miss Blob!' Hilda gasped as the woman lit the cigarette.

'Only on the odd occasion. Would you like one?'

'Gosh, no!'

'These are special, they're herbal.'

'Herbal?'

'Er . . . yes, they're made from a sort of herbal grass that comes from Colombia. I don't encourage girls to smoke, but it does help to calm the nerves – especially smoking *these* cigarettes. Are you nervous, Hilda?'

'No, not at all, Miss Blob.'

'Good. Well, I'm pleased to hear that you enjoy school. It's a fine school, but it lacks in one area – sex education. I've been taking several sixth-form girls for sex education for some time now, Hilda. Tell me, what's *your* knowledge of sex?'

'Well, I . . .'

'Come on, Hilda – you can tell me. Woman to man. I mean . . . Let's talk woman to woman.'

Shifting uneasily on the sofa, Hilda felt her face flush as she recalled the dreadful things Maxine and her gang had done in the clearing. Dare she tell Miss Blob what had happened? she wondered. In her confusion she needed to talk to someone about her experience, but if Maxine Mayhem were to find out . . . Her mind racked with guilt and the pleasure she'd derived from having another girl bring her to orgasm, Hilda hung her head.

Girl School

'Well, Hilda?' Miss Blob prompted, patting the girl's naked knee.

'I know about sex, yes. I've read books, so I know all about it,' Hilda replied sheepishly.

'What about masturbation, Hilda? Do you masturbate?'

'No, Miss Blob!'

'Most girls do. It's quite normal to masturbate, it's nothing to be ashamed about. You must have experimented with masturbation, Hilda?'

'Well, I . . . I have done it, yes,' Hilda confessed, recalling her nights beneath the sheets in the dormitory, her slender fingers massaging illicit orgasms from her erect clitoris. 'But I don't want anyone to know. It's going to become one of our Jolly Hockey Sticks Club rules, you see. Rule Fifteen – no rubbing and having naughty goodies.'

'I see. I want you to confide in me, Hilda. How often do you masturbate?'

'Not very often.'

'Every day? Once a week?' Miss Blob probed.

'Well, on average, three or four times a week,' Hilda conceded, wondering why the woman's tight skirt was bulging at the groin.

'Before I moved onto teaching, I spent many years in nursing, Hilda. What I'm doing as part of the sex education programme is examining girls. You see, it's best to have regular checks, just to ensure that things are all right – to ensure that everything is developing properly. If you wish, I'll examine *you*, Hilda.'

'I'd rather you didn't!' the girl gasped surprisedly as Miss Blob moved her hand to her inner thigh.

'Well, it's up to you. But, and I have to tell you this, if

things aren't quite right, it's best to find out now – before it's too late.'

'Too late?'

'I'm sure that you're perfectly normal *down there*, but you never know. Should there be a slight abnormality, if it's discovered early enough, then it can be put right. But, of course, if left . . . I don't mean to worry you, Hilda, but nursing taught me what to look out for in that area of the body – the signs, so to speak. Anyway, you have a think about it.'

'Yes, Miss Blob, I will. May I go now?'

'Go? Er . . . I was hoping to show you my . . . Yes, you may go, if you want to.'

'Thank you,' Hilda sighed as she rose to her feet. 'I'll give it some thought, Miss Blob,' she added, seeing herself out. 'Goodbye.'

Walking down the corridor, Hilda jumped as the fire bells resounded throughout the school. 'It's not fire practice!' she breathed, making her way to the nearest fire exit and assembling with the rest of the school on the playing field. Finding Candida and Patsy, she settled on the grass in the warmth of the evening sun to discuss excitedly where the fire might be.

'The problem was in the library, Miss Gussetpiece,' Johnson proffered as he entered the head's study. 'It was only a small fire. I've managed to put it out, but I've called the brigade just in case it flares up again.'

'Oh, well done, Jones! I hope we didn't lose too many books!'

'My name's Johnson, Headmistress. No books were damaged, thankfully.'

'How on earth did the fire start?'

Girl School

'It was in a wastepaper bin – but I don't know how it began. It spread to a table and a couple of chairs. Anyway, I'll go and wait for the fire engine to arrive.'

'Thank you, Jones.'

'Johnson, Miss Gussetpiece.'

'Oh, yes, of course.'

Holding her head as she sat at her desk, Miss Gussetpiece sighed. 'Not a good day! Not a good day at all!'

'Excuse me, Headmistress,' Miss Blob rasped, peering round the study door. 'I know that this might not be a good time, what with the fire, but I need to talk to you.'

'Not *more* problems, I hope?'

'No, not at all. I've had an idea, an idea that I'm sure you'll be delighted with, Headmistress. My brother's an eminent doctor, a gynaecologist, in fact. I thought we might start having regular medical check-ups. The girls all have their own doctors, of course, and there's the school nurse, but I thought it might be an idea to have my brother, a specialist, give the girls gynaecological examinations on a regular basis.'

'That's a very good idea, Miss Blob! But how much will he charge? Financially, things are pretty grim at the moment.'

'He won't charge anything. I've already spoken with him over the telephone. He's quite well-heeled and he's offering his services for nothing – for the good of the girls and the school.'

'That's extremely good of him, Miss Blob! If you'll arrange a meeting, I'll talk it over with him.'

'I'll see to it right away, Headmistress. Tomorrow morning, perhaps?'

'Yes, tomorrow morning will suit me perfectly. Thank

you for taking such an interest in the welfare of the girls, Miss Blob. Admirable, most admirable!'

'I try to be a good Catholic. I'll have my brother come over tomorrow morning. Good night, Headmistress.'

'Good night, Miss Blob. And thank you once again.'

Unlocking the gardener's potting shed, Maxine slipped through the door, eagerly followed by Ginger. 'Here's the stuff!' Maxine whispered, switching the light on and dragging the laundry basket out.

'Fuck my fanny!' Ginger gasped. 'There's enough here to last us for weeks!'

'I know! I couldn't believe it when I found this lot in Knickergusset's study! Let's have some vodka, shall we?'

'Ah, an old sofa!' Ginger giggled. 'I've never been in here before. This is a brilliant place!'

'If it wasn't for the bloody gardener, we could make it our HQ,' Maxine said pensively.

'Can't we get rid of the old bugger?'

'How?'

'Wank him off, and he might have a heart attack!'

'Actually, we *might* be able to get rid of him,' Maxine mused. 'You said that your brother grows cannabis, didn't you?'

'Yes, but what's that got to do with it?' Ginger asked, swigging from the bottle.

'Get a plant, and we'll have the gardener arrested for growing the stuff!'

'What's going on in here?' The girls jumped guiltily at the sight of the maintenance man peering round the door.

'Oh! You startled me!' Maxine cried, turning to face the young man.

'So *that's* where the Head's goodies got to!' he gasped, eyeing the elusive laundry basket.

'Who are you?' Maxine demanded.

'I'm new here. I'm the maintenance man,' the young man replied, walking over to the basket. 'You're going to be in a hell of a lot of trouble when . . .'

'When what?' Maxine grinned, grabbing his bulging crotch. 'You're not going to grass us up, surely?' she breathed huskily as she fell to her knees and tugged his zip down.

Pulling the young man's penis out as Ginger pushed the laundry basket beneath the bench, Maxine parted her full, red lips and took his purple knob into her hot mouth. Breathing heavily, he gazed down in disbelief at the young girl as she moved her hand up and down his veined shaft, stiffening his penis as she licked and sucked his bulbous plum.

'You're not going to say anything about our goodies, are you?' Ginger asked, taking his hand and thrusting it up her gymslip. His fingers moving her navy-blue knickers aside, he massaged her warm vaginal lips, locating the wet entrance to her tight pussy hole. 'I'm sure you'll forget that you saw our haul, won't you?'

'Yes, yes . . . Ah, that's nice!'

'Maxine's good at cock-sucking,' Ginger smiled. 'And you're pretty good at fanny-fingering. What's your name?'

'Ah, ah! Dan, my name's Dan!'

'Are you desperate, Dan?'

'Yes, ah, ah!'

As the young man's legs sagged and his penis began to pump its sperm into Maxine's gobbling mouth, the door burst open. 'This will be our new HQ!' Hilda twittered excitedly to Candida as she entered the shed. Slipping his knob from Maxine's mouth as he swung round, Dan shot his spunk down the front of Hilda's gymslip. 'Oh!' she shrieked as another white emblem of achievement flew through the air to decorate her uniform.

'Come here, pillock!' Maxine spat, grabbing the girl's arm as Ginger seized Candida. Clutching Hilda's hair and forcing her to kneel as she grasped Dan's orgasming cock, Maxine wanked his twitching penis, shooting his sperm over Hilda's pretty face. 'Open your mouth and taste it!' Maxine shrieked as she brought out the last spurt and rubbed Dan's knob over the girl's pursed lips.

'God, I'll be in trouble for this!' Dan gasped, pulling away and concealing his spent penis in his tight jeans.

'No, you won't,' Maxine asserted. 'Hilda Pillock won't tell.'

'I will!' Hilda spluttered vehemently, wiping her mouth. 'I'll tell Miss Gussetpiece that you . . .'

'Dan, how would you like to fuck Pillock's tight cunt?' Maxine asked huskily.

'I . . . I'd better not,' he replied, his dark eyes lighting up at the prospect of slipping his penis into the girl's young vagina.

'Why ever not? She could do with a good fuck. You'd like that wouldn't you?' she asked, gazing down at the delicate blonde's sperm-drenched face. 'You'd like a good fuck, wouldn't you, pillock?'

'You just dare to . . .'

'Come on, little Miss Pillock! This is the chance of a lifetime! Don't you want your tight cunt fucked?'

'Jolly well leave her alone!' Candida cried as she struggled to break free from Ginger.

'Perhaps *you* want *your* tight cunt fucked?' Ginger

asked wickedly as she tightened her grip on Candida's arm.

'Put it this way,' Maxine grinned. 'One of you is going to get fucked, so you'd better choose which one!'

Gazing at each other helplessly, Hilda and Candida knew that there was no escaping Maxine. Recalling her enforced orgasm in the woods, Hilda pondered on the prospect of having a man's penis driving into her young vagina. Candida, too, recalled her uninvited but not unpleasant climax, wondering what it would be like to have a man's organ enter her virginal pussy hole.

'Me,' Candida finally conceded. 'I'll do it.'

'Good!' Maxine cried as Ginger forced their volunteer to kneel on the floor with her face resting on the sofa.

'Are you sure . . .' Dan began, his penis stiffening, making his tight jeans bulge.

'Don't worry, they won't tell,' Maxine reassured him as she released Hilda and closed the shed door. 'Pull her knickers down!' she instructed Ginger.

Lifting Candida's gymslip, Ginger yanked the girl's knickers down, exposing her taut buttocks, her ballooning vaginal lips, as she forced the girl to project her bottom. Kneeling behind Candida, Dan slipped his rock-hard penis out and pressed his purple knob between the girl's swollen pussy lips. Her blue eyes wide with expectation, Hilda gazed at Dan's huge penis as Maxine forced her to kneel by her friend.

'You can watch!' Maxine giggled, grabbing Hilda's hair and forcing her face close to Candida's shamefully exposed girlhood. 'You can watch his cock fuck her cunt! OK, Dan, shove it right up her! When you're about to come, whip it out and you can spunk in Pillock's mouth!'

As Dan's cockhead slipped into Candida's tight vaginal tube, the girl whimpered, digging her fingernails into the sofa cushion as his knob came to rest against her young cervix. Hilda's eyes grew wide with disbelief as she gazed at her friend's taut cunny lips gripping the base of the huge male organ and she sensed her own clitoris swell. As the vaginal ramming began, she held her hand to her mouth, gasping as the wet, veined shaft repeatedly emerged, only to drive deep again into her friend's trembling young body.

'Ever seen anything like it before?' Maxine giggled, pushing Hilda's face closer to the enforced sexual coupling. Unable to utter a word as her young friend's body jolted with every pounding thrust, Hilda was stunned as Candida cried out in her coming. 'More!' the girl begged. 'Do it harder!' Suddenly slipping his penis from Candida's spasming vaginal sheath, Dan offered his knob to Hilda's open mouth.

'Suck it!' Maxine ordered, pinching the girl's nose and pushing her head forward as Dan thrust his pulsating knob into her hot mouth. Gulping down the gushing sperm, her blue eyes almost popping out of her head, Hilda ran her tongue over the silky-smooth glans, trying to conceal her obvious pleasure as she drank from the aphrodisiacal geyser.

Finally slipping his spent organ from her mouth, Dan sat back on his heels. 'That was something else!' he gasped, watching Hilda lick the sperm from her luscious lips. As Candida lifted her flushed face from the cushion and sat upright, her eyes caught Hilda's. Despite their embarrassment, they had both enjoyed their obligatory sexual couplings. Would she now be forced to take Dan's penis into her mini? Hilda wondered, the taste of sperm lingering on her awakened taste buds.

Averting her gaze as she stood and tugged her knickers up, Candida squealed as Maxine pushed her down, sitting her forcefully down on the sofa and ripping her knickers off. 'What are you doing?' the pretty blonde asked fearfully as Maxine and Ginger each took a foot and yanked her legs high into the air, opening her dripping vaginal crack.

'Lick her cunt!' Maxine ordered Hilda. 'Go on, lick her cunt out!'

'Please, Maxine, I . . .'

'Lick her cunt out, or you'll have Dan's cock up your arse!'

Kneeling between her friend's splayed thighs, Hilda tentatively moved her head forward, gazing at the girl's pinken inner folds, the creamy fluid oozing from her partially open pussy hole. Closer she moved her face, her mouth, to the luxurious velveteen slit, pushing her tongue out and reluctantly tasting the crimsoning flesh. Her eyes wide with astonishment, Candida gazed at Hilda as the girl licked the full length of her open fissure. Again, Hilda swept her tongue up the glistening sex valley, tasting the wet flesh, savouring the sticky girl-juice.

Closing her eyes as Hilda fervently licked and mouthed on her sweet inner fruit, Candida sensed her clit kernel swell and throb. Tentatively parting her fleshy lips, exposing her hardening nucleus to her friend's sweeping tongue, she gasped. 'Oh, oh! Oh, gosh!' The sensations building, shaking her young body, Candida knew she would soon have a goodie. But this was so wrong, she thought as she peeled her succulent sex lips further apart. To have another girl lick her pussy was so very wrong. But beautiful!

Maxine and Ginger said nothing as Dan slipped out of the shed, leaving Hilda to drink from Candida's young pussy hole, to stiffen her clitoris and take her to a shuddering orgasm. Dan would say nothing about the contraband, they knew. If he wanted to return to the shed to enjoy the *cordon-bleu* delights of young girls' bodies, he'd say nothing about the absent aperitifs!

'It's coming!' Candida cried as her clitoris throbbed against Hilda's snaking tongue. 'My goodie's coming!' Her body shaking uncontrollably, her face flushing, she pulled her engorged labia wide apart, gyrating her hips, grinding her open cunt into her friend's hot mouth. Wailing her appreciation as the girls opened her legs further, Candida had never experienced such incredible pleasure. Her tentative experimentation, her gentle clitoral caresses while in her bed at night, had never brought her the immense pleasure she was now experiencing.

Thrusting her fingers deep into Candida's spasming vagina, Hilda lost herself in her frenzied arousal, fingering her young friend, sucking her orgasm from her solid clitoris. But would they do this again? she wondered. After their incredible enforced sexual awakening, would they steal into each other's beds at night and pleasure each other, lick each other, finger each other?

Dropping Candida's legs and dashing out of the shed at the sound of nearing footsteps, Maxine and Ginger left the girls to enjoy their new-found lesbian pleasure.

'Someone's left the light on! This just won't do, it *really* won't!' Miss Gussetpiece complained as she opened the shed door. Staring in horror at the lewd tableau, she gasped. 'Strewth! What on earth is going on in here? Holy Mary! I have never seen anything . . .'

'She's in pain, Miss Gussetpiece!' Hilda interjected, her brain going into top gear as she leaped to her feet and wiped her salivered mouth. 'She has a terrible pain and I was just checking . . .'

'A pain?'

'Yes, inside her . . . I was trying to see what the trouble is.'

'If she has trouble with her internals, you'd better bring her inside! For a moment, I thought . . . It doesn't matter what I thought. Take her to Miss Blob's rooms. She might be able to contact her brother and have him come over and look at the girl.'

'Her brother?' Hilda echoed.

'Yes, he's an eminent gynaecologist. What's that white stuff all down the front of your gymslip, girl?'

'Er . . . It's face cream, Miss Gussetpiece,' Hilda replied guiltily.

'You are a messy girl, you really are! Come on, follow me. Face cream, indeed!'

Breathing a sigh of relief as they left the shed, the girls prayed that Miss Blob would be unable to contact her brother. 'I don't want to be examined!' Candida whispered as the headmistress strode ahead down the corridor.

'We're jolly lucky that Miss Gussetpiece didn't realize what we were up to!' Hilda breathed. 'Crikey, we could have been expelled!'

'We were naughty to do what we did,' Candida smiled with a wicked glint in her blue eyes.

'Yes, I know! But we were forced by those awful girls. What was it like, having that man . . .'

'Gosh, it was . . .'

'Right!' Miss Gussetpiece boomed as she tapped on Miss Blob's door. 'Are you still in pain, girl?'

'No, Miss Gussetpiece,' Candida smiled. 'I'm fine now.'

'Well, I think you should be examined, just in case . . . One can't be too careful with young girls' internals. Ah, Miss Blob, would you be kind enough to contact your brother and ask him whether he'd come over and examine this girl?'

'Damn right I . . . er . . . What I meant was . . . Yes, of course. Please, come in, Headmistress,' Miss Blob smiled, opening the door wide. 'What's the matter with her?'

'She has a pain, a gynaecological pain.'

'Cor! Er . . . As it happens, my brother is here. Come through to the lounge. He's in the toilet, I'll go and get him.'

'That's a coincidence!' Miss Gussetpiece exclaimed, ushering the girls through the passage.

'What is?'

'Your brother being here, in the toilet.'

'Er . . . yes, yes, it is. He doesn't often come to see me. It's *quite* a coincidence!'

Settling on the sofa, the girls frowned at each other, wondering how to escape the difficult situation. Making herself comfortable in an armchair, Miss Gussetpiece suggested that Hilda go and prepare for bed. 'It's getting late,' she said as the girl rose to her feet. 'I'll stay here with Candida, so you've no need to worry about her.'

'Yes, Miss Gussetpiece,' Hilda replied dolefully, moving to the door. 'Good night.'

As a smart grey-haired man wearing a suit, shirt and

tie entered the room, Miss Gussetpiece rose, holding her hand out to greet him. 'You're very much like your sister!' she exclaimed, shaking his hand.

'Am I? Er . . . we're twins,' he smiled. 'I'm Doctor Pouch.'

'That's an unusual name!'

'Yes, I inherited it from my father. He was Polish.'

'But, surely, your name's Blob?'

'Er . . . no, I'm Doctor Uterine Pouch. It's a long story, Headmistress, and one that I haven't got time to tell. So, this is our patient, is it?' he asked, gazing lasciviously at the delicious schoolgirl standing before him.

'Yes, this is Candida. Where's your sister got to?' Miss Gussetpiece asked.

'Er . . . she's in the toilet. She has a slight problem with her urethral . . . Well, we won't go into that now. If you'll leave us alone, Headmistress, I'll examine the patient.'

'I think I should stay,' Miss Gussetpiece returned, scrutinizing the man. 'I mean, I can't leave one of my girls alone with a strange man! I'm in a position of trust. I'm responsible for . . .'

'I'm not a strange man, Headmistress! I'm a doctor!'

'Oh, yes, I suppose you are. Mind you, I've read about doctors in the Sunday papers!'

'It's all right, Headmistress. You need have no concern for the girl's safety. Now, off you go, and I'll talk to you later,' he smiled reassuringly, placing his arm around the woman's shoulder as he led her to the door.

'You're so like your sister, Doctor Pouch. It's absolutely amazing!'

'Please, call me Uterine, Headmistress.'

'Er . . . yes . . . Uterine. If you were to wear your

sister's clothes, I don't think I'd be able to tell you apart!'

'We're identical twins.'

'Oh, how amazing! Well, I'll leave you to examine the girl, Doctor,' Miss Gussetpiece said briskly as she wandered through the passage.

Returning to the lounge, Doctor Pouch smiled at Candida. 'Slip your knickers off and lie on the sofa, please,' he ordered authoritatively.

'The pain's gone, Doctor. I'm all right now,' Candida smiled, making to leave the room.

'Candida, I *must* examine you! We don't want to upset the headmistress, do we?'

'Upset her?'

'She's asked me to examine you. We don't want to go against her wishes, do we?'

'No, I suppose not,' Candida sighed as she lifted her gymslip and tugged her knickers down her shapely legs.

Trembling as the girl lay on the sofa, the doctor dropped to his knees. Pulling her gymslip up over her smooth stomach, he gazed wide-eyed at her youthful vaginal lips, her wet dividing groove. 'Can you manage to place one foot over the back of the sofa and the other on the floor, please?' he asked.

'I can't open my legs that far!' Candida remonstrated.

'Yes, you can. Please, if I'm to examine you properly . . .'

'Well, I'll try,' the girl sighed, placing her left foot over the back of the sofa.

Her young vaginal slit opening as she stretched her other leg and placed her foot on the floor, Candida rested her head on a cushion. Moving between her splayed thighs, Doctor Pouch parted the girl's fleshy pussy lips, gazing at their pinken inner counterpart, creamy girl-come oozing from her open hole. Spreading her reddening labia further to expose her clitoris, he sighed.

'It's a good job I had the opportunity to examine you, Candida. There's something not quite right here.'

'Not quite right?' the girl echoed, lifting her head to survey her open crack.

'You're very wet. Have you recently had sexual intercourse?'

'Er . . . No, no, I haven't!' she gasped as he slipped his finger into her tight vaginal canal and began massaging her hot inner flesh. 'What's wrong with me, Doctor?'

'Well, as far as I can tell . . .' he began pensively as he caressed her clitoris with his other hand. 'As far as I can tell . . . Yes, that's the answer – shave your pubic hair off.'

'Shave my . . . But, Doctor!'

'Your dermal papillae has interacted with your epidermis, the result being irritation and inflammation of the vulval skin.'

'Dermal . . . Epidermis . . .'

'I won't bother you with the medical details, Candida,' the doctor continued, slipping his finger from her tightening pussy hole. 'Wait there and I'll see if my sister has a depilatory in the bathroom cabinet.'

As he left the room, Candida gazed down at her open pussy crack, wondering what was wrong with her skin. Finding no apparent inflammation, she began to forage around her pubic mound, frowning as she imagined some irritation there.

'Here we are!' the doctor beamed, returning with a small tube of cream. 'Just the job!' he enthused, dropping to his knees. 'Now, I'll smear the cream over your pubic hair, like this, and after about ten minutes you'll be as soft as a baby's . . . I mean, the irritation will go.'

'You won't tell anyone about this, will you, Doctor?' Candida asked as he massaged the cool lotion into her fleshy sex hillocks.

'No, of course I won't. And you must tell no one, Candida. This is between us, between doctor and patient. Now, I think that's enough – just a little more there, perhaps. Just close your eyes and relax, and I'll continue with the examination while we're waiting for the cream to do its job.'

Closing her eyes as the doctor slipped two fingers into her pussy sheath, Candida pondered on the uncanny likeness between him and his sister. *Identical twins with different surnames?* she mused, hoping to observe the pair side by side. *Miss Blob's been a long time in the toilet.*

Relaxing as her vagina tightened around the doctor's probing fingers, her clitoris stiffening as he massaged between her swollen pussy lips, she sighed. *A strange examination!* she reflected as her nubbin throbbed in response to the caressing fingertips. But, strange or not, she had to admit she was enjoying the sensations as the birth of her orgasm stirred deep within her contracting womb.

'Is this normal, doctor?' Candida gasped as he quickened his rhythm.

'Yes, it's perfectly normal to check young girls in this way. You see, I have to ensure that everything's working properly. This is known in the medical profession as CRAP – Clitoral Response Ascertainment Procedure. Now, just relax and allow the sensations to come.'

Stifling her gasps as her clitoris erupted and her vagina spasmed, Candida trembled uncontrollably. The beautiful climactic waves rolling through her young body as the doctor thrust his fingers in and out of her drenched pussy sheath, she turned her head to conceal her pleasure, wondering again at the unorthodox examination.

'That's very good!' the doctor breathed as he vigorously massaged her pulsating nub. 'Yes, everything's working very well. A perfect CRAP. Tell me, Candida, do you masturbate?'

'Yes, no, I mean . . . Ah, ah!' she wailed as her body shuddered in the wake of her climax.

'Don't you ever rub yourself and have nice feelings?' he persisted.

'Well, sometimes . . . Ah, that's . . . Ah, ah! Please, no more!'

'All right, the examination's over. You quite enjoyed it, didn't you?'

'Yes, no, I mean . . . Ah! May I go now?'

'I'd better get something to clean you up first,' the doctor smiled, rising to his feet and leaving the room.

Returning with a warm flannel, he wiped the cream from Candida's mons, her soft vaginal lips. Cleansing the girl, revealing her smooth white skin, he grinned as she gazed in awe at her hairless girl-slit.

'Oh! Oh, I look like . . .' she breathed.

'It will soon grow again, Candida,' he reassured her, stroking her hairless cunny pads. 'But you'll have to come and see me every evening for a week or so, just so that I can check that things are all right.'

'For a week? But . . .'

'Yes, every evening for a week, if not longer. You do want to get better, don't you?' he murmured, running his finger up her moist chasm.

'Well, I can't see that anything's wrong!'

'A trained eye, that's what I have. You wouldn't notice the problem, but I can see it clearly. Now, slip your knickers on and I'll see you tomorrow night.'

'Your sister's been a long time,' Candida remarked, concealing her depilated crack beneath her navy-blue knickers.

'I asked her not to disturb us. Now, off you go, Candida, and I'll see you tomorrow evening.'

'What's that big lump in your trousers, doctor?'

'Er . . . Oh, that! It's, er . . . nothing, it's nothing. Now, off you go.'

Grinning as she sat on her bed, Maxine turned to Ginger. 'We'll have some fun with this!' she giggled, wielding a huge cucumber. 'When Pillock gets here, we'll fuck her with it!'

'Where did you get it from?'

'I nicked it from the kitchens. Pillock will just love having it shoved up her cunt!'

'Yes, and her arse!' Ginger laughed, toying with several lengths of rope. 'We'll tie her down and . . . Where's she got to, anyway?'

'Fuck knows! I'll bet she's hiding somewhere, too frightened to come up here.'

'Do you reckon Knickergusset found the booze and fags in the shed?'

'Shit, I hope not, Ginger! Christ, my knickers are wet! While we're waiting for Pillock, how about giving me a good seeing-to with the cucumber?'

'OK, drop your knickers and open your legs!' Ginger giggled, lubricating the end of the vegetable phallus in her pert mouth as Maxine slipped her knickers down.

Lying on her bed with her legs spread, Maxine parted

her full vaginal lips, exposing her pinken cunny hole as Ginger settled between her thighs. Pressing the fruit between the girl's splayed inner lips, Ginger pushed and twisted the cucumber, watching in awe as the green shaft slipped into her friend's tight vaginal duct. Further she forced the huge phallus into the girl's quivering body, delighting as she watched the sensitive pink flesh stretch to accommodate the hefty intruder.

'God, that feels nice!' Maxine gasped as Ginger twisted the cucumber. 'Ah, God, I love my cunt!'

'And *I* love your cunt!' Ginger asserted, leaning over and licking Maxine's exposed clitoris. 'Mmm, you taste delectable. God, your clitty's hard!'

'Finger my bum, Ginger! Ah, please, finger-fuck my bum!' Maxine begged as her clitoris throbbed beneath her friend's sweeping tongue.

'I'll do better than that! Wait there a minute!' Ginger giggled, leaping across the room and grabbing a deodorant bottle from her bedside cabinet.

Parting Maxine's buttocks, Ginger located the girl's brown hole and pushed the rounded bottle cap against her sensitive flesh. Her cunt juice flowing, trickling between her buttocks, lubricating the plastic cap, Maxine gasped as her sphincter muscles yielded, allowing the phallus to enter her anal sheath.

'Fuck me, that's nice!' Maxine breathed as the bottle sank deep into her rectum. 'Push it right in! I . . . I love it! Oh, God, my arse! My . . . my cunt!'

'You should see it!' Ginger laughed. 'God, your bum's stretched wide open, Max!'

'Fuck my cunt with the cucumber! Really give it to me!'

Taking the green shaft in her hand, Ginger thrust the fruit in and out of her young friend's vagina, causing the girl to arch her back and gasp with delight. Licking her swollen clitoris, sucking the rubicund sex-nodule into her wet mouth, Ginger took the other girl to her desperately needed release. Shuddering, her long legs spread wide, Maxine dug her fingernails into the bedclothes, gasping, wailing in the grip of her multiple orgasm. Thrusting both phalluses in and out of the girl's abused holes, Ginger continued her licking, her clitoral mouthing and sucking, until Maxine grabbed her head.

'No more! No more! God, I've come, I've come!' Maxine cried as she tossed her head from side to side, her long black hair concealing her flushed face. Lost in her sexual delirium, she lay panting, her eyes rolling, as Ginger slowly slipped the phalluses from her tight holes. Gently massaging her wet inner flesh with her fingertips, Ginger lovingly caressed the last ripples of sex from her friend's trembling body.

'I'll lick you clean,' she whispered huskily, lowering her head to Maxine's sodden pussy. Parting the girl's bloated outer lips, she drove her tongue into her drenched canal, lapping up the flowing pussy juice. Savouring her friend's hot come, Ginger swallowed, delighting in the taste of another girl's cuntal offering. 'I love licking your cunt out!' she breathed, lapping fervently on the wet girl-flesh. 'If only I could reach my own cunt! I'd lick myself out every day!'

'Give me the cucumber,' Maxine breathed. 'I want to taste my come.'

Taking the wet vegedildo, Maxine licked the green shaft, tasting her vaginal cream as Ginger cleansed her young pussy slit. 'Mmm, my cunt cream does taste nice!' Maxine giggled. 'No wonder the boys from the Uni can't get enough of the stuff!'

'Perhaps we should bottle it and sell it!' Ginger laughed.

'That's an idea! If we got hold of some small bottles and stuffed them up our cunts, we could collect the juice.'

'Talking of cunt juice, it's my turn,' Ginger declared, sensing her navy-blue knickers filling with her slippery vaginal fluid. 'Come on, you can give me a good fucking with the cucumber.'

As the dormitory door opened, Maxine hurriedly sat up, pulling her gymslip down and concealing her inflamed pussy crack. 'Ah, little Miss Pillock!' she cried as Hilda stood in the doorway, her mouth hanging open, her eyes wide as she gazed at the wet cucumber in Maxine's hand. Leaping to her feet and locking the door, Maxine grinned. 'The rope, please, Ginger!' she demanded as she moved closer to the terrified girl. Taking two lengths of rope, Maxine ordered Hilda to lie on her bed.

'No! Please, Maxine, I . . .' Hilda squealed.

'On your bed, pillock!' Maxine growled. 'Come on, get onto your bed, or else!'

'Maxine! I don't want to . . .'

'I'm warning you, pillock! Unless you do as you're told, I'll whip you!'

Grabbing Hilda's feet as the girl lay down, Maxine bound her ankles, pulling her thighs wide apart and fastening the rope to the bed legs. Binding Hilda's wrists, Ginger pulled the girl's arms up and secured the rope to the tubular bedstead. 'Scissors, please, Ginger!' Maxine grinned. Taking a pair of scissors from her bedside cabinet, Ginger passed them to Maxine, enquiring what she was going to do. 'You'll see!' Maxine chortled, lifting her captive's gymslip. Cutting through the struggling girl's knickers, she tossed the shredded garment to the floor and contemplated her prisoner's pouting labia.

'May I?' Ginger asked Maxine as she grabbed the cucumber from the bed.

'Be my guest!' Maxine giggled.

'I'm going to fuck her cunt with this until she comes!'

Her body tethered, Hilda could do nothing to prevent Ginger parting her pussy lips and easing the cucumber deep into her tight vagina. 'No, no!' she protested as Ginger pushed it further into her hot hole. 'Argh! Take it out!' Further the green phallus sank into Hilda's trembling body as Maxine unbuttoned her victim's blouse and eased her breasts from her bra cups, gazing longingly at her brown nipples.

'Now, what shall I do with these?' Maxine asked, tweaking Hilda's erect nipples. 'I could always cut them off!'

'Please!' Hilda whimpered as the cucumber came to rest against her cervix.

'Please what? Please cut them off?' Maxine taunted, wielding the scissors.

'I'll tell Miss Gussetpiece about you, you dreadful creature!' Hilda threatened.

'Shut up, pillock, or you'll have the cucumber up your arse!'

'Let's shove it up her arse, anyway!' Ginger laughed, ramming the green shaft in and out of Hilda's tight cuntal sheath.

'After we've made her come,' Maxine replied, sucking the girl's nipple into her mouth.

The pistoning fruit blatantly distending her sex sheath, Hilda struggled, pulling on her bonds, frantically trying to escape Maxine and her evil accomplice. Finally stilling her body, she resigned herself to the fact that there was no escape. But, she mused with an exhilarating mixture of fear and excitement, this was only the beginning of the new term – the beginning of untold nights of sexual adventure.

Taking the deodorant bottle, Ginger parted Hilda's buttocks and presented the rounded cap to the girl's anal portal. 'You'll like this!' she giggled, pressing the cap past her sphincter muscles. 'I'm going to shove it right up your arse!'

'No!' Hilda screamed as the bottle entered her, stretching her rectal sheath. 'No! You can't . . . you can't do this!'

'I've done it!' the redhead returned, gazing in wonderment at the two impromptu phalluses emerging from the holes between the girl's splayed thighs.

'Don't you like it?' Maxine asked, biting on Hilda's erect nipple. 'There's nothing better than a little troilism!'

'No, I don't like it!' the girl cried. 'I hate you, you vile beasts!'

Peeling the girl's vermilion lips wide apart, Ginger sucked Hilda's clitoris into her mouth, stiffening her budling, causing her prisoner to gasp with the beautiful sensations of sex. Caressing the throbbing sex-button with her wet tongue she took the girl to her climax, mouthing and sucking as Hilda wailed in the grip of her lesbian ecstasy.

'I've got an idea!' Maxine shrieked, leaping onto the bed and sitting between Hilda's legs. 'We'll have a double fucking!' she cried, settling her legs either side of Hilda, pushing the protruding end of the cucumber into her drenched vagina.

'Fuck me!' Ginger gasped as the fruit sank into Maxine's cunny hole, her swollen pussy lips nearing Hilda's taut vaginal lips as she moved closer to the girl, driving the phallus deeper into her young love duct.

Reclining, leaning back on her hands, Maxine gyrated her hips, stirring her cuntal cream with the cucumber. 'Ram it back and forth,' she ordered Ginger. 'Give us a double fucking!'

'I hate you both!' Hilda spat as Ginger grabbed the green shaft and began her pistoning, driving the massive shaft in and out of the girls' spasming vaginas.

'I've never seen anything like it!' Ginger breathed, watching the girls' pussy lips rolling along the wet fruit. 'We'll have to do this, Max!'

'God, yes! Ah, do it faster, harder!' Maxine ordered as her vaginal muscles tightened, gripping the intruding shaft. 'Coming! I'm coming! That's it, harder, faster! More, more!'

The pistoning cucumber taking both girls closer to their illicit orgasms, Ginger virtually lost control. Forcefully ramming the fruit into the girls' quivering bodies, she delighted in watching them achieve their climaxes, gazing in awe at their swollen pussy lips, their vaginal cream spewing from their bloated sheaths. On and on she thrust the cucumber in and out of the girls' contorting bodies, ignoring their pleas for her to stop.

'God, I love your cunts!' Ginger cried, massaging each girl's pulsating clitoris in turn with her free hand. 'I want to eat your cunts, drink the come from your cunts!'

'Enough, Ginger!' Maxine cried as she pulled away. The cucumber leaving her inflamed hole, she lay back, panting, trembling in the wake of her climax. 'Fuck me, that was brilliant!'

'I hate you!' Hilda sobbed as she pulled on the ropes. 'Please, let me go!'

Pulling the fruit from Hilda's sopping vagina, Ginger sat on the edge of the bed, lapping up the cream from the green shaft, lost in her sexual delirium. Lifting her buttocks off the bed, she slipped her wet knickers down to her ankles and parted her soaked pussy lips. Pushing the cucumber deep into her vagina, she gasped. 'Oh, my cunt! My beautiful cunt!' Massaging her clitoris as Maxine released Hilda, she reached her shuddering climax, her body shaking violently, her cunt gripping the pistoning phallus like a vice as she fell to the floor. 'Oh, my beautiful cunt!' she gasped again, massaging her subsiding orgasm from her pulsating cumbud. 'Oh, God, my lovely cunt!'

'I'm glad we're girls!' Maxine giggled. 'Cucumbers, carrots, bananas ... We can shove anything up our cunts!'

Crawling beneath the bedclothes, Hilda massaged her aching vaginal cavern, wondering how many nights of enforced lesbian sex her young body could endure. Her clitoris throbbing as she allowed her fingertips to caress the sensitive tip, she brought out her orgasm. Quivering, quietly whimpering between the sheets as the girls climbed into Maxine's bed together, she wondered where Candida had got to, what the doctor had done to her. Recalling the shed, remembering licking her friend's young pussy, she fell into a deep sleep and dreamed her new dreams of lesbian sex.

Chapter Three

Up and dressed by six in the morning, Hilda was pleased to have escaped from the dormitory before Maxine and Ginger woke. Walking through the woods with Candida, she breathed in the early morning air, asking her friend what had happened with the doctor.

'He . . . Well, he examined me,' Candida replied hesitantly as the girls entered the clearing and settled on the grass.

'Crikey! And what did he say when he found nothing wrong?'

'He *did* find something wrong. Something to do with dermal epidermis or whatever. It's my skin – it's irritated. He . . . Oh, never mind.'

'He what? Crumbs, do tell me, Candy!'

'The cure, it's somewhat peculiar. He put cream on me and . . . My hair's all gone.'

'What, the hair *down there*? Your mini hair?'

'Yes.'

'Gosh! You mean you're . . .'

'Yes, there's not a hair in sight!'

'Golly! May I see?'

'Hilly, don't be so dreadful!'

'Oh, please, Candy! Just a little peek.'

'Well, all right – just a quick peek, then. The doctor

wants to see me every evening for at least a week, but I'm not going back.'

'And I don't jolly well blame you!'

Standing and pulling her gymslip up, Candida tugged her knickers down, revealing her hairless pussy to Hilda. Gazing in wonderment at her friend's smooth, pouting outer lips, Hilda tentatively reached out, stroking the soft sex hillocks with her fingertips.

'Hilly! Rule Fifteen, remember?' Candida exclaimed as she pushed Hilda's hand away and tugged her knickers up, covering her youthful crack.

'Oh, yes – Rule Fifteen. Sorry, I forgot about that. Gosh, Candy, you do look jolly queer like that! What does it feel like?'

'Sort of nice, I suppose. It feels smooth against my knickers. Yes, it's quite a nice feeling.'

'We're being awfully rude, talking about our minis like this!'

'I know we are! It's terribly exciting, isn't it, Hilly?'

'Yes, it is! Where did you get to last night? I had to endure those awful beasts, Maxine and Ginger.'

'I was chatting with some girls in the library. We went to see the fire damage. What happened to you? Did they, you know . . . did they do anything to you?'

'Yes, they jolly well did! They used a . . . Never mind what they did. I missed you last night, Candy. It was our first night back at school and I wanted to be with you.'

'I'm sorry, but I lost track of the time. Do you think Rule Fifteen is a good idea? I mean, it's a bit of a stiff one to keep, isn't it?'

'I say we abolish it!'

'The thing is, Hilly, there's only the two of us here. If Patsy was here, we'd have a quorum so we could . . .'

'Actually, Patsy and the others don't know about Rule Fifteen, so it isn't really a rule, is it?'

'No, it's not!' Candida squealed. 'Do you want to see my mini again, Hilly?'

'Do you think I should? I mean, it's terribly rude showing . . .'

'It's *very* rude! But I want to show you because . . . well, because I like showing you. I like you looking at my mini.'

Slipping her knickers down again, Candida reclined on the grass, her naked pussy slit blatantly exhibited before her friend's sparkling eyes. Parting her legs as Hilda stroked her soft vaginal lips, the girl sighed.

'Mmm, that's nice. I like you rubbing me.'

'And I like rubbing you, Candy. We should have done this last term.'

'Yes, we jolly well should have. I used to think about it, but I couldn't bring myself to talk to you about it.'

'I used to think about it, too! We are silly, not talking to each other about rubbing our mini cracks!'

'Ah, that's nice, Hilly! Do it a little harder, and faster!'

'Gosh, your clitty's so hard! It's like a pebble!'

'Oh, oh! Ah, yes, it is! Rub it faster!'

The birds singing, the early morning sun streaming through the trees, warming Candida's naked mound, the girls revelled in their new lesbian games. They had Maxine to thank, Hilda mused as she leaned over and licked her friend's cunny crack. Maxine didn't realize it, but she'd done them a favour – woken their latent lesbian desires.

'Ah, that's so good!' Candida gasped as Hilda parted her fleshy vaginal lips and sucked her clitoris. 'When you did this to me in the shed, it made me quiver all over! I'd never had anyone do this to me before yesterday.'

'And I'd never done it to anyone before yesterday! Will you lick my mini afterwards?'

'Yes, I jolly well will!'

Pressing on the soft flesh surrounding her friend's swollen clitoris, Hilda popped out the entire length of her pleasure-budling, exposing the sensitive tip to her probing tongue. Breathing in Candida's heady pussy-scent as she sensed her own clitoris swell, Hilda slipped two fingers between the girl's pouting vaginal lips and drove them deep into her tight love hole.

'Ah, the goodie, it's coming!' Candida shrilled. 'Ah, Hilly, that's lovely, don't stop! Ah, here it comes, coming, coming! Keep . . . Yes, finger me harder! More fingers, more fingers! Lick me all over!'

Thrusting with three fingers, Hilda sucked Candida's pulsating clitoris into her wet mouth and brought out the girl's orgasm. Arching her back, her smooth stomach rhythmically rising and falling, Candida looked up to the trees, crying out as wave after wave of orgasmic pleasure rolled through her quivering young body. Unbuttoning her blouse as she rode her climax, she lifted her bra clear of her firm young breasts and pinched her erect nipples, enhancing the incredible sensations emanating from her throbbing clitoris.

'I'm done!' Candida finally gasped. 'Oh, Hilly, please, do it slowly now, do it very gently – I'm done!'

'Gosh, Candy! You taste scrumptious!' Hilda cried, slipping her wet fingers from the girl's drenched hole and lapping up her vaginal cream.

'Mmm, that's nice! I like your tongue there. Ah, yes,

that's so nice! Push your tongue inside me. Lick . . . Oh, yes – lick inside my mini!'

Complying with the gasped request, Hilda peeled her friend's ripening lips wide apart, driving her tongue deep into her hot vaginal tube, lapping up her flowing honeydew. 'Mmm, that's lovely!' Candida breathed as her clitoris swelled again. 'I want to have a goodie again, but it's your turn, Hilly.'

'Yes, do it to me now!' Hilda squealed excitedly as she sat up and slipped her knickers off. 'Gosh, you've got lovely pears!' she added, eyeing her friend's firm breasts, her long, erect nipples. 'I'll kiss them afterwards!' she giggled as she reclined on the grass and parted her shapely thighs.

Closing her blue eyes as Candida stretched open her pussy lips and lapped her creamy sex-groove, Hilda sighed. 'Oh, golly, that's so nice!' The sensations building, she shuddered as she unbuttoned her blouse and pulled her bra away from her rounded breasts. Tweaking her nipples as Candida had done, she gasped. 'Oh, Candy! Oh, that's incredibly good!' Slipping a finger into the girl's drenched love duct, Candida began thrusting. 'Yes, fingers, more fingers!' Hilda pleaded. 'Oh, yes! More fingers!'

Opening her legs further, Hilda offered her girlhood completely to her young friend, delighting at the thought of another girl's tongue running up her crack, teasing her clitoris, her fingers excavating deep into her tight pussy hole. Positioning herself over Hilda's body with her gaping cunny over the girl's face, Candida buried her head between Hilda's thighs and resumed her cunny licking.

'Gosh, Candy!' Hilda cried as she gazed at the girl's

yawning crack hovering only inches above her pretty face. 'Gosh, this is terribly rude of us – but you do look nice like that! I've never seen anything so naughty! Golly, just look at all your cream pouring out!'

'Can you see my bottom-hole?' Candida panted, swivelling her hips.

'Yes, I can!' Hilda gasped, pulling her friend down and pushing her tongue into her tight vagina.

Licking, slurping, lapping up each other's juices of arousal, the girls reached their shuddering climaxes. Locked in their new-found lesbian coupling, they didn't hear the cracking of twigs as someone approached the clearing. 'Gosh! What are you two up to?' Patsy screeched as she emerged from the bushes and gazed in horror at her friends.

'Oh, er . . . Patsy, we were just . . .' Hilda began, her face flushing as Candida rolled off her trembling body.

'You *are* rude!' Patsy cried, gazing at the girl-come oozing from Candida's hairless pussy slit. 'I didn't know that you were both . . .'

'We were only playing around!' Candida protested. 'We weren't doing anything rude!'

'Yes, you were! You were kissing each other's angels!'

'You won't tell anyone will you, Patsy?' Hilda asked bashfully as she slipped her knickers up her long legs.

'No, I won't. But I still say you're both awfully rude! What have you done to your angel, Candida? Where's your hair gone?'

'The doctor did it. I have something wrong and he put some cream on me to get rid of the hair.'

'Crumbs! Fancy having no angel hair!' the girl giggled, holding her hand to her delectable mouth.

'We'd better be going or we'll miss breakfast,' Hilda

sighed, turning to Patsy. 'You can play the game with us later, if you want to,' she invited coyly.

'What, angel kissing?'

'Yes, if you want to.'

'Gosh, Hilly! I don't know whether I should. I mean, it's dreadfully naughty, isn't it? Licking each other's angel cracks is terribly wicked!'

'Yes, I know, but it's spiffing fun!'

'I might play later, I don't know. Come on, let's go – I'm famished!'

'Is it really that bad, Headmistress?' Miss Frigidus asked as she walked to the study window.

'It's worse! Financially, the school is in ruins!'

'Oh dear! What will happen to the girls?' Miss Blob asked.

'Goodness knows! We can't put the fees up again, the parents wouldn't wear it.'

'What about selling something?' Miss Frigidus suggested, turning to face the Head.

'Like what?'

'I don't know, there must be something we can sell. Perhaps we should pray?'

'We could sell a few girls,' Miss Blob suggested pensively.

'Sell a few girls? We can't sell the girls! Who would buy them, anyway?' Miss Gussetpiece asked surprisedly.

'Er . . . Well, I know a man who . . .'

'A man? Sell a few girls to a man? That's indecent, surely? How would the Pope respond to such a wicked idea?'

'He wouldn't know about it. Why not sell a few

girls? Say, half a dozen or so, just to bump up the bank balance a bit.'

'Oh, dear! What about the parents?' Miss Frigidus broke in.

'We can't sell the parents!' Miss Blob returned. 'He only likes fresh young . . .'

'No, I mean, the parents would wonder where their daughters had got to. How ever would we explain their disappearance?'

'A cover up. We could say that the girls ran away.'

'Who is this man?' Miss Gussetpiece asked, pouring a large gin. 'What's his name?'

'Er . . . I met him in London at a . . . well, at a meeting place,' Miss Blob replied hesitantly.

'A meeting place?'

'Yes, a sort of secret club where like-minded men meet.'

'Like-minded men? What were you doing in such a place, Miss Blob? It's unhealthy to hang around such places!'

'Er . . . Women meet there, too. Anyway, this man, he runs a model agency, of sorts. His name's, er . . . his name's Ivor Fetish.'

'Ivor Fetish? No, no, no – we can't sell the girls! It's ungodly!' Miss Gussetpiece returned as she downed her gin. Rubbing her chin and frowning, she gazed at Miss Blob. 'Just out of interest, how much would he pay?'

'Somewhere in the region of a couple of thousand per girl, I would imagine.'

'Excuse me, Headmistress,' Madame Fissure interrupted as she popped her head round the study door. 'There's a man here to see you. He's a priest.'

'A priest? Oh, well, you'd better send him in.'

Girl School

As the teachers left the study, Miss Gussetpiece sat at her desk and poured herself a quadruple gin. 'What would a priest be wanting with me?' she sighed, sipping her drink. *Ten girls – twenty thousand pounds!* 'A priest? Stone the crows! I could be struck down!'

'This is Father Sadcase, Miss Gussetpiece,' Madame Fissure announced as she showed the priest into the study.

'Good morning, Father,' the headmistress greeted the cleric, rising to her feet. 'Oh, Madame Fissure – will you send Maxine Mayhem to see me, please?'

'Certainly, Headmistress.'

'Now then, Father, what can I do for you?'

'Good morning, Miss Gussetpiece. I've come to your fine school to ask whether you would consider me taking the girls for confession.'

'Confession? Why, what on earth have they done?'

'Who?'

'The girls – have they sinned?'

'We're all sinners, Headmistress.'

'What are you implying?'

'Nothing!'

'Yes, you were! You were implying that I'm a sinner! What do you know of my sordid past? Er . . . I mean . . .'

'We're *all* sinners.'

'Speak for yourself, Father!'

'I speak for all God's children.'

'What *are* you talking about? Anyway, we have our own chaplain, padre, or whatever he is. Wait a minute! Don't I know you from somewhere?'

'No, Headmistress, you don't.'

'Weren't you a cleaner here?'

'A cleaner? No, never!'

'Yes, you were! Jesus! You were sent to prison for gross indecency in the lavatories! I remember it well!'

'No, I wasn't! You're mistaking me for someone else! Mistaken identity, that's what it is!'

'Well, you look awfully like the cleaner! Which church do you come from?'

'Dartmoor . . . I mean – Christ the King's Church.'

'You shouldn't take Christ's name in vain!'

'You just did.'

'That's different, I'm the Headmistress.'

'I didn't mean Christ, as in Jesus bloody Christ!'

'Father!'

'Oh, er, I'm sorry. It's the name of the church – Christ the King's Church.'

'Oh, I see. And you've come all the way from Dartmoor?'

'Yes. Er . . . No, no.'

'That's where the cleaner was sent for committing his vile crime – to Dartmoor Prison.'

'Oh, was he? It's a small world.'

'The resemblance is remarkable!'

'Er . . . Yes, well, I'll be going, Miss Gussetpiece. Would you direct me to the laundry room, please?'

'The laundry room? Why do you want to go there?'

'I know the washerwoman of old. She was a friend of my mother's, I just thought I'd look in on her.'

'Oh, right. Down the corridor and turn left. You can't miss it.'

'Thank you, Headmistress. Goodbye.'

'Goodbye, Father.'

Contemplating at her desk as the man left her study, Miss Gussetpiece frowned. 'We haven't got a washer woman! The girls do their own washing!'

'You sent for me, Miss Gussetpiece,' Maxine smiled as she approached the Head's desk.

'Did I?'

'Didn't you?'

'Didn't I what?'

'Send for me.'

'Oh, so I did! I wonder why? Ah yes, Maxine, sit down, girl. Now, something's gone missing from my study. A laundry basket full of . . . well, a laundry basket. Do you know anything about it?'

'No, Miss Gussetpiece, I don't.'

'I thought you'd say that.'

'Say what?'

'I don't.'

'Don't you?'

'Don't I what? What *are* you talking about, girl?'

'I don't know, Miss Gussetpiece.'

'Neither do I! So, you haven't seen the laundry basket?'

'No. Have you tried the laundry room, Miss Gussetpiece? I mean, someone might have returned the basket to the . . .'

'No, I haven't, Maxine. I don't suppose you know anything about the fire in the library, either?'

'I'm afraid not, Miss Gussetpiece.'

'How are you getting on with your school work, Maxine?'

'Very well, Miss Gussetpiece. I'm enjoying the work very much.'

'I'm pleased to hear it. Now that you're in the last term of the sixth form, I hope you've mended your ways.'

'Oh, yes, Miss Gussetpiece, I have! I intend to work very hard this term.'

'That's good to hear! All right, you may go, Maxine.'

Staggering down the corridor to the laundry room, Miss Gussetpiece was sure that the basket of contraband wouldn't be there. *I suppose I'd better check*, she thought as she opened the door and went in. 'Oh, Father Sadcase!' she gasped, discovering the man with a pair of navy-blue knickers pulled over his head, the stained crotch covering his face. 'What *are* you doing?'

'Oh, I, er . . . I was just trying out this balaclava, Headmistress,' he replied, slipping the garment from his head. 'I thought there might be some rain later, so . . .'

'That's a pair of knickers, Father – not a balaclava!'

'Knickers? Oh dear, I didn't realize! I thought the eyeholes were rather large!'

'And what's that other pair doing in your hand? What's all that white stuff dripping from them?'

'That's . . . that's . . . I don't know what it is. I'll be going, then. Er . . . Goodbye!' he called, clutching the knickers as he bolted through the door and sprinted down the corridor.

'What a strange man!' Miss Gussetpiece gasped as she scanned the room for her drink and cigarettes. 'I really can't be doing with all this nonsense! Now, where on earth are my goodies?'

'Ah, there you are! Good morning, Headmistress,' Doctor Pouch smiled as he entered the room. 'I was wondering when you'd like me to begin examining the pretty little girlies? I mean, the girls.'

'Good morning, Doctor Pouch.'

'Please, do call me Uterine.'

'Er . . . yes. Well, Uterine . . . You do have a most unusual Christian name.'

'It is somewhat unique, I agree. Loosely translated

from old Latin it means *home of the rampant tadpole.*'

'How strange! One lives and learns, Uterine – one lives and learns. Well, you can begin the examinations whenever you wish.'

'Oh, good! Do you have a room I could use? Preferably a room where no one can spy on me and . . . I mean, a private room, with a lock on the door.'

'You can use Sick Bay. Actually, Uterine, I have a slight problem in a certain unmentionable area. I wonder whether you'd be good enough to examine me?'

'Examine *you*? God forbid! Oh, I mean, yes, I suppose so.'

'If I have time, I'll come along after you've examined the girls. Now, you'll find Sick Bay at the far end of the corridor. Just keep walking, you can't miss it.'

'Right. So, the girls . . . When can I get my hands on the little . . . What I mean is, when will the first batch arrive?'

'Class by class, I think. Yes, I'll send the first class to you after assembly, in about half an hour.'

'Jolly good! Well, I'll go and get my KY . . . I'll prepare my instruments. Er . . . I'll talk to you later, Miss Gussetpiece.'

'Talking of assembly, I'd better make a move. Yes, I'll see you later, Doctor.'

Presiding on the school stage, Miss Gussetpiece adjusted the microphone for morning assembly. 'Good morning girls,' she slurred, clinging to the microphone stand for support as the gin took effect.

'Good morning, Miss Gussetpiece!' the girls droned in unison.

'You may be seated. Now, before we begin, there are one or two things I'd like to say. Er . . . What were they? Oh, yes. Firstly, the fire in the library last night was obviously started deliberately. I will not tolerate arseholes! I mean, arson. The girl who started the fire will be expelled when I've discovered who she is. And believe me, I *will* discover her identity! Thirdly . . . Secondly, and this only applies to the Upper Sixth, Doctor Uterine Pouch, Miss Blob's brother, has kindly offered to offer you prophylactic examination in an area where you may otherwise be too embarrassed to see your own practitioners. Class 6A will form an orderly queue outside Sick Bay immediately after assembly. The examinations will be of a gynaecol . . . gyna . . . The examinations will be of an intimate nature, just to ensure that everything's in order. Lastly, I have some sad news. The school is losing mon . . . Financially, we're in the tish. As yet, I don't know what will happen but, hopefully, God will come to our rescue. I'll be writing to your parents to explain the situation in due course, humbly asking for donations. And now for our first hymn. Hymn number 232 – May God Help Us.'

Sneaking out of assembly, Maxine turned to Ginger. 'What sort of name is Uterine Pouch?'

'A fucking stupid name!'

'What the fuck do we want a doctor fiddling with our cunts for? I'm not going!'

'Let's go, Max!' Ginger urged as they crossed the yard to the gardener's potting shed. 'It'll be a laugh! We'll embarrass the old fart!'

'Yes, that's a good idea! Come on, let's have a drink and a fag.'

Kicking the shed door open, Maxine leered at the gardener. 'What the fuck are you doing here?' she sneered.

'I work 'ere, Miss! I'm pottin' on me geraniums.'

'Well, go and pot on your pansies!'

'I can't do that, Miss! I see you've taken the stuff away.'

'What? Shit! Where the fuck's it gone?'

'Don't know, Miss. When I saw the basket 'ad gone, I thought you must 'ave cleared the stuff out.'

'You've taken it, haven't you, you old git?'

'No, I ain't!'

'Tell us where it is or I'll chew your fucking knob off!' Ginger threatened, grabbing the old man's crotch as Maxine slipped her knickers down and kicked them across the floor.

Gazing in amazement as Maxine tore the front of her blouse open, the gardener frowned. 'What you doin', Miss?' he asked as she ripped her gymslip off, tearing the garment in two before tossing it onto the sofa. Yanking her torn blouse off and kicking it across the floor, she unclipped her bra and stood naked before the stunned man.

'You'd like to finger my cunt, wouldn't you?' she asked, running her hands up her inner thighs.

'Well, I . . .'

'Of course you'd like to! Go on, shove your fingers up my cunt!'

'Me 'ands are covered in mud, Miss!'

'Yes, so I'd noticed. Now, kneel down and finger my cunt!'

Dropping to his knees as Ginger released his crotch, the old man parted Maxine's swollen pussy lips. 'You're a pretty little thing!' he chuckled as he slipped his muddy fingers into her tight vagina. 'Do you know, I ain't done nothin' like this in years?'

'Shut up and finger me!' Maxine ordered, winking at Ginger.

'I'm makin' you all muddy, Miss. You sure you don't mind?'

'I don't mind at all! That's it, that's good, shove your fingers right up my cunt!' Maxine ordered crudely as Ginger slipped out of the shed.

Cunny juice flowing down his muddy fingers, the gardener kissed Maxine's pussy slit, lapping at her clitoris as she stretched her crack wide open. 'I ain't tasted fanny juice in years!' he murmured, licking her inner folds. 'You don't arf taste good!'

'I'll sit on the sofa and you can give my cunt a good licking out,' the dark temptress grinned, squeezing the old man's fingers in place as she sat on the cushion and reclined. 'There, now really give me a good seeing-to!'

Relaxing as the gardener green-fingered her irrigating vulva and tongue-tended her flowering cherry, Maxine fondled her firm breasts. Twisting her chocolate-brown buds, she opened her legs wider, moving her hips forward and grinding her open secret garden into the old man's face.

'That's good!' the girl gasped. 'Keep licking . . . keep licking my cunt and I'll come in your mouth! Afterwards, you can fuck me!'

'I'll fuck you now, Miss!' the old man chuckled, slipping his erect penis out and stabbing between the girl's drenched vaginal lips with his purple tool. 'Ah, you ain't arf tight!'

'Christ, and you ain't arf big!' Maxine reciprocated as

his massive shaft drove into her, stretching her young vagina to capacity.

Grabbing the girl's hips, the gardener made his fucking motions, driving his swollen tool deep into her fertile cunette and withdrawing again. On and on the gasping man thrust into the girl as she massaged her orgasm from her burgeoning cherry. Her face flushed, her torso quivering uncontrollably, she threw her head back, her eyes rolling as her climax lifted her from her perspiring body.

'Coming!' the gardener eventually spluttered, whipping his distended tool out. Wanking his prize pink courgette, he splattered his seed over the girl's glistening sex-bed, the plateau of her smooth stomach. Hearing movements outside the shed, Maxine began screaming and struggling as the old man brought out the last of his gushing sperm, splattering her soft mound.

'Jesus wept! What the hell's going on in here?' Miss Blob boomed as she grabbed the wilted gardener, dragging him away from Maxine's trembling body.

'He . . . he . . .' Maxine sobbed, gazing at the pool of fertilizer running over her stomach.

'I can see what he was doing! Are you all right, child?' Miss Blob rasped as Ginger entered the shed.

'Yes, Miss Blob, I'll be all right. He forced me to . . . Look, there's the mud and sperm all over my . . . That proves it, doesn't it?'

'Yes, it does! Ginger, take Maxine to her dormitory and look after her, will you? She's somewhat distressed after her terrible ordeal.'

'May I be excused lessons today, please, Miss Blob?' Maxine asked pitifully.

'Yes, of course. I'll clear it with the Head. But first, I'll deal with this disgusting creature!' she growled, dragging the cowering old man to his feet.

Slipping the gardener's coat over Maxine's naked body, Ginger led the sobbing girl out of the shed. Closing the door, Miss Blob turned to face the old man. 'So, that's the sort of thing you get up to, is it?' she boomed. 'Well, now we're equal!'

'Oh no, we ain't! You can't prove nothin'!' the old man returned, zipping his trousers.

'I'll call the police unless you . . .'

'All right, all right! I'll keep quiet if you do.'

'Good. You swear never to threaten me again, and I'll say nothing about this.'

'Agreed.'

'At last I've got something on you, you dirty old bugger! For years you've been calling me a sad pervert and threatening to tell the Head that I'm a man! But now I've got one over on you!'

'The girl won't say nothin', will she?'

'No, I'll see to it that this is covered up.'

'They set me up, I'll 'ave you know!'

'That doesn't surprise me! What were they hoping to gain, do you know?'

'They wanted me out of this place, I reckon. They wanted it for themselves.'

'I wonder why?'

'I got a bloody good idea, but I ain't tellin' you! Now bugger off out of 'ere and leave me in peace!'

'I will, don't you worry! I'm late enough for . . . for something, as it is! Don't you forget our deal!' Miss Blob growled as she left the shed and slammed the door shut.

Dashing into her rooms, Miss Blob cast off her clothes and grabbed a suit from the wardrobe. Donning a shirt and tie, the transvestite slipped the suit on and stood before the wardrobe mirror. 'Perfect!' he breathed. 'Doctor Uterine Pouch, I presume?' Grabbing his camera, he adjusted his tie and hurriedly left his rooms.

Racing down the corridor, he smiled at the queue of fresh-faced sixth-form girls waiting outside Sick Bay. 'The first girl, please,' he called, concealing the camera as he slipped into his consulting room. 'Go behind the curtain there and remove your clothes, Melinda,' he instructed the pretty brunette as she closed the door behind her.

'How do you know my name?' the girl asked surprisedly.

'Er . . . You were pointed out to me earlier. I have a lot of girls to examine, so remove your clothes, please.'

'What, *all* of them?' she asked, slipping through the curtain concealing the examination couch.

'Yes, all of them – and then lie on the couch, please. Call me when you're ready.'

Pacing the floor as he checked his camera, Dr Pouch felt his penis stiffen as he imagined examining one naked girl after another. *A dream come true!* he mused, wondering whether he could slip his knob between the girl's pussy lips without her realizing what he was up to. *God, I daren't!*

'I'm ready, Doctor!' the girl called. Stumbling through the curtain in his eagerness to get his hands on her naked body, he almost tripped over.

'Oh, er, sorry!' he grinned, gazing at her pert breasts as he fell against the couch. 'Now then, have you had any problems with your . . . down there, have you had any problems?'

'No, I haven't,' the girl replied, crossing her long

legs and covering her small breasts with her folded arms.

'Good, good. Now, I'll start with your breasts – check for abnormalities,' he smiled as he placed her arms by her sides. 'Relax completely and uncross your legs – there's nothing to worry about.'

Gazing at her shapely young body, her smooth, flat stomach, the gentle rise of her mound, her raven pubes, the doctor could scarcely restrain himself from slipping his penis out and begging her to suck his knob. *She's only the first of many!* he chuckled inwardly as his trembling hands neared her firm breasts. Squeezing her rounded mammary spheres, he tweaked her small nipples, twisting and pulling the brown protrusions. *If only she'd allow me to suck them*, he mused, running his fingertips around her darkening areolae.

Her nipples hardening, the girl closed her eyes and turned her head away. Was she enjoying the sensations? he wondered as he pinched her milk buds again. Eyeing her young vaginal cleft, he imagined licking her there, swallowing her flowing pussy cream as he massaged her clitoris to orgasm. *My best sham in years!* he exulted, moving his attention to the girl's tightly closed crack.

Tentatively parting her fleshy cunny lips, he gazed longingly at her pinken sex folds, the wet, inviting mouth of her tight love-tunnel. His trembling fingers opening her fissure further, he gasped as her erect clitoris appeared. 'Just relax,' he murmured, slipping a finger into her tight duct. Twisting and bending his finger, massaging the wet walls of her young vagina, he noticed her stomach rising and falling, her firm breasts heaving. *The time is ripe!* he decided, gently caressing her sex-cherry with his free hand.

Concealing her gasps as best she could, the girl began to tremble. Her clitoris now solid beneath the doctor's vibrating fingertip, her vagina drenched, she was close to her climax, he knew. What she would think of his unethical examination, he had no idea. Lost in his rising arousal, he didn't care as she began to gasp. Praying that he'd be able to masturbate each girl, bring them all to rousing orgasms, he quickened his rhythm.

'Oh, oh! Do you normally . . .' the girl whimpered as her climax welled.

'Just relax, my dear,' Dr Pouch replied, thrusting his fingers in and out of her spasming cuntal sheath and rubbing her clitoris faster. 'Just relax and let it come.'

'Oh, oh! You shouldn't be . . . Oh!'

Her body trembling uncontrollably as her orgasm erupted, the girl arched her back, crying out as her vagina rhythmically tightened and relaxed. Her firm breasts heaving, her areolae darkening like the sky before a storm, she tossed her head from side to side as the tumultuous orgasmic waves rolled through her naked body. As she finally relaxed, the doctor slipped his digits from her steaming vaginal volcano and licked them clean. *Sweet nectar!* he mused, sucking on his sticky fingers and grabbing his camera.

'Turn your head away and close your eyes, please. I'm just going to check you for vaginal tilt, and then you may dress,' he said, focusing his camera on the girl's engorged cuntal crater. Taking several shots of her young crack, he hid the camera behind his back and ordered her to dress as he slipped through the curtain.

Fully clothed, the girl finally emerged. Her face flushed, her hands still trembling, she stood before the doctor. 'Do you do that to all the girls you examine?' she asked.

'I have to check for clitoral response and vaginal reaction,' he explained. 'Will you send the next girl in, please?'

'Yes, doctor. So I'm all right then, am I?'

'You're beautiful! I mean, from a gynaecological point of view, you have a beautiful pelvic floor.'

'Oh, do I?'

'Indeed you do. Now, please ask the next little beaut—, ah, girl to come in.'

'Yes, doctor,' she smiled as she left the room.

Sifting through a pile of papers, Miss Gussetpiece looked up as Hilda knocked on the open study door. 'Oh, come in, Hilda,' she smiled.

'Thank you, Miss Gussetpiece. I was wondering whether you knew the whereabouts of Miss Blob. We're waiting for our geography lesson, but she hasn't turned up.'

'That's odd. Where on earth could she have got to? Give her another ten minutes, and if she doesn't surface you'd better have a free period.'

'Yes, Miss Gussetpiece. By the way, I've had an idea for raising money for the school. I thought we could hold a fête, and a jumble sale, and . . .'

'Now that *is* a good idea, Hilda!' Miss Gussetpiece beamed. 'Yes, I'm glad I thought of that!'

'But I thought of . . . I'll organize it for this Saturday, if you wish. I'll put a sign up in the village post office.'

'Yes, excellent! I'll leave it in your capable hands, Hilda. By the way, you haven't seen a laundry basket lurking anywhere, have you?'

'No, Miss Gussetpiece, I haven't.'

'That's a pity.'

'Why, have you lost one?'

'Er . . . yes, sort of.'

'The girls have been complaining about things going missing from their lockers, Miss Gussetpiece – I thought I'd better let you know.'

'Er . . . really? Well, it would seem that we have a thief in our midst, what with that *and* the laundry basket.'

'I can't imagine who would want to steal a laundry basket, Miss Gussetpiece.'

'Er . . . no, neither can I. A most unusual item to steal!'

'I'll send a posse out to search for it if you wish, Miss Gussetpiece.'

'Er . . . yes, yes all right, Hilda. Should you find the basket, then . . . well, come straight to me.'

'Yes, Miss Gussetpiece.'

'Right, off you go, girl.'

After a shower, Maxine dressed and made her way to Sick Bay with Ginger. Pushing their way to the front of the queue, Maxine grinned. 'I'm next!' she giggled, turning to Ginger. 'I'll have a laugh with this doctor! If he wants to examine my cunt . . .'

'Will the next girl come in, please?'

Striding into the room, Maxine posed with her hands on her hips and grinned at Doctor Pouch. 'Want me to strip off?' she asked, eyeing his bulging flies.

'Yes, behind the curtain, please,' he replied. 'Call me when you're ready.'

Formulating her plan as she slipped out of her clothes, Maxine lay down with her feet straddling the sides of the couch, her young pussy slit gaping. 'Ready when you are, Doctor!' she called. Stealing through the curtain, Doctor

Pouch gazed wonderstruck at the girl's open vaginal crack, her firm young breasts.

'Tell me, my dear, have you had any problems down there?' he asked, gazing at her protruding inner lips.

'Yes, Doctor, I have. When I masturbate, I pass out. I can't think why!'

'You pass out? That's interesting. Show me, show me how you masturbate and pass out.'

'I don't think I should masturbate in front of you, Doctor!'

'But you must! This is a serious problem, and you must allow me to help you!'

Parting her swollen pussy lips, Maxine began her gentle clitoral massaging. Breathing heavily as the doctor looked on in awe, she feigned unconsciousness, her hands falling limp by her sides as the doctor shook her shoulder. 'Incredible!' he breathed as he slipped his finger into her tight vaginal duct. 'What a stroke of luck!'

Leaning over her naked body, Doctor Pouch kissed the girl's soft mound. Slipping another finger into her tightening pussy, he parted her pouting cunny lips and licked her clitoris. 'Mmm, how I love young girls' cunts!' he murmured, caressing her stiffening bud with his rough tongue.

His debased desires getting the better of him, he slipped his trousers off and climbed onto the couch. Kneeling between Maxine's spread thighs, he positioned his solid knob between her open pussy lips. 'Ah, how sweet, young girls' cunts!' he gasped as he drove his bulbous cockhead into her snug sheath. 'God, how tight!'

Resting on his hands, he began his fucking motions, repeatedly driving his solid shaft deep into the girl's hot sex-tube. Sucking on her erect nipples, he rammed his penis into her, jolting her young body with every hammering thrust. His orgasm quickly approaching as he quickened his illicit fucking, he grimaced. 'Ah, God!' he cried as his sperm jetted from his throbbing knob, filling his patient's spasming cuntal duct. 'Ah, God, you're so . . . so tight!'

Concealing a grin, Maxine suddenly lifted her naked body, resting on her elbows as she screamed in feigned horror. 'What are you doing to me?' she cried, watching the doctor's wet shaft drive between her swollen pussy lips, impaling her young body. Quickly slipping his penis out, his sperm flying through the air to anoint her smooth belly, he leapt from the couch.

Hurriedly tugging his trousers up his legs, his face flushed, he buckled his belt and began his stammered explanation. 'I . . . I, er . . . I was making sure that . . .'

'You were fucking me!' Maxine cried as she slipped off the couch. 'Look, there's spunk running all over my cunt lips! You were fucking my cunt!'

'I was only . . .'

'I'll report you for this! Wait a minute, you look remarkably like your sister! You're the same person, aren't you?'

'No, no!'

'Yes, you are! So, the rumours were true! You're a transvestite!'

'No, please, I . . .'

'Kneel before me and lick your spunk from my cunt! I've got you now, Miss fucking Blob! You're a fucking pervert posing as a geography mistress! Things are going to be very different now, Miss Blob! You're going to be my slave! Go on, lick your spunk up!'

Lapping the sperm from Maxine's soft mound, her

smooth belly, her inner thighs, Doctor Pouch cleansed her young body. He was at the girl's mercy, he knew as he licked the entire length of her tight slit and swallowed his own sperm. She'd make his life hell now!

'That's enough, slave!' Maxine ordered. 'Now, you may dress me. Go on, take my things and dress me!'

'Maxine, I . . . We can come to an amicable arrangement, can't we?'

'Arrangement? What sort of arrangement?'

'Well, if you keep quiet, then I'll . . .'

'You'll do nothing! I'll call the shots! You'll do as I say, when I say! You'll be at my beck and call! You'll pleasure me, masturbate me on demand – that's the deal, OK?'

'Yes, yes, I suppose so,' the pervert mumbled, kneeling before his mistress as she stepped into her knickers.

Dressing the girl, Doctor Pouch remained silent, wondering how to get out of the incredible situation. She'd set him up, he knew only too well as she tugged her knickers up her long legs and covered her treacherous pussy crack. Having shut the gardener up, he'd thought his terrible secret was safe. But now . . .

'OK,' Maxine declared as he finished dressing her. 'I've got one over you, and that sad old git of a gardener, so I'm going to have some real fun! This evening, you'll go into the trees by the edge of the playing field. There's a clearing there. I'll be waiting for you at seven, OK?'

'Yes, I'll be there,' he replied dolefully.

'Good. Now you can get on with your so-called examinations, you sad pervy!'

Leaving the room, Maxine grabbed Ginger's arm and marched her down the corridor. 'Have I got news for you!' she giggled as they crossed the yard to the potting shed. 'Miss Blob's a man!'

'Really?'

'Yes, he's posing as a doctor so that he can get his hands on the girls' cunts!'

'Fuck me! Are we going to grass him up?'

'No way! We've got him over a fucking barrel! We'll use the sad pervert, have some fun with his dick. But first, I want to get the booze and fags back. Now, we'll start by searching the woods. Whoever found the stuff wouldn't hide it in the school, so we'll start with the woods.'

Sitting in the clearing with Candida and Patsy, Hilda smiled. 'We've got to find the laundry basket,' she began, scribbling on her note pad. 'And then we'll organize the first fête. We'll advertise in the local post office. We'll have stalls with cakes and things, a lucky dip and . . . Every weekend, we'll have something going on – jumble sales, fêtes, coffee mornings . . .'

'Hilda,' Patsy began pensively. 'You know the games you were playing with Candy? Well, I've decided that I'd like to play, too.'

'Oh, Patsy, you are awful!' Hilda laughed. 'Here we are, planning money-raising schemes, and you want to play mini-licking!'

'So do I!' Candida giggled. 'It's such a glorious day, let's take all our clothes off and be jolly rude!'

'Candy!' Hilda gasped. 'We can't take *all* our clothes off! What if someone caught us?'

'No one will find us here. It's so hot today, I'd love to take my clothes off. Besides, I want to see Patsy's pears. They're so big!'

'Would you, Candy? Would you really like to see my pears?' Patsy giggled excitedly.

'Oh, yes!'

'All right, then,' Hilda conceded. 'We'll take all our clothes off. I did want to get things planned, but I suppose playing with each other's minis is more fun. Come on, let's jolly well strip off!'

Chapter Four

'There's a revolution in the air, Headmistress!' Miss Blob warned. 'Unless you expel Maxine Mayhem, the very infrastructure of the school will crumble!'

'A revolution? Infrastructure? What *are* you talking about, Miss Blob? Have you been drinking?'

'No, of course I haven't!'

'Jesus, I have! Er . . . Now, what's all this about?'

'I happened to overhear Maxine and her friend, Ginger. They were planning a revolution, Headmistress. They're planning the ruination of Bellend – as we speak! Do you know, they have lesbian sex sessions in their dormitory?'

'They have what?'

'Lesbian sex sessions.'

'Bellend girls don't have . . . Are you feeling ill, Miss Blob? You look awfully pale.'

'I do feel a little queer. But I'm telling you, Miss Gussetpiece – unless you act now, Maxine will bring the school down!'

'Well, I really don't know what to say! What are her plans, do you know?'

'They're going to start spreading rumours about the staff. I overheard Maxine telling her friend that she's going to spread a malicious lie concerning me. She's going to tell people that I'm a transvestite!'

'That you have a tight vest?'

'No! A transvestite. You know, a man who enjoys dressing up in women's clothes. A man who gets a sexual kick from wearing fishnet stockings and a suspender belt and tight silk panties and six-inch, red stilettoes and . . . er . . . Oh, what am I saying? They're going to put it about that I'm a man in drag!'

'Goodness me! This is dreadful! You poor badly-done-by woman!'

'I *am* rather distressed by the whole affair, I must confess.'

'If only all the girls were like Hilda Hillock,' Miss Gussetpiece sighed as she swigged from the depleting vodka bottle. 'Hilda's such a lovely girl, don't you agree?'

'Yes, I do. And her friend Candida is a right little . . . I mean, she's lovely, too.'

'Spies, Miss Blob!'

'Jesus! Where?'

'No! What I mean is, we'll send spies out to the front to gather information!'

'The front, Headmistress?'

'The front line, Miss Blob! This is war!'

'War? Who's the enemy?'

'The revolutionaries, Miss Blob – the Bellend Rebels!'

'I might be able to help you, Headmistress. I . . . Well, I know someone who's rather well in with Maxine. I'll get him to . . . I mean, I'll get *her* to gather intelligence.'

'An excellent idea! By the way, where were you this morning? You didn't take your class, they were waiting for you.'

'Take them? Where should I have taken them to?'

'Where do you normally take them?'

'Well, I take some of the girls to my rooms at night and . . . No, no, I don't!'

'You didn't teach your class, Miss Blob!'

'Teach them what?'

'Geography.'

'I've been teaching them geography on a regular basis for . . .'

'No, what I mean is – you didn't teach them this morning!'

'Didn't I? Oh, yes, I . . . I was feeling ill. I'm sorry, Headmistress.'

'And you're not feeling any better?'

'No, not really. I think it's my internals – my womb. If you don't mind, I'll take the rest of the day off to mast—, I mean, to recuperate.'

'Yes, of course, Miss Blob. Go and have a rest. Oh, if you see your brother, would you send him to me, please?'

'Yes, I will. I think he's taking a break from the gynaecological examinations so I'll ask him to come and see you straight away. By the way, I have another brother who's a rectal specialist. It might be an idea to have him check the girls on a regular basis.'

'You have quite a notable family, Miss Blob! I think it's an admirable idea, although we couldn't afford to pay him. What's his name?'

'Er . . . Doctor Anusis Rectus – he's of Latin extraction.'

'Latin? But your other brother is Polish, you're British, and he's . . .'

'Yes, my mother travelled a great deal. She was a corsetière.'

'Oh, I see. Yes, well, go ahead, Miss Blob. It's an

admirable idea! Oh, by the way, the police rang me this morning – there's a sexual pervert on the loose. He's been going around girls' schools posing as anything from a nun to a priest.'

'Really? My goodness, there *are* some mentally deranged people around!'

'Indeed there are! Anyway, keep your eyes open.'

'I am, Headmistress.'

'What?'

'Keeping my eyes open. Although I'm not feeling too well, I'm not tired.'

'No, you silly woman! I mean, keep your eyes open for perverted priests and nuns! We don't want perverts lurking around our school – it wouldn't look good. Now, I must phone the off-licence and order some more . . . I mean . . . Right, that will be all, Miss Blob, thank you.'

'I'll talk with you later, Headmistress.'

Creeping into the woods, Maxine grabbed Ginger. 'Did you hear that?' she whispered.

'Yes, it came from that direction.'

'That's not the way to the clearing, is it?'

'No, it's not. Come on, let's go!'

Peering through the bushes, the two girls gasped to behold young Fräulein Vulvahausen. Sitting on a log swigging from a vodka bottle, the German mistress was obviously drunk.

'I wonder where she got the bottle from?' Ginger whispered.

'That's exactly what I'm wondering! Come on, let's ask her.'

'We can't just go up to her and . . .'

'She's pissed, right? We'll threaten to tell Knicker-gusset unless she . . . Shush, someone's coming!'

Keeping their heads low, the girls watched in amazement as Dan emerged from the bushes and perched on the log alongside the succulent German morsel. 'Sorry I'm late, Gilda,' he smiled apologetically. 'I couldn't get away any earlier.'

'Never to vorry,' the woman slurred as she passed him the bottle. 'Here, have a drinken before ve fucken.'

'Thanks. Are you going to do one of your striptease acts for me?'

'Ja, ja!' the imported sex-doll drooled as she staggered to her feet, her long blonde hair covering her pretty face. 'There's nothing better than having a young man vatch me strippen! Jesus Christus, I'm completely fucking plastered!'

'I can see that! What a find, though! All that booze! We've enough stashed away in the basement to keep us going for months!'

'Yes, ve bloody have! Right, I'll do my act vith dee bottle for you and then you can give me a good spanken!'

Stunned, the two girls watched as the voluptuous Fräulein Vulvahausen unbuttoned her blouse. 'At least we now know where the gear is,' Maxine whispered.

'Yes, but can you believe this? Fuck me, we discover that Miss Blob's a man, and now we find out that Desperate Dan's giving it to old Frankfurter!'

'Christ, look at her tits! They're enormous!' Maxine gasped.

'Have you ever seen such whoppers?'

'Fuck me, her nipples are like miniature pricks! I'll tell you what we'll do – when they're humping each other, we'll leap out of the bushes. We've already got the gardener and old Blob under our thumbs. If we can nobble Frankfurter, too, we'll be well on top.'

'Brilliant, Max! God, my knickers are wet!'

'And mine! We'll get Dan to give us one later.'

Slipping her skirt down, Fräulein Vulvahausen staggered around trying to pull her red panties off. Falling to the ground in a fit of laughter, she managed to tug the silky garment down her shapely legs. 'Give me dee bottle!' she giggled, squatting on the grass, her plump vaginal lips pouting beneath her naked body. Passing the woman the empty vodka bottle, Dan sat down, rolling a joint as he watched her present the thick end of the bottle to her vaginal opening.

Lowering her body, gently easing the bottle into her sex entrance, Gilda shuddered with delight. Gasping as they watched the lewd spectacle, the girls clung to each other in disbelief. 'Would you credit it?' Maxine breathed.

'If I hadn't seen it with my own eyes . . . Christ, we'll have to try that! Look, it's almost disappeared up her cunt!'

'We'd never manage that! Fuck me, she must be slack!'

Bouncing up and down on the bottle, Fräulein Vulvahausen gasped with pleasure as her pussy spasmed and gripped the massive phallus. 'Shitenhausen, I vish it vas bigger!' she cried as she threw her head back and bounced faster.

'Christ, you couldn't take anything bigger!' Dan gasped.

'You'd better believe it, baby!' she panted as she lay back on the grass. 'Vell, my arsen or my cunten, vich is it to be?'

'Get on all fours and stick your bum out!' Dan chuckled as he slipped his solid penis out.

'Der Hund? You like dee doggie?' shrieked the German mistress in delight as, holding the bottle in place, she took up her position. As Dan's huge knob slipped between her ample buttocks and drove deep into her hot bowels, she began thrusting the bottle in and out of her bloated pussy sheath. 'Ja, ja, dat good!' she cried as Dan seized her hips and launched his torpedo into her anal tube. 'Give me a good bum fucken!'

Ramming his cocklength deep into her rectal barrel, Dan grimaced. 'Coming!' he gasped, his belly smacking her bucking buttocks as he thrust his weapon in to the hilt. 'Ah, coming up your arse!'

'Vunderbar, vunderbar!'

Leaping from the bushes, the girls screamed in feigned horror. 'Oh, Fräulein Vulvahausen!' Maxine gasped. 'What are you doing?'

'Er . . . Ah! Ah! Oh, mein Gott!' the trembling woman stammered, still on all fours like a laid bitch as Dan quickly slipped his knob out and showered her hindquarters with his spunk. 'Er . . . Vot are you two doing here?' she spluttered as she rolled onto her back and slipped the bottle from her sopping cavern.

'Fräulein Vulvahausen, what were you doing with that bottle?' Ginger gasped. 'Does Miss Gussetpiece know about this?'

'Er . . . Nein, nein! And if you tell her, I'll . . .' the woman began as she hurriedly dressed.

'You'll what?' Maxine grinned as Dan zipped up his jeans and made a run for it.

'I vill . . . Don't you threaten me, Maxine Mayhem!'

'Threaten you? We wouldn't do that would we, Ginger?'

'No, not if we get good reports, we wouldn't.'

'Return to dee school, both of you!' the fucked fräulein bellowed. 'How dare you intimidate me! Besides, it's your vord against mine and I rather suspect that Miss Gussetpiece vould believe me, don't you?'

'Yes, Fräulein Vulvahausen,' Maxine assented miserably as she wandered off. *But next time, I'll bring a Polaroid!*

'I say, Patsy, I've never seen such big ones!' Hilda gasped as the girl unclipped her bra and released her substantial breasts. 'Golly, compared to our little pears, they're like melons!' she added, gazing first at Candida's bumps and then her own.

'Crikey, Patsy!' Candida squealed. 'May I squeeze them?'

'Yes, if you want to,' Patsy replied as she reclined on the grass. 'You can both suck my nippies, if you want to.'

'Oh, yes!' Hilda giggled. 'I'd like to suck them! Aren't we terribly rude taking all our clothes off?'

'Yes, we jolly well are!'

Settling either side of their friend, Hilda and Candida each took a nipple into their hot mouths and gently sucked. Running their hands over Patsy's naked body, caressing her mound, her luxuriant vaginal lips, they lost themselves in their lesbian games. Panting as fingers massaged her clitoris, her sensitive inner flesh, Patsy began to tremble. 'Crumbs!' she breathed. 'I've never felt so . . . Oh, oh! That's nice! Yes, rub me just there!'

'I'll do better than that!' Hilda giggled, parting the girl's ample pussy lips. 'I'll lick your little spot for you!'

Slipping a finger deep into Patsy's tight vagina, Hilda fervently lapped at her pinken slit and sucked on her pulsating clitoris. Shuddering as Candida sucked each nipple in turn, the girl began to whimper as her climax rose from her contracting womb. 'Oh, oh! Oh, my clitty! My angel! I've never . . . Ah, the feeling's coming!'

Her orgasmic cries reverberating through the trees, the girl reached her climax. Her naked body shaking violently, her legs spread wide, her ample breasts heaving, never had she experienced such incredible sexual pleasure. Female mouths and fingers attending her most private places, she arched her back, grinding her spasming young cunt into Hilda's hot mouth as her orgasm rolled on and on. Finally pushing her friends away, she lay quivering in the aftermath of her lesbian-induced climax, her head tossing from side to side, her pretty eyes rolling.

'Gosh, Patsy, you liked that, didn't you?' Hilda asked, licking her fingers.

'Ah, yes, yes, I . . . I've never had such a good one!'

'Let's each put a finger into the next one's mini!' Candida suggested. 'We'll form a circle, each fingering the next!'

'You do think of some terribly rude things!' Hilda giggled, comparing Patsy's breasts with her own.

'Or we could put our fingers up each other's botty-holes!'

'Candy! How ever do you think of such dreadfully exciting ideas?'

'I don't know – imagination, I suppose.'

'Have you ever fingered your bottom?'

'Well . . . yes, every night I do it!'

'Crikey!'

'Sacré bleu! Comment appelle-t'on ceci?' Stumbling into the clearing, Madame Fissure gasped in amazement.

'We were just . . .' Hilda began, her face flushing as she grabbed her clothes.

'What on earth is going on here? I have never . . .'

'Please, Madame Fissure, we were only sunbathing!' Patsy cried.

'Sunbathing? Sunbathing naked? Don't lie to me, girl! I could see what you were doing! You'll all dress and report to Miss Gussetpiece within ten minutes!'

Gazing out of her study window, Miss Gussetpiece sighed. 'I can't believe it of Hilda Hillock, Madame Fissure! Naked in the woods with her friends? And what did you say they were doing?'

'They were . . . they were playing with each other, Headmistress.'

'All girls play with each other! It's an old English tradition – medieval, no doubt.'

'Not like that, they don't!'

'What were you doing in the woods, anyway?'

'I was tipped off.'

'Ripped off? Goodness me, by whom?'

'*Tipped* off, Headmistress! Maxine Mayhem told me what was going on. To be honest, I think we've misjudged Maxine. She's a changed girl this term. Unfortunately, so is Hilda Hillock – for the worse! On her first day back at school, Hilda was caught virtually naked in the locker room, behaving in a lewd and most indecent manner. Word has it that she was caught smoking and . . .'

'Actually, I caught Hilda and another girl in the gardener's potting shed. The girl, Candida, was on an old sofa with her knickers . . . Yes, you're right! Maxine has changed for the better and Hilda for the worse! But what do we do about it?'

'There's more, Headmistress. Maxine was quite distressed when she came to see me. She was obviously very concerned. She asked me to inspect Hilda's bed, whereupon I discovered a cucumber beneath her pillow.'

'She knows that it's against the rules to eat in the dormitories!'

'I don't think she intended *eating* it, Headmistress.'

'What else would she be doing with a cucumber in her bed?'

'Er . . . a phallus, Headmistress.'

'Who's callous?'

'No, a *phallus* – as in phallic symbol.'

'Phallic?'

'A *dildo*.'

'*Dildo*? What on earth is a dildo when it's at home? Goodness me, I need a drink! Pass me the gin, will you?'

'Yes, Headmistress. A dildo is a . . . It's a substitute for a penis.'

'A penis? Madame Fissure, please – this is a school for girls! I'll not have penises mentioned in this school, it's unhealthy!'

'No, what I mean is . . .'

'Who *is* your psychiatrist?'

'I don't have a . . .'

'Well, I suggest you consult one at the first opportunity! They'll be here shortly.'

'Who will?'

'The psychiatrists. God, my head's spinning! I mean, Hilda and her friends will be here shortly. You just leave it to me, I'll think of a way to deal with them.'

'Yes, Headmistress. I must get back to my class.'

Propped at her desk, Miss Gussetpiece held her head in her hands despairingly. 'I really can't take much more of this!' she sighed as Miss Frigidus knocked on the open door.

'Excuse me, Headmistress – may I have a word?' the frail woman asked.

'Yes, as long as it has nothing to do with Hilda Hillock!'

'No, it has nothing to do with Hilda. I was approached by a man.'

'A man? Good grief, first I have Madame Fissure going on about penises, and now you say you've been approached by a man!'

'It's true, Headmistress! I was walking across the playing field planning my next lesson when this man, a priest, came up to me.'

'A priest? What did he say?'

'He asked me whether I'd found God.'

'Why, has he lost Him?'

'No, I don't think so. He meant, have *I* found God.'

'And have you found God?'

'I wouldn't know if I had because I'm not sure what he looks like.'

'He's made in the image of man. No, man's made in the image of . . . I don't know what he looks like, either! Carry on, Miss Frigidus.'

'He said that I should seek God. He asked me to meet him in the woods after school this evening.'

'Who asked you, God? Have you had a vision?'

'No, the priest asked me to meet him.'

'What on earth for?'

'To find God. He said that he could take me to heaven.'

'This is all too much, it really is! Take you to heaven, for goodness sake! What happened next?'

'He asked me whether there was a vacancy for a PE mistress – he left me the mobile phone number of a highly qualified PE teacher.'

'What a coincidence, there *is* a vacancy! Give me her number, I'll ring her now.'

'Here it is, Headmistress. Her name's Miss Cueball – Coral Cueball. Do you think I should find God and heaven this evening? I mean, I'm hooked on Valium so I do need some divine guidance.'

'Yes, yes, meet God if you have to! I really must get on now, Miss Frigidus!'

'Yes, Headmistress, I'll get back to my class.'

Grabbing the phone as Miss Frigidus left the study, Miss Gussetpiece dialled the mobile phone number. 'Is that Miss Cueball?' she asked as a husky female voice answered.

'Miss who?'

'Cueball.'

'Cueball? Oh, er . . . yes, this is he . . . I mean, she.'

'This is Miss Gussetpiece speaking, headmistress of Bellend Independent School for Girls. I understand that you're a highly qualified teacher of physical education.'

'Am I?'

'Don't you know?'

'Oh, yes, of course I am! In fact, I've taught at several Swiss finishing schools. When can I come and see you?'

'Why do you want to see me?'

'I assumed you had a vacancy. Isn't that why you're ringing me?'

'Did I say there was a vacancy?'

'Well, no, not exactly.'

'I didn't give the slightest indication that there was a vacancy!'

'So there isn't, then?'

'As it happens, yes, there is. I'd be grateful if you could come over straight away. Where are you now?'

'In the laundry . . . I mean, on the M25. I'll be with you as soon as I've got this damned cassock . . . What I meant was . . . I'll be with you as soon as I can.'

'Good, I'll look forward to it.'

'To what?'

'To meeting you.'

'Oh, right, I'll see you soon. Goodbye, Miss Gussetpiece.'

'Goodbye, Miss Cueball.'

Replacing the receiver, Miss Gussetpiece poured another large gin and reclined in her swivel chair. *Money, money, money!* she mused, contemplating Miss Blob's idea of selling girls. *No, we'd never get away with it!* 'Ah, Hilda and company! You wicked, wicked girls! Right, all line up in front of my desk and explain yourselves!'

'We were in the woods, Miss Gussetpiece,' Hilda began.

'Why?'

'Why what?'

'Why were you in the woods?'

'We like nature, wildlife and . . . The sun was very hot – jolly hot, in fact! We slipped our clothes off to sunbathe and Madame Fissure stumbled across us.'

'Stumbled across you? Was she drunk?'

'No, Headmistress, I don't think so.'

'Were there any injuries?'

'No, Miss Gussetpiece.'

'You were sunbathing, naked? I've never heard of anything so disgusting! What a terrible way for young ladies to behave! There's no room for hedonism in this school!'

'We didn't think that it was wrong to . . .'

'This isn't a nudist camp, Hilda!'

'No, Miss Gussetpiece.'

'Do you know what a callous symbol is?'

'A sign of cold-heartedness?'

'Er . . . is it? Yes, yes, that's right. It has been brought to my attention that you've been eating in your bed, Hilda. Is that true?'

'Eating, Miss Gussetpiece? No, I haven't!'

'What was a cucumber doing beneath your pillow?'

'Oh, er . . . I was studying geometrical shapes for my maths lesson. Also, I was going to draw the cucumber for my art lesson and . . .'

'Oh, I see! Well, I think Madame Fissure must have got hold of the wrong end of the prick . . . I mean, stick. Anyway, please do not sunbathe naked! It's unladylike! And ungodly! You'll never get anywhere in this world by going around naked. Well, there *are* some professions that pay . . . er . . . Right, you may go.'

'Yes, Miss Gussetpiece. Thank you.'

Rummaging around the basement, Maxine shrieked as she came across several boxes packed with drink and cigarettes. 'Fuck me, I've found the gear!' she cried.

'And look what I've found!' Ginger gasped, holding up a leather whip and two pairs of handcuffs. 'Fucking hell, there's more here!' she added, snatching a huge vibrator from a box.

'Who the hell does that lot belong to?' Maxine breathed.

'I'll bet it's Dan's! I mean, it's right next to the booze and fags, isn't it?'

'Let's get all this stuff out of here. Where can we stash it?'

'I don't know, Max. What about putting it back in the gardener's shed?'

'Yes, that's a good idea. The old fart can keep an eye on it for us. We'll have to do it tonight, when it's dark. Shit, what are you *doing*?' she asked Ginger as the girl lifted her gymslip up.

Switching the vibrator on, Ginger pushed the buzzing phallus down the front of her knickers, positioning the tip between her inflating pussy lips. Gasping as the sensations stiffened her clitoris, she yanked her knickers down to her knees and parted her fleshy cunt lips with her slender fingers. 'Let me help you,' Maxine whispered as she dropped to her knees and grabbed the vibrator. Running the tip around Ginger's palpitating clitoris, she drove three fingers deep into her friend's spasming vaginal sheath. Gazing at the girl-come streaming down her hand, she smiled. 'We'll have some fun with this!' she exclaimed as Ginger's clitoris visibly swelled and pulsated. 'You can do it to me next. Shove it right up my cunt and fuck me with it!'

Leaning against the wall to steady her trembling body, Ginger closed her eyes as her orgasm stirred within her spasming sex-centre. 'God, that's incredible!' she gasped. 'Ah, God, my cunt!'

'Christ, you're so tight I can hardly move my fingers!' Maxine breathed excitedly as she thrust into the girl. 'You're crushing me!'

'I'm coming! God, I'm . . . I'm coming!' Ginger wailed as her climax erupted. 'Ah, ah, yes, I'm there!'

Pressing the vibrator harder against the girl's pulsating clitoris, Maxine fingered her young pussy hole with a vengeance, bringing out torrents of slippery come. Sustaining her friend's climax, she nibbled on her outer lips, licking the flowing girl-juice from her inner thighs. Eyeing the leather whip as Ginger's orgasm finally receded, Maxine grinned wickedly. Slipping her wet fingers from her friend's vagina, she switched the vibrator off and rose to her feet.

'I want to try something,' she declared as Ginger hung her head, panting as her quivering body began to steady. 'Turn round and face the wall,' she ordered, noticing two steel rings set in the brickwork. Grabbing the handcuffs, she quickly snapped them around Ginger's wrists. Pulling her arms up above her head, she fixed the cuffs to the steel rings before the girl had fully regained her senses.

'What are you doing?' Ginger asked fearfully, pulling on the handcuffs. 'Max, let me *go*!' she demanded as her gymslip was yanked up over her taut buttocks.

'I'm going to give you a spanking!' Maxine laughed, lightly patting her prisoner's bottom orbs as she grabbed the whip. 'I reckon Dan put the rings in the wall. He probably brings Frankfurter down here for bondage and whipping sessions!'

'I don't want the whip!' Ginger protested as Maxine ran the leather tails up her sensitive bottom crease.

'Why not? I thought you liked me spanking you.'

'I do, but not with a whip, Maxine!'

'Oh, come on – you'll love it! I'll just do it gently.'

'Make sure you do!'

The first lash caused the girl's tethered body to jolt. Maxine raised the whip above her head and landed the second, tautening her prisoner's buttocks. A little harder, the third lash caused Ginger to cry out. 'That was too hard!' she complained. As the tails continued to crack across her glowing bum cheeks, the girl protested loudly. But ignoring her friend's pleas, Maxine persisted with the thrashing, striking her buttocks progressively harder. 'I'll get you for this!' the fiery redhead warned as she sensed her crimsoning clitoris swelling. 'I'll . . . Ah, ah! God, I'm going to come!'

Losing all control, Maxine thrashed the girl's buttocks until they glowed scarlet. Shuddering as her juices of lust flooded down her inner thighs and her sex-nub pulsated in ecstasy, Ginger threw her head back. 'My clit!' she whimpered pitifully. 'Rub my clit!'

Dropping to her knees as she discarded the whip, Maxine massaged the girl's throbbing sex-button, sustaining her shuddering orgasm. Grabbing the vibrator, her mind swirling with lewd thoughts, she propelled the pink phallus deep into her friend's tight bottom-hole.

'Ah, God!' Ginger wailed as Maxine switched the vibrator on. 'Ah, that's mind-blowing! Oh, God! God!' Forcing the cylindrical device deeper into the girl's rectal sheath as she massaged her clitoris, Maxine kissed her buttocks, licking and nibbling the taut, glowing flesh. 'Oh, oh! Push it in further!' Ginger cried as her climax peaked, rocking her young body. Obeying, Maxine pushed the six-inch shaft fully home, leaving only the end visible between her friend's glowing bottom orbs. Her brown ring stretched tightly around the buzzing phallus, her clitoris solid beneath Maxine's caressing fingertips, Ginger sang out her carnal delight as Maxine slipped three fingers into her prisoner's neglected pussy sheath.

'My God!' Dan cried as he approached the precocious schoolgirls from the far end of the room. 'What the fucking hell . . .'

'Ah, your timing's perfect!' Maxine grinned, slipping the vibrator out of Ginger's bloated rectum. 'How would you like to give her one up her bum?'

'Up her bum? Fucking hell, I'd love to!'

'Maxine, I've had enough!' Ginger protested as Dan

slipped his fleshy shaft out and pushed his purple head against her tight, brown ring. 'No, no! I don't want . . .'

'You haven't got a choice, Ginger – so shut it!' Maxine returned wickedly.

His bulbous cockhead gliding into Ginger's anal tunnel, Dan gasped as Maxine dropped to her knees, gazing in awe at the illicit base coupling. 'God, you're tight and hot!' he cried, driving his purple crown further into the petite redhead's trembling body until he'd impaled her completely on his massive rod. 'Christ, you're fucking tight!' he gasped, slowly gyrating his hips, massaging her velveteen anal sheath with his solid knob.

'Bloody hell!' Maxine exclaimed as she splayed the girl's buttocks and gazed at her distended brown tissue. 'What's it like, Ginger?'

'It's . . . it's bloody wonderful! Christ, I've never known anything like it!'

'Give it to her, Dan!' Maxine ordered excitedly, fondling his weighty balls. 'Go on, give her the bum-fucking of her life! Shoot your spunk right up her arse!'

Grabbing the girl's hips, Dan thrust into Ginger's tight bottom-hole as Maxine slipped her hand beneath his swinging balls and pushed three fingers into her tightening vagina. Her tethered body rocking with every penile thrust, Ginger rapidly neared her climax. 'Oh, God!' she wailed as Maxine pressed the buzzing vibrator against her pulsating clitoris. 'God, I'm coming!' Propelling his weaponhead deep into Ginger's hot bowels, Dan grunted and jettisoned his bomb load. With spunk gushing from his throbbing knob, bathing their forbidden fusion, he rammed the girl's young body, draining his swinging balls as she cried out in her coming.

His balls emptied, Dan gently eased his spent shaft from

Ginger's bowels. Zipping his jeans, he staggered across the floor to the basement steps. 'I'll . . . I'll leave you to it!' he gasped as he climbed the stone steps. 'God, that was . . . I'll see you both again!'

'You can be sure of that!' Maxine giggled as she released her friend. 'And next time, I want your cock up *my* bum! Now, Ginger, I'll release you and you can bend over that box. I'm going to suck Dan's spunk from your bum-hole!'

'Ah, Miss Cueball, I presume?' Miss Gussetpiece greeted her visitor as she entered the study. 'You're here sooner than I'd expected.'

'Yes, there was very little traffic on the motorway,' the curious-looking woman replied, tugging her stockings up and adjusting her short skirt.

'Please, do sit down,' Miss Gussetpiece invited. 'Now, the vacancy . . . You don't have a brother, do you?'

'No, no, no – why?'

'There was someone here earlier, a priest – you look remarkably like him.'

'Oh, yes, I do have a brother in the priesthood.'

'But you just said that you didn't have a brother.'

'That's right, I didn't – but I do now.'

'How can you suddenly have a brother?'

'No, I've always had a brother, but he's only recently become a priest. I didn't have a brother in the priesthood, but I do now.'

'Most confusing! Is that a wig you're wearing? Your hair seems crooked.'

'A wig? No, this is my own head of natural blonde hair.'

'Then I suggest you find a decent hairdresser. Anyway, the position of physical education mistress is a very demanding one. We have a fine hockey team, and an excellent netball team. The girls require daily practice to keep them fit and . . .'

'I'll give them daily practice, all right! What sort of things do they wear for netball?'

'Well, the usual short skirts and sports blouses – why?'

'Do they wear knickers?'

'Knickers? Good grief, of course they do!'

'I've always found that girls play a far better game without knickers – you know, naked beneath their *very* short skirts.'

'Without knickers? But . . .'

'They're very restricting. All that running and leaping about . . . Knickers are so hot and sticky and wonderfully . . . They restrict movement. At my last school, the girls played netball naked.'

'Naked? Goodness me, we can't have that sort of thing going on at Bellend! This is a respectable establishment! Well, almost.'

'Shame. So, what other sports are they into? Do you have a large gym?'

'Yes, there's plenty left. Or would you prefer vodka?'

'No, what I meant was, do you have a gymnasium? You know, wall bars and ropes and canes . . . er . . . I mean, games.'

'Yes, we have a fine gym.'

'Are the girls any good at doing the splits?'

'Doing the splits? Why do you ask?'

'For leaping over the horse. They'll have to get their legs open as wide as they can if they're to leap over my . . . over the horse. Can they do the splits?'

'Er . . . I really have no idea!'

'What about the showers? They're communal, are they? What I mean is, the girlies all shower together – naked.'

'They certainly don't shower in their clothes!'

'Er . . . no, of course not. So they all shower together, with the PE mistress?'

'I hope you don't mind me saying so, Miss Cueball, but you seem to have an unhealthy interest in naked schoolgirls!'

'On the contrary, I have an extremely *healthy* interest in naked schoolgirls!'

'I don't like the sound of that at all!'

'No, you misunderstand, Headmistress. You see, being in physical education, I'm obliged to take an interest in the girls' bodies. PE isn't just a question of sports, it also concerns health and anatomy – naked schoolgirls.'

'Oh, yes, I understand.'

'The changing rooms – they're easily accessible and private, are they?'

'You access the changing rooms through a door, as with most rooms. And what do you mean by *private*?'

'I mean, when the girls are out on the field, would anyone be able to go sniffing around their clothes?'

'Sniffing around their clothes?'

'Yes, you know, their bras and panties – would anyone be able to steal the girls' undergarments?'

'Well, I suppose they would but . . . Why do you ask?'

'At my last school, the girls' undergarments were always being stolen. I just thought I'd better say that, should any items of clothing go missing during my time as PE mistress at Bellend, don't point the finger of blame at me.'

'Of course I wouldn't blame you!'

'Good. It's best to start off on the right foot.'

'Er . . . Yes, I suppose it is. Now, I'll need references, so . . .'

'References? Oh, I, er . . .'
'Don't you have references?'
'Yes, but they're not easily accessible just now.'
'Why, where are they?'
'Strewn across the M25, near Junction Fifteen – or was it Junction Fourteen? I had the sunroof open, you see. My references were on the passenger seat when, suddenly, there was this huge gust of wind. Whoosh! All my papers went straight through the roof!'

'How unfortunate! I hope you're not prosecuted for littering the motorway! In any event, I will need references, I'm afraid – it stands to reason. If you'll give me the full postal address of your last school, I'll . . .'

'Er . . . It's closed down.'
'Oh! Well, the school before that.'
'Ah, that one . . . that blew up.'
'Blew up?'
'Yes, there was a gas leak – a most unfortunate incident.'
'Was anyone killed?'
'Not exactly.'
'What about the establishment before that?'
'That's going back so far that I can't remember! Years and years and years!'
'Well, I'm sorry but . . .'
'Write to the landlord of the Inmates Inn, Dartmoor. He'll give references.'
'Write to a pub?'
'Yes, he was the headmaster of the school that blew up. He now runs a pub. His name's Bent-notes Charlie.'
'Bent-notes Charlie?'
'Sorry, that's his nickname. It's Charlie Hawkins.'
'I see. Right, I'll do that.'

'Do you mind if I take a wander around the school, Headmistress?'

'I'll show you round.'

'Er . . . No, no, I'd rather go alone.'

'As you wish. Actually, there's PE later on this afternoon. If you'd care for a trial run, so to speak, you can take the girls for netball.'

'Cor, I'd love to!'

'Good. They'll all be in the changing rooms at four.'

'All right, I'll be there, in my kit.'

'Excellent! Do come and see me before you leave – I'll need your address and a few other details.'

'My address? Oh, er . . . yes, right.'

'Mind you don't get lost, it's a big school!'

'It's all right, I know my way . . . Er . . . no, I won't get lost.'

Making her way down the basement steps in her search for the missing laundry basket, Hilda was mulling over her plans for a jumble sale when Maxine leaped on her from behind a pile of boxes. 'Well, if it's not Miss Pansy Pillock!' Maxine grinned, grabbing her arm. 'Fancy meeting you down here!'

'Get off me, Maxine, or I'll . . .'

'You'll what? Go running to Knickergusset, perhaps?'

'Let's get her cuffed to the metal rings!' Ginger suggested, snapping the handcuffs around Hilda's wrists and dragging her to the wall. Grappling with her struggling body, the Bellend Rebels lifted Hilda's arms above her head and secured the cuffs to the steel rings.

Standing back with their hands on their hips, the wayward girls scrutinized Hilda. 'Just look at your sensible shoes!' Maxine mocked. 'And your white ankle socks and your prefect badge! When are you going to grow up?'

'I'm eighteen!' Hilda returned.

'You look more like twelve, if you ask me!'

'You'd better let me go or . . .'

'Shut up, pillock!' Ginger hissed. 'No one ever comes down here. We might decide to leave you here for a few days and . . .'

'Ginger,' Maxine interrupted. 'I've just had a brilliant idea! We'll have some fun with her, strip her off and have a laugh, and then we'll leave her here – until tomorrow, at least.'

'And then what?'

'She goes missing, right? We tell Knickergusset that we saw her leaving the school grounds, running away. We tell her that we saw Pillock absconding – just after she'd blown the toilet block to smithereens!'

'Great! She's bound to be expelled for that!'

'There'd be no proof!' Hilda protested.

'Who needs proof?' Maxine scowled, squeezing the girl's firm breasts. 'Missing for twenty-four hours – how would you explain that?'

'I'll say that you chained me to the wall and . . .'

'Come on, who's going to believe that we captured you and handcuffed you to the wall naked? We're wasting time – let's get her stripped off!'

Lifting Hilda's feet, Ginger slipped her shoes and socks off. Hilda didn't struggle – there was little point, she knew, as her navy-blue knickers were yanked down her slender legs. Again, she was at Maxine's mercy, she pondered fearfully as her gymslip was torn from her trembling body. 'You're beastly!' she spat as Maxine unbuttoned her blouse and ripped the garment off. 'You'll pay for this, you vile beasts!' Ignoring their prisoner's threats, the assailants ripped her bra away from her pert breasts, tossing it to the floor as they shrieked with laughter.

'Let's shave her cunt hair off!' Ginger giggled, tugging on Hilda's sparse blonde curls. 'She dresses and behaves as if she's twelve years old, so let's . . .'

'You just dare!' Hilda cried. 'I'll tell . . .'

'Yes, yes, we know!' Maxine broke in. 'You'll tell Knickergusset all about it!'

'I will, Maxine Mayhem – I will!'

'Unless you shut up, I'll shave your head!' Ginger warned the frightened girl.

Kneeling before their naked prisoner, the girls licked her vaginal lips, sucking the swollen flesh pads into their wet mouths. Hilda gasped as Maxine drove a finger deep into her bottom-hole and massaged her inner flesh. With Ginger's fingers penetrating her vaginal sheath, mouths and tongues nibbling and licking her pinken sex-folds, she couldn't prevent her climax from erupting. Standing with her feet wide apart as her naked body shuddered, she imagined Candida between her legs, kissing her soft pussy folds, sucking her clitoris, bringing out her orgasm.

Suddenly, the finger massaging her rectal sheath slipped out, leaving her sensitive hole void. 'No!' she screamed as Maxine forced the buzzing vibrator into her anal duct, racking the brown tissue. 'No, please! I can't . . .' Delighting in her tortured pleas, Maxine forced the entire length of the vibrator deep into Hilda's bowels. Her clitoris swelling in Ginger's hot mouth, more tidal waves of surprise pleasure surged through the ambivalent captive's young body.

Hanging from the handcuffs, her long blonde hair dishevelled, Hilda could do nothing to stop the beautiful sexual torture. Gasping as her vagina expanded to take four fingers, she looked up to see Fukui bounding down the basement steps with Kelly.

'Fuck me!' Fukui gasped as she approached the lewd spectacle. 'What the fuck's going on?'

'Join us,' Maxine invited. 'We're having some fun with Pillock's wet cunt, and her arsehole!'

'Mmm, nice hard tits!' Kelly breathed, her green eyes sparkling devilishly as she squeezed Hilda's mammary spheres. 'Ginger's got her cunt, you've got her arse, so we'll each have a nice firm tit!'

As her erect nipples were engulfed in the girls' mouths, Hilda sensed her vagina spasm, gripping Ginger's thrusting fingers like a vice. 'No, no!' she gasped as the overwhelming sensations deep within her bowels shook her young body. 'Please, no!' Thrusting the vibrator in and out of her bottom-hole in time with Ginger's pistoning fingers, Maxine instructed the other girls to bite Hilda's nipples. 'Argh!' Hilda cried as they complied, gently sinking their teeth into her sensitive milk buds. 'Argh! Please!'

Another succession of orgasmic waves rolling through her tethered body as the four rebels crudely attended her most intimate feminine places, Hilda had never known such sexual delight. Her climax seemingly never-ending, her body trembling, her come juice pouring from her open sex portal, she felt as if she were floating on a cloud of pure carnal lust. On and on the climactic waves rolled, taking her ever higher, ever closer to her sexual heaven.

'The whip!' Maxine yelled, eyeing the thin leather tails fanning out across the floor as she twisted and thrust the vibrator. 'Let's thrash her arse!'

'Let's see how many times we can make her come

first!' Ginger declared, thrusting her fingers deep into the dangling doll's drenched cunt.

'OK, then we'll thrash her!'

'We'll take turns to whip her bum!' Ginger giggled.

Hilda's ordeal was far from over, she knew, as her multiple orgasm finally subsided, leaving her trembling body perspiring. Her nipples aching as the girls sucked like on a favourite lollipop, she grimaced. The infamous Bellend Rebels had surpassed themselves this term, she thought, as Maxine drove the vibrator deep into her inflamed bottom-sheath, causing her naked body to jolt. They couldn't get any worse – could they?

'I think someone's coming!' Kelly whispered loudly as she looked up at the basement door. Leaping up the steps, Fukui switched the light off, breathing heavily as she heard voices outside the door. Praying that they wouldn't be caught, Ginger covered Hilda's mouth with her cunny-wet hand.

'Let's get out of here!' Maxine breathed, slipping the vibrator from Hilda's sore anal sheath. 'We'll leave Pillock here and come back later.'

'Good idea,' Kelly grinned, gagging Hilda with her own knickers. 'She'll be safe enough left here.'

'Come on, let's go!'

Alone in the basement, her arms secured above her head, her knickers stuffed in her mouth, Hilda wondered when her jailers would return to further humiliate her young body. Judging by the events of its first few days, she guessed that this was going to be the worst term ever!

Chapter Five

'Hilda's missing, Miss Gussetpiece,' Candida imparted in a concerned voice as she stood before the headmistress's desk.

'Missing what?' the Head drooled, gulping a glass of neat gin.

'She's gone missing.'

'Gone and missed what, girl?'

'No, what I mean is, I can't find her.'

'Can't find her what? What's she lost?'

'*She*'s lost, Miss Gussetpiece.'

'She's lost what? Good grief, girl, you're so difficult to converse with!'

'I'll start again, Miss Gussetpiece,' Candida pursued with some exasperation. 'Hilda can't be found, we've searched everywhere for her, and we can't find her.'

Shaking her head, Miss Gussetpiece sighed as she gazed at the willowy sixth-former. Finishing her gin, she rose to her feet and tottered to the window. She was in a pensive mood, Candida surmised as she watched the headmistress gaze out across the school grounds – and drunk! About to abandon the futile conversation and resume her search for Hilda, she turned to leave the study.

'When did you last see her?' Miss Gussetpiece asked, still gazing out of the window.

'This morning. She went off in search of the missing laundry basket, and she didn't turn up for lunch or maths.'

'Miss Hairoot didn't report her absence to me!' Miss Gussetpiece complained, moving back to her desk and refilling her glass.

'She sent me.'

'Who sent you?'

'The maths mistress – Miss Hairoot.'

'Sent you where?'

'Here, Miss Gussetpiece.'

'Sent you here? What are you talking about?'

'She sent me here, to see you.'

'Why, what have you done?'

'Nothing!'

'Why would Miss Hairoot send you to see me if you'd done nothing wrong?'

'She sent me to tell you about Hilda's absence.'

'Why on earth didn't you say so, girl? Goodness me, I really can't take much more of this!' the headmistress grumbled, sipping her gin.

'What is it, Miss Gussetpiece, water?'

'Water? No! I mean, I can't take much more of these continual problems! Leave me, girl! I need to think!'

Slumped at her desk, Miss Gussetpiece finished off the half-bottle of gin. Wondering where Hilda Hillock had disappeared to as the phone rang, she lifted the receiver. 'Miss Gussetpiece drinking . . . I mean, speaking,' she slurred.

'Hallo, this is Doctor Anusis Rectus. My sister told me that you'd like me to examine the girls.'

'Examine the girls' what?'

'Examine all the girls.'

'All the girls' what?'

Girl School

'The sixth-form girls – physically examine them.'

'Oh, I see! Where are you phoning from?'

'From my rooms. I mean, I'm at home. I'm only ten minutes away from the school. If you'd like me to come over and discuss things with you, I . . .'

'Discuss things?'

'Yes, the girls.'

'Discuss the girls' what?'

'I'll ring back when you're not so . . . when you're not so indisposed.'

Replacing the receiver, Miss Gussetpiece sighed as Miss Frigidus entered the study. 'Please, Miss Frigidus, I simply cannot take any more problems today!' she warned. 'All this mental torture is . . . You couldn't spare a couple of Valium, could you?'

'I've something far better than Valium, Headmistress. Here, smoke one of these,' the slight woman smiled, opening a tobacco tin.

'Smoke? It's unhealthy! Good God, I don't smoke!'

'No, neither do I, but I had one of these earlier and it really loosened me up. Please, do try one.'

'What are they? Where did you get them from?'

'From that priest I met on the playing field. He told me that I should smoke a couple before he takes me to heaven in the woods this evening.'

'I suppose I could try one, seeing as they were a gift from a man of God. Never look a horse gift in the . . . a hift gorse . . . Jesus, my head's spinning!'

Taking the lighter from Miss Frigidus, Miss Gussetpiece ignited the cigarette and drew heavily. Coughing, she blew smoke into the air as she made for the drinks cabinet. 'Stone the bloody crows!' she cried, unscrewing the cap of a bottle of vodka. 'What on earth's in it?'

'Apparently, it's a herbal tobacco, Headmistress. He said something about Colombian grass. It's supposed to be very good for you. As I said, I tried one earlier and it made me feel wonderfully relaxed. Not even Maxine Mayhem could have distressed me!'

'Really? They *must* be good!'

Taking another drag, the headmistress reeled as her head spun. Staggering to her desk with the vodka bottle, she slumped in her chair, inhaling the scented smoke again. 'Who cares whether Hilda's lost or not?' she chuckled. 'As far as I'm concerned, the whole bloody school can get lost!'

'Miss Gussetpiece! Goodness me, it's certainly working for you! Is Hilda lost?'

'Damn right, she is! Bollocks, that's what I say!'

'Oh! Oh, dear! I don't think you should be using such distasteful language, Miss Gussetpiece! It's not natural for a headmistress to . . .'

'Why ever not?'

'Well, it's just not right. It would be deemed unethical.'

'I don't care if it is damned unethical!'

'Actually, I think I'll try another one,' the timid woman smiled, taking a roll-up from the tin and lighting it. 'Ah!' she sighed as she exhaled the smoke. 'They *are* rather good, aren't they?'

'Good? Bugger me – they're bloody brilliant! When the priest said that he'd take you to heaven, I think he meant it! Bloody hell, this is miraculous! I've found paradise!'

'Do you know, Headmistress, I've never used an expletive in my life?'

'Haven't you? I swore all the time when I was on the factory floor.'

Girl School

'The factory floor?'

'Yes, when I was . . . It was the job I had before I came here. There was this common slut of a seamstress, Violet – Vulgar Violet, we used to call her. Forever swearing, she was! By Christ, she was a dirty little slut! Anyway, I'd better not go into that. Go on, Miss Frigidus, say a naughty word!'

'Oh, I really don't think . . .'

'Go on, just one!'

'Intercourse!'

'That's no good! Intercourse? What sort of expletive is that?'

'Bugger! Oh, Headmistress! Goodness me, what have I said?'

'Excellent! Er . . . Shit!'

'Oh, dear! Er . . . Bum!'

'Sod!'

'Er . . . I can't think of any more, Headmistress. Yes, I can! Crap!'

'Fuck!'

'Arse!'

'Cunt!'

'Oh, Headmistress, I really can't think of any more.'

'I can! Tits, fart, fanny, cock, balls, wank, spunk, cunt . . . No, we've had cunt, haven't we?'

'Yes, we've had cunt, Headmistress.'

Entering the study, Madame Fissure held her hand to her mouth and gasped. 'Headmistress, what on earth . . .' Turning to Miss Frigidus, she frowned. '*You*, of all people, Miss Frigidus!'

'What about me?' Miss Frigidus giggled.

'Well, you're just not the type to use such foul language!'

'Yes I am! Fuck and cunt!'

'Oh, dear! I'll, er . . . I'll come back later when . . .'

'Yes, fucking good idea!' Miss Gussetpiece laughed. 'Fucking well get your arse back in here later!'

Taking another roll-up from the tin as Madame Fissure fled the study in disgust, Miss Gussetpiece flicked the lighter and inhaled. Swigging from the vodka bottle, her eyes rolling, she leaned heavily on the arm of the chair and crashed to the floor.

'Fucking hell!' she cried, climbing to her feet. 'Damn fucking chair! What the hell's going on with my fucking head? I feel so light, as if I'm drifting away from my body!'

'I told you they were good, didn't I?' Miss Frigidus giggled, taking another cigarette from the tin. 'Fuck! Oh! Oh, dear! I really must stop swearing.'

'Jesus Christ, I must sit down!' Miss Gussetpiece gasped as she righted her chair. 'Ah, that's better!' she breathed, flopping into it. 'Now, where was I?'

'Have you ever been married, Headmistress?' Miss Frigidus asked pensively.

'No, never.'

'Neither have I. I wonder what it's like?'

'What, being married?'

'No – you know, doing it.'

'Doing what?'

'Having . . . er . . . having intercourse.'

'Sex? Have you never been laid?'

'Laid?'

'Fucked.'

'Fucked? Oh, dear! Goodness me, what am I saying? I really don't think I should smoke any more of these!'

'I think we should smoke the whole fucking lot!'

'Fuck, so do I! What's it like, Headmistress?'
'What?'
'Getting fucked.'
'Brilliant, when you can get it! Have you honestly never done it?'
'No. I came close once, but nothing happened.'
'Came close?'
'Yes, there was this man I met at university. He . . . well, he came to my room and got it out.'
'Got what out?'
'His, you know . . . his thing.'
'What, his stiff prick?'
'Yes, his stiff prick. Oh, Headmistress! Good gracious, this is so unlike me!'
'What did he do with his stiff prick?'
'He . . . he wanted to stick it in me.'
'Did you let him?'
'No, I couldn't bring myself to allow it. It's just not in my nature, you see.'
'Shame. Well, I suppose I'd better do something about Hilda – go through the motions, at least. If one's seen to be doing the right things, one can get away with murder. Come, Miss Frigidus – the search is on!'

Creeping around the laundry room, Candida checked her watch. 'Gosh, we should have been in class ages ago!' she exclaimed, turning to Patsy. 'Miss Shaftgrinder will be livid!'
'What's more important, English Lit, or finding Hilda?'
'Yes, you're jolly well right, Patsy! Hilda is more important than anything!'
'Well, she's not in here. We've searched the woods, the potting shed, the showers, the locker room, the . . .'

'I don't think she's in school. I mean, she can't be in school, can she?'

'She must have gone down to the village or something.'

Bursting into the room, Miss Shaftgrinder stood glowering, her hands on her hips. 'So this is where you are!' she bellowed. 'What are you up to?' she demanded, her beady eyes peering over the top of her glasses.

'Looking for Hilda, Miss Shaftgrinder,' Candida replied.

'You won't find her in a laundry basket! Anyway, it's not your job to go looking for her! You've missed the English lesson, and unless you hurry up, you'll miss netball! Now, off you go and get changed, both of you!'

Wandering into the changing rooms, Candida tugged her gymslip and blouse off. 'Who's that?' Patsy asked, nudging her and nodding towards Miss Cueball.

'Must be a new PE mistress,' Candida replied, eyeing the woman's hairy legs.

'She's awfully strange, don't you think?'

'Terribly! Look at the size of her bust!'

'Gosh! I hope my titties don't get any bigger! They're huge enough as it is!' Patsy giggled as she slipped her blouse off, revealing her straining bra.

'They *are* rather large!'

'No talking, please!' Miss Cueball bellowed as she climbed onto a chair and gazed at the netball team. 'My name's Miss Cueball. Hopefully, I'm to be your new PE mistress. Now, all hurry up and get changed. Er . . . I need a volunteer. You, girl, what's your name?'

'Candida, Miss Cueball.'

'Right, Candida, stay behind after the others have changed – I want a word with you.'

'Yes, Miss Cueball.'

'Now, what do you all wear for netball?'

'Our kit,' a girl volunteered.

'Right. Er . . . do you wear special PE knickers, or do you keep your ordinary knickers on?'

'Sports knickers, Miss Cueball.'

'Good, good! Right, hurry up and get changed.'

Watching the girls file out of the changing rooms, Candida smiled as Miss Cueball approached her. Hoisting up her ample chest, the woman grinned. 'You're a pretty little thing,' she murmured, stroking Candida's golden hair. 'How would you like to be my personal assistant?'

'Personal assistant, Miss Cueball?'

'Yes, helping me to prepare for games, that sort of thing. You could be my right-hand girl.'

'Yes, all right, Miss Cueball.'

'Good. Tell me, who's the team captain?'

'Hilda Hillock. But she's gone missing.'

'Gone missing? Goodness me! Where do you think she could be?'

'I have no idea. We've searched everywhere!'

'I expect she'll turn up. You go and tell the team to get some practice in, and I'll join you shortly.'

As Candida left the room, Miss Cueball began collecting the girls' bras and knickers. 'Mmm, these are nice!' She smiled, holding a pair of knickers to her face and breathing in the girl-scented crotch. 'Bloody hell, get a load of the white stains in *this* pair! Who'd be a fucking priest when he can be a PE mistress?' Collecting all the underwear, she placed her haul in a carrier bag and stashed it behind a cupboard before joining the girls on the pitch.

'You can stuff fucking netball up your arse!' Maxine hissed as she watched the team from the bushes.

'So what's the plan?' Ginger asked, lighting a cigarette.

'Kelly's in the lab making a bomb. As soon as she's ready, we'll blow the bogs up. I've nabbed Pillock's bag. What we'll do is leave it in the boghouse as evidence. I'll break into the sanny machine and nick the money first, though!'

'So, we tell Knickergusset that we saw Pillock doing a runner just after the bomb went off?'

'Yes, and tomorrow, we'll let her go. Shush, someone's coming!'

Creeping through the undergrowth clutching a pair of navy-blue knickers, Miss Blob settled on the grass and lifted her skirt. Spying on the transvestite, Maxine and Ginger nudged each other, stifling their giggles as the man slipped his red silk panties down his stubbled, stockinged legs and revealed his rampant erection to their disbelieving eyes. Wrapping the knickers around the base of his penis as he lay down, he began wanking his huge organ.

'Sad pervert!' Maxine whispered.

'Let's pounce on him!' Ginger suggested, slipping her hand down her knickers and fingering her hot pussy hole.

'Good idea! We'll get him to frig us off!'

Leaping from the bushes, the girls stood astride the startled teacher. 'Want to look up our skirts while you wank?' Maxine asked impishly as his face flushed.

'I . . . er . . .'

'Go on, keep wanking! Spunk into the knickers!' she laughed as she squatted over his face. 'Or would you like *us* to wank you off?'

'Well. . . Yes, I would,' he smiled as Ginger knelt by his side and grabbed his penis.

'Like wanking into schoolgirls' knickers, do you?'

Maxine grinned as she lowered her body, moving her taut, bulging knickers closer to his face.

'Well, I . . .'

'You're a sad pervert, aren't you?'

'No, I'm . . .'

'Say you are, or I won't allow you to see my cunt.'

'Yes, I am.'

'Say it!'

'I'm a sad pervert.'

'Sniff my knickers – go on, push your nose into my crotch and sniff my cunt scent!'

Mouthing on the damp material covering Maxine's swelling pussy lips as Ginger wanked his erect organ, the purported 'Miss' Blob began to gasp. Leaning over, Ginger engulfed his knob in her mouth, gently sucking his throbbing glans. 'Ah, that's good!' he breathed, pulling Maxine's knickers to one side. Gazing at the girl's wet vaginal crack, her swelling pussy lips, he pushed his tongue out and began his fervent cunny licking.

'Want your cock up my cunt?' Ginger asked crudely as she slipped her wet knickers off and sat astride his trembling body. His mouth buried between Maxine's full labia, he couldn't answer, but his twitching penis signalled Ginger to impale herself on his solid shaft. Gently easing his knob into her tight vaginal sheath, she lowered her young body, sliding his cockshaft deep into her love-duct until her buttocks rested on his thighs. Gyrating her hips, stirring her creamy nectar with his rod, she tossed her head back and began to breathe deeply.

'So, Miss Blob, what's your real name?' Maxine wheedled as his tongue drove into her tight vagina. 'Come on, tell us your real name!'

'Roderick!' he panted. 'Roderick Weatherstone!'

'Well, Roderick Weatherstone, what do you think of my wet cunt?'

'Mmm! Gorgeous! Succulent! Beautiful!' he expounded through a mouthful of hot girl-flesh.

'God, I'm coming!' Ginger cried as she frigged her clitoris and bounced up and down on the huge male organ, pounding her young cervix with his pestle. 'Ah, ah! Ah, my cunt! Coming! Coming!'

'Who's a lucky geography mistress?' Maxine giggled as she ground her pinken crater into the man's hungry mouth. 'Go on, spunk up Ginger's cunt! Christ, my clit! God, that's fucking good! Don't stop!' she cried as the beautiful sensations of sex built within her quivering pelvis.

Trembling, gasping in their carnal coupling, the debased trio reached their shuddering orgasms. 'God, my cunt!' Ginger cried again as her love-mouth milked the spasming shaft's gushing sperm. 'Fucking hell, my lovely cunt!'

'And mine!' Maxine gasped as her clitoris throbbed against the man's sweeping tongue. 'God, it's . . . it's fucking beautiful! Christ, my cunt! Ah! Ah, yes!' Their orgasmic cries filling the wood, the threesome finally collapsed in a heap of quivering limbs. Rolling onto the grass, her knickers to one side, exposing her inflamed vaginal lips, Maxine gave her last shudder and sat up.

'Drink your spunk from her cunt!' she grinned wickedly as the transvestite lay trembling on the grass, his spent slug deflating over his pussy-juiced balls.

'Good idea!' Ginger shrieked, leaping up and kneeling astride the man's wet face.

'Go on, drink your come from her cunt!' Maxine ordered, gazing at Ginger's unfurling sex-folds as she settled her open pothole over his eager mouth.

Licking, sucking on the glistening cunt-flesh, Blob lapped up his sperm as it oozed from the girl's hot cuntal sheath. Shuddering as she ground the open centre of her femininity into his face, Ginger let out involuntary gasps of sexual pleasure as her clitoris swelled again, sending electrifying tingles of impending orgasm up her spine. Opening her blouse and lifting her bra away from her pert breasts, she tweaked her growing nipples, moaning as her body shook violently in her lustful desire.

'Allow me!' Maxine offered, kneeling by her friend and sucking her erect milk bud into her hungry mouth. Licking and sucking on the hardening protrusion, she slipped her finger between the girl's buttocks and located the sensitive entrance to her rectal sheath. Slipping her finger past the tight portal, Maxine massaged the velveteen walls of her friend's anal tube, causing the girl to whimper with pleasure as her clitoris throbbed in the man's mouth, taking her ever closer to her sexual heaven. Pressing a second finger into the tight anal sheath, Maxine sucked harder on the girl's nipple, gently biting the brown teat. Trembling as her climax approached, her eyes rolling, her pretty lips dry with her gasping, Ginger threw her head back. 'Coming again!' she sang out as her orgasm erupted. 'God, I'm . . . I'm coming again!'

Peeling her cunt lips apart as Maxine thrust her fingers deep into her anal canal, Ginger cried out her orgasm, shuddering as it shook the very core of her young body. 'God, don't stop!' she pleaded as Maxine quickened the rhythm of her anal thrusting. Her cunt juices decanting, flooding the transvestite's face, the girl knew she could take no more. Dizzy with sex, she fell to the ground and lay prostrate on her stomach, her friend's fingers still embedded in her bottom-hole as she quivered in the aftermath of her cosmic eruption.

'Your bum's nice and hot!' Maxine breathed as she continued to gently thrust in and out of Ginger's anal duct. 'It's at times like this that I wish I had a cock! *You*'ve got a cock, Miss Blob. Would you like to fuck Ginger's arse with it?'

'Would I? I'd give anything to . . .'

'Anything? How much have you got in your handbag?'

'Er . . . only a few pounds.'

'Yeah? Let's have a look.'

Slipping her fingers out of Ginger's dank tunnel, Maxine snatched the bag, gasping as she pulled out a wad of notes. Grinning as she counted the money, she rolled the notes up and stuffed them down the front of her bra. 'You lying bastard! Only a few pounds, my cunt!' she cried.

'That's all the money I have!' Miss Blob protested. 'There's three hundred pounds there!'

'Yes, there is – and it's mine!' Maxine laughed. 'You wouldn't want me to tell Knickergusset that you're a man, would you?'

'No,' the teacher replied despondently as he retrieved his handbag.

'Well, three hundred should just about pay for a quick one up Ginger's bum, so if you're ready. . .'

Ordering her friend to tuck her knees beneath her chest and stick her bum out, Maxine grabbed the panting man's erect penis as he knelt behind the girl. Yanking Ginger's buttocks apart, she presented his purple knob to her brown entrance and pressed it home.

'Feel good?' she asked Ginger as the bulbous knob slipped past her tightening muscles and disappeared into her anal sheath.

'God, yes!' the girl gasped as the solid shaft drove into her bowels. 'Ah, ah! Shove it all in! That's it, keep going, keep going! Ah! Oh! More, more!'

'You *do* have a hungry little bottom-hole!' Maxine giggled wickedly as the organ disappeared into her friend's trembling body, her brown ring like a vice around its base. 'There, fully home! Work your muscles, squeeze and relax, squeeze and relax. That's it, I can see your arsehole tightening around his cock! Keep it up and you'll bring out his spunk!'

'Ah, oh! God, my bum feels . . . Ah! Ah, that's good! Finger my cunt, Max! Please, finger-fuck my cunt!'

'Like this?' Maxine asked as she sank four fingers into her friend's tight vaginal sheath.

'God, yes! Now both thrust into my holes! Stretch me right open and give me a fucking good seeing-to!'

The teacher's solid shaft thrusting into the girl's tight bottom-hole in time with Maxine's pistoning fingers, Ginger laid her head on the soft grass, whimpering as the sensations of impending orgasm built within her contracting womb. The rhythmic thrusting accelerating, jolting her young body, taking her ever closer to her inevitable coming, the girl pleaded for her quick release. 'Harder, faster!' she managed to gasp as she dug her fingernails into the grass. 'More, harder, faster!'

The violent pummelling shaking her trembling body, the heavy balls slapping her bloated cunt lips, Ginger clung to the grass, panting, whimpering as her craved climax finally erupted. 'I'm there!' she wailed. 'Ah, God! I'm there!'

'Ah! Ah! So am I!' the man gasped as his sperm issued forth, filling her bowels, lubricating her anal cylinder.

'What a lovely sight!' Maxine shrieked, gazing at the

male organ as it withdrew and thrust home again. 'God, there's spunk everywhere! Do *my* arse afterwards! I want it up my arse!'

'I will! I will! I'll do your beautiful arse!'

The fierce fucking continuing, Ginger projected her bottom-orbs further, opening the very centre of her young body to her fervent defilers. Gripping her hips, the gasping transvestite made his last ramming thrusts, his solid belly smacking her buttocks until he finally withdrew his spent member and rolled to the ground. His skirt over his stomach, his drained balls rolling over his inner thigh, his limp penis glistening in the sun, Maxine couldn't help but giggle.

'You sad old bastard!' she shrieked as she slipped her fingers from Ginger's burning vaginal cavern. 'Look at your false tits, they've fallen down to your stomach!'

'God, I've never had such a good . . .' Ginger gasped as she writhed on the ground.

'Such a good bum-fuck?' Maxine giggled. 'Hey, where are you going?' she called as Miss Blob clambered to her feet and fled like a frightened rabbit into the undergrowth. 'You haven't given *me* one up the bum yet! Miserable bloody pervert! Ginger, give my cunt a good licking out, will you? After watching his cock fuck your arse, I'm aching to come!'

Working in the lab, Kelly turned to Fukui. 'Nearly there!' she grinned.

'Where the fuck did you get the uranium-235 from?' the Japanese doll asked as she tucked her gleaming jet-black hair behind her ears.

'Can't tell you, I'm afraid. I hope I've got the critical mass right. If not, the chain reaction won't be maintained.'

'So what would happen?'
'Basically, the fucking thing wouldn't blow up!'
'I still say that sugar and weedkiller would have been better.'
'Nah, course it wouldn't!'
'You might blow the whole school up with that thing!'
'Yeah, I might!'
'You might wipe the entire county off the map! What about the fallout?'
'Don't worry about that! Just leave the nuclear physics to me. Right, let's plant the thing in the lavs.'
'How will you set it off?'
'A small wedge of fissile material is fired at a larger piece and the two fuse . . . It goes bang, all right? That's all you need to know. Come on, let's go!'
'We won't kill anyone, will we?'
'Only if someone's sitting on the lav at the time! Christ, it would blow their arse clean off!'
'We'll have to make sure that the coast is clear, Kelly. I mean . . .'
'Fukui, don't worry! Everyone's in class, OK? I'll check the lavs before I set it off.'
'Well, I hope you know what you're doing.'
'Of course I fucking know! This isn't the first A-bomb I've made! Come on, we're wasting time!'

Flopping into her chair, Miss Gussetpiece held her hand to her head as she looked up at Miss Frigidus. 'I suppose we'll have to contact the police!' she sighed. 'The stupid girl could be anywhere!'
'Oh dear! We can't have girls going missing like this, Headmistress, it won't do the school's reputation any good at all!'

'What's left of the school's reputation! I'll give it a few hours more. If she's not turned up by then, I'll have to bring the police in. Hilda Hillock is causing rather too many problems this term for my liking! By the way, I rang Maxine's father, Sir Phillip Mayhem.'

'Why?'

'He's a millionaire – I thought he might help the school financially. Anyway, he's coming to see me about a deal, whatever he means by that.'

The building suddenly rocked as a thunderous explosion resounded throughout the school and Miss Gussetpiece dived beneath her desk. 'Jesus bloody Christ! What in God's name was that?' she cried as the windows blew in, showering the study with glass.

'Oh dear!' Miss Frigidus gasped as plaster dropped from the ceiling, covering the frail woman in white dust. 'Goodness me, an earthquake!' she shrieked.

'We don't have earthquakes in this country, you silly woman!'

'What was it then, thunder?'

'No, of course it wasn't!'

'Perhaps we've roused the wrath of God by swearing, Headmistress!'

'No, I'd say it was a bomb!'

'Goodness! A bomb?'

'It must have been – what else would cause the glass to blow in like that?'

'Oh dear, are we at war?'

'Of course we're not at war! Ah, Jones, what on earth was that!'

'Johnson, Miss Gussetpiece.'

'Don't start that again, I'm in no fit mental state for name games! Help me out of here, I've got myself stuck!'

Girl School

Pulling the Head out from beneath her desk, the maintenance man moved towards the shattered windows. 'The toilet block seems to have disappeared!' he gasped, eyeing the pile of smoking rubble.

'Disappeared?' Miss Gussetpiece queried, brushing her clothing. 'How can it have disappeared, for goodness sake? It's impossible for a toilet block to . . .'

'Come and see for yourself – look, razed to the ground!'

'Oh my goodness! Whatever has happened?'

'A bomb, Headmistress. And a pretty hefty one, at that!'

'This is terrible! Look, there's water shooting at least twenty feet into the air!'

'The main's burst.'

'Oh my goodness, whatever next! Look into it, Jones.'

'Johnson, Headmistress.'

'Just look into it, man! We'll have the water authority after us for wastage! We could be cut off!'

Pouring two large gins, Miss Gussetpiece passed a glass to Miss Frigidus and sat at the plaster-covered desk. 'Have you any more of those strange cigarettes?' she asked as the phone rang. 'Hallo, Miss Gussetpiece speaking,' she garbled, pressing the receiver to her ear.

'Hallo, Doctor Anusis Rectus here.'

'Who? I'm sorry, it's a bad line.'

'Anusis Rectus.'

'Anus rectum? I'm sorry, we've been bombed – it must have affected the phone lines. There's been an explosion in the toilets.'

'Then I can help you. I'm the rectal doctor!' the man bellowed impatiently. 'I'm calling about the girls' bottoms!'

'The girls' bottoms? Who is this?'

'I'm a doctor!'

'You need a doctor?'

'No, *I*'m a doctor! I spoke to you earlier about examining the girls' bottoms!'

'If that's you messing around, Jones, I'll see to it that you're dismissed from your post!'

'No, Miss Gussetpiece – this is Doctor Anusis Rectus.'

'What? Anal rectum? Are you an escaped psychopath? It's a psychiatrist you need, not a doctor!'

'I *am* a doctor, you stupid . . . Oh, for fuck's sake! Look, I'll come over and see you!'

'You'll do what?'

'I'll come and see you!'

'See my what?'

'Jesus Christ!'

'Oh, go away, you silly man!'

Slamming the phone down, Miss Gussetpiece reclined in her chair. 'Goodness knows who that was!' she sighed. 'It was some man or other going on about needing a doctor to look up his rectum! I don't know what things are coming to, I really don't!'

'Neither do I, Headmistress,' Miss Frigidus rejoined. 'What with explosions and strange men on the phone, I . . .'

'Miss Gussetpiece?' The headmistress looked up to see a man in a suit at the open study door.

'What is it, Miss Blob? Why are you dressed in men's clothing?'

'Miss Blob is my brother. No, he's not, he's my sister. I mean, *she*'s my sister. I'm Doctor Anusis Rectus.'

'All three of you are remarkably similar in appearance!'

'Yes, we're identical triplets.'

Girl School

'Miss Blob said she was an identical twin.'

'Er . . . well . . . he. . . she must have forgotten that I existed.'

'How could she forget that she has a brother?'

'I haven't seen him . . . I mean, *her* for some time.'

'It doesn't matter if you've not seen her for a thousand years, how on earth could she forget you?'

'A thousand years? We'll all be dead by then!'

'Dead? How could she forget you?'

'Er . . . she was never told about me. I arrived late.'

'But you're an identical triplet!'

'Oh, yes, so I am. I still arrived late, though.'

'It must have been a very difficult birth!'

'Yes, by all accounts it was.'

'How late were you?'

'Three years.'

'What? You were in your mother's womb for three years and nine months?'

'I didn't want to come out – it was warm and cosy in there.'

'Good grief! Your poor mother!'

'Yes, rumour has it that she was somewhat distressed. Er . . . I rang you earlier.'

'Was it you on the phone just now?'

'Yes, it was.'

'How on earth did you get here so quickly? I've only just this minute put the phone down!'

'Er . . . I was on my mobile. What's happened to your study? It looks as if a bomb's hit it!'

'A bomb *has* hit it! What is it you want?'

'I've come to ask you whether you would consider me examining the girls.'

'The exams aren't due until the end of term.'

'No, examine their bodies.'

'Examine the girls' bodies? Whatever for?'

'Because I'd love to get my hands on . . . I mean, being a doctor, I thought I'd offer the school my services.'

'Your brother, Doctor Uterine Pouch, has already examined the girls.'

'Yes, I know, but I'm an anal doctor.'

'A what doctor?'

'Uterine does the front, and I do the back. I'm a doctor of anal physiology. To put it bluntly, I examine people's bottoms.'

'Goodness me! Did you hear that, Miss Frigidus? He examines people's bottoms! Are you a sex maniac?'

'Certainly not, Headmistress!' Miss Frigidus gasped.

'No, not you, you silly woman! I'm talking to him! Well, *are* you a sex maniac?'

'Bloody right I am! What I mean is . . . No, no, of course I'm not a sex maniac! I'm a specialist in teenage girls' anal canals.'

'Why do you have this peculiar predilection for people's bottoms?'

'I don't have a predilection, it's my job.'

'You get paid to look at girls' bottoms?'

'Yes, I do. Good, isn't it?'

'Well, I'm not going to pay you!'

'I'm offering my services free of charge.'

'Oh! Well, I'm not sure that the girls would want their bottoms examined!'

'Of course they would! They'd love . . . It's not a question of whether the girls want their bottoms examined or not, they'd have no choice in the matter!'

'No choice? But it's *their* bottoms you'd be examining!'

Girl School

'Jesus! I'm offering the school my services for nothing! I really didn't expect this sort of reception!'

'What sort of reception? Are you drunk? Have you been to a wedding?'

'A wedding? Strike a light! Oh, it doesn't matter! I'll go to another school and . . . I was only trying to help!'

'Trying to help?'

'Yes, I thought that you'd appreciate my offer.'

'I do! It's just that I'm a little confused, what with you, your brother and your sister.'

'So am I!'

'Your mother was a corsetière, I believe?'

'Was she? Oh, yes, that's right – she travelled in corsets. She came from Fukien.'

'I *beg* your pardon?'

'She was Chinese.'

'But Miss Blob is British, Doctor Pouch is Polish, you're of Latin extraction – and your mother was Chinese?'

'Am I?'

'Are you what?'

'Of Latin extraction.'

'That's what Miss Blob told me!'

'Oh, yes, of course I am! I was forgetting.'

'How can you explain that?'

'I can't.'

'Do you have any other brothers or sisters?'

'I really have no idea, my mother never told me. Er . . . Well, I'll be going, seeing as I'm not wanted here.'

'All right, you may examine the girls.'

'Oh, may I? That's excellent! When? When can I get my fingers up . . . er . . . when may I begin the examinations? I'm free now if . . .'

'I don't want the girls' studies disrupted. Sunday afternoon – come and see me then.'

'Right, I will! Thank you, Miss Gussetpiece – thank you very much!'

Refilling her glass as the doctor left the study, Miss Gussetpiece held her hand to her forehead, wondering whether she should call the police about the explosion. 'I've decided that we'll have to cover this up!' she said firmly, looking at Miss Frigidus. 'We can't let it be known that the toilet block was destroyed by a bomb, it wouldn't look good. We'll get the builders in and . . . Blast, there's no money, is there? Oh, Maxine – what is it you want?' she asked as the girl knocked on the open door.

'About the explosion, Miss Gussetpiece. I thought I'd better tell you that I saw Hilda Hillock running away from the toilet block a few minutes before . . .'

'Hilda Hillock?'

'Yes. She ran across the grounds and climbed over the wall. Presumably she planted the bomb and then did a runner. I doubt that she'll come back.'

'Good gracious! Hilda Hillock, of all people! She was in line to become Head Girl this year! All right, Maxine, thank you – you may go. Wait a minute, what's that sticking out of your blouse?'

'Er . . . Nothing, Miss Gussetpiece.'

'Yes, it is! Give it to me!'

'Oh, this?' Maxine retracted, pulling out the roll of notes. 'This is money, Miss Gussetpiece.'

'I can see that! Where did you get it from?'

'Er . . . I . . .'

'Is it from a fund-raising scheme?'

'Er . . . well, sort of.'

'That's very good of you, Maxine!' Miss Gussetpiece

grinned, snatching the notes. 'Well done! You might be in line for the school captaincy! Good girl! Now, off you go!'

'Yes, Miss Gussetpiece,' Maxine groaned as she left the study.

'Come, Miss Frigidus!' the Head grinned as she stuffed the money down her cleavage. 'We must compile a damage report!'

Piling into the changing rooms after netball practice, the girls were about to take their showers when Miss Cueball interrupted them. 'Calm down, girls! Don't worry about the explosion, it was probably an electrical fault in the toilet block. Now, there's no need to shower separately. We're all girls together, so get stripped off for a jolly good rubdown.' Eyeing her charges' pert breasts, their sparse pubes and young pussy cracks as they tentatively unveiled their young bodies, Miss Cueball grinned. Her crotch bulging beneath her skirt, she knew there was no way she could join them in the shower, but she was more than happy to scrutinize the young beauties.

'What about you, Miss Cueball?' a pretty brunette asked.

'What about me?'

'Aren't you taking a shower?'

'Er . . . no, dear. I'll shower later.'

'What's that, Miss Cueball?' she asked, pointing to the woman's tented skirt.

'It's my hockey stick. Er . . . it's nothing! Off you go, now!'

'Excuse me, Miss Cueball,' Candida ventured sheepishly. 'I . . . I can't take a shower with the others.'

'Why ever not, girl?'

'My . . . you see . . . the doctor removed my pubic hair.'

'Did he? Whatever for?'

'He said that I had a skin complaint and he rubbed cream into me and . . .'

'I must see . . . I mean, follow me, girl.'

Tagging along behind Miss Cueball, Candida followed the woman to Sick Bay. Frowning as she was instructed to pull her knickers down and climb onto the examination couch, she blushed. 'It's all right,' Miss Cueball assured her. 'I used to be a nurse, so I know what I'm doing.' Lifting Candida's skirt up as the girl lay down, the woman grinned. 'Ah, yes, yes – you do have a skin complaint!'

'I can't see anything wrong,' Candida remarked, raising her head to look at her fleshy outer lips.

'I can! The trouble with this particular medical condition is that it can quickly spread. I wouldn't be at all surprised to find that it's gone internal. I'd better take a look.'

'Gone internal?'

'Yes, infected you internally. Just lie still and open your legs as wide as you can.'

Grimacing as Miss Cueball parted her pussy lips and slipped a finger into her vagina, Candida began to wonder whether or not the woman was genuine. The stubble on her chin was rather unusual, and her hands were very rough. In fact, Candida decided as the woman slipped three fingers into her young cuntal sheath, Miss Cueball had no feminine features at all!

'Bring your knees up to your chest, please,' Miss Cueball instructed. 'I do believe that you're all right internally, but I'll just check once more.' Placing her hands behind her knees, Candida brought them up to her firm breasts, exposing her bulging girl-slit to the woman's ever-widening eyes. 'That's lovely! I mean, that's fine. Oh, I've pushed my fingers all the way in! Ah, you're nice and hot and wet and . . . er . . . Right, I'll just check that your bottom's all right,' Miss Cueball breathed eagerly, slipping her wet fingers out of Candida's tightening pussy sheath and discreetly licking the slippery girl-juice from them.

Locating the girl's small brown hole, the woman slipped a finger past the tight muscles and deep into the heat of her suspicious patient's rectal sheath. 'Oh, Miss Cueball!' Candida gasped surprisedly. 'Surely, this isn't right?'

'It's perfectly right! I have to make sure that . . .'

'Yes, but you're the PE mistress, not a doctor! I've already had to endure an intimate examination by a doctor and have my mini hair removed!'

'And lovely it looks, too!'

'Lovely?'

'Yes, I mean lovely for the healing of your skin condition.'

'Ouch! Not two fingers!' Candida cried as her rectal sheath was rudely expanded.

'Right, that's that done,' Miss Cueball grinned, extracting her fingers from the girl's bottom-hole. 'Now, if you'll turn over for me, I'll just check your . . .'

'I'm not having anything else checked!' Candida protested as she climbed off the couch and pulled her knickers up. 'I'm going to Miss Gussetpiece to tell her . . .'

'No! Er . . . No, you mustn't do that!'

'Why not?'

'Er . . . Because . . . How much do you want?'

'What do you mean?'

'I'll pay you, girl.'

'Pay me for what?'

'To play with this,' Miss Cueball grinned, lifting her short skirt and exposing a massive erect penis to the shocked girl. 'Please, let me fuck you! I want to spunk up your cunt!'

'Argh! You're . . . you're a man!'

'Yes, I am. Let me fuck your beautiful cunt, please – I'll pay you!'

'Never!' Candida screamed as she fled the room. 'I'm going to the headmistress!'

Her arms hanging from the steel rings, her naked body aching, Hilda let out a low moan of despair. Having heard the explosion, she knew that Maxine would have gone running to Miss Gussetpiece with her lies. There was no way out of this one, she thought sadly as the basement door opened. She was losing the battle.

'Oh, you still here?' Maxine mocked as she switched the light on. 'I suppose you heard the bomb go off?' she giggled as she closed the door and bounded down the steps. 'Knickergusset is after your blood! I told her that I'd seen you running away from the toilets just before the explosion!' she laughed, pulling the knicker gag from Hilda's mouth.

'She'll jolly well believe me when I tell her the truth, Maxine Mayhem!'

'Of course she won't! Who in their right mind would believe that you've been chained to the basement wall, naked, for all this time? Anyway, I've put word around the whole school that you planted the bomb and then did a runner! Expulsion! At last, little Miss Hilda Pillock is going to be expelled!'

'Miss Gussetpiece will believe me! I'll bring her down here and show her . . .'

'Shut up, Pillock! I've come to the conclusion that I'd be better off keeping you down here – indefinitely! I might as well leave you to rot!'

'I'm hungry, and I need the loo!'

'Tough! Yes, I'll leave you down here until I've decided what to do with you. I don't want you running to Knickergusset and telling her the truth – there's a chance that the old bag might believe you! I'll have to keep you here, as my prisoner! Actually, I've just had a brilliant idea! I could sell you to the boys from the Uni. They'd pay well to fuck you!'

'You wouldn't dare!'

'Wouldn't I? You wouldn't like to put money on it, would you?'

'Please, Maxine, let me go! I won't say anything about the bomb or you keeping me down here if you . . .'

'Do shut up, Pillock! You're becoming boring! Right, I'll go and put word around the Uni that there's a naked girl for sale. I'm going to earn myself a small fortune from your cunt, Pillock! I've lost three hundred quid today, and you're going to replace it by selling your tight cunt! See you later!' Maxine giggled, pushing the knickers back into Hilda's pretty mouth to silence her.

Watching Maxine bound up the basement steps and slam the door shut behind her, Hilda hung her head. Her fate seemingly sealed, she knew that she could do nothing to halt the sale of her young body. Gazing down at her pert breasts, she imagined the university boys sucking on her nipples. *Please, Candida – come and rescue me!* she prayed as a tear rolled down her flushed cheek. *Please, God, I'll never play with my mini again and have a goodie if you help me to escape!*

Chapter Six

The trees cast long shadows in the evening sun as Miss Frigidus made her way into the wood in search of the priest – and heaven. Puffing on her cigarette, she cast her eyes around the undergrowth, wondering where the man of God had got to. 'Psst!' someone hissed from the bushes as she entered the clearing. 'I'm over here!'

'Oh!' Miss Frigidus exclaimed as the priest leaped out of the bushes and stood grinning before her. 'You made me jump, Father!'

'God has sent you to me!' he announced excitedly.

'Has he?'

'Oh, yes! He came to me in a vision, telling me that he'd sent you to me for hands-on healing.'

'Hands-on healing, Father?'

'How old are you?'

'Thirty-five.'

'Perfect! You must remove your shroud, Miss Frigidus.'

'Please, do call me Lavinia. What do you mean by my *shroud*?'

'Your clothes, Lavinia. You must stand naked before God – your creator!'

'Naked? Oh, dear! But I can't . . .'

'It is God's wish! You cannot defy God's wish!'

'But I can't undress in front of a man, Father! No one has ever seen me naked, not even my mother!'

'She must have done.'

'Well, a little bit, perhaps.'

'God is *here*, Lavinia! He is angry, you've roused his wrath! Quickly, before you're struck down – remove your clothes!'

Unbuttoning her dress, Miss Frigidus slipped the garment off and stood meekly before the priest in her bra and panties. Surveying her curvaceous body, he grinned. 'Have you smoked the dope? I mean, how many herbal cigarettes have you smoked?'

'I've had three in the last half-hour,' she said softly, gazing down in bewilderment at her full bra.

'Good, good! Did you tell anyone that you were coming here to meet me?'

'Only the headmistress.'

'Shit! I mean, not to worry. Hurry, Lavinia – God awaits! He is calling for you.'

'I'm not going to die, am I? I'm too young to die!'

'No, no! He awaits your complete disrobing, not your transition from this earthly plane.'

'Complete disrobing? Goodness me!'

Unclipping her bra, Miss Frigidus peeled the silk cups away from her firm, virginal breasts and tossed the lace garment to the ground. 'Ah, yes!' the priest breathed, gazing longingly at her dark areolae, her long brown nipples. 'God is pleased with your beautifully rounded and firm . . . God is pleased with your nakedness!' As she began to tug her panties down, the semi-stripped and stoned Latin mistress hesitated.

Girl School

Eyeing the priest's tented cassock, she frowned and shook her head.

'I really don't think . . .'

'God awaits!'

'Oh, dear!'

'Hurry! Remove all your clothes and offer your naked body to God for hands-on healing!'

'Oh, my goodness!'

Boldly tugging her panties down her shapely legs, Miss Frigidus stood naked before the priest. Wondering whether she really wanted to find heaven as he knelt before her and revered her pubic bush, she folded her arms, covering her delicate breasts. 'Oh!' she screamed, jumping back as the priest stroked her black pubes. 'What are you doing?'

'This is the healing hand of God!' he enlightened the quivering woman.

'But it's *your* hand!'

'God is within me, using my hand to bring you healing. Quickly, spread out on the grass! Give your body to God for hands-on groping . . . I mean, healing!'

'Oh, dear!'

Sitting on the grass, Miss Frigidus reclined and spread her limbs. Her virginal pussy crack opening before the priest's wide eyes, the effect of the Colombian grass beginning to blur her senses, she relaxed as he settled between her thighs. Sensing his finger probing between her swollen sex-cushions, she gasped. 'Oh, oh! I don't think that God would . . . Oh!'

His finger swiftly entering her hot sanctuary, the priest massaged the fleshy walls of her sex duct, placing his free hand on her smooth stomach to hold her down as she tried to raise her body on her elbows. 'Father!' she cried as a second finger slipped into her neglected pussy sheath. 'Father! Oh, my head's reeling! I feel . . . Oh dear, I feel . . .' Reclining, Miss Frigidus gazed at the canopy of green leaves high above her naked body. 'Oh, the world's spinning round!' she gasped as the priest began to massage her ripening clitoris. 'Oh, that feels . . . that feels awfully strange!'

'Relax, Lavinia, and allow the power to permeate your body!' the priest cried as he drove a third digit into her spasming vagina. 'Let there be sex! I mean, light.'

'Oh, oh! It feels . . . it feels nice!'

'Yes, it will! What you're feeling is the power! Relax and allow the sensations to build and erupt in an explosion of cosmic energy! I'm taking you to heaven!'

'Oh, gosh!'

Thrusting his fingers in and out of the spinster's uncovered pussy, the priest vigorously massaged her throbbing clitoris. Gasping, Miss Frigidus tossed her head from side to side as her climax approached. 'Oh, oh! Something's happening to me!' she cried. 'Oh, I feel . . . I can't stop trembling! Ah! Ah! What is it? What's happening to me? Oh! Ah! Yes, that's nice! Oh, don't stop doing that! Do it faster! Faster, harder, faster! Oh, what is it?'

'Heaven, Lavinia – you've found heaven!'

Discovering her sexuality as her orgasm ravished her naked body, Miss Frigidus clung to clumps of grass for dear life, her eyes rolling, her nostrils flaring, her flushed breasts heaving. Sustaining her neonate pleasure as she moaned her thanksgiving, the priest leaned over her quivering body and engulfed her magic button in his mouth. Licking, sucking the pulsating nodule, the luscious ensconcing flesh, as the frenzied woman grabbed his head and ground her open cunt into his face, he discreetly whipped out his solid penis. *Quod ore sumpsimus, Domine, pura mente capiamus:* ET DE MUNERE TEMPORALI FIAT NOBIS REMEDIUM SEMPITERNUM. *That which our mouths have taken, Lord, may we possess in purity of heart:* AND MAY THE GIFT OF THE MOMENT BECOME FOR US AN EVERLASTING REMEDY.

Bringing out the last tremblings of Lavinia's pioneer orgasm with his vibrating fingertips, the priest pulled his cassock up and knelt between her twitching thighs. Aligning his purple knob with her eager entrance, he deftly drove his love-staff deep into her virginal pussy, causing her to jolt and scream out.

'Oh, my goodness! What on earth is that? Oh, meus virginitas!'

'Dominus vobiscum!' the priest cried as he drove his weapon fully home, his solid knob pressing against her cervix, his heavy balls brushing her taut buttocks. 'The Lord be with you! This is the will of God, Lavinia! You are to surrender your virginity and take the fruits of my loins deep into your barren womb!'

'Golly!'

Thrusting his fleshpole in and out of the woman's virginal sex duct, the priest groped her firm breasts, pinching and squeezing her erect nipples, bringing her hitherto unknown sensations. Her rubicund inner lips rolling along his wet shaft as he propelled his purple knob deep into her slippery tube, he gasped as he sensed his climax nearing. Lifting her legs and placing them over his shoulders, he gazed at her full outer lips encompassing his organ, her pinken inner flesh glistening with her exotic new juices of arousal.

'Coming!' he cried as his sperm gushed into her quivering body.

'Oh, dear! Who's coming?' Miss Frigidus quavered as her vaginal sheath was unceremoniously baptized with his unholy liquid.

'I am! God, I'm coming in your beautiful cunt!'

'Ah! Ah, that's nice! Ooh! It feels . . . it feels lovely! Goodness me, I feel as if I'm leaving my body! Ah, ah! Oh, this is a truly heavenly experience!'

'God, you're tight! Christ, your cunt's hot, wet, tight . . .'

Driving his orgasming knob deep into her abused sanctuary, the priest jetted the last of his sperm over her cervix before collapsing over her heaving breasts. Quivering, panting beneath his trembling body, Miss Frigidus grabbed his buttocks, pulling him hard against her, driving his penis deep into her spasming vagina.

'More!' she begged. 'I want you to do it again! Take me to heaven again!'

'I can't, not yet!' he gasped.

'Please! Do it to me again!'

'In a minute! I need to rest first!'

'Jesus fucking Christ!' Maxine cried as she stumbled into the clearing with Ginger. 'Miss Frigidus, what *are* you doing?'

Leaping from the Latin mistress's naked body, the priest dived into the bushes, leaving the horrified woman with her thighs parted, her crimson crack open, oozing with his profane cream. Sitting up and covering her breasts with her folded arms, Miss Frigidus gazed in horror at Maxine.

'I . . . Maxine, I . . .' she stammered.

'Well, Miss Frigidus, I would never have dreamed that you . . .'

'What are you doing?' the frightened woman cried as Ginger gathered her clothes. 'Please, give me my things!'

'No, I won't!' Ginger giggled. 'You'll just have to go back to school naked!'

'Please, I can't leave the woods without my clothes!'

'Yes, you can!' Maxine laughed. 'Who was that man you were with?'

'Please, I must have my clothes! Oh dear, I need a Valium!'

'Come on, Maxine, let's go,' Ginger chortled, bundling the clothes up and leaving the clearing.

'You can't leave me like this!' Miss Frigidus sobbed pitifully as Maxine followed her friend into the bushes. 'Please, please . . .'

Rubbing her chin as she scrutinized Candida, Miss Gussetpiece frowned. 'Are you telling the truth, girl?' she asked. 'Because, if you're not . . . Candida, this is a serious allegation!'

'It's true, Miss Gussetpiece – the new PE mistress took me to Sick Bay and examined my . . . examined between my legs, and then pulled his big, stiff thing out and asked me . . .'

'Yes, yes, all right! Spare me the sordid details! On second thoughts . . . No, no. Look, we'll keep this a secret. We can't have . . .'

'But, Miss Gussetpiece! He was disguised as a woman! He was in the changing rooms with the naked girls! We must go to the police!'

'No, no! I don't want the police involved! As it is, the

toilets have been blown up, Hilda has gone off, and the girls have had their underwear stolen from the changing rooms.'

'That'll be *him*!' Candida asserted. 'He must have taken the clothes from the changing rooms! We *must* tell the police, Miss Gussetpiece!'

'Calm yourself, girl! Nothing happened to you, he didn't actually . . .'

'He put his fingers in me!'

'There's no harm done! Look, go and have a rest and I'll talk to you later.'

Gazing out of the shattered window as Candida flounced from the study, Miss Gussetpiece strained her eyes, trying to make out a distant figure running towards the school. 'Who on earth . . .' she gasped. 'Oh, my goodness, Miss Frigidus! Miss Frigidus, come here at once!' she bellowed to the naked woman streaking across the grass. 'Come here this instant!'

'I'll be with you when I'm dressed, Headmistress!' Miss Frigidus called as she rounded the building and disappeared from view.

Flopping into her chair and swigging neat vodka from the bottle, Miss Gussetpiece shook her head in despair. Gazing around her wrecked study, she grabbed the phone and dialled maintenance. 'Jones, is that you?' she asked as a man answered.

'This is Smith, who's that?'

'Smith? This is Miss Gussetpiece, where's Jones?'

'Who's Jones?'

'The maintenance man. Who are you?'

'Smith.'

'I've never heard of you! What are you doing in maintenance?'

'I'm on the phone.'
'On the phone? Why are you on the phone?'
'It rang.'
'Come to my study at once!'
'I can't.'
'You'll come here immediately or I'll ring the police! Right, that's it!' she yelled as the man hung up. 'I'm not having this sort of behaviour going on!'

Leaving her study, Miss Gussetpiece walked briskly down the corridor to maintenance and flung the door open. 'Who are you?' she demanded of a middle-aged man sitting at a bench.

'I'm Smith. Who are you?'

'I'm the headmistress, Miss Gussetpiece! What are you doing here?'

'I'm a carpenter. Mr Johnson sent for me.'

'A carpenter? What firm are you with? I'll have to check your credentials!'

'Measure Once Cut Twice Limited.'

'Measure Once Cut . . . Why couldn't you come to my study?'

'I don't know where it is.'

'What's your business here?'

'I'm to board up the broken windows. The glazier can't get here until tomorrow.'

'Oh, I see. Where's Jones?'

'Miss Gussetpiece!' Miss Frigidus called through the doorway. 'A policeman's here to see you! He's waiting in your study.'

'A policeman? Oh, my goodness! All right, I'm coming! You, Smith or whoever you are – stop sitting around and get on with your work!'

Following Miss Frigidus down the corridor, Miss

Gussetpiece smiled amiably at the policeman as she entered her study. 'Good evening,' she greeted him, diving for her drinks cabinet. 'What can I do for you, Officer?'

'We've just received a report of a naked woman streaking across the school grounds, Headmistress. What's been going on in here? Your study looks as if it's been hit by a bomb!'

'Er . . . we've got the decorators in – they're rather messy.'

'Oh. What's that pile of rubble doing outside?'

'That's . . . er . . . that's a sculpture – modern art. What's all this about a naked woman?' Miss Gussetpiece asked, flashing Miss Frigidus an accusing look.

'We've just received a report of a naked woman streaking through the school grounds. I was passing the school when the message came through. Also, a girl rang the station with an allegation concerning the PE mistress, Miss Cueball.'

'Which girl?'

'Apparently she didn't give her name. Can you tell me where the PE mistress is?'

'No, I can't. I haven't seen her since . . . We don't have a PE mistress at the moment. The girl, whoever it was, must have been . . . she was probably having a wank. I mean, playing a prank.'

'I see. Did you notice anyone streaking through the school grounds?'

'No, I did not! I think someone's been playing around, Officer. I'm so sorry that you've been put to this trouble.'

'That's all right, Headmistress – girls will be girls! By the way, the bogus priest has been sighted again. He's a known sexual pervert so, if you see him, please let us know immediately.'

'Yes, of course.'

'I'll say good evening, then.'

'Will you? Oh, yes – good evening, Officer.'

Closing the door hurriedly, Miss Gussetpiece flew at the quivering, glowing Latin mistress. 'What on earth were you doing, running through the grounds naked?' she demanded.

'I lost my clothes, Headmistress!'

'Lost them?'

'I was in the woods with the priest and . . .'

'What? You took your clothes off in front of a priest?'

'Yes, to stand naked before God.'

'Don't say another word, Miss Frigidus! I really can't take any more of this nonsense! Pour me a large gin, will you?'

'Yes, Headmistress. It must be difficult for you.'

'What must?'

'All these problems.'

'Difficult? It's impossible! A bomb, a missing girl, stolen underwear, a queer PE mistress, the police – and now you, naked in the woods with a priest! And I never did get the laundry basket back! What *are* things coming to?'

'I don't know, Headmistress.'

'Neither do I! Well, did you find God?'

'No, but the priest took me to heaven.'

'I'll have to meet this man. When are you seeing him again?'

'I don't know. He ran off, you see.'

'Ran off? Wait a minute! There's a pervert on the loose,

posing as a priest. You don't think . . . What did he do to you?'

'Er . . . well, nothing, really.'

'Nothing?'

'Well, he . . . Oh, dear! I think I've been molested by a sexual pervert!'

'You are a silly woman, you really are! What did he do to you, exactly?'

'He put his thing in me! Oh, I've been molested by a sex pest! Oh, my goodness! I've lost my virginity to a sexual pervert, to a sexual deviant, to a sex maniac, to a sex fiend, to a psychopath, to a . . .'

'Shut up, Miss Frigidus! Take a grip on yourself, woman!'

'But I've been raped!'

'Of course you haven't been raped! I wonder if he's still in the grounds? I'll go and take a look. I hope he's still in the woods, I wouldn't mind a quick . . . er . . . yes, well. As for you, you'd better go to your rooms and pray for forgiveness! And don't mention a word of this to anyone!'

'But if I'm to pray, I'll have to tell God.'

'Yes, I hadn't thought of that. On second thoughts, you'd better not pray. If God knew that you'd . . . What the hell am I talking about?'

'Oh, dear! I don't know, Headmistress!'

'Repair to your rooms, Miss Frigidus!'

Squatting on the floor, Maxine focused her camera on Hilda's swollen pussy lips and clicked the shutter. 'We'll charge a fiver for each picture,' she told Ginger. 'We can develop them in the lab.'

'You're beastly!' Hilda spat as Ginger slipped a huge

cucumber between her prisoner's pouting pussy and drove it deep into her tight vagina. 'I hate you, you vile beasts!'

'Shut up, Pillock!' Maxine returned, taking several shots of the girl's taut cunny lips encompassing the phallus. 'We never did shave your fanny, did we? Ginger, go and get a razor and some shaving foam.'

'Where from?'

'I don't know! What about hair-removing cream? Someone must have some!'

'All right, I'll see you soon.'

'I'll tell my father about you, Maxine Mayhem!' Hilda warned.

'Yeah? What's he like? What's he do for a living?'

'He's a nice, decent man! He's a doctor.'

'Oh, a doctor! Examine women's cunts, does he?'

'I've never known anyone so dreadfully . . .'

'Fucking hell, here we go again! Look, Pillock, I've just had an idea. I'll let you go if you pay me.'

'How much?'

'Fifty quid.'

'I haven't got fifty pounds!'

'I heard that you're organizing a jumble sale or something, you can pay me out of the money you make from that.'

'I can't steal from the takings!'

'All right, I'll shave your cunt and leave you here all night!'

'All right, all right! Let me go, and I'll give you fifty pounds.'

Releasing the girl's aching arms, Maxine ordered her to dress. Watching as she slipped her knickers up her long legs, concealing her abused pussy, she grinned. Hilda was in big trouble, she mused. Miss Gussetpiece would probably expel her for blowing up the toilet block. She'd certainly be suspended, she thought as she watched the girl race up the basement steps and fling the door open.

Hiding the handcuffs and whip, the evidence of Hilda's enforced bondage, Maxine grabbed a bottle of vodka from the box and unscrewed the top. 'When she pays me, I'll shave her cunt anyway!' she giggled, swigging from the bottle.

Deciding to go for a walk, Hilda stepped out of the building, breathing in the warm evening air as she stretched her sore limbs. Although dusk was falling, she needed to get away from the school and relax before her confrontation with Miss Gussetpiece. *The woods*, she decided. *I wonder if the badger's still around?*

Creeping through the undergrowth on her nature trail, she dived into the bushes as she heard voices. Crawling across the ground, she peered into the clearing, her mouth falling open as she gazed at Miss Gussetpiece.

'I'm a cleaner at the school,' the headmistress was saying. 'I might look like the headmistress, but I'm not.'

'And I might look like the PE mistress, but I'm not – I'm a priest,' the man dressed in a cassock replied.

'There's a vile, filthy, disgusting, debauched sexual pervert on the loose posing as a priest – it's not you, is it?' Miss Gussetpiece asked hopefully.

'Certainly not! I'm a man of God!'

'Are you, now? That's not what I heard from Miss Frigidus! You're the priest who came to the school asking to take the girls for confession, aren't you?'

'No, I'm not. I only arrived from the Vatican today.'

'Really? That's an awfully long way to come! How's the Pope?'

'He . . . he's fine. He sent me out into the world to enlighten women – to take them to heaven.'

'Well, I never! Miss Frigidus told me that you took her to heaven – will you take me to heaven?'

'Perish the thought!'

'I'll pay you.'

'How much?'

'Fifty pounds.'

'You're on! Take your knickers off!'

Stunned, Hilda watched the headmistress slip her bloomers down and lie on the grass with her legs splayed. Lifting his cassock, revealing his rampant erection, the priest knelt between the Head's legs and drove his penis deep into her vaginal canal. Holding her hand to her mouth, Hilda couldn't believe what she was seeing, or what her headmistress was saying.

'Ah, really give it to me!' Miss Gussetpiece gasped. 'That's it, shove it all in and give it to me rotten!'

'You like a good fuck now and then, do you?' the priest grunted.

'God, yes! I haven't been laid for thirty years! Since I was on the factory floor, in fact!'

'We'll have to meet again and fuck!'

'Oh, yes, yes! Ah, God, that's nice! Do it harder! That's it, ram your stiff cock into me!'

'It'll cost you fifty quid a fuck.'

'Yes, anything, anything!'

Shocked, Hilda crept away from the clearing, cringing as the woman's cries of sexual satisfaction filled the wood. Her heroine, her mentor, she thought sadly, was no better than Maxine Mayhem! *How could Miss*

Gussetpiece behave like that? she wondered as she entered the school.

'Hilly!' Candida cried joyfully as she sprinted down the corridor towards her friend. 'Where have you been? We've searched everywhere for you!'

'I've been . . . I'll tell you all about it later. Miss Gussetpiece is . . . Oh, I don't know, Candida! Things are different now that we're nearing the end of the sixth form. Bellend used to be my life, I loved it, but now . . .'

'Let's go to the potting shed and talk,' the girl suggested, taking Hilda's hand and leading her down the corridor. 'You look pale, tired.'

'I *am* tired. I've been chained to the basement wall, naked, for hours!'

'It wasn't . . . it wasn't Maxine Mayhem, was it?'

'Yes, and her beastly friend, Ginger.'

Entering the potting shed, Hilda gasped, gazing openmouthed at Patsy. Her young body naked, tied to the sofa with rope, her thighs spread, her vaginal lips taut around a huge cucumber, she was a pitiful sight. 'What are you doing here, Pillock?' Ginger hissed as she emerged from the shadows. 'Maxine should never have let you go!'

'What have you been doing to Patsy?' Hilda yelled, pulling the cucumber from her friend's distended sheath and releasing her.

'This is a stroke of luck!' Candida grinned as she grabbed Ginger's arm. 'All alone, without your friends to protect you – this *is* a stroke of luck!'

'Fucking well get off me!' Ginger spat as Candida twisted her arm. 'When Maxine hears about this, she'll . . .'

'She'll what?' Patsy sneered, rising to her feet and grabbing the girl's other arm. 'Now you're *my* prisoner – and I'm going to do to you exactly what you did to me!'

Yanking Ginger's gymslip off, Patsy ripped the girl's blouse from her trembling body. 'Revenge is sweet!' she cried, pulling her prisoner's bra off, exposing her firm, rounded breasts, her long, brown nipples. 'I'm going to . . .'

'Patsy!' Hilda interjected. 'I don't think you should . . .'

'What? You don't think I should what? I want revenge!' the girl hissed, a wicked glint in her brown eyes. 'I've had enough of Maxine Mayhem and her gang and this is our chance to get at one of them! I would have thought that you'd be all for it, Hilda!'

'Two wrongs don't make a right!'

'Leave, if you don't like it!' Patsy growled, ripping Ginger's knickers down her long legs.

'I'm staying!' Candida giggled. 'I want revenge, too!'

'All right, then,' Hilda conceded reluctantly. 'But there'll be repercussions, I know that!'

'Fucking right there will!' Ginger hissed, standing naked before her captors.

'So, Ginger, you stuffed a cucumber up my mini, and now I'll jolly well stuff it up yours!'

Pushing the girl over the sofa to display her comfortably rounded buttocks, her full vaginal lips nestling beneath her bottom-hole, Patsy grinned. Taking the cucumber as Candida held their prisoner down, she forced it deep into the girl's tight vaginal sheath, giggling uncontrollably as she appeared to lose her senses. Twisting and pushing the fruit, marinating the green shaft in the girl's exquisite juices, Patsy soon slipped it from her gaping pussy. Presenting the rounded end to her struggling prisoner's bottom-hole, she pushed the cucumber past the girl's tightening muscles, her wide eyes sparkling as Ginger wailed her protests.

'What's the matter?' Patsy mocked. 'Don't you like the taste of your own medicine?'

'Maxine will get you for this! You just wait and see!' Ginger sobbed as the cucumber sank into her hot bowels. 'Argh! No, no! Please, don't do this to me!'

'Oh, she's crying!' Patsy scorned. 'The big bully's crying, how sad!'

'Maxine will . . .'

'I don't think we should be doing this!' Hilda gasped as the fruit sank deeper into the girl's dank receptacle. 'You're hurting her!'

'Hurting her? I don't care if I rip her bum open!' Patsy squealed as she drove the fruit even further into the girl's squirming body.

'Fucking hell!' Maxine gasped as she burst into the shed, the devil mirrored in her fiery eyes. 'What the fucking hell's going on? Right, you two, get out of here!' she ordered Patsy and Candida. Turning her satanic glare to Hilda, she grinned. '*You* are staying!'

Scampering out of the shed like frightened rabbits, Candida and Patsy had no choice other than to leave Hilda to her dreadful fate. Satan's daughter was in no mood for God's children – but they'd return with help, Hilda was sure as Maxine grabbed her arm. 'So, Pillock, we meet yet again – and yet again, you're my prisoner!'

'Max, get the bloody cucumber out of my arse!' Ginger shrieked.

'I will, but I'll just make sure that those bitches have gone,' Maxine breathed, releasing Hilda and stepping out of the shed.

Trying to pull the fruity phallus from her bottom-hole, Ginger grimaced, ordering Hilda to help her. Kneeling behind the impaled girl, Hilda grabbed the cucumber, slowly pulling and twisting the fruit. 'Holy Mary, Mother of God!' Miss Gussetpiece cried as she entered the shed to confront the lewd spectacle. 'Stone the crows! Hilda, what have you done to the poor girl?'

'No, Miss Gussetpiece, it wasn't . . .'

'Go to my study and wait for me! I have never known such distasteful and disgusting behaviour! Are you all right, girl?' the headmistress asked Ginger, finally tugging the cucumber from the girl's bottom as Hilda fled in tears.

'Yes, I think so,' Ginger sobbed, staggering to her feet and covering her pert breasts. 'Hilda tore my clothes off and . . . Oh, Miss Gussetpiece, I was so terribly frightened!'

'Calm yourself, girl! Go and have a shower and get into bed – while I deal with Hilda Hillock!'

Waiting in the wrecked study, Hilda hung her head in shame. This was it, she thought fearfully – expulsion! No matter what she said in defence, Miss Gussetpiece would never believe her. *Attack*! she suddenly decided, recalling the headmistress in the woods with the priest. *Drop the defence and attack!*

'Well, Hilda!' Miss Gussetpiece roared as she flung the study door open and stood before the girl with her clenched fists on her ample hips. 'I have never witnessed such rude, disgusting, filthy, debauched . . .'

'No, Miss Gussetpiece, and neither had I witnessed such debauched behaviour before walking in the woods earlier this evening!' Hilda returned.

'In the woods?' the headmistress echoed, her face paling.

'Yes. I was walking in the woods looking for badgers when . . . Well, there's no need to tell you what I saw and heard. Anyway, I didn't do that to Ginger, it was her friend, Maxine.'

'Er . . . I . . . I think I need a drink!' Miss Gussetpiece stammered. 'I . . . In the woods earlier, I was just . . .'

'I know what you were doing, Miss Gussetpiece – I saw you! And those dreadful things you said to that priest were . . .'

'Yes, well . . . er . . . that pervert stole the three hundred pounds Maxine had given me! I'd offered him fifty and he . . . er . . . Go to bed, Hilda. We'll not mention this again. Go to bed and sleep well.'

'Yes, Miss Gussetpiece, thank you.'

Flopping into her chair, Miss Gussetpiece swigged from her vodka bottle, wondering why things were going so terribly wrong. *I'd better be more careful!* she thought, recalling her beautiful experience with the priest. *Bastard! Fancy robbing me of my three hundred! I'll bloody well have him for that!* Finishing the vodka, she slumped forward, her head thumping onto the plaster-covered desk as the empty bottle smashed to the floor. *Better be more care . . .* – Drifting in her alcoholic haze, the woman fell into a deep sleep – well and truly plastered.

The weekend finally arriving, Hilda rose early to organize the fête. 'You do the food stall,' she instructed Candida. 'And Patsy, you be in charge of teas and coffees. Shirley, you can manage the tombola. Right, it's ten o'clock, the people should be arriving soon. Maria, go and man the lucky dip. Julie, you can organize the other girls – make sure that all the stalls are covered. I'll be round every half-hour or so to collect the money.'

'Gosh, this is jolly good fun!' Candida giggled. 'You are a clever old thing, Hilly, you really are!'

'Yes, I am rather! Let's hope that Maxine and her beastly friends don't spoil things. Right, off you all go!'

Staggering across the field with Madame Fissure and Véronique, Miss Gussetpiece wished Hilda luck. 'I hope you take a lot of money! I need . . . er . . . Bring the cash to my study after the fête and I'll pocket it . . . I mean, I'll count it,' she drooled.

'Bonne chance, girls!' Madame Fissure smiled. 'Will someone take care of Véronique? She's a new girl, and very shy and sensitive.'

'I will, Madame Fissure!' Hilda volunteered eagerly.

'What a con!' Miss Gussetpiece slurred, gazing at the price of the teas.

'Miss Gussetpiece!' Madame Fissure gasped, her dark eyes wide with disgust. 'Please, Véronique is young and vulnerable!'

'What do you mean? What have I done?'

'Your language, Headmistress! Please, don't swear in front of Véronique!'

'I didn't swear!'

Taking the befuddled woman to one side, Madame Fissure whispered urgently in her ear. 'Headmistress, your disgusting conversation with Miss Frigidus in your study the other day stunned me, it really did! And now you're swearing in front of the girls!'

'I didn't swear! All I said was *what a con*!'

'Shush! What's got into you, Headmistress?'

'The refreshments were a con!'

'A cunt? *Con* is French for cunt.'

'Shush! Goodness me! Do you think the girl understood?'

'Look at her, she's crying, she must have done!'

'Crying? That's all I need! Where's her chaperone, that German woman?'

'She had to go away for the weekend. She's French, by the way.'

'Don't start all that again! Goodness me, listen to the stupid girl wailing! This is ridiculous! Hilda will have to calm her! I really can't be doing with sodding girls! I mean, sobbing girls! Jesus, my head's spinning, I must go and have a rest!'

'Yes, all right, I'll see you later, Headmistress,' Madame Fissure sighed as the Head staggered off across the grass.

Consoling Véronique, Hilda put her arm around the girl's shoulder. 'Miss Gussetpiece didn't mean to swear,' she said softly. 'The word *con* is short for . . .' Tears streaming down her face, the girl ran off towards the trees, wailing for her mother. 'Golly! Now *I*'ve upset her!' Hilda exclaimed. 'I was only trying to . . .'

'She'll be all right,' Madame Fissure consoled, watching the girl run away. 'I have things to do – good luck, girls!' she smiled as she walked towards the school.

'Right!' Maxine grinned, addressing her friends as they settled in the clearing. 'What we'll do is this. We'll ambush Hillock when she takes the money to Knickergusset. Fuck me, talk about daylight robbery! I've laced the lemonade heavily with vodka, so we'll have dozens of drunks staggering around. When the police arrive . . .'

'The police?' Ginger echoed fearfully.

'Yes, at the appropriate time I'll call them. Now, I want you all to wander around the fête, mingle with the crowd. Ginger, take the bag of dirty knickers and spread them out over the clothes stall. They're really dirty, cunt-stained to hell! There'll be a few complaints, I can tell you! Kelly, take the bag of condoms and drop them all over the playing field. The flour-and-water mix looks realistic enough, just like spunk! People will be slipping over everywhere! Fukui, take the bag of dirty mags and drop them around the stalls. You know, one here, one there – all open at the centrefold, of course. I'm going to take the photos I took of Pillock's cunt and pin them up everywhere. Oh, fuck, I almost forgot – I'll take the sack of litter and chuck it all over the field. There's no way Hilda Hillock will ever be allowed to hold another bloody fête – not as long as she lives! Right, into action, girls!'

Frowning at the man from British Telecom, Miss Gussetpiece shook her head. 'Why you couldn't come earlier, I really don't know!' she complained. 'The phone's not been working properly for ages!'

'Pressure of work, Headmistress,' the man replied, fiddling with the wiring.

'Yes, I know the feeling! How long will you be on the job?'

'About five years.'

'Five years! I can't wait that long! What sort of service is that? It's despicable, it really is! I blame the government for . . .'

'No, I've been doing this job for five years!'

'Oh, right! So, how long will it take?'

'It's hard to say. There's considerable damage to the outside lines. Why are the windows boarded up? What on earth happened here?'

'Er . . . I don't know, I wasn't here at the time of the ex— When the fault occurred. Ah, Miss Frigidus. What is it?'

'The glazier's here, Headmistress – he's outside, assessing the damage.'

'Good, I'll go and tell him off!'

'Oh, dear! Why?'

'Why not? You have to treat these tradespeople badly, be rude to them – it's all they understand!'

Approaching the young man, Miss Gussetpiece wagged her finger at him. 'You should have been here days ago!' she admonished.

'Why?' he asked.

'Because you were called days ago!'

'No, I wasn't!'

'Yes, you were! Anyway, you're here now, so stop hanging around and get on with it!'

'I can't do that, lady.'

'Why ever not? And don't call me lady!'

'These old leaded light windows aren't easy to . . .'

'Don't make excuses!'

'I'm not! Anyway, the lintel's cracked, it'll have to be replaced before I can . . .'

'Lintel?'

'You'll need an RSJ.'

'Everything all right?' Johnson asked as he approached.

'No, the lintel's cracked, mate. You'll need new frames, and I can't do that until the lintel's been replaced.'

'That's that, then. OK, I'll call you when I've had the lintel replaced.'

'Right, see you, mate.'

'Where's he going?' Miss Gussetpiece asked angrily as the glazier climbed into his van and drove off.

'Home, I would imagine.'

'He can't go home! What's he gone home for?'

'Because he lives there, I suppose.'

'It's not good enough!'

'How do you know, Miss Gussetpiece? Have you ever seen his home?'

'Of course I haven't! He was to come here and do a job of work and now he's . . . It's no wonder this country is going down the drain!'

'He can't fit new windows until the builders have been in to . . .'

'We can't afford all this work!'

'The insurance company will pay. I'll go and see the bursar and . . .'

'Er . . . We no longer have a bursar. I had to . . . I had to dismiss him and do the job myself. And I can't tell the insurance company about it. I don't want word getting out that there was a bomb. Besides, I had to use the insurance premium money to . . . er . . . I won't go into that.'

'You mean, the building's not insured?'

'Yes, sort of. Well, not exactly. So what can you do about the . . . about the lintel, or whatever it is?'

'Well, I suppose I could fill the crack in, cover up the broken lintel, but it won't be very safe.'

'Good, do it now, Jones.'

'Johns – Never mind.'

'Right, I must go and have a drink. Tea, I mean – a drink of tea. Hey, where do you think you're going – not home, I hope?' she called to the BT man.

'I'm going up the pole.'

'And I'm going round the bend!'

'No, no! I have to climb the pole to repair the wires.'

'Well, be quick about it! I can't have strange men climbing poles, it's not natural!'

Pacing her office floor, swigging from the gin bottle,

Miss Gussetpiece sighed as someone knocked on the door. 'Jesus, now what? Come in!' she called, sitting at her desk.

'Miss Gussetpiece?' a youngish nun asked demurely as she entered the study.

'Yes.'

'Sorry to trouble you, but I wondered whether you'd allow me to talk to the girls.'

'Talk to the girls? What about?'

'About the virgin . . .'

'Ah, you have a good disguise – but not good enough! You can't fool me, I know that you're the sexual pervert!'

'I'm a nun, Headmistress!'

'Yes, and I'm the bloody Pope! You're the man who fucked me in the woods and then stole my money, aren't you? I'm going to have you locked up! Ah, Miss Frigidus, a timely entrance, I must say. Help me to remove this pervert's habit!'

'Oh, dear! Is that wise?'

'Just help me to expose this so-called nun for the sad pervert he really is!'

Tackling the screaming nun, Miss Gussetpiece managed to pull her to the floor and tear her habit from her struggling body. Grappling with her arms, Miss Frigidus sat on the sister's chest, pinning her down as Miss Gussetpiece yanked her petticoat off. 'Got you now!' the headmistress cried, trying to yank the woman's knickers down. 'You'll do ten years for this!'

'Oh, oh! Please!' the nun wailed. 'God, help me!'

'God won't help you! You're going to prison, you sad pervert!'

'What the hell's going on in here?' Miss Blob cried as she entered the study, gazing in horror at the affray.

'We've caught the pervert!' Miss Gussetpiece declared, tugging the nun's thick, woollen knickers down. 'Look, she's not a woman at all! Oh! Oh, my God! She *is* a woman!' she gasped, gazing at the nun's blatant vaginal crack.

'Oh, dear, we've raped a real nun!' Miss Frigidus gasped.

'Jesus Christ!' Miss Blob cried. 'Jesus bloody Christ!'

Leaping to her feet as Miss Blob and Miss Frigidus fled the study, Miss Gussetpiece sat at her desk and straightened her clothing. Pulling her knickers up, the nun stood and gathered up her shredded habit. 'I have never been so . . .' she sobbed.

'A simple mistake,' the Head smiled nonchalantly. 'We'll say no more about the incident.'

'We will! I shall report you to the police!'

'What for?'

'Attempted rape!'

'Don't be so silly!'

'You tried to rape me!'

'Now you're being ridiculous! I was only trying to see your penis!'

'I don't have a . . . You need help! I'll see to it that you're removed from your post as headmistress!'

'It was a simple mistake, woman! I thought that you were a man, a sad pervert. All I was trying to do was prove that you were a man.'

'I'm going straight to the Mother Superior – and the police!' the distraught woman cried as she fled the study.

Pacing the floor, Detective Inspector Puckit turned to face the group of police officers seated in the briefing room.

'The Intelligence boys working on Operation Monk have assured me that our perverted priest is in the area of Bellend School. I want all nuns and priests apprehended and brought in for questioning. Now on to Operation Gymslip,' he said, pointing to a map pinned to the wall. 'We'll come in through the school grounds. The first group will come in from the north and the second from the south. The river blocks any potential escape route to the west so the third group will enter from the east. One of our main targets is the headmistress's study. I'll lead the raid on the study, backed up by Smith, Higgins and Baker. The reports of drunkenness suggest that there's a large haul of alcohol somewhere in the school. Jenkins, Clifton and Simpson will locate and search the basement. If you find nothing there, try the grounds – the gardener's shed and any other outbuildings. Bear in mind that we're also after pornographic material. Several people attending the fête have rung us reporting pornographic photographs and magazines, amongst other things, strewn around the playing field and stalls. There's also the question of the alleged explosion, so keep your eyes peeled for bomb-making equipment. Right, any questions? No? Right – go, go, go!'

Chapter Seven

'So you see, Sir Phillip, we're in dire financial trouble,' Miss Gussetpiece confessed to the eccentric millionaire. 'I'm not asking for millions, just a contribution to see us through these most difficult times.'

'Is that what the fête's all about?' the balding, middle-aged man asked.

'Yes, to raise money. My study windows need replacing, as you'll have no doubt noticed. We need a new toilet block and . . .'

'What happened to the toilet block?'

'Er . . . An explosion. An electrical fault caused an explosion.'

'I see. How's my beautiful daughter Maxine getting on?'

Pouring the man a large gin and tonic, Miss Gussetpiece bit her lip. She daren't complain of Maxine's appalling record if she wanted help from the girl's father. But it was hardly a closed secret that Maxine was a rebellious, uncontrollable she-devil who did nothing but wreak havoc. She could hardly paint a glowing picture of the girl!

'She's doing fairly well,' Miss Gussetpiece smiled. 'She misses quite a few lessons, which doesn't help her academically. She doesn't always concentrate to the full, either, but she's progressing satisfactorily.'

'She's an ideal candidate for Head Girl, don't you agree?' Sir Phillip smirked as he adjusted his yellow polka-dot bow tie.

'Head Girl? Er . . . well, Maxine did earn three hundred pounds from a fund-raising scheme, so . . . Yes, yes, I agree. Maxine is an admirable choice to lead the girls.'

'Good! She's a bright girl, Headmistress – she'll go far. If she leaves Bellend school with an excellent report and top grades, she'll go *very* far.'

'Top grades? *Maxine*, top grades?'

'Yes, A-plus in all subjects.'

'A-plus? Er . . . Well, I honestly don't think she's capable of . . .'

'Whether she's capable or not doesn't really come into it, if you get my meaning. You *do* require financial assistance, don't you?'

'Yes, yes, I do. But . . .'

'That's settled, then. Head Girl, Head Prefect, Netball and Hockey Captain, top grades, excellent reports, preferential treatment . . .'

'Sir Phillip, your demands are rather . . .'

'One hundred thousand pounds, Headmistress. Yes or no?'

'Er . . . Yes, thank you very much!' Miss Gussetpiece conceded as the man took his cheque book from his jacket pocket. 'Er . . . To save complications with the Inland Revenue, would you please make the cheque out to Wendy Ellen Thelma Gussetpiece.'

'Yes, of course. W.E.T. Gussetpiece.'

'Thank you, Sir Phillip.'

Seeing the millionaire out, the headmistress breathed a sigh of relief. 'Yes!' she cried, punching the air with her clenched fist as she sat at her desk and swigged from the gin bottle. 'A hundred grand!'

'Excuse me, Miss Gussetpiece,' a bedraggled-looking Hilda Hillock panted as she careered into the study.

'Ah, Hilda, you've brought me the fête money, have you?'

'Maxine Mayhem robbed me, Miss Gussetpiece! She ambushed me and stole the takings!'

'Is that true, Maxine?' Miss Gussetpiece demanded as the dark girl appeared at the door.

'Of course it's not, Miss Gussetpiece! I don't know what Hilda's done with *her* takings, but here's the fifty pounds entrance money I've collected.'

'There *was* no entrance money!' Hilda protested. 'Entry to the fête was free!'

'You've done well, Maxine! Hilda, why didn't you think of charging an entrance fee?' Miss Gussetpiece asked surprisedly.

'Well, I . . . I thought . . .'

'That shows initiative, Maxine. I like to see that in a girl – well done!'

'Thank you, Miss Gussetpiece. May I go now?'

'Yes, of course. By the way, you'll be pleased to hear that I've decided to make you Head Girl. I'll talk to you about it later.'

'Head Girl? Oh, thank you, Miss Gussetpiece!'

'Now, Hilda!' the headmistress began sternly as Maxine skipped out. 'You've had a dreadful start to the term! What with the demolition of the toilet block, absconding, smoking, eating cucumbers in bed, the disgusting and most lewd incident in the potting shed and . . .'

'And there was the incident involving you and a strange man in the woods, Miss Gussetpiece,' Hilda returned.

'Hilda, we agreed to forget all about that!'

'Yes, but what about . . .'

'Ah, that reminds me. Was it you who rang the police and . . .'

'No, it wasn't. But I *will* ring them unless . . .'

'Let's make a fresh start, Hilda. Let's put all this behind us and start again.'

'But I've been robbed!'

'Then you should be more careful! Let it be a lesson to you. Now, go back to the fête and see if you can make some more money. I have things to do, so off you go.'

Wandering dejectedly down the corridor, Hilda contemplated running away. With Maxine stealing the money *and* the acclaim for her hard efforts, there was little point in her trying to help the school. *Head Girl*, she reflected derisively as she left the building and made her way to the potting shed. *Maxine Mayhem – Head Girl!*

Flopping onto the old sofa, Hilda rubbed her tearful eyes with her fists, wondering what to do. This was all-out war! she thought as the gardener entered the shed and enquired as to her business. 'I'm getting away from it all,' the blonde beauty replied sullenly.

'Gettin' away from what?' the old-timer asked as he joined her on the sofa.

'Oh, I don't know! I used to be so happy at Bellend, but now . . . Maxine Mayhem is destroying me, my life!'

'Ah, that young Maxine! D'ya know, when I was at school, there was this bully. Frankie Tiddleworth, 'is name was. Always causin' trouble, 'e was! One day, we was all in class when 'e come in and lay into this kid. Give 'im a right goin' over, 'e did! Anyway, a few of us got together an' made Frankie out to be a star pupil.'

'Why?' Hilda asked surprisedly. 'I would have thought . . .'

'Well, you see, in front of 'is mates, 'e was an 'ero – king o' the villains! We used to collect litter off of the playin' field and clean the blackboard an' the like – and then tell the teacher that Frankie done it. We made sure that 'e got praised for everything. It weren't long afore 'is mates turned against 'im. In the end, 'e weren't only replaced as leader of 'is own gang, but 'e was thrown out of the gang!'

'That's a jolly good plan! I wonder whether I could . . . Thank you, you've helped me no end!' Hilda cried, flinging her arms around the old man and hugging him as the door burst open.

Gazing up in astonishment at the police officer towering above her, Hilda released the gardener and pulled her gymslip down to cover her young thighs. 'I was just . . .' she began awkwardly. 'We were just . . .'

'I can see what you were doing, Miss!' the police officer bellowed. 'You'd better give me your name and form number!'

More trouble! Hilda mused despondently. The gardener, too, would be in trouble, she knew – big trouble! On the sofa, her arms wrapped tightly around the wrinklie, her gymslip revealing her shapely thighs, she daren't imagine the picture the odd couple had presented. *Gosh, shades of Lady Chatterley!* she reflected. But what was a policeman doing dambusting the potting shed?

'It weren't like what it looked!' the gardener protested as he rose to his feet. 'I was 'elpin' the girl to . . .'

'Helping yourself, more like! Anyway, we'll let the courts decide what you were doing!' the officer boomed.

'I *am* eighteen!' Hilda returned haughtily. 'Not that we were up to anything naughty.'

'You'd better get out of here, Miss. And I'll deal with this pervert!'

'What *is* this all about?' Miss Gussetpiece asked Detective Inspector Puckit, looking suitably bewildered. 'It's not to do with the toilet block, is it?'

'We've surrounded the school!' the detective revealed triumphantly. 'My men have discovered pornographic material scattered around the playing field, disgusting items of girls' soiled undergarments for sale on the clothes stall, and lemonade laced with alcohol being consumed by juveniles. There was the incident concerning a naked woman running across the grounds, allegations involving the PE mistress – and an explosion! We've discovered a haul of alcohol and cigarettes in the basement . . . Need I continue, Headmistress?'

'But, but . . .'

'My men are gathering the evidence now. There were no less than fifty used condoms collected from the fête area! There's litter strewn everywhere! This, Headmistress, is no way to run an independent boarding school for girls! What the Minister for Education will say, God only knows! I'd like you to accompany me to the police station, Miss Gussetpiece.'

'But I can't leave the school!'

'We'll only keep you at the station for a short time, just long enough to take your statement and establish exactly what's been going on here. I'll need a list of your staff, their names and addresses and so on. Now, if you'd be good enough to follow me.'

'Yes, yes, all right!'

Watching Miss Gussetpiece being bundled into the back of a police car, Maxine grinned. 'That'll teach the old hag!' she laughed, turning to Ginger.

'Yes, but look what they're loading into the police van!' Ginger gasped.

'All our booze and fags! Shit, that's bloody great!'

'I think we went too far!' Ginger sighed. 'We went over the top trying to wreck the bloody fête!'

'Look, there goes Pillock with that new French girl. What's she up to, sneaking off into the woods?'

'I blame *her* for all this! Let's go and get her!'

Sitting in the clearing, Hilda placed her arm around Véronique's shoulder and smiled sweetly. 'Are you all right now?' she asked concernedly.

'Yes, I 'ave been all right now,' the girl replied, brushing her black hair away from her dark eyes.

'I *am* all right now,' Hilda corrected.

'That is good – I am all right, also. Will you be my friend, 'ilda?'

'Yes, of course I will! It must be difficult for you, being at a new school in a foreign country.'

'Yes, it is. I am missing my friends and my family. I am missing one friend very much. At the institution, my old school in Paris, I was very 'appy. I shared a bed with my friend. I am missing 'er very much.'

'You shared a bed with another girl?' Hilda asked surprisedly.

'Yes, we make *amour* in bed. I am missing 'er very much.'

'You made love? Gosh! Why were you so upset when Miss Gussetpiece said . . .'

'Because it remind me of my friend. She 'ad a lovely . . .'

Placing her hand on Hilda's inner thigh, Véronique smiled. Affectionately squeezing the delicate blonde's warm flesh, she moved her hand nearer to her swelling knickers. 'I like you very much,' she breathed as she pressed her fingers into the softness of Hilda's moistening crotch. 'You remember me of my friend in Paris. I am, 'ow you say? I am lesbienne. I like your body, 'ilda.'

'Gosh!' Hilda gasped as the girl's fingers rubbed her navy-blue knickers. Moving the damp material aside, Véronique pinched Hilda's outer pussy lips, swelling the soft, fleshy pads. Breathing heavily as she tried to push her finger into the heat of the blonde girl's vaginal cavern, Véronique leaned forward and kissed Hilda's full, red lips.

Succumbing to her rising arousal as Véronique slipped her finger deep into her young pussy sheath, massaging her wet inner vaginal flesh, Hilda reclined on the grass and parted her thighs. 'Mmm, c'est bon!' Véronique gasped as she slipped another finger into the girl's tightening cunny hole.

'Wait a minute,' Hilda panted, pushing the girl away and tugging her knickers down. 'Let me take my knickers off.'

Her slender thighs splayed, her wet pussy crack open, bared before Véronique's not-so-innocent eyes, Hilda reclined, offering the open centre of her young body to the pretty French girl. Settling between Hilda's thighs, Véronique kissed her mound, breathing in her new young friend's cunny-scent. Tentatively licking Hilda's rubicund crack, tasting her lubricious girl-juice, she slipped three fingers into the girl's love-sheath. 'Mmm, c'est trop bon!' she gasped as she exposed Hilda's ripening clitoris and sucked the swollen protrusion into her hot mouth.

Licking, mouthing on Hilda's sex-button as she fingered her tightening cunny sheath, Véronique brought out the girl's orgasm. Shuddering as she lay beneath the trees, Hilda tossed her head, her body contorting, writhing as the waves of pure lesbian ecstasy invaded her.

Sinking her fingernails into the soft grass as Véronique pushed her tongue deep into her drenched vagina and massaged her clitoris with her wet fingertips, Hilda cried out in her lesbian coming. 'Oh, yes! Ah, Véronique! Don't stop! Ah, yes, yes! Ah, my mini!' Heightening Hilda's climax, Véronique engulfed the girl's pulsating clitoris in her hot mouth again, sucking out her climax to the accompaniment of her appreciative wails.

'Oh, oh!' Hilda whimpered as her climax gently receded. 'Oh, Véronique, I have never felt so . . . Ah, stop now! No more!'

'You like?' Véronique asked as she licked Hilda's come from her sticky fingers.

'Yes, I like!'

'You do me, now?'

'Yes, yes, I do you now.'

Jumping to her feet, Véronique tore off her gymslip and blouse. Unclipping her bra, revealing her full breasts to Hilda's expectant eyes, she tossed the garment to the ground. 'You like my *sein*, my titties?' she giggled, cupping her rounded mammary spheres and licking each milk bud in turn.

'Yes, I do!' Hilda replied eagerly, gazing covetously at the girl's tongue sweeping over her burgeoning brown buds.

'And now my cunette!' Véronique breathed sensually as she tugged her knickers down.

Her sparse black pubes springing to life, her pink

vaginal crack opening before Hilda's sparkling eyes, the girl squatted, exposing her inner flesh as her slit opened fully. 'You can see in my *con* like this – inside my – 'ow you say? Inside my cunt!' she giggled, leaning forward and viewing her distended inner lips. 'I sit like this over the face of my friend and she lick me inside. You lick me like this, 'ilda. It is nice, licking like this.'

Crawling beneath the girl and lying on her back, Hilda gazed at her wet, pinken sex-folds. Opening her mouth as Véronique lowered her naked body, Hilda sucked on her inner flesh, lapping up her *crème de fille*. 'Mmm, magnifique!' Véronique gasped as Hilda's tongue swept over her ripening clitoris. 'Ah, ma chérie! Mmm, encore, encore!'

Hiding in the bushes with Ginger, Maxine gazed in disbelief at Hilda and her young French friend. 'Would you believe it?' she asked Ginger. 'Hilda fucking Pillock, of all people! Christ, that French girl's got lovely tits!'

'Dirty cow!' Ginger whispered, gazing in wonderment at Véronique's magnificent erect nipples. 'Let's join them. Let's give the French tart a real seeing-to.'

'No, not while Pillock's here. We'll have her later, when she's alone. We'll introduce her to some of our quaint English ways, such as cucumber sandwiches, except the cucumber won't be between two slices of bread!'

'Ah, ah! Ma chatte!' Véronique cried as her orgasm approached.

'What's she saying?' Ginger asked.

'She's going on about her pussy. I wouldn't mind licking her pussy out!'

'Neither would I!'

Swallowing Véronique's *crème de sexe*, Hilda located the girl's tight bottom-hole and pushed her finger deep into her rectal sheath. Gasping with the lewd sensations, Véronique threw her head back, crying out in her lesbian pleasure as her orgasm rose and erupted in her pulsating clitoris. Sustaining her friend's incredible climax, Hilda sucked harder on her throbbing budlette, bringing out wave after wave of pure sexual euphoria until Véronique collapsed to the ground, quivering, panting, writhing in the wake of her cosmic release.

'Ah, ah, 'ilda!' she gasped as she brought her knees up to her chest. 'Ah, mon clito! Ma chatte!'

'You liked it?' Hilda smiled, stroking the girl's projectile nipples.

'Very much! We will done it again later!'

'We will *do* it again later.'

'Oui, oui! Again, we do it later!'

'You'd better get dressed, Véronique,' Hilda murmured as she slipped her knickers on, concealing her drenched vaginal slit. 'I'll meet you here this evening and we'll do it again. Be here at eight o'clock.'

'Oui, oui! Eight o'clock. And we have soixante-neuf, oui?'

'Yes, we'll have soixante-neuf. Don't tell anyone about it, not even my close friends, all right?'

'All right, I tell no one.'

Creeping out of the woods, Maxine turned to Ginger and offered her a cigarette. 'Eight o'clock,' she repeated pensively, a wicked glint in her dark eyes. 'What we'll do is get Pillock out of the way and have the frog bitch all to ourselves.'

'Mmm,' Ginger acquiesced as she drew on the cigarette. 'We'll tie Pillock up in the basement and have a bloody good evening in the woods. What about the boys from the Uni? It's about time they came over, and came over us!'

'They'll come over the little frog, too!' Maxine laughed as she walked across the playing field towards the school. 'If I can, I'll get word to them. We'll have a damn good orgy!'

'Knickergusset's at the police station, we've got that transvestite Blob where we want him, and we've got one over on Fräulein Frankfurter. We're doing well, Max!'

'Yes, we are. We also have that old fart the gardener where we want him. And don't forget old frigid face! We've really got something on her!'

'That leaves Madame-cunt Fissure and Shaftgrinder. I don't think we'll ever get anything on Fissure, Max – she's squeaky-clean!'

'I'm surprised that Shaftgrinder's not sussed anything yet, what with her bloody beady eyes and all the fucking that's been going on in the woods lately. Let's set a trap for her – lure her into the woods and have her discover Pillock and the frog licking each other's cunts out.'

'Yeah, nice one, Max! Let's go and finish off the last bottle of vodka.'

'OK. We'll have to do the local off-licence and stock up on booze and fags now that the bloody coppers have nabbed it all!'

'We'll rob the village offee, and make sure that Pillock takes the rap!'

'Brilliant! Come on, let's go and get pissed!'

* * *

Casting her eyes around the staff assembled in the headmistress's study, Madame Fissure tapped on the desk. 'If you'd all be seated, please, we'll get started!' she began authoritatively. 'Now, I've called this meeting to discuss the recent events at the school and to try to discover exactly what's been going on. The police have taken away boxes of drink and cigarettes. Does anyone know anything about the goods – where they came from or who's responsible for . . .'

'Miss Gussetpiece confiscated the goods from the girls' lockers,' Johnson enlightened the woman.

'Right, so she must have put it into storage in the basement for safekeeping. Once they know that, the police won't ask further questions. Now, what about the alleged streaker, the naked woman seen running through the grounds? Can anyone throw any light on that incident?'

'Er . . . it must have been one of the sixth-formers,' Miss Frigidus proffered, wringing her hands.

'Yes, you're probably right. OK, does anyone know anything about the pornographic material that was discovered at the fête?'

'I don't know why you're asking us about that!' Miss Blob objected. 'You should be questioning the girls, not the staff!'

'Yes, I realize that, Miss Blob. But there's been some collusion with certain sixth-form girls by certain members of staff – of that, I'm sure! The rumours concerning . . . well, concerning indecent sexual activities in the wooded area edging the playing field are rife. The things I've heard would make your hair curl! Which reminds me, Miss Blob. These brothers of yours sound somewhat suspicious to me!'

'Suspicious? Why?'

'Their names, for a start! Doctor Uterine Pouch and Doctor Anusis Rectus? Come on, who are they trying to fool?'

'They're not trying to fool anyone! They've been good enough to offer their services free of charge – I don't think you should put them down for that!'

'Maybe not, but I'm still very suspicious. The school's reputation is rapidly declining. If word got out that two strange men had been examining the girls and . . .'

'They're perfectly genuine. Just because their names are rather unusual . . . Anyway, word won't get out!'

'The Minister for Education is bound to send someone down here to discover exactly what's been going on. I have no doubt that we will all be interviewed, not only by a ministerial representative but by the police. We must find out what's been happening before . . .'

'This is ridiculous!' Miss Shaftgrinder interjected. 'We can't hold a meeting without Miss Gussetpiece!'

'That's another point I was coming to!' Madame Fissure returned. 'In my considered opinion, Miss Gussetpiece is unfit for the post of headmistress! As we all know, she's a rampant alcoholic, she . . .'

'I think you'd better take a vote on that one!' Miss Blob interrupted. 'And a vote on who should lead this so-called meeting!'

'All right, all those for me to lead the meeting say *aye*,' Madame Fissure ventured. 'Oh, no one! Fair enough, I'll stand down!'

'I vote for Miss Blob!' Miss Frigidus ventured boldly.

'I'll second that,' Fräulein Vulvahausen rejoined.

'Right!' Miss Blob proposed, rising to her feet. 'Let's all down a few gins!'

'You can't do that!' Miss Shaftgrinder protested. 'All those in favour of postponing the meeting until Miss Gussetpiece has returned, say *aye*. No one? This is stupidity!' she complained as she flounced out of the study and slammed the door shut.

Pouring several glasses of neat gin, Miss Blob passed them around before assuming authority behind the Head's desk. 'I think we're all agreed that the school is in trouble,' she began. 'But we shouldn't blame Miss Gussetpiece. We're all guilty, to a greater or lesser degree. We'll hold a meeting when the headmistress returns from the police station. In the meantime, I think we should all pull our weight and get on with the job.'

'Here, here!' Miss Frigidus called, knocking back her gin. 'If the headmistress is an alcoholic, then so am I!'

'Er . . . yes, all right, Miss Frigidus! The important thing is to ensure that the school remains open. To do that, we need to be seen, at least, to be running a decent establishment. If anyone from the Minister for Education's office does visit us, we'll have to ensure that we receive a glowing report.'

'Did you hear that?' Maxine asked Ginger as they crouched beneath the open window. 'The Minister for Education! Fucking hell, if we play our cards right, we can have this dump closed down – permanently!'

'I think we should . . .'

'Shush! Blob's talking again.'

'Another suggestion I have is to talk Miss Gussetpiece into expelling Maxine Mayhem. The girl knows far too much about me . . . I mean, she's been spreading malicious lies concerning me, and other members of staff. The girl is nothing but trouble!'

'Here, here!' Miss Frigidus broke in.

'I heard that the Head intends to make Maxine the Head Girl,' Johnson volunteered. 'Although I can't believe it!'

'Yes, I've heard that rumour, too!' Miss Blob laughed. 'Obviously, it's not true! I'd like to see Maxine *and* her friends expelled! The Bellend Rebels, as they call themselves, have been causing trouble for several years and it's high time they were dealt with. I also want to replace the gardener. He's too old and he knows about my . . . he's too old for the job.'

'Here, here!' Miss Frigidus interrupted.

'Yes, all right, Miss Frigidus! You don't have to second everything I say! As for my brothers – personally, I believe that they're in clover . . . that they're an overt asset to the school.'

'Here . . . Sorry.'

'It's not every day that we have the services of highly qualified doctors offered free of charge. Now, going back to the toilet block . . .'

'That sounds like a jolly good idea, Hilly!' Candida beamed as she flopped onto her bed. 'You do think of some awfully good ideas!'

'Yes, I do, don't I? Maxine will be praised for all the good we do. Her friends, those horrid Bellend Rebels, will hate her for it! She's going to be Head Girl, they'll hate her for that!'

'Let's clear the playing field up, and then tell Miss Gussetpiece that Maxine did it!'

'Good idea! And we'll clean all the blackboards, thoroughly wash them, ready for Monday morning. We'll put every effort into the plan, Candy. We'll make Maxine out to be a glowing example of perfection to the whole school!'

Applying the finishing touches to the Head's study, Hilda and Candida were surprised by the appearance of Miss Gussetpiece. 'Goodness me!' the headmistress exclaimed. 'You *have* done well, girls!'

'It wasn't us, Miss Gussetpiece,' Hilda smiled. 'Maxine did it – and she's cleared the rubbish from the playing field and washed all the blackboards.'

'She *is* keen!' Candida grinned. 'She must be looking forward to becoming Head Girl.'

'I believe she'll make an excellent leader!' Miss Gussetpiece enthused, running her fingers over her highly-polished desk. 'Maxine certainly has changed for the better! I only wish I could say the same of you, Hilda.'

'Yes, Miss Gussetpiece.'

'I shall post news of Maxine's school leadership on the notice board for all to see. She's a wonderful example to the school, Hilda – unlike you! Now, I have things to do.'

'Yes, Miss Gussetpiece,' Hilda murmured demurely as she retreated from the study with Candida.

Wandering down the corridor, Hilda sighed. 'I hope we're doing the right thing,' she said, checking her watch.

'So do I! You do realize that this could backfire on us, don't you, Hilly?'

'Yes, I do. It's a quarter to eight and I'm . . . I'm going for a walk. I'll see you later, Candy.'

'Can't I come with you?'

'No, no. I need to be alone. I need to be alone to think. I'll see you later,' Hilda smiled as she left the building.

Walking across the playing field, the girl checked her watch again. 'I hope Véronique's there,' she breathed as she neared the trees. *This is dreadfully naughty of me!* she giggled inwardly as she recalled licking the young French girl's pussy-slit. Turning and checking that she wasn't being followed, she slipped into the wood and made her way through the undergrowth, unaware that Maxine and Ginger were lying in wait.

'Got you, Pillock!' Maxine cried as she leaped out of the bushes and grabbed Hilda's arm. 'Tie her up, Ginger!' she ordered her friend. 'Tie her to that tree!' Struggling helplessly, Hilda could do nothing to save herself as her arms were forced behind her back and her wrists bound with heavy rope. 'We're going to fuck your French friend!' Maxine giggled as she helped Ginger tie their prisoner to the tree. 'We watched you lick her cunt out, you dirty cow!'

'You'll pay for this, Maxine!' Hilda protested as her captors walked away.

'Yeah, yeah!' Maxine mocked. 'I've heard your threats before!'

'You won't be Head Girl when Miss Gussetpiece . . .'

'Bye, Pillock!'

Moving towards the clearing, Ginger turned to Maxine and frowned. 'I still don't like the idea of you becoming Head Girl,' she said pensively. 'The leader of the Bellend Rebels – Head Girl? It's just not right, Max!'

'I don't know why Knickergusset chose me. But I'll use the position to help us bring the school down.'

'I hope so! Kelly and Fukui weren't at all happy about

it when I told them. In fact, Fukui suggested that we vote for a new leader.'

'Mutinous, slit-eyed bitch! I'll deal with her, Ginger, don't worry. Shush! Look, there's the French tart. Christ, she's naked!'

'Let's grab her!'

'Right! Did you bring the cream with you?'

'Yes, everything we need is in my bag.'

'OK, let's go for it! *Vivent les filles francaises!*'

Leaping out of the bushes, Maxine and Ginger grabbed Véronique's naked body. 'Sacré bleu!' Véronique cried as Maxine squeezed her firm breast. 'Non!' she screamed at Ginger, her dark eyes wide with fear as the redhead cupped her full vaginal lips in her palm. 'Je . . . je . . . Non, non! Argh!'

'Shut it, frog!' Maxine hissed, squeezing the girl's nipple. 'Get her onto the ground, Ginger, and we'll tie her up! String her up like a bunch of onions!'

Forcing the wriggling girl onto the grass, Ginger bound her wrists while Maxine drove stakes into the ground. Taking Véronique's left foot, Maxine secured her ankle to one stake before grabbing her other foot and yanking her legs wide open. 'Keep her still!' she ordered Ginger as she bound her right ankle to the other stake. 'That's got it! You might as well stop struggling, you'll never break free!' she laughed as the captive girl pulled on her bonds.

Trying to conceal her open intimacy with her bound wrists, Véronique cried out as Maxine grabbed her hands and pulled them above her head. 'Non, non!'

'Mais oui, oui!' Maxine taunted, pulling the girl's arms behind her head and tying her hands to the third stake.

'Non! Ne me faites pas de mal . . .'

'Unless you shut your trap, I'll gag your French gob with my wet knickers!'

Stilling her trembling body, Véronique gazed up at her captors as they stood either side of her and slipped their clothes off. Settling between her prisoner's splayed thighs, Ginger took the depilating cream from her bag. 'I'm going to remove your fanny fur!' she giggled, spreading the cream over the quaking girl's mound with a plastic spatula.

'Non! You 'orrid girl! Oh, quelle honte! I tell Madame Gussetpiss!'

'You're telling no one!' Maxine warned as she knelt astride the girl's head and lowered the open centre of her young body. 'You'll lick my cunt out while Ginger gets rid of your pubes!' she ordered crudely as she pressed her swollen vaginal lips to the girl's gasping mouth.

Rocking her hips, Maxine ground her open vulva into Véronique's mouth, gasping as her clitoris swelled and her juices of lesbian lust flowed from her inner nectaries. Pushing her tongue out in her arousal, Véronique lapped at her captor's crimsoning cunt flesh, swallowing her slippery cream, stiffening her clitoris.

Slipping three fingers into Véronique's tight vaginal sheath, Ginger gasped. 'Fuck me, she's wet! Look at her cunt juice, it's flooding out!'

'I . . . I can't look!' Maxine breathed as her orgasm rose from her contracting womb. 'God, I . . . I'm coming already!'

'Ah! Je mouille!' Véronique gasped as her vagina overflowed with her lust juices.

'Come in her mouth and I'll finger her lovely cunt!' Ginger cried excitedly as the French girl's vagina tightened around her thrusting fingers.

Quivering uncontrollably as Ginger pistoned her fingers in and out of her young pussy, Véronique lapped at Maxine's open vaginal entrance, tonguing the drenched pussy folds, swallowing hard as her mouth filled with the girl's hot come. Mouthing on the wet girl-flesh as her own orgasm stirred deep within her swirling pelvis, she lifted her buttocks off the soft grass, meeting Ginger's thrusts to bring out her shuddering climax. Massaging Véronique's pulsating clitoris as she finger-fucked her pussy, Ginger leaned over and sucked the girl's stiffening nipple into her wet mouth.

'Mmm, I like your tits!' Ginger breathed, licking the girl's darkening areola. 'When your cunt hair has gone, I'll lick your cunt out, suck your clitty to orgasm!'

'Ah, oui, oui!' Véronique gasped as Maxine fell to the ground, writhing as her orgasm waned. 'Ah, oh! Encore! Encore!'

'You'll look nice without your cunt hair!' Ginger giggled, biting the girl's nipple. 'Just like a naughty schoolgirl!'

'Ah, oui, oui!'

'Let me help you,' Maxine grinned as she crawled across the grass. 'God, she's got a bloody good body! I wish I had a cock, I'd fuck her rotten with it!'

'Look in the bag!' Ginger laughed. 'I've come fully prepared!'

Opening the bag, Maxine pulled out a huge dildo and gasped. 'Christ, it's far too big! Where the hell did you get it from?'

'I found it with the whips and stuff in the basement.'

'Right, wipe that cream away and get her ready for the fucking of her life!'

Strapping the dildo on, Maxine gazed in awe at the

thick plastic shaft, waving from side to side as she walked on her knees towards her prey. 'There!' Ginger giggled, wiping the residue of cream from Véronique's smooth vaginal lips 'No cunt hair!'

'Holy shit, she's got big cunt lips!' Maxine shrieked, eyeing her prisoner's bloated sex hillocks rising either side of her wet groove. 'Talk about the Cheddar Gorge!'

'Fuck her, Max!' Ginger urged. 'Go on, shove the dildo right up her cunt and fuck her rotten!'

Presenting the rounded end of the phallus to the girl's open vaginal entrance, Maxine thrust her hips forward, driving the massive shaft deep into Véronique's tight cuntal sheath. 'Non!' the girl cried as Maxine withdrew and propelled the dildo deep into her cunt again, jolting her tethered body. Repeatedly thrusting into the girl's delectable pussy-hole, Maxine ordered Ginger to sit on her face. 'Give her your cunt juices!' she gasped as she propelled her hips again and again. 'Go on, fill her mouth with your hot come!'

Whimpering as she tried desperately to free herself, Hilda stilled her young body and held her breath as she heard someone stealing through the undergrowth. Praying that it was Candida or Patsy, she gasped as a priest sprang from the bushes. 'Please, help me!' she pleaded as the man of God stood before her. 'Some horrible girls tied me to the tree and . . . No! What are you doing?' she sobbed as the man knelt before her, lifted her gymslip and yanked her navy-blue knickers down to her knees. 'No! Please, you can't do this!'

Grinning, the perverted priest parted Hilda's fleshy pussy lips and thrust two fingers deep into her quivering sheath. 'I can do what I like!' he breathed wickedly, peeling her outer cunny lips wide apart. 'God has sent me to defile you, my child!'

'Defile me? What are you . . . No, please, not there!' Hilda begged as a finger drove deep into her hot rectum.

'Yes, there! God has sent me to defile your beautiful young body, your cunt and your tight arsehole!'

'Argh! Stop . . . Ah! Satan . . . Satan has sent you!'

'God, Satan, what the hell? The point is, I'm here!'

Slipping his fingers from Hilda's tight sex-holes, the priest rose to his feet and lifted his cassock, exposing his rampant erection, his bulbous knob, to her wide eyes. 'I am to fuck you!' he laughed uncontrollably, stabbing his purple knob between her bloated pussy lips. 'Ah, yes! Hot, tight, wet . . . God, yes!' he gasped as his knob drove deep into the girl's drenched sex duct. 'I am to fuck your cunt and fill you with my seed!'

'You're mad!' Hilda sobbed. 'You're possessed!'

'Yes, by the devil himself! And you are the devil's dirty little daughter! I will fuck you incestuously!'

Her young body jolting against the rough bark of the tree as the priest thrust into her hot cunt hole, Hilda thought again about running away. Apprehended by Maxine and Ginger, used and abused by a perverted priest, she knew that she couldn't take much more as the man of God gasped and pumped out his blasphemous seed.

'Fuck . . . fucking your tight cunt!' he cried, grabbing her hips and ramming her cervix with his orgasming knob. 'Jesus Christ, you're tight! Ah, God! God, how I love schoolgirls' tight cunt holes!'

'Please, leave me!' Hilda begged as her vaginal cavern filled with the man's communion offering and overflowed. 'Please! You can't . . .'

'Ah, ah! God, I needed that!' he grinned, slipping his spent penis from her pussy duct. 'Ah, look! Just look at your cunt-come glistening on my lovely cock!'

'You're beastly!' Hilda cried as the man's sperm oozed from her inflamed vagina and coursed down her inner thighs. 'You really are beastly!'

'If that's what you think, then I won't let you go!' he grinned. 'Say you're sorry, and I'll untie you.'

'Sorry? Never! You're a horrid, beastly man!'

'In that case, I'll leave you here. It's getting dark and the monsters will be out before long. Monsters with big pricks will be roaming the woods! Monsters with big pricks in need of a girl's cunt! You haven't heard about the evil monsters that roam these woods at night, have you?'

'I . . . There *are* no monsters!'

'Yes, there are! There are grotesque sex-fiends with two pricks and four balls roaming these woods! I've seen them with my own eyes! They seek out young girls' tight cunts and fuck them with their double cocks!'

'You . . . You're mad!'

'Far from it! You stay tied to that tree all night, and you'll soon find out!'

'All right! I'm sorry,' Hilda finally conceded. 'You're not a horrid man.'

'I'm a nice man, aren't I?'

'Yes, yes, I suppose so. Please, untie me!'

'Only if you show me your tits!'

'All right, anything. Just let me go!'

Slipping the rope from Hilda's hands, the priest grinned as he squeezed her firm breasts through her tight blouse. Unless she showed him her young milk buds, her rounded boobies, he'd rip her blouse off, she knew. Sighing, she unbuttoned her blouse and lifted her bra clear of her mammary spheres, revealing her erect nipples to the drooling, wild-eyed man.

'They're very hard!' he gasped as he kneaded her breasts, pressing his fingers into the warm flesh. 'You've got nice nipples, my dear. Tell me, do you suck them?'

'No, I don't!' Hilda returned angrily as she recupped her breasts in her bra and hurriedly buttoned her blouse. 'There, now you've seen my titties, so I'm going back to school!'

'I'll see you again for a fuck, no doubt?'

'Never! I'm going to call the police the minute I get back to school. They'll catch you, you'll jolly well see!' Hilda sobbed as the cassocked fiend dived into the bushes and made off.

Emerging from the woods as she adjusted her clothing and wiped the sperm from her thighs, Hilda decided not to go to back to the dormitory. The last thing she needed was a night of enforced lesbian sex with Maxine and Ginger! Making her way to the potting shed, she wondered whether she'd be safe there for the night. *Monsters with two cocks and four balls!* she thought fearfully! *No, there's no such thing – is there?*

Sitting alone in the potting shed, she sighed. Things were going from bad to worse, she reflected sadly. Véronique, no doubt, had been sexually used and abused by those dreadful girls, Maxine and Ginger. She should have gone and rescued the girl, but she hadn't dared return to the woods. 'Right, that's it!' she decided tearfully as she jumped up and fled from the shed. 'I'm running away – and I'll never come back!'

Chapter Eight

'It was a dreadful experience, Miss Frigidus!' the headmistress sighed as she opened a new bottle of vodka. 'I have never been so humiliated in all my life! Well, apart from the time I was caught on the factory floor with . . . The less said about that, the better! I was subjected to a body search! They put their fingers up . . . well, they didn't actually. I did suggest it to a good-looking young policeman, but he declined.'

'Oh, dear, you poor woman! Fancy being taken away by the police!'

'I don't fancy it at all! Christ, this vodka's strong!'

'Oh, by the way, there was a meeting yesterday, Miss Gussetpiece. There was talk of you being unfit for the post of headmistress,' Miss Frigidus enlightened the portly woman.

'Mutiny! Who said that? Who said that I was unfit?'

'Er . . . Well, I'd rather not say. I don't want to fall out with anyone.'

'Tell me, Miss Frigidus – or I'll have you flogged!'

'Flogged?'

'Horsewhipped!'

'Oh, my goodness! Well, in that case – it was Madame Fissure. She said that you're an alcoholic.'

'The sheer cheek of it! How can she possibly say that?

I've only had half a bottle of vodka today, and it's already past ten o'clock! I'll have her suspended by her French suspender belt for that! Dig some dirt up, Miss Frigidus! Find out all you can about the French cow!'

'Goodness me! You're not going to do anything rash, are you, Headmistress?'

'Rash? I'll throttle her! What else went on during my absence?' the Head demanded, gulping down the vodka.

'Well, Hilda Hillock's gone missing again, and that new French girl was caught climbing through the dormitory window last night.'

'Strewth! Hilda Hillock will be the death of me, she really will! What on earth was the French girl doing climbing through a window?'

'I really don't know, Headmistress. She . . .'

'Where was everyone last night? I couldn't find Miss Blob, Fräulein Vulvahausen, Madame Fissure – or you, for that matter! The place was deserted! I looked everywhere! Almost everywhere, anyway. I was feeling rather dizzy from . . . Where was everyone?'

'Er . . . Well, we all went to bed early, more than likely.'

'More than likely? Either you did or you didn't!'

'Well, *I* did, but I can't speak for the other members of staff. Perhaps they were planning the mutiny?'

'I'll give them mutiny! You say that Hilda's missing again? When was she last seen?'

'She didn't sleep in her bed last night and she hasn't been seen today.'

'Jesus, I need another drink! And what's all this about Véronique climbing through windows? I can't have this sort of thing going on, I *really* can't!'

'The maintenance man caught her climbing in through the window. She was half-naked, so he said.'

'Half-naked? Goodness me, I can't turn my back for five minutes without the place going to rack and ruin! Ah, Miss Shaftgrinder!' the headmistress greeted the beady owl as she entered her study. 'Did you attend this mutinous meeting during my untimely absence yesterday?'

'Good morning, Headmistress. Yes, I did attend the so-called meeting – and I walked out!'

'I'm pleased to hear it! At least I have two loyal members of staff!'

'Two?' Miss Frigidus echoed.

'Yes, Miss Shaftgrinder and you.'

'Me? Oh, why, thank you! I'm honoured, Headmistress, I *really* am!'

'Yes, yes, all right! Don't go over the top! Now then, Maxine Mayhem is to be Head Girl and . . .'

'No! You can't do that!' Miss Shaftgrinder protested angrily. 'Please, Headmistress, I implore you! The girl's nothing but a . . .'

'Do quieten down, woman! I can't be putting up with hysterics! Anyway, I have no choice in the matter! Maxine is to become Head Girl,' Miss Gussetpiece insisted, gulping from the vodka bottle. 'I can't tell you why, but I have no choice. What on earth is all that banging? Stone the crows, it's enough to wake the dead!'

'It's coming from outside!' Miss Frigidus bellowed above the noise.

'I know that! Stay here, and I'll go and investigate!'

Rushing outside, Miss Gussetpiece looked up to see Johnson atop a ladder wielding a club hammer. 'What are you doing, Jones? Don't you realize that it's Sunday morning? People are going to church and praying and doing quiet, Sunday-morning type things!'

'Yes, but I *must* get this work done, Headmistress!' Johnson called down. 'It was Miss Blob's idea that I start on the lintel this morning because there might be a man from the Minister for Education's office visiting us soon!'

'Come down here, this instant!' Miss Gussetpiece ordered. 'I can't possibly shout at men up ladders, it's not normal! Besides, I have an awful headache!'

Descending the ladder, Johnson explained that Miss Blob thought it wise to have the windows replaced as soon as possible. 'I suppose she's right!' Miss Gussetpiece sighed. 'But what are we to do with all that rubble?' she asked, pointing to the remains of the toilet block. 'Goodness me, if we *do* have a visit from the sinister for emulation . . . I mean, the ministry for defecation . . . Sorry, only I feel rather tipsy. I mean, topsy-turvy after my time at the police defecation . . . station.'

'Er . . . Yes, of course, Headmistress. Well, I've arranged for a mate of mine to take the rubble away and completely clear the site.'

'Good! I really can't be doing with all these problems! I'll go and have a word with the gardener and see if the old fool can cover the site with earth, and plant some flowers there – asters, pansies, geraniums, poppies . . . You never know, we might be able to get away with pretending that there never was a toilet block.'

'Good idea, Headmistress. The site will be cleared first thing tomorrow morning. The water supply and drains will be sealed off, so there shouldn't be any problems with covering the site with earth.'

'Good. And, please, do try not to hammer too hard,

my head's splitting!' Miss Gussetpiece complained as she walked off in the direction of the gardener's potting shed.

Approaching the shed, Miss Gussetpiece was about to open the door when she heard voices. Pressing her ear to the door, she decided to eavesdrop on the conversation. 'I slept here all night,' Hilda was confessing. 'I was going to run away, but it was dark and I was frightened of evil monsters with two big . . . well, I was frightened.'

'You shouldn't ought to 'ave done that, Miss!' the gardener admonished the girl. 'Ol' lady Knickergusset would 'ave you expelled if she knew you was in 'ere all night!'

'Yes, I know it was wrong but . . . I just don't seem to be able to do anything right these days! What with Miss Blob . . . Oh, never mind.'

'What? What's 'e done?'

'*He*?' Hilda repeated surprisedly.

'Er . . . I mean, *she*.'

'Then, why did you say *he*?' Hilda asked. 'There have been rumours concerning Miss Blob.'

'I shouldn't ought to have said nothin'. Forget about it.'

Staggering back to the school, Miss Gussetpiece frowned. *Why call Miss Blob, 'he'?* she pondered as she entered the building and made her way to Miss Blob's rooms. *Old lady Knickergusset, indeed!* Knocking on the door, the headmistress wondered why Hilda had slept in the potting shed. 'Stupid girl!' she breathed as the door opened. *Evil monsters, indeed!*

'Oh, good morning, Headmistress!' Miss Blob greeted her. 'Please, do come in.'

Sitting in the lounge, Miss Gussetpiece tried to plan her

line of questioning as she gazed at the woman's rough hands and stubbly chin. 'I'll need your birth certificate for the police,' she announced, congratulating herself for suddenly spawning the idea.

'Er . . . I'm afraid I've lost my birth certificate,' Miss Blob replied.

'Really? When did you lose it?'

'I . . . I lost it at birth.'

'At birth? What were you doing in possession of a birth certificate when you were born?'

'Well, that's why I had it – because I'd been born.'

'Fancy giving a birth certificate to a newborn baby, the idea's ludicrous! No wonder you lost it! Were you breast-fed?'

'Er . . . yes.'

'Did you enjoy it?'

'I really can't remember!'

'It's best to feed baby boys on the breast, don't you agree?'

'Boys? Er, yes, I suppose so.'

'It prepares them for certain aspects of sex later in life.'

'Does it?'

'Well, yes. Breast-feeding boys is natural – it gives them a fascination for the breasts later in life – a fixation. Do you have a fixation for girls' breasts, Miss Blob?'

'Cor! Yes, I . . . er . . . no, of course I don't have a fixation for girls' breasts, Miss Gussetpiece!'

'Oh, I see. Anyway, you can get a duplicate certificate, can't you?'

'Er . . . yes, I suppose so.'

'That's a nice camera you have,' Miss Gussetpiece observed, eyeing a Pentax on the mantlepiece. 'Is there a film in it?'

Girl School

'Yes, there is.'

'I couldn't borrow it, could I?'

'What, the film?'

'No, the camera.'

'Oh, well . . . Yes, of course.'

'Thank you. I want to take a few pictures of the toilet block before the rubble is removed.'

'There are a few shots left,' Miss Blob smiled, taking the camera from the mantlepiece and passing it to the headmistress.

'I was hoping you'd say that!' Miss Gussetpiece grinned.

'There are one or two personal pictures on the film,' Miss Blob added. 'When you've taken the pictures, I'll have the film developed and pass your photos on to you.'

'Fine!' Miss Gussetpiece smiled, clutching the camera and making for the door. 'Thank you, Miss Blob.'

Making her way back to her study, the headmistress bumped into Madame Fissure. 'Ah, I have a bone to pick with you!' she roared. 'What's all this nonsense about me being unfit for . . .'

'Headmistress, there's a man waiting in your study . . .'

'Waiting in my study? What sort of man?'

'An ordinary man, I suppose.'

'What's he doing waiting in my study? I can't have men hanging around in my study!'

'He's come to see you, Headmistress.'

'Has he? What for?'

'He's from the village off-licence. There's been a robbery.'

'A robbery? Why come to see me about it? It's the police he should see, not me!'

'He said that one of our girls raided his shop. You'd better go and talk to him.'

'All right, all right! Robberies, men up poles and ladders, the police, perverted priests and nuns . . . God, I need a drink! There's been no word from any Mothers Superior, has there?'

'Mothers Superior? No, not as far as I know.'

'That's something to be thankful for, I suppose!'

Wandering into her study, Miss Gussetpiece looked the young man up and down. 'Can I help you?' she asked, pouring a large gin.

'Yes, you can! One of your girls broke into my shop and stole a quantity of drink and cigarettes!' he bawled, banging his fist on the desk.

'Please, don't hit my desk – it's an antique! Besides, I have a headache. How do you know it was one of my girls?'

'I saw her from my lounge window above the shop! She was wearing her school uniform – a Bellend school uniform!'

'That doesn't prove anything! It's circumcisional . . . circum . . . It proves nothing!'

'It proves everything!'

'A uniform could have been stolen and used in the robbery by a girl from another school.'

'That's ridiculous!'

'Bring me a crate of gin, free of charge, and I'll not take the matter further.'

'What? *You*'ll not take the matter further? I'm the one who brought the matter up, not you! *I*'m the aggrieved!'

'I've been aggrieved all my life! ! Go away, or I'll ring my solicitor and have you taken to court for . . .'

'I'll go straight to the police, in that case! I thought

you'd appreciate my coming to you rather than going to the police, but . . .'

'Oh, all right! I'll deal with it internally. I'll have an internal examination.'

'And I'll bet I never hear another word about it! I've got evidence. The girl dropped this, a club membership card. I'll go to the police and . . .'

'Give that to me! What's this – Jolly Hockey Sticks Club? Stone the crows! Er . . . Look, I'm sorry about all this. I think I know who's responsible. I'll deal with the girl and send her to you to apologize.'

'What about the stolen goods?'

'Er . . . I'll have her return the goods. Now, if you don't mind, I'm very busy.'

'I'll give it some thought, but I can't promise anything. I might still contact the police. Good day.'

'Is it?'

Johnson's hammering reverberating throughout the building, Miss Gussetpiece lolled in her chair and covered her ears. 'Jesus Christ!' she breathed as the hammering stopped. 'I can't take any more of this!' Deciding to expel Hilda, she began writing a letter to the girl's parents.

'Excuse me, Headmistress,' Johnson interrupted as he tapped on the open door. 'Sorry to trouble you, but I forgot to tell you that I've discovered where the missing laundry basket is.'

'It doesn't really matter now, Jones. The drink and cigarettes are at the police station, so . . .'

'The basket contains something other than drink and cigarettes, Headmistress. It's full of navy-blue knickers – unwashed, heavily-soiled navy-blue knickers. And pornographic photographs of a certain member of your staff with some naked schoolgirls.'

'Satan, give me strength! Where are these photographs?'

'Still in the basket, in the woods, Headmistress. Shall I bring it to you?'

'Yes, immediately! Who is the member of staff?'

'I'm not one hundred percent certain that it's a member of staff, but it looks remarkably like it. I'll bring the basket to you and you can decide for yourself.'

'Right, and be quick about it!'

Holding Candida's hand as she walked to the far side of the playing field, Hilda sighed. 'So, I spent the night in the potting shed,' she related as they neared the perimeter wall. 'After the incident with the priest, I just couldn't face anything else!'

'Gosh! Fancy having a priest stick his thing up you! Did you like it?' Candida giggled.

'It's not funny! He made me show him my pears, too!'

'You didn't *have* to show him, did you?'

'He wouldn't have let me go unless . . .'

'Crikey! I've read about naughty priests, but I never thought . . . Did you like it?'

'Well . . . It was all right, I suppose. His thing was *ever* so big, Candy!'

'Let's go and sit on the wall and you can tell me all about it!'

'Have you seen Véronique?' Hilda asked, wondering how the girl was feeling after her evening in the woods with Maxine and Ginger.

'She climbed in through a window last night. She was very distressed and half-naked, but she wouldn't say why. She went straight to bed, crying.'

'Oh dear, the poor thing!'

Girl School

Climbing onto the wall, the girls frowned at each other as noises emanated from the woods outside the school grounds. 'What was that?' Hilda whispered, grabbing Candida's arm.

'There's someone in the woods, let's go and investigate! There's nothing I like better than having a jolly good adventure!'

'Yes, and me!' Hilda agreed, slipping off the wall. 'Come on!'

Creeping through the undergrowth, the girls held their hands to their mouths and gasped as they tentatively moved the branches of a bush aside to see a young girl with a nun. 'She's getting dressed!' Hilda breathed, watching the girl pull her gymslip on.

'Gosh, Hilly! What do you think they're up to?'

'I have no idea! What would a young girl be doing in the woods, putting her clothes on in front of a nun?'

'Crikey, I don't know. It's jolly queer, if you ask me!'

'That girl must be very young! I wonder who she is?'

'I don't know, I've never seen her before.'

'I'm going back to school, Candy. I don't like the look of this one little bit!'

'I'm going to stay here and watch.'

'You are naughty, Candy!'

'No, I'm not! I want to find out what's going on. I'll see you later, Hilly.'

As Hilda crept away, Candida turned her gaze to the pallid nun and the girl. 'We'll meet again, I hope?' the nun asked as the girl finished dressing.

'Oh, yes, Sister – we will!'

'Good! Off you go, then. I'll wait until you're out of sight before I leave. We can't be too careful. And remember, tell no one about me!'

'All right, Sister. I'll see you tomorrow – bye.'

Gosh! What strange goings-on! Candida thought as the girl wandered off, leaving the nun relaxing on the grass. Squeezing her eyes shut, trying to stop herself from sneezing, Candida held her breath. But unable to help herself, she let out a loud *atishoo,* causing the nun to cry out in horror.

'I'm sorry,' Candida smiled as she emerged from the bushes. 'I didn't mean to frighten you.'

'That's all right, my child. Come and sit beside me,' the daughter of God invited.

'Thank you, Sister,' Candida replied, sitting cross-legged on the grass.

'My name's Sister Regina Cunctus.'

'And I'm Candida. You have a most unusual name, Sister.'

'Yes, I was blessed with it by my mother – a woman of God.'

'Really? How interesting.'

'Do you often walk outside the school grounds?' the nun asked, gazing at the girl's tight navy-blue knickers.

'No, never.'

'What are you doing here then, my child?'

'I . . . Haven't we met before, Sister? Your face looks awfully familiar!'

'Er . . . No, no, we've not met before, my child.'

'You look awfully like a PE mistress we had!'

'What a coincidence.'

'The PE mistress we had at our school was a man.'

'Goodness me! What a strange affair!'

'Yes, it was, rather. What are you doing in the woods, Sister?'

'Waiting for you, my child. God has sent you to me. You're obviously distressed, and God has sent you to me for help.'

'For help, Sister?'

'I can see that you're under pressure, what with the odd PE mistress and everything. Lie back on the grass and relax. I'll heal you, my child,' the behabited woman smiled.

Reclining, Candida gazed up at the nun's face, fascinated by the lines of cracked powder and the uncanny resemblance to Miss Cueball. 'Allow me to bring you healing,' Sister Regina smiled, laying her hands on Candida's succulent breasts. 'Feel the power, my child! Feel it in your breasts!' she invoked, massaging the girl's pliant mammaries.

Closing her eyes, Candida succumbed to the healing power, relaxing as she allowed the strange nun to knead her young breasts. The woman's hands moving down, Candida opened her eyes as she massaged her stomach. 'Relax,' Sister Regina whispered as her wandering fingers probed the gentle rise of the girl's firm mons. 'Feel the power, my child, feel the power of God deep within your barren womb!'

Discreetly lifting Candida's gymslip, the nun exposed the swell of the girl's tight knickers. Cautiously lifting the gymslip higher, she gazed longingly at the damp material covering the girl's young pussy lips, the band of white flesh above the navy-blue garment. Her hands wandering ever-closer to Candida's mound, she massaged her smooth stomach.

'What are you doing?' Candida asked as the nun's fingers slipped beneath her knicker elastic and massaged her hairless pubic mound.

'Just relax, my child. Relax and allow the power of God to permeate your young body, your very being.'

'I don't think God would . . . Oh, Sister! That's my . . . You're rubbing my . . .'

'Why have you no pubic hair?' the nun asked.

'The doctor, he . . . he removed my hair and I've been shaving ever since.'

'It feels nice, very nice! You masturbate, don't you, my child?'

'No, never!'

'God is telling me that you masturbate. It is true, isn't it?'

'Well, yes, I suppose so. But . . .'

'I must heal you, heal your girlhood! It's all right, Candida, we are both females, so you need have no concern. Relax and allow the power of the great spirit to permeate your very being.'

Her fingers slipping between Candida's naked pussy lips, the nun began to chant. 'Ommm, ommm.'

'Are you all right?' the girl asked as she raised herself on her elbows.

'Yes, ommm, ommm. Relax, lie back and open your legs. Ommm. The power is beginning to work. Ommm. Can you feel it?'

'I can feel . . . Oh, that's . . . Oh, ah, yes!' Candida gasped, parting her thighs.

Vigorously massaging the girl's erect clitoris, Sister Regina continued her chanting to the accompaniment of the girl's whimpers of ecstasy. 'That's it, let it come!' the nun urged, massaging faster. 'Good girl, let it come!'

'Oh, oh! I'm . . . I'm there!' Candida cried as her orgasm swelled and erupted in her pulsating sex-bud.

'Oh, Sister! Sister, I'm . . . Ah, ah! Oh, yes! Don't . . . don't stop!'

Her young body convulsing as the waves of orgasmic pleasure flooded her quivering pelvis, Candida couldn't believe what the holy woman was doing to her. 'Keep coming!' Sister Regina urged. 'That's it, keep it coming! You're nice and wet now, keep coming!'

'Oh, Sister, I . . . Ah, God! God, it's so wonderful! No more! Please, I'm finished.'

'All right, let it fade now. The power has permeated you, my child. Allow the pleasure to subside now and I'll heal you again when you've rested,' the nun murmured, pressing two fingers into Candida's drenched pussy sheath. 'Let it fade now, let it fade.'

Massaging Candida's cunny hole, Sister Regina tentatively tugged the girl's knickers down, exposing her rubicund vaginal lips to her appreciative gaze. Slipping her fingers from Candida's pussy, she yanked the girl's knickers down to her ankles, easing them over her feet and tossing them aside. Spreading the girl's shapely legs, revealing the entire length of her hairless girl-slit, she smiled and lifted her habit.

'Look, my child! A miracle! God has given me a penis!'

'What?' Candida cried, lifting her head and gazing in awe at the huge male organ.

'I am a woman, Candida – but God has blessed me with this wondrous tool so that I may take you to heaven!'

'But . . . You mean, it's only just appeared?'

'Yes, miraculously, I have just been blessed with a fine penis! This is God's doing, his work, and we must make use of his precious gift!'

'But . . . but I don't understand!'

'Question not miracles of the Lord, my child. Hold it, Candida. Feel it, touch it, caress it!'

'Well, I don't know whether I should!'

'You must, child!' Sister Regina insisted as she knelt beside Candida with her erect penis pointing skyward. 'Take it in your hand!'

Grasping the massive organ, Candida gazed at the huge balls hanging from the broad base of the awesome weapon and frowned. 'I don't see how it can have just appeared!' she gasped as the solid member twitched in her hand.

'Anything is possible, my child. Have faith, and anything is possible. Faith the size of a masturbated . . . mustard seed, can move mountains! Now, I must enter you, penetrate your young vagina with God's gift.'

'No! I don't want . . .'

'Remember the Virgin Mary? She was blessed with a penis from the heavens. A fine penis, possibly this very one, was sent to her to fuck . . . I mean, to penetrate her virginal vagina and fill her barren womb with the seed of life. You must let me fuck . . . enter you, my child!'

'Well, all right, then. But don't hurt me! It looks so big!'

'I'll be gentle with you. Open wide and hang on for dear life! Heaven, here we come!'

Settling between Candida's splayed thighs, the nun aligned the purple knob of the huge organ with the girl's wet pussy hole and drove it deep into the heat of her tight sheath. 'Argh!' Candida cried as the knob struck her cervix. 'Argh! It's too big!'

'No, it's not! Ah, you're so tight, so young, so fresh, so wet! Meet my thrusts, Candida! Work your hips and meet my holy thrusts!'

Lifting her buttocks, Candida found her rhythm, taking the beautiful penile thrusting as she gasped her pleasure.

Her body quivering, her clitoris forced from its fleshy bonnet, she opened her legs as wide as she could, taking the entire length of the love-staff into her tightening channel. Her muscles gripping the pistoning penis, she tossed her head from side to side as her orgasm exploded, taking her to her sexual heaven.

'God, I'm there!' she cried as the solid knob deep within her cuntal sheath exploded, filling her creamy sex duct with sperm. Grunting, thrusting, Sister Regina drove harder into the girl's perspiring body, fucking her, filling her tight cunt with sperm until she collapsed over Candida in the wake of her ecstasy.

'That was beautiful!' the nun gasped. 'Christ, that was fucking . . . I mean, that was heaven! We must do this again, my child!'

'Oh, yes! We must do this again! But what if you become a woman again?'

'Of course I won't! What I mean is, I will be blessed with a penis whenever you come to me. Fear not, this beautiful penis will always be here to penetrate your vagina, to fuck . . . to enter you and fill your barren womb.'

'Oh, that's good!' Candida giggled as the organ slipped out of her inflamed pussy. 'I'll meet you here again, Sister! Every day, I'll come and meet you!'

'Yes, every day you'll come . . . Rest now, my child. Relax and allow the seed to enter your very womb.'

Sifting through the pile of pornographic photographs, Miss Gussetpiece gasped. 'This is disgusting, Jones! I can't work out who's doing what to whom!'

'Er . . . No, neither can I, Headmistress!' Johnson replied, stifling a laugh.

'I agree with you, this definitely looks like Miss Blob! Goodness me, whatever next? All right, Jones, you may go. I'll carry on looking through the pictures for further evidence of Miss Blob's vile behaviour. And keep this to yourself, you hear?'

'Yes, Headmistress. I'll get back to work.'

'All right. But, please, don't start hammering again!'

'No, Headmistress, I won't.'

Opening a folder, Miss Gussetpiece shook out the contents, spreading dozens of photographs across her desk. Gasping as she caught sight of a huge purple knob pumping sperm over a young girl's shaved pussy crack, she grinned. 'These are worth keeping!' she exclaimed aloud.

'What are worth keeping?' Miss Frigidus asked as she entered the study.

'Oh! Oh, Miss Frigidus!' the Head breathed, leaning over her desk in an attempt to conceal the photographs.

'Goodness me! What . . . Oh, dear! What are all those disgusting pictures?'

'I . . . They were discovered in the woods by Jones. He brought them to me so that I could . . . so that I could destroy them, Miss Frigidus.'

'Oh! What's that one? I can't see who's . . . Gosh! It's a man's thing up a lady's bottom! Goodness me, I didn't think that was possible!'

'Anything's possible if you know how! Good grief, I wouldn't mind trying . . . What I mean is . . . Oh, look at this one! Jesus! It's a man's stiff thing in a girl's mouth! Who is that girl? I almost recognize her but I can't quite see who she is with her eyes popping out of her head and her cheeks ballooning. My God, it's . . . it's absolutely . . .'

'Disgusting, Headmistress?'

'Beautiful! Er . . . Yes, that's what I meant – it's absolutely disgusting! Stone the crows, look at that!'

'What is it?'

'A man's thing being licked by two girls! Who are those girls? I'm sure I've seen them somewhere! Look at this one! Where's it gone? Ah, here it is! Who would you say that man is, Miss Frigidus?'

'Well, if Miss Blob were a man, then I'd say it was him.'

'Miss Blob *is* a man!' Miss Gussetpiece enlightened the stunned woman as she poured herself a quadruple gin.

'Oh, dear! Miss Blob, a man?'

'Yes, I'm fairly sure he is. I'm going to have to deal with him most severely, Miss Frigidus! Go and find him and send him to me this instant!'

'Oh, oh! Good gracious! Yes, Headmistress – right away!'

Turning the pages of a magazine, Miss Gussetpiece could hardly believe the centrefold spread. 'Two men and one woman!' she gasped. 'Strewth! The common slut! One up her front and the other up her back! I'm going to have to take these to my rooms and study them closer, I can see that!'

'You wanted to see me, Headmistress?' Miss Blob smiled as she entered the study.

'Ah, Miss Blob! Or, should I say, *Mr* Blob?'

'Er . . . What do you mean, Headmistress?'

'Come on, off with your skirt! I know that you're a man!'

'Oh, Headmistress! I have never been so insulted in all my life!'

'Do you deny that this is you in this vile photograph?'

'Jesus bloody Christ! Where the hell did you . . . I

mean, yes, I emphatically deny it! I'm all woman, I'll have you know!'

'Oh. But it looks so much like you!'

'That's as maybe, but it's *not* me – of that, I can assure you!'

'Mistaken identity on my part, Miss Blob. Please, do accept my apologies. But I'd like you to show me your . . . Lift your skirt and pull the front of your knickers down, Miss Blob! I must be certain that you're not a man!'

Lifting her tweed skirt, Miss Blob pulled the front of her silk panties down, revealing a thick bush of pubic hair. Careful not to expose the root of her penis, she pressed her fatty mons flesh together, forming two hillocks and a dividing groove.

'You see, Headmistress, I *am* a woman.'

'Oh, yes, so you are. What a relief! For a minute, I thought you were some kind of perverted sexual deviant!'

'Certainly not! If that's all, I'll return to the girl . . . I'll return to my rooms.'

'Yes, Miss Blob. I'm sorry for the slight misunderstanding. Here, you might as well take your camera back, seeing as I don't need to develop the . . . Seeing as I won't be needing it now.'

'Thank you, Headmistress. Goodbye.'

'Goodbye, Miss Blob.'

Refilling her glass, Miss Gussetpiece waited until the teacher had disappeared before clearing the photographs away. 'I'll need a safe place for these,' she breathed, collecting the pornographic material and placing it in the filing cabinet. 'And then I must see Hilda Hillock about the dreadful business at the local off-licence. I can't have my girls involved in robberies, I really can't! I wonder where the stolen goods are?'

'Ah, Miss Gussetpiece!' Doctor Anusis Rectus boomed as he entered the study. 'It's Sunday afternoon!'

'Yes, I do realize that! What about it?'

'I'm here.'

'I can see that!'

'As arranged!'

'As arranged? What are you talking about, man?'

'The other day you told me to come and see you on Sunday afternoon.'

'Did I?'

'Yes.'

'What for?'

'To examine the girls.'

'Wait a minute, you've not been posing for pornographic photographs, have you?'

'We've just been through all that! I mean, you've just been through all that with my brother – my sister.'

'How do you know the details of the conversation I had with your sister?'

'I just passed her in the corridor. She told me all about it.'

'Oh. Well, have you?'

'What?'

'Been posing . . .'

'Of course I haven't! I'm a respectable doctor of anal physiology! Got any nice, juicy, plump girls at your school?'

'Nice, juicy, plump girls? What are you, some kind of . . .'

'It's a sign, Headmistress!'

'Don't say that God has sent you, please! I can't be doing with everyone having visions!'

'God?'

'You're not a witness, are you?'

'A witness to what?'

'Jehovah.'

'Who's he, Headmistress?'

'I don't know who he is! Some man who did something and had witnesses to prove that he did it, I suppose.'

'Was it legal?'

'What?'

'Whatever this Jehovah man did.'

'How do I know? I wasn't there!'

'You're not a witness, then?'

'No, I'm not!'

'Well, there you go.'

'Where do I go?'

'I wasn't there, either – so I'm not a witness to whatever it was that he did – legal or illegal.'

'What? Oh, do be quiet, you silly man! If you've not been sent by God, then what's all this nonsense about a sign?'

'No, no! It's a sign of anal abnormality. Plumpness in schoolgirlies, it's a sign.'

'Is it? Well, I didn't know that! As it happens, there *are* one or two plump girls at this school.'

'Send for them and I'll meet them in Sick Bay. Er . . . assuming you have a Sick Bay, that is.'

'Yes, as it happens, we have.'

'Good! Send them to Sick Bay, Headmistress, and I'll get started on the little . . . I'll get started with the anal examinations. Got any foreign birds here?'

'Foreign birds? No, we have no birds, but there are some sheep in the farming area.'

'Really? I like a nice bit of fresh lamb on a Sunday,

or any day of the week, for that matter! Er . . . to eat, I mean.'

'To eat? What else would you do with a lamb?'

'Er . . . Not a lot.'

'What are you suggesting?'

'Nothing, nothing! Anyway, foreign girls – do you have any?'

'There are lots of foreign girls at Bellend. This school has a reputation throughout the world!'

'Yes, I'll bet it has!'

'Why do you ask about foreign girls, in particular?'

'Er . . . Well, because they should be examined first.'

'Why?'

'For foreign bodies. No, no! Er . . . Anal disorders are far more common in young foreign girls. It must be something to do with the climate.'

'Well, we have a new girl who's just started at Bellend. She's German. No, she's not – she's French. I'll send her along to Sick Bay right away.'

'Oui, oui, mon chéri! Er, I mean . . .'

'What are you talking about now?'

'Nothing. I'll go straight to Sick Bay, Headmistress! And, thank you!'

Relaxing on her bed, Hilda smiled at Véronique. 'I'm sorry about last night,' she said softly. 'Had I known that those dreadful Bellend Rebels were going to be in the woods, I'd have never suggested we meet there.'

'It is all right. There was no 'arm done. I . . . I enjoy my experience.'

'Did you? Gosh!'

'I also enjoy my experience with you, 'ilda. We do again, oui?'

'Oui, oui! We do again! I wonder what's taking Candy so long? Do you know, there are some awfully queer things going on in the woods of late!'

'Homosexuel?'

'Who is?'

'I don't know! You say, queer – that means, homosexuel, n'est-ce pas?'

'Yes, but it . . . Never mind. Oh, good afternoon, Miss Gussetpiece!' Hilda grinned, leaping to her feet as the woman entered the dormitory.

'Good afternoon, Hilda. Now, why did I want to see you? Ah, yes, the robbery. Come straight to my study, girl!'

'Why, Miss Gussetpiece? What have I done?'

'You know very well what you've done! Now, Véronique, you are going to see the doctor in Sick Bay.'

'I 'ave not see the doctor!'

'I know you haven't, that's why you're going to see him.'

'Non! I don't see the doctor!'

'Of course you don't see the doctor, he's not here! Just go to Sick Bay, girl!'

'But, Miss Gussetpiss . . .'

'I'll tell your chaperone!'

'Oui, oui, I go!' Véronique sighed as she mooched from the room.

'I *am* going! Good grief, your English is getting worse! I'll have a word with Miss Shaftgrinder about giving you extra tuition. Right, Hilda – follow me!' Miss Gussetpiece ordered.

Following the headmistress down the corridor, Hilda sighed. Again, she was in trouble, she thought sadly as she entered the Head's study and stood before her desk. 'Now, Hilda, tell me all about the off-licence!' Miss Gussetpiece demanded angrily.

'Well, they sell alcohol and tobacco. Oh, and some sweets, I believe.'

'"Sell", being the operative word, Hilda!'

'Yes, I suppose so.'

'Sell!'

'Yes, Miss Gussetpiece.'

'What does the word *sell* mean, Hilda?'

'To exchange goods for money, Miss Gussetpiece.'

'Then why didn't you pay for the goods that you took from the off-licence?'

'I've not been anywhere near the off-licence, Miss Gussetpiece!'

'You were seen, girl! And you dropped this!' the Head declared triumphantly, brandishing the club card. 'Do you deny that this is a Jolly Hockey Sticks Club membership card?'

'No, I don't deny it.'

'I'm writing to your parents to inform them of your imminent expulsion!'

'But, Miss Gussetpiece, it wasn't me! Anyone could have dropped the card. And there must be dozens of Bellend girls with . . .'

'Enough! Go to your dormitory and stay there until further notice!'

'Yes, Miss Gussetpiece.'

Grinning at Dan as she sat on the work bench, Maxine unbuttoned her blouse and eased her taut breasts from her tight bra. 'I'm sure you can manage it!' she coaxed huskily, tweaking her erect nipple. 'Just think, you can have my tits and my lovely wet cunt whenever you want – if you succeed.'

'But I can't! There's no way I could seduce Madame Fissure! Why do you want me to seduce her, anyway?' the young man asked, moving across the maintenance room towards the pretty brunette.

'Because I want her under my thumb. You're screwing Madame Fissure, right? You've got her knickers off, her legs wide open, and you're screwing her rotten, really giving her a good fucking! And I come along and catch you – voilà!'

'I can't just pull women to order! What if she doesn't fancy me?'

'Any woman in her right mind would fancy you! Then, when we've screwed Fissure, we'll do the same with Shaftgrinder.'

'I don't know if . . .'

'You do like my tits, don't you? Suck my nipple, have a taste of what could be yours whenever you want it.'

Leaning forward, Dan sucked Maxine's long nipple into his mouth. Slipping his hand up her gymslip, he kneaded the damp material covering her swelling vaginal lips and breathed heavily through his nose. 'Mmm, you taste good!' he grinned, slipping her burgeoning bud from his mouth and licking the darkening surrounding earth-flesh.

'My cunt tastes even better!' Maxine breathed. 'So, will you try to seduce them?'

'Yes, I will. Can I . . .'

'No!' Maxine giggled, pushing him away as he tried to pull her knickers to one side and gain access to her pussy. 'You're not having my cunt until you've seduced Fissure and Shaftgrinder! OK, this is the plan. Go to Fissure's room with some excuse about repairing something – and fuck her!'

'Jesus! It won't be easy! Where will you be?'

'Outside her lounge window with a Polaroid camera. I've often spied on her. There's a good view of her lounge from the bushes by the window. I'll let you know when to do it.'

'Christ! I'll try but . . . I'm not putting my job on the line!'

'If there's trouble, I'll be your alibi. I'll say that you were outside, doing something in the grounds. I'll have several witnesses, OK?'

'OK. Can I just have a little taste of what's to be mine whenever I want it?'

'All right, you can lick my cunt,' Maxine grinned, reclining on the bench and tugging her knickers down.

Parting the girl's juicy labia as she opened her legs wide, Johnson licked her sex groove, tasting her slippery girl-juice as it oozed from her hot cuntal sheath. 'Finger me!' Maxine gasped as his tongue swept across her ripening clitoris. 'Ah, that's it! Push it right in!' she sighed as he massaged her velveteen inner flesh. 'Ah, God, that's good! Make me come with your tongue!'

Fingering her tight pussy sheath as he sucked her stiffening clitoris into his mouth, Dan brought out the girl's orgasm. Gasping her delight, Maxine shuddered as she sensed a finger enter her rectal duct and massage her sensitive anal flesh, enhancing her incredible base pleasure. 'Give me your prick!' she panted. 'I want to suck your knob!' Unzipping his jeans, Dan stood by Maxine's head and offered his purple plum to her open mouth as he continued fingering her tight love holes. 'Mmm!' she purred as she took his knob into her mouth and gently sucked and licked.

Overwhelmed with carnal desire, Dan released his sperm, flooding the girl's mouth, filling her cheeks with his come. Swallowing hard, Maxine drank from his geysering fountainhead as her clitoris pulsated, nearing another sexual peak. Gulping down his cream, she rubbed her solid sex-button to another shattering climax as he fingered her hot holes. Shuddering as his knob slipped from her sperm-drenched mouth, Maxine gasped.

'Fuck! Fuck, that's . . . God, my cunt! Don't stop! Finger-fuck me!' Quickening his rhythm, Dan watched as Maxine vibrated her fingertips over her pulsating clitoris, man and schoolgirl orchestrating her pleasure until she fell limp, her hands dropping by her sides, her mouth open, gasping – spermed. 'No more!' she cried as her cunt spasmed, gripping Dan's pistoning fingers like a velvet-jawed vice. 'That's enough!'

Slipping his wet fingers from the girl's trembling body, Dan zipped his jeans up. 'You're a bloody horny little tart!' he chuckled, eyeing Maxine's inflamed pussy lips as she caressed her receding clitoris. 'I'd love to fuck your beautiful cunt!'

'You will!' Maxine promised, slipping her knickers up her long legs and jumping off the bench. 'Once you've screwed Fissure and Shaftgrinder, you *can* fuck my lovely tight cunt – and arse!'

'Have you always been a dirty little tart?' Dan asked as Maxine moved towards the door.

'Ever since my cunt sprouted hairs!' she grinned. 'Ever since I discovered my pussy had a hole hiding between my cunt lips! I'll see you later and we'll plan the seduction in more detail. Until then, Mr Fixit!'

Chapter Nine

'Hilda, when did you last see Véronique?' Miss Shaftgrinder asked as she stood behind her desk and peered over her glasses.

'The last I saw of her was when Miss Gussetpiece sent her to Sick Bay to see the doctor yesterday.'

'I'll have to mark her as absent, then. This is a fine way to begin Monday morning, I must say! Hilda, go to Miss Gussetpiece and tell her that Véronique is absent, please. I thought she had a chaperone to supervise her – goodness knows what's happened to *her*!'

Finding Miss Gussetpiece sprawled across her desk clutching an upturned empty vodka bottle, Hilda reported Véronique's absence. 'Not another one!' Miss Gussetpiece slurred, dragging herself to an upright position. 'Why on earth do girls keep pissadearing? I mean, disappearing? Did she bleep in her sed – sleep in her bed last night?'

'I don't know, Miss Gussetpiece, she's not in my dorm.'

'Wait a minute while I ring Miss Blob and ask if her brother examined the girl,' the Head sighed, lifting the telephone and punching the buttons. 'Ah, Miss Blob, I need to contact your brother, Doctor Rectus, about the German girl. How can I get hold of him?'

'Er . . . What a stroke of luck, he's with me at the moment! I'll send him to see you, Headmistress.'

'Thank you. Er . . . Miss Blob – you haven't sold anything, have you?'

'Sold anything, Headmistress?'

'Yes. Last week, you were talking about selling off a few . . . a few things.'

'Oh, the girls. No, no, I haven't sold any.'

'Are you sure?'

'Quite sure!'

'You're not mistaken, are you? I mean, you could have inadvertently sold some. These things do happen.'

'Of course I haven't inadvertently sold any girls! I'd know if I'd sold any girls, wouldn't I? It stands to reason.'

'Yes, I suppose it does. All right, goodbye. Right, Hilda, go back to your class and I'll deal with this.'

'Yes, Miss Gussetpiece.'

Answering the phone as Hilda left the study, Miss Gussetpiece gasped. 'Minister for Education? Er . . . Oh, good morning, sir!'

'Good morning, Miss Gussetpiece. I've received reports, disturbing reports, concerning Bellend School.'

'Have you? Oh, dear!'

'Yes, I have. One – allegedly, a naked woman was seen running through the grounds. Two – the police deemed it necessary to raid the school . . . What's been going on, Headmistress?'

'Er . . . Yes, I can explain that. The naked woman was a . . .'

'Three – there was an explosion.'

'Oh, you know about that?'

'Yes, I do!'

'Er . . . It was an electrical fault – it's been taken care of.'

'Four – there was a fire.'

'Yes, a paste waper bin in the . . .'

'Five – pornography was discovered at your fête on Saturday.'

'I don't know anything about that.'

'Six – there were used condoms scattered across the playing field.'

'Er . . .'

'Seven – there were soiled knickers for sale at the fête.'

'Were there?'

'Eight – the PE mistress allegedly sexually interfered with a schoolgirl.'

'Er . . .'

'Nine – there's a rumour, and only a rumour at this stage, that a Bellend girl robbed an off-licence.'

'Ah, yes, that was . . .'

'Ten – the police removed a large quantity of alcohol and cigarettes from the school's basement.'

'Yes, I confiscated . . .'

'Eleven – there's been a report of a nun who was physically assaulted by you, Miss Gussetpiece. *Attempted rape*, it says here on the report.'

'Ah, yes, I can explain that.'

'This is a catalogue of disasters, Miss Gussetpiece! I'm sending a representative to see you. He'll inspect the school and report his findings to me. I will then decide which course of action to take. He'll be with you in a couple of hours or so.'

'Oh, dear!'

'His name's Probe.'

'Mr Probe. All right, sir, I'll be here to beat him . . . to meet him.'

'Have you been drinking, Miss Gussetpiece?'

'Drinking? Certainly not! It's not in my nature to

drink! I'll have you know that I've had a decent Catholic upbringing!'

'That explains it! Right you are, Miss Gussetpiece – I'll be in touch. Goodbye.'

'Goodbye, sir.'

Banging the receiver down, Miss Gussetpiece grabbed the vodka bottle. 'Holy Mother of God!' she gasped as Doctor Rectus entered the study. 'Jesus bloody Christ!'

'I *beg* your pardon, Headmistress?'

'I said . . . never mind! What do you want?'

'You sent for me.'

'Oh, yes. Did you examine the German girl yesterday?'

'No, I didn't.'

'But I sent her to you!'

'No, you didn't.'

'Yes, I did! I sent her to Sick Bay! Are you suffering from memory loss?'

'Memory loss? Not that I'm aware of. Unless my knowledge of Europeans is grossly deficient, I'll swear on your mother's grave that I interfered with a . . . I mean, that I examined a French girl!'

'You can't swear on my mother's grave, she's a Catholic! It's not decent! Besides, she's not dead. God, my head's spinning! Ah, yes, that's what I meant.'

'What did you mean?'

'She *was* a French girl.'

'Who was, your mother?'

'No! The girl I sent to Sick Bay.'

'Thank God that we can agree on that, at least! Most distressed, she was!'

'Who, my mother?'

'The French girl you sent to see me!'

'Why?'

'You sent her to see me for an examination.'

'Yes, I know that! But why was she distressed?'

'She didn't like the way I . . . She rambled on in French, I don't know what she was complaining about. You know what these foreign girls can be like!'

'This is a matter for grave concern, Doctor Rectus! She's not been seen since she went to Sick Bay! How was she when she left you? What was her state of mind?'

'She was in tears so I presume she was in a poor state of mind. From the physical aspect . . . Well, she ran off with her knickers round her knees.'

'Goodness me! She must have been brought up in the gutter to behave in such a lewd manner! Bloody foreigners! What her parents would say, I dread to think! Mind you, it was probably their fault. Blame the parents, that's what I say. I'd better call an urgent meeting. Get your sister in here, and your brother, will you?'

'Er . . . I can't do that.'

'Why ever not?'

'My brother was called away on urgent gynaecological business, and my sister . . . I'll go and find her.'

'All right. There's a man from the Minister for Education's office coming to the school – he'll be here in a couple of hours so we must act fast.'

'Jesus Christ!'

'My sentiments exactly, Doctor Rectus! God, I really must sober up!'

Pacing the floor as the doctor left the study, Miss Gussetpiece gazed at the boarded-up windows. There was no way to explain that! she thought anxiously. Lifting the phone, she rang Miss Blob and instructed her to round up the staff. 'And be quick about it!' she snapped. 'There's a problem, a huge problem!' Banging the phone down, she sat at her desk and held her head in her hands. 'I'll be rumbled!' she moaned. 'God help me, I'll be rumbled!'

Entering the study, Miss Blob and Madame Fissure seated themselves as the other members of staff filed in. 'Right, settle down!' Miss Gussetpiece ordered before agitatedly explaining the situation. 'Any bright ideas?' she asked the assembled mob of teachers. 'We have to put on a good show. We've got to fool this man from London into thinking that this is a fine school, a decently-run educational establishment.'

'It *is* a fine school!' Miss Frigidus broke in.

'Of course it's not!' the Head bellowed. 'There's been nothing but trouble . . .'

'All right, let's not argue!' Miss Blob interrupted. 'We'll get nowhere by bickering like a bunch of senile old hens! Now, what we need to do is search the school for foreign bodies.'

'Foreign bodies?' the Head echoed. 'The school's full of foreign bodies!'

'Jesus! Is it really?'

'Yes, we have dozens of foreign girls.'

'No, not foreign bodies as in foreigners! Things that might be incriminating – alcohol, cigarettes, condoms, drugs, guns, knives and the like.'

'Oh, dear! Drugs, guns, knives . . . Oh, my goodness, what are we to do?' Miss Frigidus cried hysterically. 'We could all be drugged or shot or stabbed!'

'Control yourself, woman!' Miss Gussetpiece snapped. 'You don't know what you're saying! Mentally, you seem to be in a steady state of decline!'

'I'm sorry, Headmistress. It's just that . . .'

'Oh, do shut up! Take a couple of Valium to steady your nerves! You'll have us all going over the edge if you carry

Girl School

on like this! Right, Miss Blob, you organize the search in the main building. Miss Frigidus, check the grounds and outbuildings for perverted priests in possession of herbal cigarettes – if you're mentally fit for the job, that is! Madame Fissure, clean up the laundry room, and the locker and changing rooms.'

'Sacré bleu! I'm not a charlady!' the French mistress hissed, brushing her black hair away from her angry face.

'I didn't say you were a charlady! Just do it, or we'll all be out of work, and probably imprisoned for . . . That reminds me, Madame Fissure, I'm going to suspend you by your French suspender belt when all this is over! Unfit for my post, indeed! And how dare you call me an alcoholic, you silly frog!'

'I'll report you to the race relations . . .'

'Shut up! Now, Fräulein Vulvahausen, tidy the girls up. Some of them look as if they've been dragged through the bushes backwards!'

'Some of them have!' Miss Blob laughed. 'Er . . . What I meant was . . .'

'Do be quiet, Miss Blob! Jones, I want the maintenance room and basement in pristine condition, do you understand?'

'Yes, Miss Gussetpiece, I'll see to it right away.'

'When you've done that, check to make sure that the frog's done a good job in the laundry room.'

'If you call me a frog again, I'll . . .'

'Do be quiet! Miss Shaftgrinder, help Fräulein Vulvahausen to tidy the girls up, the sixth-formers in particular. Miss Hairoot, check the classrooms and notice boards for disgusting literature. Right, off you all go!'

'What are you going to do, Headmistress?' Miss Frigidus asked anxiously.

'I'm going to have a drink!'

'Oh, dear! I really don't think you should be drinking heavily at a time like this!'

'I have to man headquarters, Miss Frigidus! Look upon me as the admiral of the fleet. And it's a well-known fact that sailors break out the rum when they're about to go into battle. Just look at the armada – men were drinking heavily for days on end!'

'Battle? Are the Spanish . . .'

'Miss Frigidus, please! Go and check the grounds and outbuildings for perverted priests in possession of herbal cigarettes!'

'Yes, Headmistress, right away.'

Winking at Ginger as they stole out of the classroom, Maxine grinned. 'If it's true, and there *is* some geezer coming down from London, then this is our chance!'

'Fucking hell, we'll never have a better chance to close the school!' Ginger giggled as they made their way to the potting shed. 'What shall we do?'

'We'll make our plans in a minute,' Maxine replied. Kicking the shed door open, she ordered the gardener to clear off. 'We need this place!' she menaced. 'Go on, fuck off out of it!'

'Now you look 'ere, Miss!' the old man returned angrily. 'I've just 'bout 'ad enough of you and your cheek!'

'Now you listen to me, you old fart – we need this place to plan our attack! So you can fucking well . . .'

'What you attackin'?'

'Mind your own business!'

'I ain't goin' nowhere until you . . .'

'Right! Ginger, rip your clothes off and cry rape!'

Girl School

'You got it, Max!'

Watching the girl tear her clothes off, the gardener sat on the sofa and grinned. 'I knows sumfink you don't!' he chuckled, eyeing Ginger's pert breasts as she tossed her bra to the floor.

'What?' Maxine asked.

'You all thinks I'm a silly ol' fart. But what you don't know is that I knows more 'bout this school than the lot of you put together!'

'Tell me what you know, or I'll chew your balls off!' Maxine threatened, gnashing her teeth.

'Well, for starters, I knows that ol' lady Gussetpiece ain't got no qualifications. She lied to get the job 'ere.'

'Did she, now?' Maxine grinned pensively.

'Yeah! She were nowt more than a common factory worker. And I'll tell you sumfink else. Miss Blob is a man!'

'We already know that!' Ginger sneered, slipping her thumbs between her knicker elastic and her shapely hips.

'There's more! That frigid woman, the hysterical woman what learns you foreign and the like – she was 'avin' it off in the woods with a priest!'

'Fuck me! How do you know that?' Maxine gasped.

'I seen her with me own eyes! Walkin' in the woods, I was – and I come across 'er 'avin' it off on the grass with a priest.'

'You're lying, you old git!' Ginger spat. 'Old Frigid screwing a priest?'

'No, I ain't lyin'! Ol' lady Gussetpiece 'ad it off with the priest 'n' all!'

'Now I *know* you're lying! The headmistress, getting herself fucked by a priest?'

'I'm tellin' you! Seen 'er with me own eyes, I did! The

priest was on top of 'er, really givin' it to 'er! There was someone else lurkin' in the woods, but I couldn't see 'oo it was.'

'Why are you telling us all this?' Maxine asked as Ginger kicked her knickers aside and stood with her feet apart before the wide-eyed old man.

'I'm tellin' you 'cause I wants to 'elp you,' he replied, gazing at Ginger's pinken inner flesh as she peeled her outer vaginal lips wide open.

'Why do you want to help us? You don't even know what we're doing.'

'You're tryin' to close the school down. I knows everythin' what goes on round 'ere.'

'How do you propose to help us?' Maxine asked. 'What can an old fart like you do to help us?'

'Holy Jesus Christ!' Miss Gussetpiece screamed as she staggered into the shed and slipped over, crashing to the floor. 'Stone the bleedin' crows, who left that cucumber there? Ginger, what *are* you doing without your clothes on, girl?' she gasped, clambering to her feet.

'Oh, Miss Gussetpiece! I was just . . .'

'Get dressed and go to my study, this instant! There are more naked girls on the loose in this school than . . . than is decent! Maxine, what's going on here?'

'We were . . . The gardener – I came in and found him raping Ginger!'

'How could an old fool like him rape a healthy girl of eighteen? Look at him, there's nothing of him! He couldn't even rape me!'

'If you doesn't mind me sayin' so, 'eadmistress – never in a million years would I dream of rapin' . . .'

'Shut up, you old fool – or I'll have you flogged and keel hauled! I'm the admiral of the fleet, I'll have you know! Maxine, get out of here and do something useful! And you, you dirty old man – the toilet block site is being cleared of rubble. When they've finished, cover the site with earth and plant some flowers there.'

'But I'm in the middle of . . .'

'You've got two hours at the most, so get on with it!'

'Whatever you say, 'eadmistress.'

'Ginger, you wicked, wicked girl – follow me!'

Following the Head into her study, Ginger stood before the mahogany desk in her torn clothing, awaiting the inevitable lecture. 'Ginger, I have never . . . What on earth happened, girl?' Miss Gussetpiece asked angrily. 'Why were you standing in the potting shed with . . . with all you have blatantly displayed to the gardener?'

'Well, I . . .' Ginger began as the phone rang.

'Wait a minute, girl!' the Head snapped as she lifted the receiver. 'Miss Gussetpiece speaking.'

'Greenhouse To Bulletproof Limited, here,' a man said.

'What? Who is this?'

'The glazier. I work for Greenhouse To Bulletproof Limited.'

'Yes, you've already told me that! What do you want? I can't have strange men ringing a boarding school for girls! It's not natural!'

'Johnson just rang me about the windows.'

'Johnson? What about the windows?'

'He said that they had to be replaced within two hours. I can patch up the frames, now that he's bodged the lintel, and bung some new glass in tout de suite.'

'Tout de what?'

'In a jiffy.'

'What?'

'In a flash. Bish, bash, bosh – all done!'

'What *are* you talking about, you silly man?'

'Wham, bam, thank you, ma'am.'

'Are you mentally insane?'

'That's quite possible, yes'

'You need psychiatric help! What is it you want? I'm a very busy woman, I'll have you know! I can't be doing with time wasters.'

'I can do the windows in no time at all.'

'What, now?'

'Yes, within two shakes of a lamb's tail. I'm in my van, on my mobile. I'll be there in five.'

'Five? How much will all this cost?'

'I'll do it for a monkey – and I'm losing money.'

'A monkey?'

'Five hundred, OK?'

'Yes, yes, just be quick about it!' Miss Gussetpiece snapped as she banged the receiver down.

Turning to Ginger, the headmistress frowned. 'Now, what on earth were you doing in the potting shed without . . .' Her words tailing off as the phone rang again, she lifted the receiver. 'Giss Muffitpiece speaking,' she drooled.

'Who?' a woman asked.

'Sorry – Miss Gussetpiece. It was a spoonerism.'

'A what?'

'A spoonerism – you know, where you inadvertently swap the first two letters . . . Oh, never mind! Who are you? I'm busy, what do you want?'

'This is the Reverend Mother Nihilist from Our Lady Of The Doomed speaking.'

'Oh, my God! I mean . . . Jesus! Er . . . Good morning, your Most Holiness.'

'I'm calling about Sister Lucipharian. She came to see

you the other day to suggest that she talk to the girls about the Blessed Virgin Mary, and she was subjected to a horrendous indecent assault. What have you to say for yourself, Miss Gussetpiece?'

'Er . . . Hold on, please,' the flustered woman replied, covering the mouthpiece and waving Ginger out of the room. 'Sorry about that. An indecent assault, you say?'

'Yes, a sexual assault of a most indecent nature. Our dear sister told me that you dragged her to the floor and ripped her . . . that you indecently assaulted her.'

'No, no, no! It wasn't like that at all!'

'Then what *was* it like?'

'Er . . . Mistaken identity. I thought she was a man.'

'You thought that a nun was a man?'

'Yes, that's right – a man.'

'How could you ever mistake a . . . Men don't wear habits!'

'You'd be surprised by the things men . . . Er . . . Oh, is that the time? I really must be going! It's been nice talking to you, Mother Annihilist – goodbye.'

Hanging up, Miss Gussetpiece sighed. 'Let's hope that's that minor problem nipped in the bud! Now, what next? Ah, yes, the off-licence,' she breathed, grabbing the phone and asking directory enquiries for the number. 'I hate machines!' she complained as the computer intoned the number. Dialling, she waited impatiently, checking her watch, wondering when the man from London would arrive. 'Are you the off-licence?' she asked as a man answered.

'*I'm* not an off-licence, I'm a human being!'

'You know very well what I mean! Don't play games with me!'

'Games? I never play games!'

'Who are you? To whom do I have the displeasure of speaking?'

'The name's Grouse – Arthur Grouse. What do you want?'

'Well, Mr Grouse, this is Miss Gussetpiece from Bellend . . .'

'Ah, it's Gussetpiece, is it?'

'I just told you that it's me! Why ask if it's me when I've just told you it's me?'

'What?'

'Now, you listen to me, Grouse! You drop the charges and I'll . . .'

'Too late – I've already been to the police. They should be paying you a visit this morning. I wouldn't be surprised if your school was . . .'

'I'll pay *you* a visit unless you shut up and listen! Now, you'll drop the charges and make an official apology and . . .'

'I'll do no such thing!'

'Will you hear me out, Mouse, or whatever your name is? Now, listen! You drop the charges and make an official apology in writing, and I'll give you one thousand pounds in cash.'

'Shit, a grand? Right, you're on!'

'Don't swear down the phone, it's against BT's rules! Now listen to me, you nasty little man, ring the police this instant and tell them that you were mistaken about the robbery, and then write me a letter of apology. I want the letter here within one hour – along with a free crate of gin! Litre bottles, mind! Now, get on with it!'

Hanging up, Miss Gussetpiece reclined in her chair, swigging from the vodka bottle as she planned her next move. 'Stone the crows!' she cried as the boarding was ripped away from the broken windows. Shielding her bloodshot eyes from the bright sun, she called out to the glazier. 'You there, I want a professional job – and be quick about it! And make sure you clear up after yourself! I know you tradesmen-types of old!'

'I always do, lady!' he replied, smashing chips of glass from the window frame.

'And don't call me lady!'

'I'll call you what I like!'

'What was that?'

'I said, I'll make it all right!'

'You see that you do!'

Leaving her study, Miss Gussetpiece made her way to the gardener's potting shed. 'Where are you, man?' she bellowed as she entered the empty shed. 'Goodness me, there's Ginger's torn knickers on the floor! If the man from London sees those, he'll . . . If you want a job doing properly, do it yourself!' she complained, grabbing the navy-blue knickers and returning to her study.

'Right!' Maxine grinned as she passed Ginger a pair of wire cutters. 'Bare those two wires and pass them to me.'

'I hope you know what you're doing, Max!' Ginger cautioned.

'Of course I do! Now, if I connect these wires to these terminals, the fire alarm will go off instead of the school bell. At break time, the whole school will have to be evacuated, giving us the chance to start a fire.'

'Great! What else shall we do?'

'Nothing, for now. Kelly's going to streak across the grounds in full view of Knickergusset's window. That should turn the education man's head! Right, let's go and hang out in the woods until we hear the fire bells!' the girl giggled, dashing out of the switchgear cupboard. 'We'll have a drink and a fag. The bottle's still there, isn't it?'

'Yes, under the bush with the ciggies.'

'Good! Let's go!'

In the woods, Maxine and Ginger rolled about on the grass in the clearing, giggling uncontrollably as they imagined the fire alarm going off and the entire school assembling on the playing field. 'Is the man from the ministry going to have a long report to write up, or what?' Maxine chortled.

'Let's set fire to the woods!' Ginger suggested. 'There's been no rain for weeks, this lot will go up in no time!'

'Good idea! Hang on, someone's coming!'

Peering through the bushes, Maxine held her hand to her mouth and gasped as a young man in a smart suit made his way through the undergrowth. 'Who the fuck's that?' she asked Ginger.

'Fuck knows! I've never seen him before. Look out, he's coming this way!'

'Shit, he's seen us!'

'Morning, girls!' the man smiled, entering the clearing.

'Morning,' the girls replied in unison as he sat beside them.

'I've just moved into the cottage down the lane. I was taking a stroll and I seem to have got myself lost.'

'Well, you're in the school grounds,' Ginger smiled, eyeing his crotch.

'Oh! Er . . . I'd better be going, then!'

'It's all right!' Maxine smiled. 'You're safe enough here. We always come here for a drink and a smoke. Ginger, get the vodka and fags from beneath the bush.'

'A drink and a smoke, eh?' the man frowned. 'Is that allowed?'

Girl School

'Nah, of course it isn't! But we don't give a toss!' Maxine laughed.

'Here, have a swig,' Ginger invited, passing the man the bottle.

'Thank you, but no. Shouldn't you two be in class?'

'S'pose so,' Maxine returned nonchalantly. 'You're the man from the education place, aren't you?'

'Yes, I am, and I have never . . .'

'Want a fag?'

'Certainly not! I want your names, please! You'll be expelled for this!'

'Oh, that's good!' Ginger giggled, sitting with her legs crossed, the thin strip of navy-blue material barely concealing her swollen outer pussy lips. 'I've had enough of this dump!'

'Good God!' the man gasped. 'I have never . . .'

'Yeah, so you said,' Maxine interjected, swigging from the vodka bottle. 'You here to inspect the place, then?'

'Yes, yes, I am!'

'Miss Blob, the geography mistress, is a man in drag.'

'What?'

'And old Knickergusset has no qualifications.'

'But . . .'

'There's a pervert on the loose posing as a priest and fucking all the girls and . . .'

'I'm going straight to Miss Gussetpiece!' the man cried, leaping to his feet. 'Your names, please.'

'Hilda Hillock and Candida Coombs,' Maxine smiled helpfully as the man strode off.

'We're almost ready!' Miss Gussetpiece grinned, breaking out a new bottle of vodka and offering Miss Frigidus a drink.

'Oh, dear! My hormones are all over the place and my nerves are shot to pieces! I hope all goes well, Headmistress, I really do!'

'Of course it will. Look, the windows are done, the gardener's just about done his bit with the geraniums – everything's spick and span! Er . . . Come in!' she called to a knock on the door.

'Miss Gussetpiece? My name's Probe, I'm from . . .'

'Ah, Mr Probe, do come in and sit down! I've been regretting you . . . I've been expecting you. That will be all, Miss Frigidus, thank you.'

'Oh, dear! Good luck, Headmistress!' the frail woman smiled as she knocked back her vodka and reeled out of the study.

'What was that she was drinking?' Probe asked as he took his seat opposite the Head.

'It was water. She has to drink a lot to flush out her urinary pipes. Now, Mr Probe, welcome to Bellend School. Where would you like to begin your guided tour?'

'It's not a guided tour, Headmistress! This is an official visit! I've just met two girls in the wooded area edging the playing field. They were drinking and smoking and their language was disgusting! Their names are Hilda Hillock and Candida Coombs. What do you have to say about that?'

'I don't recognize the names. No, no, I'm certain that they're not Bellend girls.'

'They were in the grounds, wearing Bellend uniforms!'

'Yes, we've had a spate of thefts . . . some uniforms were stolen recently. A most unpleasant business, I must say! It's local girls from the village, I'm afraid. Terrible they are – no proper upbringing, that's their problem. You know the scenario – dishevelled mothers permanently pregnant and in the pub every afternoon. Scruffy fathers, perpetually out of work, always drunk and . . .'

'Yes, yes, all right! What about the . . . My God! What on earth . . . ?' the man cried, rising to his feet and staring out of the window in astonishment. 'Look, there's a naked girl running through the grounds!'

'Bloody . . . I mean, it's an apparition, Mr Probe. Nothing to concern yourself with, I can assure you.'

'An apparition?'

'Yes, she's known as the Naughty Naked Masturbator. Legendary, she is – been haunting the school for over one hundred years.'

'The Naughty Naked Masturbator? I can't believe that she's a ghost, she looks so real! I shall have to report this, Miss Gussetpiece! Look, you can see it's a schoolgirl by the size and shape of her . . . of her body!'

'She's a ghost, Mr Probe! Back in the nineteenth century, one of the village girls was discovered naked in a field. She was caught by the vicar, masturbating. It was a terrible business, by all accounts. The wretched child died of shame. Legend has it that she runs about looking for her clothes.'

'Died of shame? I don't believe in ghosts! It's one of your Bellend girls, more than likely! I'm going to take a walk around the school, Miss Gussetpiece!'

'Oh, er, yes. I'll accompany you, Mr Probe.'

Following the confused man down the corridor, Miss Gussetpiece prayed that there'd be no more horrendous incidents. *I'll discover who that wicked girl was and have her horsewhipped!* she thought, trying to keep pace with Probe as he strode down the basement steps. 'There's nothing of interest down here, Mr Probe!' she asserted, almost tumbling down the steps. 'Just old junk, relics from Bellend's ancient past and . . .'

'I'd like to check for myself, Miss Gussetpiece – seeing as the police discovered alcohol and tobacco stashed down here.'

Holy Mary! I hope Jones has done his business!

'Ah, now, what's all this, then?' the man asked, taking a vibrator from a cardboard box.

'I've no idea! What it is, a plastic candle? Yes, it must be one of the plastic candles we use at Christmas for . . .'

'It's not a plastic candle – it's a vibrator!'

'What does it do?'

'It's for . . . What's this? My God! A whip, handcuffs, KY gel, leather bondage straps, nipple clamps, butt plugs, lengths of rubber tubing, a cucumber . . . Can you explain what this equipment is doing down here?'

'Er . . . We were putting on a play. It was going to be called . . . er . . . *The French Prostitute's Private Life*. No, no, it wasn't! Er . . . It was going to be called *Female Carnality Explored*.'

'Female carnality . . . What sort of play would require props such as these?'

'It was all part of our sociology studies. We were exploring female sexuality in the twentieth century.'

'A play like that would be deemed . . . What are these steel rings in the wall used for?'

'They've been there since the late eighteen hundreds. They were used for . . .'

'Why are there handcuffs attached to them?'

'Er . . . As far as I know, back in Bellend's early days . . .'

'Why is the floor beneath the rings wet and stained?'

'Er . . .'

'These are signs of recent sexual activity – perverted sexual activity, I'd say! I'd better check the rest of the school! Show me to the laundry room!'

'The laundry room? Oh, er . . . yes, Mr Probe, this way.'

Leading the way to the laundry room, Miss Gussetpiece sighed. She'd failed in her mission, she knew as she decided to wring Jones's neck. *If there's anything wrong in the laundry room, I'll . . .*

'My God!' Probe gasped as he opened the door to confront a nun holding a handful of navy-blue knickers to her face. 'What *are* you doing? And what's that sticking out beneath your habit?' As the nun fled in the wake of a trail of stained navy knickers, Probe turned to the headmistress. 'This is all too much, it really is! I have never . . . Take me to Sick Bay!'

'Are you ill?'

'I'm mentally disturbed by my findings!'

'If you need a psychiatrist, I can give you the name of a good . . .'

'I do *not* need a psychiatrist! Take me to Sick Bay!'

'Oh, my goodness! I need a drink!'

'A drink?'

'Er . . . Yes, I'm thirsty – I need a drink of water.'

'Take me to Sick Bay – I wish to inspect your medical facilities!'

'Er . . . This way, Mr Probe.'

Leading the horrified man to Sick Bay, Miss Gussetpiece opened the door, ushering him in before her. 'You'll find everything in order,' she smiled confidently. 'We have a fine range of modern facilities. Facilities that the local hospital would be envious of. In fact . . .'

'What in God's name are you doing to that naked girl?' Confronting Doctor Anusis Rectus, the man from the ministry gasped. 'Why have you got your fingers up her bottom?'

'I'm examining her.'

'Why is your penis poking out of your trousers? My God, it's erect!'

'Jesus! Er . . .'

Slipping his fingers from the naked girl's bottom, the doctor hurriedly left the room. 'Come back here!' Probe called after the fleeing man.

'Sorry, I have an urgent anal appointment!'

'Come here or I'll . . . My God, what sort of establishment are you running here, Miss Gussetpiece?'

'Cover yourself!' the headmistress ordered the naked girl as she leaped from the examination couch, her firm young breasts and vaginal crack blatantly on display. 'Mr Probe, we pride ourselves . . .'

'This is disgusting! What sort of establishment *is* this?'

'We have the services of two fine doctors,' the Head began as the girl grabbed her clothes and ran out of the room. 'There's nothing wrong with a highly qualified doctor giving the girl a medical examination.'

'What, with his erect penis sticking out of his trousers? I've seen enough, Miss Gussetpiece! I shall return to London on the next train and report my findings to the Minister for Education! No doubt he'll have the school closed down immediately! Never in all my years in this job have I come across such . . . such . . . You'll be hearing from the Minister in due course!'

Resignedly following Probe into the corridor, Miss Gussetpiece watched him leave the building. Shaking her head and sighing, she made her way to her study and

Girl School

flopped into her chair. 'Well, that's that!' she breathed, taking a swig from the vodka bottle. 'The end of Bellend!'

'Good news, Headmistress!' Miss Frigidus cried as she entered the study. 'Véronique has been found!'

'Oh, that's something I suppose. Where had she been?'

'According to her, she'd been sleeping rough in the woods.'

'Good grief! What *are* things coming to? Give her ten thousand lines!'

'Ten thousand? But the poor girl's already distressed enough with an irritable bottom.'

'An irritable bottom?'

'I gather that's her problem. She's moaning about *mal* to her *derrière*.'

'I'll have her see the doctor again. Ten thousand lines! *I will not sleep rough in the woods again.* Leave me now, Miss Frigidus. I need to be alone.'

'Oh dear! Er . . . yes, Headmistress.'

Standing by the trees, Maxine nudged Ginger's arm. 'There he is!' she exclaimed excitedly.

'Right, I'm off to prepare to drive the last nail into Bellend's coffin! See you in the clearing.'

'Excuse me!' Maxine called to Probe as he marched down the school drive. Turning, the man made his way across the playing field.

'What is it?' he asked impatiently as he approached the girl.

'I want to show you something,' Maxine smiled. 'Follow me, you must see this!'

'I have a train to catch!' he snapped, following the girl through the wood. 'I haven't got the time to . . .'

'It won't take long. Come on, this way.'

Emerging from the bushes into the clearing, Probe gasped as he discovered Ginger sprawled out on the grass, naked. Gasping, her head rolling from side to side, her fingers massaging between her swollen vaginal lips, she was close to orgasm. 'Bloody hell!' Probe cried as Ginger eased a huge cucumber into her tight vagina and whimpered in her coming. 'What the hell's going on here?'

'Want to join in?' Maxine asked devilishly as she pulled her gymslip off and unbuttoned her blouse. 'I'm sure you could do with some relaxation after inspecting our school!'

'Good God! I . . . This is terrible! I have never . . .'

'Oh, come on!' Maxine coaxed, slipping her blouse off and peeling her bra away from her firm breasts. 'Don't you like my tits?' she grinned, tweaking her erect nipples. 'Would you like to suck my nipples? Come on, suck my tits!'

'I don't believe this!' Probe breathed, gazing at Maxine's moist vaginal crack as she tugged her damp knickers down her slender legs.

'Look at my cunt!' she giggled. 'It's all wet and juicy, all ready for your stiff cock! Ever fucked a schoolgirl? We're tight, you know. Really hot and wet and tight!'

Dropping to her knees, Maxine tugged the astonished man's zip down and hauled his stiffening penis out. 'You're big!' she gasped, watching the excited member swell. Peeling his foreskin back, she licked his purple knob, fully stiffening his magnificent weapon. 'I like a nice big cock! Want me to suck you off?' she asked wickedly.

'Ah! Ah, I . . .' Probe gasped as the girl sucked his

bulbous plum into her hot mouth to the accompaniment of Ginger's orgasmic cries and vaginal squelches as she thrust the wet cucumber in and out of her tight love-mouth. Gazing down in amazement as Maxine licked and sucked on his twitching knob, Probe held the girl's head and rocked his hips back and forth. 'God, you're good!' he gasped as she tugged his trousers down and cupped his heavy balls. 'Ah, ah! You certainly know how to . . . Ah, God, that's good!'

'Want to fuck me?' Maxine smiled, slipping his plum from her wet mouth and reclining on the grass with her legs open wide. 'Want to slip your lovely tool into my hungry cunt?'

'There's no need to ask me that!' the man from the ministry cried, grabbing his rock-hard penis and kneeling between the girl's splayed thighs.

Slipping his knob between her swollen cunt lips, he drove his solid shaft deep into her tight pussy sheath. 'Christ, you *are* big!' Maxine cried. 'Bloody hell, I'm going to split open!'

'And you're tight!' Probe gasped, ramming into her young body.

'What about me?' Ginger asked, crawling across the grass. 'Can I join in?'

'Of course!' Maxine giggled. 'Help yourself to whatever you want!'

Crouching behind Probe, Ginger cupped his swinging balls in her hand. 'You can do me afterwards!' she giggled, slipping her finger into Maxine's bloated vagina alongside the man's shafting penis. 'Can you manage to fuck two girls, one after the other?'

'I'll do my best!' the pistoning Probe panted. 'Christ, I'm going to come already!'

'Come up her cunt and I'll drink your sperm from her afterwards!'

'God, you're . . . you're amazing! Ah, here it comes! Ah, ah!'

Thrusting his orgasming knob deep into the girl's spasming cunt, Probe grimaced, his body becoming rigid as he pumped out his sperm. Her fingers between Maxine's splayed thighs, holding her swollen pussy lips apart, Ginger gazed at the man's wet penis as it glided in and out of her friend's vaginal cavern. On and on, the man drove his huge member into the trembling girl, draining his heavy balls, filling her cuntal cavern, until he finally collapsed over her heaving breasts.

'Christ, that was good!' he gasped, pulling himself up and nibbling on Maxine's long milk buds. 'God, that was brilliant!'

'It was!' Maxine gasped, pushing the man off her naked body. 'You'll have to close the school now, won't you? I mean, after all that you've seen and heard, you'll have to call it a day.'

'Well, I . . . I'll have to report my findings to the Minister.'

'You can't allow a terrible school like this to remain open!' Ginger declared as she reclined on the grass and spread her limbs. 'The things that go on here are . . .'

'God, you've got a beautiful cunt!' Probe drooled as she parted her fleshy vaginal lips with her slender fingers. 'I'm going to give you the fucking of your life!'

Hurriedly positioning himself between Ginger's thighs, he grabbed his solid penis and drove his ballooning cockhead deep into her tight cuntal duct. 'Christ, you're wet!' he exclaimed as she grabbed his hips, pulling him close and driving his shaft in to the hilt. 'God, you bloody Bellend girls are something else!'

'That we are!' Ginger gasped as Maxine knelt astride her head, positioning her dripping pussy crack over Ginger's open mouth. 'Come on, Ginger, suck his spunk out of my cunt!' she giggled, pressing her yawning slit over the girl's mouth. 'Mmm, that's it, lick inside my cunt! Ah, ah, yes!'

Their cries of ecstasy drifting through the summer air as Probe's sperm gushed into Ginger's spasming cunt and Maxine's orgasmic blend filled her mouth, Ginger was sure that their devious plan had succeeded. As her orgasm rose from the depths of her quivering womb and erupted in her clitoris, she emitted a cry of euphoria through a mouthful of her friend's luscious flesh-folds. 'Ah, my cunt! My cunt! I'm coming! The school's going! Ah, yes, fuck my cunt! Fuck Bellend!' Lapping between Maxine's vaginal folds as Probe made his last pummelling thrusts into her inflamed cunt, Ginger pushed her finger deep into her friend's bottom-hole and sucked her pulsating clitoris into her wet mouth.

'Come . . . coming!' Maxine wailed as her cunt decanted its orgasmic spend. 'Keep licking! My clit . . . my clitoris! Ah, ah!' Standing, Probe slipped his wet knob into Maxine's mouth and gripped her head. Sliding his knob over her tongue as she shuddered in her orgasm, he decided he would pay the girls another visit. The school would be condemned, but that would take time, he knew.

His knob slipping from the girl's mouth as she rolled off Ginger, he stood gazing at the gymslip beauties as they lay quivering on the grass. Zipping his trousers, he grinned. 'Well, you're quite a pair!' he laughed. 'I'll meet you again, I hope!'

'Whenever you're down this way, you can enjoy our cunts!' Maxine giggled. Determined to complete her mission successfully, she looked up at Probe and peeled open her inflamed pussy lips. 'See this?' she asked. 'See inside my cunt? Well, it's yours whenever you want it.'

'And mine!' Ginger squealed as she parted her sopping girl-folds, exposing the entrance to her crimsoned love-sheath. 'Whenever you want it, it's yours!'

'When will the school close?' Maxine asked as Probe made to depart.

'Very soon, but . . .'

'You can still meet us after the school's closed, can't you?'

'Well . . . It might not be easy. I'd not have an excuse to come down from London, you see.'

'What about the weekends?' Ginger suggested.

'My . . . my wife . . .'

'Oh, who's a naughty boy, then?' Maxine laughed. 'In that case, you'll just have to find an excuse to leave your office.'

'I must be going. I'll . . . I'll contact you.'

'When you phone, ask for Maxine or Ginger.'

'But I thought your names were . . .'

'Maxine and Ginger.'

'Right, well, I'd better be going,' the bemused ministry man smiled, taking a last lingering look at the girls' yawning sex-slits before creeping from the clearing.

Watching the besuited ministry man disappear, the girls grinned at each other as they dressed. 'Well, that's the last nail in the coffin!' Ginger laughed.

'There's no way the school will survive now!' Maxine agreed, slipping her sex-flushed breasts into her bra cups.

'Why didn't the fire bells go off?'

'Fuck knows! I must have fucked up the wiring job. Let's spend the rest of the day here and get pissed!'

'Yes, why not? Nothing matters anymore, does it? With the school closing, it doesn't matter what Knickergusset knows. We can sit here all day without a care in the world! She can hardly expel us, can she?'

'Hardly!' Maxine laughed. 'Now that the Bellend Rebels have won – hardly!'

Chapter Ten

'I don't understand it, Miss Frigidus!' Miss Gussetpiece sighed as she propped her elbows on her desk. 'It's been two weeks since that man came probing around here, and I've heard nothing at all! Ha! Probing, get it? Mr Probe . . .'

'No, I'm afraid I don't, Headmistress.'

'Never mind.'

'Perhaps he's forgotten about us?'

'How could he forget? One would assume that he has a memory. Unless he's lost it, of course. I think something sinister's going on. After his visit, I thought we'd be outlawed within a day or two! I don't like being left in the dark.'

'I don't like the dark, either. My fear of the dark stems from a horrifying incident that occurred during my childhood.'

'What was that?'

'I can't talk about it, it pains me.'

'Then why mention it?'

'I tried not to.'

'You are a silly woman! Something's going on somewhere in a London office, I can feel it in my water – but what?'

'Phone the Minister for . . .'

'Good God, no! I don't want to stir things up! Let

sleeping dogs lie, Miss Frigidus, that's what I say. Pass me the gin, will you?'

'The bottle's empty, Headmistress.'

'Take another one from the box, then!'

'Oh, there's only one left!'

'Only one? Jesus, I'm going to have to do something about drying out! Right, what's the time? Oh, nearly four! What are your plans for this evening?' the headmistress asked, sifting through a pile of bills.

'I'm meeting the priest again this evening,' Miss Frigidus smiled sheepishly.

'I thought you'd steer well clear of him after . . .'

'Yes, I know, but . . . Temptation, Headmistress, that's what it is. I've succumbed.'

'Beckford: 26, 18.'

'I'm not too well up on the Bible, Headmistress.'

'Not the Bible, the Penguin Dictionary of Quotations, Miss Frigidus. Page twenty-six, quote eighteen – *I am not over-fond of resisting temptation.*'

'Neither am I! I seem to be drawn to the man after . . . well, after he took me to heaven again yesterday.'

'Yesterday? You didn't tell me that you'd seen him again.'

'I was going to mention it, but I couldn't bring myself to. It's my dreadful secret, you see. I'm not used to harbouring dreadful secrets.'

'But the man's a sexual pervert!'

'Yes, I know. But he's also a priest, he showed me his documentation. The terrible thing is, I do believe that I'm one, too.'

'You're a priest?'

'No, not a priest, a . . .'

'What? You're a sexual pervert?'

'Yes, Headmistress – isn't it awful of me?'

'It's abominable! But I suppose someone has to play the role of sexual pervert in life's tragic play. What makes you think that you're a . . .'

'I don't know how to tell you this, but . . . I'll just come straight out with it. I've been touching myself in bed at night. Do you think there's something terribly wrong with me, Headmistress?'

'I can't be the judge of that until I have more knowledge of your *touching*.'

'Well, it's not touching so much as rubbing, I suppose.'

'Masturbate, Miss Frigidus!'

'Oh, dear! What, now?'

'No, you silly woman! That's what you do in bed at night.'

'Goodness me, do I?'

'Well, don't you?'

'Yes, I suppose I do. I've discovered my sexual identity.'

'Where was it?'

'I don't know. It came to me in a rush of passionate desire when the priest took me to heaven. I've been sexually woken, Headmistress.'

'Were you asleep?'

'Dormant.'

'What is?'

'My sexuality, it was latent.'

'Your sexuality was latent? Well, I don't know what to say, Miss Frigidus. I do hope that this awakening of yours won't affect your teaching at Bellend!'

'I'll try to suppress my inner desires and concentrate on teaching, Headmistress. It won't be easy, but I'll try.'

'I'm pleased to hear it! Now, I'd better go and change. And I must visit the gardener and ask him why the geraniums he planted on the toilet block site are all dead.'

'Yes, Headmistress. I'll see you at dinner.'

Entering the potting shed, Miss Gussetpiece was surprised to find Miss Blob talking to the gardener. 'Have you no class, Miss Blob?' she asked.

'I've had a pagan upbringing by a middle-class family, I'll have you know!' Miss Blob returned indignantly.

'No, you silly woman! What I meant was, have you no geography class?'

'Oh, I see. Er . . . yes, they're having a quiet study period. It's my last class today so I thought I'd . . .'

'They're far from quiet, from what I heard as I passed your classroom just now! You'd better get back and try to control the little . . . the little darlings.'

'Yes, Headmistress.'

'Now!' Miss Gussetpiece growled, glaring at the gardener as Miss Blob left the shed. 'I want to know why the geraniums are all dead. Have you not watered them? Can't you do a simple task without me having to . . .'

'I've watered 'em every day!' the old man protested.

'Why are they dead, then? Plants don't die for no reason.'

'It's a mystery to me! I've put several other flowerin' plants there, but they've died 'n' all!'

'How odd! Well, we can't be doing with a patch of barren ground. In my position as principal I must ensure that the girls remain barren. In your position as gardener you must ensure that the land remains fruitful. Look into it, will you?'

'Yes, 'eadmistress. Oh, by the way, you might consider callin' the police.'

'Why? Are you suggesting that the flowers have been murdered? Goodness me, we can't have botanicide at Bellend!'

'No, no! There's a tramp livin' in the woods. I come across a makeshift 'ut earlier. It's by the school wall. Go right through the woods and you'll see it.'

'Goodness gracious! All right, I'll go and investigate. A tramp, indeed! Whatever next?'

Hiking through the woods, Miss Gussetpiece located the wooden hut and frowned. 'Odd, most odd!' she breathed, pulling a sheet of polythene aside and going in. 'What's this? A cassock, a nun's habit, navy-blue knickers . . . Goodness me! Dozens of pairs of knickers! And bras! Right, this needs investigating!' the headmistress cried, striding back to the school.

'Crikey! I don't understand it!' Hilda complained to Candida. 'Maxine's Head Girl, *and* hockey and netball captain!'

'I know,' Candida sighed despondently as she toyed with her pen. 'It's an impossible situation.'

'I wonder where Miss Blob's got to? Some geography lesson this is!'

'I don't know. To be honest, I'm not in the mood for a geography lesson.'

'Shall we sneak off and have a chat, Candy?'

'Yes, jolly good idea. You go first, and I'll meet you in the woods at the far end of the playing field where we saw that nun with that young girl.'

'Right, see you soon.'

Meeting in the woods, the girls reclined on the grass and relaxed. 'Hilly, there's something I didn't tell you,' Candida confessed pensively.

'What's that?'

'Well, the nun we saw here, I . . . I spoke to her.'

'Why didn't you tell me?'

'Because I . . . I was too embarrassed to talk about it. She rubbed me, Hilly – and I had a goodie.'

'Candy! But she's a nun! How could . . .'

'Yes, she is a nun. But I . . . I had a divine experience with her. If I tell you what happened, promise me that you'll keep it a secret.'

'Yes, I promise.'

'Well, she was giving me healing, massaging my pears, and then she moved down to my stomach and then down to my . . . Anyway, a miracle happened.'

'Gosh, a miracle?'

'Yes. God gave her a penis.'

'Crumbs! Did she show it to you?'

'She did more than show it to me – she put it into my mini!'

'Truly, that *is* miraculous! Oh, Candy, you *are* lucky!'

'Yes, I know. I haven't been back here to meet her because I was too afraid.'

'And so you should be! It's best to be God-fearing. What's the nun's name?'

'Sister Regina Cunctus.'

'Perhaps she was an angel, sent by God.'

'Perhaps. She said that God had blessed her with a penis so that she could take me to heaven.'

'And did she take you to heaven?'

'Oh, yes – it was absolutely heavenly!'

'But – a penis, appearing just like that?'

'She said that anything was possible with faith. She said that the Virgin Mary was blessed with a penis from heaven. Possibly the very same one that she'd been blessed with. It must be a divine penis, kept for special occasions.'

'Crikey! And she put that very same penis into your mini and did it to you?'

'Yes, she did. You won't tell anyone, will you, Hilly?'

'No, I won't – Jolly Hockey Sticks honour!'

'Many times I've thought of coming here to see the nun, but . . . The reason that I suggested we come here was . . . I met the nun yesterday as I was walking across the playing field. She asked me to meet her here this afternoon. What with classes, I didn't think I'd be able to, but I told her that I'd try.'

'Crumbs, Candy!'

'And I'm pleased that you were able to come to me, my child!' The friends froze as a soft celestial voice emanated behind them from the bushes.

Turning, Hilda gazed open-mouthed at the apparition, a sense of reverence overwhelming her fear as the nun moved closer to her. 'Are you an angel?' she asked the black spectre incredulously.

'No, my child, but I have been sent by the Lord to heal you,' the nun smiled.

'Allow her to heal you,' Candida urged, holding Hilda's arm. 'Allow her to take you to heaven, Hilly.'

'Well, I don't know. Have . . . have you got a penis?'

'Yes, the Holy Organ – it came to me as I was walking through the trees. Slip your clothes off and I'll heal you, my child.'

Kicking her shoes off and removing her gymslip, Hilda unbuttoned her blouse. The day was hot, becoming hotter by the minute, and the girl was relieved to be free of her clothing. 'I feel so much cooler now,' she smiled, sitting in her bra and knickers. Unsure about revealing her pert breasts to the stranger as she reached behind her back to unclip her bra, she turned to Candida. Giving her friend a reassuring smile, Candida lifted Hilda's bra away from her breasts, exposing her darkening areolae, her lengthening nipples to the watchful nun.

Reclining on the grass, Hilda slipped her thumbs between the elastic waistband of her navy-blue knickers and her shapely hips, watching the nun as she slowly tugged the garment down. 'Hilda, your mini hair . . . Where's you mini hair gone?' Candida gasped, eyeing the girl's blatantly smooth vaginal lips.

'I . . . I shaved it off. I wanted to be like you so . . .' Hilda confessed as the nun knelt beside her.

'You have a beautiful body, my child. I am pleased that you've removed your pubic vestige – God is pleased.'

'Oh!' Hilda exclaimed, proud to think that she'd pleased God. 'We'll have to shave our mini hair off for ever and ever, Candy!'

'Yes, we will! For ever and ever!'

'You must both come to me in the woods,' the nun soothed, massaging Hilda's firm breasts. 'Come every day for healing. Candida, you may remove your clothes, my child. Remove them all and expose your beaut— . . . your body for healing.'

Standing, Candida pulled her gymslip over her head, dishevelling her golden locks. Slipping her blouse over her smooth shoulders, she smiled at Hilda. 'You'll enjoy the healing,' she promised, removing her bra and displaying her pert breasts.

'Indeed you will!' the nun agreed, reaching beneath a bush and pulling out a canvas bag. 'I've brought my healing candle with me,' she smiled, plunging her hand into the bag. 'This is a church candle, from the altar. It has been anointed for the occasion.' Gripping the candle between her palms, she looked up to the trees and closed her eyes. 'Our candle who art in my hand, hallowed be thy shaft. These girls will come, they will be done – on the grass and taken to heaven.'

'Crikey! What are you going to do with it?' Hilda asked, gazing in awe at the huge phallus.

'You are both good friends, are you not?' Sister Regina asked.

'We're best friends!' Candida expounded, kicking her knickers from her feet.

'Then I shall seal your friendship. I want you to kneel on all fours, with your bottoms touching,' the nun instructed. 'I will join you in everlasting friendship with the healing candle.'

Taking up their positions with their buttocks pressed together, the girls waited for the nun to join them in everlasting friendship. Wondering why they had to take up their peculiar postures, Hilda gasped as the nun reached between her thighs, pushing the candle between her smooth pussy lips. 'Oh! Oh, what are you doing?' she cried as the waxen phallus glided into her slippery pussy sheath, stretching her sex duct to the limit.

'Joining you in friendship,' the nun murmured, easing the other end of the candle into Candida's tight vagina. 'This will seal your friendship, for life. Now, push your bottoms together, that's it! A little more and . . . That's very good! Your wombs are now as one!'

'How long do we have to stay like this?' Candida gasped as she rested her head on the grass and peered at Hilda between their parted thighs.

'Only for a while,' the nun smiled, plunging her hand into her bag again.

Watching with bated breath, Hila's eyes opened wide as the nun moved towards her, wielding a second long, thin candle. 'Now, I must connect your bowels to complete the spiritual coupling,' Sister Regina Cunctus smiled, slipping one end of the candle between Hilda's buttocks and gently easing the waxen shaft into her rectal sheath.

'Oh! Argh! No, not there!' Hilda protested as the shaft slipped ever deeper into her anal duct.

'Quiet!' the nun ordered. 'You'll upset the fine balance of the healing forces! Move apart slightly so that I can . . . That's it, good girls!'

Parting Candida's buttocks, Sister Regina slipped the other end of the candle into the girl's tight bottom-hole. 'Now, I want you to rock back and forth so that your bottoms slap together,' she instructed, grinning at the waxen phalluses joining the two girls. 'That's it, back and forth, back and forth! Ommm! Ommm!'

Gasping as their vaginal muscles tightened around the candle, the girls continued their rocking. Their buttocks slapping, their clitorises stiffening, they quickened their rhythm. 'Oh, oh!' Hilda gasped as the nun reached between her thighs and massaged her blossoming bud. 'Oh, that's . . . that's nice!' Stroking Candida's ripening budlette with her free hand, the nun intoned:

'Give us this day our daily head, and forgive us for not coming earlier, as we don't forgive those who don't come at all. Lead us into temptation and deliver us into evil.'

The girls' sex juices glistening on the waxen shaft, dripping and pooling on the grass, the nun knew they were almost ready to be taken to heaven. Gasping as they rhythmically rocked, slapping their bottom-orbs together, they began to tremble. 'Oh! Oh, I'm going to . . .' Candida cried. 'I'm going to have a goodie!'

'And so . . . Ah, ah! So am I!' Hilda gasped.

Their clitorises pulsating beneath the nun's vibrating fingertips, the girls' orgasms exploded, orbiting them to their sexual heavens. 'Ommm! Ommm!' the nun chanted as she rubbed the girls' throbbing sex-buttons. 'Ommm! Ommm!'

'Ah, ah!' the girls chanted in reply. 'Ah, oh, ah!'

Collapsing to the ground, the candles slipping from their tight sex holes, the friends lay panting, trembling in the aftermath of paradise. 'Lie on your back with your legs open as wide as you can and you shall receive the holy penis!' the nun cried, lifting her habit and displaying the magnificent organ. Kneeling between Hilda's thighs, Sister Regina grabbed the staff of lust in her hand and drove the purple crown deep into the girl's spasming vagina. 'Deliver us into filth!' she gasped, resting her weight on her hands and rocking her hips. 'Deliver my spunk into the girl's cunt! Oh, I mean . . .'

'Ah, it's too big!' Hilda protested as her young naked body jolted with every hammering thrust. 'Ah, oh! Rule Fifteen . . . Ah, yes, yes!'

Quietly witnessing the divine coupling, Candida massaged her erect clitoris, eagerly awaiting her turn as the nun gasped, her body becoming rigid as she ascended to her climax. 'Ah, God! God, I'm coming!' the sister gasped. 'My spunk's filling your unholy cunt!'

'Oh!' Hilda cried as her climax shook her very soul. 'A goodie, a goodie!'

'Swallow the spunk from my loins!'

'Oh, yes, yes!'

'Fill thy barren womb with my gushing spunk!'

'Ah, ah!'

Collapsing over Hilda's heaving breasts, the nun lay

panting, trembling, as she absorbed the wet heat of the girl's sperm-drenched vagina. Finally rolling off the girl's naked body, she lay on her back, the blasphemous penis snaking across the rolling balls, glistening in the evening sunlight. Her hands between her thighs, her fingers twisting and pulling on her inner girl-lips, Hilda gazed up to the foliage high above her and smiled.

'I've found heaven,' she breathed, dragging the sperm from her inflamed hole up her sex-valley and rubbing the cream into her fire-red clitoris.

'Is it my turn now?' Candida asked the nun like a petulant brat, reclining and spreading her shapely thighs.

'Give me a moment to rest, my child,' Sister Regina smiled as she sat up.

'The penis won't go away, will it?'

'No, no, not until it has penetrated you and filled your barren womb with its holy seed. Ah, a miracle! Look, the penis is rising! Now it is your turn to find heaven!' she cried, settling between Candida's thighs.

Sinking the purple penis-head deep into the girl's quivering body, Sister Regina smiled. 'You're tight, my child! But you've managed to accept the holy shaft fully. God is pleased, very pleased!'

'Oh! Oh, good!' Candida gasped as the nun began thrusting. 'Ah, ah! It's . . . it's too big!'

'Never! You've taken it into the hilt! Open your legs wider, do the splits and allow your vaginal throat to swallow its heavenly gift!'

Ramming into the girl's young cuntal sheath, the sister's sperm rose quickly, spurting from the bubbling fountainhead to lubricate the shafting. 'God, I've come again!' the nun cried, pistoning the girl with such force that her young body glided across the grass. 'Ah! Jesus, I've come up your tight cunt!'

'Oh, Sister!' Candida wailed in her coming. 'Oh, oh, my . . . Ah, a goodie!'

'A baddy!' the nun chuckled, making her last thrusts, filling the girl's spasming cunt with the unholy seed. 'Ah, ah! You're . . . your cunt's so tight!'

Frowning as the nun fell limp, collapsing over Candida's trembling body, Hilda wondered at the daughter of God's language. 'Where do you come from?' she asked as Sister Regina climbed to her feet.

'I . . . I'm from the Nunnery of The Sacred Orgasmus. Which reminds me, I must be going. I have to tend the herb garden.'

'Won't you stay a while longer?' Candida asked as Sister Regina replaced the candles in her bag.

'God calls, girls! Meet me here again tomorrow, and I'll fuck . . . I'll take you to heaven again.'

'Has the penis gone yet?' Hilda called as the nun dived into the bushes and ran off. 'What a queer nun!' she remarked, turning to Candida. 'She used some awfully bad language!'

'Yes, perhaps she has permission from God to use such dreadful words. We'd better dress and get back to school before we're missed.'

'Yes, I suppose you're right, Candy. It's been terribly exciting, hasn't it?'

'Terribly! Shall we bring Patsy along tomorrow?'

'Yes, it's only fair that we allow her a share of the healing forces.'

Eyeing Madame Fissure's lithe, suntanned legs, Johnson grinned. It was the first opportunity he'd had to try to seduce the French mistress and, with Maxine and Ginger hiding outside the lounge window with a Polaroid camera, he was determined to succeed.

'There you go, all working again,' he smiled, switching the standard lamp on.

'Thank you,' Madame Fissure replied. 'I read by that lamp, so I'm very grateful to you. It'll be dark before long, so you might as well leave it on. Would you like some tea or coffee, Mr Johnson?'

'Er . . . no, thanks. Please, call me Dan. So, how long have you been teaching at Bellend?'

'Too long, I'm afraid. I came here ten years . . .'

'Madame Fissure, I'm going to come straight out with it!' Johnson interrupted.

'Straight out with what?' the slender woman asked, her dark eyes frowning.

'I'm in love.'

'Oh! In love? Who with?'

'You, Madame Fissure! God only knows how I've endured the pain of loving a woman who doesn't even acknowledge the fact that I exist!'

'But I *have* acknowledged your existence, Dan! I've seen you just about every day since you first came here.'

'Yes, but you've not known of my burning love for you, have you?'

'Oh, well, put like that – no, I suppose I haven't.'

'Madame Fissure . . .'

'Michèle.'

'Michèle, allow me to make love to you!'

'What? Now? Here? In my lounge?'

Shit, what was that other line? Oh, yes! 'Anywhere! I'm desperate to feel the heat of your womb close to my maleness!'

'My womb? Sacré bleu!'

'Look, I'm on bended knee! I shall die without your love!'

'I can't have men dying in my lounge, it wouldn't be right!'

'Then, allow me to make love to you! Quickly, Michèle, the angel of death is near!'

'Well, in that case, I suppose . . . Just let me draw the curtains.'

'No, no! We must make love beneath the stars!'

'What, go outside, you mean? Someone might see us!'

'No, leave the curtains open so we can be seen by the stars!'

'I hope only the stars see us! Shall I take my clothes off?'

'Yes. I will stay here, kneeling at your feet, and watch you unveil your beautiful body!'

Eagerly unbuttoning her blouse, Madame Fissure slipped the garment off her shoulders and tossed it onto the sofa. Tugging her long skirt down and displaying her bulging red silk panties, she smiled at Johnson. 'This is very naughty, I must say! But it's fun!'

'Your bra, Michèle – remove your bra and free your beautiful breasts!'

'Do you like my breasts?' the woman asked as they tumbled from her bra cups.

'God, they're the epitome of beauty! You must allow me to suckle your nipples. Your skin is so beautifully bronzed, your body so shapely, your . . . Please, your panties!'

Peeling her panties away from her mound, Madame Fissure pointed to a large cupboard in the corner of the room. 'Look in there,' she whispered. 'You'll find some things of interest.' Crawling across the carpet, Johnson opened the cupboard and gasped. Taking out a whip and several pairs of handcuffs, he turned to the French mistress.

'I would never have dreamed that you . . .'

'That I'm what? Into bondage and whipping? You'd be surprised what I'm into, Dan!' she laughed throatily as she stepped out of her lace panties and stood with her feet asunder. 'Come over here and kneel before me, slave!' she ordered unexpectedly.

'Christ, you've shaved your pubic hair off!'

'Do you like it, my *con*, my firm cunt lips?'

'God, yes! They're so full, swollen! I've never seen such big cunt lips!'

'Lick me, slave!' Madame Fissure instructed, jutting her hips and towering over the handyman.

Kneeling before his mistress, Johnson licked her irrigating sex groove and sucked on her distended inner labia. 'Mmm!' she sighed, peeling her luxuriant cunny lips apart. 'C'est trop bon! Quelle langue! Lick inside my cunt!' His tongue snaking into the woman's pinken portal, his eyes caught Maxine's and Ginger's through the window. His plan to seduce Madame Fissure had worked well, he reflected happily, lapping up the lust-liquid flowing from her formidable crack. Or had she seduced him? he wondered as she grasped his head and ground her feminine intimacy into his hungry male mouth.

His mistress's clitoris swelling, hard against his tongue, Johnson thrust three fingers deep into her hot vaginal sheath. 'Ah, oui, oui!' she gasped, gyrating her hips. 'Ah, mon Dieu! More, more!' Pistoning his fingers in and out of her tightening cunt, sucking hard on her blossoming bud, he transported the quivering woman to her celestial climax. Shuddering, clinging to his head to steady herself, she finally collapsed to the floor, writhing in her ecstasy.

'God, that was good!' she gasped, her head rolling from side to side as she massaged her inflamed clitoris. 'You *are* a good slave! Now I want you to remove all your clothes and join me on the floor,' she instructed. Kicking his shoes aside and slipping his shirt and jeans off, Johnson yanked his socks and boxer shorts off and stood over the French mistress. 'On all fours!' she ordered, gazing at his erect penis. 'Lick my *con* again and I'll suck you off.'

Kneeling astride the woman's head, Johnson trembled as she took the entire length of his solid penis into her hot mouth. Burying his face between her swollen vaginal lips, he began his fervent licking. Drinking her flowing come-juice, sweeping his tongue round her glistening sex entrance, he wondered why he'd not approached the delectable morsel earlier. *A most delicious French tart!* he mused, lapping up the lashings of sex-cream oozing from her juicy hole.

'Bloody hell!' Maxine whispered to Ginger. 'We've got some bloody good shots of Fissure's shaved cunt! Look at her taking Dan's cock into her mouth!'

'Christ, I feel really horny watching those two. I'd love to join in!'

'So would I, but we can't. I've a good mind to tell Knickergusset about Fissure.'

'No, you'll drop Dan in it if you do that, Max!'

'Yeah, I hadn't thought of that. Look, she's taken his cock out of her mouth. She's wanking him! Christ, he's going to come all over her face!'

Kneeling with her thighs apart, slipping her hand down the front of her knickers, Maxine pressed her fingertips between her inflamed pussy lips and massaged her erect clitoris as Johnson's knob exploded, showering Madame Fissure's face with his sperm. Her full red lips open wide, the French mistress directed the gushing come into her mouth. Licking and sucking the throbbing knob, the woman opened her thighs wide and gyrated her hips, forcing her pulsating clitoris into the man's mouth as her orgasm gripped her quivering body.

Massaging her clitoris faster, reaching her own mind-blowing climax, Maxine gasped. 'Ah, ah! Ah, God, that's heavenly!'

'You should have let *me* frig you off!' Ginger laughed, watching her friend's face contort with ecstasy.

'Ah, God, my cunt!' Maxine breathed, massaging the last waves of orgasm from her throbbing nub. 'You can lap up my juicy come if you want to.'

'Take your knickers off, then,' Ginger smiled, licking her pouting red lips in anticipation.

Sitting on the ground, Maxine tugged her wet knickers down, revealing her yawning vaginal crack to Ginger's appreciative gaze. Reclining, opening her legs wide, displaying her inner folds to her friend as the girl settled between her thighs and kissed her warm mound, Maxine grinned.

'There's nothing I like better than having my pussy licked out,' she purred as Ginger's tongue swept up her glistening sex groove. 'Ah, that's nice! That's it, lick my clitty!'

'What's going on in there?' Ginger gasped as Madame Fissure cried out. 'Hang on, I'm going to take a look.'

Peering through the window, the girl held her hand to her mouth. On all fours, her hands cuffed, her knees wide apart, Madame Fissure's buttocks twitched as the whip struck her rounded orbs. 'Harder!' she cried as Johnson thrashed her. 'God, that's good! You'll whip me every evening, slave!'

'Max, come and see this!' Ginger cried.

'I . . . I can't! I'm coming!' Maxine wailed as her clitoris pulsated beneath her vibrating fingertips. 'Ginger! Quickly, lick my cunt!'

Lapping at Maxine's throbbing button, Ginger thrust two fingers into the girl's vagina. Massaging the creamy walls of her pussy sheath as she sucked on her clitoris, Ginger frowned. 'What's that in your cunt?' she asked in astonishment.

'An apple! I . . . Lick me! I stuffed it up there earlier!'

'You randy bitch!' Ginger giggled, massaging her friend's swollen clitoris with her wet tongue.

'God, that's good!' Maxine gasped as Ginger sustained her shuddering climax with her caressing tongue. 'Ah, my lovely cunt! I can feel the apple! My cunt's gripping the . . . Ah, ah, yes!'

Crushing Ginger's head between her thighs, Maxine shook violently in her coming. Her sex juices flowing in torrents, her clitoris sending electrifying pulses of sex through her quivering womb, she finally fell limp, writhing in the wake of her girl-induced climax. Leaving her friend to recover, Ginger gazed through the window to see Johnson thrashing Madame Fissure's crimson buttocks.

'God, they're still at it!' she gasped, eyeing the crisscrossed weals fanning out across the French mistress's tensed bottom-orbs. Gazing longingly at Johnson's erect penis, Ginger grinned as he discarded the whip and knelt behind his mistress. Parting her glowing buttocks, he pushed his purple knob against the woman's brown portal, his face grimacing as his plum disappeared into her dank bowels. 'He's fucking her arse!' Ginger exclaimed excitedly, looking down at Maxine's grimacing face as the girl vigorously massaged her clitoris. 'Max, leave your cunt alone and come and see what Fissure's doing!'

Ignoring her friend, Maxine continued to masturbate, emitting gasps of satisfaction as her clitoris sent overwhelming currents of sex coursing through her young body. Turning her head, Ginger focused on Johnson's cock shafting the French woman's tight anal sheath. She was obviously lost in her debauchery, Ginger mused, gazing now at her gasping mouth, twisted in her act of rampant fornication. Taking several more photographs of the lewd scene, Ginger watched Johnson slip his penis from the woman's tight bottom-hole and wank his solid shaft, spraying her burning buttocks with his jetting jism.

'We've enough pictures now,' Ginger grinned as Maxine slipped her wet knickers up her long legs. 'Come on, let's get out of here!'

'I missed most of it!' Maxine complained.

'Your decision. If you want to spend your time frigging, it's your fault! Anyway, I've got some cracking shots of old Fissure.'

'OK, we'll go to the potting shed and look through them – cut them up so no one recognizes Dan.'

'I've been careful not to get his face in the shots, so he'll be safe. Fissure won't, though! We've really got one over on her now!'

'Right, let's fuck off out of here before we're caught!' Maxine grinned as she crept away. 'To the shed, Ginger! I want you to suck my cunt!'

'I can't wait! Sixty-nine, OK?'

'Definitely!'

*   *   *

Quivering on the floor, Madame Fissure gazed up at Johnson and smiled. 'That was brilliant!' she breathed, sitting up with her cuffed hands between her thighs. 'I only wish we'd met sooner!'

'Christ, so do I!' Johnson agreed, wishing that he'd never set the woman up. Aware that the scheming girls had gone, he decided to get hold of the photographs before they had the chance to blackmail his new-found French delicacy. 'I'll see you later,' he smiled, releasing the handcuffs before grabbing his clothes and dressing. 'There's something I have to do.'

'But I've not finished with you!' Madame Fissure complained. 'We've barely started!'

'I'll be back, don't worry. I promise you, I'll be back!'

Guessing Maxine and Ginger's whereabouts, Johnson was making his way to the gardener's potting shed when he bumped into Miss Gussetpiece. 'Ah, Jones!' the headmistress greeted him. 'I've been looking everywhere for you! Where have you been?'

'Well, I finish work at five o'clock, so . . .'

'We none of us ever finish work, Jones! During our every waking moment, we must work for the good of the school!'

'Yes, Headmistress, but . . .'

'There are no buts! Now, I want you to remove a makeshift hut from the wooded area.'

'But I . . .'

'I haven't forgotten about the things the education man discovered in the basement, Jones! I'm still in two minds as to whether to dismiss you or not! Now, remove the hut!'

'Yes, Headmistress.'

'Follow me and I'll show you where it is.'

Entering the woods, Miss Gussetpiece stopped and turned to Johnson. 'Did you hear that?' she asked.

'Hear what?'

'I thought I heard a sort of low whimpering sound. There it is again! Right, the hut's in that direction, by the perimeter wall. You go and remove the hut and I'll go this way and investigate,' the headmistress ordered as she wandered off.

Suddenly remembering that Miss Frigidus was meeting the priest that evening, Miss Gussetpiece grinned. *Better leave her in peace to find heaven!* she giggled inwardly as she made her way through the wood. Hearing twigs cracking underfoot, she stopped and turned. Moving the branches of a bush to one side, she held her hand to her mouth. *What on earth is Véronique up to?* she thought, discovering the girl on her knees, gazing at something through the undergrowth. Circling Véronique to position herself where she could see what the girl was looking at, Miss Gussetpiece peered through a bush edging the clearing.

Lying naked on the ground, her limbs spread, her wrists and ankles roped to wooden stakes, Miss Frigidus was the picture of depravity. There was no sign of the priest, which Miss Gussetpiece thought odd. Should she free the stupid woman? she wondered. Or was the priest returning to take her to heaven again? As Véronique emerged from her hide and stood over Miss Frigidus, the headmistress frowned. *Stone the crows! Surely, the girl and Miss Frigidus aren't . . .*

'Why the holy man leave you like this?' Véronique asked, gazing down at the Latin teacher's naked body.

'Oh, dear! Oh, my goodness, how embarrassing! Please, untie the ropes!'

'I like you, your body,' the girl smiled, kneeling between the flustered woman's parted thighs. 'I finger your pussy for you, oui?'

'No! Goodness me! Please, untie me!'

'Non! I finger your pussy or I tell Miss Gussetpiss of you and religious man! I tell 'er 'ow I see the church man fuck your *con*!'

'Oh, dear!'

'Why 'e leave you like this?'

'He's coming back. He's gone to get . . .'

Slipping her slender finger between the woman's swollen cunny lips, Véronique massaged her inner vaginal flesh. 'Your pussy is full with sperm!' she giggled, gazing at her drenched finger. 'Naughty Latin lady! I tell Miss Gusset— . . .'

'What are you doing, girl?' Miss Frigidus cried, struggling to break free. 'Leave me alone! You mustn't . . .'

'You no liking your pussy fingered?'

'Yes, I . . . No, I don't! You're a girl! Good gracious, this is wrong! I'm not a lesbian!'

'I am lesbienne! I like girls' pussies more than I am liking men's!'

'Men don't have . . .'

'Men's willies! Big, stiff, 'orrible willies! Argh, spunking everywhere! I am liking girls' pussies!'

'You're a terrible girl! Unless you untie me, you'll be expelled!' Miss Frigidus threatened, pulling on the ropes as Véronique slipped a second finger into her hot cunny sheath. 'Let me go!'

'Non! I play with you, then I let you go! And I am not being expelled because if I am I tell of you and man of the church!'

Kneeling behind the bush, Miss Gussetpiece gazed

open-mouthed as Véronique parted her prisoner's bloated vaginal lips and began licking her inner sex folds. Quivering, her areolae darkening, her nipples rocketing skyward, Miss Frigidus closed her eyes, obviously lost in her lesbian arousal. *Well, I never!* the headmistress thought as Véronique ran her fingers over the slight swell of the tethered woman's naked body and kneaded her firm breasts. *What is this school coming to?*

'Oh, oh, dear!' Miss Frigidus gasped as her clitoris throbbed in response to the female tongue sweeping over its sensitive tip. Her vaginal muscles gripping the girl's thrusting fingers, she cried out as her orgasm welled. 'Oh, heaven is coming! I can feel it coming!' Her black bob concealing her pretty face, Véronique continued her fervent lesbian licking, caressing the woman's inner thighs, stiffening her sex budling, taking her ever higher to her sexual heaven. 'Ah, I'm there!' Miss Frigidus finally sang as her orgasm erupted and ripped through her shaking body. 'Oh, oh, I'm there! Ah, don't stop! It's . . . it's heavenly!'

Watching the lewd lesbian coupling, Miss Gussetpiece shook her head, wondering whether it had been such a good idea for the Latin mistress to have been introduced to sex. Creeping away from the clearing she made her way back to the school, hoping she'd bump into the priest. 'I could do with another trip to heaven!' she sighed, entering the old building.

Installed back at her desk, she poured herself a large gin, wondering whether Véronique would release Miss Frigidus or leave the poor woman there all night. 'Ah, Jones!' she exclaimed as Johnson knocked on the open study door. 'Did you locate and dismantle the hut?'

'No, headmistress. You see . . .'

'Could you not find it?'

'I found the hut, yes. There was a nun inside. I crept up to the hut and peered through a crack in the planking.'

'A nun? Wanking? You should have asked her what on earth she thought she was doing! We can't have wanking nuns hiding in huts in the school grounds!'

'Planking, Headmistress. But as it happens, she *was*, well. . .'

'She was what?'

'There was a light on in the hut, and I could clearly see the nun masturbating.'

'A nun masturbating! My God, whatever next? I hope you didn't hang around and watch the ungodly act, Jones!'

'I did, actually.'

'My God – you disgusting man! Watching a woman masturbate . . . It's despicable! Have you had no upbringing?'

'It wasn't a woman, Headmistress.'

'The nun wasn't a woman? How can a nun possibly be anything other than a woman?'

'She . . . I mean, he wasn't a nun.'

'But you just said that there was a nun in the hut. What *are* you talking about, man?'

'It was a nun's habit . . .'

'I have no interest in the nun's despicable habits!'

'No, I mean, her clothing was a habit. She was wearing a habit.'

'It was a man wearing a nun's habit, is that what you're trying to say?'

'Yes, it was a man dressed in a nun's habit – and he was masturbating.'

'Jesus! It's the sexual pervert, Jones! That bastard . . . I mean, that pervert who stole my money! The very sexual pervert the police are seeking has been living in a hut in the school grounds!'

'Shall I call the police, Headmistress?'

'Er . . . no, no,' the Head replied pensively. 'I'll deal with this. I'll . . . I'll, er, go and have a word with the nun . . . I mean, the man. Right, off you go, Jones!' she ordered, knocking back her gin and staggering to her feet. 'Nuns living in huts, indeed!'

'We can't have none of that!' Johnson chuckled as he left the study.

'We certainly can't!' Miss Gussetpiece echoed, following him down the corridor. 'I'm going to have to order this sexual pervert to deal most severely with me! I mean, I'll deal most severely with him! I'll start off by getting him to give me a jolly good . . . Yes, well . . . Off you go, Jones! And say nothing about this to anyone!'

'Yes, Headmistress. I'll see you tomorrow.'

'What about? Why will you see me tomorrow?'

'Because I work here, as you do.'

'I know you work here!'

'You work here, too, so . . .'

'I know I work here! Oh, go away, you silly man! You work here, I work here . . . Madness, sheer madness! Report to a psychiatrist at your earliest convenience!'

Chapter Eleven

'Thank goodness there are only a few days left before the end of term!' Miss Gussetpiece sighed, wandering down the corridor with Madame Fissure. 'I really don't think I can take much more of this school! Unless we make it to the end of term without a hitch, I'll end up in a home for mentally deranged headmistresses!'

'I'm sure you won't!' Madame Fissure laughed.

'I only wish I had your positive attitude! The pervert's still on the loose, fortunately.'

'Fortunately, Headmistress?'

'Er . . . What I mean is . . . Oh, never mind. Hilda Hillock has done nothing but cause trouble, Miss Frigidus is a changed woman . . . And not for the better, I might add!'

'Yes, I've noticed the change in her. She used to be so . . .'

'She's found God, that's what's she's gone and done. She's always taking trips to heaven, daft woman that she is!'

'Taking trips to heaven, Headmistress?'

'Yes, in the woods. She . . . nothing. No wonder she's taken to her sick bed for the last few days! She's probably worn out!'

'Worn out?'

'Er . . . Tired, I mean.'

'Oh, I see. By the way, I saw Maxine Mayhem skulking in the trees earlier. I think the wooded area should be out of bounds to the girls.'

'You might be right, there. And to the staff! Maxine Mayhem has surprised me. She's been doing so well of late. She seems to have stepped into Hilda Hillock's shoes.'

'Doesn't Hilda mind?'

'Mind what?'

'Well, Maxine taking her shoes?'

'Has she? Good God, she can't do that!' the Head returned.

'What?'

'Take another girl's shoes! It's despicable! When you next see her, send her to my study, will you?'

'Er . . . yes, of course. I must say that Maxine's recent work is excellent!'

'Yes, it's strange how she's doing so well in every subject except English. I don't understand why Miss Shaftgrinder disagrees with the other teachers. She says that Maxine's behaviour is worse than ever! Perhaps Maxine genuinely can't cope with English. Apparently, her grammar is appalling, her spelling non-existent, her . . . I wonder if, somehow, Maxine has managed to get a hold on everyone, except for Miss Shaftgrinder?'

'A hold, Headmistress?' Madame Fissure echoed as she stopped and turned to face Miss Gussetpiece.

'Yes, it's as if everyone is afraid of Maxine. As if she's blackmailing everyone to give her top marks and excellent reports.'

'Blackmail? Er . . . I'm sure she's not!'

'It all seems rather strange to me. In fact, the more I

think about it, the stranger it is! I've not received one bad report concerning Maxine from anyone – apart from Miss Shaftgrinder. It's all rather mystifying.'

'We should be pleased that Maxine's a changed girl – not mystified, Headmistress.'

'Yes, I suppose you're right. Her report will please her father. I'd better not mention the shoe-stealing episode. At least I won't have to fiddle . . . Er . . .'

'Fiddle what?'

'Nothing, nothing. Talking about people changing, Madame Fissure, I've noticed a dramatic change in you.'

'Er . . . oh, have you, Headmistress?'

'Yes, you seem worried. You look pale and drawn of late. Is there something troubling you? Money? Or personal problems, perhaps?'

'No.'

'No what?'

'No, Headmistress.'

'No Headmistress? But *I'm* the Headmistress!'

'I meant, no, there's nothing worrying me.'

'And I meant – did you say "no" to money problems, or "no" to personal problems? Your internals aren't playing you up, are they?'

'Goodness me, no!'

'Mine are. I think I must have something wrong with my . . . I'd better get Doctor Uterine Pouch to check me over. Oh, I've been meaning to ask you – what did you mean the other day when you asked me whether I'd seen any photographs of you?'

'Er . . . holiday snaps. I've lost some, you see.'

'They'll turn up, no doubt – these things always do. Was it nice?'

'No, I went to Paris.'

'No, you silly woman. Not Nice – was your holiday nice?'

'Oh, yes, thank you.'

'So, there's nothing else bothering you?'

'No, not at all.'

'Well, I'm pleased that we've had this little chat. I'm also pleased that you no longer consider me unfit for the post of headmistress.'

'Yes, Miss Gussetpiece. I'm sorry, it was wrong of me to call you an alcoholic.'

'Yes, it was. *Me*, alcoholic! Goodness, it couldn't be further from the truth! And I'm sorry that I called you a frog.'

'Oh, I wonder who that is?' Madame Fissure asked as a middle-aged man approached the women.

'I have no idea. I hope it's not more trouble! Oh dear, he's carrying a briefcase! I don't like suited men with briefcases, they unnerve me. They bring back dreadful memories of bailiffs and . . . Oh, he might be from the Minister for Education!'

'I hope not! I'll see you later, Headmistress,' Madame Fissure half-grinned, hurriedly slipping into her classroom and closing the door.

'Can I help you?' Miss Gussetpiece asked the good-looking man.

'Good morning. I'm looking for the headmistress.'

'And who would you be?'

'Who would I be? Well, I've never really thought about it.'

'You've never thought about it? I find that difficult to believe!'

'All right, I'll give it some thought now. Er . . . Mick Jagger.'

'Mick Jagger?'
'Yes – fame, fortune . . .'
'Oh! Well, what an honour! What brings you to Bellend?'
'I've come to see the headmistress. Would you direct me to her office, please?'
'Yes, of course – follow me,' Miss Gussetpiece smiled, striding down the corridor. 'So, are you still running around and singing?'
'Singing? Well, I sing in the bath,' the man replied, frowning as he followed the Head into her study. 'I also go jogging.'
'How's Marianne?'
'Marianne?'
'Haven't you seen her recently?'
'Er . . . No, no, I haven't.'
'She's a lovely girl. It's a shame the two of you didn't . . . Didn't she like the Mars Bar? Anyway, sit down and have a drink,' Miss Gussetpiece invited as she flopped into her chair and grabbed the vodka bottle.
'I don't drink, thank you.'
'Er . . . Oh, no, neither do I. I'm the headmistress, by the way – Miss Gussetpiece.'
'Ah, right! I'm pleased to meet you. Now, the reason I'm here is . . .'
'We've never had a celebrity visit the school before.'
'A celebrity? What makes you say that?'
'Say what?'
'That you've never had a celebrity visit your school.'
'Because it's true! In my thirty years as principal of this school we've never had a celebrity visit us. It's quite an honour, I must say! The girls would be frenzied and

uncontrollably excited if they knew who was here, in my very study.'

'Would they?'

'Oh, yes! Goodness knows what they'd do. May I kiss your hand?'

'Kiss my hand? What ever for?'

'How about your autograph? Or a signed photo, perhaps? I'll hang it in my study, on the far wall, there.'

'I really don't . . . Look, I'm from the . . .'

'I'm sorry to fluster you – I'm not being fair, am I? It's just that I feel all unnecessary in your presence. My hormones are going wild, I can tell you! I suppose you're used to having women flocking around you. I'm a great fan, you know. I particularly liked *Ferry Across The Mersey*. How are the others?'

'The others?'

'The band – Pete Townsend, Ringo McCartney and the others, how are they?'

'Excuse me, Headmistress,' Miss Frigidus interrupted as she popped her head round the study door. 'The parents are arriving. I thought I'd better let you know.'

'Oh, is that the time already?'

'I can see you're busy,' the man interrupted, checking his watch. 'But I have some serious business to discuss with you so, if you don't mind, I'll wait here until . . .'

'I'm so sorry about this, Mr Jagger – it's Parents' Day, you see.'

'My name's Hardrock, Headmistress – Jonathan Hardrock.'

'Hardrock? Oh, I see – a pseudonym! Yes, very wise. A man in your position can't be too careful. Well, Mr Hardrock, it's an honour meeting you. You're more than welcome to wait here. I might be a little while, but . . .'

'Might I look through your books while I'm waiting?'

'Certainly, Mick . . . Whoops! I mean, Mr Hardrock. The library's down the corridor.'

'No, I mean your accounts, Miss Gussetpiece. I'm from the Inland Revenue.'

'Jesus, a bloody tax man! Er . . . ah, *those* books? Er . . . I must be going, the parents await!'

'I'll need to see your accounts for the last five . . .'

'Must dash, sorry!' Miss Gussetpiece called, bolting out of her study and slamming the door shut.

Slipping into the assembly hall, Miss Gussetpiece ordered Miss Frigidus to get rid of the unwelcome visitor. 'I can't have tax men lurking in my study, it's frightening! Strewth, my stomach's churning and my hands are trembling!'

'Oh dear, a tax man! How shall I get rid of him?' Miss Frigidus asked.

'I don't know – just get rid of him! Lie, or something!'

'Lie? But I've been ill of late and I . . .'

'You took to your bed to masturbate, more than likely!'

'Oh! Masturbate? How did you know?'

'I know more than you think, Miss Frigidus! Especially about French connections!'

'French . . .'

'We're wasting time! Tell the tax man that he'd better get out of the building as quickly as possible as there's been a typhoid outbreak.'

'Oh, dear – has there?'

'No, of course there hasn't!'

'But you just said . . .'

'A bomb!'

'Goodness me – where?'

'Tell him that there's a bomb scare. Go on – quickly!'

'Er . . . Very well, Headmistress.'

Approaching a group of parents, Miss Gussetpiece donned her aristocratic smile. 'Good morning, good morning!' she trilled, patting her blue-rinsed curls down. 'Ah, Lord and Lady Tawdry-Trollops, how absolutely divine to see you!'

'Yes, it is,' Lord Tawdry-Trollops grunted, twisting his waxed moustache. 'Well, Gussetpiece, how's one's daughter faring?'

'I don't have a daughter, your Lordshit . . . ship.'

'My daughter, not yours!'

'Oh, of course. Your daughter is faring very well, Lord Tawdry-Trollops.'

'Good, good – pleased to hear it! Top of the jolly old class, is she?'

'Not quite, but she's getting there.'

'You'll have to work the young filly harder, Gussetpiece! One won't get anywhere in life unless one's worked like a horse. Bring back the birch, that's what I say! What, what!'

'I didn't say anything.'

'What? You didn't say anything?'

'No, I didn't.'

'I know you didn't say anything! Yes, well, er . . . So, her maths is top hole? What!'

'What?'

'Her mathematics – top hole, eh?'

'Er . . . Yes, yes, she's doing very well,' Miss Gussetpiece smiled.

'Good, good! She was a mistake, you know. Turned up rather late in one's life. The blasted condom split on one's world cruise! Right in the middle of the confounded Atlantic! What, what!'

'What?'

'Oh, Gregory!' Lady Tawdry-Trollops gasped, holding her hand to her wrinkled, powder-plastered face.

'Don't fuss, old girl! So, Gussetpiece, my daughter's prepared for the world, is she?'

'Yes, Lord Tawdry-Trollops, she is.'

'Good, good! How's her grammar? What!'

'What? Oh, er . . . her grandma? I have no idea how her grandma is.'

'In that case, as head of this school, I think you should make it your business to find out! What!'

'What? Don't *you* know how her . . .'

'Damn it! If I knew, I wouldn't be asking you, would I?'

'Er . . . No, I suppose not.'

'Find out and write to me! Well, excuse us, one must mingle, don't you know!'

'Don't I know what?'

'What?'

'What don't I know?'

'I don't know what you don't know!'

'Er, I'm sorry – I'm a little confused. I'll see you before you go.'

'Yes, yes. Come on, old girl – there's mingling to be done!' Lord Tawdry-Trollops boomed, taking his wife's hand and marching her away.

Smiling as a young designer-dressed couple approached her, Miss Gussetpiece curtsied. 'Ah, Baron and Baroness Marijuana – good morning!'

'Mornin', love!' the man grinned, adjusting his white tie. 'How goes it?'

'Very well, thank you.'

'Good. Look, we can't hang about – things are a bit hot at the moment. How's my little Morphinette doin'?'

'Your daughter is doing well, Baron Marijuana. What do you mean, *things are a bit hot?*'

'Godda duck and dive, if you get my drift.'

'Duck and dive?'

'Yeah, keep the old head low, and the lugs to the ground.'

'I'm sorry, I don't understand.'

'In my business, you've godda keep your eyes peeled all the time. Ain't that right, Poppy?' he asked the young woman by his side.

'Yeah. You see, Caine reckons we were followed here,' she confided, tossing her long blonde hair over her naked shoulder.

'Followed? Who by?'

'Micky Snort's thugs, I reckon,' the young man whispered. 'Anyway, if the girl's OK, we'll shoot off.'

'But . . .'

'Listen, tell Morphinette that I've bunged a couple of grand in her bank account.'

'Wouldn't you like to see your daughter?'

'No, I can't hang about. I've a flight booked to Brazil. I'm seeing Castro about . . . about a deal. Must split.'

'Well, it's been a pleasure talking to you,' the Head smiled as the couple sidled off.

Spotting Miss Frigidus dashing across the hall towards her, Miss Gussetpiece frowned. 'What's the matter?' she asked the distraught woman on her agitated approach.

'It's that man, Headmistress!' Miss Frigidus panted. 'He won't go away.'

'What's he doing?'

'Going through the books.'

'Stone the crows! How did he get hold of them?'

'Well, I . . . I gave them to him.'

'You gave them to him? Jesus Christ! Are you mad, woman?'

'Well, I don't think so.'

'Don't you know?'

'As far as I know, there's no history of madness in my family.'

'You surprise me, Miss Frigidus!'

'I did smoke one of those cigarettes earlier, but . . .'

'Give me one. I need to relax!'

'Yes, Headmistress – here we are,' the trembling woman replied, taking a cigarette from her bag. 'I hope I haven't caused too much trouble.'

'You've signed my death certificate, that's what you've done! Give me your lighter!'

'Oh, yes – here you are. I didn't sign anything, Headmistress, I can assure you!'

'Oh, do be quiet! You're a changed woman since you met that priest! And the things you get up to with that young French girl are . . .'

'Oh, you know about that?'

'Yes, I do, Miss Frigidus! Think yourself lucky that I've turned a blind eye to your vile escapades! Right, I'd better go and face the music.'

'He's not listening to music, he's . . .'

'Be quiet! Oh, no, here comes Earl Nipplethwart! That's all I need! You'll have to deal with him, Miss Frigidus.'

'Oh, yes, of course, Headmistress.'

Entering her study, Miss Gussetpiece lit the roll-up and inhaled the aromatic smoke. 'Ah, you're still here,' she smiled as the tax man looked up from the books spread out on the desk.

'Yes, I am. There are too many discrepancies here for my liking!' he said accusingly. 'For example, what's this entry?'

'Er . . . oh, yes, cleaning materials,' Miss Gussetpiece replied as her head began to spin.

'Cleaning materials? Purchased from an off-licence?'

'Er . . . yes, alcohol – for cleaning purposes.'

'But the receipts that tally with this entry are for gin and vodka.'

'Are they? Well, I . . .'

'And what about this entry? Five hundred pounds spent on wine?'

'Er . . . that was for the Christmas party.'

'Purchased in March?'

'March? Ah, yes, I remember – there was a special offer on at the time. Buy two and get one free. Or was it buy three and only pay for two? It was something along those lines, anyway. There's a baked bean war on at the moment.'

'A baked bean war? I'm going to have to take these books away with me, I'm afraid, Miss Gussetpiece. Look at this! Two thousand pounds spent on building works, and no invoices or receipts at all! Plumbing – three thousand pounds! Electrical work – five thousand pounds! Grounds maintenance – six thousand pounds! No invoices, no receipts, no nothing!'

'Oh dear, I must have lost them.'

'Lost them, my . . .'

'No, no, I haven't lost them. They're in the drawer over there – but I've lost the key.'

'Well, you'd better find the key and forward the receipts and invoices to me!'

'Yes, yes, I will.'

'And what's happened to the staff's PAYE deductions?'

'Er . . .'

'Their contributions have been deducted from their earnings, but we've not received a penny!'

'Ah, yes, you see . . .'

'Fraud, Miss Gussetpiece!'

'Bloody hell, where?'

'Right here, in these falsified books!'

Dragging on her cigarette, Miss Gussetpiece grabbed the bottle of vodka and unscrewed the top. Watching the tax man gather the books up and make to leave, she gulped the vodka down, wondering what the penalty was for cooking the books.

'There's no mention of buildings insurance premiums listed in your expenditures,' the man said, turning in the doorway. 'I presume you *have* buildings insurance?'

'Er . . . yes, I presume I have!' the Head giggled, dragging on the roll-up again.

'Are you feeling ill?'

'Feeling ill? No, no, just comfortably blown away!'

'Blown away?'

'Blown away on the wind of confusion! It's at times like this that one realizes just how much life stinks, don't you agree?'

'Er . . . no, I don't.'

'I couldn't agree more! The Inland Revenue, sexually perverted priests and nuns, bombs, the education man, the police . . . Do you know, they found no less than fifty used condoms on the playing field?'

'I beg your pardon?'

'Why, what have you done?'

'Used condoms . . .'

'You've used condoms?'

'No, I haven't!'

'Well, you should! Particularly when having anal sex. Oh, what *am* I saying?'

'Do you see a psychiatrist?' the tax man asked, perplexed by the woman's behaviour.

'Er . . . No, no, I can't see one, can you?' Miss Gussetpiece replied, looking around the study as she dragged on her cigarette. 'Is there one here?'

'You should have a resident psychiatrist, if you ask me!'

'I don't resent psychiatrists! What are you talking about? Oh, go away, you silly man!'

Staggering to her desk as the man from the Revenue strode down the corridor, Miss Gussetpiece collapsed into her chair. Inhaling the intoxicating smoke again, she looked up and grinned as Miss Blob came in. 'Ah, Blow Job . . . I mean, Jo Blob. How are things in the history department?'

'Geography, Miss Gussetpiece.'

'Geography?'

'I teach geography.'

'Er . . . do you? Yes, yes, I know that!'

'Then why ask about history?'

'Er . . . I simply asked how things were in the history department, I didn't say that you taught history! Do you think me stupid?'

'I'd rather not answer that question.'

'You don't have the right to silence in *my* study – answer the question!'

'Er . . . no, I don't think you're stupid, Headmistress,' Miss Blob muttered. 'I think you're a retard.'

'I'm a what? What did you call me?'

'I think you work hard.'

'Good! Anyway, what is it I want?'

'I really have no idea.'

'I mean, what do *you* want?'

'Given a choice, a nice villa in the sun and enough money to . . .'

'No, no! What are you doing here?'

'Talking to you, Headmistress.'

'Yes, but what about?'

'I haven't got a clue!'

'Then I suggest you return to your class.'

'But I came to see you.'

'What about, woman?'

'In all this confusion, I can't remember. Oh, yes I can. Madame Fissure tells me that Maxine Mayhem's been stealing shoes.'

'Yes, apparently. The stupid girl!'

'You asked Madame Fissure to send Maxine to see you, but she can't find her.'

'Good grief! Not another missing girl! Actually, Miss Blob, I've been meaning to have a word with you about Maxine's geography . . .'

'She hasn't said anything about me, has she?'

'Said anything?'

'Mentioned anything about transvestites or cross-dressing or . . .'

'Why would she mention transvestites? What's cross-dressing?'

'Er . . . I don't know.'

'She did say that she knew something about you that would shock me but I put it down to adolescence.'

'Er . . . yes, more than likely. She's renowned for spreading rumours, I wouldn't take any notice of her if I were you.'

'Come to think of it, the other day the girl's friend Ginger was on about a man called Roderick something or other. I was somewhat drunk . . . somewhat *tired* at the time and didn't understand what she was talking about. She mentioned this man's name in connection with you, which I found extremely odd. I must speak to Maxine and Ginger and establish . . .'

'I wouldn't bother, Headmistress. You know what adolescent girls are like, making up stories about men in drag and transvestite geography masters . . . I mean, mistresses.'

'You've nothing to hide, have you, Miss Blob? No guilty secrets or anything?'

'Er . . . Certainly not!'

'Good. Wait a minute, Maxine was skulking in the trees earlier. Perhaps she's still there. Take a look, will you?'

'Yes, Headmistress.'

Reclining on the grass in the clearing, Maxine parted her thighs, exposing her yawning pussy-slit to Ginger's wide eyes. 'Come on, Ginger!' she coaxed. 'Just because I'm Head Girl now, it doesn't mean to say that we can't . . .'

'The Bellend Rebels have voted you out!' Ginger returned angrily. 'They're going to send you to Coventry.'

'Why? For fuck's sake, just because I can't put a foot wrong lately with the sodding teachers, the Rebels aren't going to speak to me?'

'A foot wrong? Christ, Max, you're getting top marks in just about everything you do! You're hockey and netball captain, you arse-licked Knickergusset by cleaning her study and washing all the blackboards, you . . .'

'I didn't do those things! I keep telling you, it wasn't me!'

'The girls have decided that unless you start behaving like your old self again, they'll tie you down and sexually torture you. If I were you, I'd start rebelling against the system this very minute!'

'All right!' Maxine conceded, jumping up and pulling her knickers up. 'I'll go and set fire to Knickergusset's study!'

Grinning as Maxine took her lighter from her breast pocket and wandered off, Ginger lay back and slipped her hand down the front of her knickers. Massaging her erect clitoris, she closed her eyes and sighed. 'Ah, that's nice! Might as well do it properly, though.' Slipping her knickers down, she parted her swollen cunny lips and dragged her girl-juice up her moist valley to lubricate her fingertips. 'Ah, God, that's . . .'

'I heard what Maxine said!' Miss Blob growled as she dived into the clearing.

'Oh, it's you!' Ginger spat, parting her thighs further and slipping a finger into her tight vaginal sheath.

'Yes, it's me! You two have something on me, but when the fire starts I'll have something on *you*!' Miss Blob grinned, dumping a large bag on the ground.

'No one will believe that Max started the fire!'

'Yes, they will. The headmistress will . . .'

'Bugger off, you sad, perverted, sex-starved old tosser of a transvestite!'

Taking a pair of handcuffs from her bag, Miss Blob

pounced on Ginger, rolling her over and cuffing her hands behind her back. 'I'll teach you a lesson!' she raged, rolling the girl onto her back and ripping her gymslip from her struggling body. 'I've just about had enough of you and your threats to expose me! The Head's been telling me that you've bandied the name "Roderick" to her. And apparently Maxine's alleging that she knows something about me that would shock her.'

'Yes, that's right! We're going to expose you, Blob!'

'I can't have naughty little girls threaten me! You've been the bane of my life at Bellend School! It's time you were brought down a peg or two, my girl! I'm going to give you the thrashing of your life!'

'You touch me and I'll go straight to Knickergusset and . . .'

'Save your breath! Miss Gussetpiece said that Maxine would be here. She sent me to take the girl to her study.' Taking several lengths of rope from her bag, Miss Blob grinned. 'Knowing she'd be here, I've come prepared!' she bellowed. 'I was going to thrash Maxine but, as she's gone, I'll thrash you instead!'

Tying ropes to Ginger's ankles, Miss Blob reached up and fastened one to the branch of a nearby tree. Slinging the other rope over the high branch of another tree, she grabbed the dangling end and pulled, forcibly opening the girl's legs as wide as she could. Pulling again, lifting the girl's buttocks clear of the ground, the sexual deviant made the rope fast. 'There, get out of that one!' she cried triumphantly, dropping to her knees and tearing off the remainder of the girl's clothing.

Naked, her young body defenceless, Ginger screamed for help as Miss Blob took a huge vibrator from her bag and pushed the rounded tip between the girl's splayed buttocks. 'You bastard!' she shrieked as the pink vibrator dilated her tight bottom-hole and entered her rectal sheath. 'I'll fucking well . . .'

'Unless you shut up, I'll stuff your knickers in your mouth!' the he-woman warned.

'You'll pay for this, you bent old git! I'll chew your fucking balls off!'

'And I'll chew your fucking nipples off! You and your interfering little friend have gone too far, pushed me to the edge – and now you'll receive your just reward!'

Sinking the vibrator deep into the girl's tight anal sheath, Miss Blob grabbed a pair of nipple clamps from her bag. Grinning wickedly, she moved to Ginger's side and squeezed her pert breasts. 'You have nice tits!' she chuckled. Lifting her head, her mouth hanging open, Ginger gazed in terror as Miss Blob clamped her nipples, tightening the screws until the girl grimaced and cried out.

'Argh! That hurts!' the redhead complained as the clamps tightened around her erect nipples, painfully pinching the brown protrusions. 'Please . . . please, no!' Ignoring her prisoner's protests, Miss Blob plunged her hand into her bag and pulled out a pair of scissors and an electric razor.

'Let's get rid of these ginger curls, shall we?' she grinned, moving between the girl's thighs and snipping her pubic hair.

'I'll get you for this!' Ginger spat as her captor worked the scissors over her sex-mound. 'You just wait until . . .'

'When I've finished with you, I'm going to grab Maxine bloody Mayhem and put her through the same treatment!' Miss Blob growled. 'I'll put an end to these threats, my girl – if it's the last thing I do!'

Bounding into the clearing, Maxine gasped in disbelief as she gazed at her friend's naked, tethered body. 'Ah, Blob!' she screeched, grabbing the geography mistress's arm. 'I've been waiting for an opportunity like this!'

'And so have I!' the burly transvestite returned, breaking free and ripping Maxine's gymslip from her curvaceous young body.

Struggling to overpower the sex-fiend as the fire bells rang out, Maxine could do nothing to save herself from the enforced disrobing. Her blouse torn off, her bra and knickers yanked from her writhing body, she finally lay naked on the ground, pinned down by her captor. Grabbing more rope from her bag, Miss Blob tied the girl's hands behind her back before standing and towering over her cowering prisoner.

'So, I now have *two* Bellend Rebels!' she laughed. 'Ah, the fire bells! You've set fire to the headmistress's study, then?'

'Yes, I have!' Maxine grinned. 'With any luck, the whole fucking school will go up in smoke!'

'No, I doubt it,' Miss Blob smiled taking more rope from her bag. 'Ever been thrashed, Maxine? Ever had your buttocks whipped until they've burned with fire and you've begged for your very life?'

'I'll get you for . . .'

'Yes, so Ginger keeps saying. Right, let's get these ropes tied to your feet and string you up next to your friend so that your bum's in position for a whipping!' she laughed, binding the girl's ankles.

'You just wait, Blob!' Ginger hissed.

'Oh no, not again! Right, you've asked for this!' the school pervert cried, grabbing the girl's stained knickers and stuffing them into her mouth. 'There, that's better!'

she laughed as Ginger tried to eject the garment. 'I like peace and quiet.'

Looking up to a tree branch, Miss Blob grinned. Taking the rope attached to Maxine's left ankle, she threw it over the branch and pulled it tight. 'That's one leg airborne!' she chuckled, securing the rope. 'And now for the other!' Moving to another tree, she tossed the rope over a branch and tugged, opening the girl's legs until she was doing the splits, her buttocks raised clear of the ground.

'Just you wait, Blob!' Maxine cursed as her captor fastened the rope. 'You'll regret ever meeting us when . . .'

'Now, what else do I have in my bag?' Miss Blob muttered, ignoring Maxine's threats. 'Ah, a big thick cucumber! Yes, the very thing to shove up your cunt!'

'When you let us go . . .' Ginger began, spitting her knickers out of her mouth and watching Miss Blob ease the fruit between Maxine's shaved pussy lips and drive it deep into her tight cuntal sheath.

'*When* I let you go? Who said anything about *ever* letting you go? If you think I'm stupid enough to release you, you have another think coming! You'll enjoy the night, the creepy crawlies, the owls, the bats . . . Just look at you both, side by side, naked, your legs straddled, your cunts open, your bottoms ready for the leather strap! Now, let's delve into the goodies bag again.'

Pulling out another pair of nipple clamps and a second vibrator, Miss Blob settled between Maxine's splayed thighs and parted her taut buttocks. Twisting and pushing the vibrator against the girl's brown portal, she grinned as the pink shaft slipped deep into her rectum. Dismissing Maxine's expletives, she pushed the plastic phallus in to the hilt, leaving only half an inch protruding from the girl's stretched bottom-hole. Taking the nipple clamps, she moved to her prisoner's side and tweaked her long milk-buds.

'You have fine nipples!' she complimented Maxine, attaching the clamps and tightening the screws until the girl grimaced. 'A little tighter, perhaps?' she grinned, turning the screws.

'Argh, that hurts! You just wait, Blob!' Maxine spat.

'I *am* waiting – waiting to fuck you both and then thrash you until you beg for mercy! Now, let me see – you both have your nipples clamped, you have vibrators up your bottoms, Maxine has a cucumber up her cunt . . . Ah, yes, I must finish shaving your little friend!'

Taking the electric razor, Miss Blob shaved the stubble from Ginger's pert mound, her fleshy outer pussy lips. 'Just a little more around the edges!' she chuckled, working the buzzing razor between the girl's full lips and the creases at the top of her thighs, exposing baby-smooth white skin. 'You have a lovely cunt, Ginger – nice pink fleshy lips. And you seem to be aroused! Look at your girlie-come, oozing from your young cunt! I'm going to enjoy wanking up your cunt, filling your tight cunt-hole with spunk! Right, all done! And now for this!' she cried jubilantly, lifting her skirt and displaying a huge male organ. 'Hold tight, girl – you're about to be fucked rotten!'

Stabbing his solid purple knob between Ginger's hairless pussy lips, the transvestite drove his veined shaft deep into her wriggling body. 'Ah, yes! Hot, tight, wet!' he cried, repeatedly withdrawing and thrusting into the girl's vaginal sheath. 'Where do you want my sperm, up your cunt or all over your stomach? Or in your mouth, perhaps?' he chuckled, quickening his penile thrusting.

Turning her head as her naked body jolted with the vaginal pummelling, Ginger winked at Maxine. Their day of revenge would come, they both knew as Miss Blob gasped and filled Ginger's spasming cunny hole with her treacherous sperm. Eventually, they'd escape and hunt down the pervert – and when they caught him . . .

'I could fuck you both all day long!' Miss Blob gasped, driving the huge male organ deep into Ginger's aching cunt, bathing her young cervix with the last of his gushing jism. 'And I could thrash your beautiful bottoms all day long!' His heavy balls slapping the girl's taut bottom-orbs, he finally collapsed over her firm stomach, panting in the wake of his climax. 'Ah, ah, that was good! Christ, that was good!'

Hearing twigs cracking underfoot, the transvestite quickly withdrew his spent penis from Ginger's sperm-drenched vagina and scanned the bushes. Calling for help, the girls exchanged joyous looks at the prospect of their imminent rescue – and Miss Blob's downfall. But the debauched participants gasped as a nun entered the clearing. Confronting the lewd spectacle, she gazed at the sperm oozing from Ginger's hairless sex-groove, the vibrators embedded in the girls' bottom-holes.

'Fuck me, a nun!' Miss Blob bellowed. 'Sorry, your ungodliness, I mean . . .'

'What's going on here?' the daughter of God enquired softly.

'Er . . . We were just . . .'

'Are these little beauties your prisoners?'

'No, no. Well, not exactly, you see . . .' Miss Blob stammered.

The school sex-assembly gasped as the nun ripped her habit off to display a rampant erection. 'Jesus Christ!'

Miss Blob breathed, eyeing the long, thick weapon. 'You're a man!'

'How observant of you!' the nun laughed, hoisting up her fishnet stockings and adjusting her suspender belt. 'My name's. . . er . . . you can call me Sister Satanic.'

'Please to meet you, Sister – my name's Miss Blob – Josephine Blob.'

'What a lovely name.'

'Yes, I like it.'

Fondling his penis, his heavy balls, Sister Satanic asked Miss Blob whether he'd be allowed to join in the sexy fun. 'You have them tied up in such wonderful positions, I'd love to sink my cock into their wet cunts!'

'And why not, Sister?' Miss Blob chuckled. 'Take your pick. Oh, I've just done that one's tight cunt,' she added, pointing to Ginger's shorn pussy.

'Then I shall take this delectable little beauty!' Sister Satanic intoned lustfully, moving towards Maxine's vulnerable pussy-hole with his flesh-rod in his hand.

'You keep away from me!' Maxine cried as the man's bulbous cockhead ran up her drenched pussy crack. 'I'm warning you . . .'

'Ah, that feels good!' he sighed, driving his veined shaft deep into the girl's hot vaginal canal. 'God, you're beautiful! Ah, ah, yes!'

'I'll get you!' Maxine cried as her young body jolted with the Sister's fucking motions. 'I'll bloody well . . .'

'I've had an idea!' Miss Blob laughed. 'If I can position myself here on the ground, by her bum . . . That's it!' she cried, slipping the vibrator from the girl's anal sheath. 'Although I'm sideways on, I'm sure I can slip my cock up her arse!'

'No, you'll never do it,' the nun replied. 'You'll be in

my way if you . . . Let's turn her over, lay her on her stomach so . . .'

'Better still, if she were on all fours, you could crawl beneath her and slip your cock up her cunt, and I could fuck her arse!' Miss Blob laughed.

Slipping his wet penis from Maxine's tight cunt, Sister Satanic helped Miss Blob position the girl's struggling body. On her hands and knees, ropes fanning out in all directions from her wrists, knees and ankles, tied to the trees, Maxine was powerless to move. Cursing as Miss Blob ran a length of rope around her middle, she wondered what sexual debauchery she'd be forced to endure. Her back arching as Miss Blob tossed the rope over an overhanging branch and pulled it tight, she became fearful, wishing that she'd never threatened to reveal the transvestite's secret.

As the nun manoeuvred himself beneath her naked body and gazed up at her flushed face, Maxine knew that she was about to be fucked as she'd never been fucked before. But it was the prospect of a merciless thrashing that really frightened her.

'That's it!' Sister Satanic cried, driving his penis deep into the girl's cunt. 'Perfect! Now, Miss Blob, you can kneel between my legs and shove your cock up her arse!'

'Ah, what a lovely sight!' Miss Blob chuckled, eyeing Maxine's bloated pussy lips, taut around the broad base of the nun's erect penis. 'And your bottom-hole looks so inviting, Maxine! You'd like my cock pushed deep into your tight bum, wouldn't you?'

Maxine said nothing as the transvestite's penis glided into her rectal sheath. Grimacing as her pelvic cavity bloated, she turned her head and gazed at Ginger. The girl was watching, open-mouthed, obviously wondering what it was like to have two solid penises in her tight holes. Winking at Ginger, Maxine offered her a reassuring smile.

'Let the fucking begin!' Miss Blob hailed, thrusting her rock-hard penis in and out of Maxine's tight anus.

'Let the double-fucking commence!' Sister Satanic rejoined, thrusting deep into the girl's drenched vagina.

Her body rocking as the male shafts thrust into her tight love-holes, Maxine gasped, her eyes rolling as her clitoris responded to the enforced double pistoning. Her juices flowing, her nipples rock-hard, pinched by the clamps, she whimpered as her climax stirred within her contracting womb. Ginger could see that her friend was enjoying the two thrusting penises, and she wondered hopefully whether the perverts would have the energy to double-fuck her own tight holes.

'Come together!' Maxine cried involuntarily as the penises swelled within her bloated sex-sheaths. 'Both spunk up me together!'

'God, I'm coming!' Sister Satanic gasped. 'My spunk's coming!'

'And mine!' Miss Blob breathed. 'My sperm . . . my sperm's coming! Going to . . . Ah! Going to sperm up your arse!'

Gasping as the profane spunk gushed into her perspiring body, Maxine reached her own mind-blowing climax. Her clitoris throbbing, sending wave upon wave of electrifying sex-tingles through her quivering womb, she had never experienced such an incredible multiple orgasm. Imagining a third penis thrusting into her gasping mouth, bathing her tongue with luscious male cream, she wailed her appreciation, filling the wood with her orgasmic cries.

'More, more! Fuck me harder!' she screamed as the men drained their heavy balls, filling her inflamed holes to the brim with their climactic spend. The pistoning knobs finally coming to rest deep inside her creamy love-ducts, Maxine hung her head, panting for air. Her cunt spasming, her anal sphincter convulsing, the girl was well and truly fucked.

'And now for the thrashing!' Miss Blob cried, slipping her shrinking organ from the girl's rectal sheath. 'Come on, Sister Satanic! Pull your cock out of her cunt and help me thrash the girl! I want to see her arse-cheeks glowing a fire-red!'

'And so do I!' Sister Satanic panted eagerly, slipping his penis from Maxine's cuntal sheath and joining the crazed teacher.

'This leather strap will bring you both pain and pleasure, Maxine!' Miss Blob laughed, pulling the thick leather belt from her bag.

'Please!' Maxine gasped. 'Please, no!'

'Look at the spunk pouring from her holes!' the teacher chuckled, raising the strap above her head and bringing it down with a loud crack.

'No!' Maxine screamed as the strap lashed her twitching buttocks again.

Watching the incredibly arousing spectacle, Ginger sensed her clitoris swell and throb and her love juices ooze between her pinken inner lips. Praying that she'd be given the same gruelling punishment, she grinned as the men's penises stiffened. *One up each hole*, she mused as her cunt muscles tightened. *I want three cocks – in my mouth, my bum and my cunt!* she thought in her rising wickedness.

'Someone's coming!' Sister Satanic suddenly whispered, holding Miss Blob's arm to halt the thrashing. 'Quickly, let's get out of here!'

'Christ, if it's the Head, I'm done for!' Miss Blob exclaimed, dropping the leather strap and diving into the bushes.

Wandering into the clearing with Candida, Hilda grinned. 'Oh, what have we here?' she giggled. 'The Bellend Rebels, tied up ready for a good spanking!'

'Let us go, Pillock!' Maxine hissed.

'Let you go?' Candida laughed. 'We didn't tie you up, so why should we let you go? I bags we spank them with this leather belt, Hilly!'

'Yes, jolly good idea, Candy! You go first, and then I'll take my turn. We know that you set fire to Miss Gussetpiece's study, and we've told her. We saw you, Maxine Mayhem – we saw you start the fire. Miss Gussetpiece is after your blood, I can tell you!'

'You'll pay for this, Pillock!' Ginger spat as she struggled to break free.

'Damn right you will!' Maxine rejoined.

Thrashing Maxine's already burning buttocks, Candida allowed her prisoner no quarter. Again and again she lashed the girl's naked orbs, grinning as broad weals decorated the rapidly reddening flesh-canvas. Maxine's pathetic cries and Ginger's wails as Hilda spanked her taut buttocks drifting through the wood unnoticed, the gymslip assailants were in their element as they administered their punishment.

'Show no mercy, Mr Christian!' Hilda cried, spanking Ginger's glowing orbs with the palm of her hand.

'No mercy, Captain Bligh!' Candida giggled, bringing the belt down with a loud crack.

Girl School

A scream suddenly rending the blue air, the girls halted their thrashing and turned on their heels to see Miss Gussetpiece staring at them in horror. 'Jesus bloody Christ!' the Head bellowed. 'What the fuck . . . I mean . . . Hilda, Candida, I have never . . .'

'Maxine set fire to your study, Miss Gussetpiece!' Hilda interjected. 'We were punishing her for . . .'

'You, Maxine? You set fire to my study?'

'Please, Miss Gussetpiece, I . . .'

'Don't say another word, Maxine! You've done me a favour, my girl – a big favour! The receipts and invoices have been destroyed! Or they would have been if they had existed. This is the perfect answer for the tax man!'

'That's why I did it, Miss Gussetpiece,' Maxine smirked. 'I was assisting you.'

'Excellent, Maxine! I couldn't have done a better job myself. Hilda, release these poor girls and then report to my study – what's left of it, anyway.'

'Please, Miss Gussetpiece – Maxine's fooling you! She knew nothing about any receipts or invoices!' Hilda protested.

'Yes, I did!' Maxine returned as Hilda untied the ropes. 'I was helping Miss Gussetpiece in her time of need – unlike you!'

'Admirable, Maxine – most admirable!' Miss Gussetpiece enthused. 'I shall now return to the school and I want to see you, Hilda, and you, Candida, in my study in five minutes flat! Excellent, Maxine!' the beaming woman rambled on as she wandered into the bushes. 'What a refreshingly bright, intelligent girl!'

Chapter Twelve

'It's the last day of term tomorrow, the end of my schooldays – and I've been expelled!' Hilda sighed despondently as she packed her suitcase.

'I don't know how things turned out this way,' Candida said gloomily as she wandered into the dormitory and flopped onto her bed. 'Fancy Miss Gussetpiece expelling you when you're leaving Bellend tomorrow anyway! It's incredible – Maxine Mayhem the Head's pet, and you've been expelled!'

'My father's really mad at me! He rang me this morning. The letter Miss Gussetpiece sent him lists all the terrible things that Maxine has done – and blames me! The fire in the library, the toilet block explosion, the awful trouble at the fête . . . I've even been blamed for spreading rumours about Miss Blob being a man! When my mother read the bit about me spanking Ginger in the woods and the incident in the potting shed with the cucumber, she jolly well fainted!'

'Gosh, Hilly – you are in a sticky spot!'

'I wanted to go to university and teacher training college, but now . . .'

'I know you did – and you will! You *will* go to the ball!'

'They'll never allow me to . . .'

'Look!' Candida beamed, holding up several sheets of paper. 'A glowing report and excellent references from Miss Gussetpiece!'

'But how . . .'

'I sneaked into her study during the night and typed it on the school's headed paper.'

'Crumbs! You *are* clever, Candy. Do you think I'll get away with it?'

'Yes, why not?'

Striding into the dormitory, her hands on her hips, Miss Blob ordered Hilda to report to the Head's study. 'Miss Gussetpiece wants a word with you!' she imparted sternly. 'A lecture, more than likely!'

'*Now* what have I done?' Hilda sighed, slamming her suitcase shut and flouncing out of the room. What could follow expulsion? she mused, making her way down the corridor. Nothing worse, surely?

'Hilda!' Miss Blob called, striding after the girl. 'Hilda, what would you give to leave Bellend without an expulsion order hanging over you?'

'Anything, Miss Blob! To be expelled is an insufferable nightmare! For the rest of my days, it will be with me. It will haunt me forever!'

'I'll be blunt, Hilda. I'm not going to beat about the bush, I'll just come straight out with what I have to say. If you come to my rooms and sexually pleasure me . . .'

'Oh, Miss Blob!' Hilda gasped, her blue eyes mirroring her shock.

'I can save you, Hilda!' Miss Blob said, nervously scanning the corridor. 'You sexually pleasure me, do what I ask, when I ask, and in return, I'll save you from expulsion.'

'But . . .'

'You did say you'd give *anything*.'

'I know, but . . .'

'The choice is yours,' Miss Blob smiled, scanning the corridor again before lifting her skirt and displaying a rampant erection.

'Argh! You *are* a man!' Hilda gasped in horror, gazing at the huge purple knob, the long, veined shaft, the heavy balls. 'You're a . . . you're a . . . I'll tell Miss Gussetpiece that you're a man!'

'She won't believe you, Hilda. The things you've done, the lies you've told, I doubt very much whether she'll believe anything you say!'

'I'd rather be expelled than . . .'

'Would you, Hilda? As you said, it will haunt you for the rest of your days. The nightmare will never leave you. Is that what you want?'

'No, but . . .'

'The choice is simple. Pleasure this, my penis – or leave Bellend having been expelled. I don't know what your future employer would say if . . .'

'What would I have to do, exactly?' Hilda asked pensively.

'Suck it, lick it . . . Anything I demand of you,' Miss Blob grinned, massaging the veined shaft.

'This is blackmail!'

'Yes, it is! So, what's it to be? I can save you, Hilda – save you from the horrific shame of expulsion.'

Realizing that she had no choice, Hilda reluctantly conceded. 'All right, I'll do it,' she mumbled as Miss Blob lowered her skirt and concealed her formidable weapon.

Entering the study, Hilda stood cowering before the Head's desk, wondering how Miss Blob was going to save her from expulsion. 'Hilda, you have been involved in too many horrendous incidents,' Miss Gussetpiece began. 'I had no choice other than to write to your father informing him that, even though tomorrow is your last day at Bellend, you will be leaving with the cloud of expulsion forever hanging over you.'

'The incidents were . . .'

'Hilda, the incidents are too numerous to list! The bomb, the fire in the library . . .'

'That wasn't me!' Hilda protested, praying that she could save herself without Miss Blob's intervention – without the intervention of Miss Blob's penis.

'Fukui and Kelly saw you, Hilda. They saw you setting fire to the waste paper bin! You were also seen running away from the toilet block just before . . .'

'What about our deal? You in the woods with that priest . . .'

'The deal's off, Hilda! No one in their right mind would believe that I was in the woods with a priest having it . . . Look at the times I've caught you in the potting shed! The fête was a complete disaster! The letters of complaint I've received from the people who attended the fête are . . . And as for the letter from the local vicar! From day one of this term, you've been in trouble. Why, Hilda? Why have you done these dreadful things?'

'I didn't, Miss Gussetpiece!'

'Hilda, there's no point in continuing with your lies. In all my years at this school, I've never known anyone to behave as you have. Well, that's not strictly true. Ah, Miss Blob, come in! I was just telling Hilda about . . .'

'Yes, Headmistress, I know. I feel that I have to say something,' Miss Blob said, standing by the Head's desk.

'Don't waste your breath, Miss Blob!' Miss Gussetpiece laughed sarcastically. 'Hilda's appalling record speaks for itself!'

'What I have to say is in Hilda's defence, Miss Gussetpiece. I didn't come forward earlier because . . . well, because I . . .'

'Hilda, will you leave us, please?' Miss Gussetpiece asked. 'And close the door behind you. I'll send for you later.'

'Yes, Miss Gussetpiece,' Hilda sighed, pictures of an orgasming knob sperming over her tongue looming in her tormented mind as she left the study.

'Well, that's Pillock dealt with!' Maxine grinned as she entered the potting shed and lit a cigarette.

'We've won!' Ginger exclaimed triumphantly, flopping onto the sofa. 'The Bellend Rebels have defeated The Jolly Hockey Sticks Club!'

'Yes, but there's Blob to pay back for what he did to us.'

'Yeah, you're right! What's your plan?'

'Apart from chewing Blob's balls off, I don't have a plan, as yet. But I'm working on a way to expose him for what he really is – a perverted transvestite! I'm taking the pictures of Madame Fissure's shaved cunt to Knickergusset later. When she sees Dan's fucking great prick stuck up Fissure's cunt-hole, it'll be instant dismissal for the frog! Dan's face isn't in the pictures, so he'll be OK. And then, I'll . . .'

'It's Knickergusset that we need something on, Max.'

'I know, but that's not going to be easy. Oh, Christ, what do you want?' Maxine snarled as the gardener pottered into the shed.

Grinning, the old man said nothing as he grabbed a can of paraffin from the bench and unscrewed the top. Splashing the liquid over the wooden floor, he tossed the can into the corner of the shed and slipped a box of matches from his jacket pocket.

'Bloody hell!' Ginger cried as he struck a match and dropped it on the floor.

'Jesus! What the hell are you doing?' Maxine gasped, following the gardener and Ginger through the door as the flames quickly spread.

'That'll go up nicely!' the old man chuckled, standing between the stunned girls and watching the flames licking around the doorframe.

'Why the fucking hell did you do that?' Maxine asked. 'Are you fucking mad?'

'I'm leavin' this dump! Tomorrow is me last day and I thought I might as well 'ave you blamed for burnin' me pottin' shed down!'

'You bastard! I thought you said that you wanted to help us?'

'I lied! Ah, 'ere comes the 'eadmistress!' the old man laughed, gleefully rubbing his hands together. 'You've been gettin' that poor 'ilda 'illock into trouble, and now I 'ear that she's bein' expelled. I 'ope you're kicked out now!'

Striding towards the burning shed with Miss Blob in tow, Miss Gussetpiece asked the gardener how the fire had started. 'She done it!' he replied, pointing to Maxine. 'I seen 'er with me own eyes! She covered the floor with paraffin and set fire to the place!'

'To my study, Maxine Mayhem!' Miss Gussetpiece bellowed. 'And you, Ginger – this instant! Miss Blob, call the fire brigade, will you?'

Girl School

'Er . . . There's little point, Headmistress,' Miss Blob replied as the flames swirled through the roof. 'By the time they get here, the shed will no longer be in existence.'

'Yes, I suppose you're right!' she roared, turning to the gardener. 'You stay here and make sure that the fire doesn't get out of control and burn those bushes! Right, I'll deal with Maxine Mayhem and her friend. Miss Blob, will you tell Hilda of my decision concerning her expulsion, please?'

'Yes, I'd be delighted, Headmistress! I'll . . . er . . . I'll take her to my rooms and give her a good . . . What I mean is, I'll have a good talk with her.'

'Good idea. Yes, take her to your rooms. If only all my staff were like you, Miss Blob. You're keen, willing, helpful . . . Yes, take the girl to your rooms and comfort her.'

'Oh, I *will*, Headmistress! I'll have her . . . I'll comfort her.' Closing the door behind her, Hilda wandered through the narrow passage to Miss Blob's lounge, wondering whether or not she'd been saved from expulsion. 'Good news, Hilda!' Miss Blob grinned, closing the door and ogling the girl's shapely thighs. 'You won't be expelled. Miss Gussetpiece is writing to your father to say that she mixed your name up with someone else's. It wasn't easy, but you're completely off the hook – thanks to me.'

'Yippee!' Hilda cried. 'You don't know how pleased . . .' Her joyous face suddenly paling, she frowned and hung her head. 'So, now I have to . . .'

'Yes, now you have to keep your side of the bargain. Take all your clothes off, please,' Miss Blob grinned, sitting on the sofa.

Standing before her lone audience, Hilda tugged her

gymslip over her head and unbuttoned her blouse. Slipping the garment over her shoulders, she hesitated as she reached behind her back to unclip her bra. 'Carry on,' Miss Blob smiled. 'A deal's a deal. I could always have another word with Miss Gussetpiece and . . .' Removing her bra, peeling the cups away from her firm breasts, her erect nipples, Hilda pondered on the deal she'd made. *A choice between the devil and the deep blue sea*, she reflected, her face flushing as she tugged her knickers down her slender legs, revealing her full, hairless pussy lips. *And it has to be the devil!* Kicking her shoes off she stepped out of her knickers, averting her gaze as the leering Miss Blob scrutinized her fresh young body.

'What do you want me to do now?' the girl asked, wearing only her white ankle socks.

'Stand on the sofa with your feet either side of my legs so that I can examine your beautiful girlie-crack properly.'

'Like this?' Hilda asked bashfully, balancing on the sofa, her feet wide apart, the gentle swell of her hairless mound, her fleshy outer lips, only inches from Miss Blob's sparkling eyes.

'Yes, that's perfect! You have a lovely cunt, Hilda. You have a beautiful young body, gorgeous tits, succulent nipples . . . You're the epitome of female sexuality. Ask me to kiss your cunt.'

'Kiss me,' Hilda murmured sheepishly.

'Kiss your what?'

'Kiss my . . . kiss my cunt.'

'Please.'

'Please, kiss my cunt.'

Clutching Hilda's taut buttocks and kissing her soft mons, Miss Blob licked her dividing groove, her protruding inner lips. 'You taste nice, Hilda – very nice! There's nothing I like more than licking a teenaged girl's cunt out.' Releasing her buttocks and parting her fleshy pussy lips, Miss Blob examined the humiliated girl's pink inner folds, her rosebud clitoris – the wet entrance to her inner sanctum. 'A finger, I think!' the geography mistress grinned, parting Hilda's luxuriant inner lips further and peering into her vaginal sheath. 'Ask me to finger your cunt, Hilda.'

'Please finger my cunt, Miss Blob.'

'Try and be a little more affirmative, Hilda! A little more assertive, as if you really mean it.'

'Please push your finger up my cunt, Miss Blob!'

'That's better!'

The erotic sensations causing her womb to flutter, Hilda felt that she'd made the right decision. Although she felt terribly disgraced, this really wasn't so bad after all. *Definitely the devil!* she mused as Miss Blob's finger massaged her spasming cunt. But, she reminded herself, beneath this she-devil's skirt lurked a hideous monster – a rock-hard penis!

'Open your cunt lips for me,' the gender-bender instructed as she thrust her finger in and out of Hilda's tightening vaginal sheath. Peeling her swollen outer lips wide apart, Hilda exposed her most intimate flesh to Miss Blob's wistful gaze. 'That's very good! Now I'll lick your wet cunt flesh, lick your clitoris. Beg me to lick your cunt out.'

'Please lick my cunt out,' Hilda whispered.

'Assertion, Hilda!'

'I want your tongue up my cunt!'

'And?'

'I want your tongue up my wet cunt, licking my wet cunt out!'

'Good girl!'

The hot tongue sweeping over her throbbing clitoris, Hilda let out an involuntary yelp of delight. 'Ah! Golly! Ah, that's . . .' Too embarrassed to admit that she was enjoying the intimate attention, she held her breath, closing her eyes as her magical bud pulsated. How many times would she be called upon to commit degrading sexual acts during her last two days at school? she wondered as another finger crudely invaded her bottom-hole. Dozens of times! she decided as Miss Blob frenziedly licked her solid clitoris.

Taking Hilda to her shuddering climax, Miss Blob continued licking and sucking the girl's clitoris, fingering her spasming cunt-sheath, her tight bottom-hole, maintaining the incredible waves of pure sexual lust. Clinging to her abuser's head for support, Hilda gasped, her nostrils flaring, her eyes rolling as her orgasm ripped through her quivering body. *A cross-dressed devil – an angel?* she speculated wildly in her blurred sexual haze. But still the snake-like monster skulked beneath Miss Blob's short skirt, eagerly awaiting its goal – Hilda's hot, wet, tight vagina.

Dizzy in her coming as the fingers slipped from her tight holes, Hilda stepped off the sofa and stood trembling, panting, in the wake of her orgasm. Her warm girl-come trickling down her inner thighs, her swollen inner labia inflamed, her nipples on full alert, she awaited her next instruction. *The monster!* she thought as Miss Blob lifted her short skirt, revealing her huge erection, her heavy, rolling balls to the girl's fearful eyes.

'Kneel between my legs and suck my knob,' came the inevitable order. Kneeling and leaning forward, Hilda sucked the huge purple knob into her hot mouth and rolled her tongue over the silky surface. She might as well go for it, she decided. There was no point in hesitating, delaying the inevitable – the gushing sperm. *Take the bull by the bollocks,* she thought, thanking God that this was the penultimate day of term.

Taking the huge balls in her hand and gently kneading them, she moved her head down, sucking half the length of the man's penis into her mouth. Gasping, Miss Blob grabbed Hilda's head, thrusting his shaft up and down, mouth-fucking the young girl, bringing his climax closer. Opening his legs wide, the pervert ordered Hilda to wank him, keeping only his throbbing glans between her full, red lips. Complying, Hilda rolled her wet lips over his glans, wanking his hard shaft with her hand, waiting for the gush of his sperm to fill her cheeks.

'God, that's good!' Miss Blob cried, his seed coursing its way up his shaft. 'Here it comes!' he gasped as his spunk jetted into Hilda's mouth, bathing her tongue. 'Drink it, girl! Swallow my spunk! That's it! Ah, ah! Take it out and lick it, I want to spurt over your lips!' Slipping the jetting glans from her mouth, Hilda licked as the male cream splattered her lips, her nose, her chin. 'Lick faster, lick all over!' Miss Blob demanded as the girl continued her frenzied wanking.

Finally falling limp, Miss Blob grabbed Hilda's hand, halting her massaging. Panting, gasping as the girl lapped up the sperm running down his softening shaft, Miss Blob gazed at her rosebud lips, her pink tongue, glistening with his male come. Hilda was good, he mused, deciding to use her for sex as often as he could while he had the chance.

'Was that all right?' Hilda asked coyly, licking her lips.

'That was very good, Hilda – very good!'

'What do you want me to do now?'

'I need to rest for a while so I'd like you to lie across my lap with your legs open and masturbate.'

'But, Miss Blob, I . . .'

'Come on, Hilda! Full length on the sofa with your bum on my lap and bring yourself off!'

Taking up her position, Hilda wondered where it would all end – how long she'd have to endure the teacher's sexual exploitation of her. At least by tomorrow night she'd be away from the school – for good! His stiffening penis between her thighs, resting against her swollen cunt lips, the girl parted her fleshy folds and began her slow clitoral massaging, thinking of the glorious hours she'd spend bird-watching once she'd left Bellend.

Gazing in wonderment, Miss Blob watched the beautiful exhibition of female masturbation, the girl's slender, caressing fingers, her solid clitoris, her moistening vaginal entrance. Pushing his knob into her drenched, yawning sex-valley, he rubbed his glans against her glistening, pinken folds as she quickened her masturbation rhythm.

Wanking his shaft, his throbbing glans just inside her vaginal opening, Miss Blob elicited his second coming in unison with the girl's climax. His sperm jetting over her hand, lubricating her masturbating fingertips, splashing her gaping crack, he wanked his shaft faster, gasping as he sustained his orgasm. Crying out as her own climax gripped her shuddering young body, Hilda wriggled her hips, slipping the head of Miss Blob's penis into her hungry cavern.

'Fuck my cunt!' the girl cried in her spiralling arousal. 'Your cock, I want it sperming up my cunt!' Bending his veined shaft, Miss Blob eased his knob into the girl's vagina, absorbing her inner heat, bathing her velveteen walls with his gushing cream to the accompaniment of her orgasmic cries. Massaging the last of his sperm from his ballooning cockhead as Hilda slowed her clitoral caressing, the geography mistress and his pupil lay panting, their genitals locked in lust, glued with a blasphemous blend of sperm and sticky girl-come.

'Now, Maxine!' Miss Gussetpiece stormed as she barged into her study to find the girl staring out of the window. 'What on earth did you think you were . . . Where's Ginger?'

'She couldn't wait any longer, Miss Gussetpiece.'

'Couldn't wait? How dare she leave when I'd ordered her to . . .'

'She had to go to the bog house.'

'Goodness me, have you no etiquette at all? You'll never get anywhere in life unless you speak the Queen's English! The lavatory, Maxine.'

'What about it?'

'The ladies' room.'

'Where?'

'That's what it's called.'

'I know, Miss Gussetpiece.'

'Then don't call it the bog house! Now, where was I? Oh, yes – why did you set fire to the potting shed?'

'I didn't, Miss Gussetpiece – the gardener did it.'

'Of course he didn't! Why would he set fire to his own potting shed? That shed was his life, his existence revolved around it! I thought you were doing so well, Maxine. A changed girl, that's what I thought you were. This has blotted what was to be an excellent final report. What your father will say, I . . . ah, yes, your father. Er . . . we'll forget the incident. Right, off you go.'

'Forget it, Miss Gussetpiece? But . . .'

'One hundred grand is . . . The less said about the matter, the better.'

'Is that it, then? I set fire to the shed, and you . . .'

'So you *did* start the fire! Er . . . the shed needed replacing, anyway. You've done me a favour by burning it down.'

'A favour!' Maxine gasped surprisedly. 'I can't do anything wrong, can I?'

'Wrong? You don't *want* to do anything wrong, do you?'

'Yes, I do! I mean, no, I suppose not.'

'That's that, then. Off you go, girl,' Miss Gussetpiece ordered as Maxine flounced off, pushing Johnson aside as he entered the study. 'Ah, Jones – what is it?'

'What, Headmistress?' Johnson asked.

'What do you mean, *what*?'

'What do I mean, *what*? I'm not with you, Headmistress.'

'Not with me? Where are you if you're not standing next to me in my study? Are you an apparition, a ghost – a mirage, perhaps?'

'A mirage, Headmistress?'

'If you're not here then, where are you, man?'

'Er . . . I'm not anywhere.'

'You must be somewhere! You think, therefore you are.'

'Am I?'

'Yes, of course!'

'I'm in your study.'

'I can see that! Good grief! Pass me that bottle of gin, will you?'

'Yes, Headmistress,' Johnson replied, shaking his head in despair as he took the bottle from the shelf. 'One of the girls told me that you wanted to see me.'

'Do I?'

'Apparently.'

'Who?'

'I'm sorry, Headmistress?'

'Who?'

'Who what?'

'Who said that I wanted to see you?'

'A girl – I don't know her name.'

'Well, now that you're here . . . The potting shed has been burnt down.'

'So I noticed, Headmistress.'

'Fire! Fire!' Miss Frigidus screamed, tripping over as she dashed into the study.

'Jesus! Where?' Miss Gussetpiece asked, picking the woman up.

'The chapel! The chapel's on fire!'

'Right, Jones, go and see what you can do. I'll ring the fire brigade!'

'What about me?' Miss Frigidus asked.

'What about you?' Miss Gussetpiece snapped, grabbing the phone and dialling 999.

'What shall I do?'

'Go away, you silly woman! Oh, no, sorry – I didn't mean you,' Miss Gussetpiece garbled to the operator. 'Fire! Fire!'

'Another one?' Miss Frigidus gasped.

'No, I'm talking to the woman on the phone! What? No, I don't want a service, I want the fire brigade! Why would I be wanting a service at a time like this? Ah, are you the fire brigade? Good. Yes, Bellend School. Be quick about it!'

Banging the phone down, the Head gulped down half the bottle of gin and left her study, bolting down the corridor to the chapel. 'The altar's gone up, and there's nothing I can do to stop the fire spreading!' Johnson shouted as Miss Gussetpiece approached the chapel doors.

'The fire brigade's on the way,' she announced, gazing through the doors at the flames licking up the walls. 'The Virgin!'

'A virgin? Where?'

'The Virgin Mary! You must save her!' Miss Gussetpiece gasped, pointing to a statuette on a side table in the chapel. 'She'll be sullied!'

'I'm not going in there to get it!' Johnson remonstrated as several hundred wittering girls filed out of the building.

'Jesus!'

'The fire brigade can help us, Headmistress! Keep calm!'

'No, you silly man! The statue of Jesus is in there too! Right, I'll check to see if Miss Blob and Hilda have left the building.'

Using her skeleton key, Miss Gussetpiece burst into Miss Blob's rooms to find the man naked, kneeling on the floor behind Hilda Hillock with his solid penis embedded deep in the girl's bottom-hole. Looking up, his face flushing, Miss Blob grinned. 'Ah, Headmistress! I . . . I was just checking this girl's anal sphincter muscles for . . .'

'Miss Blob! I have never . . .'

Girl School

'No, no – I'm Doctor Anusis Rectus, Miss Blob's brother!' he replied, slipping his penis out of the girl's anal sheath and standing before the Head.

'That's right,' Hilda rejoined, climbing to her feet and covering her naked body with her gymslip. 'I had a pain, you see, Miss Gussetpiece.'

'A pain? I have never known a doctor put his . . . put his thing into a young girl's bottom and . . .'

'It's a new treatment, Headmistress,' Doctor Rectus smiled, slipping his skirt on. 'You can't get it on the NHS, it's only available privately.'

'Privately? Why are you wearing a skirt?'

'Ah, how silly of me! Er . . . Where are my trousers? I'm always making that mistake. I blame it on my childhood. I had a very difficult upbringing, being an only child. My mother wanted a girl, you see.'

'I thought you were a triplet?'

'Am I? Ah, yes, so I am! It must be the heat.'

'What must?'

'The heat of the day, it must be affecting my memory.'

'This is all rather peculiar, if you ask me! There's a fire in the chapel so we must evacuate the building. You'll both report to my study when the fire's out!' Miss Gussetpiece bellowed, leaving the room.

Finding Candida in the woods with Véronique, Hilda settled herself on the grass beside them. 'I'm not going to be expelled after all,' she sighed wistfully.

'But I thought . . .' Candida began, her blue eyes frowning.

'Expelled?' Véronique echoed.

'Yes, I was going to be expelled, thrown out of the school, but now . . . I did a deal with Miss Blob.'

'A deal?'

'It's a long story. At least Miss Gussetpiece can't blame me for setting fire to the chapel. She knows that it wasn't me because she caught me . . . Sirens! That must be the fire engine.'

'Yes, it must,' Candida replied. 'I wonder how the fire started?'

'I will going to 'ave a look to see the fire,' Véronique said, rising to her feet and brushing grass from her gymslip.

'I'll come with you,' Candida smiled. 'Coming, Hilly?'

'No, no, I'll stay here. I've got some thinking to do.'

'OK, see you later.'

Alone in the clearing, Hilda thought of the summer. *One more day*, she mused, picturing the hide her father had built at the end of the garden. *One more day, and then I'll be free to go bird-watching and badger-spotting and . . .*

'I thought I'd find you here!' Maxine grinned fiendishly as she led three university boys into the clearing. 'This is the girl,' she declared, turning to the young men. 'I want to watch you fuck her! One up her arse, one up her cunt, and one in her mouth! I want you to fill her with spunk!'

Hilda didn't resist as the young men ran their hands over her nubile body, molesting her firm breasts, her shapely thighs, her taut, rounded buttocks. There was little point, she decided as her gymslip was tugged over her head and her blouse torn off. Her bra tossed to the ground, she looked down as two men squeezed her breasts and sucked on her erect nipples. As her knickers were yanked down her long legs and her smooth vaginal lips massaged, she gasped. Her arousal rising swiftly, the familiar sensations her young body was now bringing her caused her to tremble. Her libido had increased dramatically in the wake of her enforced sexual awakening and illicit orgasms. Now, delighting in the exquisite sensations emanating from her swelling clitoris, she craved sexual satisfaction. A finger massaging her solid cumbud, she closed her eyes, surrendering her curvaceous young body to her assailants as they explored her female mounds and crevices.

'Come on, then!' Maxine ordered impatiently. 'Get her on the ground and fuck her!' Concealing a grin as she was pulled to the ground, Hilda wondered at the prospect of having three penises pumping their sperm into her orifices. This was an opportunity that might never arise again, she mused as the men slipped their jeans and T-shirts off, scattering the garments around the clearing in their eagerness to begin the orgy. An experience of a lifetime! she reflected as, sitting naked on the grass, gazing up at the three solid male organs, her stomach somersaulted.

The students were good-looking, their bodies muscular, firm with youth. Eyeing their heavy balls, their solid shafts, their purple knobs, Hilda wondered which one she'd have to suck. *All of them!* she found herself hoping as one man lay on his back, his penis pointing skyward.

'Squat over his cock and stick it up your cunt!' Maxine ordered crudely. Taking her position, kneeling astride the stranger, Hilda lowered the open centre of her femininity, guiding the solid knob into her juicing vaginal sheath. Gasping as his shaft stretched her spasming cunt, Hilda wondered again at the prospect of three penises entering her young body. 'Right, that's her cunt done!' Maxine giggled. 'Now for her arse!'

Obediently projecting her buttocks, Hilda grimaced as a young man knelt behind her and pressed his knob against her tight anal portal. Screwing her eyes shut as her sphincter muscles yielded, allowing the intruding knob to slip into her hot duct, she shuddered. Her pelvic cavity bloating as the rock-hard organ glided deep into her bottom-hole, she gazed in awe as the third man knelt before her, his awesome shaft erect before her wide eyes. *Number three*, she thought in awe as he pressed his plum to her red lips. Opening her mouth, she took the knob inside, tasting the salty glans, rolling her tongue over the hard, silky surface. Gasping, all three men began their pistoning, bringing the girl incredible sensations of lewd sex as their shafts glided in and out of her hot orifices.

'That's brilliant!' Maxine giggled, watching Hilda's young body rocking with the three thrusting penises. 'All come in her at once!' she cried, taking her Polaroid camera from beneath a bush and focusing on Hilda's pretty face, her bloated cheeks. As Maxine clicked the shutter, Hilda opened her eyes and gazed at the girl. The last thing she'd expected was to be photographed in her debauched coupling! But it was too late, she knew, as the she-devil took her position behind her and focused on the two ivory shafts driving into the tight holes between her splayed thighs.

The man driving his knob into Hilda's mouth suddenly gasping, she sucked harder, excitedly awaiting his sperm as the other men began panting. 'All come at the same time!' Maxine reminded her young studs as their bodies became rigid. Grunting as they thrust into Hilda's shaking body, the men loosed their sperm, filling her orifices, abusing her young body, satisfying their male lust. Her tongue sweeping over the orgasming glans filling her mouth, Hilda savoured the man's spunk as it flowed, bloating her cheeks. Her bottom-sheath expanding to take the swelling male organ, she sensed the seed discharging from the thrusting glans, lubricating her inflamed anal tube as her rhythmically contracting pussy sheath filled with spunk.

In her sexual heaven, Hilda moaned through her nose as her own climax erupted. Her clitoris throbbing, transmitting electrifying shock waves of lust through her quivering pelvis, she mouthed on the throbbing glans, swallowing the spurting liquid until she'd drained the heavy balls swinging beneath her chin. The men finally halting their pistoning, her trembling body calmed slowly. Her breathing heavy, her clitoris gently pulsating as her orgasm receded, she knew that she'd experienced the ultimate sexual coupling. There could be nothing to surpass three solid cocks, throbbing in orgasm, filling her orifices with sperm, she mused – nothing!

The click of the shutter brought her down to earth as she opened her eyes to see Maxine focus the camera on the penises withdrawing from her aching bottom-hole, her drenched vagina. *The photographs! Blackmail!* Hilda thought fearfully as her inflamed sex sheaths contracted, her once-private portals oozing with sperm.

Licking her lips as the spent glans slipped from her mouth, she wondered whether or not her ordeal was over. Would she be forced to endure a thrashing? Recalling Candida whipping Maxine's glowing buttocks with the leather strap, she knew that the girl would seek revenge.

'That was brilliant!' Maxine giggled as Hilda rolled off the young man beneath her perspiring body. Climbing to their feet and dressing, the three studs laughed and joked about their experience, talking about their lay as if she wasn't there while Maxine took more shots of the girl's abused body. *Used for sex*, Hilda thought as she lay on her back, her body aching, her holes burning, bubbling with sperm. But was her bitter-sweet ordeal yet over?

'Right, twenty pounds each, as agreed,' Maxine demanded excitedly. As the men handed over their payment and panted their breathless farewells, Hilda climbed to her feet, covering her young breasts with her folded arms. 'The pictures have come out well!' Maxine shrieked, thrusting the photographs beneath the girl's nose. 'Now I've really got you stitched up!'

Watching the wicked girl dive into the bushes and make her getaway with the stark evidence, Hilda picked her panties up and covered her glistening, rubicund pussy lips. *Crikey, I've been sold for sex!* she thought woefully. Slipping her bra on, she finished her dressing before silently leaving the clearing, her head spinning with her wonderfully wicked ordeal. She dared not tell her friends, she decided, wondering who Maxine would threaten to show the photographs to. *Gosh, if mummy sees them!*

'I suppose it could have been worse!' Miss Gussetpiece sighed, looking around the charred chapel as the firemen left. 'The poor Virgin Mary's had a roasting!'

'I'll clean her up, Headmistress,' Johnson obliged, grabbing the statuette.

'Mind where you touch her!' the Head warned, noticing the man's hand between the Virgin's thighs.

'It's only stone, not the real thing!'

'That's not the point. We must treat her with the respect she deserves. It's immoral, carrying her with your hand between her legs! And mind her breasts!'

'How am I going to clean her if I'm not allowed to touch her?'

'Clean her with your eyes closed and your mind on something else, something far removed from wicked, sinful acts.'

'Yes, Headmistress.'

'Give Jesus a good going over, too. He looks as if he's from Jamaica!'

'Right you are.'

'When you've cleaned them, bring them to my study for inspection,' Miss Gussetpiece ordered as she left the chapel. 'And mind your language in front of them! Utter only Godly words. Better still, say nothing.'

Making her way to her study, Miss Gussetpiece thought about the following day, the last day of term – the last time she'd ever see Maxine Mayhem and Hilda Hillock. 'If I can just get through tomorrow!' she sighed, entering her study. 'Jesus Christ!' she gasped, noticing several pornographic photographs neatly laid out on her desk. 'What the hell . . . Madame Fissure! My God, the woman's shaved her . . .'

'Ah, Miss Gussetpiece,' Madame Fissure smiled as she entered the study. 'One of the girls said that you wanted to see me.'

'I didn't send for you, but I'm glad you're here! What have you to say about these?'

Gasping as she cast her eyes over the sordid photographs, Madame Fissure shook her head. Stunned, she stood speechless as Miss Gussetpiece picked up a picture of the French mistress bending over, her taut buttocks criss-crossed with thin weals, her full, hairless vaginal lips bulging between her slender thighs.

'Well?' Miss Gussetpiece asked. 'You can't deny the fact that this is you in this disgusting pose!'

'No, no, I don't deny it, Headmistress. I really don't know what to say.'

'Who on earth took these pictures?'

'I . . . I don't know.'

'What with Miss Frigidus and that young French . . . I can't believe this of you, Madame Fissure! This is a respectable independent boarding school for girls! I can't have this sort of repugnant behaviour going on! It's not natural! What would the parents say? What would the girls say if they knew that their French teacher . . . I will not tolerate this wanton behaviour!'

'No, Headmistress.'

'Look at this one! Who's that man with his thing up your bottom? Good grief, that's illegal!'

'I don't know who he is.'

'You don't know? You mean to say that a man pushed his penis into your bottom, and you have no idea who he is?'

'Well, I do know, Headmistress, but . . .'

'Ah, honour amongst thieves! All right, I respect your judgment. Give me a clue, something to work on, if you don't want to reveal his identity.'

'I can't say anything, Headmistress. He's not to blame for the pictures.'

'The pictures aren't the issue in question, it's what they depict! I'll decide how to deal with you later, Madame Fissure! I'm hanging on to these pictures as evidence of your vulgar and most debased behaviour! You'd better return to your duties!'

'Yes, Headmistress.'

Flopping into her chair as Madame Fissure scurried out of the study, Miss Gussetpiece swigged from the vodka bottle, wondering who the man in the photographs was. Studying the man's penis, she noticed a small mole near the base. 'That will identify him!' she breathed. 'It can only be the gardener or Jones. They're the only two males in the school. Unless it was the glazier or the BT man.'

'What about the BT man?' Miss Frigidus queried, creeping into the study.

'Nothing!' the Head snapped, slipping the photographs into her desk drawer. 'Mind your own business!'

'Oh! Er . . . Headmistress, I was wondering, would I be able to drive your car?'

'You would be able, yes.'

'Oh, thank you.'

'I didn't say you could borrow it! I said that you'd be able to drive it.'

'Oh, I thought you meant . . .'

'You'd probably be able to drive the Queen's Rolls Royce, but I doubt that she'd lend it to you!'

'So the answer is no, then?'

'Yes.'

'I *can* borrow it?'

'No! I meant, yes, the answer is no. What do you want my car for, anyway?'

'I can't tell you.'

'Then don't ask! Now I have some end of term preparations to be getting on with.'

'There was one other thing, Headmistress.'

'What?'

'I'm leaving Bellend tomorrow.'

'I know that. It's the end of term, we're all leaving.'

'I'm leaving for good. I wish to hand in my resignation.'

'Request denied! You'll be teaching French as well as Latin next term.'

'But Madame Fissure teaches . . .'

'I might have to dismiss her for gross misconduct of a most lewd and debased nature. Go and see if Jones has given the Virgin Mary and Jesus a good rub down.'

'Blasphemy!'

'No, you silly woman! I'm talking about cleaning the statuettes. They were blackened by the fire.'

'Oh, I see. Yes, right away, Headmistress.'

Answering the phone as Miss Frigidus left the study, Miss Gussetpiece gasped to hear the abrupt tone of a prominent school governor. 'What's been going on, Gussetpiece?' Lord Snodgrass asked sternly.

'Er . . . going on, Lord Snodgrass?'

'I've had the Inland Revenue contact me. Put me on to the bursar!'

'Ah, the bursar, yes. He's indisposed at the moment.'

'Indisposed? Where is he? What's he doing?'

'Er . . . he left, your Lordship.'

'Left? Good grief, woman, why wasn't I told?'

'I've only just found out myself.'

'When did he leave?'

'Er . . . two months ago.'

'And you've only just found out?'

'Yes, he's the secretive type, you see. He didn't tell anyone that he was leaving.'

'Sex, Gussetpiece!'

'Oh, my goodness! Where, your Lordship?'

'At Bellend School! I've had reports of orgies! Schoolgirls having sex with nuns and priests! This is dreadful!

I'm coming over to the school to discover exactly what has been going on, Gussetpiece!'

'Oh, there's no need to . . .'

The dialling tone purring in her ear, Miss Gussetpiece replaced the receiver and sighed. Wondering when Lord Snodgrass would arrive, and how he knew about the priest, she grabbed the vodka bottle. Answering the phone again as she gulped from the bottle, she almost choked.

'Snodgrass here! Is that you, Gussetpiece?'

'Er . . . no. I'm afraid Miss Gussetpiece has passed away.'

'Passed away? What, died?'

'Yes, I'm a nurse. I was just passing through, and I noticed the headmistress on the floor – dead.'

'How did she die? I was speaking with her only minutes ago!'

'Er . . . acute malnutrition.'

'That's ridiculous! Are you sure she's dead? Have you called a doctor?'

'Yes, he's on his way. She's dead, all right! Not breathing, not moving – stone cold dead!'

'Good God! Right, I'm one of the school governors – I'll be there tomorrow morning to sort things out.'

'Right you are. Goodbye.'

'Jesus Christ! Why did I tell him that I'd died?' Miss Gussetpiece breathed, wondering what she should do when Lord Snodgrass arrived at Bellend. 'Cross that bridge when I come to it, I suppose. The important thing to do is to get absolutely pissed!' she told herself, pillaging the vodka. 'Absolutely bloody pissed!'

Chapter Thirteen

'Hurrah! The last day of school!' Candida cried as she chased down the corridor after Hilda. 'Wait for me, Hilly! I've just overheard Maxine saying that she's going to get you today! She said that, as it's the last day of term, she'd really put you through hell.'

'Oh, great! That's all I need, what with . . .'

'Where are you going?'

'I've got to see Miss Gussetpiece about . . . about something I did yesterday in Miss Blob's rooms,' Hilda replied dolefully.

'Gosh! What did you do?' Candida asked, brushing her blonde hair away from her pretty face as she tried to keep up with her friend.

'I can't tell you, Candy. I'm too ashamed to talk about it. Oh dear, Miss Blob . . . I mean Doctor Rectus has just gone into the Head's study. I'll see you later, Candy. Wish me luck.'

'Good luck, Hilly, old girl – whatever you might need it for.'

Tentatively entering the study, Hilda stood next to Doctor Anusis Rectus, wondering why Miss Gussetpiece hadn't twigged Miss Blob's perverted alter ego. Frowning at the doctor, the headmistress rose from her chair and walked to the window. Then, her hands on her ample hips, she turned on her heels to confront the guilty pair.

'Tell me about this new treatment,' she challenged the doctor, staring into his fathomless brown eyes.

'It's . . . er . . . as I said yesterday, Headmistress, it's not available on the NHS.'

'Good grief, I'm not surprised!'

'Yes, quite. The idea is . . .'

'The idea is grossly indecent, to say the least!'

'No, no! You see . . . Ah, yes! Sperm contains testosterone which helps to relieve anal inflammation. Sperm . . .'

'Don't use such filthy words in my study!'

'Sperm isn't a filthy word, Headmistress.'

'Yes, it is! Is that what you had, Hilda, anal inflammation?'

'Er . . . yes, yes I did, Miss Gussetpiece,' Hilda stammered, confused as to whether or not to expose Miss Blob.

'Doctor Rectus, I find the whole thing most disturbing. Anal sex . . . I'm sorry I have to use such vile words in front of you, Hilda, but . . . anal sex is illegal and . . .'

'I don't look upon administration of the cure as having anal sex, Headmistress,' the doctor broke in. 'The act is a simple and most effective cure for a medical condition.'

'What would the girl's father say if he came to you, a doctor, complaining of anal inflammation – and you suggested buggery as a cure? Sorry, Hilda, another vulgar but necessary word, I'm afraid.'

'Christ, I don't do it to men!' the doctor gasped.

'Why not? Surely, if it's an effective cure, you'd help men as well as young girls?'

'Perish the thought! I mean . . . you see . . . er . . . It only cures young girls.'

'Why does it only cure young girls?' Miss Gussetpiece asked agitatedly. 'I don't see the reasoning, the logic.'

'Well, they're hot and tight . . . No, no they're not. Er . . . yes, that's it! It's because they have different hormones. Women have different hormones.'

'What did you think of this most unorthodox remedy, Hilda?'

'It worked, Miss Gussetpiece. I'm fine now.'

'What were the symptoms?'

'A pain. Discomfort.'

'And it's completely gone?'

'Yes, completely.'

'All right, girl, you may go,' Miss Gussetpiece smiled. Waiting until Hilda had left the study, she turned to the doctor. 'Doctor Rectus, I've been having some anal discomfort of late. Would you be good enough to administer me your unusual remedy?'

'Jesus bloody . . . er . . .'

'Don't swear! Is there a problem?'

'Well, no . . . er . . .'

'I'm a woman with female hormones so your cure would be effective, would it not?'

'Yes, I suppose so. All right, I'll do it. This evening, I'll be visiting my sister in her rooms so . . .'

'Good! I'll be there at eight. Thank you, doctor.'

'Thank *you*, Headmistress. For nothing,' the doctor muttered under his breath.

'What did you say?'

'I said, until this evening.'

'Oh, yes – until this evening.'

Wandering down the corridor, Hilda prayed that she'd get through the last day of term without running into Maxine

Mayhem and her gang. *I hope I never see the wicked girl again!* she thought as she slipped into the laundry room. She knew that she couldn't spend the rest of the day in hiding, but the more she restricted her movements, the less likely she was to bump into the beastly Bellend Rebels.

Sitting on a bench by the washing machines, Hilda looked up as Doctor Rectus entered the room. 'Ah, Hilda, I thought I saw you sneak in here,' he smirked, a wicked glint in his eyes. The girl knew what was coming next as the doctor gazed hungrily at her shapely thighs. 'I'd like you to come to my rooms, please.'

'But . . . but, Miss Blob . . .'

'Now then, Hilda! We have a deal, remember? I had quite a job convincing the headmistress that you were innocent of the charges brought against you. I had to lie, Hilda, and lying isn't in my nature. Masturbating . . . masquerading, perhaps, but not lying.'

'Masquerading? Is that what you call . . .'

'I'll see you in my rooms in five minutes, Hilda! Be there, or else!'

Sighing as the geography mistress strode off, Hilda decided that there was no better hiding place than Miss Blob's rooms. She'd be far better off committing vile sexual acts with Miss Blob than falling into Maxine's hands. Checking to see if the coast was clear, she dashed down the corridor to the teacher's rooms and closed the door behind her. *So far, so good!* she thought, navigating the passage and entering the lounge.

'Oh, Miss Blob!' Hilda cried in horror, discovering the man standing naked beside a large table, his penis erect, his heavy balls rolling.

'Ah, Hilda, my little beauty. Remove all your clothes and then come over here,' he smiled as the girl pulled her gymslip over her head. 'I'm a bottom man, Hilda. Some men are into legs, others are into tits or cunts, but my particular interest is girls' bottoms. There are nipple men, cunt men, feet men – and I'm a bottom man. I like spanking young girls' bottoms, kissing them, nibbling their buttocks, fingering their tight arseholes, licking them – fucking them. Did you enjoy me fucking your bottom yesterday?'

'Well, I . . . I don't . . .' Hilda stammered as she slipped her blouse off, revealing her tight bra, her smooth stomach, her bulging panties.

'You either liked it or you didn't.'

'Yes, I suppose I did.'

'Good, then you shall enjoy it again.'

'I'd rather . . .'

'You'll love me spunking up your bottom, Hilda. Because Miss Gussetpiece interrupted us yesterday, I didn't get the chance to come up your bum, to shoot my sperm deep into your tight arsehole. Do you like me talking dirty, Hilda?'

'No, I don't.'

'Good, then I shall talk in an absolutely disgusting and filthy manner. Now, bring your delicious cunt over here and stand by the table. That's it, bend over and stretch your arms across the table. I want to see your arse cheeks, your beautiful bottom-hole, your swollen cunt lips.'

Meekly complying, Hilda stood with her feet apart. Leaning over, squashing her firm breasts against the polished table top, she spread her arms. As Miss Blob cuffed her ankles to the table legs, the girl became fearful. 'What are you going to do to me?' she asked shakily.

'Fuck your bottom, as I told you. Fuck your bum and spunk up your tight arse.'

'But there's no need to . . .'

'And then I'm going to give you a little light caning, Hilda. You'll enjoy the cane. It'll bring colour to your cheeks!' the sex-fiend laughed.

'No, please don't cane me!' Hilda cried as Miss Blob bound her wrists with rope, pulling her hands to the far corners of the table and tying the rope to the legs.

'A *light* caning, Hilda – nothing severe, I promise you.'

'But . . .'

'There are no "buts", Hilda! Schoolgirls like you should be caned regularly. That's what their bottoms are for – for caning. And for fucking!'

Moving behind the deliciously spreadeagled blonde, Miss Blob parted his prisoner's buttocks. Kneeling and examining the tightly-closed brown entrance to her anal sheath, licking the sensitive tissue, the depraved teacher splayed the girl's buttocks further. 'Mmm, you taste nice!' he breathed, nibbling her tensed bottom-orbs, licking the full length of her dank dividing crease. 'I think I'll cane you *before* I fuck you, just to warm you up. Do you prefer a thin bamboo cane, or this?' he asked, holding up a wooden paddle as he moved around the table. 'The cane is sharper, stinging – whereas the paddle covers a far greater area and is less . . .'

'I don't want either!' Hilda protested, eyeing the huge, flat paddle.

'The paddle it is, then!' Miss Blob grinned, moving behind her young prisoner again. 'What a beautiful bottom you have! I'm going to enjoy this!'

Grimacing, tensing her buttocks, Hilda waited anxiously for the first slap of the wooden paddle – praying for the day to end, for her parents to arrive and take her home. 'Argh!' she cried as the paddle slapped her right buttock, reddening her taut flesh. 'Ouch!' she screamed as her left buttock received a stinging smack. Thrashing each buttock in turn, causing the girl to cry out and beg for mercy, the sadist lost himself in his spiralling sexual arousal, beating the girl's crimson bottom cheeks progressively harder with each lashing.

Her clitoris responding as her own carnal pleasure heightened, Hilda sensed her vaginal muscles tightening, yearning to grip on a throbbing, pistoning penis. The merciless thrashing bringing her ever closer to her climax, she closed her eyes, conjuring images of the three penises that had driven in and out of her hot orifices in the clearing, pumped her trembling body full of sperm. She had changed, she knew, as her clitoris throbbed, sending tingles of crude sex through her pelvis. Far removed from the innocent young girl she had been at the beginning of term, she now craved sex with both male and female partners. Her enforced sexual awakening had left her hungry – hungry for sex and orgasm.

His penis standing to attention, yearning for the heat of the girl's bowels, Miss Blob finally discarded the paddle and grabbed a tube of cooling cream. 'Is that nice?' he asked huskily, massaging the cream between the girl's engorged vaginal lips.

'My . . . my clitty!' Hilda gasped.

'You want me to rub the cream into your clitty, do you?'

'Yes, yes! I . . . I'm going to have a goodie!'

Lovingly massaging Hilda's solid sex-budlette, Miss Blob masturbated the girl to her climax. Her girl-juice flowing from her inner nectaries, blending with the cooling cream, Hilda's body shook violently as her orgasm peaked. 'Oh, oh, that's nice!' she gasped, her fingernails scratching the table-top. 'Ah, yes, yes! Don't stop!' Her multiple orgasm seemingly lifting her from her shuddering body, she sensed her nipples stiffening against the table-top, enhancing the incredible pleasure emanating from her pulsating clitoris.

As Hilda relaxed in the aftermath of her incredible climax, Miss Blob filled the palm of his hand with cream. Smearing the girl's burning buttocks, wiping a good quantity of the cooling cream around her tight brown hole, he took his penis in his hand. Grinning as he pressed his knob against the sensitive brown tissue, he gasped. 'Ah, it's slipping in so easily! Ah, yes! God, you're a tight young schoolgirlie!'

As the solid shaft sank further into Hilda's bottom-hole, opening her anal tube, filling her pelvic cavity, she recalled again the three studs she'd enjoyed in the clearing. This was nothing in comparison, she decided as Miss Blob began his fucking rhythm. But it was beautiful, all the same!

The male shaft gliding in and out of her tightening rectal sheath as she clung to the table, Hilda knew that she was going to miss the sex at Bellend. Recalling licking Candida's pussy-crack, taking the young girl to orgasm, she vowed to stay close to her friend. She'd keep in intimate contact with Patsy, too – suck on her beautiful nipples, lick her pinken crack, drink her girl-come, bring her goodies.

'Coming!' Miss Blob cried urgently, breaking the girl's reverie. 'Coming up your arse!' His sperm bubbling from his throbbing glans, lubricating the illicit coupling, he grabbed Hilda's hips and drove his cockhead deep into her anal tube with a vengeance. Gasping as her body rocked with the rectal pummelling, Hilda felt her clitoris throb, yearning for a massaging fingertip – a wet, caressing tongue. 'God, your arse is so tight!' the bugger gasped, spurting the last of his orgasmic cream into the girl's bowels. 'How I love fucking your tight arse!'

The solid penis finally withdrawing from her inflamed anal canal, Hilda lay panting across the table, her body trembling, her clitoris throbbing, close to orgasm. What sexual delight would she have to endure next? she wondered, hearing the man moving about behind her. Her buttocks suddenly yanked apart, she gasped as the maniac presented the rounded end of a candle to her chestnut portal. 'You'll like this!' he chuckled, twisting and pushing the candle, gently sinking the waxen shaft into the girl's sperm-filled anal sheath. Further the candle drove into her quivering young body, bringing her delightful sensations of crude sex. 'There, all the way in!' Miss Blob cried triumphantly. 'What a beautiful sight! You should see your brown ring stretched around the candle!'

Taking a second, larger candle, the beast parted Hilda's drenched vaginal lips, pushing the huge wax shaft deep into the girl's cunny hole – stretching her almost to capacity. 'You do look nice with two candles stuffed up your holes!' he chuckled. 'And now I'm going to push my cock up your cunt, too! Do you reckon I'll be able to get it in?'

'No!' Hilda protested. 'Please, you'll split me open!'

'No, you'll be all right. Hold on, here we go!'

Clinging to the table, Hilda grimaced as the solid penis slipped alongside the candle, opening her cunt, filling her pelvic cavity to capacity. 'Ah!' the pothole-plunderer gasped. 'Yes, yes, it's in! And now I'll fuck your tight cunt, Hilda! Sperm up your hot girlie cunt!'

'Please, take it out!' Hilda begged. 'I . . . I can't take it! I'm going to . . .'

'You *have* taken it! Your holes are stretched to the limit with my cock and the candles! What's it like?'

'Ah! Oh, it's . . .'

Grabbing the end of the candle nestling between Hilda's burning buttocks, the demented teacher began his thrusting, driving his penis deep into the girl's distended vagina, thrusting the candle into her hot bowels, causing her to tremble, whimper in her enforced double-fucking. 'Golly, my mini!' Hilda gasped as her clitoris swelled and throbbed. 'Rub me, rub my clitty!'

Reaching beneath the girl, Miss Blob managed to locate her pulsating clitoris. Massaging the throbbing budlette, he continued his vaginal fucking, his anal shafting, taking the girl to her shuddering climax as he pumped out his sperm, lubricating his pistoning glans. 'A goodie!' Hilda shrieked, her long blonde hair dishevelled, matted with the perspiration of sex.

'The cane!' the teacher chuckled as he jetted the last of his sperm into the girl's tight cuntal sheath. 'I'll cane you next! Thrash your tight bum-cheeks until you scream for mercy!'

'No, please!'

'Yes! Ah, God! Feel my spunk, Hilda! Feel it spurting up your tight cunt!'

'Miss Gussetpiece, there's someone to see you,' Miss Frigidus announced as she tiptoed into the study, followed by Lord Snodgrass.

'Ah . . . er . . . Good morning, I'm the headmistress's sister,' Miss Gussetpiece smiled, shaking the ageing man's hand.

'By Jove! Her sister? I didn't know she had a sister! You're amazingly like her! My name's Snodgrass, by the way – I'm on the board of governors. I'm awfully sorry to hear of Miss Gussetpiece's untimely demise. A damn' rough time for you, what?'

'Yes, it was so sudden. Er . . . all right, Miss Frigidus, you may go.'

'Yes, Headmistress,' Miss Frigidus obliged, frowning as she left the study and closed the door.

'Why did she call you headmistress?' Lord Snodgrass enquired.

'Because . . . er . . . we're identical twins. She's mixing us up, I would imagine.'

'I say! Mixing you up with a dead woman?'

'She's distressed by the loss of my sister, mentally confused. It stands to reason. Actually, I've taken the liberty of replacing my sister, on a temporary basis. I'm acting headmistress.'

'That's jolly good of you. Have you had experience?'

'Oh, yes! It was bloody marvellous with the priest before the bast— . . . er . . . I was headmistress of a Swiss finishing school for fifteen years. I'm presently looking for a similar permanent position in England.'

'Are you? By gad, what a coincidence! Well, if you'll stay on as acting headmistress, I'm sure the board of governors would be delighted to employ you on a permanent basis. We'll need references, of course. Character references and what have you. Being an identical twin, there'll be . . .'

'Wait a minute!' Miss Gussetpiece breathed in a flash of inspiration. 'Identical triplets? Two doctors and Miss Blob . . .'

'I'm sorry, I'm not with you,' Lord Snodgrass frowned, scratching his balding head.

'No, and I won't be with *you* for a while! Excuse me!'

'But . . .'

Striding down the corridor, Miss Gussetpiece used her skeleton key to enter Miss Blob's rooms. Bursting into the lounge, she stood flabbergasted, staring in disbelief at Hilda Hillock's crimson buttocks, a massive candle emerging from her stretched bottom-hole. Dropping the cane, his penis solid, pointing skyward, Miss Blob's face flushed as Miss Gussetpiece moved towards him.

'Miss Blob!' the Head yelled, eyeing his stallion-like penis, his wet, purple knob.

'No, I'm Doctor Rectus!'

'The most vile, unholy trinity! Doctor Anusis Rectus, Doctor Uterine Pouch, and you, Miss Blob, are all one and the same!'

'No, I swear, Headmistress!'

'You'll do nothing of the sort! There's been enough bad language in this school of late! Release the girl this instant! Pack your things – you're dismissed from your post as geography mistress at Bellend!'

'But . . .'

'Release the girl this instant! I have never known such rampant debauchery, such indecent behaviour, such an immoral act!'

Pulling the candles from Hilda's inflamed sex holes, Miss Blob freed the girl, helping her to her feet as Miss Gussetpiece looked on in anger. There was no way he'd change the Head's mind, he knew – his time at Bellend was over. Slipping his trousers on as Hilda dressed, Miss Blob turned to the headmistress.

'I . . . I'm sorry about all this,' he said, offering a faint smile. 'I can't help myself.'

'And I'm sorry too, Miss Blob! You were a good teacher, one of the best. Hilda, go to my study and wait for me. I have to talk to Miss Blob.'

'Yes, Miss Gussetpiece,' Hilda replied sheepishly as she finished dressing and scurried out of the room.

'Right!' Miss Gussetpiece bellowed as Hilda closed the door. 'I don't have the time to discuss your disgusting perversity now because Lord Snodgrass is waiting in my study. It's a long story, but I've told him that I'm my sister.'

'You're your sister?'

'Yes, I told him that the headmistress has died. I can't explain now, there's no time. Put your women's clothes on and come to my study as soon as you can. Appear distressed by the loss of the headmistress and . . .'

'But you've just sacked me!'

'I might change my mind – if you come to my study and tell Snodgrass that you were there when I died . . . when my sister died.'

'All right, but only if you increase my salary.'

'Stone the crows! I haven't decided whether you're staying on at Bellend yet! Don't push your luck, woman! I mean, man!'

'Sorry.'

'You will be! Hurry up, Snodgrass has been waiting long enough as it is! You are a sad pervert, Miss Blob, you really are! A complete and utter depraved sexual deviant!'

'Yes, Headmistress.'

'We'll have a long talk about your deep-seated sexual problems when Snodgrass has gone. Now, hurry up!'

'Might we also have a long talk about the one hundred thousand pounds Sir Phillip Mayhem gave you?'

'Er . . . I . . .'

'Going back to my salary, I think . . .'

'We'll discuss this later!' Miss Gussetpiece snapped, wondering how the dubious woman knew about the money as she strode out of the room.

Entering her study, Miss Gussetpiece frowned at Hilda. 'Where's the man?' she asked.

'The man?' Hilda echoed, her blue eyes frowning.

'Don't tell me you don't know what a man is! Jesus, you've had enough sexual experience with . . . There was a man in here, Hilda – Lord Snodgrass.'

'There was no man here when I came in.'

'Damn and blast it! He must have gone! Hilda, I want to know what you were doing with those candles pushed up your . . .'

'Miss Blob made me do it! I'm young and impressionable, Miss Gussetpiece. I'm easily led, easily influenced and . . .'

'Don't talk rot, girl! You're eighteen, you have free will! Young and impressionable, my fanny! I mean . . .'

'Will you expel me, Headmistress?'

'I don't know, Hilda. Your disgusting behaviour with Miss Blob leaves me speechless! What sort of girl are you?'

'I don't know, Headmistress.'

'Well, find out! Write me an essay on the sort of girl you think you are. Go and do it now and bring it directly to me!'

'Yes, Headmistress.'

Pouring herself a large gin, Miss Gussetpiece gazed

Girl School

out of the window and sighed, wondering where she'd gone wrong, why the school was rife with sexual perverts. Snodgrass would be back, she knew. But she'd not be blamed for cooking the books – not as long as she could convince people that she was the Head's sister.

'A funeral,' Miss Gussetpiece breathed thoughtfully. 'Yes, I'll arrange a quiet funeral.'

'A funeral?' Miss Frigidus echoed as she peeked her head round the door.

'Ah, Miss Frigidus. You'll be teaching French as well as Latin next term. I've decided that I will have to dismiss Madame Fissure.'

'Oh, dear. I really wanted to leave Bellend and . . .'

'Don't talk nonsense! Of course you don't want to leave Bellend! By the way, I'm the headmistress's sister.'

'How can you be your own sister, Miss Gussetpiece? Are you your mother, too?'

'My mother? What *are* you talking about, you silly woman?'

'I'm not sure, Headmistress. How can you be your own sister?'

'My sister's dead. I'm arranging a quiet funeral.'

'Oh, I see! For a moment, I thought you meant that *you* were your sister.'

'Miss Gussetpiece, the headmistress of Bellend is dead.'

'But you're here, Miss Gussetpiece – alive and kicking!'

'No, I'm not! I'm her sister! I'm taking over as headmistress.'

'But you *are* the headmistress! You've been the head— . . .'

'Good grief, Miss Frigidus! Look, just try and accept

that I'm the Head's sister. You can carry on calling me Miss Gussetpiece, because that's my name.'

'I know it's your name, Miss Gussetpiece!'

'God, give me strength! What on earth is the matter with your brain? Pass me the vodka, will you?'

'I'm sorry, but I'm terribly confused,' Miss Frigidus sighed as she grabbed the bottle and passed it to the headmistress. 'I'm not used to all this confusion and having to harbour dark secrets.'

'Dark secrets? What have you done now? What dreadful things have you been up to now?'

'I've fallen in love,' Miss Frigidus whispered, taking a handkerchief from her cardigan sleeve and blowing her nose.

'Good grief! In love? Who with?'

'With Véronique. We're running away together.'

'Running away? You'll do no such thing! She's only a young girl, it's indecent!'

'She's eighteen, Headmistress.'

'I don't care *how* old she is, you're not running away with her!'

'But I'm old enough to do . . .'

'You'll do as I say! Latin mistresses don't run off with pupils! And they certainly don't fall in love with them!'

'But I *have* fallen in love! It was when Véronique was shaving me that I . . .'

'Shaving you?'

'Er . . .'

'*Where* did she shave you?'

'In my rooms, Headmistress.'

'Where on your *body*?'

'She shaved my . . . down there, between my legs.'

'Miss Frigidus! I . . . I really don't know what to say

about your debauched behaviour! Give me a cigarette! You'll fall out of love this instant, do you hear?'

'I can't do that, Headmistress,' the timid woman quavered, passing her a roll-up. 'You see, I'm deeply in love.'

'You'll be deeply in the shit in a minute!'

'Oh, Headmistress! Goodness me, what awful language!'

'You'll hear worse than that unless you . . . Shaving, indeed! You'll grow your pubic hair and never shave again, and that's an order!' Miss Gussetpiece bellowed, lighting the cigarette and inhaling the befuddling smoke. 'Ah, that's better! Now, let's have no more of this "love" nonsense. What about the priest? I thought you'd found heaven with him?'

'I still go to him on the odd occasion. Even though I'm in love, I still have to visit heaven. He says that it's God's wish.'

'What is?'

'My shaving – it's God's wish.'

'God's wish? You are a silly, gullible woman, you really are! You'll keep away from the woods!'

'But I have to go there to get my supply of herbal cigarettes.'

'These cigarettes *are* rather good, I must say. All right, you may visit the woods to collect the cigarettes, but I don't want you . . . Ah, Madame Fissure!' Miss Gussetpiece growled as the French mistress knocked on the door and entered the study.

'Headmistress, I was wondering . . .' Madame Fissure began, clutching a large brown envelope.

'You're dismissed! Sacked! Fired! You've got the big E!'

'The big *con*? The big cunt? Dan said I had the tightest cunt in Brest!'

'Not the big C, you silly woman, the big E! For your debased and most vile behaviour you are dismissed from employment, Madame Fissure!'

'Oh, dear! Might I have a word in private, Miss Gussetpiece?'

'All right. Miss Frigidus, will you leave us?'

'Oh, yes, of course, Headmistress.'

Miss Frigidus closing the door behind her, Miss Gussetpiece drew hard on her cigarette, gazing into Madame Fissure's dark eyes as she inhaled the intoxicating smoke. *Should* she dismiss the woman? she wondered. After all, the French mistress wasn't the only one who'd been indulging in rampant sex sessions. Even the headmistress had had her share of sex with the priest in the woods!

'Madame Fissure, I might change my mind and allow you to stay on at Bellend,' Miss Gussetpiece began, swigging from the vodka bottle. 'You've been teaching German here for what, five years?'

'French for ten years, Headmistress.'

'Ah, yes, of course.'

'Headmistress, I wanted to talk to you about some photographs . . .'

'They're in safe keeping, Madame Fissure. The vile, disgusting, perverted pictures of you are . . .'

'No, not the ones of me. I . . . I found these.'

Pulling several photographs from the envelope, Madame Fissure spread them out on the mahogany desk. Her eyes wide, her mouth hanging open, Miss Gussetpiece gazed in horror at a picture of Hilda Hillock with a huge penis embedded in her bottom-hole and another massive male organ buried deep within her vaginal sheath. Looking at another picture of Hilda sucking on an erect penis, sperm dribbling down her chin, the headmistress gasped.

'Where on earth did you find this most sordid and disgusting pornography?' she asked Madame Fissure.

'Beneath Hilda's pillow, Headmistress. Maxine Mayhem tipped me off. I know I can't speak, what with the pictures you have of me, but . . . Well, I thought I ought to show you.'

'Yes, quite right! These are absolutely . . . I really can't think what's got into Hilda Hillock of late. She's become a raving nymphomaniac! What with the pictures of you, and now these! Bellend School appears to have become the home of lewd sex sessions! Miss Frigidus has fallen in love with a female frog, I've discovered that Miss Blob is a bloody . . . er . . . right, I'll have this out with Hilda later.'

'So I'm staying on at Bellend, Headmistress?'

'Yes, yes, of course you are. It would seem that you're not alone when it comes to committing indecent acts of sexual debauchery, Madame Fissure. The place is rife with filthy perverts!'

'Yes, Headmistress, it does seem to be. I'll be going, then.'

'Yes, all right.'

Reclining in her chair and swigging from the vodka bottle as the French mistress retreated, Miss Gussetpiece sighed. 'Where the hell have I gone wrong?' she asked herself as she gulped the vodka. 'Ah, Jones, I've been meaning to have a word with you!' she boomed as Johnson popped his head round the door. 'Come in, man – come in!'

'Yes, Miss Gussetpiece.'

'I'm going to ask you a question, an embarrassing question. But you must answer me truthfully.'

'Whatever you say, Headmistress.'

'Do you have a mole near the base of your penis?'

'Headmistress! I . . .'

'Tell me the truth, man!'

'I don't know! I've never looked!'

'Then look now. I'll turn my back.'

'I'd rather not, Miss Gussetpiece. If it's all the same to you . . .'

'It's not all the same to me! Have a look, man!' the inebriated woman ordered, lurching to the window and gazing out across the grounds.

Tugging his zip down, Johnson pretended to examine his penis. Realizing the implication of the question, he didn't intend giving himself away by revealing that he did indeed sport a mole at the root of his penis. 'Not a mole in sight, Headmistress,' he pronounced as, concealing a grin, he zipped his jeans up.

'Oh!' Miss Gussetpiece sighed disappointedly. 'In that case, you may go. I wonder whether it was the gardener who . . .'

'Excuse me, Miss Gussetpiece,' Miss Blob interrupted.

'Yes, what is it?' the Head asked as Johnson left the room.

'I've come to see you about a strange phenomenon. There's been a supernatural happening in the basement.'

'A supernatural happening?'

'A ghost, Miss Gussetpiece.'

'What are you talking about, man? I mean, woman.'

'I went down to the basement to have a quick . . . There was a naked woman drifting across the floor. She disappeared behind some boxes, and I couldn't find her. She was an apparition.'

'Rubbish! There are no such things as ghosts!'

'The basement was cold, freezing – and there was an eerie light and a strange smell in the air. There were noises, too. Ghostly noises – whimpering, moaning, wailing noises.'

'Stone the crows, whatever next? I'd better go and investigate. There's probably a simple explanation.'

'Shall I come with you?'

'No, I'll go alone. Get back to whatever it is you're supposed to be doing.'

'Yes, Headmistress. I'll return to my rooms and continue with my packing. There's so much to do on the last day of term.'

'Indeed there is! All I need are ghosts haunting the school! It's probably the girls having an end of term wank . . . prank.'

'Yes, I hope so.'

Gingerly opening the basement door, Miss Gussetpiece switched the light on and descended the steps. 'Ghosts, I ask you!' she mumbled as she moved behind a pile of boxes. Peering into a dark corner, she gasped as the light went out. 'Who's there?' she called, groping her way around the boxes. 'Switch the light on this instant!'

'Headmistress!' an eerie voice echoed around the basement. 'Headmistress!'

'Jesus bloody Christ! Who . . . who is it?' Miss Gussetpiece asked shakily.

'I am the ghost of Bellend. You will report to Miss Blob's rooms and beg for your punishment!'

'Punishment? Who are you? What's that strange smell? If that's you, Jones . . .'

'You will beg Miss Blob to punish you for your wickedness!'

'Wickedness? But I . . . What's that blue light?'

'You have taken one hundred thousand pounds. The money was for the school, and you have taken it. You shall be punished!'

'Please, I don't want to be punished!'

'Then I shall forever haunt you! I am Miss Thrashings, the original headmistress of Bellend.'

'Oh, my goodness! I've heard the stories about you! What . . . what sort of punishment will I have to . . .'

'The cane!'

'Jesus, the stories *are* true!'

'Yes, they are. Beg Miss Blob for your penalty, or I shall forever haunt you – and let it be known that you took the money!'

The light coming on, Miss Gussetpiece looked around the basement. Searching behind boxes, in cupboards, she could find no evidence of trickery. 'Goodness me!' she breathed as she climbed the steps, her hands trembling, her face pale, her heart racing. 'Miss Blob's rooms . . . Yes, I'd better go to Miss Blob. Bloody hell, I've had a visitation from Miss Thrashings!'

Knocking on the door, Miss Gussetpiece tried to compose herself as she waited for Miss Blob to answer. The eerie light, the strange smell, the uncanny voice . . . *Goodness me, I've had a ghostly visitation!* she thought again as Miss Blob opened the door and bid her enter.

'Did you see the ghost?' Miss Blob asked.

'No, but I heard her! I . . . I wonder, Miss Blob, whether you'd . . . No, this is ridiculous! Punishment, indeed!'

'Punishment? What were you going to ask me?'

Girl School

'Nothing. What was that?'

'What, Headmistress?'

'Listen, there's a voice!'

Her mouth hanging open, Miss Gussetpiece grabbed the geography mistress's arm as the wailing grew louder.

'I shall forever haunt you!'

'Did you hear that, Miss Blob?'

'No, I heard nothing.'

'Forever haunt you!'

'Goodness me! What am I to do? Miss Blob, do you have a cane handy?'

'A cane? Well, yes, as it happens, I have.'

'You must cane me! Please, cane me for my sins!'

'Cane you for your sins? Are you feeling all right, Miss Gussetpiece?'

'No, I'm not! You must cane me, I beg you!'

'Well, if you insist, Headmistress,' Miss Blob replied, concealing a grin. 'Lean over the table and bare your buttocks, and I'll cane you for your sins.'

Hoisting her skirt up and tugging her bloomers down to her knees, the headmistress leaned over the table, exposing her fleshy buttocks in readiness for the thrashing. *I'll take my punishment*, she thought apprehensively as Miss Blob moved behind her, flexing the thin bamboo cane. *But I'm keeping the money!*

'Are you sure that you want me to do this, Miss Gussetpiece?'

'Yes, Miss Blob – positive!'

'It's somewhat unusual for a headmistress to receive the cane!'

'That's as may be, but I have good reason. You may begin the thrashing, Miss Blob. Only half a dozen strokes, mind. Six of the best, and no more.'

Grinning, Miss Blob gazed at the Head's full buttocks, her mature, pouting vaginal lips nestling beneath her deep bottom-crease. His penis stiffening, tenting his skirt, he raised the cane above his head and brought it down as hard as he could. 'Argh!' the headmistress cried as the thin bamboo struck her tensed buttocks. 'Carry on, Miss Blob!'

Bringing the cane down again, leaving a thin pink stripe across the woman's rippling flesh, the sadist stifled a laugh. His ghost scam had worked perfectly, he reflected. Since the headmistress had discovered his secret, his transvestism, he'd longed to thrash her, to bare her bountiful buttocks and cane her wobbling bottom-orbs. Rigging up a blue light, spraying the air with perfume and talking through a hidden loudspeaker, he'd scared the life out of the poor woman. But he hadn't finished yet – the tape recorder concealed behind the sofa was set to make the next ghostly announcement.

Bringing the cane down again, lashing the Head's twitching buttocks, Miss Blob continued the thrashing. 'Number six!' he finally cried, landing the cane on the hillocks of swollen, reddening flesh for the last time. 'There, six of the best!'

'One more, I think!' Miss Gussetpiece quavered. 'Or two, just to be on the safe side.'

'Whatever you say,' Miss Blob grinned, flogging the woman again. 'Now this is the last one!' he said, landing the cane with such force that it broke in two.

'Oh, oh!' Miss Gussetpiece cried. 'That was quite . . . er . . . quite an experience! I wouldn't mind having another six.'

'The cane's broken, but . . .'

'Not to worry, Miss Blob. We must get a supply of

canes for future spanking sessions . . . er . . . no, I don't mean spanking sessions.'

As the headmistress stood and pulled her bloomers up, the tape recorder burst into life. 'You will be taken from behind to complete your punishment!' the eerie voice decreed.

'Jesus! Did you hear that, Miss Blob?' Miss Gussetpiece asked fearfully.

'Hear what?'

'A ghostly voice!'

'You will bare your bottom and be taken from behind!'

'Bloody hell! Quickly, take me from behind!'

'But, Headmistress!'

'Just do it!'

Tugging her bloomers down again, the headmistress kicked the garment aside and leaned over the table with her feet wide apart. Moving behind the terrified woman, Miss Blob lifted his skirt and grabbed his solid penis. Grinning, pressing his bulbous knob between the woman's swollen vaginal lips, he drove his shaft deep into her hot cunny hole. Grabbing her hips he began his thrusting into her vagina, jolting the woman's body, causing her to gasp and pant.

'My bottom!' she cried. 'You must do it up my bottom!'

'In a minute!' the pistoning pervert gasped, driving his rod deep into her trembling body.

'No, you must do it now! You must save me from a life of perpetual hauntings by taking me anally from behind!'

'All right, all right!' the beskirted man acquiesced, slipping his penis out of the frantic woman's spasming vagina.

Pressing his well-oiled purple knob against the headmistress's tight bottom-ring, he eased his plum past her sphincter muscles. His shaft gliding into her rectal sheath, he gasped as his heavy balls came to rest against her ample labia. 'God, you're hot! You're so hot and . . .'

'Jesus! And you're big!'

Making his thrusting motions, Miss Blob rammed his glans deep into the woman's bowels, heightening her arousal, stiffening her clitoris. Gasping, Miss Gussetpiece reached between her legs and massaged her stiffening sex-nodule, wetting her vaginal tube, tightening her bottom-sheath as she climbed ever closer to her sexual peak. As her climax neared, she massaged faster between her pussy lips, masturbating her pulsating clitoris to fruition in unison with Miss Blob's exploding glans.

The gushing sperm filling her bowels as she gasped and rocked her hips to meet the penile thrusts, Miss Gussetpiece shuddered in her coming. Her clitoris ballooning beneath her massaging fingertips, her vagina spasming, her sphincter muscles convulsing, gripping the intruding penis, she'd reached her sexual heaven. On and on the transvestite thrust his orgasming glans into the headmistress's bottom-hole until his swinging balls had drained and he collapsed, gasping, across her back.

'That was good!' Miss Blob breathed, his penis absorbing the fiery heat of Miss Gussetpiece's bowels. 'God, that was bloody good!'

'I've been saved!' the Head cried as he slipped his veined shaft from her sperm-drenched anal canal. 'I've been saved!'

Slipping her bloomers up, concealing her swollen vaginal crack, her inflamed bottom-hole, Miss Gussetpiece thanked the geography mistress for delivering her from

Girl School

evil. 'I'm eternally grateful,' she smiled as she adjusted her clothing. Composing herself before leaving, she wondered whether to suggest that Miss Blob take her from behind on a regular basis. 'I might come to your rooms again for . . .' Changing her mind, she thanked him again and made her way to her study.

Pouring herself a large vodka as several cars pulled up outside the study window, she grinned. 'The end of the last day of term!' she sighed contentedly. Gazing out of the window as she sipped her drink, she watched the teenaged girls hugging their parents and climbing into cars. 'I've done it! I've made it! Despite the ghost of Miss Thrashings, I've made it to the end of term!'

'Goodbye, Miss Gussetpiece,' Hilda smiled as she stood bashfully in the doorway.

'Goodbye, Hilda, and good luck,' the headmistress beamed. 'I'd better go and show my face, I suppose. Right, off you go, Hilda! I'll say nothing about you in the woods with three big . . . with the three young men.'

'Oh!' Hilda gasped. 'You know about that?'

'Yes, I do! I have never seen such disgusting photographs in my life! Well, that's not true, actually. School's over, Hilda, so I can hardly expel you. Right, off you go – out into the big wide world.'

Outside the old school, Miss Gussetpiece waved her pupils goodbye. *Maxine, Hilda, Ginger, Kelly, Patsy, Fukui, Véronique, Candida – hopefully, I'll never see them again!* she thought as the girls climbed into their parents' cars. *They're not a bad lot, really*, she reflected. 'Yes, they bloody well are!'

Seeing the staff off, the headmistress returned to her study and sat at her desk. The chatter of young girls, the scraping of chairs across the parquet flooring, the shouting of frustrated teachers . . . All was quiet now – ghostly quiet. But after two months, the school would be full of life again. Another set of sixth-form girls would rise through the ranks and, no doubt, terrify Miss Frigidus.

'I must make the wooded area out of bounds,' she murmured pensively, recalling the priest and the sexual antics of not only the sixth-form girls but of certain members of her staff. 'Yes, out of bounds.' Finishing off the vodka, Miss Gussetpiece slumped over her desk in an alcoholic haze, and passed out.

Chapter Fourteen

Driving along the winding lane to Bellend School, Hilda wondered what changes had taken place during the years she'd spent at university and teacher training college. Parking her car, she smiled as she gazed up at the quaint Victorian building. Memories flooding back as she entered the school by the main door, the young woman lugged her cases along the familiar corridor to the Head's study.

'Miss Gussetpiece!' Hilda beamed as she breezed into the study and dumped her cases on the floor.

'Well, if it's not Candida Coombes!' Miss Gussetpiece grinned, rising from her seat and shaking the young woman's hand.

'Hilda, Miss Gussetpiece – Hilda Hillock,' Hilda corrected, shaking her head in despair as she eyed a half-bottle of Russian vodka on the desk.

'Oh yes, of course – how silly of me! Hilda Hillock.'

'It's awfully nice to see you, Miss Gussetpiece!'

'And you, Hilda – welcome back! I must also extend a most warm welcome to you as the new history mistress.'

'Er . . . I'm the new PE mistress, Miss Gussetpiece.'

'Are you? Oh yes, of course you are.'

'Thank you so much for taking me on.'

'Not at all! You have your university degrees and a glowing report from the catering . . . I mean, the teacher training college. I'm delighted to have you as a member of my staff, Hilda.'

'Thank you. I must say that it's good to be back after all these years,' Hilda smiled as the headmistress swigged from the bottle.

'Nothing's changed, Hilda. Miss Blob is still here, and so are Miss Frigidus, Miss Hairoot, Miss Shaftgrinder, Madame Fissure, Fräulein Vulvahausen, Jones the maintenance man . . . Sadly, the gardener died shortly after you left. His grandson has taken his place.'

'Died? Oh, that's sad!'

'He *was* getting on in years. God, this vodka's strong! I mean, mineral water.'

'How are the school's finances these days?'

'I had a dreadful time with the Inland Revenue, but it's all been sorted out now that they think that I'm my sister . . . Yes, well, the less said about . . . On the financial front, things have changed, Hilda – for the better, I might add.'

'Gosh! It's so good to be back, Miss Gussetpiece!'

'It's good to have you back! I'm glad you're early because, being the first day of term, we've had an influx of new girls and I need all the staff I can get to settle them into their dormitories and so on. Your rooms are ready for you so, if you'll unpack and settle in as quickly as possible, we'll get started.'

'Yes, of course, Miss Gussetpiece,' Hilda grinned as she grabbed her cases and bounced out of the study. *Gosh, she's still on the bottle!*

Marching down the corridor, Hilda couldn't stop grinning. *A dream come true!* she rejoiced as a young girl sprinted towards her. 'You there! No running!' the young woman admonished the girl.

'Yes, Miss. Sorry, Miss.'

'Are you a new girl?'

'Yes, Miss.'

'In that case, I'll let you off this time.' *Gosh, I'm a real teacher!* Hilda reflected happily as the girl mooched down the corridor. Unlocking her bedroom door, she lugged her cases inside. *A real teacher!*

Hurriedly unpacking her belongings, Hilda recalled her darker days at Bellend – the times when Maxine Mayhem and her friends had forced her to strip and commit degrading sexual acts. But, she consoled herself, there had been many good times – times spent in the woods with Candida and Patsy. And there were going to be even better times now that the Bellend Rebels had gone. Taking a deep breath, Hilda thought of the new term, the netball team, the hockey team. *We'll win match after match!* she smiled inwardly.

'Well, if it's not little Miss fucking Pillock!' a frighteningly familiar voice emanated from across the room. Turning on her heels, Hilda gazed open-mouthed at Maxine Mayhem leaning in the doorway. 'Still shave your cunt hairs, Pillock?' the young woman asked crudely.

'Maxine!' Hilda gasped. 'What are you . . .'

'I'm the English mistress. I got fed up with working as a stripper in fucking seedy bars, so I falsified some credentials and I'm now the English teacher at Bellend. I've been here for a year now. I'm aiming for the Head's job, you'll be pleased to hear.'

'But . . .'

'Ginger's working here, too. She's the history mistress.

It's going to be just like old times, isn't it? Ginger and me making your life hell and . . .'

'Things are different now, Maxine,' Hilda smiled sweetly. 'We're grown women now, so let's not act like silly schoolgirls.'

'Nothing's different as far as I'm concerned! You can finger-fuck my cunt this evening, Pillock! You can lick my cunt out and make me come! Yes, just like old times! Let the war resume! And may the Bellend Rebels win!'

'Maxine, please, I . . .' Hilda stammered as the girl walked towards her with the devil in her eyes.

'Show me your cunt, Pillock!'

'No, Maxine!'

'Show me your cunt!' Maxine hissed, taking a lighter from her breast pocket.

Shaking her head defeatedly, Hilda recalled the first day of her last term at Bellend when Maxine had threatened to set fire to her locker. This was the last thing she'd expected on her first day as a teacher! As the she-devil ignited the lighter, Hilda knew that she'd have to do as the beastly girl ordered or . . .

'Come on, Pillock! Show me your cunt or I'll . . .'

'Maxine, we're not silly schoolgirls anymore! Can't we make a fresh start?'

'I *am* making a fresh start! And I'm starting by taking a look at your cunt! These your books?' Maxine grinned, holding the lighter close to a pile of Hilda's PE text books. 'Well, what's it to be, Pillock?'

Lifting her tight, short skirt, Hilda revealed her bulging silk panties to Maxine's appreciative gaze. Pulling them down, she exposed her sparse blonde pubes, her pinken vaginal crack. 'Finger your cunt!' Maxine giggled, still holding the lighter close to Hilda's books. Slipping a finger between her pouting cunny lips, Hilda pushed it into her wet vagina. Her face flushing, her heart racing as her adversary focused on her intimacy, she extracted her finger from her tight love-duct and tugged her panties up.

'Very good!' Maxine giggled, slipping her lighter into her pocket. 'I'm pleased to see that you're going to cooperate. I wouldn't want to have to set fire to your things now, would I? I'll be seeing you later, Pillock! Oh, before I go – suck your cunt juice from your finger.'

Sucking her finger, Hilda savoured her pussy juice, wondering what life at Bellend had in store for her as Maxine swaggered from the room. Flopping onto her bed, her stomach sinking, her hands trembling, her face pale with shock, she sighed despairingly. Gulping as she realized that her dream had been shattered, she did her best to finish unpacking.

Maxine hadn't changed at all! she reflected anxiously. Her black hair was still long and dishevelled, her dark eyes still reflecting her evil thoughts. 'Of all the jolly bad luck!' Hilda sobbed, tears rolling down her cheeks as she placed her favourite teddy bear on her pillow. 'Oh well, I suppose we've got to make the jolly best of it, Ted, old boy!'

Donning her sports kit after morning assembly, Hilda sauntered across the playing field to the hockey pitch. *I'll keep out of Maxine's way*, she decided. *I'll be safe enough in my rooms at night and* . . . Hearing a scream, she stopped and turned to face the wood. *Crikey! What was that?* she wondered, walking briskly towards the trees. Tramping through the undergrowth in the direction of the clearing, she recalled her erotic times with Candida and Patsy. *We were very naughty!* she reminisced, peering through the bushes into the clearing.

Spying Maxine and Ginger, Hilda froze. Gazing at several photographs as they swigged from a vodka bottle, the terrible twosome burst out laughing. 'Look at this one of Hillock having her bum and her cunt shafted by two fucking great cocks!' Maxine giggled. 'God, those were the days!'

'I'm surprised you kept the pictures,' Ginger smiled, lighting a cigarette.

'Oh, I didn't! I found these in Knickergusset's drawer, beneath a load of old papers. She must have forgotten about them. I also found the ones we took of Madame Fissure with Dan's cock shoved up her cunt.'

'Would you believe it? Here we all are, back at Bellend, just like the old days, and we have the pictures of old Fissure – *and* Hilda bloody Hillock!'

'I know! It's incredible, isn't it? We'll use the photos, Ginger!' Maxine declared. 'We'll have copies made and blackmail Hillock and Fissure! Right, I have a class to take. I'd better be going.'

'Oh, I thought we were going to frig each other off,' Ginger complained, sitting cross-legged and pulling her red silk panties aside.

'Later, Ginger,' Maxine smiled, gazing at her friend's open vaginal crack. 'After my class, I'll lick your cunt out and bring you off.'

'Sixty-nine!' Ginger giggled.

'Yes, sixty-nine! See you later.'

Creeping away from the clearing, Hilda wandered back towards the school, her stomach churning, her face pale. The war had indeed resumed! But the odds were far worse than ever before. As the last remaining member of the Jolly Hockey Sticks Club, she was alone in the fight. Passing the new potting shed, she decided to peer inside. Apart from her rooms, she needed a retreat outside the main building, somewhere she could make a dash for should Maxine give chase. Opening the shed door, she cautiously wandered inside.

'And who might you be?' a well-spoken young man enquired.

'I'm Hilda Hillock, the new PE mistress,' Hilda smiled.

'Pleased to meet you – my name's Tod. I'm the gardener.'

'I hear the old gardener died.'

'Yes, my grandfather. He died from exposure to radioactive material, although no one has a clue as to how he was subjected to a lethal dose of radiation.'

'Oh dear, how sad!'

'Yes, it was. Knew him, did you?'

'Yes, he was the gardener when I attended Bellend as a schoolgirl.'

'Oh, I see. This your first day back, then?'

'Yes, it is,' Hilda replied a little sadly, gazing at the young man's black hair, his dark eyes, his rugged, suntanned face.

'You're a pretty little thing,' he smiled.

'Oh, thank you. I think you're rather . . .'

'Look, I'm a bit busy just now but . . .'

'Oh, I don't want to disturb your work.'

'We'll meet again, no doubt.'

'Yes, I hope so!' Hilda enthused, moving to the door. 'It's . . . it's been nice meeting you,' she smiled as she left the shed. *A nice young man*, she mused, walking across the yard to the school, her stomach somersaulting.

Things might not be so bad after all. I must get to know him.

Exploring the dormitories, Hilda reflected again on her days as a Bellend schoolgirl. 'That was my bed!' she breathed nostalgically as she entered her old dormitory. But as much as she tried to push it from her mind, the thought of Maxine Mayhem and her wicked threats marred her happiness. 'This is silly!' she spat through gritted teeth, stamping her foot. 'I'm a teacher now! I won't be intimidated by Maxine Mayhem!' Striding down the corridor to her enemy's classroom, she decided to confront her.

'Oh, Hilda!' Miss Gussetpiece called as she meandered down the corridor, leaning on the wall to support her swaying body. 'Hilda, might I have a word?'

'Yes, of course, Headmistress.'

'As you've not got a class until this afternoon, would you be so good as to man my study for a while? I have to pop out to the off-licence . . . to the village, for supplies. Would you remain in my study to answer the visitors and receive the phone? Er . . . to phone the visitors and . . .'

'Certainly, Miss Gussetpiece.'

'Good. I'll just let Maxine know that I'm going out. Oh, you don't know that she works here, do you?'

'Yes, Headmistress, I'm afraid I do!' Hilda sighed.

'Just like old times!' Miss Gussetpiece giggled in her drunken stupor as she staggered down the corridor. 'I'll see you later, Hilda!'

'Surely you're not driving your car?' Hilda called as the headmistress almost fell over.

'Not until I get in it, I'm not!'

* * *

Girl School

Sitting behind the Head's desk, Hilda grinned. 'Gosh, this is jolly exciting!' she breathed, imagining herself as headmistress. Noticing a light flashing on the telephone, she picked the receiver up and pressed the button to find herself listening to Maxine. 'So that's what we'll do, Dan. I want the Head's job, and with Hillock nosing around Knickergusset's study . . . Must go, someone's coming!'

Frowning, Hilda replaced the receiver. 'Why on earth are Johnson and Maxine . . .' Hearing footsteps in the corridor she reclined in the chair, wondering who her visitor was. 'Oh, Dan! How are you?' she smiled as Johnson entered the study.

'Hi, Hilda! I heard you were back. How are things?'

'Fine!'

'I've got to fix the light switch in here so . . .'

'Don't mind me. I'm manning the study while Miss Gussetpiece goes down to the village for supplies.'

'I'll take over for a while, if you like.'

'All right, I'll take a walk around the school. I won't be long,' Hilda smiled, wondering what Maxine's plan was.

Slipping into the study the minute Hilda had gone, Maxine grinned at Dan. 'Well, done!' she giggled, sitting at the desk as the phone rang. 'What a stroke of luck! Er . . . Good morning, Bellend School,' she replied, grabbing the receiver.

'Is that Miss Gussetpiece?' a woman asked.

'No, this is Hilda Hillock. The headmistress is out, can I help you?'

'Yes, this is Lady Tawdry-Trollops. One's daughter will arrive at Bellend this afternoon. She's been delayed at . . .'

'You mean, she's going to be late for school?'

'Yes, it can't jolly well be helped, one's afraid.'

'Well, it's not fucking good enough!'

'I *beg* your pardon?' the stunned woman gasped.

'We can't have the fucking little tart rolling in when she fucking well feels like it!'

'Good gracious! I have never . . .'

'What's she think this is, a fucking hotel? I'll have her fucking knickers ripped off and her cunt hairs shaved for this!'

Laughing uncontrollably as the shocked caller hung up, Maxine rolled off the chair, crashing to the floor, her skirt riding up her shapely thighs, her bulging panties blatantly displayed to Dan's appreciative gaze. 'Fuck me!' she gasped, climbing to her feet as the phone rang again. 'Er . . . Good morning, Bellend School,' she replied, flopping into the chair.

'Miss Gussetpiece?' a man enquired.

'No, this is Hilda Hillock. The headmistress isn't available at the moment, may I take a message?' Maxine asked, watching Dan cringe in the corner as she swigged from the vodka bottle.

'Yes, if you'd be so kind. This is Sir Rearend-Shaftings. I have a daughter, Amy, and I'd like her to attend Bellend school as from the beginning of next term.'

'Why?'

'Er . . . Because I hear that Bellend is a fine school.'

'Jesus Christ! What daft cunt told you that?'

'I'm sorry?'

'Bellend is the fucking pits, mate! I wouldn't send my daughter here. All the girls are fucking lesbians, licking each other's cunts out every night in the dorms and fingering each other's tight arseholes. And they all get fucked rotten by the university boys! They're into arse-fucking, cunt-fucking, cock-sucking . . . Oh, he's hung up!' Maxine exclaimed in mock dismay as she replaced the receiver. 'Right, I'd better bugger off! I've had my fun. See you later, Dan.'

'Yes, tonight in your rooms.'

'OK, we'll have some fun with the vibrator. I'll bring Ginger along, too.'

'Great, I'll look forward to that!'

'Shit, might as well take one more call!' Maxine breathed as the phone rang again. 'Good morning, Bellend school, can I help you?'

'Miss Gussetpiece?' a well-spoken woman asked.

'No, this is Hilda Hillock.'

'Oh, I see. I wonder whether you'd tell Miss Gussetpiece . . .'

'Shall I tell her to fuck off?' Maxine giggled.

'Oh! Oh, whatever . . .'

'Why don't you stick a cucumber up your wet cunt and fuck yourself silly?'

'Oh, my goodness!'

'You could stick it up your arse and give yourself a rear-ender and then shave your cunt hairs off and . . . Oh, now *she*'s hung up! Oh well, see you later, Dan!' Maxine grinned, banging the phone down and flouncing out of the study.

'Crikey, where's Dan got to?' Hilda exclaimed as she returned to the empty study. Flopping into the Head's chair, she sighed. 'Is there no one reliable? It's a good job Miss Gussetpiece didn't come back and find the place deserted! What a dreadful start that would have been!' Resting her elbows on the desk, she looked up and smiled sweetly as Miss Gussetpiece lurched in. 'You were quick!'

'My car wouldn't fart . . . I mean, start. It's probably just as well as I'm way over the limit and . . . Yes, well. Thank you for folding the hort . . . holding the fort. Were there any calls?'

'No, Miss Gussetpiece,' Hilda smiled as she stood and walked to the door. 'No calls or visitors. I'll leave you to it.'

'Thank you, Hilda. I'll see you at lunch, no doubt.'

Wandering into maintenance, Hilda glared at Dan. 'You deserted the Head's study, you dreadful man!' she snapped. 'It's a jolly good job she didn't come back and find . . .'

'Got you, Pillock!' Maxine grinned, leaping out from behind the door and grabbing Hilda's arm. Dashing from the corner of the room, Ginger closed and locked the door, giggling as she yanked Hilda's other arm and instructed Dan to strip their prisoner.

'No!' Hilda shrieked as Dan tore her blouse from her trembling body.

'Come on, Pillock, you know you like being stripped and fucked!' Maxine laughed as Dan wrenched the girl's bra off, exposing her ample breasts, her elongated milk-buds.

Hilda stopped struggling as her skirt was tugged down her slender legs. It was futile to fight Maxine and her friends, she knew from bitter experience. Her face flushing as her panties were unceremoniously yanked down to disclose her full vaginal lips, she gasped as Dan's finger slipped into her tight love-mouth.

'That's it, Dan!' Ginger coaxed. 'Get her cunt nice and wet, ready for your cock!'

'Let's put her on the bench!' Maxine suggested, dragging Hilda across the floor as Dan slipped his finger from the girl's tight hole. Her naked body lifted off the floor and dumped on the bench, Hilda lay shamefully naked with her three captors standing over her. Grinning as they ran their hands over her breasts, her thighs, her pussy-crack, the girls ordered Dan to climb on the bench and kneel between Hilda's thighs.

'You'll love this, Pillock!' Maxine sniggered as Dan took his position and yanked his solid penis out of his tight jeans. Lifting her head and focusing her eyes on the man's ballooning purple knob, Hilda reclined, resigning herself to the fact that her young curvaceous body was going to be fucked and sexually abused every day. Squeezing her eyes shut as Dan's huge weapon parted her pussy lips and glided into her wet vaginal sheath, she again recalled her schooldays at Bellend. *Nothing's changed*, she reflected sadly as the girls sucked on her long nipples, gently biting, teasing the brown protrusions. *Nothing will ever change at Bellend!*

Her body jolting with Dan's penile thrusts, Hilda sensed her clitoris throb, her vagina tighten, as her enforced climax neared. Gasping as Maxine and Ginger mouthed on her long milk-buds and massaged her clitoris, she cried out, her body trembling uncontrollably as her orgasm erupted. 'Oh, oh!' she gasped as her nipples were sucked into the girls' hot orifices. 'Ah, that's . . . Ah, ah!'

Dan's sperm gushing from his throbbing glans, bathing her cervix, Hilda arched her back, tossing her head from side to side as she was taken to her paradise. *This isn't so bad*, she surmised in her sexual delirium, clinging to the sides of the bench, recalling the three stallions pumping their sperm into her mouth, her tight anal tube, her wet cunt.

'God, that was good!' Dan gasped, slipping his wet penis from Hilda's inflamed cunny-hole, his sperm oozing from his knob-slit, dripping over her inflamed vaginal lips, trickling down her pink crack. 'Christ, that was fucking good!'

'We'd better get out of here!' Maxine whispered, hearing Miss Gussetpiece shrieking in the distance.

'Yeah, let's go!' Ginger rejoined, grabbing Hilda's clothes and following her friends through the door.

Her naked body still quivering, Hilda lay on the bench in the wake of her beautiful climax. Sperm oozing from her splayed, pinken inner lips and trickling down to her bottom-crease, she lifted her exhausted body and staggered onto her sagging legs. 'My clothes!' she gasped, wiping sperm from her inner thighs. 'Gosh, they've taken my clothes!'

'Hilda, where are you?' Miss Gussetpiece shrieked outside the door. 'Come here immediately!' The door bursting open, Hilda folded her arms, covering her flushed breasts, her glistening nipples. 'Hilda!' the astonished Head cried, gazing at the young woman's dripping pussy-slit. 'My God! What have you . . .'

'Miss Gussetpiece, I . . .'

'Stone the clothes . . . I mean . . . Where are your crows? And what's that running down your legs?'

'Oh, I . . .'

'You've not changed at all! And I thought . . . I put you in charge of my office for five minutes and I've had a string of complaints about your vile telephone manner! And now I find you naked in maintenance! Put your clothes on and report to my study this instant!' the woman bellowed as she slammed the door and stomped down the corridor.

Cringing in the corner, Hilda slid down the wall to the floor. 'I can hardly go to my rooms like this!' she sobbed as she buried her face between her knees. 'I wish I'd never come back to this dreadful place!' Looking up at the sound of voices outside the door, she noticed a boiler suit hanging in the far corner of the room. 'That's it!' she cried leaping to her feet and slipping into the suit.

Dashing down the corridor, Hilda almost fell into her rooms as she slammed the door behind her. 'Safe at last!' she gasped breathlessly. 'And now I shall pack my things and leave this dreadful place forever!'

'Are you all right, Headmistress?' Maxine asked as she peered round the study door and gazed at the red-faced woman.

'No, I am not all right! Come, in, Maxine – come in.'

'What is it? What's the matter?'

'It's that Hilda Hillock! Quick, pass me my heart pills, will you?'

'These?' Maxine asked, taking a small brown bottle from a shelf and unscrewing the cap.

'Yes, give me one. I feel . . . Goodness me, I feel quite overwrought!'

'Oh, I've dropped the bottle!' Maxine gasped, concealing a wicked grin as the glass shattered and the pills rolled across the floor.

'Stupid woman! God, I feel . . . I'm going out for some fresh air. Take charge here, will you?'

'Yes, of course, Miss Gussetpiece. You take your time, there's no need to hurry back.'

'Thank you, Maxine,' the headmistress smiled as she staggered into the corridor.

Installed at the Head's desk, Maxine grinned as she reclined in the chair. 'Soon, Maxine – soon this will be *your* chair!'

'Hi, Max!' Ginger smiled as she breezed into the study. 'Where's the old bag?'

'Having a heart attack, with any luck!'

'You just can't wait, can you?'

'Nope! Imagine me as the headmistress, Ginger! I've received a reply to the letter I forged from the old hag. The governors are all for me acting as temporary headmistress, should anything happen to Knickergusset. And what with the bogus letter of recommendation, I'll be in this chair as soon as she pops off!'

'Yes, but you still haven't got her signature, have you?'

'That's where you're wrong! I got her to sign it when she was half-pissed the other day. She thought she was signing for a delivery of text books, the stupid fucking cow!'

'Fuck me, you've as good as got your feet under her desk already!'

'Once I'm temporary Head, it'll just be a matter of doing a brilliant job and convincing the board of governors that I'm ideal for the post. I wonder whether Pillock's still naked in maintenance?'

'More than likely!'

'Where did you put her clothes?'

'In the bin!' Ginger laughed.

'We should take all her clothes from her rooms and burn them!'

'Yeah, that's a good idea!'

'I've got to go out for a while. Can you hang on here until I get back?' Maxine asked as she rose from the chair.

'Yeah, sure. I'll see you later, Max. I mean, Headmistress!'

'Don't speak too soon, Ginger! See you later.'

Gazing out of her bedroom window as she packed her things, Hilda frowned. 'What's Miss Gussetpiece doing?' she breathed, watching the woman disappear into the trees edging the far side of the playing field. 'And there's someone watching her from the bushes! How strange!'

Leaving her rooms, Hilda made her way across the playing field, wondering whether Miss Gussetpiece was still having lewd sex sessions in the woods with the priest. *Gosh, nothing's changed at all! Is the miraculous nun still lurking in the woods?* she wondered, recalling the divine penis.

Tramping through the wood, Hilda walked into the clearing, but there was no sign of the headmistress. 'Gosh!' she cried, noticing the woman's clothes beneath a bush. 'She must have gone off with someone to . . . I'd better get back to school.' Turning to leave the clearing, she remained rooted to the spot in shock as Miss Blob emerged from the bushes and stood menacingly before her.

Grinning perversely, the geography mistress eyed Hilda's firm breasts ballooning her tight blouse, her toned thighs, her streamlined legs. Staring at the bender's short skirt and false breasts, Hilda recalled her last day of term – the enforced, degrading sexual acts she'd had to commit with the masquerading teacher.

'I saved you, Hilda,' Miss Blob smiled treacherously.

'You'd never have got a job had you been expelled from Bellend. How about offering me a little something to show your appreciation?'

'No!' the girl returned stoutly. 'If you think I'm going to . . .'

'Hilda, Hilda! Don't tell me that you didn't enjoy our encounters just before you left school! From what I remember, you loved every minute of it.'

Recalling the pervert's solid penis buried deep within her tight bottom-hole, Hilda's stomach somersaulted. She *had* enjoyed herself, she had to admit. As she'd predicted she would before she left Bellend, she'd missed the sex. Since leaving school, Patsy had gone to work abroad and Candida had moved to Scotland to teach, leaving her alone. While the boys at university had seemed only to take an interest in the tarty young girls, the students at the teacher training college had been mainly women. Yes, in her celibate existence, she'd missed the sex. Regular masturbation, utilizing candles and deodorant bottles to appease her deprived vagina during her clitoral massaging, had quelled her sexual force. But she'd been denied a stiff penis, gushing sperm – and other girls' young bodies. Dan had roused her libido with his enforced fucking, she now reflected, her clitoris swelling, her vagina convulsing at the very memory of his sperm filling her neglected pussy.

'Well, you did, didn't you?' Miss Blob persisted, breaking Hilda's reverie.

'I did what?'

'Enjoy your encounters with me.'

'I . . . I don't . . .'

'Hilda,' the transvestite smiled, lifting his skirt and displaying his erect penis, his silky glans. 'Kneel before me and suck my knob, or I'll be forced to have a word with Miss Gussetpiece about you exposing your cunt to a young schoolgirl.'

'But I didn't!' Hilda returned angrily.

'You know that, and I know that, but . . .'

Kneeling before Miss Blob, Hilda took his formidable penis in her hand. Examining the veined shaft, the purple plum, she closed her eyes and took him into her hot mouth. Gently sucking, licking his solid cockhead, she emitted an involuntary low moan of sensual pleasure through her nose. This was the first penis she'd sucked in years, she mused. In fact, this very organ had been the last penis she'd sucked.

As Miss Blob took Hilda's head in his hands and rocked his hips, mouth-fucking the young woman, Hilda cupped his swinging balls. Her full red lips rolling over his glans, she eagerly awaited his sperm – the first taste of sperm she'd had in years. As the man towering above her gasped, the sex-starved girl rolled her tongue over his throbbing knob, desperate for his orgasmic spend to bathe her tongue, fill her cheeks. Her cunt spasming, her clitoris pulsating, she prayed that he'd fulfil her feminine desires, satisfy her insatiable craving for lust, force his penis deep into her tight cunt and fuck her.

'Coming!' the man breathed as his sperm flooded the girl's mouth. 'Ah! Ah, God, that's . . . that's . . . Ah, yes!' Savouring his salty offering, Hilda licked and mouthed on his orgasming knob, suckling like a babe at the breast, swallowing hard as his seemingly never-ending flow of male come flooded her mouth.

His balls finally drained, his cockshaft deflating, Miss Blob slipped his glans from Hilda's mouth. 'You're very good!' he grinned, looking down at the sperm trickling down her chin. 'And now I'd like you to strip off and show me how you've developed into a woman.'

Standing as Miss Blob sat on the grass, Hilda unbuttoned her blouse. Slipping the garment off and unclipping her bra, she thought of her future at Bellend – if she were to stay. The sex was good, very good, she mused. But with Maxine and Ginger? Peeling her bra cups away from her pert breasts, she sensed her stomach somersault as her nipples grew erect and her areolae darkened. Unzipping her skirt and tugging it down her long legs, she kicked it aside and stood in her red silk panties, displaying a damp patch covering the bulging crotch.

'Carry on,' Miss Blob smiled, gazing at the enveloping wetness. 'Life will be good at Bellend with you around!' he chuckled as Hilda peeled the silk away from her mound, revealing her swollen cunt lips. 'Ah, yes! Life will be very good! Now stand with your feet wide apart and allow me to drink from your beautiful cunt!' he ordered, kneeling before the girl's naked body.

Her arousal rising at an alarming rate, Hilda stood meekly before the teacher and peeled her engorging labia wide apart. Closing her eyes, tossing her head back as she sensed his hot breath teasing her glistening inner flesh, she shuddered. Her carnal desire rampant as the man's tongue swept over her solid clitoris, she decided to remain at Bellend – Miss Gussetpiece permitting!

'You have a lovely cunt, Hilda!' Miss Blob breathed. 'Look at your clitoris peeking out at me from beneath its little pink hood! Yes, life will be good!'

'Lick me!' Hilda gasped involuntarily as she tweaked her solid nipples.

'Please!' Miss Blob chuckled, pushing three fingers into her tightening pussy sheath.

Girl School

'Please lick my cunt out!'

'That's better! Just like old times, Hilda – just like old times!'

His tongue sweeping up her rubicund sex-valley, Miss Blob took Hilda ever closer to her long-overdue climax. Gasping as she pinched and twisted her sensitive nipples, Hilda began to tremble, her vaginal juices flowing, bathing the frenzied man's thrusting fingers. 'Coming!' she breathed as her cunt tightened around the pistoning fingers and her clitoris ballooned. 'Ah, ah, I'm . . . I'm coming!'

Grabbing his head to support her quivering body, she grimaced as her orgasm erupted. Shaking violently, gasping her orgasmic gasps, she rocked her hips to meet the thrusting fingers, the lapping tongue. On and on her orgasm rolled, ripping through her nervous system, gripping her very soul until she finally collapsed to the ground.

'Oh, Miss Blob! Oh, that was . . . Ah, that was exquisite!'

'There's more to come, Hilda!' Miss Blob cried, grabbing his rock-hard penis and kneeling between the girl's thighs. 'Now I'm going to fuck your hot, wet, tight cunt!'

'Oh, oh, Miss Blob!' Hilda gasped as his cockhead glided through her love tunnel and pressed against her cervix. 'Oh, you're so big!'

'The bigger the better, Hilda – the bigger the better!'

Taking the beautiful vaginal fucking, Hilda recalled the man slipping his knob deep into her bowels. Praying that he'd roll her over and repeat the beautiful act as her clitoris swelled and pulsated again, she wondered at herself, the incredible metamorphosis she'd undergone.

As her climax approached, she decided to play Maxine at her own game, order the girl to pull her panties down and expose her wet cunt, command her to finger-fuck herself. Her vaginal canal filling with her molester's sperm, her climax exploded. Her pulsating clitoris sending electrifying trembles throughout her young body, her cries filled the woods, her orgasmic sirening sending the birds flying from the trees as she sang out in her coming.

Finally collapsing over the girl's perspiring body, Miss Blob rolled to one side, his penis slipping from her sperm-drenched cuntal sheath as he hit the ground, trembling in the aftermath of his release. Sitting up, Hilda gazed at her inflamed pussy-crack, her clitoris peeping out from its hide – erect, swollen with its recent coming.

Hurriedly slipping her clothes on as Miss Blob lay back recovering, Hilda decided that he was in no fit state to take her bottom-hole. Creeping away from the clearing, she walked through the trees, wondering at her wanton act of debauchery – and where Miss Gussetpiece had got to. Slipping into the school, she made her way down the corridor, determined to stay on in her school post – despite the Bellend Rebels! Hearing giggling as she passed the laundry room, she stopped in her tracks.

Kneeling, Hilda spied through the keyhole to see two sixth-form girls, their hands down each other's knickers. 'Gosh!' she gasped, jumping up and bursting into the room. 'What on earth are you two doing?' she asked angrily as the girls withdrew their hands and stood to attention.

'Oh, Miss . . . We were just . . .'

Smiling inwardly, Hilda again recalled her days of sexual discovery, sexual exploration with her young school friends. *They're young, learning about their bodies, about sex*, she mused as she mirrored their wide eyes. 'You will both come with me to my rooms to receive your punishment!' she scolded, wondering what on earth she had in mind as she gazed longingly at the swell of their pert breasts. 'Come on, follow me!'

Ordering the girls to sit on the sofa in her lounge, Hilda paced the floor, wondering what to say. She'd missed Candida and Patsy terribly – more than she'd realized, she reflected, picturing the young sixth-formers' pussy-cracks, their erect nipples. Gazing at their girlish thighs, their coltish legs, Hilda became aware of her rising arousal. Dare she suggest that she show them how to masturbate properly? she wondered. Dare she introduce them to the delights of a cucumber?

'Girls of your age often touch each other,' she began, her heart racing, her clitoris swelling – her mind swimming with delicious thoughts of lesbian sex. 'But . . .'

'Please, Miss . . .' the pretty auburn-haired girl began.

'Miss Hillock,' Hilda smiled. 'I'm the new PE mistress.'

'Please, Miss Hillock, we were only . . .'

'Show me what you were doing, exactly.'

Their faces flushing, the pretty girls gazed at each other, obviously wondering why the PE mistress had suggested such an odd thing. 'It's all right,' Hilda smiled. 'I was your age once, and I remember experimenting with my friends. Come on, don't be shy.' Her hands trembling as the auburn-haired girl lifted her friend's gymslip up and slipped her hand down her knickers, Hilda's stomach somersaulted. Watching the girl recline as her friend massaged her clitoris, she realized that she could no longer hold back. 'No, no, not like that!' she admonished the stunned girls. 'Like this!'

Falling to her knees, Hilda tugged the girl's knickers down to her ankles, exposing her young vaginal slit. Parting the startled sixth-former's thighs and leaning forward, she licked the length of the girl's crack, tasting her cunny cream, breathing in her intoxicating girl-scent. 'Like this,' she whispered again, peeling the girl's soft labia apart and licking her glistening inner flesh.

'Are you a lesbian, Miss Hillock?' the other girl asked as she gazed in astonishment at the PE mistress licking her friend's cuntal crack.

'I'm . . .' Hilda began, catching the girl's wide eyes, wondering what answer to give her. 'Yes, I am.'

'Oh! So are we, Miss Hillock. Is that dreadfully awful of us?'

'No, it's not dreadfully awful at all! What's your name?'

'I'm Emily.'

'And I'm Nikkie!' the other girl gasped as Hilda slipped a finger into her vaginal cavern. 'Ah, that's nice, Miss Hillock!'

'Listen, girls,' Hilda smiled as she slipped a second finger into Nikkie's tight vagina. 'When I was a sixth-former, we had a club – the Jolly Hockey Sticks Club. I'm the only remaining member so . . . If you'd like to, you may join my club.'

'What's the club for, Miss Hillock?' Emily asked, gazing at her friend's crimsoning vaginal lips, taut around Hilda's fingers.

'All sorts of things. We were a group of girls who organized fêtes, among other things, to raise money for the school. We were dedicated to working hard, to achieving good results, to sports and . . . well, we were dedicated to the good of the school.'

Girl School

'Were your friends lesbians?' Emily asked.

'Yes, one or two. We used to . . .' Hilda began as someone knocked on the door.

Slipping her fingers from Nikkie's tight vagina, Hilda ordered the girl to pull her knickers up. Walking through the hall to open the door, she frowned. *I wonder who that could be?* 'Oh, Miss Blob! I'm rather busy at the moment so . . .'

'I've come to tell you that Miss Gussetpiece has passed away, Hilda,' Miss Blob imparted solemnly.

'What? Miss Gussetpiece – dead?'

'Yes, she was found naked in the woods with a candle stuck up . . . er . . . well, she'd been masturbating with a candle, from what the police said. Presumably, her heart couldn't take it.'

'Oh, dear!' Hilda gasped, recalling seeing someone watching the headmistress from the trees. 'So who will take her place?'

'I rang the governors and . . . well, Maxine Mayhem will be temporary headmistress – of all people!'

'Maxine . . . Oh, no! Anyone but her!'

'It's an odd choice, I must say. She's only been here for a year and . . . The other staff members aren't at all happy, but there's little we can do. Well, I'd better go and find Maxine and tell her the news.'

'All right, Miss Blob. I'll see you later.'

'Later?' Miss Blob grinned, gazing at Hilda's straining blouse. 'Why will you see me later? Have you . . . er . . . have you anything interesting in mind?'

'No, not for that!' Hilda laughed, her clitoris throbbing at the prospect of sex.

'Oh, I see.'

'Well, it might be for that!' Hilda smiled, flashing her

blue bedroom eyes, wondering at her ever-increasing libido. 'We'll have to see, you naughty man!'

'Great! Until later, Hilda.'

Closing the door, Hilda couldn't believe that Miss Gussetpiece had gone. But more, she couldn't believe that Maxine Mayhem was taking over as headmistress! Returning to the lounge, she told Emily and Nikkie the bad news. 'So, Miss Mayhem is acting headmistress, I'm afraid. She was leader of the Bellend Rebels, so we'll have to watch her.'

'Crikey! Leader of the Bellend Rebels? I've heard of the Bellend Rebels – they're legendary! Who were they? What did they do?' Nikkie asked.

'They did nothing but cause trouble, I'm afraid. And they're doing it again, it would seem! Look, the Jolly Hockey Sticks Club will be our secret. The three of us will meet here, in my rooms, every evening for . . . This must remain our secret!'

'It will, Miss Hillock!' Emily grinned.

'You may call me Hilda – only when we're alone, though. Now, shall we have some fun together?'

'Oh, yes, Hilda!' the girls shrieked in unison as they tugged their gymslips over their heads and slipped their blouses off, revealing their curvaceous young bodies.

'I'll have to initiate you,' Hilda smiled, squeezing the girls' firm breasts through their full bras. 'Come on, take all your clothes off, and I'll initiate you into the Jolly Hockey Sticks Club! Strip off for the initiation.'

Sitting at the mahogany desk as Miss Blob left the study, Maxine grinned at Ginger. 'So I'm in the chair, at last!' she giggled.

Girl School

'Yes, but what happened to Knickergusset? I mean, she wouldn't die from an orgasm, would she?'

'Death by orgasm! Sounds like a chocolate dessert, doesn't it?'

'I can't believe that an orgasm killed her!' Ginger persisted. 'Christ, it must have been a massive one to finish her off!'

'It wasn't an orgasm that killed her,' Maxine grinned.

'What? You mean that you . . .'

'Forget about it. Knickergusset has gone, and I'm in charge now! There are two of us, Ginger – and Pillock's all alone. Two against one – we'll cause some real trouble for the last remaining member of the Jolly Hockey Sticks Club, we really will!'

Reclining on the floor with her two young friends sucking on her erect nipples and massaging her solid clitoris, Hilda sighed. 'Ah, this takes me back!'

'Hilly?' Emily began. 'Hilly, there are three other girls who I'm sure would like to join our club and . . . well, and come to your rooms every evening.'

'Good, that'll be six of us. Six against two – we'll cause some real trouble for the last remaining members of the Bellend Rebels, we really will!'

II

Sextro

Chapter One

Gazing up at the night sky, Grant Wesley, amateur photographer and ardent UFO investigator, shook his head. 'Not a bloody thing!' he sighed despairingly. 'I'd have been better off going to the pub! Or having a damn good wank!' Wishing he'd brought a battery-operated electric vagina with him, he cast his eyes across the dark void of space and focused on the stars forming the Plough. *If there's life out there, then there's fucking!* he reflected logically, imagining a female alien with two pussy holes and four clitorises.

Star Trek and *Blake's Seven* had sparked Grant's interest in aliens. His interest in sex had been ignited by Emma Golding, an ugly schoolgirl with a maniacal fascination with the penis who'd paid him two pounds to take him into her mouth and suck him to his first orgasm. From that day forward he'd wanked almost daily and thought of little other than girls' damp panties, their wet pussies and hot mouths. And, of course, flying saucers.

Do Martians wank? Grant mused idly, scanning the heavens through his binoculars for a UFO. Becoming bored, he was about to give up his quest when he heard what sounded like whimpering female voices drifting through the warm night air. *The whimpers of female orgasm?* he speculated optimistically, his penis twitching in expectation. Curious, he turned in the direction of the suggestive sound and, focusing on a clump of trees silhouetted by the full moon, trod his way towards the wood.

Cautiously stealing through the undergrowth towards the unmistakable echoes of wailing women, Grant imagined spying on an orgy of young couples making wild and passionate love. *Those were the days!* he reflected nostalgically as he crouched behind a large bush. *Whatever happened to Emma Golding?*

Stifling a gasp as he moved the branches aside, he stared in disbelief at the incredible scene that met his eyes. *Curiosity killed the bloody cat!* he cursed himself, his heart pounding, his breathing unsteady.

Dancing round a fire, a group of stunningly beautiful naked young women were performing what Grant assumed to be an occult ritual. Their fresh, lithe bodies the epitome of female sexuality, their full vaginal lips swollen, hairless, their pert breasts peaks of perfection, he gazed in wonderment at the blonde angels. *God, they're fucking gorgeous!* he breathed, ogling the girls' gaping pinken vaginal cracks.

Two naked Adonises sitting on a fallen tree eagerly watched the erotic dancers, their sparkling eyes reflecting their appreciation for the female form. Clearly visible in the flickering yellow firelight, the young men's remarkably large penises stood erect, rising proudly between their legs as exemplary monuments to the male species. *Lucky bastards!* Grant thought enviously, admiring their huge organs.

Fearful, and yet highly aroused, he wiped beads of sweat from his brow, feverishly brushing his black hair away from his face. To which idol were the sect offering their naked bodies? he pondered. Were they witches – or devil worshippers? Suddenly, the bizarre dance came to an abrupt halt as one young man rose and raised his hands above his head.

Grant watched with bated breath as the two men grabbed one of the goddesses and dragged her away from the group. His penis twitched involuntarily as, hauled across the clearing, her legs kicking, he noticed that the size of her succulent vaginal lips was greatly out of proportion to the rest of her body. Her milk teats, too, were grossly exaggerated – at least five times larger than average nipples.

As the girl's struggling body was hauled over the fallen tree, Grant realized with horror that she might well be going to be offered as a sacrifice. Wondering whether to intervene, he bit his lip. Although he was six feet tall, fit and fairly strong, he doubted that he could overpower the rippling-muscled young Adonises. And should the women join in the struggle and help take him prisoner, there was no telling what might happen. *I might end up as the bloody sacrifice!* he thought apprehensively as he gazed at the girl's exposed squirming body. No, for the time being, there was nothing he could do, other than observe.

Lying with her stomach against the rough bark, her slender legs spread wide, her buttocks and full vaginal lips blatantly exposed, the girl finally gave up her futile fight, permitting the men to bind her wrists and ankles with rope and secure her trembling body to the tree. Her rounded buttocks taut, the pinken opening to her vaginal shaft crudely bared, her naked body defenceless, Grant felt his arousal, and his fear for the girl's safety, sharply rising.

She'd seemed willing enough to participate in the dance, he reflected. Had she not known that she might be chosen as the sacrifice? Perhaps she'd been tricked into joining the group? Maybe she'd been led to believe that the invitation was to a party – an orgy in the woods? His mouth hanging open, he watched one of the men position himself behind the tethered girl, his massive penis in his hand, his heavy balls rolling, fully laden. *Perhaps he's only going to give her a good fuck?* Grant thought with some relief, a slight smile furling his lips as the girl projected her taut buttocks, apparently offering her feminine intimacy to the male.

The girl's vaginal lips visibly swelling, parting as the man's ballooning knob ran up and down her drenched crevice, Grant thought of his girlfriend, Karen, wishing she was more adventurous in bed. An extremely attractive girl in her early twenties, Karen was shy and reserved when it came to sharing her body with him. Although he'd gently coaxed her, encouraged her to relax and open herself to him, she'd always remained stilted, uneasy with her nakedness. He'd even bought her a vibrator in an effort to awaken her sexuality, but she'd shunned the idea of female masturbation – especially with the aid of a sex-toy.

Karen had never experienced an orgasm, so she'd told him when they'd first met. 'Women don't have to climax during sex,' she'd said by way of an excuse for what she obviously saw as her failing. He'd laughed, sure that he'd bring her one multiple orgasm after another once he'd lured her into his bed. But his clitoral licking, his vaginal tonguing, seemed to have fallen on barren ground. She hadn't even bothered faking an orgasm, which had not only disappointed him but left him wondering at his own sexual ability. Karen's idea of sex was to lie on her back with her legs parted just enough for him to penetrate her tight vagina. She'd gasp a little, make the odd murmuring noise, but they were gasps and murmurs of displeasure. She'd grimace, waiting for him to finish with her body, to slip his penis from her unaccommodating vagina and leave her to sleep.

Perhaps she was too beautiful, too sexually attractive,

for her own good, Grant reflected. She'd unwittingly rouse men's base instincts with her big blue eyes, her pink tongue, as she provocatively licked her full red lips. Her breasts were firm, conical, crowned with long nipples that stood proud through her blouse. She usually wore short skirts, unthinkingly showing off her long legs, her shapely thighs. In her sweet naivety, she was blissfully unaware of the men's eyes ogling her curvaceous young body as she walked innocently along the street. Unaware of their male thoughts of sex.

'Veneris!' the men chanted, breaking Grant's reverie as the young man's penis drove into the whimpering girl's vagina. 'Veneris! Come unto us, Veneris, our Goddess of Carnality! We invite you to witness this enforced sexual coupling to show our allegiance to you!'

Frowning as he watched the man's solid organ sink further into the young girl's naked body, Grant's penis suddenly ballooned, becoming painfully hard within his tight jeans. Grimacing, he manipulated his crotch, desperately trying to manoeuvre his swollen member into a comfortable position. His eyes widening with terror, he stared, dumbstruck, as finger-like shafts of green light reached down from the trees and touched each member of the group.

Adrenalin coursing through his veins, he was about to creep away from his hide and make his escape from whatever evil had been called upon when a shaft of light meandered towards him, bathing his trembling body with its green hue. Sperm suddenly gushing from his orgasming penis as the light played around his crotch, his climax painfully intensified. His sperm drenching his balls, soaking his jeans, he fell back, clutching his solid organ, virtually unable to bear the immense pleasure emanating from his throbbing glans. The girl suddenly crying out as her enforced orgasm rocked her leashed body, Grant jumped to his feet, dropping his binoculars as he bolted through the undergrowth as fast as he could.

Well away from the wood, he stopped running, leaning over and resting his hands on his knees, panting for breath. 'Jesus!' he gasped, gripping his still-solid penis through his saturated jeans. 'God, I've never come like that in my life!' Finally composing himself, he walked down the moonlit hill to his car, wondering whether he'd imagined the uncanny green light. 'I didn't imagine my spunk!' he muttered, climbing into his car and adjusting the wet crotch of his jeans as he drove off.

Grant's penis was still erect as he quietly opened the front door and crept upstairs to the bathroom. Slipping his shoes and jeans off, he gazed at his rigid organ, wondering whether it would ever deflate. *I can't walk around like this!* he thought, imagining that his cock had increased in size. Examining the veined shaft, he frowned, sure that his organ was indeed bigger. *Why the hell is it so stiff?*

Deciding not to tell Karen of his extraordinary experience, he contemplated the bizarre gathering he'd stumbled across, wondering how often they met in the woods. 'I didn't imagine the light,' he murmured pensively as he washed his still-erect penis, his rolling balls. 'I know I didn't!'

'Grant, is that you?' Karen called from the bedroom.

'Yes, I'll be with you in a minute!' he replied, slipping his shirt off and lovingly drying his painfully hard penis.

'How many UFOs did you see?' Karen giggled mockingly.

'None, as bloody usual!' *But I spotted a few shaved cunts!*

Karen was propped up in bed reading a magazine, her

long blonde hair fanning out across the pillow, her mouth alluring – inviting. Raising her eyes as Grant entered the room, she focused on his muscular body, his rock-hard penis, his heavy balls. 'Why are you like that?' she asked almost fearfully, obviously dreading the thought of his male hardness penetrating her sacrosanct vagina.

Because I've been watching a young girl having her cunt fucked from behind.

'Grant, I hope you're not expecting . . .'

'I'm not expecting anything!' he snapped as he climbed in beside her. 'I never expect anything these days!' *Apart from a good wank when you're not around!*

'Don't be so nasty! You know that I don't want sex all the time!' she returned irritably, yanking the quilt from him.

All the time? Christ, once a month is hardly all the time!

'Why are you stiff? God, your dick's got bigger!' Karen declared, catching a glimpse of his mighty member as he lifted the quilt. 'What have you been up to?'

Watching an orgy. 'I haven't been up to anything! I suppose it's been so long since we last did it that I'm frustrated! Sex-starved!'

'It was only two weeks ago, Grant!' Karen snapped, tugging on the quilt again. 'Sex isn't everything!'

It is to me! 'No, obviously not. Anyway, two weeks is a bloody long time!'

Pulling the quilt over his shoulder, Grant breathed in Karen's aphrodisiacal female scent, wishing she'd use her mouth, her wet tongue, to bring out his sperm. Many times he'd begged her to let herself go, to free herself of inhibitions and suck his penis and swallow his jism. But she'd always shied away from the idea, telling him that if it was a common slut he wanted, then he should leave her and go and find one. *My fault, I suppose*, he reflected. *I should have taken up with a rampant tart.*

As he tentatively ran his fingers over her smooth stomach, praying for her to gobble his knob, to drink his sperm, to relieve his dangerously high sexual tension, Grant jumped. 'Well, that's a turn-up for the books!' he chuckled as Karen lovingly squeezed his twitching organ in her warm hand. Without a word, she slipped beneath the quilt and took his silky glans into her mouth, gently sucking, running her tongue around his pulsating knob.

'Ah! Ah, that's nice!' he gasped as she took the swollen crown of his penis to the back of her throat. 'God, Karen, what's come over you?'

'I . . . I don't know,' she murmured as she slipped his purple plum out of her mouth and began licking and nibbling his rolling balls. 'I can't think why I'm doing this!'

'Christ, I've never known you to be so horny!'

'Neither have I!' Karen returned, her long blonde hair tickling his balls as she took his knob into her wet mouth again and lovingly wanked his fleshy lance with both hands.

Lifting the quilt, Grant gazed at his girlfriend's generous red lips rolling over his wet, veined fleshpole as she moved her head up and down, almost taking his entire length into her fiery mouth. His sperm rapidly rising, he took her head in his hands, praying for her to swallow his liquid offering. Moaning through her nose, Karen seemed to lose herself in her new-found excitation as Grant let out an involuntary gasp and filled her cheeks with his spouting come. Grimacing as his incredible orgasm rode on, he thrust his hips, ramming his knob in and out of her overflowing mouth as she gulped down his male milk like a starving babe at the breast. This wasn't at all like Karen, he reflected, wondering why she'd suddenly changed.

Grant's copious flow finally ceasing, Karen slipped his knob from her mouth and fervently lapped up the spilt nectar from his balls. Amazed by his girlfriend's incredible transformation, Grant lay trembling in the wake of his climax, watching her frenzied licking. Not letting one drop of spunk go to waste, Karen cleansed his balls, his shaft, his lower stomach. Sucking globules of sperm from his pubic hairs, she finally lifted her head and curled her sperm-wet lips into an unfamiliar, impish grin.

'Was that OK?' she asked huskily, kissing his purple-headed warrior as if worshipping his male hardness.

'It was great!' Grant smiled, still unable to believe the remarkable act his girlfriend had so lovingly performed. 'Whatever made you do it?'

'I don't know. Something came over me and . . .'

'And I came in you!' he laughed.

'Seriously, Grant – I can't understand why I did it!' she declared, her blue eyes frowning as she shook her head in puzzlement. She was obviously stunned by her uncharacteristic behaviour as she settled on the pillow and gazed into Grant's dark eyes. 'I really don't know what made me do it!' she repeated anxiously. 'The thought came into my head, and I knew that I had to suck you.'

'Well, whatever the reason, I'm glad you did it!' Grant smiled, kissing her cheek.

Hoping Karen was sexually aroused enough to allow him to lick her pussy folds, her clitoris, he pushed the quilt down and gazed at her curvaceous body, the swell of her breasts, her brown milk teats. Casting his eyes over her smooth stomach, the neat indent of her navel, he focused on her pink inner lips protruding enticingly from her long vaginal slit. Gently but firmly parting her thighs, he kissed her swollen pussy lips, breathing in the aphrodisiacal perfume of her girl-scented golden pubes, wondering again at the incredible change in her character.

As his tongue snaked between her swelling sex-hillocks and swept over her erect clitoris, Karen moaned and pitched her head from side to side. It was like being with another woman, Grant mused as he peeled her rubicund labia apart and lapped up the slippery cream pouring from her vaginal entrance. Whatever it was that had brought about the change, he didn't care. This was the new Karen – and he wasn't complaining!

Slipping three fingers into her tightening love-sheath as he sucked on her pulsating clitoris, he realized to his amazement that she was close to her first orgasm. 'Ah, yes, finger me!' she begged huskily, wickedly, opening her legs and offering her femininity. 'Lick my cunt!' Her unfamiliar words of female lust bubbling from her gasping lips, her fingers wandering over her rounded breasts, toying with her sensitive milk buds, Karen arched her back and opened her long legs as wide as she could. 'Coming!' she cried, a hint of fear in her quavering voice as her pioneering orgasm rose from her contracting womb. 'Oh, God! I'm coming! Grant, I'm coming!'

Her body shaking violently as her climax exploded, Karen sang out her appreciation for her new-found sexual satisfaction. Her eyes rolling, her nostrils flaring, her legs twitching, she peeled her pussy lips wide apart, stretching her innermost flesh, unveiling her throbbing clitoris to Grant's caressing tongue. Her exquisite climax rocking her trembling body, reaching out and tightening every muscle, stimulating every nerve ending, she lifted her head. 'Lick harder, faster!' she ordered, gazing at Grant's mouth, his

tongue, working fervently between her inflamed cuntal lips.
'Finger my cunt faster!'

His tongue aching, Grant did his best to sustain Karen's incredible pleasure, wondering yet again at her amazing U-turn. If she was going to demand rampant sex night after night, he'd give up UFO-spotting and remain at home! he decided as her climax finally began to diminish. This was far more fun than stargazing! Lapping up her creamy come as he slipped his fingers from her drenched love-hole, Grant felt his insatiable penis twitch, aching for another orgasm. Wondering whether Karen would beg him to fuck her as he swallowed the last of her pussy juice and lay by her side, he was amazed as she hauled herself upright and sat astride his naked body.

'God, you can't get enough, can you?' he grinned as she grabbed his penis, lowering her body and guiding his cock-head deep into her fiery cunt.

'No, I can't!' she giggled wickedly, frenziedly bouncing up and down, digging her fingernails into his hard chest. 'God, I'll never get enough of your beautiful cock!'

Shades of Emma Golding!

Riding her stud with frightening vehemence, ramming his shaft in and out of her convulsing cunt, Karen climbed to another mind-blowing orgasm. Grant's sperm gushing from his throbbing glans, lubricating his piston as she rocked and gyrated her hips, he grasped her breasts, kneading her firm mammary spheres, tweaking her erect nipples, adding to her incredible pleasure.

The perspiration of sex matting her dishevelled blonde tresses, Karen finally slowed her rhythm, gently stirring her vaginal cream with Grant's fleshy rod, massaging her pulsating clitoris against his hard shaft. *This is incredible!* Grant thought, lifting his head and eyeing her bloated pussy lips, taut around the base of his penis. *God, I'd like to get my tongue into her cunt!*

'Now I want you to lick your spunk out of my cunt!' Karen cried as her orgasm receded. Slipping Grant's consumed penis from her inflamed love-hole, she climbed up his naked body and positioned her gaping vaginal crack over his astonished face. Lowering her drenched intimacy, she settled her full pussy lips over his mouth, ordering him to lick inside her cunt as she gazed down at his dark eyes. 'Drink!' she rasped in her lechery. 'Drink from my cunt!'

Stunned by her crude words, Grant eagerly complied with his mistress's instruction, pushing his tongue as far as he could into her steaming sex-duct. A blend of hot cunt milk and sperm pouring into his mouth as his tongue curled inside her heaving body, he looked up between her long nipples at the obvious pleasure depicted on her pretty face. Cupping her taut buttocks, caressing her sensitive brown hole, wondering when she'd finally announce that she'd had enough, he raised his eyebrows in surprise as she ordered him to finger her bottom-hole. 'Put your finger into my bum!' she gasped. 'Finger my bum!'

Parting her taut buttocks, Grant eased his finger into his prim girlfriend's anal duct, staggered by the satisfaction revealed in her expression as her head flopped forward. Her mouth open, gasping as he continued his rectal fingering, his vaginal tonguing, Grant wondered whether she'd been with another man. She must have learned of the pleasures her body had to offer from someone, he mused as she slid her gaping pussy crack back and forth over his wet mouth, decanting her maiden-juice. There was no way she'd discovered the joys of crude sex on her own!

Quivering, panting, Karen finally lifted the open centre of her exhausted body from Grant's flushed face. His finger slipping out of her anal duct as she raised her leg and moved aside, she fell onto the bed, lying beside him, running her hands between her thighs as her trembling flesh began to calm. Gazing at his young girlfriend as she drifted into a deep sleep, her hair matted, dishevelled, Grant frowned. *Has she been with someone else?* he wondered as he turned over and closed his eyes. Someone had brought about the incredible change. Someone had transformed Karen from a virtual prude into an insatiable nymphomaniac!

Waking to the sun streaming in through the window, his penis stiff, yearning for Karen's tight vagina again, Grant turned his head and gazed longingly at his sleeping girlfriend. He'd return to the woods that night, he decided, wondering whether the eerie green light had somehow increased his staying power. Fondling his manhood, squeezing his painfully rock-hard shaft, he remembered the young men calling on Veneris. *Don't be stupid, Grant!* he chided himself as he slipped out of bed and wandered into the bathroom. *A Goddess of Carnality? Don't be fucking ridiculous!*

Taking a shower, Grant wondered whether he'd permanently quenched Karen's uncharacteristic thirst for sex. *A one-off?* he pondered, picturing her masturbating with a vibrator. Grinning as he recalled the young women in the woods, he imagined Karen without pubic hair, her vaginal lips smooth, soft, alluring in their pubescent-like nakedness. He'd never bothered asking her to shave – with her attitude towards sex, there'd been little point! But now? *No, one step at a time. Ease her gently into the delights of perverted sex*, he mused.

Returning to the bedroom, he smiled as Karen propped herself up on her elbows. 'And how are you this morning, my horny little angel?' he asked, eyeing her long, lush nipples. *Hot, wet, tight and ready for another good fucking?*

'Sore!' she complained, her expression one of annoyance.

'We had a good time last night, didn't we?' Grant chuckled as he dressed, feigning obliviousness to her bad mood. 'We had a bloody good time!' *Well, I did!*

'I don't know why I did those awful things, Grant! I certainly don't want to do anything like that again!' she spat. 'What I did was . . . was disgusting!'

'But I thought . . .'

Shaking his head in disbelief as Karen threw the quilt back and leaped out of bed, Grant reached out to put his arms around her naked body. Ignoring his gesture, she walked past him and strode out of the room. Slamming the bathroom door shut and turning the key, she ran a bath, disregarding his pleas to open the door and tell him what was wrong. 'Please yourself!' he finally shouted as he bounded downstairs. 'Please your bloody self!' *There are plenty more fish in the sea – and birds in the woods!*

After a boring sales meeting that dragged on into the evening, Grant didn't bother to go home. The last thing he needed was one of Karen's moods. Parking his car and climbing the cowslip-covered hill to the woods, hoping he'd have the pleasure of watching the angelic young women being taken by the well-endowed men, he wondered whether they'd allow him to join their raunchy games. No, he thought – he'd learn more about the sect before revealing himself. There was no telling what danger he might encounter if he were to make himself known too soon.

The orange sun setting over the hills to the west, silhouetting a man walking his dog, Grant recalled the eerie green light, wondering whether it was wise to return to the wood. 'I've got to get my binoculars back,' he murmured, tramping through the undergrowth. *The moonlight reflected off the leaves?* he pondered. *Possibly*, he decided, crouching behind the bush and tentatively moving the branches aside – although it wasn't a particularly credible explanation. *Of course it wasn't fucking moonlight!*

To his great surprise, the young men and women were there, standing naked in a circle around the fire, the men's arms raised high above their heads. Making himself comfortable as dusk blanketed the wood, Grant gazed in awe at the young men's penises. Their bollocks like tennis balls hanging in wrinkled leather pouches, their ballooning knobs mimicking large, purple nectarines, the length and width of their shafts was incredible. *If only!* he mused enviously as his own minor member stiffened. *God, if only!*

As on the previous night, one of the girls was forcibly dragged away from the group by the two men. The females being remarkably similar in appearance, Grant couldn't determine whether or not she was the girl who'd been tied over the tree the night before. Her long blonde hair covering her angelic face as she fought to save herself, Grant again wondered why the girls had joined the group if they'd known that one would be chosen for sexual abuse – or worse. *Perhaps it's all part of their games?* he pondered as the girl was thrown over the tree and her naked body secured with ropes. *Perhaps the little tart enjoys a bit of rough treatment!*

As he watched one of the men take a length of rope and run it through his hands, he realized that none of the group had spoken. Apart from the chanting, the calling of the Goddess Veneris, not one word had passed their lips.

The girl suddenly screaming, sending bats flapping from the trees, Grant bit his lip, gazing at the weals appearing across her twitching buttocks as the rope lashed her. Wincing as the rope swished through the air and cracked loudly across her taut bottom-orbs again, he was sure that she was far from enjoying the beating. Fearful for her, he decided to creep away and return with the police. There was nothing he could do to save her, he reflected as he grabbed his binoculars from the ground where he'd dropped them the night before and began to crawl away from his hide.

'Veneris, our Goddess of Carnality!' the men chanted, stopping Grant in his tracks. 'Veneris, come unto us and charge our genitals with your great sexual power!' Peering through the bush again, Grant waited in trepidation. His hands trembling, his heart pounding hard against his chest, he stared in terror as fingers of green light snaked down from the trees and sought each member of the group. This wasn't imagination, he knew! The light playing between their legs, Grant backed away as a shaft of light, seemingly aware of his presence, slowly wove its way towards him.

Bathing his suit trousers, the eerie light played between his thighs, stiffening his penis, ballooning his throbbing glans. Stunned as he realized that he was about to come, he gasped, desperately trying to pull his organ out and masturbate. His sperm suddenly gushing, spurting from his pulsating knob, he fell to the ground, trying to tug his zip down and haul out his geyser. Writhing in the delicious agony of a violent orgasm, he rolled about on the ground, his hands between his legs as his sperm flooded his balls, his pubes, his inner thighs.

The seemingly perpetual climax intensifying as the light flickered between his legs, he thought he'd pass out with the immense pleasure emanating from his gushing cock.

His body rigid, his sperm still flowing in torrents, he lay on his back shaking uncontrollably, praying for his climax to subside as his penis swelled to an incredible size. 'God, no more!' he hissed through gritted teeth as the last of his sperm pumped into his drenched trousers. 'Christ, no more!'

Finally released from his sexual apoplexy, he lay gasping, trembling, wondering fearfully about the Goddess of Carnality, the uncanny green light. The girl's screams filling the wood as the merciless thrashing continued, his body weak, his mouth dry, he crawled across the ground to make his escape. Finally emerging from the wood, he rested his aching body on the grass. 'Jesus Christ!' he breathed, clutching the huge bulge in his wet trousers as the tethered girl's blood-curdling screams drifted through the night air. 'What the hell *is* all this?'

He couldn't go to the police wearing sperm-drenched trousers! Besides, he thought wickedly as he descended the hill, there might well be a chance that he'd be able to join in with the incredible sex sessions, the orgies. His thoughts on the girl, his conscience nagged him as he climbed into his car. But, he decided, he wouldn't jeopardize the chance of becoming a member of the sect and enjoying the young girls' cunts. Wrong though it was, he'd leave the girl to her terrible fate.

Karen was in the lounge watching television when Grant slipped through the front door and tiptoed upstairs. There was no way he could explain his spunked trousers, he thought as he closed and locked the bathroom door. She'd never believe it if he were to tell her the truth. As he slipped out of his clothes and looked down at his erect organ, his eyes widened with shock. His penis had grown, the shaft now nearing twelve inches long, the purple glans as big as a snooker ball. Gripping the incredible inflated member with both hands, his shock subsided into a smug grin as he realized that this was a dream come true.

Wherever the strange light had come from, whatever mystical goddess the young men had called upon to charge their genitals with sexual power, he realized he too had been charged – and the result was unbelievable! His purple-headed warrior waving from side to side as he bounded downstairs, he wondered at Karen's reaction to the phenomenon. No woman could deny herself the pleasure of such a fine male organ! he thought as he opened the lounge door and charged into the room. Standing proudly before his girlfriend as she looked up and gazed into his dark eyes, he eagerly waited for her to focus on his magical truncheon.

'Grant, I told you this morning that I don't want . . .' Karen's words tailed off as she moved to the edge of the sofa, her eyes almost popping out of her head as he walked towards her with his weapon in his hand. Reaching out and grasping his broad shaft, she was speechless for several seconds. 'Grant, what . . . what's happened to you?' she finally managed to stammer.

'Like it?' he asked smugly.

'I've never seen . . . how did you do it?'

A good question, Grant thought wryly. How could he explain his suddenly magnificent organ? What lies could he concoct? 'I . . . I bought some special cream,' he began hesitantly, realizing that the idea of cream enlarging his penis was ridiculous. 'I really didn't think it would work, but it did.'

'But cream can't do *that*!' Karen gasped, stroking his silky-smooth glans with her fingertips. 'It's just not possible!'

Grant knew Karen wasn't stupid – but she *was* gullible, naive. 'I've also been doing genital exercises to improve my manhood for your benefit,' he laughed, hoping she'd suck his prize knob into her hot mouth and swallow his sperm. 'Now you can see for yourself that it's worked! I've been exercising for several weeks, and using the cream.' *And wanking!*

'But it wasn't that big yesterday! It was bigger than usual, but not that big!'

'Whatever it was or wasn't yesterday, it's big now! You're holding the proof in your hand!'

'It's amazing!' Karen cried, examining the purple knob. 'But, as I said this morning, I don't want . . .'

'What was wrong this morning?' Grant asked, sensually brushing her cheek, wondering at her strange mood swings, praying for her to suck his proud cock. *Christ, if I were a woman I'd want my cunt fucked hourly by an organ like this!* 'I'd have thought that, after last night, you would have . . .'

Noticing a burning passion in Karen's eyes as she engulfed his bulbous cock-head in her mouth, Grant frowned. These weren't mood swings, he reflected. They were complete changes of character! Gazing at her full lips, taut around his deep purple bulb, he noticed a green hue glowing around his shaft. Straining his eyes, he watched the eerie light spread to Karen's mouth, bathing her lips and creeping over her face. Shaking his head and blinking several times, he looked again, but saw nothing. As his glans throbbed against the girl's sweeping tongue, the stark reality of the unbelievable events finally hit him.

The naked men must have called upon some supernatural power, he contemplated fearfully. *The Goddess Veneris?* Was he possessed by some horrendous evil spirit? No, he decided.

Nothing had changed, other than the size of his penis – and Karen's attitude towards sex! How she'd been affected, her sexuality suddenly woken, he didn't know. Unless, he thought pensively, his penis had somehow influenced her. *Christ, perhaps my knob's possessed?* But did it really matter what had happened? he rationalized as Karen moved her head forward, taking his massive purple crown to the back of her throat, her eyes rolling as she lost herself in her rising arousal. No, it didn't matter at all!

There'd be no more mood swings, personality changes, he was sure. This was the new Karen, the insatiable nymphomaniac who craved his magnificent male organ, yearned for his gushing sperm. As he watched her suck and mouth his monumental knob, he imagined her taking her blouse and bra off and rubbing his glans over her young breasts, her erect nipples. He pictured his huge cock-head spurting his spunk over her areolae, her long milk buds – and Karen lapping up his male cream from her firm breasts.

As she slipped her blouse off while continuing her mouthing and sucking, Grant frowned. *It's as if she's heard my thoughts!* he mused as she unclipped her bra and tossed the silk garment to the floor. Pulling away and taking his formidable weapon in her small hands, Karen ran his knob around her nipples, stiffening her brown protrusions. Wanking him, her eyes aglow with a strange inner lust for sexual satisfaction, she uttered her uncharacteristic words of crude sex. 'I want your spunk all over my tits! Come over my tits!'

Unable to reply as his climax erupted, Grant watched his knob swell, his sperm spray from his slit and shower her firm mammary glands. On and on his milk spurted, covering her rounded breasts, her hard nipples, running down her smooth stomach, dripping onto her skirt. Gasping as she sucked him into her mouth again and drank from his fountainhead, Grant couldn't believe what was happening.

His intense orgasm seemingly unceasing as Karen slipped his knob from her mouth and continued her wanking motions, spurting his come over her breasts, her erect nipples, he imagined her on all fours, projecting her bottom-orbs, begging him to come up her tight bum.

At last, his flow stemming, Karen sucked the remnants of sperm from his purple plum, savouring his salty offering, licking her full red lips. Taking her breasts in her hands and licking the taut flesh, Grant watched his girlfriend take each nipple into her mouth and lap up his spunk. This was incredible! Karen, the shy, reserved prude, lapping up sperm from her tits? This was unbelievable! But he couldn't have been happier with his new, fulfilling relationship – or more stunned when the girl entreated him to take her from behind.

'Please, Grant!' she begged, slipping off the sofa. 'I want you to fuck me!' Pulling her wet knickers down, she positioned herself on all fours. 'I want you to fuck my arse!' she ordered crudely, lifting her skirt and revealing her rounded buttocks, her dripping vaginal slit nestling deliciously between her smooth thighs.

Gazing at her tight bottom-hole as she rested her head on the carpet and projected her taut buttocks, Grant was sure that, inexplicable though it was, she'd somehow heard his thoughts. He'd put her to the test later, he decided, taking his weapon in his hand and kneeling behind her. To determine whether or not she was able to read his mind would be easy enough – but not now. *There are more important things to do!*

Cupping her bottom-orbs, he slipped his huge knob into

her drenched vaginal sheath to lubricate his piston in readiness to comply with her incredible demand. Driving his rod deep into her tight cunt, his shaft opening her, stretching her fleshy vaginal walls, he made several hard thrusts before sliding his well-oiled cock out of her hot duct. Eyeing her tight bottom-hole, he wondered whether he'd manage to push his huge knob past her defending muscles and sink his shaft into the dank heat of her bowels. He was big, and her arse so small, so tight. But he'd endeavour to gain entry.

Dragging Karen's cuntal cream from her pussy hole with his fingers, Grant lubricated her sensitive brown tissue, praying that she'd not have a change of mind the minute she sensed his hardness trying to penetrate her private cavern. He'd dreamed of this, fantasized about fucking her from behind, taking her bottom-sheath, spunking into her bowels – and now his dream, his fantasy, was about to become reality.

'Fuck my arse!' Karen pleaded impatiently in her rising lust, reaching behind her back and peeling her buttocks apart, opening her brown hole. Without hesitation, Grant presented his knob to her anal entrance and began pushing against her twitching muscles. 'That's it! Go on, push it in!' the impassioned girl urged as her inlet opened and sucked his bulbous knob into the darkness of her rectal duct. 'More, more!' she pleaded to his astonishment. Gripping her hips and gently pulling her towards him, Grant watched with bated breath as his cock-head disappeared into her quivering young body. Gasping, Karen was obviously delighting in the crude coupling, desperately awaiting her first anal fucking. But what had brought about the incredible change in the girl? Grant wondered.

Sinking his shaft deeper into her perspiring body, he

closed his eyes, his glans absorbing the inner heat of her bowels as his shaft drove further into her hot posterior duct. Whimpering as she manoeuvred her hips, aligning her anal tube with his indriving cockshaft, Karen reached between her legs and massaged her erect clitoris.

'Finger my cunt while I masturbate!' she cried as her clitoris pulsated and her vaginal muscles spasmed, spewing out hot cunt milk. Driving his penis in to the root, his heavy balls resting against her swollen cunny lips, Grant located her dripping love-mouth and drove three fingers deep into her velvety pussy sheath. In her sexual heaven, Karen continued her clitoral masturbation, rocking her shaking body to meet Grant's anal thrusts. Her orgasm quickly rising from her contracting womb as she quivered and gasped in her sexual delirium, she begged Grant to come.

'Please!' she whimpered as her climax erupted in her pulsating sex-nodule. 'Please, spunk up my arse!'

'What the hell's got into you?' Grant gasped, driving his massive tool deep into her bowels as he sensed his own orgasm building. 'What the hell's changed you, Karen?'

'Oh, God! God, I'm coming! Please, you must come with me!'

Thrusting into the girl with such force that she glided across the carpet, Grant released his sperm, filling her bowels, lubricating their debased coupling. Both shuddering, crying out as their incredible climaxes gripped them, they fell to the floor, locked in their soaring lust. Still driving his cock into her tight arse, his sperm continuing to fill her bowels, Grant persisted with his anal fucking, using the girl's quivering body to satisfy his perverted sexual craving until he'd drained his huge balls and collapsed.

Resting on Karen's heaving body, he lay still, his knob buried deep within her bowels, the root of his shaft lovingly gripped by her tight anal ring. 'God, that was something else!' he breathed, pulling his fingers from her spasming cunny hole. 'Christ, Karen, you're something else! You were brilliant!'

'You were pretty good, too!' she giggled impishly as he hauled his body up and slowly slipped his long tool out of her anal sheath. 'Ah! Ah, slowly! Pull it out slowly!'

His purple plum finally emerging from the clammy heat of her used body, Grant pulled himself up and flopped onto the sofa, wondering yet again about Karen's incredible transformation. As she rolled over and lay on her back with her legs spread, her cunt crack yawning, he wondered whether she really had heard his thoughts. *I want her to shave her pubic curls*, he decided, imagining Karen's sex-mound, her cunny lips, smooth, soft and hairless. *Shave your cunt!* he urged her in his mind as he gazed at her matted, blonde pubic bush. *Get a razor and shave your cunt!*

Watching Karen drag her exhausted body up, Grant waited in expectation, his stomach somersaulting, his hands trembling, his heart pounding with anticipation. Had it worked? Could his wicked thoughts really influence her actions? As she moved to the door, she turned to face him.

'I'm going to bed, Grant. I'm absolutely knackered!' she sighed, tossing her dishevelled hair away from her flushed face.

'Oh, right. Er . . . yes, I'll come up with you,' he replied disappointedly.

As they climbed the stairs together, Grant began to doubt his theory. Even if Karen were able to read his mind, his lewd thoughts wouldn't drive her to beg for anal intercourse! he mused. Something, or someone, had influenced her to behave as she had – but what or who?

Lying in bed thinking about the naked young women in the woods, his penis stiffened painfully, swelling almost to bursting point. *Christ, I need to come again!* Massaging his solid knob, he wondered at his staying power, his ability to enjoy orgasm after orgasm. But what had happened to him? What had happened to Karen? Was it the eerie green light?

He was determined to discover more about the mysterious sect – who they were, where they lived and worked, what sort of people they were. And as for the Goddess Veneris and the uncanny fingers of green light! There was a strange power in the woods – a power capable of enlarging his penis, increasing the duration and intensity of his orgasms. As yet, it was an inexplicable power, but he would unravel the sect's enigma, discover what the power was, from where it originated.

I'll follow them, he decided. *Follow one of them home and use some excuse or other to make contact.* Wondering about the tethered girl's fate, he became uneasy. He should have helped her, but his base sexual desires had got the better of him. Finally convincing himself that the girl was all right, that she'd enjoyed the games, he turned and faced Karen.

Fondling her pussy crack as she lay sleeping by his side, he slipped a finger into her drenched vagina, delighted that she'd become an insatiable nymphomaniac. Or had she? he wondered, recalling her strange change of character that morning. As he slipped a second finger into her tight cunt, he wondered what he'd wake up to the following day. Little Miss Prissy – or a raving nympho?

Chapter Two

Deciding to take the day off work, Grant slipped out of bed, leaving Karen sleeping as he crept into the bathroom. Gazing at his ever-erect penis, he grinned. 'I look like a bloody stallion!' he chuckled, standing sideways-on to the mirror and eyeing his huge curved member. *I could star in porn videos with a fucking great tool like this!*

Suddenly, he became fearful. The things he'd done with Karen, his penis growing to an incredible size, the strangers in the wood . . . *What's going on?* he wondered, pulling his foreskin back and examining his ballooning purple knob. His orgasms were now incredible, the strength and duration amazing. And after years of virtually no sexual response, Karen was able to achieve staggering multiple orgasms! *What the hell's happened to us?*

He'd read about occult groups calling on Satan to increase the pleasure derived from their orgasms, but he'd never believed it could work. *Christ, is that what I've stumbled across?* he reflected anxiously. *Satan?* His sex life with Karen now better than he could ever have dreamed, he decided to steer well clear of the occult group. *Get out while the going's good*, he mused, scrutinizing his magnificent penis.

Washing before dressing in his blue jeans and open-neck shirt, Grant descended the stairs to the kitchen and made himself a cup of coffee. Daydreaming, he wondered whether Karen would demand rampant sex the minute she woke, beg him to open her pussy folds and lick her clitoris to a mind-blowing climax. *I could give her a good fuck on the lawn!* he thought wickedly, staring at the unkempt garden through the kitchen window, imagining her naked body sprawled out on the long grass. Hearing movement upstairs, he pondered on his girlfriend's alluring fresh body, her hot pussy, her tight bottom-hole. *Or give her one over the kitchen table!* he thought, picturing the girl leaning over the table, her rounded buttocks taut, her vaginal lips inflated between her splayed thighs.

Finishing his coffee, wondering what was taking Karen so long, he wandered out into the garden and inhaled the flower-scented summer air. Praying that she'd not had another weird character change, reverted to a prude, he sat on a patio chair in the warmth of the morning sun. Imagining tying Karen to a tree and whipping her naked buttocks, his penis stiff, bulging his jeans, he pondered on his voracious lust for perverted sex. *Thanks, Veneris!* he laughed inwardly as he gazed up to the clear blue sky – to the heavens. 'Oh, Goddess of Carnality, send unto me woman after woman to enjoy the pleasures of my fucking great cock!' he chuckled, wondering whether it was heaven he should be looking to – or hell. *Shit, I'd better be careful!*

Hearing the front door slam shut, Grant leaped to his feet and dashed into the house. 'Oh, that's great! She's bloody well gone out!' he cursed as he looked out of the lounge window to see Karen climb into her red Mini and drive off. 'Sod it! She must have thought that I'd gone to work!' Returning to the garden, he cursed again as the front doorbell rang. 'Who the fuck's that?'

Opening the door, Grant smiled at the tall, attractive girl poised on the step. 'Hi, Jackie!' he greeted her, his eyes focusing on her young breasts, her deep cleavage. 'Karen's out, I'm afraid – you've just missed her.' *But I'm here!*

'Yes, I saw her drive off. I knew you were in because I noticed your car outside. How long will Karen be, do you know?' the auburn-haired girl asked, her hazel eyes sparkling, her complexion youthful, her body curvaceous – fuckable.

'To be honest, I've no idea where she's gone! You can come in and wait if you want to, but I don't know how long she'll be.'

'Well, I've nothing else to do so ... are you sure you don't mind?'

'Of course I don't mind! Come in and have a coffee.' *Or something.*

Closing the door and following the ravishing girl into the kitchen, Grant surveyed her shapely thighs, the globular swell of her buttocks accentuated by her tight red miniskirt. *I wonder what she'd think of my superb cock?* he thought as he filled the kettle, envisaging her sucking on his bulbous knob, guzzling his jetting spunk. His mind-reading theory was definitely wrong, he decided, as he unsuccessfully willed the girl to plead for his cock, to beg for his sperm – definitely wrong!

'No work today, then?' Jackie asked, sitting at the pine table and crossing her lissome legs, her auburn bob framing her fresh face.

'No, I decided to take the day off. I had to endure a boring sales meeting yesterday which dragged on into the evening, so I reckon I deserve a day off!'

'What's that?' the pretty girl asked, her eyes frowning, focusing on his hand.

'What's what?'

'That green stain or whatever it is. Look, there, on your right hand.'

'I can't see anything.' Perplexed, he held his hand up. 'I can't see anything at all!'

Grasping his fingers, Jackie carefully examined the back of his hand. 'Oh, I must have been imagining it!' she gasped surprisedly. 'I was sure I saw something!'

I know what I'd like to see! Grant mused, squeezing her fingers as he gazed down her cleavage, revealed by her partially open blouse. *I'd like to see your tits!*

Releasing his hand as Grant moved away to make the coffee, Jackie unbuttoned her white silk blouse and slipped it over her shoulders. Watching in amazement as she unclipped her bra and peeled the silk cups away from her ample breasts, Grant gasped.

'Jackie, what *are* you doing?' *Christ, you horny little tart!*

'I . . . I don't . . . I really don't know!' she stammered, gazing down at her long, wedge-shaped nipples, the darkening discs of her areolae.

'God, you're an attractive woman!' Grant beamed excitedly, his penis swelling, tenting his jeans. Grabbing the opportunity, he reached out and cupped her warm breasts in his palms as if to weigh them. *God, did my thoughts make her do this?* Imagining sucking her beautiful milk buds into his mouth, he gazed into her wide eyes as he pinched and twisted her sensitive nipples.

Making no attempt to shroud her nakedness as Grant knelt before her and gazed at her lavish breasts, Jackie sighed as he closed his lips over her nipple and sucked the erect protrusion into his mouth. Her head reclining, her eyes closed, she licked her succulent red lips as Grant moved to her other breast and gently nibbled the sensitive chocolate-brown bud.

'That's nice!' Jackie breathed, as her nipple stiffened in response to Grant's circling tongue. 'Suck me harder, bite me!' Gently nibbling the sensitive protuberance as he tweaked her other nipple with his finger and thumb, Grant breathed in her female scent, wondering at the girl's sudden disrobing. 'Harder!' she gasped in her arousal. This was incredible! Grant thought, sinking his teeth into her solid nipple. 'Bite harder!'

Why she'd slipped her blouse and bra off, Grant could only hazard a guess. *It must be some form of telepathy or thought transference*, he pondered. But why hadn't Karen shaved her blonde pubes when he'd willed her so strongly in his mind? Perhaps it only worked when the conditions were right? But what *were* the conditions? Slipping Jackie's nipple from his mouth, he sat back on his heels, willing the girl to beg to suck his penis. *Nothing!* he thought perplexedly, gazing at her appealing lips, praying that the day would come when *he*'d come – in her mouth.

His eyes smiling as he again sucked on her brown teat and kneaded her full breasts, he was happy that he'd at least got this far with her. But how to get into her knickers? he wondered as he released her breasts and focused on her shapely thighs – how to get into her hot, tight, wet cunt? *Stand up and take your skirt and panties off!* he urged her mentally. *Jackie, I want your cunt!*

Looking down at Grant, Jackie frowned. 'Why have you stopped?' she asked, cupping her breast and offering her erect milk bud to his mouth. 'Please, suck me again.'

Take your skirt and knickers off! I want your cunt!

'Grant? Grant, what's the matter, what are you thinking? Don't you like my breasts?' she asked, taking his hand and placing his fingers over her nipple. 'I like you doing that!' she sighed amorously as he pinched her sensitive teat. 'Squeeze them, squeeze them hard!'

One last try, Grant decided, rolling her nipple between his finger and thumb. *Stand up and take your skirt and panties off!*

Pushing her chair back as she rose to her feet, Jackie kicked her shoes off and unzipped her skirt, pulling it down her long, naked legs, revealing her bulging red panties to Grant's stunned eyes. The V of her tight panties clearly defining her sex-groove, Grant waited in anticipation, imagining her yawning cunt slit, her succulent inner lips. Tugging her panties down with her thumbs, exposing her thick black bush, her gaping pink slit, she stepped out of the garment and stood naked before him.

'God, you're beautiful!' Grant gasped, sensually stroking her milk-white inner thighs with his fingertips, still unable to believe that his thoughts had enticed the girl to strip. *No, it's not possible – is it?* Moving his finger up her thigh, stroking the swell of her full vaginal lips, he imagined slipping his tongue into her love sheath, lapping up her decanting girl-come.

Her face flushing, Jackie looked down between her breasts at her pubic bush as Grant ran his finger up and down her opening crack. 'Grant, I . . . God, why am I doing this? I don't know what I'm thinking of!'

I know what I'm thinking of! 'You've a beautiful body!' he grinned, suddenly realizing what the conditions were, how to use his strange power. 'I've got it!' he cried, parting her full cunny lips and easing a finger into her moist vagina, knowing that she'd not try to halt the invasion of her most private place. *Jackie, ask me to finger you.*

'You've got what?' she asked, standing with her feet

further apart and massaging her breasts, pinching her roused nipples. 'Ah, yes, that's nice! Finger me, Grant! Finger me!'

Grinning wickedly as he realized the potential of his incredible power, Grant decided to put Jackie to the test. Slipping another finger into her tightening cunt, thrusting deep into her hot hole, he closed his eyes and concentrated his thoughts. *Beg to suck my knob! Jackie, beg to suck my knob. Plead for me to come in your mouth!* Sitting on the chair as Grant slipped his wet fingers from her drenched vagina, Jackie grinned salaciously.

'Stand up, Grant,' she ordered huskily, moving forward on the chair and provocatively licking her full red lips. 'Please, I want to suck your knob.'

'And what else do you want?' he asked as he rose to his feet and stood before her, amazed by the apparent control he had over her mind, her actions.

'I want you to come in my mouth. Please, I want your sperm in my mouth!'

'Then you shall have it!' he grinned, tugging his jeans down. *Christ, this is too good to be true! But how the bloody hell does it work?*

Gasping, staring in awe as his huge penis catapulted to attention before her disbelieving eyes, Jackie parted her lips, gripping his hard shaft by the base and taking his swollen glans into her hot mouth. 'Mmm,' she moaned through her nose in her sexual delirium, her eyes closing, her tongue licking, savouring his salty plum. 'You taste lovely,' she breathed, slipping his glans out and licking his twitching shaft. 'I want you to come in my mouth, Grant. Fuck my mouth!' Moving her head forward, she took his ballooning knob to the back of her throat, kneading his heavy balls with one hand and wanking his solid shaft with the other.

Grinning, Grant thought again of the potential of his power. *Make physical contact with any woman, tell her what to do in my mind, and she'll do it!* he thought, incredible as the idea was. Recalling the previous evening when he'd willed Karen to shave her pussy hairs, there'd been no physical contact. That was the secret, he mused – physical contact! Should he put Jackie to another test? he wondered – ask her to shave her cunt? *Yes*, he decided in his wickedness. *But not until she's swallowed my spunk!*

Mouthing, sucking, fervently licking Grant's throbbing knob, Jackie's lust soared to fever-pitch. She couldn't get enough of his massive penis, kissing and adoring his huge weapon as if it was the first she'd ever seen. *Dirty little bitch!* Grant smiled inwardly. *I'll bet you frig your clitty to orgasm in bed at night!*

Yes, frig.

Paralysed as the unspoken words echoed through Grant's mind, he couldn't believe that he'd actually heard her thoughts. *How often do you masturbate?* he asked her mentally, wondering whether he was going mad.

Three . . . three times . . . week.

This was incredible! he contemplated as he watched her move her head back and forward, repeatedly taking his throbbing glans to the back of her throat. Realizing that he could discover Jackie's innermost secrets, he thought of Karen, wondering what skeletons she had in the cupboard. *I'll soon find out!*

Was Jackie aware that she was answering his intimate questions? he wondered. Or was he able to delve into her mind and discover her secrets without her knowledge? He was probably picking up her subconscious thoughts. But why were her thoughts coming across as broken words? Why not complete sentences? Blissfully unaware that her subconscious was revealing her darkest secrets, she'd never know of Grant's power, his ability to trespass in the murky alcoves of her mind. *Her subconscious can hear my thoughts*, he realized. That was the reason she'd followed his instructions, because he'd somehow gained direct access to her subconscious. *Suggestion, the power of suggestion!*

When did you discover masturbation? he asked in his mind.

Teens . . . early teens. Young . . . in bed.
Do you finger your cunt?
Handle. Hairbrush . . . long, nice, hard.

This was fantastic! Grant thought, watching the girl suckle his pulsating glans.

Fantastic, the girl's thoughts replied. Close to orgasm, Grant turned his attention to his penis, his throbbing knob – Jackie's hot mouth, her caressing tongue.

As his knob exploded in her mouth, filling her cheeks with sperm, Grant grabbed her head, rocking his hips, sliding his pulsating glans over her sweeping tongue. Gasping, he looked at her full lips, straining to stretch around the sheer girth of his extraordinary penis. How many women would enjoy his gushing sperm? he wondered as Jackie did her best to swallow the copious flow jetting from his throbbing glans. But what would Jackie think later, when she was at home? What would she think when she recalled what she'd done? Would she come back for more? Grant wondered as the last of his sperm shot to the back of her throat.

Slipping his knob from her sperm-drenched mouth, Jackie licked and kissed his shaft, worshipping his organ as Karen had done. But there was more to this than met the eye, Grant pondered as he watched his slave idolize his monument to male prowess. He desperately wanted to make contact with the strangers in the wood and discover exactly how his new-found domination over women worked. He had so many unanswered questions – but did he dare return to the woods?

Becoming bored with Jackie's penis-worshipping, he pulled away and tugged his jeans up, concealing his erect organ from the disappointed girl. 'Did you like that?' he asked as she looked up at him, a yearning in her big eyes, sperm running down her chin. *You loved it, didn't you?* he thought, brushing her cheek.

Sperm. Nice. Tastes nice. 'I loved it, Grant!' she grinned. 'I . . . I don't know what made me do it, but I loved it!' There was a strange innocence reflected in her eyes now, Grant noticed, but also confusion, conflict between the conscious and subconscious. 'You won't tell Karen, will you?' she asked anxiously.

'Christ! Of course I won't tell Karen!' he laughed, brushing her fringe away from her eyes. *I'm not mad!*

Not mad. Sperm, nice. 'I've never done that before,' she confessed, licking the spunk from her glistening lips. 'That was the first time I've ever . . .'

'You've still not got a boyfriend, then?' Grant asked hopefully as she dressed.

'No, no, I haven't.'

'You don't need one now that you have me, do you?'

'But you're Karen's partner! She's one of my best friends, Grant! I can't . . . I'd better go. I shouldn't have done what I did – it was wrong.'

It was brilliant!

Taking her hand as she finished dressing, Grant smiled and gazed into her pretty eyes, thinking his wicked thoughts. *Go to the bathroom and shave your pubic hairs off.* He hoped that he was right and she wouldn't be conscious of his thoughts as he willed her to shave her pubes. Christ, if she knew his game! he thought fearfully. But no, she wasn't consciously aware, he was sure.

This was the ultimate test! he thought gleefully, wickedly. If she followed his instruction without hesitation, then he had real power not only over Jackie and Karen but, possibly, all women he came into contact with. The possibilities were endless! he mused.

Shave. Pubic hair . . . shave.

Yes, Jackie, shave your pubic hair off. Go to the bathroom and use the razor.

Yes, shave. 'May I use the bathroom?' she asked as Grant squeezed her hand and reiterated his sinful thoughts.

'Yes, of course. You know where it is, don't you?'

Upstairs. 'Yes, I do. Grant, I . . .'

'What?'

'Oh, it doesn't matter.'

'Tell me, Jackie.'

'I'm . . . I'm having strange thoughts.' *Shave.* 'They're not my thoughts, though. That doesn't make sense, I know, but . . .'

'What sort of strange thoughts?'

Shave, pubic . . . 'I don't know how to explain it. I've always been sensitive, I can easily pick up people's moods, their emotions, but . . . I'm not sure what I'm picking up now!'

'Go to the bathroom, Jackie, and then go home. You're probably tired. Either that, or you've been out in the sun for too long.'

'No, it's not that!'

Go to the bathroom and shave your pubic hair.

Shave. 'I'll just go up to the bathroom and . . . I won't be long.'

Releasing her hand, Grant sat on the edge of the table as the girl left the room. Would he be able to pick up *any*one's thoughts? he pondered. *Christ, I'll discover everyone's darkest secrets!* But how powerful were his thoughts? Were they strong enough to coerce Jackie to shave her pussy, against her will? Would she change her mind once she was in the bathroom, clutching the razor? Without the physical contact, there was no point in sending out his encouraging thoughts. All he could do was wait, wait and pray – pray that Karen wouldn't come back!

Finally wandering into the kitchen, her face flushed, her hands trembling, Jackie sighed. 'I'd better be going, Grant.'

'Are you all right?' he asked, squeezing her hand.

'I'm confused.' *Shaved . . . shaved my hair.* 'I don't seem to know what I'm doing!'

Show me your cunt, Jackie. Lift your skirt, pull your knickers down, and show me your cunt!

Show Grant. 'Grant, I . . .' Jackie began as she lifted her skirt and tugged the front of her panties down. 'Grant, look what I've done.' *Show Grant.*

'God, you look beautiful!' he praised her, gazing longingly at her full, hairless vaginal lips, her open pussy crack, her smooth, baby-soft mound. 'But what on earth made you do it?'

'I don't know what made me do it! I really don't know what's come over me!'

'You obviously did it because you wanted to!' he laughed, still clutching her hand. 'I think you look lovely without any pussy hair!'

'It looks awful!' *Schoolgirl. Looks like . . . like schoolgirl.* 'Never in my life have I dreamed of shaving my . . .'

You think it looks lovely, Jackie. You like your pussy like that and you'll shave every day.

Shave pussy. 'Actually,' she smiled, bending over and gazing at her hairless vaginal lips. 'I quite like the idea of having a hairless pussy.' *Schoolgirl.*

'You look wonderful, you really do.'

'I don't understand any of this, Grant! It's as if someone else's thoughts are filtering into my head.' *Must go home.*

Are you conscious of my thoughts, Jackie?

No. Conscious, no.

Grant squeezed the girl's hand a little tighter. *You crave sex with me, Jackie.*

Crave . . . crave sex . . . 'I'd better be going!' she sighed, pulling her hand from his and adjusting her clothing. Walking into the hall, she turned on her heels. 'I don't understand all this. It's so unlike me to . . .'

'May I see you again?' he asked.

'I don't know, Grant. God, I can't stop thinking about you, your body, your . . . I just don't know what to do! My thinking's gone haywire! I don't want to break up your relationship with Karen, but . . . I must go home.'

'Yes, I understand,' Grant smiled, knowing that all he had to do when he wanted to get his hands on her naked body, his cock up her hairless cunt, was to hold her hand and think his thoughts of sex. 'Don't worry,' he reassured her. 'Everything's fine.'

'I *am* worried! I don't know what's happened to me! I've behaved like a tart, and now I've gone and shaved my . . . God, I don't know! You won't tell Karen that I called, will you?'

'No, I won't,' he smiled as he opened the front door. 'I'll ring you.'

'OK, Grant. Bye,' she replied as she stepped outside.

Grinning as he closed the door, Grant wandered through

the hall to the lounge, flopping onto the sofa and contemplating his fascinating domination over women, his ability to listen to Jackie's thoughts. Desperate to use his new power, to discover its true potential, his mind swirled with ideas. By shaking a woman's hand, a total stranger's hand, would he be able to influence her? Would he have the power to will strangers to strip and offer their naked bodies to him for sex? The power of the subconscious was formidable, he reflected. And he had direct access!

'Oh, what are you doing here?' Karen asked surprisedly as she entered the lounge and dumped her shopping bag on the floor. 'Why aren't you at work?'

Because I've been pumping sperm down Jackie's throat! 'I decided to take the day off. Where have you been?' he asked, admiring her tousled blonde hair, her sensual mouth.

'I've been shopping. Grant, I want to talk to you about the things we did last night.'

Christ, here we go again! 'Come and sit down, love,' he smiled, patting the sofa.

Sitting next to Grant, Karen frowned. 'I've been trying to think why I asked you to . . . well, you know, to do what you did to me last night. I don't know what happened to me, why I begged you to do it!'

'You liked it, didn't you?' Grant asked, taking her hand.

'Whether I liked it or not is beside the point!' *Liked it. Nice, sexy, rude.* 'It's just not like me to do that sort of thing!' *Sore bum. Nice.* 'I don't want you thinking that I'm a slut, Grant!' *Whore, tart, slut.*

'I don't think you're a slut!' he returned. *Karen, do you masturbate?*

Masturbate . . . no. 'I behaved like a slut!'

'Of course you didn't!'

'I really can't think what came over me.'

'I wouldn't worry about it if I were you. We enjoyed sex together, so what's wrong with that?' *Karen, take your clothes off. You feel horny, sexy.*

Clothes off . . . horny, sexy. 'I just don't understand it!'

'There's nothing *to* understand! You enjoyed it, and that's that!' *Have you ever been unfaithful to me?*

Unfaithful. No.

Is there anyone you fancy, anyone you fantasise about?

Next door. Man next . . . Chris.

Take your clothes off. You feel sexy, randy, horny.

Sexy. Clothes off.

Rising to her feet, Karen slipped her dress off and stood before Grant in her bra and panties. Grinning, she unclipped her bra, her breasts tumbling from the cups, her nipples growing as she peeled the silk garment from her firm mammary spheres. Silently tugging her panties down her long legs and kicking them across the room, she gazed at Grant with confusion reflected in her blue eyes. *Her conscious battling with her subconscious*, Grant concluded. *This is weird!*

'I feel so randy!' she breathed, gazing down at her naked body. 'Christ, what's happened to me? I feel really horny!'

Reaching out and taking her hand, Grant smiled reassuringly. 'There's nothing wrong with feeling horny!' *Turn round and stand with your feet wide apart and bend over!*

See my . . . pussy . . . see lips.

Do it, Karen. Stand with your feet wide apart and bend over as far as you can.

Following his unspoken instruction, Karen turned and bent over, her hands resting on the carpet, her feet wide apart. Gazing at the swell of her full pussy lips bulging between her parted thighs, Grant smiled, admiring the girl's pinken inner lips protruding invitingly from her vaginal groove. Kneeling behind her and stroking her swollen sex-hillocks, he planted a kiss on her buttock, licking her warm flesh.

'You're a sexy little thing!' he breathed, holding her leg. 'You look great, bending over like this!'

Dirty, rude. 'I must get dressed, Grant!' she sighed, slowly bringing her naked body upright. 'Julie's coming round soon so . . .'

Don't get up! Stay as you are! 'When did you see Julie?'

Julie . . . clothes, must dress. 'In town this morning,' Karen replied, bending over again. 'Grant, I must get dressed. Why on earth am I doing this?' *Humiliated.*

'To show me your beautiful cunt, that's why.' *Finger your cunt.*

Finger . . . cunt . . . 'God, I feel so randy!' she breathed, parting her pussy lips and sliding three fingers deep into her wet vaginal sheath. 'Ah, that's nice!'

Tell me how much you like fingering your wet cunt.

'God, I really love doing this! My cunt's so wet, so hot! Why am I feeling like this? Why am I doing this?' *Embarrassed.*

'Because you love it!'

Nice. Love it. Wet cunt. 'But I've never even dreamed of doing anything like this before!'

'There's always a first time!'

Masturbating. Bad girl!

Stunned by his amazing control over the girl, Grant released her leg. *Can't have her listening to my thoughts!*

She was sexually aroused beyond belief, he observed as she thrust three fingers in and out of her young pussy. Was it merely his thoughts that had transformed her? Turning into a tart, an insatiable whore, she was becoming someone else – another woman! Or was this the real Karen flooding through? Had her dormant sexuality, her latent feminine desires, somehow been woken?

Watching the beautiful sight, Karen's cunny-drenched fingers thrusting in and out of her tight vaginal duct, Grant shook his head disbelievingly and grinned. *I've got myself a real live nympho!* he thought, eyeing her inner lips clinging to her pistoning fingers. *I've also got Jackie and her shaved cunt!* Focusing on Karen's taut buttocks, her tight bottom-hole, he felt his penis swell painfully. Picturing her tight brown ring opening to allow his knob entry to her hot bowels, he wondered what other debauched act he could will her to allow him to commit. Bondage, whipping, caning, spanking . . .

Suddenly having a wicked idea, Grant rubbed his chin, grinning as he pictured another man's cock fucking his vulnerable girlfriend's tight cunt. To watch another man's swollen knob slip into her fanny, spunk up her cunt, would be incredible! Tie her down, legs wide apart, cunt lips gaping, rolling along the shaft of an intruding penis . . . Almost spunking in his jeans as he pictured the adulterous sight, his mind filled with lewd thoughts. *Sell her for sex! No, best not to go too far!* But he was sure she'd not be able to resist his powerful thoughts and protect her pussy, her anal canal, her pretty mouth, from penetration by another man's cock!

Go and get the vibrator I bought you and lie on the floor and masturbate, he urged, gripping her leg. As she slipped her cunny-wet fingers out of her vagina and left the room, Grant sat on the sofa, again contemplating his power. Why was she feeling so horny? he wondered. Picking up his thoughts was one thing, but what was turning her into a nympho?

Returning with the vibrator, Karen lay on the floor and spread her long legs. 'I'm going to use this,' she announced nonchalantly, switching the vibrator on and parting her swollen cuntal lips as if she were doing nothing out of the ordinary.

'Have you ever used the vibro before?' Grant asked, perching himself on the edge of the sofa for a better view.

'No, never! God, I'm feeling so randy, Grant!'

'Then bring yourself off with the vibro!'

Gasping as she pressed the tip of the buzzing phallus against her erect clitoris, she tossed her head from side to side, lost in the beautiful sensations emanating between her engorged pussy lips. 'God, I need to come!' she gasped. 'Ah, ah! Why am I feeling like this?'

'It doesn't matter why, just enjoy yourself, your cunt!'

'Ah! Ah, yes – my cunt!'

Moving between her legs, Grant thrust three fingers deep into her spasming vagina and transmitted his dirty thoughts. *Ask me to finger your bum.*

My bum. Finger bum. 'Ah, that's nice! God, it feels nice! Finger my bum, Grant!'

'Like this?' he chuckled, slipping his wet fingers from her tightening vagina and parting her taut buttocks. Pressing a finger deep into her rectal duct, he watched her contorting face, her gasping mouth, as the sensations from his anal massaging mingled with the pleasure throbbing within her erect clitoris.

Beautiful. Bum, beautiful. 'God, yes! Like that!' she cried as he managed to slide a second finger into her tight bottom-hole. 'Yes, like that!'

Are you sure you've never used the vibrator before?

No, never. Dirty. Rude. Nice.

Again, Grant pondered on returning to the woods. Having the greatest power over women he could imagine wasn't enough, he needed to learn more about it. He felt compelled to return to the sect. As if a powerful force were acting upon him, drawing him like a magnet, he sensed an irresistible desire to return. But there was danger lurking there, he was sure.

'Oh, Grant! Grant, I'm coming!' Karen wailed as her clitoris swelled and pulsated. *Fingers, want fingers.* 'Finger both holes!' she ordered crudely, much to Grant's delight. Parting her vaginal lips with his free hand, he drove three fingers into her drenched cavern. Two fingers pistoning in and out of her anal sheath, three driving into her contracting pussy hole, the vibrator transmitting incredible sensations deep into her pelvis, Karen rolled her eyes, crying as her multiple orgasm peaked, shaking her young body, rocking her very soul.

Never in his life had Grant seen a woman become virtually unconscious with sexual pleasure. Her body shaking violently, Karen brought her knees up, ballooning her engorged cunny lips between her thighs, tightening her grip on Grant's thrusting fingers as her orgasm rolled on. 'God, I can't stop coming!' she grimaced, lifting her head off the carpet as her body became rigid with lust, locked in orgasm. *Love my cunt.* 'God, I can't . . . I can't take any more!' *Fingers . . . wet cunt.*

Finally relaxing as her incredible pleasure subsided, Karen dropped the vibrator and lay quivering, perspiring, gasping, as Grant slipped his fingers from her love-sheaths. 'You certainly enjoyed that!' he laughed, eyeing the sticky girl-come pouring from her inflamed pussy hole. 'I've never seen anything like it!'

'Oh, God! Christ, that was . . . that was heavenly! I didn't know what I'd been missing! God, if only I'd discovered masturbation years ago!'

Clutching Karen's leg as the front doorbell rang, Grant sent out his wicked thoughts, willing her to allow her friend Julie to finger her cunt, to vibrate her clitoris, to tongue her vaginal crack. He'd grab Julie's hand and place thoughts of lesbian sex in her mind before she entered the room, will her to commit vile lesbian acts. But would it work? he wondered as Karen tried to lift her aching body off the floor.

'Stay there,' he smiled, still gripping her leg. 'I'll go and see who it is.'

Julie! Naked, no! 'It'll be Julie! I can't let her see me like this!' *Clothes!*

You want *her to see you naked, Karen! You* want *her to use the vibrator on your clitty. When you see her, you'll yearn for her to finger your cunt! Sit on the sofa. Don't dress, you* want *her to see your naked body!*

Lesbian. Girl, naked, pussy. 'I suppose I've got nothing that she hasn't got,' Karen conceded as she hauled her trembling body up and sat on the sofa, her legs open, her vaginal crack inflamed, drenched. 'We're both women, so . . .'

'I'll go and let Julie in,' Grant interrupted, rather too eagerly, praying for his evil plan to work.

Opening the door, he smiled at the attractive young girl and invited her in. *I could have a harem!* he pondered. Wondering what the hell he was trying to do, how far he'd go in his quest for debauched sex, he took the girl's hand in his. Sensing a pang of guilt stab his conscience, he knew that this was wrong, but he couldn't suppress his male desires, his rising lust, his unquenchable thirst for sexual deviance. He couldn't ignore or deny the amazing domination he now had over women.

'How are you, Grant?' Julie asked, kissing his cheek. Her miniskirt was tight, too tight, faithfully following the slight swell of her stomach, revealing her curvaceous thighs. Her T-shirt ballooning, the white material stretched tautly over her pointed breasts, Grant couldn't take his eyes off her delectable young body.

'I'm fine, Julie. Actually, I'm just going out. Karen's in the lounge,' he smiled, gripping the petite girl's hand a little harder. *You want lesbian sex with Karen. When you go into the lounge and see her naked body, you'll want to finger her, lick her cunt, suck her tits. You'll beg her to lick your cunt and make you come with her vibrator.*

Lesbian. No, not . . . masturbate. 'OK, I'll see you around sometime,' she replied, her dark eyes suddenly mirroring her anxiety as Grant's powerful thoughts permeated her subconscious. *Masturbate.*

Do you masturbate, Julie?
Masturbate. Nice, coming, fingers.
Where do you masturbate?
Bath, bed.
How often?
Day. Every day.

Still clutching the pretty girl's hand, dizzy with the power he had over her, Grant reiterated his thoughts, willing her to fall into a state of frenzied lesbian lust the minute she set eyes on Karen's naked body. 'Go through to the lounge, she's waiting for you,' he said, releasing her hand, imagining her masturbating in the bath. *No one can keep their dirty secrets from me!* 'I won't be long – I'll see you later, perhaps.'

Julie was eighteen, feminine in the extreme, her long dark hair shining in the light, her full red lips glistening invitingly as her pink tongue emerged from her mouth and swept over them. Would they soon glisten with sperm? Grant wondered. Would she fall prey to his debased thoughts and drink the gushing sperm from his knob after she'd enjoyed lewd lesbian sex with Karen? Yes! he decided. He'd have her, take her young body – fuck her pretty mouth and shoot his spunk down her throat!

Opening the front door as if about to leave the house, he watched the girl walk down the hall, wondering what colour her panties were, whether they were stained, cunny juice-stained. Imagining her naked, doing the splits, her cunt crack open wide, her fingers thrusting in and out of her hot hole, he shuddered. *Christ, I'm sex-mad!* he thought, imagining her kneeling before him, her naked body bound with leather straps, his penis throbbing in orgasm, pumping sperm over her tongue, filling her cheeks.

His erect organ twitching, he desperately wanted to learn how his power over women worked, what the power was, where it came from. Whatever evil lurked in the woods, he knew that he'd return. He couldn't resist the overwhelming urge to return and show himself, make himself known to the group. Dangerous though it was, he *had* to return!

Closing the front door as Julie entered the lounge, Grant tiptoed down the hall and took up his position of voyeur. Gazing through the crack in the door as the young girl sat beside Karen, he listened intently, again praying for his plan to work. Could his thoughts turn two straight women into rampant lesbians? *Christ, they might remain lezzies! No, I have the power to turn them into anything I wish!*

'Where's Grant?' Karen asked, seemingly having no concern for her nakedness, no shame, no embarrassment.

'He's gone out,' Julie replied, reaching for Karen's breast and squeezing her erect nipple. 'Karen, you're beautiful!' she breathed sensually, huskily, as she tweaked the girl's sensitive brown protrusion.

'Julie!' Karen cried, apparently shocked by her friend's uncharacteristic action.

Shit, it's not going to work! Why the hell . . .

'What are you . . .' Karen gasped as Julie leaned forward and sucked the naked girl's nipple into her pretty mouth. 'Julie . . . ah, that's nice! God, your mouth's hot! Suck harder, bite me! You like me feeding you, don't you? Lie on the sofa, on my lap, and I'll breast-feed you properly.'

His penis solid, bulging his jeans, Grant watched the girl lie with her head cradled in Karen's arms. *This is unbelievable!* he thought as Karen offered her distended nipple to Julie's hungry mouth. Closing her eyes and sucking on the tender milk bud, Julie parted her thighs as Karen pulled her skirt up over her stomach and slipped her hand down the front of the girl's pink panties. From Grant's vantage point, he could clearly see Julie's swelling vaginal lips as Karen moved her wet panties aside and gently massaged her young clitoris.

His thoughts returning to the debauched acts he could will Karen to commit, he decided that he'd invite a male friend to the house. *She fancies Chris!* he reflected wickedly, imagining his next-door neighbour easing his penis into Karen's tight anal sheath. In his increasing corruption, he pictured Karen bound with rope, her naked body draped over the kitchen table with another man pushing his solid cock deep into her drenched vagina. *Have I the same power over men as I have over women?* A life of debauchery stretched out before him, Grant smiled and concentrated on the girls' lesbian activities.

Karen's finger gliding in and out of Julie's wet cunt, her nipple in the girl's hungry mouth, the lesbian scene was highly arousing. Lovingly suckling at the breast, Julie's body visibly trembled, quivering as Karen dragged her friend's slippery pussy juice up her pink crack and lubricated her erect clitoris. Karen's expert massaging, her female masturbation taking Julie ever closer to her climax, Grant wondered whether he should enter the room and join the girls. Julie's cunt would be tight with youth, he knew – her bottom-hole even tighter! Should he show himself, display his massive cock, to the lust-struck lesbians?

Karen's nipple slipping out of Julie's mouth as the girl gasped with the pleasure building within her clitoris, Grant held his breath, gazing in awe at the young girl writhing in her orgasm. 'Ah, ah, don't stop!' she wailed as Karen quickened her massaging rhythm, bringing out the girl's orgasm with her vibrating fingertips, taking her to amazing heights of lesbian lust. 'That's heavenly! Rub me faster!'

This was too much for Grant! His penis craving a tight, hot, wet vagina, he slipped into the room and knelt before the girls. Clutching Karen's leg with one hand and Julie's arm with the other, he willed them to allow him to join in. *Julie, beg me to fuck you. Karen, beg me to fuck Julie. You want to watch me fucking another girl, you want to help, you want to guide my cock into Julie's cunt and watch me fuck her.*

As Julie's orgasm began to subside, the girl opened her eyes and gazed longingly at Grant. Hauling her quivering body upright, she slipped her wet panties off and reclined on the sofa with her skirt up over her stomach and her legs spread wide – her cunny crack inflamed, drenched.

'Fuck me, Grant!' she sighed, peeling her pussy lips wide apart and moving forward on the sofa as Karen lifted the girl's T-shirt up and yanked her bra away from her firm, pointed teenage breasts. 'Fuck me, Grant – please!'

Unzipping his jeans and releasing his weapon, Grant offered his solid shaft to Karen, instructing her to guide his knob into Julie's wet cunt. Obeying, Karen leaned forward, sucking Grant's ballooning glans into her mouth, wetting his penis before presenting his cock-head to her young friend's open vagina. Mouthing, sucking, Karen finally slipped the male organ from her mouth and ordered Grant to fuck her friend. 'I want to watch you fuck her!' she gasped. Moving forward on his knees as his plum gently slipped into the girl's fiery cunt, he sighed, shuddering in ecstasy as his tool absorbed the dank heat of her tight love duct.

Sucking Julie's erect nipple into her hot mouth, Karen massaged the girl's pulsating clitoris as Grant made his fucking motions, driving his weaponhead deep into her tightening love-mouth, stretching her young sex cavern open with the sheer girth of his rod. Gasping with the incredible pleasures her body was bringing her, Julie's eyes rolled, her head lolling from side to side as she was quickly taken to another mind-blowing orgasm.

His sperm suddenly jetting from his throbbing cock, Grant filled Julie's spasming cunt as she, too, climbed to the peak of her coming. Both shuddering, gasping as their climaxes rolled on, their bodies locked in orgasm, they thrust their hips, finding their rhythm and sustaining their pleasure. Biting on Julie's nipple, massaging her pulsating clitoris, Karen took Grant's hand in hers, pushing his fingers against the swell of her drenched pussy lips, desperate for him to massage her inner vaginal flesh. Slipping three fingers into his girlfriend's dripping cunt and massaging her clitoris with her thumb as he thrust his tool into Julie's gripping cunt, his head flopped forward, his face grimacing as his sperm continued to pump into the girl's sex cavern.

All three gasping, moaning, they finally collapsed into a heap of trembling limbs, their genitals hot, fiery, wet with sex. 'Christ!' Grant gasped as he finally slipped his massive tool from Julie's tight vagina and ran his purple knob up and down her yawning crack. 'Christ, that was . . .'

Come with me! Come with me to the woods!

The words echoing around Grant's mind, he looked at each girl in turn. They hadn't sent out the thought, so who had? he wondered as the girls kissed, locking their mouths, their tongues entwining in their new-found lesbian lust. Turning to the window, Grant stared in disbelief at a young blonde girl's face as she peered through the glass. Her blue eyes beckoning, Grant knew she was one of the strange sect. But how had she found him? What did she want?

Concealing his wet penis and zipping his jeans, Grant left the lust-hungry girls to lick, suck, masturbate, and finger each other. Dashing out of the house, he looked about him, but the mysterious girl had gone, vanished into thin air. Whimpers of lesbian sex emanating from the house, Grant shook his head as he stepped into the hall and closed the front door. 'How the hell did she find me?' he breathed as he recalled the girl's words. *Come with me to the woods*.

Grabbing his camera from the hall table, he left the house, closing the door behind him as Karen cried out in her female tongue-induced orgasm. He could always instigate the lesbian sex again, he mused as he climbed into his car and drove off. Now he had Karen and Julie under his control, he could use them for sex whenever he wished, and Jackie! But now, he had to return to the woods and discover . . . discover what? he wondered fearfully. *Discover what? Satan?*

Chapter Three

Closing the front door as Julie left the house, Karen pondered on her incomprehensible act of lesbian sex, her debauched session with Grant and Julie. Julie had left the house as bemused as Karen, wondering why she'd allowed the couple to use her young body for illicit sex. Confused, the girls had agreed to meet again after they'd had time to take in what they'd done, and tried to understand why they'd done it.

Recalling guiding Grant's penis into Julie's young love-mouth, Karen couldn't comprehend why she'd condoned his blatantly adulterous act, let alone helped him commit it! Contemplating the recent events, the changes both in herself and Grant, she pondered on the fact that her first night of lust had been triggered when Grant had returned from his UFO-spotting trip. Her second evening of wanton debauchery, of crude anal sex, had also followed one of his expeditions to the hill. *I wonder whether he's meeting another woman?* she mused, deciding to go to the hill the next time he went UFO-spotting and check that he really was there. But, even if he had been seeing someone else, that wouldn't account for the change in herself.

Sitting on the sofa, her nude body glowing in the aftermath of lesbian sex, Karen eyed the sticky vibrator she'd allowed Julie to bring her to orgasm with. Picking the device up and switching it on, she pressed the buzzing tip to her nipple, shuddering as her sensitive brown protrusion responded, distending, darkening in arousal. Opening her legs wide and massaging her solid clitoris with her fingertips, she closed her eyes, lost in her lust, her wanton act of self-loving. The sensations of orgasm quickly building, rhythmically contracting her young womb, she gasped, massaging her cumbud faster and tossing her head from side to side. Pressing the vibrator against her clitoris, the beautiful eruption came, gripping her very being, taking her to her sexual heaven. Waves of orgasm crashing through her young body, her breasts heaving, her stomach rising and falling, she could barely endure the awesome climax of her female masturbation.

As her sexual exhilaration began to subside, Karen lay trembling, wondering why she'd changed beyond recognition. Slipping the vibrator down her yawning pussy crack and into her hot cunt, she shuddered as the sensations permeated her pelvis, transmitting pre-orgasmic ripples of sex into her trembling womb. Her thighs splayed, the vibrator deep within her tightening cunt, she relaxed, savouring the gentle sensations of her rhythmically contracting vaginal muscles. The exquisite vibrations holding her on the threshold of orgasm, inducing her cunt milk to flow, she closed her eyes, rousing her nipples with her inquisitive fingertips, stiffening the aching protrusions.

Sex was good, she concluded as her clitoris palpitated, sending a jolt of pleasure deep into her pelvis, causing her womb to flutter. But she'd never imagined that it could be *this* good! As she lay quivering, teetering on the verge of orgasm, her body shaking in her sexual paradise, she wondered where Grant had got to, why he'd suddenly left the house without a word.

'God, I can't take any more!' she breathed as her aching

cunt spasmed and decanted its creamy lubricant. Slipping the wet vibrator from her tight, yearning vagina, she sighed. 'What's happened to me? Why am I behaving like this?' Leaping to her feet and pulling her dress on over her head, shrouding her naked body, her erect nipples, her matted blonde pubes, she moved to the window to see whether Grant's car was parked outside. 'Where is he?' she whispered, noticing his car across the road.

'I'm here!' he announced, followed into the room by Chris, their next-door neighbour.

'Where have you been?' Karen asked, aware of warm pussy juice oozing from her inflamed vagina and trickling down her inner thighs.

'I was going up to the hill, but I . . . I changed my mind. I might go this evening.'

Her heart fluttering, Karen turned to Chris, the man she'd fantasized about, trying not to show her emotions, her heady lust for his muscular body. 'Hi, Chris,' she smiled, her stomach somersaulting as she recalled her uncharacteristic fantasy as she'd watched him working in his garden, of Chris's bronzed naked body heaving on top of her.

'Hi, Karen, how are you?' he asked, his dark eyes catching hers as he swept his black hair back.

'Fine, fine,' she replied, aware of her sensitive nipples brushing against her dress.

Offering him a seat, she deftly slipped the wet vibrator beneath the sofa cushion and gathered up her bra and panties from the floor, wondering what he'd think if he knew what she'd been doing, how she'd spent the afternoon. Her mind still reeling with her wanton act of lesbian lust, she scrutinized Chris, imagining his muscular body naked, his penis stiff, hard in readiness to penetrate her sex.

In his mid-twenties, single and good-looking, Chris would

make a good catch for some young girl, Karen mused. She'd often gazed out of the bedroom window and watched him working in his garden with his shirt off, his muscles rippling. He worked from home, designing company logos, so he'd said when they'd first met over the garden fence. But he'd only moved in a month ago and Karen didn't know him very well – yet!

Taking Karen's hand as Chris reclined on the sofa, Grant smiled. 'Would you like some tea, love?' he asked, an evil glint in his eyes as his lust for perverted sex reared its beautiful head. *You want Chris to fuck you, Karen. You'll wank and suck him, and beg him to fuck you.*

'I'll make the tea, Grant. Would you like some, Chris?' she asked, turning her head to face her neighbour.

'Mmm, please,' he replied, noticing Karen's eyes focused on the bulging crotch of his tight trousers.

You'll beg Chris to fuck you, Karen. You'll ignore me and beg him to fuck you. You'll be crude, act as a common slut.

Releasing Karen's hand as she turned and left the room, Grant wondered how to make physical contact with Chris. He could hardly hold his hand! he mused as he sat beside him. 'I think I will go and search for UFOs this evening,' he said, tentatively brushing the back of the man's hand. *You want to fuck Karen. You desperately want to fuck her, Chris.*

'You and your UFO-spotting! I don't know why you bother!' Chris laughed. 'I reckon that . . .' His smiling eyes turning to a frown as Grant's thoughts drifted into his subconscious, he took a deep breath. 'Er . . . as I was saying, I don't know why you bother.'

When you're alone with Karen, she'll suck and wank you. Then you'll fuck her. 'One of these days, I'll see one. I know they're out there – the aliens.'

'There might well be life on other planets, but flying saucers?' Chris smiled, trying to keep up with the conversation as his subconscious swirled with Grant's powerful thoughts – thoughts of Karen's naked body, her hot cunt.

'Why not? Why shouldn't there be life, more intelligent life, further advanced than us?' *You want Karen's cunt!*

'Right, tea's up!' Karen smiled as she entered the room and placed the tray on the table. 'Sugar, Chris?'

'Two, please.'

'I'm just nipping upstairs,' Grant murmured, rising to his feet. His heart thumping hard against his chest, his hands trembling with expectation, with guilt, he left the door ajar and stood motionless in the hall. Spying, listening, he waited with bated breath. *God, what the hell am I doing?* he wondered, all too aware of his rising thirst for crude sex. *Why am I enticing Karen to be unfaithful?*

Glimpsing Chris's bulging trousers again as she passed him his tea, Karen caught his eyes and smiled. 'I can offer you more than tea,' she breathed huskily, wickedly.

'More than tea?' Chris repeated, placing his cup on the coffee table beside the sofa. 'What do you mean?'

Sitting next to him, Karen placed her hand on his knee. 'I like you, Chris – I like you very much. We should get to know each other a little better, don't you agree?'

'Yes, I do!' Chris replied eagerly, gazing down at Karen's hand as she manipulated his crotch. 'God, you . . . you don't waste any time, do you?'

'Why waste time when we both know what we want? I want your knob, and you want my cunt.'

'What about Grant?'

'Grant's not here, is he? Anyway, he won't mind sharing me with you,' Karen grinned, unzipping Chris's trousers and hauling his erect penis out. 'You don't mind sharing me with him, do you?' she asked, pulling his foreskin back as she leaned forward and took his purple glans into her hot mouth.

'God, that's nice! No, I don't, I . . . ah! Ah, your mouth's nice and hot! I can feel your tongue! I don't mind sharing you with him.'

Watching Karen take Chris's knob deeper into her hungry mouth, Grant wondered about his plan. This was Karen, supposedly his girlfriend – and he'd influenced her, willed her to become unfaithful! But his rising perversion had changed his relationship with the girl. In his debauchery, he desperately wanted to watch another man screw his girlfriend, to see her writhe in orgasm as another man's cock fucked her and filled her tight cunt with sperm. But would his plan work? Would they ignore him when he entered the room and watched their illicit fucking? Or would they feel embarrassment, shame, guilt, for their debauched act?

Making his move, Grant took a deep breath and sidled into the room. Sitting in the armchair, he watched Karen slip Chris's cock from her mouth and lift her dress, revealing her knickerless pussy to the man's wide eyes. 'You do want to fuck me, don't you, Chris?' she asked, looking down at her sparse blonde pubes. 'You do want to shoot your spunk into my wet cunt, don't you?'

'God, yes!' Chris replied eagerly, gazing at her pinken vaginal slit, her protruding inner lips – wet, glistening, inviting. 'God, you're a horny tart!'

Kneeling on the floor, Karen rested her head on the sofa, her dress high over her back, her buttocks taut, her pussy lips parted, wet in readiness for her adulterous fucking. Moving behind the girl, his rock-hard penis in his hand, Chris pushed his solid plum between her bulging cunny lips and into the welcoming warmth of her nest. Gasping as the veined shaft drove into her spasming vagina, Karen moved her knees further apart and reached between her legs, grabbing Chris's swinging balls.

'Fuck me hard, Chris!' she ordered in her unfamiliar depravity. 'Fuck me really hard!'

'You're a dirty little thing, aren't you?' Chris chuckled as he grabbed her hips and began his fucking. 'A right dirty little bitch!'

'Yes, yes, I am! Ah, God, that's good! Shaft me! Ram your cock deep into my tight cunt!'

Watching his girlfriend's faithless act, Grant again imagined selling her young body for sex. With the power he had over her thinking, her actions, he could will her to do anything! he mused as he moved behind Chris and touched Karen's foot. *Ask him to fuck your bum!* he thought wickedly. *Karen, beg Chris to fuck your arse!*

'Chris, I want your beautiful cock up my bum!' Karen gasped as her young body jolted with his vaginal pummelling. 'Fuck my arse!'

'Christ, do you really want me . . .'

'Yes! Push your cock deep into my arse and fill me with your spunk!'

Stunned, Chris slipped his shaft from Karen's hot vaginal sheath and presented his swollen knob to her small anal entrance. Easing her buttocks apart, he pressed his glans against her tight ring, gasping as her muscles yielded and his plum glided into her hot duct. Grabbing her hips, he gently pulled her closer to him, watching his shaft sink deeper into her tight rectum until he'd impaled her completely on his love staff.

His penis solid as he reclined in the armchair, Grant stared wide-eyed at the lewd spectacle, wondering what the young couple would think after they'd committed their illicit act.

How would they react when their obscene coupling was over, when Karen's bowels were swimming with Chris's spunk? How could they face Grant?

They had ignored him, as he'd willed them to, but did they know he was there? he wondered. Were they aware of their voyeur? Imagining slipping his penis into Karen's tight pussy as Chris fucked her bum, Grant's perversity was now running dangerously wild. Was there nothing he wouldn't do in his quest for more and more obscene sex? he wondered, picturing Karen bound to a tree, her bottom-orbs bared, whipped with a cat-of-nine-tails until they glowed crimson and she begged for mercy. *I'll transform the bitch into a sex machine!* he laughed inwardly, imagining a dozen men standing over her naked body, wanking, splattering her with their gushing spunk.

'Coming!' Chris cried, driving his pulsating shaft-head deep into Karen's inflamed rectal sheath. 'God, I'm coming!' Pumping his sperm into the whimpering girl's spasming anal canal, Chris peeled her buttocks wide apart, affording Grant a perfect view of his girlfriend's tight anal ring stretched around the thrusting penis. Crying out in her lust as she groped between her swollen cunt lips and vigorously massaged her pulsating clitoris, Karen's transformation was complete. Now she was Grant's slave, a woman with whom he could do what he wanted, when he wanted.

As the couple continued their anal fucking, Grant's mind swirled with the evil acts he could will Karen to commit. He'd build a structure to bind her naked young body to. Create a framework with leather straps to secure her in lewd positions, some form of arrangement where she could sit with her legs open, her cuntal lips exposed, gaping. A high chair, he mused, with arms and leather straps and wooden extension pieces to secure her open legs. Her thighs splayed, her cunt would be yawning, open, vulnerable – her body defenceless to his every perverted whim.

'God, that was good!' Chris cried as he extracted his spent penis from Karen's tight anal duct and sat on his heels.

'That was amazing!' Karen giggled, bringing her exhausted body upright and turning to face Chris. Standing before him and lifting her skirt, she peeled open her wet cunny lips, exposing her pinken feminine intimacy, her swollen clitoris to his wide eyes. 'I want your tongue up my cunt!' she ordered in her wickedness. 'Lick my cunt out!'

There had been no subconscious instruction to trigger *that* request! Grant thought. Perhaps she was becoming nymphomaniacal in her own right, without his prompting thoughts? Watching as Chris knelt before Karen and licked the full length of her wet vaginal slit, Grant wondered again whether they were aware that he was there, watching their intimate act. There was definitely more to all this than suggestion, he knew. Karen had instigated the vaginal licking herself – why? Was it simply her arousal that had impelled her to order Chris to lick her?

Confused, Grant hoped that the character changes were over at last. Now, this really *was* the new Karen, the nymphomaniac, the insatiable tart, the sex-crazed whore. 'Do you like Chris licking your cunt?' Grant asked, watching the man's tongue sweep up her drenched sex-slit.

'God, yes!' Karen breathed, tossing her head back and clinging to tufts of Chris's black hair as his tongue swept over her erect clitoris.

'You don't mind me watching?'

'No, I don't mind. I like you watching.'

His thoughts turning to the young girl he'd seen at the window, Grant became uneasy. Rising to his feet, he moved towards the door and slipped into the hall. Dusk was falling, and the woods beckoned. Karen and Chris were happy enough revelling in their new-found lust, he mused as he opened the front door. *Might as well leave them to it!*

Images of the young blonde haunting him, Grant climbed into his car and drove to the foot of the hill. He hadn't visited the woods earlier during daylight as he'd felt that the group would only meet there at night. He'd also been fearful, as he still was! *How did that girl know where I lived?* Telepathy, he mused. She'd somehow locked on to his subconscious and traced him to the house.

Parking his car and grabbing his camera from the passenger seat, Grant climbed the hill. Were they there? he wondered. Were they expecting him? *Jesus, I must be mad!* Imagining Satan waiting for him, he entered the wood and trod his way through the undergrowth, again thinking that he must be completely insane to return to the clearing, to whatever danger lurked.

Welcome. The unspoken word echoing through his mind as he approached the clearing, he knew it was the girl he'd seen at the window. Placing his camera on the ground as he hid behind the familiar bush, he peered through the branches at the naked girls. *Come, join us*, the speechless invitation reverberated through his mind. His adrenalin flowing, Grant stood and moved around the bush, revealing himself to the sect. *Do not be afraid*, one of the young men communicated telepathically.

Can you hear me? Grant thought, his dark eyes frowning.
Yes, we can all hear you. Join us. Remove your clothing and join us.

Slipping out of his clothes, the flickering flames of the fire mesmerizing him, Grant felt a little easier. The two young men were like identical twins, and there was no visible difference between the pretty girls. Surely, they weren't all brothers and sisters? Their bodies were perfect, unblemished, beautiful in the extreme, almost unreal. But there was evil lurking, Grant could feel it!

His breathing unsteady as he stood naked before the group, he looked down at his erect penis. He felt no shame, no embarrassment, only an overwhelming sexual urge. Raising his eyes to the girls' bloated pussy lips, he frowned. *Are those their clitorises emerging from their cracks?* he wondered, focusing on the swollen pink protrusions.

Yes, our clitorises, a female voice echoed in his head as one of the girls parted her vaginal lips, revealing her inch-long penis-like clitoris to Grant's wide eyes. *Your penis has enlarged. Veneris caught you with her light, did she not?*

Yes, she did, Grant replied mentally as a young blonde stepped forward.

Kneeling before him, she took the bulbous head of his penis into her mouth and gently sucked. As another girl stood before him, Grant wondered at the telepathy, the clarity of the thoughts as they filtered into his mind.

How does it work? he wondered.

You do not understand, do you? one of the men asked.

No, I don't.

Do not try. Be happy with your power, but do not abuse it as you have already done!

Who are you? Grant asked as the girl kneeling before him slipped his knob from her hot mouth and stood, her deep blue eyes gazing up to the trees.

We are friends of males.

'Veneris!' the men chanted, their hands high above their

heads as they looked up to the trees. 'Veneris, come unto us and charge this man's genitals with your great sexual power!'

Becoming increasingly afraid, Grant looked up to the trees, wondering about the green light that had previously sought him and played between his thighs. *Will it hurt?* he pondered as a ball of eerie green light began to form high above the clearing.

No, it will not hurt you. Stand still, do not move. Veneris is here.

Snaking down from the shimmering ball, finger-like shafts of light reached out, touching each member's genitalia. Looking down at his penis as the light flickered between his legs, Grant grimaced, his organ swelling, becoming painfully hard. *Stand still!* someone instructed as he squeezed his eyes shut. *Do not move!*

The fingers of light finally retracting into the ball, Grant opened his eyes, gazing at his huge organ, sure that it had grown. *Choose. Which female do you want?* The male words filtered into Grant's mind as he raised his head and looked at the pretty young girls.

They all look the same!

They are different in many ways. Choose.

As Grant pointed to a girl, the men grabbed her, dragging her struggling body across the clearing to the fallen tree. Slapping her buttocks with the palms of their hands as she desperately fought to escape, the men laid her on her back over the tree, her legs spread, her vaginal lips swelling, parting. Slapping her inner thighs, reddening her pale flesh, they quickly bound her struggling body with rope.

She is yours to use for your sexual pleasure!

Why do you hurt her? Grant asked, gazing at the girl's

body arched over the tree, her arms painfully outstretched, her wrists bound with rope.

She is yours, take her!

Standing between the girl's thighs, Grant pressed his knob into her gaping pussy slit, locating her wet vaginal entrance and pushing his penis deep into her tight cunt. Gazing at her incredibly long clitoris as her vagina tightened around him, gripping his penis like a velvet-jawed vice, Grant cast his eyes over her curved body to her breasts, her amazingly huge nipples. She was a rare beauty, he mused as he slipped his penis out of her gripping vagina and drove into her again. But why had they treated her so cruelly?

Making his fucking motions, driving his knob deep into her fiery cunt, Grant wondered whether he'd be allowed to join the orgies every night. He imagined taking each girl in turn, using his massive penis, his incredible staying power to fuck each girl in turn. Were they all as hot and tight as the little beauty he was fucking? he wondered. The girl's cunt was becoming tighter than any he'd fucked, her clitoris the largest he'd seen, visibly throbbing as she cried out in her enforced pleasure.

This was a unique find, he thought as his sperm suddenly gushed, drenching her vaginal cavern. Wailing as her own climax ripped through her quivering body, the girl's cunt rhythmically contracted, almost painfully crushing Grant's throbbing knob as he repeatedly thrust into her. On and on Grant's sperm gushed, overflowing from her hot vagina, spewing from her trembling body, drenching her inner thighs as the endless fucking took her ever higher to her sexual heaven.

His heavy balls slapping her sperm-drenched taut buttocks as he made his final thrusts, Grant gazed in amazement at the girl's clitoris, twitching, pumping like a miniature penis in orgasm. *I'd love to suck her clit!* he thought as she whimpered in her coming.

You may. She is yours, her body is yours to do with as you wish. When you have had your pleasure, you will whip her!

Whip her?

Yes, whip her until she screams and begs for mercy.

Slipping his wet penis from her increasingly tightening pussy hole, Grant knelt with his head between her thighs, wondering why the girl should be whipped. It was as if she was to be punished, he mused – used, fucked, and then punished. Gazing in awe at her full vaginal lips, her long clitoris, stiff, pulsating, standing proud from her sex-groove, he moved forward and sucked the pink protrusion into his mouth. The girl's body jolting as he ran his tongue over the sensitive tip of her erectile sex-button, he quickly took her to another shuddering orgasm.

Her vaginal lips engorged, becoming red in her arousal as her climax shook her young body, he thought she was going to pass out with the incredible pleasure he was bringing her. Her girl-come spewing from her open vaginal entrance, splattering his chin, his neck, Grant had never witnessed a girl experience what was obviously a multiple orgasm of such amazing intensity and duration. Her cunt milk pumped from her love-mouth like sperm from a penis, her clitoris throbbed, pulsated violently, as he sucked out her orgasm, sustaining her sexual pleasure.

The girl finally letting out a long sigh, her naked body calming, Grant slipped her solid clitoris from his mouth and stood between her thighs. Turning, he smiled at the young men, wondering what was going to happen next. *You must whip her!* The cruel words seeping into his mind as the men released the girl and turned her struggling body over, Grant became fearful again. *Why treat the girl as if she were an animal?* he pondered. It was as if the males were taking their revenge on the females, but why?

Handed a length of rope, Grant looked at his prisoner's taut buttocks as she was tied over the tree in preparation for the beating. Lit by the flickering fire, her bottom-orbs taut in youth, unblemished, he ran his fingertips up her dividing crease. Her body was trembling uncontrollably, her smooth buttocks tensed in her fear. She was terrified, he knew as he hesitantly turned to face the men. *You must whip her! Having taken her for your pleasure, it is expected!* Facing the girl again, Grant raised the rope above his head and brought it down with a loud crack across her twitching buttocks. The girl's body jolting in response, she cried out, filling the wood with her screams as the rope lashed her again. *Whip her harder!*

Again, Grant brought the rope down, lashing her twitching buttocks, gazing at the pink weals spreading out across her crimson flesh as he continued the cruel thrashing. His penis still solid, he wondered again whether he'd be allowed the pleasure of the other young girls' bodies, given permission to fuck each one in turn.

The quaking girl begging for mercy, Grant carried on the lashing, turning her pale buttocks a fire-red, her screams becoming louder, blood-curdling. *Enough!* Halting the beating, Grant dropped the rope and turned to face the bizarre group, asking how they'd discovered where he lived.

We located you by your thoughts.
I don't understand. Is this really telepathy?
Yes. When you were spying on us, Veneris reached out and charged you – that should not have happened. But as it did, and your penis grew, enlarged, we have had to ask Veneris to complete the process. This has been done.

How long have you been having your occult meetings here?

Go now! Do not return, never return!

But . . .

Clothe yourself and go, never to return! And remember, do not abuse the power you have. If you do, then . . . go now!

Hurriedly dressing as the trembling girl was released, Grant smiled at each member of the group before slipping into the undergrowth. Kneeling behind the bush, he grabbed his camera and secretly took several shots of the naked girls, praying that there was enough light from the fire for his camera to work properly. They were a weird bunch, he mused, watching two girls kneel before the men and suck their bulbous knobs into their mouths – a weird bunch!

Stealing through the undergrowth, wondering why he'd been ordered never to return, Grant finally emerged from the wood and sat on the grass. *I'll develop the film later*, he decided. His experience hadn't really sunk in, he mused, wondering at Veneris, the Goddess of Carnality. *The whole thing's bloody weird!* But, he reflected gratefully, weird though it was, his penis had enlarged incredibly, and the girls' clitorises were amazing! Was there really a Goddess of Carnality? he wondered fearfully. 'I'll never go back!' he asserted, climbing to his feet and running down the moonlit hill to his car. He'd been lucky this time, but next time . . .

Noticing a car parked next to his, Grant frowned. *Must belong to one of the sect*, he mused, taking a mental note of the registration number. *Shame I don't know any coppers!* he thought, wondering how to discover the owner's identity. But the car hadn't been there when he'd arrived, and no one had entered the clearing while he'd been there. 'Some young couple screwing beneath the stars!' he chuckled.

Wondering whether Karen was still fucking with Chris as he drove off, Grant pondered again on the green light. He'd seen the light creeping over Karen's face when she'd sucked his knob. Was that the reason Karen's libido had dramatically rocketed? Yes, it must be, he concluded. The power, whatever it was, had flowed from his penis and charged Karen. *Christ, what if she were to go to the wood and have a full blast of the power?* he thought, imagining her having an inch-long clitoris and huge nipples.

Chris had gone by the time Grant breezed into the lounge and flopped onto the sofa beside Karen. Noticing a green shimmer playing around his fingers, he clasped Karen's hand in the hope that she'd be charged with the strange power, become even more nymphomaniacal.

'I've been up to the hill,' he smiled, wondering what she thought of her lewd sex session with Chris.

'I wondered where you'd got to,' she replied. 'Chris left ages ago.'

'Did you enjoy screwing him?'

'Yes, very much. But I don't understand why you're not jealous, and why I don't feel guilty. It was as if it was the natural thing to do, to allow Chris to screw me. God, right here in the lounge, I let Chris screw my bum! And you were watching!'

'But you enjoyed it, didn't you?'

'Yes, I did. Anyway, I've given up trying to work it all out. I've been sitting here for ages trying to make sense of it all, why I feel the way I do about Chris and everything. But I've given up now and accepted that, whatever has happened to me, it's here to stay.'

'Will you screw Chris again?' Grant asked, desperate to watch his girlfriend used for crude sex.

'Yes, if you don't mind.'

'I don't mind at all. Perhaps I'll join in next time!'

'God, two men at once!' Karen exclaimed, holding her hand to her mouth as she imagined two penises entering her love holes.

'Yes, why not?'

'I suppose it might be interesting,' she murmured, obviously confused by her thinking, her desire to enjoy the intimate attention of two men – two rock-hard penises. 'By the way, a man rang for you earlier.'

'Who?'

'He didn't say. He asked if you were up the hill, in the wood.'

'In the wood?'

'Yes. Any idea who it was?'

'No, none at all!' Grant frowned, wondering who knew about the wood. *Unless it was one of the sect?*

'I expect he'll ring again,' Karen smiled. 'God, two men at once!' she breathed, imagining two solid penises entering her tight love holes.

Again, Grant thought about shaking a stranger's hand and thinking his wicked thoughts. Releasing Karen's hand as he had an idea, he stood up, desperate to try out his power. 'I'm just going over the road for a pint,' he said. 'I won't be too long.'

'OK. I think I'll go up to bed, I'm completely knackered! Don't get pissed, will you?'

'Of course I won't! I'll try not to wake you when I get back. See you later,' Grant said, affectionately kissing Karen's forehead before leaving the room. 'By the way, where's the vibrator?'

'It's . . . it's beneath my pillow,' she replied bashfully.
'Great! See you later.'

Ten-thirty, he mused, checking his watch as he closed the front door behind him and walked the short distance to the local pub. If this worked, and he could pull the barmaid, there wouldn't be a woman in the world that he couldn't fuck! he thought happily as he entered the deserted pub. 'John Smith's, please,' he said, catching the young barmaid's blue eyes as he approached the bar. *If she's got her own flat, I'll get her to invite me back for a fuck!* he thought wickedly as she placed his beer on the counter.

'You're new here, aren't you?' he asked.

'Yes, I started last night,' she replied, a smile curling her full red lips.

Her breasts heaving, straining the tight material of her blouse, Grant was desperate to knead her heavy mammary spheres, to suck on her erect nipples. Suddenly having an idea as he paid for his pint, he smiled at the girl, crossing his fingers, praying for his wicked plan to work.

'I'm a professional psychic,' he announced without introducing himself.

'I don't believe in all that rubbish!' she laughed, her long blonde hair falling over her pretty face as she leaned on the bar. 'I've heard some chat-up lines in my time, but that one's crazy!'

'Here, give me your hand and I'll prove it to you.' Taking the girl's hand, Grant delved into her subconscious, pried into the darkest corners of her mind to discover her secrets. 'Well, Diana, firstly . . .'

'How do you know my name?' she asked as he gripped her hand a little tighter. 'I only started working here last night! How could you possibly . . .'

'Does your boyfriend know that you're seeing his brother?'

'How . . . how do you . . .' she stammered, her blue eyes widening.

'His name's Ian – your boyfriend, I mean.'

'You must have been speaking to someone who . . . all right, tell me something that no one could possibly know about me. Oh, hang on, I'll just serve this customer,' she said as a man entered the pub.

This was fun! Grant reflected, watching the pretty girl pull a pint for the man standing at the other end of the bar. Gazing at her long blonde hair cascading over her ample breasts, he felt his penis stiffen. *I'll fuck her tight cunt if it's the last thing I do!* he asserted as she returned.

'This evening, before you came here, you had a bath,' Grant began, taking her hand in his.

'Yes, but that's nothing special! Most people . . .'

'But it's what you did in the bath,' he smiled, gazing into her astonished eyes.

'I . . . I washed, that was all!' she returned apprehensively.

'You did more than wash, Diana! It's OK, I won't embarrass you with the details.'

'There *are* no details! All I did was wash!'

'You've got a small vibrator, haven't you?'

Pulling away, her hands visibly trembling, the girl grabbed a glass and shoved it under an optic, filling it with two measures of vodka. Topping her drink up with lime, she dropped two ice cubes into the glass and gazed at Grant. What was she thinking? he wondered, desperate to touch her hand again. She must think it amazing!

'You're wrong!' she finally announced. 'Completely wrong!'

'Am I? Give me your hand again and I'll tell you more about yourself.'

Tentatively placing her hand on the bar, she watched Grant lay his fingers on her warm skin. Taking a deep breath and closing his eyes, he sighed. 'Ah, yes, yes,' he whispered mysteriously. 'You got the vibrator from a company you saw advertised in a magazine. It's small, black in colour and . . .'

'Can't you tell me anything else?' she interrupted, her face flushing with embarrassment, guilt.

'Yes, I can tell you anything.'

'Tell me what I'm thinking about now.'

'You're thinking about your car. You've been having trouble with it and . . .'

'Yes, that's right! But . . .'

'You did masturbate in the bath, didn't you?'

'Shush! That man will hear you! Anyway, you got that bit wrong.'

'All right, have it your way.' *You want to see me again. You want to meet me.* 'Your television is on the blink, isn't it?' *Ask me to meet you tomorrow afternoon.*

'Yes, it is! What are . . . what are you doing tomorrow afternoon?'

'Not much, why?' *Meet me in the car park at the foot of Horstead Hill.*

'I just wondered whether you'd like to meet me.'

'Yes, why not? How about going for a walk in the country?' *The car park.*

'OK. Do you know Horstead Hill? I'll meet you in the car park by the hill at three.'

'Great, I'll look forward to it! My name's Grant, by the way.'

'OK, Grant. You must tell me more about this mind-reading thing, it's fascinating! I'll bet you can't tell me my phone number.'

'Two five . . . er . . . two five four, seven nine eight.'

'Yes, that's incredible! Oh, I have a customer to serve, excuse me for a minute,' she said as a young couple entered the pub.

Gulping his beer, Grant pondered on the possibilities of making money from his 'mind-reading' act. *As much sex as I want, with whom I want, plenty of money . . .* The sky was the limit, he mused, deciding to give up his job and spend his life screwing women and earning cash from his act. Finishing his beer as the girl returned and leaned on the counter, Grant reached out and held her hand.

Invite me back to your place for coffee, he thought, gazing into her blue eyes.

'Would you like to come back for a coffee after I've finished here?' she asked, her smiling eyes now frowning, mirroring her confusion.

'What about your boyfriend, and his brother?' Grant asked. *Invite me back. You fancy me, you fancy me rotten!*

'I have my own place. I'd really like you to come back with me.'

'OK. How long will you be here?' *You really fancy me, Diana!*

'My boss will be down to close up soon. Give me about ten minutes.'

'OK. I'll have another John Smith's while I'm waiting,' he smiled, releasing her hand.

Gazing at the girl's long legs, her tight miniskirt hugging her rounded buttocks as she pulled his pint, Grant grinned, his stomach somersaulting at the prospect of slipping his penis deep into her tight vagina. The full potential of his power finally sinking in, he pondered on the future. Should he stay with Karen? he wondered. Yes, for the time being, anyway. He needed a base, and someone to do the cooking and washing while he was out screwing young girls! Downing his second pint as the landlord entered the bar and spoke to Diana, Grant thought of the night ahead. *Screw her senseless!* he laughed inwardly as she grabbed her bag and walked around the bar towards him.

'Ready when you are,' she smiled, slinging her bag over her shoulder. 'He's let me off early.'

'Right, let's go!' Grant replied eagerly as he placed his empty glass on the bar. 'How far is your place?'

'My flat's just round the corner. I only moved in last week so I'm not properly organized yet. It's rather messy, I'm afraid.'

'That's OK.' *It's your wet cunt I want, not your flat!*

Taking her hand as they left the pub, Grant thought his wicked thoughts. *You'll want to get straight down to sex when you're home. You'll stand in front of me and strip. You'll want to strip and show me your naked body.*

'Actually,' Diana began as she approached a front door between two shops and pulled a key from her bag. 'I know I said that I had my own place, but I share with another girl.'

Damn! Grant thought, following her through the door and up the stairs. 'Is she in?' he asked, suddenly realizing that he could screw both of them.

'Yes, she should be. Come through to the lounge, you can do your mind-reading thing on her,' Diana smiled, opening a door on the landing. 'You'll have to excuse the mess, I'm afraid. Hi, Mandy! Grant, this is my flatmate, Mandy,' she said as Grant followed her into the room and gazed at a delectable girl perched on the sofa.

Her long black hair framing her pretty face, her eyes sparkling, her curvaceous young body swathed in a tight, pink silk gown, she stood and held her hand out. 'Hi, Grant,' she smiled. 'Pleased to meet you.'

'Don't touch him!' Diana squealed excitedly, holding her hand to her mouth. 'He's a mind-reader!'

'A mind-reader?' the girl echoed, shaking Grant's hand. 'Well, how interesting. Tell me, Grant, what's on my mind?'

'Coffee. You're wondering who should make the coffee, you or Diana.'

'Incredible!' she gasped.

Take your dressing gown off. It's a very hot night. You feel very hot. You want to show me your beautiful body, Mandy. Take your dressing gown off. 'You're also wondering whether to go to your room and leave us alone.'

'That's amazing! How do you do it?'

Take your dressing gown off and show me your naked body. 'I can't explain. It's rather like riding a bicycle, you know how to do it, but you can't explain it.'

Releasing the girl's hand as Diana invited him to sit on the sofa, Grant wondered whether she'd picked up his wicked thoughts. Sitting down as Diana left the room, announcing that she'd make the coffee, he gazed at the girl's tight robe, praying that she'd open it, slip it off her shoulders and stand naked before him.

'It's so hot tonight,' she smiled, slipping the gown over her shoulders and dropping it to the floor. Her expression was one of bewilderment as she gazed at her pert breasts, her elongated nipples. Smiling, Grant agreed that it was hot, very hot, as he scrutinized her well-trimmed black pubes, her pinken vaginal slit, her protruding inner petals.

'Do you mind if I sit beside you?' she asked. 'I want you to tell me my future.'

'Be my guest!' Grant said, stunned by her beautiful body, and by his ability to influence women to strip, to have sex with him.

'So, what's in store for me?' she asked as she sat beside him and took his hand in hers. 'Anything interesting, such as a few million pounds?'

'Er . . . I'm not really a fortune teller.' *You want me, Mandy. You want my body, my cock.* 'But I can tell you that you don't have a boyfriend at the moment. Brian, that was his name – he left you for another girl.'

'That really is incredible!'

'Mandy!' Diana cried as she entered the room. 'Mandy, what *are* you doing?'

'Talking to Grant,' the girl replied, nonchalantly turning to face Diana.

'But, you've taken your dressing gown off!'

'I was hot.'

'Come and sit down,' Grant invited, smiling at Diana. 'I'll read your mind again.'

Sandwiched between the two girls as Diana sat down, Grant pondered on the incredible situation. Two beautiful young girls at his disposal! Life was good, bloody good! he mused. *Right, let's get started!* Holding Diana's hand, he turned to face her. 'Let's see what I can get for you.' *Diana, you're feeling hot and horny. Stand up and strip off. Do it now, you're hot and horny. You want sex with me, and with Mandy.* Releasing her hand as she rose to her feet, he clasped Mandy's hand. *Mandy, you want sex with Diana and me. When she's naked, you'll kneel before her and lick her pussy crack.*

His eyes locked on Diana's hands as she stood before

her audience and unbuttoned her blouse, Grant sensed his penis ballooning painfully within his tight jeans. What a night this was going to be! he thought, imagining the girls doing sixty-nine, licking each other's dripping pussy slits out. His lust rising fast, he placed his hand between Mandy's parted thighs and ran a finger up and down her sex-groove.

'Mmm, that's nice,' she breathed, parting her thighs and reclining. 'That's it, just there!' she gasped as he located her erect clitoris with his cunny-wet fingertip. Watching Diana toss her blouse to the floor and unclip her bra, Grant waited in expectation. Her breasts were ample, he observed as her bra cups fell away from her mammary globes, revealing her dark areolae, her long brown milk buds – more than ample!

Running his fingertip around Mandy's throbbing clitoris as she closed her eyes and sighed, lost in her arousal, Grant didn't take his eyes off Diana. Tugging her miniskirt down her long legs, revealing her bulging pink panties to his hungry eyes, she kicked the garment aside along with her shoes. Silently gazing at Grant as she stood before him in her panties, she peeled the pink material away from her young mound, exposing her bloated vaginal lips, her yawning dividing groove, her protruding pinken inner lips.

Diana was a real beauty! Grant decided, still massaging Mandy's solid cumbud. *Mandy, kneel before your flatmate and lick her pussy slit*, he urged in his mind. Slipping off the sofa as Grant retrieved his fingers from her cunny slit, Mandy knelt before Diana. *I could video scenes such as this and earn myself a fortune!* Grant thought wickedly as Mandy peeled Diana's pouting labia open and licked her inner flesh. Standing, his penis twitching, solid, Grant decided that he wanted some of the action as

Diana began to gasp in response to the caressing female tongue.

'Diana, stand with your feet as far apart as you can,' Grant instructed the girl as he placed his hand on her shoulder. *Do as I say, Diana.* Obediently complying, she moved her feet apart, her cunny groove opening, allowing Mandy access to her innermost fleshy folds. Slipping his jeans off as the girls enjoyed their lesbian coupling, Grant grabbed his solid penis, gazing at the monster, sure that it had grown even more. 'OK, Diana,' he said, holding her shoulder again. 'Bend over and rest your hands on the floor.' *Do it, Diana. Bend over and touch the floor.* 'Mandy, you can guide my cock into her wet cunt,' he ordered crudely, grinning as the girls immediately took their positions.

Diana's pussy lips bulging between her milk-white thighs as Grant stood behind her and offered his huge organ to Mandy, he knew that this was going to be one of the best fucks he'd ever had. 'Guide me in!' he instructed Mandy. His bulbous knob stretching her pussy folds wide open as Mandy grabbed his solid shaft and guided it in, Diana gasped, her young curvaceous body trembling as his knob drove deep into her hot, tight cunt. 'Ah, that's good!' Grant breathed, her taut lips gripping the base of his cock, his glans pressing hard against her cervix.

You like it, Diana. You like it very much! Grant suggested silently. 'Do you like it, Diana?'

'God, yes! You're . . . you're so big!'

'You're a lucky girl having my magnificent cock to fuck you.' *Beg me to fuck you hard.*

'I want you, Grant! I want you to fuck me hard!'

Driving his massive weapon in and out of the girl's gripping vagina, Grant ordered Mandy to frig her friend's clitty. Pressing his thumb into Diana's tight bum hole, bringing her new and lewd sensations of depraved sex, Grant was in his sexual heaven. *Girls, girls, girls!* he thought in his debauchery as he fucked. *I can have any girl in the world!*

'Ah, ah! I'm coming!' Diana gasped as her clitoris pulsated beneath Mandy's massaging fingertips. 'Oh, God! Don't stop! Don't stop!' Grabbing her hips and fucking her in his wild and frenzied lust, Grant massaged the velveteen inner flesh of the girl's tight bottom-hole, pushing his thumb deeper into her anal tube. His sperm suddenly gushing, filling her spasming cunt, he rammed his cock-head into her, his belly slapping loudly against her taut bottom-globes as he thrust. 'God, that's heavenly!' Diana cooed in her coming, her cuntal muscles rhythmically squeezing Grant's pistoning tool. 'Ah, I've never been fucked like this before!'

Supporting Diana's sagging body, Grant made his final thrusts, pumping the last of his sperm deep into her brimming pussy hole. 'God, you're good!' he gasped, eyeing her taut cunt lips rolling along the wet surface of his pistoning cock. 'You're a bloody good fuck!'

Sliding his knob from the girl's gripping cunt, Grant gazed appreciatively at her distended inner lips, dripping with a blend of girl-come and sperm. Taking Mandy's hand, halting her masturbating, he mentally transmitted his instruction to the girl. *Kneel behind Diana and lick her cunt clean. Drink my spunk from her cunt.*

Obediently taking her position, Mandy peeled Diana's full vaginal lips apart and fervently lapped up the heady cocktail of sperm and vaginal juice, swallowing hard as the blend oozed from Diana's yawning love-mouth. Grant would take Mandy next, he decided, and then fuck the girls' bottom-holes, fill their bowels with spunk, and then he'd spank them until they . . .

The doorbell ringing, breaking Grant's reverie, he checked his watch. 'Are you expecting anyone?' he asked concernedly.

'It'll be my boyfriend,' Diana murmured, her fingers massaging her solid clitoris as Mandy licked and sucked her friend's inner sex petals. 'He often calls after I've finished at the pub.'

'Christ, I'd better get out of here!' Pulling his jeans on as Mandy slipped into her gown and Diana hurriedly dressed, Grant suggested that they pretend that he was Mandy's boyfriend. 'I don't want to cause you any problems, Diana!' he said, tugging his zip up.

'God, if Ian knew what I'd been doing!' Diana gasped as she pulled her panties up her long legs, concealing her wet, inflamed pussy crack. 'Why did I . . . I don't understand why I . . .'

'Don't worry. I've just called round to see Mandy, OK? He'll have no reason to doubt that.'

'Yes, but . . .'

'I'll be in touch,' Grant smiled, taking Diana's hand as she finished dressing. *Diana, I'll meet you tomorrow, as we arranged. Bring Mandy with you and we'll have a bloody good time.*

Descending the stairs with Mandy as the bell rang again, Grant opened the front door and smiled at the young man waiting on the step. 'Hi, I'm Grant, Mandy's boyfriend,' he said, walking past the man into the street.

'Oh, pleased to meet you. I'm Ian, Diana's . . .'

'Yes, I know. Look, it's nice to have met you, but I must dash. We'll meet again, no doubt. I'll see you tomorrow, Mandy.'

'Yes, OK, Grant,' the girl smiled as the young man entered the hall. 'I'll look forward to it.'

Christ, that was dodgy! Grant reflected as he walked down the street. *I don't want to get involved in any punch-ups!* Walking home, he pondered on his female lovers. Karen, Julie, Jackie, Diana, Mandy ... He was doing well, he mused, but his voracious lust for females was still rising, and he desperately wanted to get his hands on more and more young women, his cock up more hot cunts. 'Tomorrow's another day, another day for pulling young girls!' he chuckled as he opened his front door, his head spinning with his evil plans of seduction. *Another day of fucking young girls!*

But he was becoming fearful of his ever-rising lust to commit sinful acts. Where would it all end? he wondered, flopping onto the sofa. It was as if he was being driven by an evil power, a power so strong it might completely engulf him, use him for its own debased craving for the female form. Where did the path he'd taken lead to? he wondered anxiously. *To hell?*

Chapter Four

Parking her car next to Grant's at the bottom of the hill, Karen silently cursed him. She hadn't believed his story about him having been UFO-spotting half the night. She knew Grant, she knew that he was up to something – and she was determined to discover what it was.

After resigning from his job, which had surprised and annoyed her, he'd left the house at two-thirty that afternoon and not returned. He wasn't usually so elusive, she reflected. He'd often spent entire nights searching the heavens for alien craft, but this was different. And he'd never disappeared without a trace.

Intrigue gripped her rather than suspicion. After watching Grant screw Julie, Karen wasn't bothered whether he was secretly meeting another woman or not. She felt no jealousy where Grant was concerned and, strangely, no remorse for begging Chris to screw her. If Grant was seeing someone else for sex, then she wanted to join in rather than be left out. In her ever-rising thirst for sex, she craved orgasm, longed to be taken, brought to orgasm by both men and women. But still nagging thoughts haunted her – what had happened to her? Why had she changed, become a ravenous nymphomaniac?

Dusk rapidly falling as she climbed the hill to Grant's usual spot, she stopped and looked about her. *Where the hell is he?* she wondered agitatedly as she walked towards the trees, aware of her clitoris inflating between her swelling vaginal lips, her cunt milk seeping from her hot love mouth. Sitting on the grass, watching a man walking his dog, she wondered about her relationship, the sudden and dramatic changes. The way she'd behaved was inexplicable, she mused as she cast her mind back over the last few days.

She still couldn't comprehend the things she'd done with Chris and Julie, she couldn't understand what had driven her to behave so immorally. Although she'd told Grant that she'd accepted the mysterious changes, her out-of-character conduct, her mind was still troubled. She craved sex, orgasms, and she desperately needed to understand the extraordinary transformations, her uncharacteristic hunger for lewd sex.

Wondering whether Grant had slipped a drug into her tea or coffee to heighten her libido, she recalled reading an article on testosterone, how small doses spectacularly increased the sexual urge in women. *Surely, he wouldn't drug me?* she wondered. *If he had, than he must have drugged Julie, too.* But Grant wouldn't resort to drugs! His hunger for sexual satisfaction was rampant, but he'd never resort to drugs!

The smell of burning wood filling her nostrils, Karen rose to her feet and gingerly made her way through the trees, wondering who had lit a fire. *Perhaps it's Grant?* the thought crossed her mind. Tramping through the undergrowth, unaware that she was nearing the naked men and women, the occult sect, she spotted the firelight flickering through the bushes. *Grant? What the hell is he up to?* she wondered, tentatively emerging from the thick bushes and entering the clearing.

'Oh!' she gasped, gazing in surprise at the young women's beautiful naked bodies, the men's huge penises. 'I . . . I'm sorry, I didn't realize . . .'

'Welcome,' one of the men greeted her, reaching out and firmly gripping her arm. Petrified as he turned to the women and unashamedly instructed them to remove their guest's clothes, Karen prayed for Grant to leap from the bushes and save her from . . .

From what? she questioned, staring in awe at the man's bulbous knob, his huge penile shaft. Shaking uncontrollably, she knew what she'd have to endure as the women surrounded her, running their hands over her breasts.

Although she struggled desperately as her skirt was yanked down her legs, she couldn't move. Her body seemed to be locked, paralysed, as hands moved about her, exploring her, disrobing her. Gazing at the men's erect penises as her panties were ungraciously tugged down, unveiling her femininity, she imagined the huge shafts stretching her vagina open, the men taking it in turns to abuse her young body.

She should never have gone to the hill, but it was too late, she reflected, as the women completed the disrobing, squeezing her firm breasts, venturing between her thighs, her full vaginal lips. This was Grant's fault! she thought, her body trembling uncontrollably, her stomach sinking with fear. He should never have resigned from his job, he should never have . . . A finger entering her pussy hole, delving deep into her vagina, she squeezed her eyes shut, again praying for Grant to rescue her.

Lifting her naked body as the finger slipped out of her tight sex duct, the women laid her on her back over the rough bark of the tree, spreading her legs wide, tying her limbs with rope – exposing the vulnerable pinken entrance to her tight vagina. As mouths and tongues moved about her breasts, her nipples, her inner thighs, she realized, to her horror, that she couldn't speak or cry out. It was if she was under a spell, she thought, closing her eyes as the bulbous head of a penis trespassed between the wet softness of her cunny lips.

As someone gently turned her head to one side, she opened her eyes to see another huge penis only inches from her face. Again, she tried to cry out, to protest, but the words wouldn't come. As the man between her legs pushed his solid knob into her love mouth, stretching her vaginal walls to capacity with his massive shaft, the other man offered his purple glans to her pretty mouth. Aware of her swelling clitoris, her rising libido, Karen opened her mouth and eagerly took the magnificent cock-head inside. Her fear fading fast, her uncanny thirst for sexual satisfaction rising rapidly again, she couldn't understand the changes she'd been through, why she was delighting in sucking on a stranger's bulbous knob as another man fucked her tight cunt.

Running her tongue over the silky-smooth penile crown, savouring the salty glans, she moaned through her nose, fervently mouthing on the pulsating organ. Desperately suckling like a starving babe at the breast, she rocked her head back and forth, repeatedly taking the huge glans to the back of her throat and then between her full red lips as she awaited her prize – his salty sperm.

Throbbing, transmitting wonderful sensations of sex deep into her contracting womb before the young man between her legs had even begun his vaginal fucking, her clitoris swelled and pulsated as never before. Her body alive with sensations of crude sex as her nipples were sucked into hot mouths and her bloated cunt spasmed, Karen couldn't believe the incredible pleasure her tethered young body was bringing her, the amazing sensations coursing through her tingling flesh. The two penises driving into her orifices, fucking her, she lost herself in her frightening arousal, her staggering hunger for perverted sex.

Her tethered body jolting with the crude double pistoning, Karen's orgasm suddenly welled up from her contracting womb and erupted between her legs, her swollen cunt lips. Quivering as one fleshpole thrust deep into her tight vagina and another crudely fucked her wet mouth, bloating her cheeks, her young body became rigid as her climax soared. Her nipples being sucked harder, nibbled, tongues snaking over her smooth stomach, her mound, her clitoris, she felt as if her entire self had been engulfed in her incredible climax, her very soul enveloped within her pulsating clitoris.

On and on the man thrust into her gripping vagina, taking her to dizzy heights of sexual arousal as his penis swelled and exploded in a gush of sperm. Sensing the male liquid filling her sex cavern, gushing from her pussy hole and streaming down between her buttocks, she thought her acute climax would never end. The pulsating knob within her mouth erupting, filling her cheeks with sperm, Karen swallowed hard, desperately trying not to waste a drop of the male nectar as it gushed from the rock-hard penis. Her mouth overflowing, sperm bubbling from her lips, she lifted her head, taking the orgasming glans to the back of her throat and sinking her teeth lightly into the veined shaft to hold the throbbing organ there as she drank.

Her clitoris pulsating within a wet mouth as the man's penis slipped out of her brimming vagina, she grimaced as the second man withdrew from her sperm-drenched mouth and quickly moved between her thighs. Penetrating her, stretching her pussy hole to the limit again, he thrust his saliva-covered knob into her tight cunt. The beautiful cervical pounding causing her womb to contract, the clitoral licking sustaining her mind-blowing climax, she sank her fingernails into the tree bark, praying for release from a multiple orgasm so intense that she felt that she'd die from the exquisite pleasure.

Another orgasmic explosion of sperm gushing into her spasming cunt, Karen tossed her head from side to side as the spunk jetted from her stretched cunny hole and sprayed her inner thighs. The open centre of her naked body inflamed, overflowing with male come, her clitoris pulsating violently beneath a sweeping tongue, at last she finally managed to cry out in her coming. Her wails of pleasure rocking the wood as the exquisite vaginal fucking continued, sperm bubbling from her inflamed cunt, orgasmic shockwaves painfully swelling her pulsating clitoris, she desperately fought to cling to consciousness, wondering if the ecstasy would ever end.

Her young perspiring body finally calming, breathing deeply, her breasts heaving, her stomach rising and falling as the huge penis glided out of her sperm-filled love duct, she closed her eyes. For several minutes she wallowed in the aftermath of her incredible climax, her body serene, sexually satisfied as never before as a tongue snaked into her hot vagina and lapped up the creamy products of sex.

Her limbs aching as she was finally released and helped to her feet, she staggered across the clearing, collapsing to the ground as her legs sagged, crumpling beneath her. The smell of the damp grass filling her nostrils as she lay on her back, she sensed sperm oozing from her hot pussy hole and trickling between her buttocks. Her nipples hard and sore, her cunt burning, she opened her eyes and looked up at the angelic faces peering down at her.

Closing her eyes as a shudder of sex ran through her pelvis, she became aware of hands lifting her naked body off the ground. The strangers dressing her, cupping her breasts in her bra, concealing her inflamed, sperm-drenched pussy crack within her silk panties, she finally stood before her audience, her captors, wondering what was to become of her, what they had planned for her.

Focusing on the young women as they gazed at her flushed face, Karen steadied her wavering body and tried to speak, but the words wouldn't come. As if under a spell, she could only stand trembling before the naked sect. Who were they? she wondered, staring in awe at the young women's swollen vaginal lips, the men's incredibly large cunny-wet penises. Would they allow her to leave? Her head spinning as she tried to take in her extraordinary experience, she prayed for her captors to free her. But if they let her go, then they would be endangering themselves, risking her talking, exposing them. They couldn't release her – could they?

'Go now!' one young man ordered, much to Karen's relief. Quickly leaving the clearing in case he changed his mind, staggering through the undergrowth, ripping her clothing on branches in her haste, she finally emerged from the woods and collapsed on the moonlit hillside, still quivering from her unmatchable climax. Her racked mind swirling with thoughts of crude sex, she lay on the soft grass to rest her exhausted young body, recalling the man's massive penis coming in her mouth, filling her cheeks with sperm. Pushing her tongue out and licking her chin, she smiled. No, it hadn't been a dream! she realized, savouring the salty sperm. Slipping her hand between her thighs, she massaged her inflamed cunt lips through her drenched panties, recalling the shafting penises pumping sperm deep into her tight vagina. The nightmare, the beautiful dream, had been only too real!

* * *

Grant's car was still there, parked alongside another, when Karen finally managed to haul her aching body up and descend the hill. Driving down the lane, thoughts of her enforced fucking fading from her mind, she began to wonder where the time had gone. Try as she did as she reached the house and parked, she couldn't remember what had happened to her – her mind was a blank.

'Why are my clothes torn?' she gasped as she entered the lounge and switched the light on. 'What's happened to me?' Even when she slipped her soaked panties down her legs and kicked them aside, she recalled nothing of her experience in the wood. 'God, is that sperm?' she cried, gazing at the white liquid pooling on the carpet between her feet as the phone rang.

'Is Grant there, please?' a man asked as Karen lifted the receiver.

'No, he's out. Who's calling?'

'It doesn't matter, I'll ring again when he's back from the . . . I'll ring again.'

'May I tell him who called?'

'He doesn't know me. I'll ring again.'

Frowning as she replaced the receiver, Karen wondered whether it was the same man who'd called before. Wondering who he was, what he wanted, she retrieved her soaked panties from the floor and left the room. The blend of girl-juice and sperm coursing down her inner thighs, Karen climbed the stairs and ran a bath, desperately trying to recall where she'd been, what she'd done. Slipping out of her clothes, her head spinning with confusion, she caught sight of her curvaceous naked body in the mirror and froze.

Gazing at her nipples, her blue eyes wide with shock, she shook her head in disbelief. Her brown milk buds had enlarged, quadrupled in size. Running her finger round her nipples, over the dark brown discs of her areolae, the delightful sensations coursing through her body, swelling her clitoris, she discovered that her milk teats had also become acutely sensitive.

Looking down at her pussy slit, Karen's eyes widened with astonishment as she gazed at her clitoris. Protruding between her swollen lips, her erect pleasure bud was almost an inch long. 'My God!' she cried, peeling her wet cunny lips apart and examining the sensitive organ protruding from its fleshy hood. 'God, what's happened to me?'

'Karen!' Grant called as he slammed the front door shut. 'Karen, where are you?'

'I'm up here, in the bathroom!' she replied, leaping into the bath and concealing her body beneath the swirling bubbles.

'Hi!' he grinned as he entered the room and brushed his black hair away from his forehead. 'Sorry I've been so long.'

'I've only just got in myself,' she smiled, again trying to recall where she'd been, where the time had gone.

'Where have you been?' Grant asked, sitting on the edge of the bath.

'I drove to the hill to look for you, and then ... I can't remember what happened after that. I parked my car next to yours and ... I don't know, I must have dozed off!'

'I was round the other side of the hill, UFO-spotting. Not that I saw any!'

'That man rang again, by the way.'

'Did he say who he was?'

'No, but he said he'd ring again.'

'That's strange! I wonder who it was?'

'I've no idea.'

Grant suddenly frowned, noticing the anxiety mirrored in

Karen's blue eyes. 'Are you all right?' he asked concernedly. 'You look a bit pale.'

'I'm OK.' she replied softly, trying to conceal her anguish behind a sweet smile.

'Christ, what's happened to your tits?' Grant asked surprisedly as the water lapped around Karen's pointed breasts, washing the bubbles away – her areolae and her long nipples now islands of sensitive brown flesh.

'I . . . I don't know, Grant,' she replied hesitantly, gazing in awe at her long mammary buds glistening in the light.

'Christ, they're huge! What the hell have you done to them?'

'I haven't done anything! I've only just noticed them myself!' She hesitated, wondering whether to reveal her clitoris to Grant's staring eyes. 'It's not only my nipples that have grown,' she finally confessed, lifting her buttocks, exposing her mound. 'Look, my clitty's grown, too.'

Gazing in awe at her long clitoris emerging from her rubicund sex valley like a miniature penis, Grant immediately knew that she'd been to the wood and visited the sect. Somehow they'd erased the visit from her memory, he mused, asking her whether she'd entered the wood. Recalling nothing, Karen lowered her buttocks, concealing her inflamed pussy slit beneath the soapy water. The realization suddenly striking Grant that Karen might now be able to hear his thoughts, he placed his hand on her shoulder.

Karen, can you hear me? he asked in his mind. *Are you consciously aware of my thoughts?*

No, not conscious of your thoughts.

Did you meet the people in the wood?

Yes, I met them.

Was there a green light?

No.

What happened to you, what did they do?

The men . . . the men fucked me. My pussy, my mouth – they fucked me.

OK, I'm going downstairs. When I've gone, shave your pussy. Use my razor and shave off every pubic hair. When you've done it, come into the lounge, naked, and show me.

'I can't understand what's happened to my body!' Karen sighed as she took the soap and lathered her firm breasts, her aching milk buds.

'No, neither can I!' Grant chuckled, wondering whether she'd shave her pussy. 'It doesn't matter what caused your nipples and clit to grow like that, I think you look great!'

'You would! What *did* I do? I remember driving to the hill, and then . . .'

'Perhaps you'll remember in the morning,' Grant smiled as he rose to his feet.

'Perhaps.'

'I'm going downstairs, love. I'll leave you to . . . to wash.'

Praying for Karen to denude her young pussy, Grant bounded downstairs to the lounge and flopped onto the sofa. This was getting better, he mused. Able to hear Karen's subconscious thoughts perfectly now, there'd be nothing she could hide from him. *As for her nipples and clitoris growing like that!* he contemplated. 'She'll become sex-crazed now!'

Wondering how intense her orgasms would be now that her clitoris was bigger, more sensitive, his thoughts turned to the green fingers of light. Why hadn't the Goddess Veneris bathed Karen's cunt with her strange light and bestowed upon her the gift of telepathy? he wondered. Why had her clit grown if the light hadn't played between her legs, caressed her pussy?

Hearing movement upstairs, Grant adjusted his bulging jeans, eagerly awaiting Karen's shaved pussy – and wondering why Diana and Mandy hadn't turned up at the car park to suckle on his gigantic glans, to swallow his sperm! Contemplating calling at their flat later, his heart leaped as he heard Karen descending the stairs. This was it, the revelation!

'I've shaved my pussy,' Karen announced almost proudly as she breezed into the room and stood naked before Grant, displaying her hairless crack. 'Do you like it?'

'Yes, very much!' he replied, scrutinizing the swell of the girl's smooth cunny lips, her naked vaginal slit, her amazing clitoris. 'You look great!'

'I don't know what made me do it! The thought just came into my head and . . .'

'Christ, it's taken fifteen years off you! Off your pussy, anyway!' he laughed, stroking her swollen sex hillocks with his fingertips. 'Come and sit next to me.'

'It's strange, the thought entered my head from nowhere! The idea surfaced and I knew that I had to shave! It's weird, isn't it?' she asked, sitting next to Grant.

'Weird or not, I love it!'

'Do you? I'm not sure that *I* like it! What on earth made me do it, I'll never know. I really don't understand what's been happening lately. What with my nipples, my clitty, and now shaving my . . . God, all these problems!'

'They're not problems, Karen! Don't worry about it, you look fantastic – all girl!'

'I'm glad *you* think so! By the way, Grant – what are we going to do for money now that you've resigned?' she sighed, reclining on the sofa. 'Don't you think I'd better look for a job now that you're not . . .'

'I have plans! Don't you worry, I'll make some *real* money now that I have . . . now that I have the time.'

'I hope so!' Karen breathed as Grant held her hand. 'I wish you hadn't resigned.'

'Well, I have, so that's that!'

Karen was his sex slave, Grant mused as he gazed at her amazingly firm breasts, her incredibly long nipples – and he'd make money by using her, selling her for sex. From shaving her pussy to offering him her bottom-hole for fucking, she really was his sex slave! Squeezing her hand, he sent out his decadent thoughts, willing the girl to get some rope. His perversity raging, his mind swirling with devilish ideas, he was going to put Karen to the ultimate test. *Go and get some rope*, he urged mentally, sensing Satan lurking within him. *There's a length of rope hanging up in the garage. Bring it to me.*

Obediently rising to her feet and silently leaving the room, Karen returned with the rope and handed it to Grant. 'I got this from the garage,' she said softly, her eyes frowning as she wondered what she was doing.

'Why bring me a length of rope?' he asked, standing before her and placing his hand on her naked shoulder.

'I don't know. I . . . I thought you wanted me to.'

Ask me to tie you up, Karen. Ask me to tie your wrists and use you for perverted sex.

'Why don't you tie me up, Grant? Tie my wrists with the rope and . . . and use me for . . . for sex,' she breathed, almost repeating his instruction word for word.

Ask me to whip you, Karen.

'Whip me. Tie me up and . . . and whip me.'

'Whip you? Do you really want me to tie you up and . . .'

'Yes, I want you to whip me.'

'OK, you're the boss!'

Dragging the armchair to the centre of the room, Grant instructed Karen to stand behind it and bend over. Arching her back, her feet wide apart, she dutifully laid her naked body over the back of the chair. Eyeing her rounded bottom-orbs, his heart racing as he imagined thrashing her naked buttocks, Grant took the rope and bound one of her ankles. Running the rope around the base of the chair, he secured her other ankle, ensuring that she couldn't close her legs to protect her love holes. Hauling the rope round the side of the chair, he tied her wrists together, asking whether she was comfortable.

'Yes,' she replied softly, her long blonde hair fanning out as she rested her forehead on the cushion.

'Good. Now I'm going to whip your bum with my leather belt. You really do want that, don't you?'

'Yes, I do. Grant, I . . .'

Placing his hand on her back, he grinned. *Beg me to whip you with my leather belt.*

'Whip me, Grant. Please, whip me with your leather belt!'

Removing his belt, Grant stood behind his prisoner, gazing at her hairless vaginal lips ballooning beneath her yawning bottom-crease. His penis stiff, he focused on her tight anal hole, imagining forcing his massive tool into her rectum and fucking her there, filling her hot bowels with his spunk. But first, the thrashing of her life!

The leather belt cracking loudly as it landed across her taut buttocks, Karen yelped, her young body jolting in response to the stinging pain. Again, Grant lashed her tensed orbs, reddening her pale flesh. In his frenzy, he lost control, thrashing the girl as hard as he could, ignoring her pitiful pleas for mercy. Her bum cheeks glowing, burning, her young body shaking violently, he continued the merciless beating, delighting in her whimpers between each lash, her screams as the belt struck her.

Her buttocks turning a fire-red, her juices of arousal oozing between her bulging vaginal lips as Grant persisted with the lashing, Karen was discovering the new and exciting pleasures her young body had to offer. Coaxed by Grant's unspoken thoughts, she was becoming an insatiable, sex-crazed tart – an object to be used for sexual gratification!

Bringing the belt down for the twentieth time, causing her to scream out as the pain and pleasure mingled, Grant was forced to halt the punishment as his painfully hard penis threatened to burst his tight jeans. Discarding the belt, he dragged his jeans down and ran the purple crown of his solid penis up and down Karen's drenched pussy slit, lubricating his weaponhead to ease the penetration of her tight brown ring. His bulbous glans glistening with her pussy juice, he was ready, oiled for entering her defenceless anal portal and driving his veined shaft deep into her dank bowels.

'Grant!' Karen cried as he pressed his knob against her sensitive brown tissue. 'Grant, untie me now!'

You want me to fuck your arse! Beg me to spunk up your bum!

'Grant! I . . . I want you to fuck my arse, spunk up my bum!' she whimpered pathetically in a swirling cloud of arousal and confusion.

Tell me that you want your arse fucked every day!

'I . . . I want my arse fucked every day!'

Grinning, he grabbed his sex slave's hips and, inch by inch, eased the entire length of his solid penis into her yielding anal duct. His balls pressing against her wet cunt lips, he rested, his knob throbbing within the fiery heat of her bowels, the base of his penis gripped by her tight anal aperture.

'Would you like two cocks up you, one up each hole?' he asked in his deepening depravity. 'Chris up your cunt and me up your arse?'

'No, no, I . . .'

Yes, you would, Karen! Tell me that you want to have both your holes fucked!

'I want both my holes fucked. Yes, you and Chris . . .'

'Shall I go and get him now?'

'No, no . . . Grant, I'm uncomfortable!'

'Good, then you will enjoy this even more! The ultimate – pain mingling with pleasure!'

As if possessed by some incensed demon, Grant began his violent anal thrusting, shaking the young girl's naked body as he repeatedly rammed his knob deep into her tightening rectal sheath. His craving for debased sex now climbing to frightening heights, he spanked her burning buttocks with his palm as he drove his cock-head in and out of her hot tube, stinging her already smarting flesh. Whimper and beg for mercy as his prisoner did, nothing was going to stop Grant – nothing!

Tell me you love it! he instructed her mentally. *Come on, bitch, tell me how much you love being tied up and fucked and thrashed!*

'Ah, Grant! Ah, please! I love being tied up and fucked and . . . fucked and thrashed!'

'I'll fuck you every day, Karen! Fuck your tight arse every day!'

'Grant, stop now!' she cried in her puzzlement. 'Stop spanking me!'

Her transformation from prude to nympho wasn't quite complete, Grant mused as he spanked and fucked her inflamed bottom. But soon, he was sure she'd crave anal sex, beg to be thrashed without his inducing thoughts.

Halting the spanking, wondering what she was thinking, he slowed his thrusting, listening for her thoughts in his mind, concentrating on her subconscious. *Oh, my bum! Ah, nice! Faster. No more smacking.* The pleasing words from Karen's subconscious drifting through his mind, he smiled. She was enjoying the anal fucking! But, whether she was enjoying it or not, Grant realized that he didn't care. He was treating her like an animal, there was no compassion, no love any more – only cruel, cold sex!

Increasing his rhythm, he decided not to thrash her any more, not yet, anyway. Driving his knob deep into her tightening anus, his sperm suddenly gushed, flooding her bowels as her orgasm welled deep within her quivering pelvis. Sensing her approaching climax, he reached beneath his swinging balls and located her pulsating clitoris, massaging the solid protuberance, bringing out her shuddering orgasm.

This was the first climax she'd had since her enforced awakening in the wood, and it was the best she'd ever experienced. Her tethered body shaking fiercely, her mouth open, gasping, she wailed her appreciation as Grant's sperm gushed into her contracting rectum. On and on he pistoned his throbbing glans into her perspiring body, massaged her throbbing cumbud, taking her ever higher to her sexual paradise, ever deeper into the dark depths of depraved sex.

Finally slowing his rectal pummelling, Grant stilled his trembling body, gazing at the girl's taut anal ring gripping the base of his solid organ as he massaged the last shudders of orgasm from her distended clitoris. Tethered and under his complete control, she could do nothing to prevent him living out his debauched fantasies, and his mind swirled with lewd ideas. A cucumber thrust up her wet cunt? Yes, why not? *Ask me to push a cucumber up your wet cunt.*

'Use a cucumber, Grant!' Karen breathed as her body recovered from her multiple orgasm. 'I want a cucumber up my wet cunt.'

'If that's what you want, then that's what you shall have!' he replied eagerly, slowly sliding his penis from her tight anal canal. *Half the cucumber up your cunt, and the other half up your arsehole!*

'Half and half,' she echoed, much to his delight as he pictured her holes stretched wide open by the cool fruit. 'Half up my ... up my cunt, and the other half up my bum.'

'Don't go away!' he laughed, his huge cock pointing skywards, wavering from side to side as he left the room.

Returning with the halved fruit, Grant knelt behind his naked girlfriend, grinning wickedly as he parted her inflamed buttocks. 'I dipped each half into the butter dish,' he said, twisting and pushing the cut end of one half against her inflamed, sperm-drenched bottom-hole. 'It'll help it slip into your arse.'

'God, it's big!' she cried as her brown hole suddenly opened, allowing the cooling green shaft to enter her anal duct. 'Ah, ah! God! Don't ... don't push it in too far!'

'What's it feel like?' he asked as he pushed and twisted the fruit, stretching her sensitive brown tissue to the limit.

'Cold, very cold! Ah! Grant, not too far!'

'There, it's right in! God, you should see your bum hole!'

'It feels as if I'm splitting open!'

'And now for your cunt!' he chuckled, parting her ballooning pussy lips with his fingers, opening the pinken entrance to her drenched vaginal duct.

The cucumber gliding into her hot love duct, filling her pelvic cavity, Grant wondered at his girlfriend's depravity. She was becoming increasingly sex-crazed as time passed, he mused. Picking up her thoughts, her delight for the ecstatic sensations of crude sex emanating from her bloated love holes, he wondered how deep she'd sink into the murky pool of debauchery, how far she'd slip into the dark depths of debased sex. This was more than a dream come true: he had a real live girl-slave at his disposal!

Gazing at the broad weals fanning out across her fiery buttocks, he contemplated giving his slave another disciplinary thrashing, strapping her taut flesh with his leather belt until she begged for mercy. In his lechery, he decided to thrash her again, lash her burning buttocks to ensure her loyalty to him, to force her further into the bottomless pit of sexual corruption.

'Another thrashing!' he cried, grabbing the belt.

'No, Grant! Please, no more!' she protested futilely.

Beg me to whip you, he urged, clutching her leg as he pushed the cucumber deeper into her tight bottom-hole, leaving only half an inch emerging between her glowing anal globes.

'Grant, I . . . I want you to . . .'

Beg me to lash your buttocks!

'Whip me! I want you to lash my buttocks!'

Bringing the leather belt down across Karen's twitching bottom-orbs with a deafening crack, Grant resumed his merciless thrashing. Her muscles tightening, spasming with each lash, the cucumber shot from her bottom-hole like a bullet, landing the other side of the room.

'Now that was naughty!' he admonished her, retrieving the fruit and forcing it deep into her inflamed rectal duct. 'Control your muscles or I'll thrash you harder!'

'Grant!' Karen whimpered. 'Untie me now. Please, I . . .'

'Untie you? But I haven't finished with you yet!'

'Please, Grant! I can't take any more! I'll pass out if you . . .'

'All right, I'll release you,' he finally conceded, wondering what vile act to force her to endure next.

Freeing her ankles and helping to bring her aching body upright, Grant left the cucumber halves in place, grinning as he eyed her swollen vaginal lips – inflamed, taut around the emerging green shaft. Raising his head, he gazed at her erect nipples. Long, hard, they invited a hot mouth, he mused as he tweaked each milk bud in turn between his finger and thumb.

'Untie my hands,' Karen whimpered, stretching her arms out.

'No, you must remain my prisoner!' he chuckled, taking the end of the rope and leading her out of the room.

'Where are you taking me?'

'To bed,' he replied, pulling on the rope as he climbed the stairs.

'I can't sleep like this!' she complained. 'I'm not an animal!'

'You're my sex slave, Karen. You must . . .'

'I'll play along with your games, but I'm not sleeping with my hands tied!'

'All right, I'll untie you,' he conceded as she stood at the foot of the bed.

Freeing her hands, Grant knelt before her and grabbed the end of the cucumber emerging between her swollen pussy lips. 'No, Grant, leave it there,' she said, much to his surprise, his great delight.

'Are you sure?' he asked, pushing the green shaft

fully home and neatly folding her wet cunt lips over the end.

'Yes, it feels nice. Leave it there.'

'What about the other one?' he breathed surprisedly, rising to his feet.

'Leave that there, too.'

'Really?'

'Yes, really.'

'God, you've changed!'

Slipping out of his clothes and wandering into the bathroom as Karen climbed into bed, Grant washed his half-erect penis, his heavy balls, in readiness for the next anal or vaginal fucking. Wondering at the incredible change in Karen as he returned to the bedroom and slipped beneath the quilt, he grinned. *Karen, sleeping with cucumbers stuffed up her holes? Incredible!*

Pressing his fingertips into her swollen, hairless cuntal lips as she lay on her back and closed her eyes, he wondered whether he'd be able to pry into her mind as she slept. Concentrating on her subconscious thoughts as she sank into a deep sleep, images began to form in his mind. There were no words, only vivid images of Karen's young body, bound with rope, standing in the centre of a room. *Christ, she's dreaming!* he realized. Chris and Grant were in her erotic dream – Chris behind her, his solid shaft driving deep into her bottom-hole, and Grant pistoning his massive organ in and out of her pussy hole.

Watching the Technicolour show, Grant frowned when a third man appeared from nowhere and, drifting in the air, drove his swollen knob into Karen's mouth. The image of Karen mouthing, sucking on the man's knob, incredibly clear, Grant wondered who the stranger was. He couldn't see his face, only his body, his swinging balls, his penis driving into Karen's hungry mouth. Was this someone she knew? he wondered as the man's sperm gushed, filling her mouth, running down her chin. .

He'd discover the stranger's identity tomorrow, he decided as he turned over. *Perhaps she has someone on the side?* Sleep finally engulfed him, and he dreamed his own erotic dreams of bondage and whipping, of young girls' shaved pussies decanting cunt milk into his thirsty mouth. His penis stiff as he dreamed on, he was unaware of the phone ringing in the lounge, the stranger trying to make contact with him.

Jumping out of bed and bounding downstairs the following morning, Grant discovered that Karen had gone out. 'I should have kept the bitch tied up!' he breathed, filling the kettle for coffee. *Who was that in her dream?* Imagining leading her naked body around the house with a rope, he planned his day of sex.

Recalling as he poured his coffee his idea of building a structure to which he would bind Karen's naked body, Grant wondered which room to use as his sex dungeon. There was the spare room, but it wasn't big enough to swing a cat in, let alone a pussy! The garage was a complete mess, full of junk. But the disused summer house, a large cedar building at the end of the garden, was ideal! 'There's a power point, too,' he murmured as he climbed the stairs to dress.

After hurriedly eating overcooked egg and bacon, Grant wandered down the garden to the summer house. 'Perfect!' he grinned, imagining Karen's naked body hanging from chains attached to the roof. But what sort of structure to tie her to? he pondered. His high chair idea was no good, he decided. *A table with a big U cut in it?* It all depended on what he was going to do with Karen, he concluded. If Chris and he were both going to take her, one behind and one in front, then she'd have to be standing.

The table idea would do for starters, he decided, walking across the garden to the garage. Amid the junk, he found the old dining room table he'd intended using as a work bench and dragged it out. 'Jigsaw,' he muttered, rummaging through his tools, wondering whether to have a quick wank to relieve his ever-rising need for sexual gratification!

Karen finally arrived home at noon and searched the house for Grant. Spotting him in the garden, she opened the back door. 'What are you doing out there?' she called. 'Don't tell me that at long last we're going to have a decent garden!'

'Come and see for yourself!' he replied, entering his sex dungeon with a huge grin on his face.

Walking towards the summer house wearing the shortest miniskirt possible, her long legs naked, her breasts ballooning her pink silk blouse, Karen had obviously been shopping for new clothes. 'You look great!' Grant praised the girl, eyeing her shapely thighs.

'I decided I needed to look more sexy. I don't know why, but I've been feeling more sexy recently, so I thought I'd better look as I feel.'

'You look sexy, all right!' Grant chuckled. 'God, you're a horny little thing!'

'What have you done to the table?' she asked, gazing at the U-shaped cutout. 'And why have you painted the windows white? Are you moving your darkroom out here?'

'No, this is my sex dungeon!' Grant announced proudly. 'You see, you lie on the table with your head on the cushion and your legs open either side of the cutout section, and I . . .'

'Grant, you're sex-mad!' she giggled, perching herself on the table and reclining with her legs wide open. 'I think I am, too!'

'Perfect! Now, I sit on the chair in the middle of the cutout, like this, and I can give you a good cunt-licking in comfort! Oh, no panties!' he beamed, pushing her miniskirt up over her stomach and gazing appreciatively at her shaved pussy crack, her protruding clitoris.

'No panties, no bra – it's all part of my new image!'

Licking Karen's vaginal fissure, stiffening her long clitoris to the accompaniment of her low moans of pleasure, Grant imagined tying Julie to the table and instructing Karen to suck the girl's pussy folds into her hot mouth. *Chains*, he mused, pushing his tongue into Karen's slippery love hole as she writhed and gasped. *A whip, a riding crop, handcuffs, chains, vibrators, nipple clamps* . . . He'd make a list of everything he needed for his dungeon of perverted sex, he decided.

'Oh, Grant!' Karen whimpered, opening her thighs further. 'God, my clit! Lick it, suck it!' Peeling her cunny lips apart, Grant sucked the inch-long pulsating protrusion into his mouth, running his tongue over the sensitive tip. 'Ah, yes!' Karen gasped, gripping the sides of the table as her orgasm rose from the depths of her trembling pelvis. 'God, I'm . . . I'm coming!'

Her damsel juice pouring in torrents from her pinken vaginal sheath, Karen rolled her head from side to side as her orgasm peaked. Her rigid body shaking uncontrollably, she wailed in her incredible coming, her eyes rolling, her cunt lips inflamed, engorged, her clitoris pulsating wildly. Lifting her head off the cushion, her knuckles whitening as she gripped the sides of the table, she gazed at the beautiful sight of her swollen cunt lips spread wide, engulfing Grant's mouth.

'God, no more!' she finally breathed, her head flopping back onto the cushion as another series of orgasmic shockwaves exploded within her sexual epicentre and rolled through her perspiring body. 'Grant, please, stop now!' Slowing his rhythmical sucking and tonguing, Grant finally moved away, watching her juices of lust seeping between her engorged inner lips, her clitoris deflating as her climax gently receded.

'Well, what do you think of my sex table?' he asked, licking her girl-come from his lips.

'It's great! God, I've never known such an orgasm!'

Gripping Karen's leg, Grant gazed into her sea-blue eyes and thought his dirty thoughts of crude sex. *Beg me to fuck you, Karen. Plead with me to fuck your hot cunt.*

'God, that was incredible! Fuck me now, Grant. Please, fuck my hot cunt!'

'My pleasure!'

Moving the chair back as he stood between the girl's thighs, Grant whipped out his magnificent organ and ran his purple globe up and down her open vaginal crack. Her orgasmic spend lubricating his hammerhead, he drove into her tight cunt, filling her love channel to the brim, ramming the hard softness of her cervix. Holding her pussy lips wide apart with his thumbs, her pink flesh stretched over her pubic bone, he watched his wet shaft slide back and forth.

'You've a beautiful cunt,' he murmured as her clitoris pulsated. 'Would you like Julie to lick your cunt, suck your clit to orgasm?'

'Julie? No, no, I . . .'

You want Julie to suck your cunt, lick your clitoris to orgasm.

'I . . . ah, that's nice. Yes, Julie . . .'

'You'd like her tongue in your cunt, wouldn't you? You'd like another girl's tongue up your cunt, wouldn't you?'

'Yes, another girl's tongue . . . ah, God!'

'You'd like her to squat over your face, wouldn't you? You want to drink her cunt juice, don't you?'

'No!'

You want her to squat over your face so that you can tongue-fuck her cunt and drink her come!

'Ah, yes, yes! Tongue-fuck Julie's cunt!'

Lifting and bending Karen's legs, Grant pushed her knees against her chest, her firm breasts. Her cunt lips swelling, closing around his pistoning tool as he pressed her thighs together, he imagined her legs hanging from chains. There was a lot of work to do in the dungeon, he thought as the girl quivered in the stirring of her second multiple orgasm.

'Coming!' Karen sighed, forcing her hand between her closed thighs and massaging her stiff clitoris. 'Grant, I'm . . . I'm coming!' His sperm gushing, he quickened his fucking motion, his belly slapping the backs of her thighs as he took the whimpering girl to her sexual heaven. Watching her vaginal lips rolling along his shafting penis, he grabbed her feet and forced her legs wide apart, opening the sexual centre of her shapely young body. 'Oh, God!' Karen cried as a series of orgasmic pulses shook her. 'Ah, ah! I've . . . I've never . . . oh, God! Fuck me harder!'

Ramming into her tightening vagina, pumping her love mouth full of sperm, Grant pictured Julie tied to the sex table, her young cunt open, wet, begging for his huge cock. Making his last thrusts as Karen begged him to stop, he decided to lure Diana and Mandy to his den of sex and tether their young naked bodies. 'Please!' Karen gasped. 'Grant, I . . . I can't take any . . .' Finally halting his sexual pistoning, his tool deep within her tight sheath, he lowered her legs, grinning as she massaged the last ripples of orgasmic pleasure from her incredibly large clitoris.

'That was good!' Grant breathed, sliding his organ from her quivering cunt. 'God, it gets better every time!'

'I don't know what's happened to me!' Karen sighed as she lifted her exhausted body and sat up. 'I've never known sex to be so good!'

'Neither have I!' Grant replied excitedly, tugging his zip up. 'It doesn't matter what's happened, the point is that it's the best sex ever.'

'God, I want to come again,' she gasped, peeling her cunny lips apart and looking at her erect clitoris. 'I've turned into a nymphomaniac!'

'Why don't you give Julie a ring and ask her to come round for a drink this evening?'

'Yes, yes, that's a good idea,' Karen smiled as she slipped off the table and adjusted her miniskirt, veiling her swollen sex hillocks.

'We could bring her out here, to my sex dungeon.'

'No, Grant!'

'Well, let's just wait and see what develops.'

'Ok, I'll go and ring her now,' Karen said as she opened the door and stepped into the garden. 'But you mustn't show her the summer house!'

She didn't seem too keen on the idea of taking Julie into the sex dungeon, Grant reflected, but why ever not? Had she forgotten the lesbian sex she'd enjoyed with the young girl? Hardly! he thought, recalling Karen breast-feeding her young friend.

Julie would enjoy the sex dungeon, Grant mused as he looked up to the roof. *Chains fixed to hooks and . . .* Making his way to the garage, his mind swirling with images of young Julie naked, her body in chains and leather straps, her sweet cunt shaved, he wondered whether to return to the woods or not.

The occult sect certainly had power! Or the ability to call on some incredible sexual force. *The Goddess Veneris?* he pondered as he entered the garage and pulled several lengths of chain from a box. If he were to call on the Goddess, would she come to him? *Better not try it!* he grinned inwardly as he grabbed a box of nails and a hammer. *God, there's no telling what might happen!*

Working through the afternoon, fixing spotlights and a pulley system to the roof of the summer house, securing leather straps to the corners of the table, Grant's sex dungeon was nearing completion. Calling from the house as he worked, Karen informed him that Julie had agreed to come round that evening. Once Grant had transmitted his thoughts of crude sex, willed the girl to take part in his evening of debauchery, she'd agree to anything!

Strips of leather cut from an old jacket and secured to a wooden pole made an excellent cat-of-nine-tails. A row of candles of varying lengths and thickness lined a shelf along with home-made nipple clamps and other devices created from Grant's bottomless pit of depraved ideas. A long bamboo cane stood ominously in the corner, as if waiting for its victim's naked buttocks – Julie's buttocks! Grant had also plugged a powerful body massager into the wall socket to use on Julie's clitoris, to vibrate her sex-button to one multiple orgasm after another.

Yes, he decided jubilantly as he looked about him, Julie would definitely enjoy the sex dungeon! *I'll have to lure Jackie and her hairless pussy into my lair*, he mused. *And Diana and Mandy!* Why hadn't the girls turned up at the car park? He'd thrash them for their disobedience! He'd thrash every female he could get his hands on – thrash them to orgasm!

Again, he wondered where the path was taking him, to what terrifying depths of depravity. Treating Karen as nothing more than an animal, an object to be used for crude sex, he wondered at his relationship. *Fuck the relationship!* he thought in his evil thirst for debased sex. Was Satan lurking?

Chapter Five

Eagerly awaiting Julie's arrival, Grant leaped to his feet as the front doorbell rang. 'This is it!' he chuckled as he dashed out of the lounge and through the hall. 'Oh, Chris! How are you?' he asked surprisedly as he opened the door to his neighbour.

'I'm fine. I just wanted a quick word with you.'

'Er ... yes, yes of course, come in,' Grant invited, picturing Chris screwing Karen's tight bottom-sheath, wondering why he'd not been back for more.

'Thanks. It's about ... well, about Karen and ... Grant, I don't want you thinking that I'm going crazy, but ...'

'Why would I think that?' Grant laughed, closing the door and leading the way to the lounge.

'When I was here yesterday, did I ... do you remember what happened?'

'Yes, of course I do – why?'

'I've gone over it again and again in my mind and ... the funny thing is, it all seems like a dream!'

'What seems like a dream?'

Brushing his black hair away from his lined forehead, Chris was obviously riddled with confusion. 'I don't know how to tell you this, Grant, but ... oh, I don't know. I had this vivid dream where I screwed Karen, but then I wasn't sure if it *had* been a dream! I'm sorry, I'm not making much sense, am I?'

'Don't worry about it, Chris – we all have erotic dreams!'

'Yes, I know, but this one was so real!'

'In this dream of yours, where were you when you screwed Karen?'

'In your lounge. You were there, too – watching us!'

'Watching you? Christ, it was a dream all right! I've never watched anyone screwing Karen!'

'But it was vivid!'

'Oh, hi, Chris!' Karen smiled as she breezed into the room in her incredibly short miniskirt and stood with her feet apart, displaying her shapely inner thighs.

'Hi, Karen. I just came round to ask Grant . . . actually, I'd better be going, I have things to do.'

'Why not stay for a while?' Grant suggested, imagining Chris screwing Julie's tight bottom-hole again, his solid penis driving in and out of her hot anal sheath.

'I've arranged to see someone this evening,' Chris replied. 'If I'm back early enough, perhaps I'll drop by.'

'It would be nice to see you, Chris. Do try and pop in later. Oh, that'll be Julie,' Karen said, leaving the room as the doorbell rang.

'Chris, do try and come back,' Grant urged, wondering why Chris had thought he'd been dreaming about Karen.

'I'll try. I don't know what time I'll . . .'

'Chris, this is Julie,' Karen introduced, leading her friend into the room.

'Hi, Julie!' Chris smiled, eyeing the girl's pert breasts ballooning her tight blouse.

'Hallo, Chris – pleased to meet you!' she trilled, shaking his hand as she gazed into his dark eyes.

'Sorry, but I can't stay. I might be back later, though. Are you staying for the evening?'

'Yes, I am,' Julie replied, tossing her long dark hair over her shoulder and innocently licking her full red lips.

'OK, perhaps I'll see you later.'

'I'll look forward to it.'

Seeing Chris out, Grant made his plans. The sex dungeon was ready, the spotlights switched on, the vibrator plugged in, the stage set . . . All he had to do was touch Julie and think his magical thoughts and the night of perverted sex would begin! *Why had Chris thought it a dream?* As he entered the lounge, he held his hand out, grinning as he approached the vulnerable young girl.

'So, Julie, how are things?' he asked, taking her hand in his. *You want sex with Karen and me.*

'I'm OK,' she replied as Grant squeezed her hand a little harder. *I want sex with Karen and . . .*

When I suggest going to the summer house, you'll come with me and crave sex. You'll take all your clothes off and beg me to fuck you.

Take my clothes off. I want sex. Fuck me.

Julie's thoughts filtering into Grant's mind, he grinned. 'How about grabbing a bottle of wine from the fridge, Karen?' he suggested, releasing Julie's hand. 'Julie, come and see what I've done to the summer house. I think you'll be quite surprised.'

'Grant, I . . . I don't think . . .' Karen began hesitantly.

'I didn't know you had a summer house!' Julie interrupted excitedly, following Grant into the hall. Was Karen going to try to stop him taking the girl to his sex dungeon? he wondered. No, he had power over Karen – over all women! No one could stop him!

Grant could feel her arousal, sense her rising lust as the girl became aware of her pussy lips swelling within her tight silk panties, her erect clitoris throbbing within her vaginal crack. Her subconscious swirling with Grant's suggestions, was she aroused by the prospect of lesbian sex with Karen? he wondered.

But what had she thought when she'd come face to face with Karen, the girl she'd committed her indecent act of lesbianism with? There seemed to be no embarrassment, no remorse or guilt – no recollection of the lewd act! After enjoying anal sex, Chris and Karen had faced each other, said hallo as if nothing had happened, and Grant wondered whether their memories were fading. Chris had seemed vague, for some reason thinking that he'd dreamed about screwing Karen. Karen couldn't recall her time in the wood, so perhaps she couldn't recall Chris fucking her?

If their memories faded after committing their debased sexual acts, then Grant could use people for immoral sex without having to worry about repercussions, without having to answer awkward questions. Did Julie remember her lesbian sex session with Karen? Could she recall Karen guiding Grant's solid penis into her tight pussy sheath? Grant reflected pensively.

'We've never really made use of the summer house, until now,' Grant smiled, leading Julie through the kitchen and opening the back door. 'Come on, this way!' he chuckled enthusiastically as Karen took a bottle of wine from the fridge, grabbing three glasses and following the pair into the garden.

Her dark eyes frowning as she entered the summer house and stared at the cutout in the table, the chains hanging from the roof, the candles and leather straps, Julie turned to face Grant. 'What's all this stuff for?' she asked apprehensively, her expression betraying her anxiety.

You want sex with me, Julie! Slip your clothes off and lie on the table, Grant willed the girl as he held her wrist. *Strip off and beg Karen and me to bring you to orgasm.*

'Grant, I . . . I . . .' Julie stammered as she slipped her hand from his, her slender fingers automatically unbuttoning her silk blouse.

Turning to Karen, Grant wondered whether she'd join in the debauchery without the need for him to send out his inducing thoughts. Her blue eyes widening as she placed the bottle of wine and the glasses on the table, she watched Julie slip her blouse over her shoulders. What was she thinking? Was she going to join in? he wondered as he took her hand in his. Better not take any risks! *Karen, help Julie to undress and then take your clothes off. When she's on the table, you're going to sit on the chair between her legs and lick her pussy, drink from her wet cunt!*

Gazing at Julie's firm breasts, her young milk budlettes as the girl slipped her bra off, Karen dropped to her knees and tugged her young friend's miniskirt down. Gazing at his victim's bulging red panties, Grant sensed his penis twitch and stiffen. This was going to be a night to remember! he thought, taking the bottle of wine and glasses from the table and placing them on the shelf. *Wonder if I could get the wine bottle up her tight cunt? Or up her arse!*

Slipping Julie's panties down, revealing her thick pubic bush, her soft mound, Karen tugged the garment down the girl's shapely legs, gazing longingly at her closed vaginal slit. Her naked curvaceous body glowing beneath the spotlights as she kicked her shoes and panties aside, Julie was a real beauty – and Grant couldn't wait for the debauched sex to begin! And if she remembered nothing about it the following day . . . The possibilities were endless, Grant thought, eyeing Julie's firm breasts, the slight swell of her soft stomach, the gentle rise of her mons, her pinken pussy crack. He could use her every day, and she'd know nothing about it, forget the perverted acts she'd committed, ask no awkward questions! *A life of beautifully depraved sex!*

'Lie on the table and rest your head on the cushion, Julie,' he ordered softly as Karen slipped out of her clothes.

'Yes, I . . . I will,' Julie stammered. 'Grant, I . . .'

'What is it?' he smiled, realizing that her thinking was confused. 'Don't you want us to finger your beautiful pussy and massage your clitty to orgasm?'

'Yes, no, I mean . . . God, I feel dazed! I don't know what . . .'

'Just lie on the table and relax,' Grant gently coaxed, grasping her naked arm. *Lie on the table and beg Karen to lick your cunt*.

As the girl climbed onto the table and laid her naked body down, Grant stretched her arms out behind her head and bound her wrists with the leather straps secured to the corners of the table. Moving to the other end of the table as Karen stood naked by his side, he placed his prisoner's ankles in the leather slings attached to the chains hanging down from the roof.

Julie had said nothing as Grant had secured her young body. What was she thinking? he wondered as he instructed Karen to sit on the chair between the girl's splayed thighs. Whatever she was thinking, it didn't matter, he mused, pulling on a chain hanging down by the wall. All that mattered was that he'd lured the girl into his sex den, sent out his thoughts of sex – and now had her defenceless naked body strapped to the table.

The system of pulleys squeaking as the chains lifted and parted Julie's legs, Grant grinned. *Perfect!* he thought triumphantly, gazing at the girl's opening vaginal crack as he heaved on the chain, almost lifting her buttocks clear of the table as her legs opened further, exposing the very centre of her feminine beauty. Securing the chain to a hook on the wall, the actresses poised, the stage set, he was ready to begin the night of lewd sex.

'Give Julie's cunt a good licking-out,' he ordered Karen crudely. 'She'll like a female tongue licking her cunt, her clitty. She wants to come in your mouth, don't you, Julie?'

'Yes, I want to come!' she gasped in her rising arousal as Grant squeezed her firm breasts, running his fingers round her erect nipples.

Beg Karen to lick your cunt. When you're ready, beg me to fuck you.

'Karen, please – I want you to lick my cunt!'

Moving forward, her open mouth level with Julie's gaping pussy slit, Karen pushed her tongue out and licked the girl's swollen sex hillocks, savouring the taste of her female honeydew. 'Finger her cunt,' Grant ordered as he leaned over Julie's naked body and sucked her nipple into his mouth. Silently complying, Karen parted her young friend's vaginal lips and drove three fingers into her hot pussy canal. 'Lick her clit!' Grant instructed excitedly, slipping the erect nipple from his mouth and licking the girl's darkening areola. 'Suck her clitoris into your mouth and bring her off!'

Hearing a noise in the garden, Grant slipped through the door, leaving the girls to enjoy their lesbian coupling, their cunt-licking. Perhaps it was Chris? he wondered, walking towards the house. *Chris spunking up Julie's arse and me coming up her wet cunt!* he mused, picturing the lewd scene. Dusk rapidly falling, he couldn't quite make out who the figure was standing in the shadows beneath the trees.

'Chris, is that you?' he asked, straining his eyes to focus on the dark shape.

Veneris has discovered that you have abused your power! the young naked man communicated telepathically as he emerged from the shadows and stood before Grant.

'No, I . . .'

You were warned!

'But I only . . .'

I cannot help you. I cannot save you from your fate!

'What fate?' Grant asked fearfully as the young man turned to leave.

You were warned! he replied, the shadows cloaking his naked body as he moved away. *Unless you stop abusing your gift, then your fate will be sealed.*

'But I haven't . . .' Grant's words tailed off as the young man disappeared round the side of the house. 'Wait! Come back!'

Returning to the girls, Grant watched Karen mouthing and sucking on Julie's clitoris. *What fate?* he wondered, gazing at Karen's pink tongue lapping between her friend's splayed cunt lips. *Did he walk here naked?* Close to orgasm, Julie gasped, her eyes rolling in her sexual delirium, her naked body quivering uncontrollably.

'Coming!' she wailed as Karen thrust her fingers in and out of the girl's open cunt and swept her tongue over her pulsating clitoris.

Julie's orgasmic cries filling the summer house, the sex dungeon, Grant rubbed his chin, pondering on the young man's unspoken words, why he'd come to the house naked. *What fate?* he thought again, imagining Veneris coming after him, her green fingers of light snaking around his neck – strangling him. Grant *had* abused his power, he knew as he gazed at Julie's tethered body. But what was the power for if it wasn't to be used? Why had his penis enlarged to an incredible size and his orgasms intensified beyond belief if he wasn't to enjoy sex? *Perhaps I shouldn't have got Chris to fuck Karen?* he pondered. *I used Diana and Mandy – and Jackie.*

'Grant, please fuck me!' Julie cried as Karen swept her tongue up the girl's drenched vaginal slit. 'Please, fuck me!' Standing between his prisoner's legs as Karen rose to her feet and moved the chair away, Grant slipped his jeans off. He couldn't allow opportunities like this to slip through his fingers! he thought as his penis sprang to attention. Instructing Karen to guide his weaponhead into the girl's vaginal tube, he decided to ignore the warning, whatever the consequences, and enjoy a life of debauched sex with as many young girls as he could get his hands on – fuck as many tight, wet cunts as he could thrust his solid cock into.

Taking Grant's penis in her hand, Karen aligned his bulbous purple knob with Julie's open vaginal portal, pressing his glans against her wet pink flesh. Moving forward slightly, his knob slipping between the girl's hot cunny folds, her decanting cunt milk running over his glistening plum, oiling his piston-head, he was ready to give her the fucking of her young life. Projecting his hips forward, he drove his tool deep into her quivering body, stretching her inner flesh, filling her vaginal cavity with the sheer girth of his manhood.

'Karen, kneel over Julie's face. I want to watch her lick your hairless cunt crack while I fuck her,' Grant ordered as he drove his shaft fully home. Climbing onto the table with her back to Grant, Karen knelt astride her friend's face and lowered her gaping slit, settling her swollen cunny lips over the girl's gasping mouth. 'Julie, lick Karen's cunt,' Grant instructed as Karen leaned forward, projecting her buttocks, the broad weals fanning out across her taut bottom-orbs, displaying her full pussy lips nestling beneath her small brown hole to Grant's appreciative gaze. 'Give her cunt a good tongue-fucking!'

Falling deeper into his well of depravity as he watched Julie's tongue snaking between Karen's bulging vaginal lips, Grant began his penile thrusting, sliding his massive fleshpole in and out of the tethered girl's tightening love mouth. Swivelling her hips to align her long clitoris with Julie's sweeping tongue, Karen began her gasping – her body quivering, her cunt milk decanting, running down Julie's chin.

But this wasn't enough, Grant mused in his deepening perversity, grabbing the vibrator from the nearby shelf – this wasn't nearly enough! Switching the device on, turning the control to full power, he pressed the buzzing vibrator against Julie's erect clitoris as he continued his fucking motions. The vibrations permeating her pelvis, transmitting through her engorged inner flesh to play on Grant's throbbing knob, he gasped, his eyes rolling as the pleasure spread through his trembling body.

The beautiful sensations causing the girl to cry out through a mouthful of Karen's pussy flesh as her tethered body became rigid in lust, Grant drove his solid penis deep into her vibrating love sheath, fucking her tight cunt. Her smooth stomach rising and falling as Grant thrust his massive organ in and out of her hot hole, Julie squirmed and writhed, pulling on her bonds as Karen slid her drenched pussy crack back and forth over the girl's cunny-wet mouth. Grant's sperm finally jetting from his throbbing glans, filling the young girl's rhythmically gripping love sheath, he pressed the vibrator harder against her pulsating clitoris and drove his huge organ into her hot cunt with a vengeance, sustaining their pleasure, their shuddering climaxes.

The girls crying out as their simultaneous orgasms gripped them, all three wailed in their coming, their bodies rigid, their muscles twitching as waves of pure sexual ecstasy crashed over them. This was the ultimate, Grant reflected – coming in a chained girl's cunt whilst he held a vibrator against her clit and his girlfriend came in her mouth, this was, indeed, the ultimate! With his amazing domination over women, he'd devote his entire life to sex, sexual conquests, sexual encounters of the most vile kind.

Pumping the last of his sperm into the quivering girl's tight vagina, he finally stilled his rocking body, his knob glowing within the wet heat of her inflamed pussy as he switched the vibrator off. Halting her gyrating hips, pressing her swollen vulval lips against Julie's open mouth, Karen rested her exhausted body, delighting in the post-orgasmic ripples of sex emanating from her engorged clitoris.

Withdrawing his veined shaft from the trembling girl's vaginal sheath, Grant gazed at the blend of spunk and girl-come flowing from her open hole. *Can't let it go to waste!* he mused as Karen climbed off the table, her cunt milk trickling down her inner thighs. Holding her arm, steadying her sagging body, Grant mentally instructed the flushed-faced girl to drink from Julie's love-mouth, to cleanse her in readiness for his next debauched act.

Placing the chair between her friend's legs, Karen sat down and pressed her open mouth against Julie's splayed sex-hillocks. Lapping the wet inner flesh, her tongue snaking into the girl's love tunnel, Karen swallowed hard, drinking the heady cocktail, draining her friend's hot vaginal cavern as Grant watched excitedly. Peeling the girl's rubicund cunny lips wide apart, exposing her intimate folds, Karen lost herself in her act of oral lesbian sex, savouring the heady juices of lust.

Moving to the head of the table, Grant gazed at the sheer satisfaction depicted in Julie's expression as her young body quivered spasmodically in the aftermath of her incredible multiple orgasm. His mind swirling with lewd thoughts as Karen peeled their prisoner's pussy lips further apart and continued her vaginal licking, Grant pulled down two thin cords from the ceiling. Taking the clothes pegs attached to the ends of the cords, he clipped them to Julie's erect milk buds, pinching the sensitive protrusions. Moving to the wall, he slowly pulled on a cord hanging down from a pulley, his eyes mirroring his evil thoughts. Grinning wickedly as he gently drew the cord down, he watched Julie's nipples rise, her breasts becoming taut cones of flesh.

Her face grimacing as her nipples rose higher, he pulled a little harder, wondering when she'd cry out in pain. 'Argh! No, Grant!' she finally protested, the pegs biting into her sore nipples as he continued to pull on the cord. Satisfied with the shape of her painfully stretched breasts, he wound the cord round a hook on the wall and moved to his prisoner's side.

'How does that feel?' he asked the whimpering girl.

'I . . . ah, I . . . I don't know!'

'I think a good whipping is in order, don't you?'

'No, please . . .'

Beg me to whip your buttocks, Julie, he urged her in his mind as he placed his hand on her smooth palpitating stomach.

'Grant . . . I . . . I want you to whip my buttocks!'

'Anything you say!' he laughed, grabbing the home-made cat-of-nine-tails from the corner of his sex dungeon, his mind now brimming with evil ideas.

Sextro

Instructing Karen to move aside, Grant unhooked the chain from the wall and pulled it downwards, lifting Julie's legs high into the air, her buttocks clear of the table. Moving to the opposite wall, he pulled on another chain, a sinful grin twisting his face as he watched the rising fear in his prisoner's expression. The pulleys rattling, he continued to pull on the chain, folding her naked body until her feet were high over her painfully taut breasts. Her young body contorted, her taut buttocks, her yawning vaginal crack were fully exposed, vulnerable, defenceless to Grant's every debased dream.

Glimpsing the girl's anguish depicted in her expression, Grant wondered what she was thinking as he passed the whip to Karen and ordered her to begin the thrashing. Holding Julie's arm, he listened to her inner thoughts as Karen raised the whip high above her head. *No, not the whip! Argh, no!* The leather tails lashing her tensed bottom-orbs, Julie's thoughts became louder. *God, no! Please, stop!*

You like it, Julie, Grant thought, gripping her arm tighter. *Enjoy the sensations.*

No, yes, I like it. It hurts! Argh! Nice! Argh, it hurts!

Ask me to put my knob into your mouth, Julie. You want to suck my knob, you want me to come in your mouth.

'Grant, I want to suck your knob! I want your knob in my mouth! Come in my mouth!'

Pulling his foreskin back, exposing his pussy-wet purple glans as Julie turned her head to face him, Grant slipped his huge plum into her accommodating mouth. 'Ah, that's nice!' he gasped as her tongue swept over his silky-smooth knobhead. 'Karen, grab two candles from the shelf and push them deep into her tight holes!' he ordered his girlfriend.

As if inspired by some horrendous sexual demon, Grant's lewdness knew no bounds, no limits. Although his depravity was deepening by the day, by the hour, he seemed to have no concern. His morals gone, his scruples nonexistent, nothing could stop him diving into the cloudy depths of sexual corruption – nothing!

'Do it, Karen!' Grant commanded. Julie's eyes almost popping out of her head as Karen presented a huge candle to her gaping vaginal opening and eased it deep into her love sheath, she tried to turn her head and slip Grant's knob out of her mouth. *Keep sucking!* Grant urged, holding her head still. *You love sucking my cock! You want to drink my spunk!* Working silently, Karen took the second candle and pressed the pointed end against Julie's tight anal ring, causing the girl's tethered body to jolt, her eyes to bulge again. As Grant watched Karen gently ease the waxen shaft deep into her friend's hot rectal duct, his craving for perverted sex soaring, he sensed his orgasm approaching.

'Whip the little bitch again!' he cried. 'God, I'm going to come in the tart's mouth! Whip the whore again!' The beautiful lashing resuming, Grant loosed his sperm, flooding the squirming girl's cheeks as he thrust his penis back and forth, fucking her pretty mouth. This was better! he thought as he grimaced and pumped out his spunk. Her love holes full, stretched and bloated by two candles, her mouth fucked and filled with male come, her taut buttocks burning a fire-red as the lashing continued – this was debauchery at its finest!

Julie's body shook uncontrollably, her vaginal muscles spasming, gripping the candle as Grant shot the last of his sperm down her throat and Karen lashed her crimson buttocks with the thin leather tails. Never in her sweet short life had the girl known such pleasures of the flesh, never had she realized the incredible sensations her young body, her tight cunt, could bring her. But this was only the beginning!

Swallowing the remnants of Grant's sperm as her stinging buttocks received the final and hardest lash, Julie gasped for air as the purple glans slipped from her sperm-wet mouth. Quivering, the centre of her sexuality crudely bared, exposed to her audience, Julie closed her eyes, breathing deeply as her body calmed.

'What next?' Grant chuckled in his inexorable quest for total debasement, moving to the end of the table and eyeing the candle emerging from Julie's exposed bottom-hole. 'Yes, a good bum-fucking, I think!' he laughed, slipping the candle out.

'No!' Julie protested. 'Not there!'

'Yes!' Grant laughed. 'I want to fuck your bum!'

'Grant, please!'

Taking his ever-erect penis in his hand, he pressed his purple bulb against the girl's virginal brown ring. 'Karen, stand on the table with your feet either side of Julie's bum so that I can lick your cunt while I fuck her arse,' he ordered decadently, forcing his knob into Julie's tight anal sheath as the young prisoner whimpered and squirmed in her pain and pleasure.

Taking her position as Grant slid the entire length of his solid pleasure-rod deep into Julie's tightening rectum, Karen bent her knees, aligning her yawning pussy crack with Grant's cunt-hungry mouth. Peeling her hairless vaginal lips wide apart with her slender fingers, Karen gasped as he sucked her erect clitoris into his wet mouth and ran his tongue around the pulsating tip.

Her protesting whimpers becoming wails of sexual pleasure, Julie writhed and pulled on her bonds as her inflamed anal sheath stretched to accommodate Grant's pistoning organ, her vaginal muscles tightening around the hot candle.

Grant's staying power, his ability to come again and again, was amazing, he mused as he drove his cock-head in and out of Julie's hot anal canal and sucked on Karen's pulsating clitoris. Losing himself in his debauchery, he fervently mouthed and sucked between Karen's legs, pushing three fingers deep into her wet vaginal canal as he thrust his penis deep into Julie's anal sheath. His mind swirling, dizzy with thoughts of crude sex as the girls whimpered in their own lust, Grant shot his spunk deep into Karen's bowels, lubricating his pistoning knob.

'Oh, God!' Julie cried, her eyes rolling. 'I can feel your sperm! Don't stop! Ah, yes!' Shuddering, clutching Grant's head to steady her sagging body, Karen gasped as she reached her mind-blowing climax. Her hot girl-come running down Grant's thrusting fingers as her cunt tightened and her clitoris swelled within his mouth, Karen reached between her legs with her free hand and peeled her girl-lips wide open, exposing her sensitive inner vaginal folds to his sweeping tongue. All three gasping in their lewd coupling, their orgasms finally receded, leaving them quivering, the perspiration of sex matting their hair, running down their flushed faces.

'Bloody hell!' Grant breathed as he slipped his swollen penile shaft from Julie's inflamed bottom-hole and helped Karen down from the table. 'Jesus, I've never had such a good fuck!'

'Please, let me go now, Grant!' Julie cried, the centre of her girlhood crudely exposed to her captors, sperm oozing from her small brown hole.

'Let you go?' he chuckled, slipping the candle from his prisoner's drenched vagina. 'Let you go?'

'Yes, please, please . . . I'm uncomfortable, Grant.'

'But we haven't finished with you yet! The night is but

young! Karen, what would you like to do to our guest? What pleasure would you like to bring her?'

'I don't know, Grant. I can't think why I'm . . . I think we should release her.'

Taking Karen's arm, Grant smiled. *You don't want to release her, Karen. You want to play with her, finger her bum, push a candle up her bum*. Releasing Karen, Grant unhooked the chain from the wall and pulled it downwards. Positioning Julie's feet higher above her head, splaying her buttocks, crudely exposing her yawning bottom-crease, her vaginal entrance, he secured the chain to the hook.

'Grant, please!' Julie cried, lifting her head off the cushion and gazing at her painfully stretched breasts, her yawning vaginal crack. 'Please, I . . .'

'What's the matter?' he asked the girl, resting his hand on her taut buttock. *Beg Karen to fuck your bum with a candle. You want her to fuck your bottom-hole with the biggest candle she can find. Beg her to do it!*

'Karen . . . I . . . I want you to fuck my . . . to fuck my bottom with a candle,' Julie stammered in her confusion as she rested her head on the cushion.

'If that's really what you want,' Karen replied, her blue eyes frowning as she tried to find some reason, some logic in her unfamiliar thinking, her uncharacteristic behaviour.

'Here, use this,' Grant smiled, taking a huge candle from the shelf. 'And you'll need this,' he added, grabbing a jar of Vaseline.

Sitting on the chair before Julie's obscenely splayed buttocks, Karen smeared Vaseline over her brown anal ring. Dipping her finger into the jar, she gently massaged the sensitive tissue surrounding the small opening to the girl's inner sanctum, relaxing her anal sphincter. Pressing against the tight anal iris, she slipped her finger inside, caressing the velvety walls of Julie's sperm-filled rectal sheath, stimulating her most private nerve endings. Trembling with the new-found sensations emanating from her sensitive inner flesh, Julie whimpered, squirming as Karen pushed her finger fully home, greasing her anal duct in preparation for the massive candle.

Rotating her finger within the tight duct, Karen slowly slipped it out, watching as the brown tissue closed, sealing the entrance to the girl's bowels. Grabbing the candle, her eyes catching Grant's, she frowned. 'This won't go in, it's far too big!' she gasped, returning her gaze to the candle that expanded from an inch at one end to three inches in diameter at the other.

'Yes, it will,' Grant reassured her. 'Go on, pointed end first, and it'll easily slip into her bum.'

'How big is it?' Julie asked fearfully, raising her head to see the candle.

'Just lie back and relax,' Grant ordered his prisoner, placing his hand on her leg. *Relax and enjoy it. You're going to enjoy the sensations in your bum as Karen fucks you with the candle.*

Massaging Julie's clitoris as Karen pressed the pointed end of the candle into the girl's anal rose, Grant watched with bated breath. The narrower end opening her tight hole as Karen pushed, the brown tissue yielding, he was sure the girl's bottom-hole could accommodate the massive waxen shaft. Further Karen pushed and twisted the phallus, opening the girl's anal entrance, stretching her tight ring as she gasped and writhed. The chestnut tissue taut, gripping the wax shaft, surrendering as the candle entered her, Julie begged for mercy.

'Keep going!' Grant ordered Karen as she looked up at him, her blue eyes wide with apprehension. Focusing on her friend's anal tissue stretched open to at least two inches, she pushed and twisted the candle to the accompaniment of Julie's gasps and whimpers. 'Keep going, you're halfway there!' Grant coaxed as he massaged Julie's solid clitoris. Her bottom-hole opening to three inches as the shaft sank deeper into her hot bowels, the sensations causing her young body to tremble, Julie tossed her head from side to side. Her dark hair matted, concealing her pretty face, her mouth open, gasping as the candle widened her anal portal further, she cried out.

'No, no more! Please, no more!'

'A little more, Karen,' Grant instructed her calmly.

'But, Grant, I don't think . . .' Karen began.

'More, Karen!' he returned angrily. 'And remember, it's your turn next!'

'Grant, I . . .'

Do as I say, Karen. Push the candle in as far as you can, Grant thought, holding Karen's naked arm. *Go on, push it right in and then push another candle up her fanny.*

Ignoring Julie's pleas, Karen eased the candle further into her rectal duct, only stopping when barely an inch was left protruding between her splayed bottom-orbs. 'That's good, Karen!' Grant praised her. 'God, her bum hole's stretched wide! It's beautiful! Now take another candle from the shelf and ease it into her hot cunt.'

Gasping, her nostrils flaring, her young body rigid, Julie couldn't utter her words of protest as Karen began to force another candle into her young vaginal cavern. A good three inches across, the huge shaft opened her pinken pussy folds, stretching her inner flesh as it slowly sank into her quivering body. Pushing the phallus fully home, the girl's cunt flesh painfully taut, Karen looked up at Grant as if awaiting her next instruction.

'How does it feel?' Grant asked, a devilish grin across his face as he turned to look at Julie.

'It . . . it hurts, but it's nice!' she whimpered, lifting her head to look at the huge candle emerging from her vaginal sheath. 'God, look at my . . . at my . . .'

'Karen, pass me that plank of wood from the corner, please,' Grant instructed the girl, releasing Julie's sore nipples from the clothes pegs.

Kneading his prisoner's firm breasts, Grant smiled as Karen passed him the small wooden plank with short legs set in each corner. Positioning the legs either side of Julie's shoulders with the plank running just above her neck, he ordered Karen to sit on the wooden seat with her cunt slit facing Julie's mouth. 'You'll have to get yourself between her feet,' he said, helping her onto the table. Taking her position, sitting between Julie's chained legs with her feet either side of her head, her gaping vaginal fissure only inches from the girl's mouth, she rested her arms on her knees.

'Right!' Grant said eagerly, lifting Julie's head and forcing her mouth against Karen's bulging pussy lips as he stuffed a second cushion beneath her head. 'There! Now you can lick her pussy out in comfort! Karen, reach beneath your legs and open your cunt as wide as you can for our guest.'

Taking the vibrator as Julie began her vaginal licking, Grant switched the device on and pressed the buzzing tip against his prisoner's exposed clitoris. Immediately swelling, visibly throbbing in response to the powerful vibrations, her sex-button quickly erupted in orgasm. Her vaginal muscles gripping the candle buried deep within her inflamed sex sheath, her anal sphincter spasming, squeezing the huge candle filling her bowels, the girl moaned her moans of sexual satisfaction as she snaked her tongue inside Karen's wet pussy hole.

Both girls moaning, writhing as their bodies shuddered in orgasm, Grant's mind swirled with more debauched ideas. Massaging Julie's pulsating clitoris with the vibrator as he thrust the candle in and out of her bloated cunny hole, he grinned. After the girls had enjoyed their orgasms, he'd will them to commit the most perverted act he could dream up. His mind awash with immoral thoughts, evil ideas, he moved the vibrator away from Julie's swollen clitoris and slipped the candle out of her bloated vagina.

'OK!' he said excitedly as Karen's cunt milk poured from her spasming vagina, flowing into Julie's thirsty mouth. 'Karen, get off the table and I'll release Julie.' Dragging her exhausted body from the table, Karen sat on the chair, quivering, watching her perverted boyfriend release their prisoner. 'Now, Karen, it's your turn to lie on the table,' he said, turning to his naked girlfriend.

'Grant, please . . .' Karen began, rising to her feet and standing beside him.

Climb onto the table and lie on your back, he ordered her mentally as he squeezed her arm.

Laying her naked body on the sex table, Karen gazed up at the roof, at the chains and pulleys, wondering what vile act her boyfriend had in mind. 'OK, drop your legs over the sides of the table,' Grant instructed, parting her thighs.

'I can't open my legs that far!' Karen complained.

'Yes, you can. That's it, you're nearly there. Now bend your knees and let your feet hang down,' he grinned, eyeing the girl's yawning pussy crack as she contorted her young body. 'The splits! Perfect! Julie, I want you to lie on top of Karen, on your stomach with your head between her thighs.'

'Grant, my legs hurt!' Karen protested.

'You're all right,' Grant smiled reassuringly, helping Julie onto the table. 'That's it, down a bit so that you can lick each other's cunts!' he chuckled as Julie rested her naked body on Karen's. 'Now, let's get you doing the splits, too!'

Opening Julie's legs as wide as he could, exposing the girl's creamy pinken slit to Karen's wide eyes, Grant took a length of rope from the shelf and tossed it over Julie's back. Pulling the rope taut beneath the table, he tied the ends together, securing his young prisoners in their lesbian coupling.

'OK, both lick each other's cunts!' he laughed, placing Julie's feet in the leather slings and pulling on the chain. Raising and parting the girl's legs, he secured the chain to the wall hook and stood by the table, watching Karen's tongue sweeping around Julie's drenched vaginal entrance. Kneeling on the table astride Karen's head, he took his erect penis in his hand and ran his purple knob up and down Julie's bottom-crease.

'While you're giving Julie a cunt licking, I'll give her another bum fucking!' he laughed evilly, his heavy balls brushing Karen's face as he pressed his plum against Julie's inflamed anal entrance.

'Not again, Grant!' Julie protested through Karen's wet cunt flesh. 'Please, not my bum again!'

'Yes, your bum again!'

His knob gliding into Julie's rectal duct as she wriggled, trying to escape her second anal fucking, Grant grabbed her hips and drove his weapon fully home. As the girls licked, sucking on each other's pulsating clitorises, Grant withdrew his organ and thrust deep into Julie's spasming anal sheath again, causing her to whimper through mouthfuls of wet pussy flesh.

'You can drink my spunk from her bum afterwards, Karen!' he breathed as he continued his thrusting. His balls slapping Karen's nose as she snaked her tongue into her friend's drenched pussy hole, Grant increased his rhythm, repeatedly propelling his knob deep into Julie's quivering body. The girls gasping, letting out low moans of pleasure as they neared their orally-induced climaxes, Grant loosed his sperm, bathing Julie's velveteen inner flesh.

'Ah, don't stop!' Karen cried as Julie's sweeping tongue massaged her pulsating clitoris, bringing out her orgasm.

'God, I'm there!' Julie wailed, mouthing for all she was worth between Karen's swollen vaginal lips as her bowels filled with sperm again.

'Ah! Ah, me too!' Grant grimaced as his spunk gushed.

Fucking Julie's bottom-sheath with a vengeance as Karen sucked and licked her throbbing clitoris, Grant slipped his penis out and wanked his huge shaft, splattering Karen's face with his spunk. Opening her mouth wide, she caught the white liquid and then moved back to Julie's engorged cunt. Her taste buds alive as she savoured the heady blend of sperm and girl-juice, her eyes rolling, Karen teased the last ripples of orgasm from her friend's solid clitoris before swallowing her liquid offering.

'I think I'll leave you both there all night!' Grant laughed, massaging the last of his sperm from his knob and splattering Karen's blonde hair, her pretty face. 'You can lick each other's cunts all night long!'

'Grant, please!' Julie cried, resting her head on Karen's hairless mound as Grant climbed off the table. 'Please, let me go!'

'And me, Grant!' Karen rejoined, her face running with spunk and cunny juice.

'All right, enough's enough, I suppose,' he conceded, untying the rope.

Helping the exhausted girls from the table, Grant

suggested that they dress. He'd enjoyed his debauched evening, he reflected, but it was only the first evening of many to come! Diana and Mandy would enjoy the sex dungeon, as would the many other girls he'd lure there. Life was good, he thought, tugging his jeans up as the girls dressed, concealed their aching bodies, their inflamed love mouths. *Shame Chris didn't make it*, he smiled inwardly, again imagining his neighbour screwing Karen's tight bottom-hole while Grant drove his penis deep into her pussy.

'I must go!' Julie sighed as she finished dressing. 'I'm sore and I ache all over! And it's getting late!'

'We didn't have the wine,' Grant said, observing the bottle, wondering again whether to force it deep into Julie's drenched pussy duct. 'Still, there's always tomorrow night!'

'I'm not . . .' Julie began as Grant held her hand.

Come back tomorrow evening. Tell Karen that you want to come back for more sexy fun.

'I'll . . . I'll be back tomorrow for some more sexy fun,' Julie said softly as Grant's words reverberated around her subconscious.

'Er . . . yes, tomorrow,' Karen replied, puzzled by her thoughts of wanton lesbian sex as she licked the aphrodisiacal orgasmic blend from her glistening lips.

The girls were confused, Grant observed as he released Julie's hand and opened the door. But that wasn't a problem. They had no control over their actions, no defence to protect their young bodies – not when he was around! Walking across the garden followed by his obedient sex slaves, he wondered whether they'd recall their debauched evening. *How long before they'll forget?* he pondered as they entered the house.

Taking Julie's hand again and willing her to return for a session of depraved sex the following evening, Grant said goodbye. 'Until tomorrow!' he chuckled, his eyes mirroring his horrendous lust for evil as they walked to the front door.

'Yes, until tomorrow,' Julie replied softly, brushing her dishevelled hair away from her flushed face.

'We'll have the wine tomorrow,' Karen smiled as she opened the front door.

'We certainly will!' Grant laughed, imagining the bottle slipping into Julie's tight vagina – her anal sheath.

Walking into the lounge, leaving Karen to say goodbye to her lesbian partner in lust, Grant sat on the sofa. The evening had gone well, he reflected. His amazing power over women was, indeed, a gift! A gift from the Goddess Veneris? Or from Satan? As Karen joined him on the sofa, he wondered again about her memory, whether she'd forgotten Chris fucking her bottom-hole.

'Do you remember Chris coming round?' he asked.

'What, this evening, you mean?' she replied, trying to wipe the sperm from her matted golden locks.

'No, yesterday. Do you remember what happened when Chris came round?'

'No, I don't,' she frowned. 'I remember him coming round, but . . . that's right, you went out and he . . . he must have gone, too. Yes, he left with you, didn't he?'

'Yes, that's right. How did you feel after he'd gone?'

'How did I feel? I really can't remember! What's all this about, anyway?'

'Oh, nothing. So, did you enjoy yourself this evening?'

'Well, I . . . Grant, why have we become like this?'

'Like what?'

'Well, sex-mad! We never used to . . .'

'Don't you like it?'

'Yes, I suppose so. It's just that I don't understand it. And as for the things I did with Julie! God, I didn't realize that she was like that! I didn't realize that *I* was like that!'

'Well, I love it! Having the two of you naked in my sex dungeon was great!'

'Sex dungeon? Whatever next? God, I'm knackered, Grant! I'm going to have a bath and wash your sperm and Julie's . . . I'm going to have a wash – and then I'm going to bed! My God, the things I've done!' she cried as she leaped to her feet and left the room.

Pondering on his incredible sex life, Grant rose to his feet and walked to the kitchen. Grabbing a beer from the fridge and noticing that the spotlights were still on in his den, he left the house and walked down the garden. Tidying his equipment, placing the candles and vibrator on the shelf, he turned to switch the light off – and froze.

You were warned! The naked girl's thoughts reverberated around Grant's mind as she stood in the doorway, her naked body shimmering, bathed with an eerie green light.

'What's all this about?' Grant asked, eyeing her firm breasts, her incredible nipples – her pouting vaginal lips.

Abusing the power you have.

'Yes, so the young man said earlier! Do you lot always walk around naked?' he asked nonchalantly, his fear gone.

The consequences are . . .

'I don't give a toss about the consequences! The only thing that matters is that I now have the biggest cock imaginable, and the staying power of a . . .'

Then I will go. If you will not heed my words, I must leave you to your fate.

'What fate? Christ, all I'm doing is making good use

of the power your Goddess, or whatever she is, gave me! What's wrong with that?'

Watching the girl leave, Grant rubbed his chin. *To hell with the lot of them!* he thought, switching the spotlights off and returning to the house. *I wish they'd bugger off and leave me alone!* Swigging his beer, he pondered on the future. *Tomorrow, I'll visit Diana and Mandy and lure them into my den!* 'Sex, sex and more sex!'

Switching the kitchen light off as he made his way to the lounge, he didn't notice the ball of green light hovering ominously over the sex dungeon. 'Fuck the consequences!' he breathed as he sat down with his beer. 'Fuck them!' *Fuck Satan?*

Chapter Six

Answering the door to find Jackie perched on the step, Karen beamed. 'Jackie, come in! I haven't seen you for ages!'

'Morning, Karen,' the girl replied with a hint of despondency in her voice as she stepped into the hall.

'Are you OK?'

'Yes, I'm fine. A little confused, but fine.'

'Confused?'

'Yes, I . . .'

'Come through and tell me all about it,' Karen invited, closing the door.

Sitting at the kitchen table, her hazel eyes gazing blankly across the room, her long auburn hair shining, well-groomed, Jackie wrung her hands. 'I need to talk to someone,' she sighed, turning to face Karen. 'Something's happened to me, and I'm worried.'

'What's happened?' Karen asked, sitting opposite her friend, eagerly awaiting the girl's news.

'I've . . .'

'Hi, Jackie!' Grant smiled as he entered the kitchen. 'How are you?'

'Grant, if you don't mind, Jackie and I want a private chat!' Karen interrupted, irritably.

'Oh, I see,' Grant replied, placing his hand on the back of Jackie's neck. 'In that case, I'll go and sit in the garden.

Talk to you later, Jackie.' *Say nothing about your shaved pussy. Don't tell Karen anything.*

Leaving through the back door, Grant was sure that Jackie was going to tell Karen about her mysteriously hairless pussy. Although the girl had probably forgotten her time with Grant, sucking his knob and shaving her pubes, she'd still be bewildered – she'd wonder where the hell her pussy hair had gone! Slipping around the side of the house, Grant opened the front door and crept through the hall, listening to the girls' conversation as he stood outside the kitchen door.

'You can't remember?' Karen asked surprisedly.

'No, I can't remember what I was going to tell you! My mind's gone blank!'

'Well, it couldn't have been very important!'

'It was! I've been worrying about it for ages, and now I don't know what I was worrying about! God, I must be going mad!'

'I've forgotten something that happened the other day. Our neighbour, Chris, came round and then ... then I don't know what happened. I made some tea, took it into the lounge, Grant said he was going somewhere, and I can't remember anything after that! Grant said that Chris had left with him, but I don't recall it. And there's more. I drove to the hill where Grant goes to look for flying saucers, and I can't remember anything that happened after I'd parked the car. I suppose I must have fallen asleep, but I don't remember it.'

'That's strange!' Jackie giggled, her mood lifting slightly. 'Perhaps we're both going crazy!'

'Perhaps! A lot of things have been happening lately. God knows why, but Grant went and resigned from his job, leaving us with no income. Last night I . . . God, now last night's becoming vague! And I'll tell you something else, I took a shower and noticed that my . . .'

No! Don't say anything! Grant thought, praying that the girls wouldn't discover that they'd both shaved their cunts. *Don't say anything about shaving your pussy!*

'And what?' Jackie asked, leaning forward expectantly.

'Now I can't remember what I was going to say! God, I *must* be going mad! I think I need a bloody holiday!'

Wondering whether Karen had somehow picked up his thoughts without him touching her, Grant frowned. If that *was* the case, then his power was increasing. Grinning as he pondered on the fun he could have, he directed his thoughts to the girls to test his theory. *Karen, who was the man in your dream?* he asked mentally, recalling a man's knob sperming into the girl's mouth.

No one, just a fantasy.

OK, talk about masturbation. Ask Jackie when she first discovered masturbation.

'Do you masturbate?' Karen asked nonchalantly, almost giving Grant a heart attack as her words echoed round his mind.

'Yes, quite often,' Jackie replied unashamedly.

'When did you first discover it?'

'I was about thirteen years old. I remember fiddling with my pussy in bed one morning. I began rubbing between my lips and I had this lovely feeling. I didn't know what I was doing, of course, but I kept rubbing and, suddenly, whoosh!'

'I never did it when I was young. I suppose it was because I didn't discover it. When I was older, I did it once or twice, but then stopped. I should have carried on!' Karen giggled.

'When I was about fourteen, my mother bought an electric

toothbrush. I was having a bath, fiddling about with the thing, and I slipped it between my pussy lips. I don't know why I did it, curiosity, I suppose – but it was heavenly! I remember having a terrific orgasm. I must have made quite a noise because my mother knocked on the door and asked me if I was all right!'

'You were only fourteen?' Karen asked excitedly.

'Yes. And the batteries I got through!'

Grant's head was spinning with evil ideas as he slipped though the front door and climbed into his car. *If I can influence people without physically touching them* . . . The possibilities were endless! Driving into town, unable to believe the incredible power he had, he parked and made his way to the bank. *This will be the supreme test!* he thought excitedly as he entered the bank and approached the pretty girl perched on her chair behind the glass partition.

'Good morning,' she smiled, displaying a perfect row of white teeth.

Better be careful what I think about! 'Good morning. I'd like to make an appointment to see the manager,' Grant said. *Give me one thousand pounds. You'll remember nothing about it after you've handed me the money.*

'Certainly, sir,' she replied, taking bundles of twenty-pound notes from the drawer beside her. Counting the money, she passed the wad of notes to Grant. 'I'll go and find out when he can fit you in,' she smiled, wandering away, obviously clueless as to what she'd just done.

Clutching the money, Grant left the bank quickly, his mind swirling, his heart thumping hard against his chest. *Jesus! I could be a rich man!* he thought as he climbed into his car and gazed at the notes. Wondering whether he'd been caught on video as he stuffed the money into his pocket and drove off, he laughed. 'No, they won't be looking for bank robbers! Shit, they might sack the poor girl!'

Pulling up by the recreation ground, Grant climbed out of his car and wandered across the grass, wondering how Karen and Jackie were getting on, whether they were talking about their shaved cunts. Shaking his head in disbelief, he sat on a bench pondering on the riches, the lewd sex, his incredible power could bring him. 'God, now I've *really* abused my power!' he breathed, the money bulging his pocket. *One thousand pounds, just like that!*

Desperate to use his gift again, he focused on a young woman walking some distance away. Concentrating, he tried to pick up her thoughts, delve into her subconscious. *I don't care if he isn't seeing her any more!* The words filtering into Grant's mind, he gazed at the woman, locking on to her thoughts, listening intently. *Bastard! He needn't think I'll take him back again!*

Come and sit on the bench. Sending out his unspoken instruction, Grant smiled as the woman turned and walked towards him. *Come and sit next to me.*

As she joined him, crossing her long legs and reclining, her red miniskirt riding high, Grant eyed her shapely thighs. She was in her early thirties, he reckoned. With long dark hair framing her pretty face, her ample breasts billowing her blouse, she was an attractive woman. But what now? he wondered. Ask her to strip off in the middle of the park? *Talk to me.*

'Don't mind me joining you, do you?' she asked, turning to face him.

'No, not at all. My name's Grant.'

'Hi, I'm Jane.'

'Nice day for a walk,' Grant smiled, picturing her naked.

'Is it?' she snapped. 'Sorry, I'm not in a particularly good mood at the moment.'

'That's OK. Boyfriend trouble?'

'Yes, but how . . .'

'A lucky guess, I suppose. What's he done?'

'Cheated on me – again!'

'Well, there are plenty more fish in the sea!' *Pull your skirt up!*

'Yes, I suppose so,' she sighed, hoisting her skirt up, exposing her bulging pink panties. 'Although I don't know whether I want any more fish!'

'Give it time and you'll feel better.' *Pull your skirt up over your stomach and sit with your legs wide apart.*

'Time heals, does it?' she asked, lifting her buttocks clear of the bench and yanking her skirt up over her stomach.

'Yes, time does heal.'

She seemed to be unaware of what she was doing, Grant mused, gazing at the swell of her panties, the dividing groove between her outer lips forming a deep crease in the material as she sat with her thighs parted. *She must be consciously aware that she's sitting like that!*

She only seemed to pick up his thoughts when he directed them to her – which was just as well! he laughed inwardly, imagining seeing a line of schoolgirls at a bus stop and thinking about them stripping off. *God, they'd all stand in the queue naked if they picked up my thoughts!*

'Oh!' Jane cried, gazing down between her legs. 'Why am I . . .'

Pull your panties off and sit with your legs wide apart.

'Why . . . why am I . . .' she stammered again, lifting her buttocks and tugging her panties down. 'I'm sorry,' she began, kicking the garment off her ankles and reclining

with her milk-white thighs splayed, her pussy slit gaping.
'I . . . I don't usually do this sort of thing! I don't know why . . .'

'Don't mind me!' Grant laughed, gazing longingly at her moist inner lips protruding between her full sex-hillocks. 'You've a beautiful body, Jane, why hide it?'

'Yes, but . . .'

Talk to me about sex, what you enjoy doing. Tell me all about your sex life.

'I don't want my boyfriend back, but I'll miss the sex,' she confessed, parting her legs further. 'He was good at oral sex. God, he really knew how to lick my clitty! But what I didn't know was that he was also licking someone else's clit, the bastard!'

'Did you like sucking him off?'

'Yes. For me, that was the best part of our sex life. He used to like watching me masturbate, so he'd get on all fours with his cock over my face so that I could milk him with my mouth, as he put it, and I'd masturbate while he watched.'

'Sounds great!'

'It was! Christ, why am I telling you all this?'

'I don't know – but carry on.' *Tell me more.*

'I loved swallowing his spunk!' she giggled. 'There's nothing I like more than cock-sucking and swallowing spunk!'

Ask to suck me off. You want to suck my cock and swallow my spunk.

'Grant, I . . . I'd like to suck you off,' she said hesitantly.

'What, here, now?'

'Yes, there's no one around so . . .'

'OK!' Grant smiled, unzipping his jeans and easing his erect penis out.

'God, you're big!' she cried, leaning over and eagerly taking his massive plum into her hot mouth.

A stranger walking in the park, and Grant could will her not only to show him her pussy, but to suck him off? This was incredible! he reflected. *A grand in my pocket and my knob in a woman's mouth!* Did he really need Karen now? he wondered as Jane snaked her tongue around his ballooning glans. He'd thought of ditching her when he'd picked Diana up in the pub – perhaps the time had come to get rid of Karen? But she wasn't a problem, he mused. If she didn't mind him bringing girls home and luring them into the sex dungeon, then he'd keep her on. There again, of course she wouldn't mind! All he had to do was to send out his thoughts and she'd join in with him and any girls he happened to take home!

'God, you've a lovely cock!' Jane cried, examining his purple knob before taking it to the back of her throat.

Grinning, Grant glanced about him. *Not a soul in sight*, he thought, reclining and closing his eyes. His orgasm approaching, he took Jane's head in his hands and gently thrust his penis in and out of her wet mouth.

'I want your spunk!' she cried, his knob between her full red lips. 'Come in my mouth, I want to swallow your spunk!'

As his sperm jetted from his throbbing glans, filling Jane's gobbling mouth, he thrust deeper, forcing his cock-head to the back of her throat. She was good, well practised, he mused as she lowered her head, expertly taking his glans down her throat, her lips closing tightly around his swollen shaft. He'd arrange to meet her again, to fuck her mouth again, he decided. But, there again, why bother? He could pull any woman, anywhere, anytime!

His flow of sperm finally ceasing, he lay quivering

beneath the hot summer sun, delighting in the sensations emanating from his twitching cock as she slipped his knob out and licked his shaft, lovingly cleansing him with her sperm-covered pink tongue. Gazing at her full mouth, her sweeping tongue, Grant recalled Jackie taking him into her mouth, swallowing his spunk. *Women worship my magnificent cock!* he thought happily as she sat upright, still clutching his wet shaft.

'That was something else!' Grant cried as she ran her tongue over her glistening, sperm-drenched lips.

'I've never seen such a big cock!' she giggled. 'And I've never swallowed so much spunk in all my life! God, you're certainly all man!'

'We must meet again,' Grant smiled as she stood and slipped into her panties.

'Yes, we ... Christ, I know nothing about you!' she gasped, wiping sperm from her chin. 'I know nothing about you and I've ...'

'Yes, you do. You know my name, you know my cock ...'

'But, we're complete strangers!'

You want to come here again and suck me off.

'I'll see you again, I hope. I'd like to ... to suck you off again.'

'Definitely!' he grinned, zipping his jeans.

'Well, I'd better be going. I have some serious thinking to do about my uncharacteristic behaviour! I'll see you again, Grant. Bye.'

'Bye, Jane. And thanks!'

'Thank *you*!'

Returning to his car, Grant drove home, his head swimming with the incredible things he could get up to. But he had to make serious plans, do something useful with his life – apart from screw anything in a miniskirt! Money was no object now, he reflected, wondering whether to call in at another bank and ask for a few thousand pounds. *Later, maybe*, he thought as he parked outside his house. *There's no rush!*

Jackie and Karen had gone by the time Grant arrived home. He'd no idea where they'd gone, but he wasn't bothered – he had his plans to make! His insatiable penis solid within his tight jeans as he recalled Jane sucking his knob, swallowing his gushing spunk, he wandered out into the front garden in search of vulnerable female neighbours. *I need another sexy woman*, he thought, adjusting his bulging crotch. *God, this is too easy!* Watching a pretty blonde walk past, he directed his thoughts to her. *Stop and talk to me!*

'Hi!' the girl smiled, turning and leaning on the wall.

'Hi! Nice day, isn't it?'

'It is. Er . . . sorry, I don't know your name.'

'Grant,' he replied, walking across the garden and shaking her hand.

'I'm Emily, pleased to meet you. It's funny, I don't know you and yet . . . I don't want you getting the wrong idea. I mean, I don't usually talk to strange men!' she giggled.

'I'm not strange!' Grant laughed, wondering whether to abuse his power again, abuse the young girl's delectable body – her fresh cunt.

He'd exploited his strange gift so many times now that it didn't matter, he reflected, recalling the young man and woman warning him of his fate. And he'd robbed a bank! *God, she's a beautiful little tart!* he observed, gazing into the girl's sparkling eyes. *I'll bet she's got a tight pussy! Fuck my fate – and her pussy!*

'Well, I'd better be going,' she smiled, hooking her golden tresses behind her ear.

Dare I fuck her? 'Where do you live, Emily?' he asked, wondering whether to demonstrate his mind-reading act.

'Round the corner, in Lancaster Road.'

'Something's bothering you, isn't it?'

'Er . . . how do you mean?' she frowned.

'You've something on your mind. You're worried about . . . about your job.'

'Yes, I am, but how on earth do you know that?'

'I'm a professional psychic. It's a girl – Mary, I think. She's been causing you problems at work.'

'God, that's amazing!'

'Yes, I suppose it is. To be honest, I tend to be somewhat blasé about it.'

'Well, you shouldn't be! It's an incredible gift! What else can you tell me?'

'Er . . . let me think. Look, why don't you come into the house? It's not easy doing this over the garden wall.'

'Well . . . I'll be late for work if I . . .' *Mary will cause more problems if I'm late again.* 'I've a few minutes to spare, I suppose.'

'Good!' Grant smiled, opening the gate and leading the girl down the garden path. *Literally!* he mused as they stepped through the doorway into the hall. 'Come and sit in the lounge, we'll be more comfortable in there.' *Candy from a baby!*

Settling in the armchair, Emily leaned forward, no doubt wondering, Grant mused, what he was going to reveal about her. Sitting opposite on the sofa, he gazed between her thighs, willing her to open her legs. Obediently complying, she reclined, relaxing with her thighs parted, the V of her white panties bulging with her young sex. *Eighteen?* Grant pondered. *Certainly no older!*

'You live with your boyfriend,' Grant began, holding his head to bring authenticity to his mind-reading act – not that he needed to! 'You've an older sister, Joan, I think – no, her name's Jill.'

'Yes, that's right!' she squealed excitedly, eagerly leaning forward again.

'Going back to your boyfriend . . . I don't know whether I should say this but, he's not the one for you, Emily.'

'That's true!'

'You're unhappy living with him, but you've nowhere else to go.'

'Right again!'

Scrutinizing the young girl's curvaceous body, her damp panties, Grant suddenly had an idea – get her to move into the house as his sex slave. Karen wouldn't object, not once Grant had delved into her subconscious, willed her to believe that it had been Karen's idea. With money being no object, he could easily afford to keep Emily. She was the most beautiful young girl he'd seen in years, and he was determined not to lose her!

'Emily, I've just had an idea. I'm looking for an assistant for my mind-reading act. You know the type of thing, a beautiful girl to walk around the audience and hold people's belongings while I'm blindfolded, telling the punters their darkest secrets. You could leave your boyfriend, move in here and . . .'

'Move in here, with you?' she gasped.

'Not *with* me! There's a spare room so . . .'

'I'd have to leave my job.'

'Yes, but I'd pay you well. You're not happy at your present job, you're not getting on with your boyfriend . . .'

'But, to turn my life upside down like that would be . . .'

'It's the best way, I reckon. When changes need to be made, make them in a big way!' *Say yes. You want to move in and work for me. Say yes!*

'Yes, OK! You're right, make changes in a big way. I'll have to give my notice in, though. Shall I start next month?'

'Next month? Er . . . well, I need someone right away. Just leave your job. Go home now and pack, and move in today. A big way, Emily – a big way!' *Agree! Go home and pack. Be as quick as you can and tell no one where you're moving to!*

'OK, I'll do it!' she shrieked, leaping to her feet. 'I'll be as quick as I can.'

'I thought you'd say that!' Grant laughed, following the girl through the hall and seeing her out. 'See you soon, Emily.'

'OK, Grant. Bye!'

Closing the front door, Grant gleefully rubbed his hands together. 'Life's great!' he cried, punching the air with his fist and jumping up and down at the prospect of rampant sex and riches. Calming himself, he wandered into the kitchen and gazed at the summer house. 'First of all, deal with Karen,' he breathed. *I'd better prepare the spare room.* 'No, Emily can sleep in my bed and Karen can move into the spare room!' *No, we'll all sleep in my bed!*

Walking down the garden, Grant entered the sex dungeon, wondering what improvements or additions he could make to his equipment. 'A bloody great rubber cock attached to a machine!' he laughed, picturing a huge phallus thrusting in and out of a young girl's pussy. Switching to debauch mode, he imagined a naked girl strapped over the table. *One cock up her bum and another up her cunny*, he mused, trying to work out how to position his victim for the double fucking.

'Oh, there you are,' Karen said as she entered the dungeon. 'Where did you get to?'

'I've been to the bank.'

'That man rang again while you were out. It's strange, he knew my name, but wouldn't say who he was!'

'He knew your name? That's weird!'

'He mentioned the hill, the wood, asking whether you were there.'

'I can't think who he is!' Grant frowned. 'Anyway, where have you been?'

'After Jackie left, I went to a local church to see a priest.'

'A priest? Why the hell go to see a priest?'

'Because I need some answers, Grant. Not that he could explain what's happened to me, but ... I needed to talk to someone. I'm losing my memory. I've shaved my pussy and I don't remember doing it, or why I did it! My clitoris has grown, my nipples are huge, and this sex dungeon of yours is ...'

'You don't need a priest!'

'I've become a nymphomaniac! I can't keep my eyes off men's crotches – or girls' legs and tits!'

'You've discovered sex, what's wrong with that?'

'Oh, I don't know! And another thing, why did you leave your job? What's happening, Grant?'

'Nothing's happening! You didn't tell this priest about shaving your pussy, did you?'

'No, of course not! I talked about losing my memory.'

'What did he say?'

'He wants to see you. He said that we should get together for a chat.'

'I don't want a chat with a bloody priest! You shouldn't have told him anything, Karen!'

'He's coming here. I . . . I invited him.'

'Christ! When?'

'He'll be here any time now. Grant, I need to talk to someone, I need to understand!'

'There's nothing *to* understand! We've got a great sex life, a good future – there's nothing to understand! Jesus Christ, a fucking priest! You do realize that they're all homosexual, incestuous fucking perverts, don't you?'

'Of course they're not!'

'They bloody well are! Pick up any Sunday tabloid and you'll . . .'

'I'm not interested in tabloid crap! What I want to know is, why has my clitoris grown? There must be something wrong with me, don't you agree?'

'No, I don't. It's hormones, more than likely. Now we've got a good sex life, I expect your hormones have . . . God, you can't ask a priest why your clitoris has grown!'

'I'm not going to! I just want . . . I don't know what I want. Why did I shave my pussy? I don't even remember doing it, let alone *why* I did it!'

Scrutinizing his girlfriend, Grant wondered what to do. The pussy shaving hadn't been a good idea, he mused as he gazed at her young thighs. But what the hell? He had control over her, over her thoughts and actions – and control over the priest. When the holy man, the perverted choirboy-hungry pervert, arrived, Grant would have a private chat with him, tell him that Karen had been under stress recently. *I could always get him to fuck her!* he thought in his rising wickedness. *He's probably well into hot, tight bottom-holes!*

'I don't know why you shaved your pussy,' Grant smiled. 'But I like it.' *Are you wearing your bra and panties? Yes, I am.*

Go to the lounge and take all your clothes off except for your bra and panties. 'Let's go into the house and wait for him. We'll have this chat, if you think it will help you.'

'OK. I really do need to talk to someone, Grant. I'm becoming so confused lately.'

'I know. Come on, we'll go and wait for him.' *When you're in the lounge, take everything off except for your bra and panties.*

As with the pussy shaving, this probably wasn't a good idea! Grant thought as he followed Karen to the house. But what an opportunity! A local priest, fucking Karen in the lounge – what an opportunity! *Jesus fucking Christ! I could take pictures and send them to a newspaper!*

Sitting on the sofa, Grant watched Karen unbutton her blouse and slip the garment off her shoulders. She had a fine body, he observed as she dragged her skirt down her long legs, revealing her swelling panties – a fine body, and it was his to use, his for the taking! Stepping out of her skirt, Karen kicked her shoes off and stood before Grant.

'Grant, why am I . . .' she began, looking down at her near-naked young body as if she had no recollection of undressing.

'It's a hot day, you'll feel much cooler without your clothes,' Grant smiled.

'But . . . but the priest . . .'

'He won't mind!' Grant laughed, rising and gathering Karen's clothes. *Sit on the sofa with your legs wide open.* 'I'll go and hang these up. Just sit down and relax.'

'But I'm half-naked! I don't understand . . .'

Forget that you're half-naked. Just relax. The priest really turns you on. You want him to fuck you. You crave his body, his cock. When he walks into the room, you'll become desperate for him to fuck you. 'Ah, that'll be him,' Grant said as the doorbell rang. 'Sit down and relax. We'll all have a good chat about you losing your memory or whatever.'

Hiding her clothes behind the sofa, Grant glanced at Karen as he left the room. A perfect picture of feminine beauty, he thought, walking through the hall and opening the front door – the perfect seductress! 'Hallo, Father,' he greeted the greying priest. *You fucking sad pervy!* 'My name's Grant. Please, come in.'

'Thank you. I'm Father Gerald. Your wife's told you about her talk with me, I take it?'

Wife? 'Yes, yes. She's been under some stress lately,' Grant replied, closing the door. 'We're going through some financial problems and she's been worried.'

'She told me that she's losing her memory,' the priest said, rubbing his chin and frowning at Grant.

'It's the effect of stress. It's not that she's losing her memory, it's just that, with her mind being muddled with all our problems, she's become a little forgetful.'

'I see. Well, it's at times like this that some guidance will be helpful. A problem shared is a problem halved.'

'Yes, there's nothing like a little guidance to . . .' *When you go into the lounge, you'll want to fuck Karen. You'll have an erection, and you'll become desperate for her young body. You won't comment on the way she's dressed. You'll become desperate to use her body, desperate for her cunt.*

'She said that you've resigned from your job, Grant.'

'Yes, I'm . . . I'm working for myself now. Karen's waiting in the lounge – please, come through.'

His cassock billowing behind him as he walked down the hall, the priest entered the lounge and smiled at Karen, ogling her half-naked body, but seemingly thinking nothing of it. Her cunny-wet panties bulging between her splayed thighs, clearly defining her sex-groove, Karen displayed no signs of embarrassment or shame.

'Hallo, Father,' she smiled. 'Thank you for coming. Please, sit down.'

'Thank you. I was just telling your husband that some guidance will be helpful, helpful during your time of need.'

'Yes, I think it will,' she replied as Grant sat in the armchair opposite, eager for the unholy lechery to commence.

Gazing at the tight strip of red material hugging Karen's ballooning pussy lips, Grant sent out his thoughts, willing the priest to slip his hand into her panties and massage her clitoris. *Slip your hand down her panties. She'll love it. Finger her wet cunt, rub her clitty. You're desperate for her juicy cunt!*

His eyes wide as he watched the priest talking to Karen, Grant grinned as the sinful man tentatively moved his hand towards the girl's bulging panties. *Go on, do it!* Grant urged him again. Moving his hand away, the priest frowned. Grant was getting through to him, but his thoughts weren't strong enough, it seemed. No doubt things would have been very different if Karen had been a choirboy! *Put your hand down the front of her panties and masturbate her!*

Hesitating, the priest finally pulled the girl's panties away from her smooth stomach and slipped his hand inside. 'Oh! Er . . . what am I doing?' he gasped, cupping her warm, swollen vaginal lips in his palm. 'I'm so sorry! I . . .'

Tell him that you like it, Karen!

'Don't stop, I like it!' Karen breathed, parting her thighs

further and pressing his hand against her crotch. 'I like your hand there.'

'I . . . I don't know what's come over me!' Father Gerald cried as he located the wet entrance to the girl's hairless pussy and drove a finger deep into her hot vagina. 'What am I . . .'

'Ah, that's nice! Finger me, Father, make me come! I'm desperate to come!' Karen gasped without Grant's prompting.

'And I'm . . . I'm desperate for your cunt!'

Grant was again amazed by his incredible power as he watched his girlfriend close her eyes and breathe deeply. But why hadn't the priest followed Grant's instructions immediately? Why had he hesitated? *Perhaps I'm losing my touch?* Grant wondered. *Lift her bra away from her tits and suck her nipples!* Sending the thought out, Grant waited but there was no response. *Suck her nipples!* he ordered again, wondering whether the power was fading. Perhaps the priest was so strong-willed that he could restrain even his deep-seated subconscious desires? *Lift her bra away from her tits and suck her nipples!*

As the priest lifted Karen's bra away from her pert breasts and sucked her huge nipple into his mouth, Grant gave a sigh of relief. Again, he wondered about the subconscious mind and the power of suggestion – if it was suggestion. This was telepathy, but how did it work? The bundle of bank notes bulging his pocket, he sat back, pleased with his gift, his power over others, even though he didn't understand it. But the word *fate* still played on his mind, nagging like perpetual toothache.

His debauched thoughts swirling, he pushed the warnings he'd had from the members of the group to the back of his mind and pondered on the priest. *Get him to fuck her bum?*

he thought in his evilness, picturing Karen on all fours with the man of God driving his unholy penis deep into her tight bottom-hole. *Yes, he'll love that!* But first, he'd instruct Karen to take the man's penis into her mouth.

Massaging Karen's pulsating clitoris as he fervently sucked on her sensitive nipple, the priest was obviously delighting in breaking his vows. *Stand up and lift your cassock up*, Grant ordered silently, grinning as his instructions were followed obediently. The man's admirable penis standing to attention as he lifted his cassock and pulled his undershorts down, Grant ordered Karen to kneel before him and suck his knob.

'Ah, ah! That's good!' the priest breathed as she knelt on the floor and sucked his purple knob into her hungry mouth. Gripping the base of his solid shaft with both hands, she moved her head back and forth, taking his glans to the back of her throat. 'I . . . I don't know why I'm doing this!' the priest stammered, his rolling eyes looking up to the ceiling, to heaven, as his long-neglected penis throbbed in the girl's mouth. 'Ah, I'm . . . I'm . . .'

His sperm quickly rising and gushing over her snaking tongue, she slipped his knob from her mouth and eagerly licked his pulsating glans. Fired by lust as the white liquid jetted, splattering her pretty face, she rolled her tongue round his plum before taking him deep into her mouth again and swallowing his fruits. Grinning, Grant watched the trembling priest commit his sinful act, wondering what he'd think when he left the house and returned to his church. But the memory would soon fade and his guilt slip away. He'd recall nothing of his sin, Grant mused – but God would!

His legs sagging as his head lolled forward, the unholy man clung to Karen's head, gasping as his heavy balls drained, his celibacy crudely forsaken. Which was worse, Grant wondered – taking the money from the bank, or destroying a priest's vows? Both were equally as bad, he decided – equally brilliant! The randy old git was probably already fucking half his parishioners – and the choirboys!

As Karen slipped the spent penis from her sperm-drenched mouth, Grant silently ordered her to slip her panties and bra off. Complying, she stood naked before her guest, displaying her feminine beauty, her gentle curves and crevices to his wide eyes as he let his cassock fall into place, concealing his manhood. Provocatively pinching her long nipples and licking her sperm-covered lips with her pink tongue, Karen ran her hand down her stomach and over her smooth mound. Parting her swollen pussy lips, exposing her inner female flesh, she was the epitome of seduction. *She's mine, all mine!* Grant thought excitedly.

'I really should be going,' Father Gerald breathed, gazing at the girl's shaved pussy lips, her gaping vaginal slit. 'I don't know why I . . . I'm sorry, I shouldn't have come here.'

Karen, get on all fours and beg him to fuck you!

'Don't go!' Karen smiled as she turned and took her position on the floor, projecting her buttocks, the weals still visible from the thrashing Grant had given her, displaying her swollen pussy lips – wet, glistening, inviting. 'Please, I want you to fuck me.'

'My child, I . . .'

'Please, you've come in my mouth, so now come in my pussy. I want to feel your cock deep inside my hot cunt.'

Succumbing to temptation, and to Grant's penetrating thoughts, the priest fell to his knees and positioned himself behind Karen. Lifting his cassock, he presented his solid glans to her drenched vaginal crack as she rested her head on the carpet, breathing deeply in anticipation. *Go on, push your cock right up her tight cunt!* Grant ordered mentally. Taking his penis in his hand, the priest drove his knob deep into Karen's spasming vaginal sheath, gasping as his glans pressed against the welcoming warmth of her wet cervix. *Now give her the fucking of her life!*

Sliding his organ in and out of Karen's tight vagina, the ungodly man closed his eyes, muttering his words of sex, revelling in his illicit act. 'You're so hot and tight! I can feel your quim lips, gripping me, your cunt . . .'

'Sperm in me!' Karen gasped, reaching between her thighs and massaging her erect clitoris. 'Come in my cunt! Shoot your spunk deep into my tight cunt!'

'I will, I will! Ah, it's been so long since . . . God, how I love your cunt!'

Grant's penis now rock-hard, aching for relief, he stood and slipped his jeans off. *Why let her mouth go to waste?* he thought as he knelt on the floor and lifted Karen's head. Gasping as she supported her rocking body on her arms, she gazed at Grant's bulbous purple knob hovering before her flushed face. *Suck it!* Grant ordered the girl, wondering what the priest would think of the double-ended fucking.

Taking his cock-head deep into her hot mouth, Karen moaned through her nose. Her stomach somersaulting with the sensations of debased sex as the two penises glided in and out of her wet orifices, she shuddered in her new-found ecstasy as she gobbled Grant's ballooning glans, eager for his spunk. Never had Grant imagined his prudish girlfriend committing such a vile and beautiful act! But there was so much more he'd do with her, he mused – so much more perverted sex!

As she began to rock her body back and forth, the men stilled their thrusting cocks, allowing her to do the work. Taking first one solid penis deep into her drenched vaginal sheath, and then the other to the back of her throat, she quickened her rhythm, slapping her taut buttocks against the priest's stomach, taking the gasping men ever closer to their climaxes.

A third man shafting Karen's tight anal tube would be the ultimate in sexual depravity! Grant thought as he gazed at the trembling girl's popping eyes, her billowing cheeks. His quest for debased sex soaring, he imagined the girl strapped to the table in the sex dungeon with twenty men queuing up to screw her. *God, am I going to have some fun with the bitch!*

Gasping, the priest grabbed Karen's hips and drove his throbbing knob deep into her tightening cunt as his sperm gushed, filling the girl's spasming vaginal cavern. Grimacing, Grant loosed his spunk, filling her cheeks as she rolled her tongue around his pulsating glans. Her own climax exploding within her solid clitoris, she let out a low moan through her nose as her orgasm gripped her, engulfing her very being.

Ignoring the front doorbell as his sperm flowed from his throbbing penis, Grant thrust his knob to the back of Karen's throat, taking her head in his hands and stilling her. Gently rocking his hips, massaging her tongue with his pulsating glans, he grimaced as the last of his spunk jetted down her throat. Slipping his huge knob out of her mouth, he grinned as she licked his shaft, gasping as her own climax began to recede. Mouths, cunts, anal sheaths . . . Grant was going to use every female orifice for his debased pleasure, he mused, watching her tongue curl round his shining plum.

The doorbell ringing incessantly, Grant guessed that it was Emily. God, I haven't told Karen yet! he thought as the girl licked and mouthed his knob. Slipping his spent penis from her wet mouth, he watched the priest make his last penile thrusts into the girl's sperm-drenched vagina. *Emily could join in!* Grant thought, picturing the girl with one cock thrusting into her young cunt and another shafting her tight rectum. But no, the time wasn't right, he mused as he zipped his jeans.

Both dress now, Grant ordered as the priest withdrew his organ from Karen's inflamed love-mouth and sat on his heels, panting in his debauchery. *Karen, your clothes are behind the sofa. Both dress and sit on the sofa.* Answering the door to Emily, Grant smiled to see the girl standing on the step between two suitcases. 'Hi!' he smiled, eyeing the pretty girl's shapely thighs, longing to get at her tight pussy.

'Hi, Grant! Well, here I am!'

'You are, indeed! Come in, come in.'

'My boyfriend doesn't know I've left him yet,' she said as Grant grabbed her cases. 'He's out, but he'll have quite a shock when he gets home!'

'What about your work?'

'I rang them and told them what they could do with their job!' she giggled.

'So, you're free to begin your new life, then?'

'Yes – at last!'

Leaving the suitcases in the hall and leading her into the lounge, Grant introduced her to Father Gerald and Karen. 'This is Emily. She's come to stay with us for a while.'

'Stay with us?' Karen echoed, her blue eyes glaring at Grant, her hair dishevelled from her double fucking.

'Er . . . I'll be going now,' the priest said shakily, moving towards the door. 'I . . . I hope things turn out all right for you both.'

'I'm sure they will, Father,' Grant smiled. 'Did you enjoy your visit?'

'Er . . . yes, yes, very much,' he smiled, his face flushing, his mind confused. 'I'll see myself out. Goodbye.'

'Goodbye, Father,' Karen said. 'Thank you for calling.'

Did he recall what he'd just done? Grant wondered as the man left the room. It was strange, he mused – the priest had just committed an indecent sexual act, broken his vows, and then said goodbye as if nothing had happened! But his face had flushed, so he must have recalled screwing Karen. Or was Grant's power becoming stronger and his victims losing all recollection of their debauched acts within minutes? *Whatever's going on*, Grant thought, gazing at Emily, her sweet smile, *I'm enjoying myself!*

Inviting Emily to sit down, Grant turned to face Karen. 'Emily is going to live with us,' he began. *You like the idea, Karen. You want her to stay here.* 'She's going to move in with us and . . .'

'I'm sorry, Grant, but I'm not having someone move in . . .'

'Karen, if you'll just listen to me for a moment.' *You want her to stay with us! Tell her that you'd love her to move in!*

'Grant, I'm not having you making arrangements for people to move into our house behind my back! The idea's ridiculous!' Turning to the girl, Karen forced a smile. 'I'm sorry, Emily, but I wasn't consulted about this. You do understand, don't you?'

'I thought Grant lived alone. I'm sorry, I didn't realize that he . . .'

'Karen, I want to speak to you in private. Will you excuse us, Emily?' Grant asked the bewildered girl as he opened the door. 'Sit down, we won't be long.'

'Er . . . yes, yes, of course.'

'Come into the kitchen, Karen. I want to explain things.'

'There is nothing *to* explain!'

'Yes, there is. Please, come into the kitchen.'

Leaning back on the worktop with her arms folded, Karen glared at Grant as he closed the kitchen door behind him. 'What's all this about, Grant?' she asked angrily.

You want her to stay here!

'You invite some young girl to move into our house without even mentioning it to me, and then you expect me to . . .'

It's not working! 'Karen, I . . .' *Tell me that you want her to live with us!*

'I don't know who or what she is, Grant! I don't know why you . . .'

'Do you remember what the priest did?' Grant asked, fearful now that his power had gone.

'What the priest did? What do you mean?'

'When he was here, do you remember what happened?'

'We talked and . . . I don't know what you're getting at, Grant! Forget about the bloody priest! What I want to know is, why did you ask that girl to move in without even mentioning it to me?'

'I thought that . . .'

'That's a terrible thing to do! How would you feel if I'd asked some young man to move in with us?'

'Karen, I . . .'

Shaking his head as Karen stormed upstairs, Grant sighed. Was this the fate he'd been warned about? he wondered. Losing his power, was that the fate? The power had worked with the priest, and with Karen, up until a few minutes ago, so what had happened? he wondered as he walked through the hall and entered the lounge. *Test it on Emily*, he decided, sitting opposite the girl. *Sit with your legs wide apart. Pull your skirt up over your stomach and sit with your legs wide apart!*

'Grant,' she began as she crossed her legs. 'I didn't know that you were living with someone! I thought . . . I don't know what I thought!'

'I'm sorry, Emily. I didn't think Karen would take it the way she did. Look, you're here now, so I'll show you up to the spare room and you can unpack.' *Pull your skirt up and show me your knickers!*

'I don't think it's a good idea to move in, Grant. My boyfriend doesn't know I've left yet, so I think I'll go back to the flat. And as for my job . . . well, I don't know what to do about that!'

You want to stay here! Open your legs and show me your knickers! 'Well, if that's what you want to do, it would seem that I can't change your mind.'

'I'll call round tomorrow and see you,' she smiled as she rose to her feet and moved towards the door.

'OK,' Grant sighed, standing and following her into the hall. 'I'm sorry about all this.'

'You should have said that you were with someone.'

'I'm not *with* her. She's not my girlfriend or my wife, she's . . . won't you change your mind?'

'No. Whatever she is or isn't, I can't move in,' she replied, grabbing her cases as Grant opened the front door. 'Tomorrow, perhaps – I might see you tomorrow. Bye, Grant.'

Saying nothing as the pretty girl lugged her cases down the path, Grant closed the front door and returned to the lounge, his mind reeling with confusion and disappointment. 'I suppose I went too far!' he sighed, flopping onto the sofa. 'Shit, I had everything! And now I've blown it!' *I'll go back to the wood this evening!* he suddenly thought. *I must return to the wood and talk to the people!*

He doubted very much that they'd bestow the gift upon him again, but it was worth trying. Veneris? he wondered. Had she snatched the gift? Had she been aware of his debauched behaviour with the priest and Karen and taken the gift away from him? He *had* to return to the wood! He wasn't sure what to say to the sect, but he had to return to the wood – there was no other way!

Chapter Seven

Dusk rapidly blanketing the wood, Grant made his way through the undergrowth in search of the sect, praying that they'd restore his power and allow him domination over women. The future had looked so good, but now? Now all he had was a redundant sex dungeon and one thousand pounds to show for his efforts! Karen had gone, Emily had gone ... What was the use of having a magnificent penis without a constant supply of women?

Emerging from the bushes, Grant stood in the small clearing, gazing at the curvaceous young girls, their elongated nipples, their full vaginal lips. They were beyond beauty, he observed. Their skin taut in youth, not even blemished by a small mole, their teeth brilliant white, perfect, they reminded Grant of angels. *The Devil's angels?* His heart racing, he forced a smile as one of the young men approached and stood before him as if awaiting an explanation for his uninvited arrival.

'I ... I came back because ...' Grant began hesitantly.

You were told never to return!

'Yes, I know, but ...'

You have lost your power?

'Yes, I have.'

You were warned not to abuse your power. Had you heeded ...

'Please, I want the power back! I'll do anything, anything!'

It is too late! We cannot help you.

'Is there nothing I can do to put things right?' Grant asked despairingly, gazing at the man's huge erect penis. 'I don't even know what I'm supposed to have done, apart from enjoy my gift.'

It is not for us to decide whether you should be blessed with the gift or not. It is the Goddess Veneris who makes such decisions. You have betrayed Veneris!

'No, I . . . please, call on her. Please, I need . . .'

Should Veneris decide to bestow the gift upon you again, which I doubt she will, then she'll require something in return.

'Anything! I'll do anything!'

Remove your clothing.

Moving away, the young man raised his arms and looked up to the trees. Joining him, the other male raised his arms, his eyes closed as if in some kind of trance. The girls kneeling before the men, gazing at their solid penises glowing in the firelight, Grant wondered whether their intimate attention was part of the ritual as they took turns to suck on their bulbous knobs. Calling upon their Goddess of Carnality, the males began their strange chanting as the girls fervently mouthed and sucked their huge organs, quickly bringing out their gushing sperm, each drinking in turn until they'd drained their heavy balls.

Slipping out of his clothes, Grant again prayed that the power would be returned to him. He couldn't live without the control he'd had over women, the incredibly debauched sex life he'd become used to. But what would Veneris require in return for restoring his gift? he wondered as he stood naked, his penis sadly limp. The girls licking the men's solid shafts, lapping up the spilt come, Grant wondered why the arousing sight hadn't caused his penis to swell and stand proudly to attention.

A shimmering ball of green light materializing and hovering high above the clearing, Grant waited in fear and anticipation. This was it! he thought anxiously as a finger of light snaked down from the ball and played on his penis, caressing his glans, stiffening his huge organ. Looking down at the eerie glow surrounding his painfully solid member, he froze. He shouldn't have returned, he thought, watching his aching knob balloon as the green light bathed his twitching penis.

The supernatural, unseen worlds, the occult . . . It wasn't wise to dabble with dark powers, no matter how much he craved the strange gift! But his unquenchable thirst for sex had plunged him into the darkest depths of depravity, and he realized that he'd offer his very soul to the Devil in exchange for domination over women!

His penis twitching as a young girl knelt before him and sucked his knob into her pretty mouth, Grant closed his eyes. Rolling her tongue over his glans, the girl quickly brought out his sperm, her mouth filling with the product of his orgasm, her cheeks ballooning as the light played around Grant's heavy balls. Yes, he decided, he'd offer his very soul to the Devil in return for complete domination over women!

His sperm gushing, bathing the young girl's tongue, Grant thought his incredible climax would never end. On and on his spunk flowed, his glans pulsating, his shaft painfully swelling as his balls finally drained, leaving him gasping for breath. Was his power returning? he wondered as the girl slipped his plum from her mouth and licked his shaft, lovingly cleansing his purple knob with her wet tongue.

You wish for the power? The music-like voice echoing in his mind, Grant knew that this was the Goddess of Carnality communicating with him as he looked up to the ball of light. *You wish for the power?*

'Yes, yes, I . . .' he began as the girl at his feet scurried across the clearing like a frightened animal.

But you used your power on your own kind, your own sex! You betrayed your own sex!

'No, all I did was . . .'

You have influenced a priest, willed him to commit a sexual act against his conscious will! You did this for your own pleasure, you took pleasure in using a member of your own sex!

'Yes, I did. But I thought . . .'

You used your gift to entice a male to take a woman. The power you had over the subconscious mind was only to be used to control the opposite sex, the weaker sex.

'I didn't know that.'

If I bless you with the gift and you use your powers on your own sex, you will be punished with eternal impotency.

'Yes, yes, I understand.'

Man is the stronger sex, the leader, the ruler. Women are to be slaves to men. The power is not to be used to control the male species.

'But aren't *you* female?'

I am both male and female. I am the cumulation of many millions of orgasms.

'The cumulation of orgasms?'

Telepathy is communicating by sending and receiving thoughts. Orgasm produces thoughts, powerful thought forces, which have combined and built to create a supreme sexual force. I was created from many millions of orgasms over millions of years – I am the supreme sexual force!

'Why not give women the power to . . .'

Woman has deprived man of sexual pleasure since the beginning of time. Woman, with her sacrosanct vagina, has ruled man. Now, woman will become the slave to man, give her body to man, the superior sex.

'But I don't understand . . .'

Before I endow you with the power, the females will fire your lust, provoke your anger, your craving to abuse their young bodies. And then, to show your allegiance to me, the Goddess of Carnality, you will tether and whip the females until they beg for mercy, until they recognize you, a man, as the all-powerful species.

'Whip them? But . . .'

You will whip them until they cry and plead for mercy!

'But . . .'

Do you not want power over women, domination over the cruel sex who have denied men sexual pleasure for aeons?

'Yes, I do.'

Women have sold their bodies to men, and they blame men for exploiting them! Women have used their bodies, their vaginas, to exploit men, and they will be punished! Will you prove your allegiance to me by punishing women, using them for your own sexual pleasure?

'Yes, I will.'

You must prove your competence to dominate females, to treat the selfish females for what they are – slaves to mankind. The females will now fire your lust, provoke your anger, your craving to abuse their young bodies.

The green light fading, leaving Grant's penis, he looked at the young girls, their pert breasts, their full, pouting labia. *Provoke my anger?* he pondered as the two men approached him. *What the hell are they going to do?* he wondered anxiously as they grabbed his arms and dragged him across the clearing.

Laying him on his back over the tree, the men grinned as the girls spread his limbs, ran their hands over his inner thighs, his heavy balls. His arms outstretched, his legs wide, the men held him in place as the girls bound his wrists and ankles to the tree with rope. Caressing his naked body, his rolling balls, his solid cock, his ballooning glans, they gathered around Grant – around their male victim.

They want revenge! the young men communicated in unison. *The females want revenge!*

'Revenge?' Grant frowned, his fear rising as he pulled on his bonds. 'Revenge for what?'

Revenge for the way males are treating them, using them, abusing them. They are the weaker sex, they are used by males as slaves, as sex objects. Now they seek revenge – and you are their victim! It is the will of Veneris!

'But I thought . . .'

To prove your allegiance to Veneris, you will give your body to the females. When they have done with you, fired your anger, roused your wrath, you will crave vengeance and beat them by way of punishment!

The girls' pretty mouths grinning, twisting as their blue eyes widened and sparkled with an inner desire, Grant's fear soared. *Revenge!* The word haunted him, echoed around the murky depths of his depraved mind as he wondered how they would attain their vengeance, what dreadful acts they would commit against his naked body.

Taking a length of thin rope, a wicked glint in her eyes, one of the females tied it around the shaft of Grant's penis. His body curved over the rough bark of the tree, he raised his head to see his penis jerking as the rope was pulled this way and that. They were playing with him, he knew, as another girl yanked his foreskin back, giggling as she exposed his bulbous purple knob. *This isn't so bad!* he thought, reclining his head as a young girl stood with her thighs either side of his face, her gaping vaginal crack pressed to his mouth.

Lapping up the honeydew oozing from the girl's hot sex valley, Grant grimaced as teeth nibbled the shaft of his solid penis. His heavy balls sucked into a wet mouth, teeth biting his nipples, the rope tugging on his swollen organ, he wondered how far the girls would go in their quest for revenge against mankind. Would the teasing, the toying, become frenzied and develop into sexual torture? he pondered fearfully.

The yawning cuntal fissure fervently sliding over his mouth, bathing his face with slippery girl-juice, Grant spluttered, barely able to breathe. The girl was close to her climax, he knew, as she aligned her long clitoris with his open mouth, pushing the erect protrusion against his snaking tongue. His cock-head licked by two wet tongues as he turned his head to one side and gasped for air, Grant was quickly nearing his own desperately needed climax.

His body alive with lust as the trembling girl ground her open cunt into his gasping mouth, whimpering as her orgasm rose from her quivering womb and peaked in her pulsating clitoris, Grant sucked on her girl-bud, sweeping his tongue over the sensitive tip, sustaining her mind-blowing climax. Her cunt milk decanting, filling his mouth, running over his flushed face, he swallowed hard, wondering whether her copious flow would ever cease.

His penis twitching, on the threshold of orgasm, the girls ceased their licking, leaving him trembling, desperate to come, to loose his spunk. Was this their revenge? he wondered as his mouth again filled with the slippery product of the girl's climax. Swallowing hard, his penis on the verge of exploding in ecstasy, Grant prayed for a mouth, a tight cunt to envelop his yearning knob and take him to his sexual ecstasy. Was this their cruel vengeance?

'Please!' he gasped through a mouthful of wet girl-flesh. 'Please, I need to come!' But his desperate appeal was maliciously denied by the giggling girls. His impending climax finally receding, his knob swollen, his shaft twitching, Grant swallowed the last of the girl's orgasmic spend as she swivelled her hips, massaging her inflamed vaginal lips against his protruding tongue.

Moving her gaping sex groove away from Grant's mouth, the girl gazed at his cunny-wet face, her blue eyes sparkling, reflecting the flickering yellow light from the fire. She'd decanted her vaginal juice, quickly brought out her orgasm, used Grant for her sexual pleasure – and left him teetering on the brink of orgasm. How long would this go on? he wondered as a tongue teased his silky glans, licked his sensitive knob-slit. How long could he endure the sexual torture?

Another girl standing with her thighs either side of his head and pressing her open vaginal entrance against his mouth, Grant resumed his licking, drinking from her hot cunt as she gasped her pleasure. Didn't they want to sink his solid shaft into their love sheaths? he wondered as his rolling balls were licked, teased by two tongues. Didn't they want his gushing sperm filling their cunts, their thirsty mouths?

His penis aching for relief as the girl swivelled her hips, aligning her tight bottom-hole with Grant's probing tongue, he thought about Diana and Mandy – luring them into his sex dungeon and enjoying a night of wanton lust. With his power, he'd lure girl after girl into his den, and use their young bodies, their cunts, their tight anal canals for his debased pleasure. He'd thrust his massive penis deep into

Julie's hot bottom-hole, into Jackie's shaved cunt, into Karen's wet mouth – and satisfy his craving for perverted sex. *And* prove his allegiance to Veneris!

The tip of his tongue pushing against the girl's anal iris, she reached behind her back and yanked her taut buttocks apart, opening the small entrance to her very core. His tongue slipping into her rectal duct, inciting her sensitive nerve endings, Grant gasped as a hot mouth engulfed his swollen glans. Would he now be allowed the relief he desperately craved? No. His cock-head leaving the girl's mouth, twitching, so near to an incredible climax, Grant wasn't to be permitted the shuddering relief of orgasm.

More tongues licked his naked body, his balls, his inner thighs, his nipples, sending terrific sensations of sex through his quivering flesh. As he lapped between the girl's open crack, swallowing her copious flow of girl-come, he silently swore to get even with his female tormentors – with all females! Karen would suffer, he decided, as would the other girls he'd snare. His sex dungeon would become his sexual torture chamber, his den of lust – of revenge! But first, he was to suffer at the hands of the young females!

Releasing his feet, the two young men grabbed his legs, pressing his knees against his chest and securing them with rope. His erect penis and his heavy balls exposed, he was defenceless, powerless to halt the girls as they fingered his bottom-hole, tugged on the rope tied to his solid organ, kneaded his rolling balls. Craving orgasm as he pushed his tongue further into the girl's anal sheath, Grant sensed rope being tied round the neck of his heavy ball bag and the base of his throbbing penis.

The tree bark biting into his back, the cold reality hit him, the stark realization gripped him – revenge in the form of torture! What were they going to do? he wondered anxiously as the rope was pulled tight, his balls dragged away from his taut buttocks, his crudely violated bottom-hole. The finger withdrawing from his anal sheath, the rope pulled tighter, his fear soared again.

The first stinging lash of the rope striking his tensed buttocks and causing Grant's tethered body to jolt, he squeezed his eyes shut. *That's why they tied my balls up, in preparation for the whipping!* he thought with slight relief as the rope lashed his stinging buttocks again, the pain permeating his burning flesh. His tongue slipping out of the girl's bottom-hole as she swivelled her hips and presented her gaping vaginal entrance to his mouth, he cried out as the rope cracked loudly across his crimson flesh again.

This was their revenge against mankind! But would it stop there? Would a thrashing satisfy their frightening lust for vengeance? *Do unto others as they have done unto you!* Grant didn't know which girl's thoughts he'd heard, but he realized that they were using his body as their bodies had been used and abused by men. They had been thrashed, whipped, tethered with rope and abused, and now . . .

The thrashing halting as the girl towering above him reached her climax, draining her cuntal fluid into his gasping mouth, Grant wondered what punishment he'd be forced to endure next. Would it end there? What else could they do to his naked body, how would they vent their anger?

His buttocks crudely yanked apart, he grimaced as a large cylindrical object was forced into his anal duct, stretching the sensitive inner flesh to capacity. Further the object drove into his bowels, opening him as he'd opened girls' rectal sheaths, abused their young bottoms. The girl's dripping cunt finally leaving Grant's wet mouth, he breathed uneasily as the phallus sank deeper into his quivering body.

His anal ring painfully taut around the solid object, the thrashing resumed, reddening his quivering buttocks, sending shockwaves of pain and pleasure through his restrained body. *Revenge is sweet! Man will suffer! Thrash him harder!* His racked mind picking up the girls' thoughts, Grant again swore to get even with them. As they took their revenge, revelled in their retaliation, they knew that their turn was coming, that they'd be thrashed, their buttocks whipped, their bottom-holes violated with his huge penis. The young man was right, Grant reflected, he *did* crave vengeance – he *would* beat the girls by way of punishment!

The rope jolting his naked body, the tree bark gnawing his back, he longed to shoot his spunk into a girl's tight vaginal sheath, he craved to have his penis sucked to orgasm. But he was to endure the whipping before he was awarded the pleasure he yearned for, if he was allowed the pleasure at all! Finally, the giggling girl wielding the rope halted the cruel lashing. Was it someone else's turn to thrash him now? he wondered. Or had they planned something worse?

Hands grabbing his painfully solid penis, he gasped as a hot mouth engulfed his purple knob. *Please, I need to come!* he begged inwardly as the girl's tongue wound its way around his painfully ballooning glans. More hands moved between his thighs, releasing the rope from his penis, his scrotum, allowing his heavy balls to roll freely. The girl taking his knob to the back of her throat and gently sinking her teeth into his veined shaft, Grant was sure that the time had come to spunk into her mouth, bathe her pink tongue and find release from his sexual torment.

As someone slipped the object out of his bottom-hole, the girl moved her head away, pulling his knob from her hot mouth. *Please!* Grant urged, his organ twitching, dangerously close to shooting its come. Raising his head, he gazed between his knees to see a young female lifted high off the ground by the men. Sitting her on the backs of Grant's thighs, they held her there as another girl guided Grant's penis deep into her tight vagina.

Gasping as the welcoming warmth of her wet cunt engulfed his rock-hard weapon, he closed his eyes, breathing deeply. At last, this was it! he thought as the men bounced the girl up and down, repeatedly impaling her young body on his throbbing cock, pummelling her cervix with his solid knob.

A finger entering his anal canal, massaging the inner, velveteen flesh, Grant moaned as the intense pleasure permeated his body, his very being. Achingly close to his long-awaited climax, he pushed his tongue out as a girl stood astride his head, offering her open cunt to his thirsty mouth. Licking, tongue-fucking the girl's drenched vagina, his sperm finally gushed, filling the bouncing girl's gripping cunt as she cried out in her enforced orgasm.

This was the best climax he'd ever had, the duration and intensity incredible! Veneris had caressed his genitalia with her eerie light, heightened his pleasure, increased his staying power, he reflected thankfully as his orgasm rode on and his spunk flowed in torrents into the whimpering girl's rhythmically tightening cunt.

His tongue winding its way into the girl's hot vaginal sheath as she stood with her feet wider apart, Grant swallowed her warm sex-liquid, drinking from her inflamed cunt as she massaged her solid clitoris and reached her shuddering orgasm. All three writhing in their simultaneous climaxes, filling the wood with their orgasmic cries, they finally relaxed their exhausted bodies, revelling in the sensations of sex rippling through their trembling flesh.

Lifting the girl, slipping Grant's erect penis from her

inflamed pussy hole, the men laid her on the ground before releasing Grant and helping him to his feet. *Choose a female!* The words permeating Grant's mind as he stood upright and stretched his aching limbs, he grinned, pointing to a girl who had been quietly sitting by the fire. *Take her, she is yours!*

Forcing the girl over the tree, her stomach against the rough bark, her buttocks splayed, they bound her wrists and ankles with rope and moved away. *She is to be whipped!* Grabbing the length of rope, Grant raised his arm above his head, bringing the rope down with a loud crack across her taut bottom-orbs. Whimpering, her vaginal crack open, oozing with her sex lubricant, her body jolted with every horrendously powerful lash of the rope.

Revenge is sweet! Grant thought wickedly as he watched thin weals fan out across her taut flesh. Although she hadn't been the girl who'd whipped him, she was a female, and females were to be whipped, fucked and used by males, he reflected as he brought the rope down again with a deafening crack.

Bent on using women to satisfy his ever-rising perverted lust, his ever-deepening sexual depravity, Grant made his plans as he continued with the merciless thrashing. If there was time, he'd go to the pub and will the barmaid to ask him back to her flat. The night was but young, and there were tight cunts, hot bottom-sheaths, wet mouths, to be fucked and filled with spunk by the superior sex – the male, the leader, the ruler!

Diana, the beautiful young barmaid with her long blonde hair, deep blue eyes, firm breasts, tight wet cunt . . . She'd pleasure Grant, suck his knob, beg him to drink her warm girl-come, plead with him to fuck her tight bottom-hole – and then he'd thrash the bitch! Mandy would lick between

Diana's cunt folds, suck her pulsating clitoris into her wet mouth, bring her to orgasm with her sweeping tongue. Under Grant's influence, the girls would commit lewd acts, give the best lesbian show ever. And then he'd whip them until they begged Grant to show compassion!

But what about men? Grant pondered as whipped the tethered girl's glowing bottom-orbs, her screams filling the wood. If he couldn't enlist other men to join him in his debauchery, to fuck the girls' bottoms, their mouths, as Grant fucked their cunts . . . But there were plenty of men who'd be only too willing to join in! he reflected. And he could charge them, make money from his debauched ways. Money and rampant sex would be rife now that he had the gift, the power over women – complete domination of the weaker sex!

Finally discarding the rope, Grant yanked the girl's buttocks apart, exposing the private entrance to her innermost sanctum, the tight portal to the fiery heat of her very core. Pressing his purple plum against the brown tissue, he let out a long sigh of pleasure as his knob slipped past her defending muscles and drove deep into her tight anal tube. Slowly moving forward, he propelled his organ further into the girl's quivering body until his belly pressed against her crimson buttocks, his heavy balls resting against her dripping cunt lips.

Whimpering, the harnessed girl began to tremble as Grant slowly withdrew his fleshpole forcefully and drove into her tight rectal duct, his belly slapping her bottom-globes, his swinging balls pounding her swollen labia with every powerful thrust. Not only did he have complete dominance over women, not only had Veneris endowed him with a massive penis, with incredible staying power – but his libido had risen to frightening heights. Now, he craved perverted sex, yearned for girls' fresh young bodies, hungered for their beautiful cunts. And he was gripped by an evil passion to thrash and whip their pretty bottom-cheeks!

Driving his throbbing knob deep into the girl's quivering body, Grant finally loosed his spunk, bathing her smooth inner flesh, lubricating her anal cylinder as he repeatedly propelled his cock into her young body. His face contorting as his intense orgasm rode on, he grabbed her hips, fucking her bottom-hole with a vengeance, using the girl for his own debased pleasure, abusing her – his slave. All women were his slaves now! They'd worship him, his magnificent penis, beg for his sperm, crave his masculine body – and offer their buttocks to the whip!

Making his last thrusts, draining his swinging balls, Grant finally withdrew his weaponhead from the trembling girl's sperm-drenched bowels. Turning to the young men, his penis solid, glistening in the firelight, he smiled. Had he passed the test? he wondered. Had the thrashing, the anal fucking, proved his allegiance to Veneris? He couldn't hear their thoughts as he grabbed his clothes and dressed. Were they silently discussing him? Was Veneris close, lurking? Was he to take all the girls, thrash all the females before he'd be allowed to leave?

You have done well! Grant knew that the words swirling through his mind had been transmitted by the Goddess of Carnality. *You now have the gift, use it wisely.*

'Thank you,' he replied, looking up to the trees, to the unearthly ball of green light as he finished dressing.

Go now, and enjoy your power. Do not return to this place. And remember that you will be punished with eternal impotency should you abuse your power. Do not even attempt to listen to the thoughts of males. Never return to this place – never!

'I understand,' Grant replied fearfully.

Here, take this. You will need it for your girl-slave, one of the men smiled, handing Grant a studded dog collar and chain. *Use it to control your girl-slaves.*

'Yes, I will. Thank you.'

Go now!

Glancing at the young girls, their fresh bodies, their long nipples and gaping vaginal cracks, Grant quickly left the clearing. He'd done it! he reflected as he dashed through the undergrowth and emerged from the wood. Bounding down the hill, his heart racing, his adrenalin flowing, his mind swirled with thoughts of debauchery, thoughts of perverted sex. The incredible power, the beautiful gift, was again his! He'd done it!

There was still time to go to the pub, time to meet Diana and . . . *Take her home with me!* he suddenly thought as he climbed into his car. Glancing at another car parked next to his, he grinned. *Some young bloke having his end away beneath the moon!* he thought as he drove off. *I hope he thrashes the tart!*

His stomach somersaulting with excitement, Grant made his plans. *Take Diana home with me. Send my thoughts out to Karen – and enjoy a night of depraved lust!* Karen wouldn't present a problem now, he pondered happily, evilly. She was under his complete control – she was his sex slave!

Parking his car outside his house, Grant began to walk the short distance to the pub, praying that Diana would be there. His penis twitching at the prospect of penetrating the girl's tight sex sheath, his lips curled into a wicked grin as an attractive middle-aged woman approached. *Stop and pull your knickers down!* Obediently standing before Grant, the woman lifted her long dress up over her stomach and yanked her panties down, the light from a lamp post revealing her thick pubic bush to Grant's evil stare.

Open your cunt lips. When were you last fucked? he asked mentally as she peeled her fleshy vaginal cushions apart, exposing her glistening inner flesh.

This morning.
Who fucked you?
My husband's friend.
Having an affair, are you?
Yes, I am.
Did you come when he spunked up your cunt?
Yes.
What's your name?
Elizabeth. Elizabeth Miles.
OK, Elizabeth, you'd better be on your way before I fuck you against the wall! Where do you live?
Forty-nine Rochester Street.
Forty-nine Rochester Street. OK, off you go!

Watching the woman tug her panties up and walk down the street, Grant thanked Veneris for his power. *I could have had that woman suck my knob!* he mused happily as he crossed the road to the pub. *I can have any woman, anywhere, any time!* He also realized that he could blackmail people such as the woman who was having an affair with her husband's friend. *But why bother?* he reflected. *I can walk into any bank and ask for cash!* Was that abusing his power? No, he decided – it wasn't!

But blackmail would be fun, he thought in his deepening wickedness. Able to pry into the mire of people's subconscious minds, he could discover their darkest secrets. He could toy with his victims, play with them, put the fear of God into them – the fear of the Devil! Was this Satan's thinking? he wondered fearfully. *What the hell am I becoming?*

Diana was standing behind the bar cleaning glasses as Grant pushed the swing doors open and entered the pub. Her blue eyes smiling as she looked up, she tossed her long blonde locks over her shoulder and provocatively licked her full red lips with her wet tongue. She was obviously pleased to see him, he observed, but did she remember him visiting her flat? Did she remember the fucking, the lesbian cunt licking?

'I couldn't make it to the car park the other day,' she said softly. 'Mandy was supposed to meet me after I'd finished the lunchtime session, but . . .'

'Don't worry,' Grant interrupted, leaning on the bar and gazing longingly between her full breasts at her deep cleavage. 'You'll be finishing here soon, won't you?'

'Yes, in about ten minutes.'

Ask to come home with me. You want to come back to my place for coffee.

'How about inviting me back to your place for coffee, Grant?'

Perfect! 'Yes, good idea. I think wine would be better than coffee though, don't you?'

'Definitely! Just let me finish here, and I'll be right with you.'

'I'll have a pint of John Smith's while I'm waiting.' *And don't charge me for it!*

Watching the girl pour his beer, Grant pondered on the future. He had to hold on to his amazing gift. Life wouldn't be worth living if he lost his domination over women again. He'd lost the power once, had a taste of life without it, had a frightener, and was now determined to keep it.

Smiling as Diana passed him his beer, he wondered whether to call in at her flat on the way home and pick Mandy up. *Three girls!* he thought, picturing Karen licking between Mandy's cunt lips as Diana licked and sucked Karen's pussy folds. *Each girl licking another girl's cunt, completing the lesbian triangle!*

'Where do you live?' Diana asked, resting her elbows on the bar, her chin on her fists. 'It's not too far, is it?'

'Five minutes away, just down the road,' he replied, gazing into her sea-blue eyes. *What colour are your knickers?*
Red.
Did you masturbate today?
This morning, in bed with my vibrator.
How many times did you come?
Twice.
Did you finger your cunt?
Yes.

Sipping his beer, Grant nodded towards Diana's boss as he entered the bar. 'You'd better look as if you're busy,' he whispered.

'I can't look busy with only one customer!' she sighed. 'The time really drags when the place is so quiet. The last pub I worked in was always packed.'

'You've got two customers,' Grant whispered, nodding his head towards a man sitting in a shadowy corner.

'He's only been there for a while. He came in just before you arrived, and he's not stopped staring at me!'

Ever had your bum fucked?
No.
Do you like sucking knobs?
Yes, very much.
What do you like most, sexually?
Being licked. Having a tongue up my pussy.

'What's Mandy up to this evening?'

'She went to the cinema with a friend. I'll just do the ashtrays and then I'll get my bag.'

Wondering what sort of mood Karen would be in as he finished his beer, Grant planned the night ahead. *I wonder whether Chris would like to join in?* he mused. Grant still hadn't experienced his ultimate whim, to give a girl a fanny shafting as another man screwed her bum. *Three men?* he pondered as Diana approached with her handbag slung over her shoulder, her ample breasts ballooning her tight blouse.

Eyeing her miniskirt, imagining her tight red panties hugging her swollen sex lips, he again pictured two cocks, one thrusting deep into the girl's rectal sheath and the other driving into her tight cunt. *I can't use my power on Chris, but I can ask him whether he'd like to join in.*

'Shall we go?' Diana asked, waving goodbye to her boss as Grant placed his empty glass on the bar.

'OK!' he replied eagerly, wondering whether Karen was in bed as he checked his watch. Walking out into the dark street, he took Diana's hand in his as his penis swelled within his tight jeans. 'You're very attractive,' he said. 'Extremely pretty.'

'Thank you! You're not so bad yourself.'

'Do you remember when I went back to your flat with you the other night?'

'Yes, of course I do!' she giggled. 'Why would I forget?'

'Do you remember what happened?'

'We had coffee with Mandy. Why do you ask?'

'No reason. My place is just over there, across the road.'

Grabbing the collar and chain from his car, he led Diana up the path to the house, picturing the girl naked, the collar around her neck, leading her around the house on all fours like an animal. Opening the front door, he ushered her into the hall as Karen emerged from the lounge.

'Grant, where have you been?' Karen asked, her expression one of anger as she glared at Diana.

'Sorry I left you alone for so long, but . . .'

'I wasn't alone, Julie's been round.'

'Oh, God! I forgot about that! Damn it, I wanted to . . .'

'That man rang again. What's going on, Grant?'

'Nothing! I've no idea who he is! Er . . . Karen, this is a friend of mine, Diana,' he introduced. *You want her to stay and have a drink. She's a friend of mine. You want her young body, you want to lick her cunt!*

'Hi, Diana! Pleased to meet you. Any friend of Grant's is a friend of mine,' Karen trilled. 'Go through to the lounge and I'll get you a drink.'

'Thanks. Er . . . Grant, I . . .' Diana began, her blue eyes mirroring her confusion as she watched Karen walk away. 'Grant, you didn't tell me that . . .'

Come into the lounge. Don't ask any questions, just come into the lounge and sit down.

Sitting in the armchair as Diana made herself comfortable on the sofa, Grant pondered ringing Chris and inviting him round. No, he decided, toying with the dog collar, there was plenty of time to bring Chris in on the fun. Tonight, he wanted the girls to himself!

Karen was to be his slave, not Diana, he mused as his girlfriend entered the room with a bottle of wine and three glasses. *Diana, stand up and remove Karen's clothes*, he willed the girl as Karen placed the wine and glasses on the coffee table. *Karen, you'll allow Diana to undress you and fix the collar around your neck. You're going to become my sex slave!*

This was too easy! Grant thought as Diana obediently rose to her feet and stood before Karen, unbuttoning the girl's blouse. Slipping the garment over Karen's shoulders, Diana unclipped the girl's bra, peeling the cups away from her pert breasts, revealing her elongated breast buds. *Give her nipples a little suck to stiffen them up a bit*, he willed Diana. Opening her mouth as she leaned forward, Diana took Karen's long penis-like nipple into her mouth, gently sucking the stiffening milk bud. Squeezing the girl's firm breasts, Diana closed her eyes as she suckled, moaning through her nose, obviously savouring the lesbian coupling.

Tossing her head back, her glazed eyes looking up to the ceiling as Diana sucked on her other breast bud, stiffening the brown teat, darkening her areola, Karen gasped as the pleasure permeated her mammary spheres. *Now her skirt and panties*, Grant thought, his penis threatening to burst through his jeans as he watched Diana drop to her knees and tug Karen's skirt down her shapely legs to her ankles. Her red panties already cunny-wet, Karen lowered her head, watching as Diana pulled the silk material away from her swollen, hairless pussy lips, her pink vaginal slit.

Kick your shoes and skirt off. Lifting each foot, Karen kicked her clothing aside, her curvaceous body naked before her audience. 'Diana, fix this around her neck,' Grant said, rising to his feet and passing the collar and chain to the girl.

'Grant, what . . . what am I . . .' Karen stammered as Diana slipped the collar around her neck and fastened the leather buckle. 'What . . .'

'You're my sex slave, Karen,' Grant smiled, taking the end of the chain. *You'll do anything I ask, Karen! Get on all fours like a dog!*

Obediently complying with his silent instruction, Karen

took her position, her taut buttocks weal-lined, jutting out, her cunny lips ballooning between her thighs. *Diana, take your clothes off*, Grant instructed the pretty blonde, his stomach somersaulting at the prospect of watching the lesbian sex show. Yanking the chain as Diana slipped her blouse off, Grant led Karen to the armchair and sat down, wondering again whether to ring Chris as his girl-slave settled at his feet.

Diana had large rounded breasts, Grant observed as her mammary spheres tumbled out of her bra cups. Firm with expansive areolae and long, chocolate-brown nipples, they were fine specimens – suckable. As the girl tugged her skirt down, revealing her white panties, Grant unzipped his jeans and slipped his rock-hard penis out. His knob ballooning as he gripped the monstrous weapon in his hand, he watched Diana drag her panties down, displaying her scant blonde pubes, her pinken pussy crack.

'Right, now that you're both naked, the fun can begin!' Grant chuckled, massaging his solid penile shaft. 'Diana, go to the kitchen and see what you can find to shove up Karen's cunt!' he ordered in his wickedness. Leaving the room, the naked girl returned clutching a huge aubergine. 'Perfect!' Grant cried. 'Karen, get on all fours and stick your bum out!' Her knees wide apart, Karen projected her buttocks, her pussy slit gaping, the opening to her hot vaginal sheath bared. 'OK, Diana, push the aubergine up her cunt.'

Kneeling behind the girl, Diana pushed and twisted the purple fruit, gently forcing it between Karen's swollen pussy lips and deep into her drenched vaginal cavern. 'What's it feel like?' Grant asked the girl as she rested her head on the carpet.

'Too big! It feels too big!' she gasped, her blue eyes wide.

'Diana, I want you to push as many fingers as you can into Karen's bum,' Grant ordered, pulling on the chain and lifting Karen's head off the floor. 'Try to get your fist up her bum.'

'No, Grant!' Karen cried. 'Please, you can't . . .'

You want Diana to finger your bum, Karen. You're going to enjoy it.

Yes, I'm going to enjoy it.

Licking her slender fingers, Diana parted Karen's taut buttocks and pushed her middle finger into the heat of her rectal sheath. Managing to slip a second finger into the trembling girl's anal tube, she looked at Grant. 'Go on, more fingers!' he ordered, joining the girl on the floor, his eyes transfixed on Karen's stretched anal ring. Pushing a third finger into the girl's tight duct, opening her brown ring, Diana tried to drive her fourth finger into the girl's bottom-tube.

'Please, no more!' Karen whimpered, her pelvic cavity painfully bloated.

'I can't do it!' Diana complained, trying to slip the fourth finger into the girl's bottom. 'It's just not possible to . . .'

'Yes, it is!' Grant assured the girl. 'Go on, keep trying!'

'Grant, I can't take it! I'll split open!' Karen protested as her taut brown tissue slowly stretched to capacity.

'No, you won't, Karen! You're my slave, so you'll do as you're told! Relax your muscles and she'll be able to get all her fingers up your bum.' *Relax and enjoy it. Beg her to push her fist up your bum.*

'Diana, push your fist up my bum,' Karen whimpered, her clitoris swelling in response to the lewd act.

'I'll try, but I don't think I can!'

Try as she did, pushing and twisting her hand, Diana couldn't realize Grant's vile fantasy. Ordered to piston her three fingers in and out of Karen's bottom-hole while Grant made a phone call, she held the girl's buttocks apart and began her crude anal finger-fucking to the accompaniment of the girl's wails of debased pleasure.

'God, that's nice!' Karen breathed, her vaginal muscles spasming, gripping the aubergine. 'Ah, don't stop! God, it feels . . . ah, ah!'

Grinning as he leaped to his feet, his penis proudly standing to attention through his open zip, Grant picked the phone up and dialled Chris's number. He *had* to realize his perverted fantasy, he mused as he listened to the ringing tone. Chris would grab the opportunity to join in the debauched sex, he was sure. What normal man could resist two beautifully depraved young girls?

'Chris, it's Grant,' he said as his neighbour answered. 'I know it's late, but I thought you might like to come round. I'm having what I can only describe as an orgy.'

'An orgy?' Chris laughed. 'Who with?'

'Karen and another girl. Want to come round and help me fuck them both senseless?'

'Well, I . . . I don't know. Karen's your girlfriend, Grant!'

'No, she's not – she's my sex slave!'

'Your sex slave? Christ, who's the other girl?'

'Some horny little tart I met in the pub. Come round, I'll go and open the front door for you.'

'OK, I'll see you in a minute.'

Banging the phone down, Grant turned to the girls. 'Right, take the aubergine out of her cunt!' he ordered Diana as she pistoned her fingers in and out of the girl's anal canal. 'You're both in for a double fucking!' he laughed, bounding through the hall and opening the front door. Returning to the lounge, he instructed the naked girls to stand side by side. 'When Chris gets here, you'll both crave his body, you'll suck him off, offer your cunts to him. Ah, that'll be him!' he chuckled as the front door slammed shut.

Chris let out a rush of breath as he entered the lounge to see the naked girls standing in the centre of the room. His eyes nearly popping out of his head as he gazed longingly at Karen's shaved sex hillocks, her incredibly long clitoris emerging from her pink crack, he focused on Grant's gigantic penis, his bulbous knob.

'Bloody hell!' he exclaimed. 'I've never seen such a big cock!'

'Don't worry about my cock! What do you think about the girls?' Grant asked, turning to face the naked beauties.

'They're gorgeous! What have you done, drugged them?'

'No, of course not!'

'Jesus, a collar and chain!'

'Karen's sole aim in life is to pleasure me! They want us to fuck them. They're dying for it, aren't you, girls?'

'Yes, we're dying for it!' Karen smiled, her blue eyes reflecting a burning passion for debased sex. 'Fuck us, Chris!'

Moving towards Chris, Diana dropped to her knees, following Grant's unspoken instructions and tugging the man's zip down. Hauling his erect penis out, she peeled his foreskin back, revealing his purple knob, his small slit, to her wide eyes. Looking down in amazement as the girl engulfed his silky glans within her hot mouth, Chris gasped, his thick black hair falling over his closed eyes as she took his plum to the back of her throat and gently sank her teeth into his veined shaft.

Diana or Karen? Grant pondered as Chris's gasps of male pleasure filled the room. Which girl was to endure the first double fucking? Karen! he decided, standing behind the girl. *I'll take her arse, and Chris can have her cunt!* Ordering Karen to stand with her feet as wide apart as possible, he splayed her taut buttocks. *Here it comes!* he chuckled inwardly, pressing his bulbous glans against her tight anal rosebud.

'Chris, why don't you fuck Karen's cunt?' Grant asked as his knob slipped past the girl's anal sphincter into the warmth of her tight cylinder. 'I'll fuck her bum while you fuck her cunt!'

'Christ, I've never done that before!' Chris laughed, slipping his knob from Diana's mouth and standing before Karen's trembling body.

'Neither have I!' Grant chuckled. 'Go on, shove your cock up her tight cunt and we'll give her a simultaneous fuck!'

Whimpering as Chris forced his penis deep into her vagina and Grant drove his knob into the dank heat of her bowels, Karen closed her eyes. Her young body impaled on two stiff organs, her legs sagging, she clung to Chris for support as her love holes spasmed, her pelvic cavity inflating as the double thrusting began.

The men's balls swinging, clashing as their knobs drove into the young girl's tightening love sheaths, Grant ordered Diana to massage Karen's clitoris and take her to orgasm. Kneeling beside the girl, Diana slipped her hand between her yawning pussy lips and located her solid cumbud, massaging the sensitive protrusion, taking Karen to frightening new heights of sexual ecstasy. Wailing her appreciation as her body jolted with the anal and vaginal pistoning, Karen's head lolled forward, the chain hanging between her firm breasts – her very being shuddering as her orgasm stirred within her contracting womb.

'How near are you to spunking up her?' Grant gasped crudely as he sensed his orgasm approaching.

'Nearly there!' Chris replied, his eyes rolling as the girl's cunt tightened around his thrusting shaft. 'I can feel your cock! I can feel it thrusting into her arse!'

'And I can feel yours! We'll come together!' Grant breathed excitedly. 'Now, now! Come now!'

As Karen's orgasmic explosion rocked her perspiring young body, the thrusting penises erupted deep inside her inflamed sex ducts, filling her with sperm, lubricating the swollen cock-heads. Incomprehensible words bubbling from Karen's open mouth as her clitoris pulsated beneath Diana's caressing fingertips, the girl flung her arms around Chris's neck as her knees sagged and her legs crumpled.

'God, it's beautiful!' Karen managed to gasp as sperm jetted from her distended sex holes and coursed down her inner thighs. 'Ah, my cunt! My . . . ah, that's enough now! Please, no more!' Ignoring the exhausted girl's pitiful pleas, the men continued their fucking motions, draining their heavy balls, satisfying their base desires until their legs bowed, barely able to support their quivering bodies. 'Please . . .' Karen sobbed again in her coming as Diana persisted with the clitoral massaging. 'Please, stop now!'

Gasping, the men finally stilled their thrusting shafts, their pulsating knobs resting deep within the girl's sperm-drenched canals. Slowing her masturbating rhythm, Diana brought out the last ripples of pleasure from Karen's throbbing clitoris, gently bringing the girl down from her sexual heaven, returning her to her trembling, abused body.

'Christ!' Chris gasped as he slipped his penis out of Karen's hot cunt. 'Christ, that was bloody good!'

'Good? It was fucking brilliant!' Grant cried as he slowly withdrew his penis from Karen's sperm-drenched anal sheath. 'We'll give Diana a double fucking now!' he added wickedly as Karen's consumed body dropped to the floor in a crumpled heap.

'You must be joking!' Chris returned, his penis hanging limp. 'There's no way I could do it again! Not yet, anyway!'

Looking down at his own penis, Grant smiled. 'No staying power, that's your problem,' he said, proudly displaying his erect cock. 'I could go on fucking the tarts all night!'

'You and your fucking great dick, you're putting me to shame! Anyway, I don't think the girls want any more – look, they've fallen asleep in each other's arms.'

'Oh, that's great! Diana hasn't been fucked yet!' Grant protested.

'How about tomorrow night?' Chris asked as he concealed his penis within his trousers. 'I could come round tomorrow.'

'OK, tomorrow it is. I suppose it's getting pretty late now.'

'Right, I'll leave you with your sleeping beauties. Thanks for calling me round, it was great! I'll see you tomorrow evening, about seven?'

'Yes, about seven. See you, Chris,' Grant said as his satisfied neighbour left the room.

Zipping his jeans and flopping onto the sofa, Grant smiled, gazing at Diana's full vaginal lips bulging between her thighs as she rolled over and brought her knees up to her rounded breasts. 'I'll let them sleep for an hour – and then I'll fuck them both senseless!' he breathed, lying full length on the sofa and closing his eyes. *Fuck them both rotten!* he thought happily as sleep engulfed him. *Fuck their cunts, their bums, their . . .*

Chapter Eight

Diana had gone and Karen had climbed the stairs to her bed by the time Grant woke the following morning. Stretching on the sofa, he glanced at his watch, wondering what the day would bring, how many new sexual encounters he'd enjoy. But he had to plan his life, he contemplated. It was one thing to spend a lifetime screwing young girls' tight cunts, but there was more – much more!

With his power, his money . . . *What does one do with such power?* he wondered. It was like winning the lottery, money was no object! But when you'd bought a big house, fast cars, enjoyed a world cruise . . . *Better than the lottery, I can have money* and *young girls!* But what else was there? What other excitement could his gift bring him? *Blackmail!* The word drifted through his mind, teasing him, goading him.

Recalling the unfaithful middle-aged woman he'd met in the street, he grinned. 'Elizabeth Miles, forty-nine Rochester Street!' he breathed, leaping to his feet and grabbing the phone book, his mind seething with wicked ideas. *Blackmail!* Flicking through the pages, he found the woman's number and grabbed the phone.

'Is that Elizabeth?' he asked as a soft female voice answered.

'Yes, it is.'

'Your husband's friend, the one you're having an affair . . .'

Dave! Who knows about Dave?
Christ, it works over the phone! 'Er . . . Elizabeth, I'd better come round and talk to you about the affair you're having.'

'No, no! Who is this?' *Who could it be?*

'I want to come to your house and talk to you. You see, your husband is about to discover your . . .'

Listening to the dialling tone as the woman hung up, Grant replaced the receiver. Pondering on his telepathic powers, he frowned and rubbed his chin. *Presumably, distance is no object?* he mused. *How interesting!* There was so much more to learn about his gift, it seemed! *I wonder whether I could influence people on television? Influence the news reader to tell the nation to fuck off!*

'Poor Elizabeth, that's put the fear of God up her fanny!' he laughed as he left the room and bounded upstairs to the bathroom. *Evil though it is, I'll go and see her!* he decided, running a bath. *See how far she'll go to keep her dirty secret from her betrayed husband!*

Washed and dressed, Grant hurriedly gulped down a bowl of cereal before looking in on Karen. Still sleeping, her blonde hair fanning out across the pillow, her red lips slightly parted, the dog collar around her neck, he gazed at her and smiled. 'You'll have another double fucking tonight, my horny little slave!' he whispered, kissing her cheek. 'Possibly a triple fucking! Your arse, your cunt, and your mouth!'

Leaving the house, Grant leaped into his car and drove to Rochester Street, his mind swirling with sinister thoughts, wicked ideas. He wouldn't let on about his 'mind-reading', he decided. He'd ask Elizabeth for sex in return for keeping quiet and see how she reacted, he thought as he pulled up outside the expensive detached house. *With my power, it'll be easy enough to have her invite me in!*

Opening the door as Grant rang the bell for the third time, the horrified woman stared into his dark eyes. 'Hallo, Elizabeth,' he grinned.

'Go away!' she cried, her hands visibly trembling. 'Please, leave me alone!'

Invite me in and we'll talk.

'You'd . . . you'd better come in,' she conceded shakily, falling prey to his intruding thoughts as she opened the door wider. 'How do you know about me?' she asked, entering the lounge as Grant closed the door behind him. 'How could you possibly know?'

'Your husband has employed me to discover who you've been having an affair with,' he replied, following her into the expensively furnished room. 'I'm a private detective.'

'Oh, my God!' she gasped, flopping into an armchair, her short dark hair framing her guilt-ridden face as she shook her head in disbelief. 'How on earth does he know? There's no way he could . . .'

'He's had his suspicions for some time now. He doesn't know about your affair, not yet, anyway.'

'What are you going to do? If you tell him, then . . .'

'I might not tell him. It all rather depends on . . .'

'You want money, don't you? You've come here to blackmail me, haven't you?'

'No, I'm not after your money.'

'Then, what is it you want? Why are you here?' she asked, shifting uneasily in the chair.

Playing his wicked games with the distraught woman, Grant reclined on the sofa, gazing at her long legs, her ample breasts swelling her blouse, picturing her naked at his feet, his knob pulsating within her mouth. With his gift, he could have her do anything, of course – but blackmail was more fun!

'What is it you want?' she repeated apprehensively, her bottom lip quivering as she nervously twisted her fingers together.

'I want you to strip off and show me your body!' Grant replied unashamedly.

'Please, no!'

'All I want you to do is strip off and show me your body. It's not a lot to ask in return for . . .'

'But . . . look, I have a little money.'

'I don't need money, Elizabeth.'

'But, I can't . . . not in front of a total stranger! Please, I'll . . .'

'Why can't you? Take all your clothes off and show me your body, and I won't come back. Once you've shown me your breasts, your pussy, I'll go. I promise you, I'll never come back.'

'But . . .'

'Oh well, I suppose I'd better go and talk to your husband.'

'No, no! Please . . .'

'He'll be very interested to hear about . . .'

'All right, I'll do it,' she finally conceded, biting her lip.

'Good! I knew you'd see sense. Stand in the middle of the room and take all your clothes off.'

'You . . . you only want to look, don't you?'

'Yes, Elizabeth, I only want to look.'

How unfortunate that the poor woman should happen to have passed Grant, of all people, in the street! This wasn't fair, he knew as she stood and slipped her white blouse off, revealing her straining lace bra, her smooth flat stomach.

There again, she was the one having the affair. Play with fire and you'll get burned! *I could walk into any woman's house and have them strip!* he thought as she peeled her bra cups away from her large breasts, her elongated brown nipples. *I'll just have a little fun and then leave her in peace*, he decided, guilt stabbing his conscience as she tugged her skirt down her stockinged legs and stepped out of the garment. *Better not fuck the poor cow! There again . . .*

She was around forty-five, Grant reckoned as he eyed the swell of her red panties, her black lace suspender belt. *A pretty good figure for her age! Wonder whether she shaves her cunt?* Slipping her shoes off and unclipping her black stockings, she rolled them down her shapely legs, her face flushing as she looked up and caught Grant's appreciative gaze, the wicked glint in his evil eyes. This really was unfair, he thought as she pulled her stockings off her feet and stood upright, her cheeks turning crimson, her hazel eyes mirroring her fear as she tentatively removed her suspender belt and dropped it to the floor. But it was bloody good fun!

Only her red silk panties concealed her feminine intimacy from Grant's sinister gaze now. Should he tell her to dress? he wondered as she stood trembling before him, her heavy breasts, her large wedge-shaped nipples, blatantly displayed. Should he show some mercy? Driven by Veneris, by Satan, he grinned, nodding his head, indicating for her to unveil the most intimate part of her curvaceous body. *Evil knows no mercy!*

Opening her mouth as if about to speak, she sighed. She had no choice, she knew, as she focused her tearful eyes on Grant again – she either complied with his demands, or risked a messy divorce! Slipping her thumbs between the tight elastic of her panties and her shapely hips, she hesitated before exposing the very centre of her sexuality – her pussy.

'Promise me that you'll go after I've . . .' she began nervously, tugging the silk garment down an inch or so. 'Please, you will leave, won't you?' Smiling, Grant said nothing as she gingerly peeled the material away from her mound, exposing her sparse, well-trimmed pubic bush. Pausing before revealing her vaginal crack, she looked at Grant again, trying to find a glimmer of compassion in his wide eyes. But all she saw reflected in the dark pools of his staring eyes was evil. Compassion, mercy, love, sympathy, understanding . . . No, only an unquenchable thirst for sin!

The complete domination Grant had over women had cost him dearly, he knew. Love, warmth, affection . . . All had gone, been stripped by his incessant lusting for crude sex. But this had been what he'd wanted, hadn't it? Power over the fair sex, the weaker sex, was what he'd desperately craved, prayed for. And now he had that power! *Complete domination!* he mused, realizing the horrendous depths of sexual depravity he'd fallen to.

'Promise me that you'll leave after I've . . . after I've taken my panties off,' she whimpered, a tear rolling down her cheek.

'Why cry?' Grant asked, his lips twisting into an evil grin. 'I mean, you have no qualms about cheating on your husband, screwing his friend behind his back, lying to him, betraying his trust, his loyalty . . .'

'Please, don't! It's not like that!'

'Isn't it?'

'No, no! I . . . I love my husband very much.'

'Love? I don't think you know the meaning of the word!'

Grant laughed. 'How can you say you love him when you're having another man spunking up your cunt?'

Cringing as his words echoed around the confusion in her mind, she shook her head. 'Please, you don't understand!'

'I'm not here to talk about your infidelity, to understand your cheating ways. I'm here to see your naked body, your tits, your adulterous cunt!'

Her hands trembling as another tear emerged from the corner of her eye and rolled down her cheek, she slipped her panties down her long legs and kicked them aside. Standing upright with her feet slightly parted, displaying her pinken girl-slit, she looked into Grant's leering eyes.

'Well?' she sighed, her hands by her sides, her breasts heavy with age, her long nipples pointing downwards.

'Very nice!' Grant praised her. 'God, your inner lips are big! That's one thing I like about older women, their distended inner lips, the way their heavy tits hang and . . .'

'Please, I don't want to hear! Don't you think I'm embarrassed enough?'

'No, I don't! I like your nipples, they're long, big, succulent . . . You've got pretty good tits for a woman of your age, you should be proud of them. You've a nice fleshy cunt, too.'

'Please, stop it!'

'Tell me, the man you're screwing behind your husband's back – does he lick your cunt out? Does he tongue-fuck your cunt hole and drink your come?'

'Please! I've done what you asked!'

'Does he spunk in your mouth?'

'No, no! Look, I have some money upstairs. It's not much, but . . .'

'Peel your cunny lips apart. I want you to show me your

clitoris. I want to see the clitoris your lover licks to orgasm behind your husband's back.'

Delving into her subconscious, prising out her inner secrets as she tentatively moved her hands to her black bush, Grant smiled. She masturbated, he discovered from the wreckage of her guilt strewn about the murky depths of her mind. She thought about her illicit lover, his orgasming penis driving deep into her cunt, as she secretly rubbed her clitty to orgasm. But her lover hadn't been the first! Grant discovered to his surprise. She'd had many men, cheated on her husband many times throughout their twenty-year farcical marriage.

Moving forward on the sofa as she finally conceded and parted her swollen sex hillocks, Grant nodded his head appreciatively. 'Good, very good!' he chuckled, gazing at her inner folds, her clitoris peering out from beneath its pinken bonnet. 'How many men have you had during your marriage? How many have men licked your clitoris to orgasm? How many men have spermed into your lying mouth? It's at least ten, isn't it?'

'Please, stop it!' she sobbed hysterically.

'I'd say it was fifteen or more!'

'There's only ever been one!' she cried, releasing her fleshy vaginal lips, concealing her intimate pink folds, her clitoris.

'There was your neighbour, Graham. That lasted for over two years!'

Stunned, she remained silent for a few seconds, her head shaking in disbelief again. 'How . . . how do you know so much about me?' she finally managed to blubber through her tears.

'I know everything about you! I've done my homework, Elizabeth. You masturbate, don't you? You think about

Dave's penis thrusting into your cunt while you frig yourself off, don't you?'

'Who are you?' she asked, her breasts swinging as she bent over and retrieved her panties. 'Who the hell are you?'

'Don't dress! I haven't finished with you yet!' he bellowed. 'I wouldn't want to have to tell your husband about all the affairs you've had, about all the men who have wanked themselves off in your mouth and spunked down your throat.'

'Please, stop talking like that!'

'Why? It's true, isn't it? You've had at least fifteen men fuck your mouth and sperm down your throat.'

'No! I want you to go now!'

'Yes, I'd better go and speak to your husband. After all, he did employ me to . . .'

'All right, all right – I'll do anything! Just ask, and I'll do it!' she sighed, her head dropping in her shame. 'My husband must *never* discover the truth, it would kill him! What do you want me to do?'

What indeed? Grant wondered. Ask her to masturbate, to suck his knob and swallow his spunk while she frigged her clitoris to orgasm? He was spoilt for choice! he thought, gazing at her fleshy sex groove, imagining his solid penis driving between her swollen vaginal cushions and deep into the fiery heat of her adulterous cunt.

He'd not used his gift yet, he reflected. She'd stripped, parted her pouting vaginal lips, exposed her clitoris, asked him what he'd wanted her to do – without his coercive thoughts. He'd delved into her subconscious to discover her dark secrets, but she'd stripped without him sending out his silent instructions. It was more fun this way, he concluded wickedly. Watching the trembling woman drowning in her shame, her guilt, her humiliation, her degradation, was much more fun!

'What do you want me to do?' she repeated, clasping her trembling hands, veiling her vaginal crack.

'What would you like to do?'

'I . . . I don't know. What do you mean?'

'Well, you masturbate, so how about bringing yourself off while I watch?'

'No, please!'

'What, then? What would you like to do?'

'I want to get dressed! This is inhuman! You can't do this to me!'

'You'd be surprised by the things I can do to you!'

This was her punishment, Grant thought as she wrung her hands, another tear rolling down her tortured face. For the lies, the deceit, the adultery, the broken marriage vows – this was her punishment! In his evilness, he grinned, picturing the woman bending over, her buttocks splayed, her bloated pussy lips bulging below her bottom-crease. That was it! he decided. Humiliate her, degrade and shame the bitch!

'Stand with your back to me with your feet wide apart and touch your toes,' he instructed the distraught woman.

'Haven't I done enough?' she sobbed, wiping the tears from her eyes.

'You haven't even started! Your husband, Terry . . . I'll give him a ring at work.'

'I hate you! You're evil!' she spat as she turned round.

'And what are you? Nothing but a lying, cheating adulteress!'

Her feet wide apart, she bent over, touching the carpet, displaying her yawning vaginal crack, her distended inner cunt lips. His penis solid, Grant scrutinized his victim, her rounded buttocks, her small brown hole. A damned good whipping was what she deserved! he thought, eyeing the taut, milk-white flesh of her smooth buttocks. An ideal candidate for the sex dungeon!

'Does your lover fuck your arsehole?' Grant asked crudely.

'No!'

'Have you ever had a big cock fuck your tight arse?'

'I hate you! You're crude, disgusting, vile . . .'

'He comes in your mouth, doesn't he? He wanks in your mouth and spunks over your tongue!'

'No!' she screamed hysterically, standing upright. 'I'm not going to . . .'

'Bend over! He spunked in your mouth yesterday. He came here, after your loving husband had left for work, and you sucked him off in this very room. You were sitting on the sofa and he stood before you with his cock in your mouth and . . .'

'You've been spying on me!' she gasped, resting her hands on the floor again.

'I know everything about you, Elizabeth! OK, finger your cunt. I want to see how many fingers you can push into your adulterous cunt.'

'No, I won't do it! I'm not going to have you come here and . . .'

'I have photographs of you sucking Dave's cock, drinking his spunk. There's one, in particular, of you licking his knob while it's spunking over your face.'

Sighing, reaching between her thighs, she parted her moist cuntal lips and slipped two fingers into her sex sheath. Easing a third finger into her open hole, stretching her delicate inner flesh, she closed her eyes, her face flushing with humiliation as Grant knelt behind her. 'Four fingers!' he ordered, eagerly watching as she managed to comply with his crude demand. Her pink flesh taut, wet, he instructed her to finger-fuck her cunt, to thrust her fingers in and out of her juicy love hole.

'Haven't I done enough?' she sobbed as she pistoned her fingers. 'What more do you want from me?'

'You'll find out soon enough! This is your punishment for your betrayal, your adultery!' Grant chuckled, gazing at her cunny-wet hand.

'You . . . you won't tell Terry, will you? You won't tell him, not now that I've . . .'

'No, I won't tell him – not if you do as you're told. OK, now finger your bum hole.'

'Please, I can't . . .'

'Just do it, Elizabeth! Why make things difficult for yourself? All you have to do is push a finger into your bum! What's so bad about that?'

'It's degrading!'

'Exactly! Do it, or I'll finger your arse for you!'

'I'd . . . I'd *rather* you did it,' she replied softly.

Now there's an invitation! Grant thought surprisedly as she slipped her wet fingers out of her vaginal cavern. Would she enjoy it? he wondered, slipping his middle finger into her drenched cunt and massaging her inner flesh. Withdrawing his finger, he held her buttocks apart and drove it deep into her anal sheath, causing her to whimper, her body to tremble.

The humiliation must have turned her on, he reflected as she trembled, gasped and panted – the degradation excited her, aroused her. Bending and twisting his finger, he caressed her velveteen rectal tube, wondering whether to force his massive penis deep into her hot bowels and fill her with his spunk.

'Is that nice?' he asked, thrusting his finger in and out of her tight hole.

'Yes, yes it is!' she breathed, much to Grant's astonishment.

'Would you like two fingers up your bum?'

'Yes, yes! Ah, that's good!'

Sliding a second finger into her tight bottom-hole, Grant pondered on her obvious arousal. Perhaps she was a whore at heart? he mused as she shook uncontrollably in her arousal. After all, she'd screwed at least fifteen men during her married life! Perhaps her husband was unable to satisfy her rampant lust and she'd had to seek sexual gratification elsewhere? She was nothing more than an insatiable tart!

'I want you!' she cried, reaching between her thighs and parting her swollen vaginal lips with two fingers, exposing the reddening entrance to her hot sex cavern. 'Please, I want you inside me!'

'You want me to fuck you?' Grant asked in reply to her incredible demand.

'Yes, please fuck me! Come inside me!'

Pushing his finger deeper into her anal canal, Grant rose to his feet and unzipped his jeans. Pulling his weapon out, he offered his bulbous knob to her wet pussy hole and pushed his glans into the welcoming heat of her wet sex. Gasping, she grabbed his balls, fervently kneading them as he thrust his penis into her cunt, forced his finger deep into her rectal duct. He'd not expected this! he reflected. He'd humiliated her, degraded the sobbing woman – and then she'd begged him to fuck her! *Incredible!*

'God, you're so big!' she wailed as he repeatedly drove his solid penis into her drenched cunt and pummelled her soft cervix with his hammerhead. 'I've never known a man so big!'

'Why are you unfaithful to your husband?' Grant asked, pistoning her anal-hole with his finger. 'Why cheat on him?'

'He . . . he won't give me what I need. Ah, ah, that's so good! I love him deeply, but he doesn't satisfy me!'

'So you get other men to fuck you?'

'No, no. I . . . ah, ah, yes! Harder! I need physical love. I need . . . oh, oh! Oh, God! I'm coming! Please, don't stop!'

'You need fucking regularly!'

Her naked body shaking violently as she reached her climax, Grant shot his sperm deep into her spasming cunt, bathing her cervix, filling her sex cavern with his copious flow. 'I can feel it!' she gasped. 'God, I can feel your sperm!' Shafting her naked body with a vengeance, Grant drained his heavy balls, almost passing out with the intensity, the duration of his shuddering orgasm. Watching her huge inner lips cling to his cunt-wet shaft as he thrust in and out of her convulsing love hole, he grinned.

Older women had a lot to offer! he thought, amazed by the size of her inner petals. She was a good fuck, her fanny not as tight as a young girl's, but a bloody good fuck! It might be worth visiting her again, he thought, driving his knob deep into her spasming, sperm-drenched vagina. Her husband might not be able to satisfy her sexual needs but, with his magnificent weapon, Grant certainly could!

'You're so big!' she gasped again, her face flushed, her hair brushing the carpet as her body jolted with the vaginal pummelling. 'God, you're so big! I love it! I love your cock!'

'And I love your cunt!' Grant returned, his face contorting as his climax gripped him, shaking his perspiring body. 'I'll fuck your tight arsehole next!'

His glistening member sliding out of her consumed body as she crumpled to the floor, Grant jumped as he heard a key turning the front-door lock. Concealing his wet penis, he looked around the room, desperate for a hiding place as someone stepped into the hall and closed the door. 'Who's that?' he asked the exhausted woman as she hauled her trembling body up. 'Who the bloody hell . . .'

Diving behind the sofa, Grant held his breath as the lounge door opened. 'Elizabeth!' a male voice exclaimed. 'Elizabeth, what *are* you . . .'

'Hallo, Terry,' she replied as calmly as possible. 'I was just going up to have a bath. What are you doing home at this time of the day?' she asked, gathering her clothes from the floor and holding them against her naked body, concealing her inflamed vaginal crack, her sperm-drenched inner thighs.

'I forgot my briefcase,' he replied grumpily. 'I left in such a hurry this morning! Why undress in the lounge?'

'I was in the bathroom and . . . the phone rang so . . . does it really matter?'

'It's most unusual for a woman, or a man, for that matter, to undress anywhere other than the bathroom, Elizabeth! I find it most odd, I must say! A husband doesn't expect to come home and find his wife naked in the lounge!'

'Goodness me, Terry, don't make such a fuss! I was undressing upstairs when the phone rang. I hadn't got a towel with me, so I grabbed my clothes to cover myself. Are you happy now?'

'What if someone saw you through the window?'

'No one can see in. Anyway, go and get your case and leave me to have my bath.'

As the couple left the room, Grant breathed a sigh of relief. 'Pompous old fool!' he muttered, realizing why his wife had to seek sexual satisfaction elsewhere. 'Christ, that was close!' He couldn't have used his power to influence Elizabeth's husband, he reflected. He daren't use his power on his own sex! *I don't want the gift taken away again! Jesus, eternal impotency!*

Hearing the front door close, he clambered out of his hide and smiled as Elizabeth entered the room. 'I understand now,' he said, admiring her heavy breasts as she tossed her clothes onto the sofa, her hazel eyes smiling, her naked body glowing from recent sex.

'I do love him, but . . .'

'Yes, I know. Look, I'd better be going. I'll call round . . .'

'Yes, please do. Call round any morning, it's usually safe.'

'What about your other man?' Grant asked, guilt stabbing his conscience again as he recalled the humiliation he'd caused the woman.

'I'll deal with him. I don't want to see him any more. Thank you for . . . oh, my God! I've just realized, I don't even know your name!'

'Grant, it's Grant!' he laughed, tweaking her long nipples. 'I must go. I'm sorry for the way I . . .'

'What will you tell Terry?'

'Terry?'

'My husband. What will you say when he asks you what you've discovered about me?'

'Oh, that! Er . . . I'll tell him that there is no one, that you're definitely not having an affair.'

'Thank you, Grant. I must say, you really frightened me when you arrived!'

'Yes, I'm sorry. I shouldn't have been so cruel.'

'I . . . I liked the way you spoke to me. After a while,

I realized how much it turned me on. I thought you were going to rape me. I'd have liked that.'

'Would you?'

'Yes, I . . . I like sex, Grant. Terry doesn't seem to want to know. He's very old-fashioned. He doesn't think it right for a man and wife to see each other naked.'

'God, he *is* old-fashioned!'

'I do love him, but . . .'

'Yes, I understand. I'd better be going.'

'I'll see you again, won't I?'

'Yes, you will,' he replied, giving her his phone number. 'Ring me sometime and we'll arrange to meet. I don't want to turn up here unannounced in case your husband's around. I'll see myself out and leave you to your bath, or whatever. Bye, Elizabeth.'

'How did you discover so much about me?'

'I'm a good detective!'

'What about the photographs?'

'I'll destroy them, don't worry!' he laughed as he left the room.

Driving home, Grant pondered on the morning's events. His evil plan to leave Elizabeth in dread of her future hadn't worked at all! Rather than leave her in a terrible state of anxiety, he'd left her sexually satisfied and happy! *That's not the way to dominate women!* he thought, recalling the words of Veneris. *Woman has deprived man of sexual pleasure since the beginning of time. Woman, with her sacrosanct vagina, has ruled man.*

I should have thrashed the bitch! Grant reflected, wondering whether Veneris was close by, adjudicating his actions, watching his every move. *You will whip females until they cry and plead for mercy!* The words filtering into his mind, he was about to return to Elizabeth's house and thrash her naked buttocks with his leather belt. Had they been the words of the Goddess Veneris? he wondered, pulling up by the park. Was the Goddess nearby, lurking, watching? Unless he used his gift properly, she might take it away from him again.

But there was plenty of time to thrash Elizabeth, he mused as he climbed out of his car and walked across the park to the bench, wondering whether Jane would turn up and suck on his knob, drink his spunk. There was plenty of time to lure her to the sex dungeon and whip her until she screamed for mercy!

The sun hot on his back, Grant sat down, scanning the park for women, vowing to prove himself to be worthy of the great power bestowed upon him by Veneris. He'd prove not only his allegiance to the Goddess, but his complete commitment to her cause. He'd prove himself to be the dominant sex, the male, the ruler of the inferior species!

'Ah, what have we here?' he breathed, gazing across the freshly mown grass at a young woman walking alone through the park. She was in her mid-twenties, tall, slim, attractive – ideal! *I wonder what secrets she harbours?* Concentrating his thoughts, he explored the shadowy corners of her subconscious, listening to her inner thoughts, her memories.

Names filtered through his mind – *John, Mary, Christine, Brian* . . . Her thoughts becoming clearer, Grant listened intently, desperate to discover something sordid about her past, something he could use to blackmail her. Discovering nothing, he decided that the woman must be some kind of angelic virgin. 'Shit, she doesn't even masturbate!' he sighed. She was too young, he reflected – she wasn't even married, let alone an adulteress!

Suddenly, an older woman came into view. Although she was some distance away, Grant focused his eyes on her slender body, reckoning her to be around forty. Concentrating again, he grinned as he listened to her intimate subconscious thoughts. She was married – a good start! he mused as she walked towards him. Adultery? No, damn it! She was as faithful as they come!

Money. Mr Stringer. Stolen money. One hundred pounds every week. Her mind was racked with guilt and fear. She'd been stealing from the office safe, carefully altering the accounts to conceal her thieving from her boss. No one knew her dreadful secret, not even her husband. *Thousands of pounds. Prison!*

Willing the woman to sit on the bench, Grant made his plans, checking his watch and grinning. *Eleven-thirty, must be her tea break.* The private detective scam had worked well with Elizabeth, he reflected as the woman approached and sat next to him. Yes, that was the answer – tell her that he was working for Mr Stringer, her boss.

Good-looking with well-groomed, long black hair, she was fuckable, Grant mused. Her make-up impeccable, her full red lips pursed, her green eyes frowning, she was obviously worried. In her navy-blue skirt and matching jacket, she looked like secretarial material. But she didn't look like a thief!

'Nice day,' Grant smiled, turning round to face her. *Talk to me.*

'Yes, it is,' she replied, forcing a smile.

'You on your tea break?'

'Yes, I like to get out of the office in the summer.'

'So do I! Where do you work?'

'Stringer's – just around the corner.'

'No? That's incredible! I'm working for Mr Stringer!'

'Are you?' she frowned. 'I haven't seen you around.'

'Er . . . no, no, you won't have done. Mr Stringer has employed me to . . . well, I'd better not say anything.'

'Go on, tell me!'

'I'm a private detective – he's employed me to discover who's fiddling the books.'

'Fiddling the books?' she echoed, her green eyes widening with horror.

'Yes, someone's been taking money from the safe each week. It's been going on for a long time.'

'Do you . . . do you know who it is?'

'Her name's Melinda.'

'Melinda?' she repeated, her face turning pale with shock. 'What are you going to do? I mean, will she be arrested?'

'Actually, I've been lying to you. It's not professional, I know, but . . .'

'But what?'

'It's funny, you coming to the park and joining me on the bench. Quite a coincidence, in fact!'

'Why?'

'You're the girl. You're the thief, Melinda.'

'*Me?* I haven't been taking money from . . .'

'I have proof – photographs, videotape . . . it's odd that we should meet like this after all the time I've been working on the case.'

'Please . . . please, I don't want to . . . I couldn't face prison!'

'You should have thought about that before you started stealing the cash every week!'

'I was desperate! I'll pay it back! Out of my salary, I'll . . .'

'I'm afraid it's too late for that, Melinda!'

'Does Mr Stringer know?'

'Not yet. I'm going to tell him this afternoon. I have all the evidence in my car.'

'Please, I couldn't face the humiliation! Please, don't tell him!'

'I *have* to! He's paid me well and I've done a good job, how could I say that I've not discovered the identity of the thief after all these weeks?'

Breaking down in tears, the woman buried her face in her hands, begging for forgiveness. Grinning as he reclined and stretched his legs out, Grant pondered on his next move. He felt no remorse, no regret for the pain and anguish he was putting her through. He only sensed a stimulating feeling of great triumph, immense delight! After all, she was the thief, not him!

'Please, is there nothing I can do to stop you from . . .' she sobbed uncontrollably.

'I don't know,' Grant replied pensively, shaking his head. 'I don't have a choice, do I?'

'Please! There must be something . . .'

'If you were to pay all the money back in one lump, I might be able to . . .'

'I don't have any money!'

'Look, I'll not tell Mr Stringer yet. I'll leave it a day or two so that you can get hold of some cash.'

'I can't get any money!'

'Well, I'll leave it for a day or two anyway.'

'Oh, God! God! I don't know what to do! My husband will . . . God, he'll go mad!'

'Look, come round to my place this evening and we'll talk about it, try to work something out.'

'Yes, yes, thank you! Here, I have a pen in my bag. Give me your address,' she sobbed, passing Grant the pen as she took a handkerchief from her bag and wiped her eyes.

Writing his address down, Grant told her to be there at seven o'clock, assuring her that he'd do his best to find a way out of the mess she was in. 'I can't promise anything, of course, but I'll try to help you,' he smiled as he rose to his feet.

'Thank you! Oh, God! What have I done?' she wailed as she stood and faced him.

'I'll see you this evening, Melinda. Go back to the office now and . . .'

'No, no! I can't go back! I'll . . . I'll go home.'

'All right, I'll see you this evening.'

'Yes, yes, I'll be there!' she cried as she walked away. 'Seven o'clock!'

Rubbing his hands together as he walked to his car, Grant remembered Emily saying that she might call round today. 'God, life's good!' he cried, punching the air with his fist. 'Women, money, blackmail, sex . . . I love it!'

Again, Grant thought about dumping Karen. Did he really need her? he wondered as he climbed into his car. What role was she playing in his games? What use was she? She wasn't in the way, but . . . 'I suppose I'll keep the bitch on!' he laughed as he drove off. 'If only to give her a damned good thrashing every day!'

Karen was in the hall looking into the mirror, trying to release the dog collar from her neck as Grant opened the front door. 'Grant! Did you put this bloody thing on me?' she asked angrily. 'I woke up with the bloody chain almost strangling me!'

Leave it alone! You'll wear it all the time!

'I think . . . I think I'll leave it on,' she smiled, turning away from the mirror, her pointed breasts billowing her tight T-shirt. 'Where have you been?'

'I went out for a walk. It's a nice day.'

'I've only just got up and had a bath. God, was I knackered! My body was aching all over!'

'You had a bath with the collar and chain on?'

'I didn't have any choice, I couldn't get it off!'

'I like it, it suits you.'

'Yes, it . . . it does.'

'Has anyone called?'

'Only that bloody man again!'

'Christ, who the hell *is* he?' Grant breathed.

'How do I know? If you weren't out so often, you'd be able to speak to him!'

'If it's that important, he'll keep trying, I suppose. Has anyone been round?'

'No, why?'

'I'm expecting Emily to come round today.'

'Emily?' Karen echoed.

'Yes, you know, the girl who came round yesterday – the one I said was moving in with us.'

'Oh, *her*! Grant, you're not going to . . .'

You want her to move in!

'Yes, yes, it'll be nice to have her living with us. Want some lunch?'

'Thanks, I'll join you in a minute.'

Entering the lounge as Karen made her way to the kitchen, Grant took a deep breath and closed his eyes, concentrating on Emily, trying to pick up her thoughts. Picturing the girl, her pretty face, he heard faint words drifting through his mind. *Must find a new job. I should never have left.*

Emily, go and see Grant! Go to his house now! Grant urged the girl.

Grant. Must go and see Grant.

Yes, go now!

Go to Grant's house now.

'This is fantastic!' he grinned, imagining the things he could do, the people he could communicate with – the women he could lure to his sex dungeon without even leaving the house!

'Grant, your lunch is ready!' Karen called from the kitchen.

'OK, coming!' Leaving the room, his face beaming at the prospect of licking Emily's wet cunt folds, he gleefully rubbed his hands together again.

Gazing at Karen's rounded buttocks ballooning her tight miniskirt, he willed her to take her clothes off. Passing him a cup of coffee and a plate of sandwiches, she tugged her skirt down and slipped her panties off, revealing her smooth, hairless pussy lips, her elongated clitoris emerging from the top of her long slit. Tugging her T-shirt over her head, she tossed it over the back of a chair, her pert breasts ballooning, her incredibly long nipples suckable.

'I didn't bother putting a bra on,' she smiled, the chain running down her deep cleavage.

'Good! You have nice tits, you shouldn't cover them up. Emily should be here soon,' Grant said, munching his sandwich. 'And there's a woman coming round this evening.'

'Oh, who's that?' she asked, joining Grant at the table.

'Melinda. I met her this morning, in the park. She's . . .'

'You can't bring strange women . . .'

Shut up, Karen! You want me to bring women to the house. You'll lick their cunts, whip their buttocks. You're my sex slave, you'll do as I say!

'What time is she coming round?'

'Seven o'clock. Finish your sandwich and come to the sex dungeon with me, I have to prepare you for the role of sex slave.'

'Yes, sex slave,' she smiled.

'Damn, I've just remembered that Chris will be here at seven! Look, I'll need to talk to Melinda alone for a while so, when he arrives, let him in and take him to the kitchen and ask him to wait.'

In the dungeon, Grant took a length of rope and tied Karen's hands behind her back, grinning wickedly as he imagined Emily lashing the girl's buttocks. 'I made this the other day,' he said, taking a wide leather belt from the shelf. Running the belt around Karen's body, aligning the two large holes with her nipples, he pulled it tight and fastened the buckle behind her back. 'There! Look at your nipples forced through the holes!' he beamed triumphantly, gazing at her milk buds painfully inflated through the holes in the belt. 'OK, back to the house!'

Taking the chain, Grant led his slave through the kitchen and into the lounge, his stomach somersaulting as he gazed at her bloated nipples forced through the holes in the leather belt. 'Damn!' he cursed as the phone rang. 'Who the hell's that?' Ordering Karen to sit down, he grabbed the receiver.

'Hallo,' he said, watching Karen sit on the sofa.

'Is that Grant?' a man asked, his voice soft, his words spoken slowly.

'Yes, speaking.'

'You don't know me, Grant, but . . .'

'Are you the one who's been trying to get hold of me?'

'Yes, I am. I often walk my dog on the hill and I've seen you there several times.'

'Yes?'

'I'm intrigued.'

'Why?'

'Well, I've seen you go into the woods on several evenings and . . .'

'Yes, I go for walks, what about it? How do you know my name, anyway?'

'That doesn't matter. There was a young woman . . . she went into the woods at night and came out some time later with her clothes torn. She appeared to be totally exhausted! Goodness only knows what she'd been doing!'

'So what's that got to do with me?'

'I'm the nosy type, Grant. I like to know what's going on, what people get up to. I followed her and discovered that she lives with you.'

'Look, what the hell is all this? Who are you?' Grant asked angrily.

'I was intrigued, and I decided to follow you one evening after I'd seen you come out of the woods. You might remember seeing my car parked next to yours? Anyway, I followed you and parked a short distance from your house and . . .'

'Look, I've had enough of this crap!'

'Please, hear me out. You parked and locked your car and went into your house. A short time later, you walked to the pub. If you remember, you were talking to the barmaid when I came in. I couldn't help but overhear several parts of your conversation. I was intrigued by your mind-reading, most intrigued!'

'Yes, and?'

'You went back to the barmaid's flat.'

'What's wrong with that?'

'Nothing, nothing at all! Another time, I followed you to the park. I always carry a pair of binoculars in my car and . . . well, I could clearly see what that woman did to you!'

'What are you, some kind of weirdo?'

'I spoke to the woman as she left the park. I asked her about you, Grant. She was somewhat reticent at first, but I told her that I thought you might be an old neighbour and that I didn't want to make a fool of myself by approaching you. She opened up and said that she'd only just met you. It's strange how women seem to be all over you within minutes of meeting you, isn't it?'

'What are you getting at?'

'I'm intrigued.'

'Yes, so you've said – *several* times!'

'I've been trying to work it all out, piece it together and make some sense out of it. This morning, you drove to Rochester Street and . . .'

'Look, I'm busy, I haven't got the time to listen to . . .'

'How did you get that woman to strip off and do the things she did?'

'She's a good friend of mine, not that it's any business of yours! You'll get yourself arrested for . . .'

'After you'd gone, I spoke to her, pretending that I'd recognized you as you'd driven off. I said that I was an old friend of yours and that I wanted to get in touch with you. We got chatting and she said that she'd only just met you! Again, I thought it odd that she did the things she did, having only just met you!'

'What do you want?' Grant asked uneasily, wishing he could use his power on the man, will him to forget all he'd discovered. But he daren't risk eternal impotency!

'I want to know how you do it. I visited the wood today and found a small clearing and the remains of a fire.'

'So?'

'There were some lengths of rope tied to a tree. Again, I was intrigued.'

'Your bloody intrigue will be the death of you!'

'Do you know what I think?'

'No, and I don't care!'

'I think you're using some sort of occult power to rape women.'

'You're fucking crazy!' Grant returned. 'Occult power to rape women?'

'Yes, why not?'

'You're off your head! Just because I can pull the birds . . .'

'No, there's more to it than that, Grant!'

'Who are you?'

'It doesn't matter who I am. I was in the pub again last night, sitting in the corner. You took the barmaid back to your house, which was odd as your wife was at home!'

'She's not my wife!'

'Girlfriend, then. I took the liberty of spying through a crack in the curtains.'

'You've taken too many fucking liberties for my liking!'

'What I saw was amazing! Two men, two women . . .'

'I've got a brilliant sex life! What the fuck's wrong with that?'

'I want to know how you do it.'

'Well, I'm not going to tell you so you might as well sod off!'

'OK, have it your way. I'll find out without your help, and when I do . . .'

'Why don't you just fuck off?'

'I like your garden shed, it's quite a little sex den, isn't it? Anyway, I'll always be there, watching you, your every move, learning, discovering . . .'

Banging the phone down, Grant turned to Karen. *You'll forget all you've just heard!* Lifting the phone, he punched in the dial-back number. 'The caller withheld their bloody number!' he cursed, banging the phone down again.

'What?' Karen asked, rising to her feet.

'Nothing! Look, I've got to go out for a while,' he said, removing the belt and rope from the girl's naked body. 'If Emily turns up, invite her in and tell her that I won't be long. You'd better put your clothes on.'

'Where are you going?'

'Nowhere important. I'll see you later.'

Leaving the house, Grant looked up and down the street at the parked cars, wondering who was watching him, spying on him. 'God, I'm becoming paranoid!' he breathed as he drove off, gazing into the rear-view mirror, watching a car pull out and follow him. The car turning off, Grant sighed. 'Jesus, I'm going bloody mad!'

Even if he did discover the man's identity, there was nothing he could do, he mused. *I should have used my power to get his name and address! No, perhaps not!* 'Shit, with all my power, I'm bloody powerless!' he cursed through gritted teeth. He didn't know what he was going to do as he pulled up at the foot of the hill, scanning the landscape. *I wonder if they're in the wood? They're the only people who can help me! They've got to be there!*

Chapter Nine

Having waited in the clearing for several hours, Grant finally drove home. *They probably only meet at night*, he mused as he entered the house, wondering whether Emily had arrived. Finding Karen in the kitchen, the dog collar still round her neck, the chain dangling in the valley between the mammary mounds ballooning her tight T-shirt, he smiled.

'Is she here?' he asked expectantly, his rampant penis twitching.

'Emily? No, no, she waited for a long time and then she went home,' Karen replied, brushing her golden tresses from her pretty face. 'She said she might call round this evening.'

'Damn! Oh well, let's hope she turns up later. Melinda will be here soon.'

'You say you met this Melinda in the park?'

'Yes, we got chatting and . . . she has a few problems that I might be able to help her with.'

'How old is she?'

'About forty.'

'What's her problem?'

'She's in trouble at work. She . . .'

'Oh, by the way, Chris rang while you were out.'

'Chris? What did he say? Did he mention anything about last night?'

'No, why?'

'No reason. What did he say?'

'Just that he's unable to come round this evening. He didn't say what he was supposed to be coming round for.'

'It's OK, I know what he was coming round for!' Grant laughed. 'It's probably just as well, what with Melinda . . .'

'What are you up to, Grant?'

'I'm not up to anything!'

Yet another evening of debauchery lay ahead! Grant thought wickedly, picturing Melinda enduring a double fucking. The poor woman was distraught, probably praying that Grant wouldn't reveal the truth to her boss! How far would she go to save herself? he wondered. Would she destroy a lifetime of faithfulness to her husband? Would she willingly offer her body, her cunt, to Grant in exchange for him keeping her grisly secret?

As with Elizabeth, he wouldn't use his gift – only blackmail! In Melinda's mind, she'd have no choice, she either had to give her body, her wet cunt, sacrifice her marriage vows – or face prison! The wicked plan was brilliant, Grant thought, gazing at Karen as she prepared the evening meal. Melinda, Emily, Karen, Grant – what an orgy! *Shame Chris can't make it*. But who was spying on Grant? Who was forever watching his every move? he wondered. *Lay a trap*, he mused. Perhaps, by going to the hill, he'd bring the mysterious man out into the open and then . . . and then what? There was nothing he could do.

'I'm going to the sex dungeon,' Grant announced as he opened the back door. 'I've one or two things to do.'

'OK, I'll call you when dinner's ready,' Karen smiled, her sea-blue eyes catching his. 'Grant, do you love me?'

'You know I do! Why do you ask?'

'Because . . . because things are different between us now. You've changed – we've *both* changed!'

'No, we haven't!' *Stop questioning our relationship, Karen.*

'Sorry, I'm being silly – things are fine between us! I'll call you when the meal's ready.'

'OK, love.'

Switching the spotlights on, preparing the dungeon for Melinda, adjusting the pulley system, checking the leather straps, Grant glanced at his watch – six-thirty. 'Christ, she'll be here in half an hour!' He'd take her into the lounge to begin with, he decided. Keep Karen well out of the way and chat with Melinda, prepare her, tentatively suggest how she might be able to help herself. If all else failed, he'd use his power to get his hands on her naked body, his massive penis up her hot cunt!

He'd really put Melinda though it! he thought in his evilness, recalling his failure to put the fear of God up Elizabeth's fanny! He'd spend some time telling her of the gravity of the situation, the severity of her predicament and, after he'd revelled in her agony, her tears, he'd gently take her step by step to his evil goal. *Start by suggesting that, if she shows me her tits, I'll get her off the hook*, he mused. She'd protest when he asked to see her cunt, of course, but he'd remind her of Holloway Prison!

After the meal, Grant instructed Karen to go to the bedroom and wait for him to call her. 'I need to be alone with Melinda so that we can talk about her problems,' he explained, ushering Karen through the hall as the front doorbell rang. *Don't come down until I call you.*

'OK, Grant. Good luck!' she trilled, bounding up the stairs, her miniskirt revealing her rounded buttocks, the girlie bulge of her panties between her shapely thighs.

'Right, this is it!' he grinned, walking to the front door. 'Another conquest!'

Her tear-streaked face offering a slight smile, Melinda stepped into the hall, hooking her long black hair behind her ears. Wearing a loose-fitting white blouse and a knee-length blue skirt, she wasn't bad-looking, Grant reckoned, leading her into the lounge and inviting her to sit on the sofa. Reclining in the armchair, he began the charade, shaking his head despairingly.

'I've given it a lot of thought, Melinda,' he began pensively, displaying a pained expression as she made herself comfortable. 'I'm in a very difficult situation, as you'll appreciate.'

'Yes, I realize that,' she replied softly, wiping a tear from her eye. 'I was desperate. You see, my husband doesn't earn a great deal and . . . he didn't want me to go out to work, so I told him that my salary was double the amount it really was. I had to take the money to . . .'

'*Why* you took the money doesn't really matter, does it?'

'No, I suppose it doesn't,' she snivelled pathetically. 'I love my husband very much. If he knew . . . God, it would ruin him!'

'It would ruin your marriage, wouldn't it? I mean, you spending, say, two or three years in Holloway would . . .'

'Please! I can't face prison!'

'You've a very good marriage, haven't you?'

'Yes, I have!' she sobbed, taking a handkerchief from her bag and dabbing her cheeks. 'We've been happily married for twenty-two years. It's such a strong marriage, unlike most. He was my first love, and I was his.'

'I don't know what to say, Melinda. I mean, Mr Stringer has paid me well for the work I've done. How can I say that I've discovered nothing? He'd want my fee back if I told him that I'd failed him!'

'What's the point in my coming to see you if there's nothing you can do?' she asked, clutching her handkerchief in her trembling hand.

'I might be able to help you, but what would I get out of it?'

'What do you mean?'

'Well, I'd be breaking all the rules – having wasted all my time, I'd lose my fee, and I'd be risking . . .'

'How much do you want?'

'You haven't got any money, have you?'

'No, no, I haven't. All I have is fifty pounds I'd put by for my husband's birthday present.'

Shaking his head again, Grant took a deep breath, doing his best to look as if there was no way he could save her from her terrible fate. How to bring up the subject of sex? he wondered, watching her wiping tears from her cheeks. How would she react if he suggested that she show him her tits? *Just go for it, Grant!*

'There might be a way round this,' he began, leaning forward.

'How?' she asked, her eyes widening with hope.

'Well, I'm a red-blooded male and you're a very attractive . . .'

'What . . . what are you suggesting?' she asked fearfully, wringing her hands.

'I'd like to see your breasts, Melinda – your tits, your nipples.'

'What? No, please . . .'

'The choice is yours – Holloway Prison, or show me your breasts.'

'You're a disgusting man! I thought you . . .'

'I wouldn't be rude if I were you! I hold the key to your future, to your marriage.'

Shaking her head in disbelief, the distressed woman sighed. This was *really* evil! Grant thought sinfully, imagining her baring her tits, breaking her marriage vows. She'd only ever been with her husband, he was the only man who'd ever seen her naked body, squeezed her breasts, lovingly tweaked her nipples – fucked her wet cunt! What a choice she had to make! he ruminated, relishing in her plight. His stomach somersaulting, he reminded her of her dreadful future again.

'Systematically stealing over such a long period, you might even get five years,' he warned. 'It all depends on the judge.'

'Why are you doing this to me?' she sobbed hysterically. 'Why are . . .'

'I'm trying to help you, Melinda!'

'*Help* me? No, you're not! No decent man would . . .'

'In that case, I see little point in discussing this further.'

'If I . . . if I do as you ask, how will you help me?' she asked demurely.

'I'll tell Mr Stringer that it's not a member of his staff, so it must be an outsider. I'll suggest that he keep a record of all those who . . .'

'But, my husband . . . I can't do this to him! Oh, God! I don't know what to do!'

'Show me your breasts – it's as easy as that! It's not as if I'm asking you to . . .'

'But . . . but I'm a very private woman! I've never . . .'

'All you have to do is pop your tits out and show them to me!'

Tentatively unbuttoning her blouse with her trembling fingers, the sobbing woman parted the silk material, revealing her full black lace bra. 'How do I know that you'll keep your side of the bargain?' she asked, her face flushing with embarrassment.

'You might think me disgusting, but I'm not one to go back on my word!'

'You . . . you only want to look, don't you?'

'I love women's breasts, their beautiful erect nipples, their . . .'

'Yes, all right, all right!'

Lifting her bra, her heavy breasts tumbling from the cups, her long nipples succulent, erect, she averted her gaze, looking down at the floor in her shame. 'Pinch your nipples,' Grant ordered. 'I want to see you stiffen them.'

'You said that you only wanted to look!' she returned, her fearful eyes staring at him in disgust as she raised her head.

'Lift your bra higher and open your blouse further, I can't see your tits properly.'

Complying, the distraught woman looked down at her long brown teats. 'There,' she whimpered, pinching one milk bud between her finger and thumb. 'Are you satisfied now?'

'Does your husband suck your tits?'

'Stop being so crude!' she returned, cupping her mammary spheres in her bra and pulling her blouse together.

'Don't put them away, Melinda! We haven't finished yet!'

'Please, I've shown you . . .'

'Take your blouse and bra off.'

'No, I won't be subjected to this sort of . . .'

'The choice is yours – Holloway Prison, or do as I ask!'

Slipping her blouse over her shoulders, she unclipped

her bra, tossing the garment over the arm of the sofa. Tears flowing down her crimson cheeks as she sniffled pathetically, she lowered her head in her humiliation. Wild with excitement, with evil thoughts, Grant scrutinized her naked breasts, the dark discs of her areolae surrounding her delectable milk teats. She was much more fun than Elizabeth! he reflected.

How far would Melinda go? he wondered again. When he asked her to stand with her feet apart and peel her cunt lips open, would she obey? When he crudely instructed her to finger-fuck her wet cunt, would she choose to go to prison rather than commit the degrading act?

His penis stiff within his tight jeans, he imagined spunking over her tits, fucking her deep cleavage and shooting his sperm over her neck. She deserved this, he reflected. She was a thief, she deserved all she had coming to her – and all she was going to have coming over her!

'Stand up,' Grant ordered his victim, desperate to see her bulging panties. Was the voyeur lurking outside the window? he wondered, glancing at the closed curtains. Was he spying, gazing in awe at the poor woman, desperate to learn of Grant's power?

'What are you going to do?' Melinda asked, rising to her feet, her unsupported breasts swinging.

'You've got nice nipples. Does your husband spunk over them?'

'Please, don't talk like that!'

'I only wondered whether you liked him wanking and spurting his spunk over your tits!'

'Please, don't!'

'Take your skirt off.'

'No, never!' she spat, her eyes afire with hatred. 'If you think I'm going to . . .'

'Holloway isn't a very nice place!' Grant chuckled, glancing at the curtains again.

'You're an evil man! I'm not going to . . .'

'I was talking to Mr Stringer the other day. He said that, when he found out who the culprit was, he'd make sure that it was splashed all over the front page of the local paper. I can imagine how he feels. I mean, a trusted member of his staff consistently stealing from him and . . . imagine your poor husband seeing a picture of his wife on the front page of the paper! How would the caption read? Yes, just one word – THIEF!'

'No! The humiliation would destroy him!'

'There you are, then! Take your skirt off, and you'll save him from that!'

Unzipping her skirt, she allowed the garment to fall down her naked legs and settle around her ankles. Her black panties bulging with her sex, she hung her head and gently nudged her skirt aside with her foot. She knew what would be asked of her next, Grant was sure as he gazed between her thighs, picturing her swollen cunt lips, her long sex groove. *Veneris would be proud of me!* he mused. *Satan would be proud of me!*

'That's good, Melinda – very good! Now, how about showing me your cunt?'

'No, I've gone far enough! I know what you're after! I know . . .'

'I'm not after anything! I just want to see your cunt!'

'I'd rather go to prison than . . .'

'But it's not just a case of going to prison for a few years, is it? It's the shame and humiliation your husband would have to endure. Think of the neighbours – he'd have to move house!'

'You only want to look, don't you?'

'Take your knickers off and show me your beautiful cunt.'

'Please, don't keep using that awful word!'

'OK, show me your beautiful pussy slit, your girlie crack, your fanny, your . . .'

'Stop! Please, stop it!'

Melinda was much more fun than Elizabeth! Grant reflected as she tugged her panties down to the top of her crack, revealing her thick pubic bush. He wouldn't let Melinda leave the house sexually satisfied, happy! he thought in his wickedness. This was humiliation at its best, degradation in the extreme! And he'd not used his gift to influence her at all! Her future in the balance as she tugged her panties down a little further, Grant scrutinized her fleshy vaginal groove, her distended pink inner lips.

'You've a nice body!' he praised the humiliated woman. 'Tell me, does your husband lick your cunt out?'

'I'm not going to answer any of your obscene questions!' she spat, her head hung low, her long black hair veiling her flushed face.

'I'll bet he tongue-fucks your wet cunt!' Grant laughed. 'Does he spunk in your mouth?'

'I'm going now! I'll tell my husband everything! I'd rather be honest with him than do this behind his back!'

'Yes, they say that honesty pays. But you wouldn't know about that, would you? I mean, you being a thief, you . . .'

'Yes, I *am* a thief! And I'll tell Mr Stringer and my husband!'

'What would your husband say if he knew that you'd come here and stripped off?'

'He wouldn't believe it, so you needn't try that one!' she returned, pulling her panties up and concealing her womanhood.

'Oh, Melinda – I almost forgot!' Grant laughed, holding his hand to his head. 'How silly of me not to have mentioned it earlier! There's a hidden video camera in this room. Your disrobing is on tape. I'll edit it, of course, so that when your husband sees it, he'll get the right idea! There again, if you do as I ask, I'll give you the tape and you can destroy it.'

'I don't believe you!'

'You'd better believe it! Now, take your knickers off and show me your . . . your cunt!'

Kicking her shoes off, pulling her panties down to her ankles, she stepped out of the flimsy garment and stood upright, displaying her naked body to Grant's evil gaze. This was nothing! he thought, scrutinizing her long vaginal slit. The degradation had barely begun! What next? he wondered. Have her bend over as Elizabeth had done and show him her pussy lips ballooning between her thighs? Or have Karen come in and . . . No, it wasn't time to have Karen lick the woman's cunt out – he would save that mortifying act for later!

'Pull your cunt lips apart and show me your pussy hole,' he ordered the trembling woman. 'Come on, Melinda, I want to see inside your wet cunt!'

'No! This has gone far enough! I don't care if you have got me on videotape, I'll tell my husband everything. He'll believe me!'

'Will he? It's quite a risk to take, isn't it?'

'He knows me well, he'll . . .'

'How can you say that he knows you well? You're a persistent thief, for Christ's sake! I don't think he knows you at all!'

'I'll . . . I'll explain . . .'

'It's extremely risky, Melinda! You'd not only be risking him believing that you came here behind his back because you're a two-timing tart, but there's also the prison sentence! You don't have any choice, do you?'

The evil lurking within Grant's mind was frightening! He could discover any woman's secrets and have her commit depraved sexual acts, have her do anything he asked of her! Watching the woman's slender fingers move tentatively towards her sex groove, Grant held his breath, waiting in anticipation for her to reveal her most intimate inner cunt flesh to his staring eyes. To his great annoyance, her hands fell to her sides: she'd obviously had a change of mind.

'Well, if that's the way you want it,' he sighed despairingly, shaking his head. 'It's a shame to have to . . .'

'Please, I've done everything you've asked so far!' she wailed. 'I'm standing here naked! Isn't that enough?'

'No, I'm afraid it's nowhere near enough! Melinda, why not look at it this way? No one will ever know what took place in this room, it'll be our secret. Besides, I've seen naked women before, you don't have anything that I've not seen before, so . . .'

'That's not the point! Not even my husband has seen me naked, let alone . . .'

'I'm doing you a great favour, Melinda!'

'How can you possibly say that?'

'I'm stopping you from thieving, for a start! You'll never steal money again, will you?'

'No, never!'

'There you are, then! If you think about it, I'm doing you many favours! I'm stopping you from stealing, rescuing you from a prison sentence, saving your marriage, saving your husband from the shame and humiliation of . . .'

'But you don't know how this makes me feel! The embarrassment, the . . . standing here, naked, I feel . . .'

'You feel humiliated?'

'Yes, very!'

'Utterly degraded?'

'Yes!'

'Good, because that's what I like! Call me evil, but I love revelling in your humiliation! That's what this is all about!'

'You *are* evil! You're the most vile, evil . . .'

'Yes, yes, I know! Now, are you going to pull your cunt lips apart and show me your clitoris, your fanny hole – or would you rather I went to see Mr Stringer and your husband?'

Tentatively parting her fleshy vaginal lips, Melinda closed her eyes, trying to blank out the stark reality of her lewd act. It hadn't been easy getting her this far, Grant reflected as he gazed at her clitoris, her open pussy hole. But no matter how difficult, how long it took, he had far more in store for her than parting her cunny lips! How to put it? he wondered. Finger your cunt? Thrust two fingers into your wet cunt hole? Grinning, he gazed at Melinda's sex crack as she closed her full pussy lips, pressing the swollen vaginal cushions together to veil her intimacy.

'I want to watch you finger your cunt,' Grant smiled in his decadence. 'I want to see your finger thrusting . . .'

'No! I'm not going to do anything else!' she cried, grabbing her panties from the floor. 'I have never been so . . .'

'Melinda, may I remind you that . . .'

'You can remind me of anything you like, but I'm not going to do anything else! You're a pervert, you're sick!'

'In that case, I'll see Mr Stringer first thing in the morning. I'll see your husband, too – give him a copy of the videotape and . . .'

'I don't care what you do! I have never met such a vile man as you! You're an animal! You're callous!'

'I've done my homework very well, Melinda,' Grant said nonchalantly, searching her subconscious for more clandestine information, more dreadful secrets.

'I don't care!' she returned, pulling her panties up her legs and cloaking her pussy slit. 'I'm going home!'

Her tormented mind was so racked with anguish, fear and guilt that Grant found it difficult to sift through her thoughts and find anything of value to him. Picking up a jumble of words, he asked her what other secrets she had, hoping they'd surface from her muddled mind as she thought about them – if there were any! Without replying, Melinda cupped her heavy breasts in her bra and grabbed her blouse.

Grant didn't want to use his gift to get between the woman's legs – there'd be no humiliation, no degradation if he willed her to slip her fingers into her vaginal sheath and finger herself to orgasm. There'd be no fun if he was forced to use his power! Asking her again whether she had any other dreadful secrets, he concentrated his thoughts, listening to her subconscious.

Wedding ring. Shouldn't have sold my wedding ring and said I'd lost it. Needed the money..

'As I was saying, Melinda, I've done my homework very well,' Grant began as she buttoned her blouse and grabbed her skirt. 'You sold your wedding ring, didn't you?'

'I don't know what you're talking about!' she returned. Her eyes wide with shock, she was obviously stunned by the revelation!

'You lied to your husband, told him that you'd lost it. I'd better not only tell him that you're a thief and that you came here to have sex with me, but that you sold your precious wedding ring because you were desperate for money!'

'You can't prove anything! Besides, I didn't sell it!'

'You sold it to the jeweller in the High Street. They'd have a record, of course.'

Frozen to the spot, Melinda stared into Grant's eyes, her mouth hanging open, her hands trembling. Grinning at his victim, he relaxed in the armchair and raised his eyebrows. The poor woman was beside herself with fear, he observed, as she shook her head and dropped her skirt on the floor.

'You have another dark secret, don't you, Melinda?' he asked, listening to her thoughts as they filtered into his mind. 'A secret so terrible that it would completely destroy your husband if he found out about it.' *And I'd thought she was as faithful as they came!* he reflected, wondering how she'd been able to hide her shocking secret from him.

'I don't have any other secrets!' she returned.

'Your son, he's not your husband's, is he?'

'What? I . . . I . . .'

'That fling you had all those years ago when your husband was working away . . .'

'No, you're wrong! Of course he's my husband's son!'

'Ron, that was your lover's name. So, we now have the stealing, the wedding ring, you coming here to have sex with me – and now this!'

'How could you possibly know?' she asked. 'How ever did you find out?'

'It doesn't matter how I found out, Melinda – the point is, I know. Now, if you'd be so good as to remove your clothes again.'

At last, Grant had found a direction, discovered the best way to use his gift. Playing games with Jackie, Chris, Karen,

Julie, Diana, Mandy . . . It had been fun, but blackmail was better than games – it was evil! This was true domination over women, complete control – slavery at its best! Now, in her whimpering patheticness, Melinda was his for the taking! It hadn't been easy, but Grant, the male, had won! Now he'd found his direction, he wouldn't bother with Diana, Mandy and the others. He'd concentrate on using blackmail to defile, degrade, and humiliate the weaker sex – the inferior sex! And prove his unshakable allegiance to Veneris, the Goddess of Carnality!

Watching Melinda strip and stand naked before him, he grinned. 'Right! Now we'll get down to the really dirty stuff! Come with me!' he ordered, rising to his feet and opening the lounge door.

'Where are we going?' she asked, following Grant through the hall, desperately trying to conceal her crudely bared womanhood with her trembling hands.

'You'll see. Come on, this way!' Grant chuckled, wondering what Karen was doing as he opened the back door.

As Melinda entered the sex dungeon and stared in horror at the equipment, she gasped, her eyes bulging with terror. Locking the door, his stomach somersaulting with excitement, Grant ordered the woman to lie on the table with her buttocks over the cutout, her legs spread wide – her cunt open.

'Please, you can't . . .' she sobbed.

'Melinda, I can do anything I like!' Grant laughed, adjusting the spotlights.

'This is evil! You're treating me no better than an animal! I'm a woman!'

'Yes, and you have a cunt! Now, get on the table or I'll have to . . .'

'All right, all right! But I'll tell you this – the day will come when . . .'

'Just get onto the table and cut out your futile threats!'

Shaking her head, resigned to her fate, she complied, resting her head on the cushion as Grant placed her feet in the leather slings and pulled on the chain, lifting and parting her trembling legs. The voyeur couldn't see into the sex dungeon, Grant was sure as he fixed the chain to the hook on the wall and moved to the end of the table, watching the woman's cunt milk ooze from her pussy hole.

Lay a trap, he mused again, wondering what to do when he discovered the man's identity. Go to the wood and lie in wait? Ambush the mysterious man as he followed Grant? Or invite him to join in with the debauchery? *Blackmail!* Grant thought, suddenly realizing that, if he could discover something sordid about the man's past, he could put a stop to his meddling.

'Are you comfortable?' Grant asked the tethered woman, gazing at her open cuntal crack.

'No, of course I'm not!' she spat.

'Good! Tell me, Melinda, what's it feel like to have your cunt gaping open, displayed before a total stranger?'

'I'm not answering any of your . . .'

'I'll bet you feel embarrassed!' he chuckled. 'Look at your fleshy inner bits! I'll bet you're really humiliated!'

Gazing up at the pullies as Grant strapped her wrists to the corners of the table, her naked body rudely bared, Melinda remained silent in her rising fear. She *was* humiliated! Her very femininity, always concealed, private, sacrosanct, was now crudely displayed beneath the spotlights! Her breasts, her nipples, always screened from roving eyes, were now exhibited before her evil blackmailer.

There was nothing she could do apart from pray that,

once her ordeal was over, Grant would release her, give her freedom – and keep his side of the bargain by not revealing her terrible secrets. But would he demand more from her? she wondered as he tweaked her long nipples. Would he demand that she come back and endure perverted sex again and again? He had a permanent hold over her, she knew.

As she'd taken money from the office safe and falsified the accounts, never had she dreamed that her thieving would lead to this! She'd often thought of the consequences as she slipped the notes into her bag – the sack, the court case . . . But sexual degradation, humiliation? Again, she thought about Grant demanding that she come back time and time again to satisfy his lust for perverted sex. The stealing, the wedding ring, her son . . . Grant had so much on her! Why should he keep his side of the bargain? Evil as she knew he was, he wouldn't free her and allow her to live life in peace.

Her eyes squeezed shut as Grant sat on the chair, gazing at her crudely opened vaginal lips, her yawning sex groove, her body jolted as he pressed the buzzing tip of the vibrator against her unveiled clitoris. Trembling, her stomach rising and falling as the powerful sensations permeated her pelvis, she held her breath, desperately trying to deny herself the incredible pleasure emanating from her erect pleasure nodule.

Grabbing a candle from the shelf, Grant slipped the waxen shaft deep into the woman's vaginal canal, causing her to cry out as the pleasure overwhelmed her, quickly taking her to a shuddering climax. Her wails of ecstasy filling the sex dungeon, Grant watched her clitoris pulsate, her cunt milk flowing in torrents, bathing his fingers as he thrust the candle in and out of her progressively tightening pussy hole.

Even the prudish Melinda loves sex! he mused, gazing at her reddening cunt flesh, her swollen, pulsating clitoris as her orgasm peaked. She'd said that her husband had never seen her naked, so how would she feel after her crude sexual awakening, her enforced debauchery? How would she feel the next time he drove his hard cock deep into her velveteen cunt sheath and fucked her?

Her sex life was well below average, Grant was sure of that! How often did her husband fuck her? he wondered, watching her vaginal lips engorge, swell as her orgasm rode on. Did he lick her cunt, suck her clitoris to orgasm? Had she ever had a tongue snake its way into her unaccommodating vaginal canal? Had she experienced the beautiful sensations of sex obtainable from a vibrator? *You don't miss what you haven't had*, Grant mused, gripping the wet candle and continuing the vaginal thrusting. She'd miss the vibrator now it had taken her to an incredible climax!

After her vibrator-induced orgasm, would she buy herself a body massager and secretly entice orgasms from her clitoris? Would she hide the device, only bringing it out and taking herself to her illicit climaxes after her husband had gone to work? Perhaps she'd come back to Grant and beg him for more crude sex!

'Oh, oh!' she whimpered as her climax peaked again, sustained by the incredible vibrations reverberating within her pulsating clitoris, permeating her inner cuntal flesh, her contracting womb. 'Oh, no more!'

'Don't you like it?' Grant asked, watching her rubicund vaginal lips swell to an incredible size, her clitoris throb, sending shockwaves of pleasure through her quivering body.

'Yes, yes!' she managed to reply, her head tossing from

side to side, her mouth open, gasping in her enforced sexual stimulation.

'I'll fuck you in a minute!' Grant chuckled, focusing on her erect nipples.

'No, no! No, you mustn't . . . ah, ah!'

'I'll fuck you properly, hard, the way a woman should be fucked!'

'No, no you . . . ah! Ah, I've never known such . . .'

'Keep coming, Melinda! Keep coming!' Grant urged, thrusting the candle faster, harder, into her spasming cunt.

The trembling woman's climax finally slipping away, leaving her face flushed, she lay trembling, breathing heavily in the aftermath of her pioneering orgasm. Her cunt milk flowing, matting her thick pubic bush, Grant scrutinized her elongated nipples, wondering whether to fix the clothes pegs to her mammary teats and painfully stretch them with the cord.

Shall I come in her cunt or her mouth? he wondered, turning as someone knocked on the door. 'Who is it?' he called, wondering whether it was the mysterious voyeur.

'It's me, Karen!'

'Who's Karen?' Melinda asked, lifting her head off the cushion and looking at the door.

Placing the vibrator on the shelf and unlocking the door, Grant smiled as the girl entered the sex dungeon, her wide eyes gazing at Melinda's naked body, the candle emerging from her inflamed vaginal crack. *Go and get a razor and shaving foam!* he urged the astonished girl. *You're going to shave Melinda's cunt!*

'I'll . . . I'll go and get . . .' she stammered, leaving the dungeon, the chain dangling between the swell of her breasts as she returned to the house.

'Who's that?' Melinda asked again, her eyes reflecting her fear. 'What's she going to get?'

'She's my girlfriend, my sex slave. She's bisexual, she likes licking women's cunts. She enjoys a female tongue up her cunt. She also likes . . .'

'No! How dare you . . .'

'As I was saying, she also likes her women shaved.'

'No! My husband will . . .'

'You said yourself that he's never seen you naked, so what's the problem?'

'But he'd feel me there and realize that . . .'

'Like it or not, she's going to shave your cunt hairs off!' Grant laughed, slipping the candle from the woman's vaginal sheath as Karen returned with the depilating equipment. 'Right, Karen, sit on the chair and shave Melinda's cunt! I want it looking like a schoolgirl's!'

Her eyes squeezed shut as Karen sat down and squirted shaving foam over her black bush, Melinda's fear rose, her body shaking as she wondered how to explain her denuded vulval flesh to her husband. Massaging the foam into the woman's thick pussy fleece as Grant looked on, Karen grabbed the razor and dragged it over Melinda's mound, leaving a streak of milk-white smooth flesh in its wake.

'Make sure you remove every single hair,' Grant ordered the girl. 'I want her completely free of pubes before I fuck her cunt!'

'No, please don't . . .' Melinda cried, lifting her head and focusing her tearful eyes on Grant. 'Please, isn't this enough?'

'Nothing's ever enough when it comes to perverted sex!' he laughed. 'I'm going to spunk up your cunt after Karen's shaved you!'

'My husband . . . oh, God, what will he say?'

'He'll ask why you've shaved! And you'll have to tell him that you did because you're a horny tart, because you like masturbating your shaved cunt with a vibrator!'

'You're a crude, despicable man!'

'Yes, I do believe I am! Hurry up, Karen, I need a good fuck!' he laughed, turning his head and focusing on Melinda's partially denuded vulval cushions.

Working silently, Karen repeatedly dragged the razor over the woman's mound, her swollen vaginal lips, unveiling her femininity, exposing her once-sacrosanct intimacy to Grant's appreciative gaze. Finally removing the last few pubic curls, Karen wiped Melinda's vaginal flesh with a flannel, wiping off the remnants of foam as she turned to Grant for his appraisal.

'Excellent!' Grant beamed, eyeing Melinda's baby-soft sex hillocks, her naked vaginal groove, her protruding inner lips. 'What do you think?' he asked the tethered woman as she gazed in horror at her schoolgirl-look-alike pussy.

'Oh, my God!' she shrieked. 'My God!'

'Good, isn't it?' Grant chuckled, running his fingertips over her sex cushions.

'It's awful! Oh, God! My husband will . . .'

'Sod your bloody husband! Right, Karen, I'm going to fuck Melinda. While I'm doing that, I want you to kneel either side of her head and rub your cunt over her mouth!'

'No!' Melinda protested as Karen obediently slipped her panties off and took her position, her shaved cuntal lips gaping above the woman's grimacing face. 'No, please!'

'Lick her cunt out!' Grant ordered. 'Lick her to orgasm, or you'll have the whip! And I'll tell Mr Stringer and your husband about you!'

Slipping his solid penis out, grinning as he stood between

Melinda's twitching thighs, Grant aligned his purple knob with her open hole. 'No, you can't! You mustn't!' she protested wildly through a mouthful of Karen's wet vulval flesh. 'No! Please, my husband . . . please!' she begged as his inflated glans parted her hairless pussy lips and drove deep into her vaginal tunnel. 'No, this is adultery! I can't commit . . .' she stammered, her face wet with Karen's pussy juice.

'I don't know why you keep going on about your bloody husband! You've committed adultery before, so what's the problem?' Grant asked, gazing at her ample inner petals clinging to his wet shaft as he withdrew his penis before thrusting his knob deep into her cunt again.

'No, that was . . . ah, ah! You're too big!' she gasped, his knob pummelling her soft cervix. 'I don't want this! Please!'

'Shut up!' Grant bellowed. 'You're going to have my spunk up your cunt whether you like it or not, so shut up and lick Karen's clitty to orgasm!'

Grant's attitude towards females was becoming sacrilegious in the extreme, his frightening hunger to commit vile sexual acts against the weaker sex shocking. Where would it all end? Would it ever end? As he drove his cock-head deep into the woman's hot cunt again, he knew that he'd gone far beyond the point of no return, slipped over the edge of the bottomless pit of corruption – and fallen into the mire of his own perversion.

Her feet high in the air, her legs parted, her cunt tight around Grant's shafting penis, Karen's hot girl-folds pressed against her gasping mouth, Melinda shuddered as her clitoris swelled, sending beautiful sensations through her contracting womb. Never had her wet vaginal walls been stretched to the limit before, never had she experienced such a huge penis thrusting into the sexual centre of her trembling body – never had she licked another woman's wet girl-flesh before!

Her head tossing wildly between Karen's thighs, she whimpered as she felt Grant's organ swell within her contracting vagina as her own climax erupted, exploding within her pulsating clitoris. Karen's swollen vaginal lips pressing harder against her gasping mouth, the girl's lubricious cunt milk decanting, Melinda couldn't help but swallow the liquid offering.

'Oh, God!' she cried, her face contorting as her climax peaked and Grant's sperm gushed, filling her hot pussy sheath. 'God, no! Ah, ah, no!'

'Push your cunt into her mouth to shut her up!' Grant ordered Karen, making his hardest thrust yet, massaging his throbbing knob against the fiery walls of her sex duct. 'I'm spunking up your cunt! Can you feel my spunk?'

'Yes, yes! Feel your ... your ... oh, God! I've never known ...'

Filling her sex cavern with his gushing sperm, draining his heavy balls, Grant finally slowed his rhythm, resting his glans against Melinda's hot cervix as he watched her licking between Karen's fleshy girl-lips. Was she enjoying her enforced fanny licking? he wondered as Karen shuddered and began her orgasmic gasping, massaging her pulsating clitoris against the woman's cunny-wet tongue. Was Melinda revelling in her cunt licking? Probably not – hopefully not!

Her cunt milk flowing in torrents, bathing Melinda's flushed face, Karen rocked her hips, whimpering as her orgasm peaked, taking her to her sexual heaven. This was real degradation! Grant thought, his penis twitching within Melinda's tight vagina, his insatiable knob aching for another orgasm. Gazing at Melinda's hairless pussy lips, her crimson inner petals furled around the root of his organ, Grant smiled.

'You have a nice cunt, Melinda! It's hot, wet, tight . . .'

'Please, let me go now!' she whimpered as he slipped his spunk-wet shaft out of her fiery hole and ran his knob up and down her gaping sex valley.

'Did you enjoy licking Karen's cunt?' he asked as Karen slid her inflamed crack off Melinda's wet mouth and hauled her exhausted body off the table.

'No, yes . . . I feel so . . . so degraded!'

'Why? All I've done is fuck you!'

'How will I ever face my husband again?' she sobbed, licking the girl-cream from her wet lips. 'I don't know how I'll ever be able to . . . no! Please, what are you doing?' she screamed hysterically as Grant pressed his bulbous knob between her splayed buttocks. 'God! Please, not there!'

His mouth twisting into an evil grin, Grant pressed his knob against the protesting woman's tight anal iris, gasping as his glans slipped past her defeated muscles and sank into the dank heat of her virginal rectum. Tugging on her bonds, her head thrashing from side to side as Grant's knob glided deep into her anal duct, Melinda screamed her objections, her pleas.

'Take it out! I'll do anything! Please . . .'

'God, you've a tight arsehole!' Grant sniggered, revelling in the woman's humiliation as her face flushed. 'Is this the first time you've had your arsehole fucked?'

'You're vile, obscene, disgusting! I have never . . .'

'Well, you have now! Now you can tell your friends, your husband, that you've had a bloody great cock fuck your arse! And that you've licked another woman's cunt to orgasm!'

'When I get out of here, I'm going to . . .'

'Buy yourself a vibrator and masturbate every day?'

'No! I'm going to . . .'

'Let's stop the chatter and get on with the bum-fucking!' Grant laughed. 'I'm going to spunk up your tight arsehole!'

Watching the degrading act, Karen pulled her panties up her shapely legs, her mind awash with confused thoughts as Grant ordered her to lick Melinda's clitoris. Parting the quivering woman's hairless cunny lips, Karen leaned over and tongued her swollen pleasure bud, causing her to arch her back and cry out as her body became alive with the sensations of obscene sex. Her clitoral licking taking the woman to her climax as Grant groaned and loosed his sperm, Karen slipped two fingers into Melinda's drenched cunt, thrusting them in and out of her sperm-drenched hole, sustaining her incredible climax.

'Can you feel my spunk, Melinda?' Grant breathed as he shafted her anal canal with a vengeance.

'Ah, no, yes! Oh, God! Please let me go now!' she cried, her tethered body shaking violently as her orgasm heightened. 'Please, please!'

'Christ, your arse is fucking beautiful!'

'Stop! Please stop now!'

'Never!' Grant laughed, driving his orgasming knob deep into the fiery heat of her inflamed bowels again, filling her quivering body with his gushing sperm.

Her leashed body jolting with the anal pummelling, her mouth gasping, her eyes rolling, Melinda prayed that her ordeal was finally over as Grant slipped his massive organ from her bottom-hole, leaving her rectal sheath sperm-drenched, inflamed. She couldn't take any more –

her body exhausted, her mind racked, demoralized – she couldn't take any more humiliation, any more abuse.

Karen finally stood upright, leaving the woman's cuntal flesh wet and engorged in the aftermath of her tongue-induced orgasm, her clitoris transmitting post-orgasmic ripples of pleasure deep into her quivering pelvis, her spasming womb. Licking her full red lips, she turned to Grant, confusion mirrored in her sea-blue eyes as she tugged on the dog collar.

'I think we should let her go,' Karen murmured.

'Let her go?'

'Yes, she's had enough, Grant.'

'Well, I don't know about that!' Grant sniggered, catching the woman's eyes as she turned her head to face him. 'How about me spunking in your mouth, Melinda, spurting my sperm down your throat?'

'Please, I want to go now!' Melinda sobbed.

'OK,' Grant smiled, concealing his glistening penis within his jeans and releasing her wrists. 'I suppose Karen's right, you've had enough – for one day!'

'No, please! Don't make me come back! I've done all you've asked, I've done more than . . .'

'You've not been whipped, you've not had my knob spunking in your mouth, you've not fingered Karen's cunt, you've not . . .'

'Stop it, please! I can't stand your crudity!'

Releasing the sobbing woman, his unquenchable thirst for vulgar sex raging, Grant took her arm, steadying her trembling body as she climbed off the table and stood on her sagging legs. Gazing down at her hairless pussy flesh, her naked womanhood, tears rolling down her cheeks, she opened the door and fled the sex dungeon.

'I'd better go and see her out,' Grant said, eyeing Karen's nipples pressing through her blouse.

'You shouldn't have treated her like that!' Karen admonished, following Grant to the house. 'She might go to the police and . . .'

'No, there's no way she'd do that!' he laughed, walking through the hall and entering the lounge to find Melinda dressing her violated body. 'We'll be seeing you tomorrow evening for another sex session, I hope?' he quipped, watching her tug her knickers up and veil her schoolgirl, look-alike cunt lips.

'Never! You'll never see me again!' she spat, donning her skirt and leaving the room.

'I hope you manage to explain your shaved cunt to your husband!' Grant laughed as the front door banged shut.

Relaxing on the sofa, Grant made his plans for the following day as Karen left the room and climbed the stairs to bed. He'd not had the pleasure of Emily's young vaginal sheath yet, he mused – or her tight bottom-hole! Elizabeth could do with another fucking, too! He'd sit in the park again, relax on the bench and discover the secrets of the women who passed by – and blackmail them! Life was good! he thought, leaping to his feet as the phone rang.

'Had a nice evening?' the man asked as Grant pressed the receiver to his ear.

'Oh, it's you again!' Grant bellowed. 'What is it with you? Why keep phoning?'

'I want to know how you manage to influence all these women. I saw a woman leave your house just now. She appeared to be very distressed!'

'Yes, she would – I've just fucked her arsehole! Look, if you want to know how I do it, then why not come round and we'll talk about it?'

'Oh, no, no! I'm not going to . . .'
'In that case, there's nothing I can do!'
'Tell me over the phone, Grant.'
'No, you either come round here, or forget it! You can join me, the women, and have some fun.'
'No, I'm not going to meet you, Grant. If you won't tell me over the phone, I'll find out without your help. By the way, your lounge curtains were drawn properly this evening, I couldn't see a thing!'
'Good!'
'I went to the wood this evening and . . .'
'You're playing with fire, my friend! If you . . .'
'There was no one in the clearing, but the fire was burning.'
'I know nothing about the wood! All I do is go for walks!'
'There's something about that wood, Grant, a connection with . . .'
'All right, I'll tell you how I do it – it's hypnosis.'
'No, it's not! That woman you had tied down in your shed wasn't hypnotized! I could clearly see that . . .'
'There's no way you can see into . . .'
'Karen shaved the woman's fanny, I saw the whole thing!'

Replacing the receiver, his hands trembling, his face pale, Grant flopped onto the sofa. *How the hell could he see?* he pondered. He had to visit the sect and ask for their help to rid him of the voyeur. If he could use his power once on the man, will him to forget all he'd discovered, he'd be free to carry on with his increasingly perverted life. *How the hell could he see into the dungeon?*

Chapter Ten

Standing outside the sex dungeon, the early morning sun on his back, Grant frowned. There was no way anyone could see in! he concluded, trying to look through the painted windows. The cedar tongue-and-groove boarding firmly butted, there were no cracks to spy through, and the far end of the wooden building was jammed up against the fence, leaving no space for anyone to lurk there.

'I just don't understand it!' he breathed despairingly, running his hand over the boarding. Since he'd mentioned Karen shaving Melinda's pussy, the man had obviously seen into the dungeon, but how? Entering the building and examining the inside walls, he shook his head. 'There's no way he could have seen!' he sighed, his annoyance rising.

Deciding to go to the park in the hope that the mysterious man would follow him, Grant stepped out of the dungeon and locked the door. *Force him out into the open*, he mused, entering the kitchen and hanging the key on a hook. Hearing Karen moving about in the bathroom as he wandered through the hall, he smiled, imagining two solid penises driving into her inflamed cunt. *That should be possible!* he thought, deciding to invite Chris round for the double pussy fucking.

Leaving the house and walking down the street, keeping his eyes peeled, Grant finally reached the park. There didn't appear to be anyone following him, he observed, glancing over his shoulder as he wandered across the grass towards a clump of trees. But he was there, Grant knew. The mysterious voyeur was out there, lurking, spying. Entering the trees, Grant hid behind a bush, scanning the park through a gap in the leaves, praying for the man to show himself.

After half an hour, Grant emerged from the trees and sat on the bench, recalling the man saying that he'd watched Grant through binoculars from his car. But there were only two cars parked in the road, and both were empty. *This is ridiculous!* he thought, pondering on the time he was wasting as he jumped up and walked briskly across the park.

His penis twitching, yearning for a hot, tight vagina, a pretty mouth, he walked along the street wondering where to find his next victim. But now, his craving for debauched sex soaring, even blackmail wasn't enough! There had to be more! he pondered, entering a busy coffee shop. There had to be more evil, more perverted sexual acts to experience! *Give me some ideas, Satan!*

Sitting at a corner table, Grant ordered a cup of coffee, eyeing the pretty waitress as she smiled sweetly and wandered back to the counter. There was nothing out of the ordinary in her life, he discovered by searching her subconscious thoughts. Apart from masturbating a couple of times a week, she was boringly normal!

I'd be finished if this was discovered! Gazing around the coffee shop, wondering whose thoughts he'd picked up, Grant listened intently as the waitress placed his cup of coffee on the table. *Embezzlement! I'd be struck off!* Scanning his fellow customers, he couldn't determine who the culprit was until a woman in her mid-thirties wearing a smart skirt and jacket stood up and moved towards the door. *Better get back to the office.*

Tossing a pound coin on the table and leaving his coffee, Grant tailed the woman to a firm of solicitors' offices in the high street. *Embezzlement?* he pondered. *This is a good one!* 'Excuse me,' he smiled, catching up with her and following her through the swing doors as she entered the building. 'Are you Mrs Jenkins?'

'Yes, how can I help you?'

'Embezzlement, Mrs Jenkins. Is there somewhere we can talk?'

Her blonde bob framing her guilt-ridden face, she stared in horror at Grant, her blue eyes widening as shock registered. 'This way,' she whispered, glancing nervously around the foyer as she opened a door. Following her into an office, Grant's stomach somersaulted at the prospect of scrutinizing her naked body, her breasts, her pink cuntal crack – humiliating her, degrading her.

'Embezzlement, Mr . . .' she began, closing the door after Grant.

'Er . . . Brown – Roy Brown.'

'Embezzlement, Mr Brown, is . . .'

'Yes, I know what it is!' Grant smiled, sitting on the edge of the desk. 'And, of course, *you* know only too well what it is!'

'What is it you want, Mr Brown? I'm very busy and I haven't got the time to . . .'

'The company you're dealing with, Blackthorns . . . I wonder how they'd react if they discovered that nigh on twenty thousand pounds . . .'

'I don't know who you are, where you're from, or what you know – and I'm not interested. What is it you want from me, money?'

'Oh, I don't want money, Mrs Jenkins!'
'Then what *do* you want?'
'Your body!'

Watching the woman sit at the desk, seemingly unperturbed by his crude request as she shuffled some papers around, Grant wondered whether she'd ever allowed a man to drive his cock into her tight bottom-hole and fuck her there. That would be the first thing he'd force her to endure! he decided, imagining her in his sex dungeon, her naked body strapped to the table, her legs high in the air, open.

Respectfully asking him to remove himself from the desk and take a seat, she clasped her hands together, her full red lips furling into a smile. She was obviously trying to appear composed, Grant mused as he sat opposite her. *Composed or not, I'll have her stripped off and I'll screw her tight arse!* he thought wickedly.

She was married to someone fairly big in the City, he gleaned from her thoughts. If her husband were to discover what she'd done . . . She was a good catch! he mused, his eyes catching hers. A stuck-up, elegant female solicitor, embezzling money from a big company – she would not only be struck off, but imprisoned!

'Now, Mr Brown, if that's your real name – which I very much doubt it is! You say you want my body? What, exactly, do you mean by that?'

'I want you to strip off and show me your tits, your cunt!' Grant replied unashamedly. 'I'd like to see you part your cunt lips and show me your . . .'

'There's no need to be crude! In return for my disrobing, you'll keep quiet, is that the idea?'

'Yes, that's the idea. Is there a lock on the door?'

'I do not intend to remove my clothes *here*, Mr Brown!' she replied petulantly. 'I'm free this afternoon so, if you'd care to give me your address, I'll be only too happy to comply with your request, peculiar though it is.'

'Oh!' Grant gasped surprisedly. 'Er . . . what time?'

'One o'clock, Mr Brown. Write your address down and I'll be there at one,' she said calmly, passing him a pen and a piece of paper.

What was her game? Grant wondered, scribbling his address. Was she sex-starved? Perhaps the idea of stripping before a complete stranger had turned her on? Perhaps his crude words had excited her? Taking the paper and carefully folding it, she slipped it into her jacket pocket and smiled amicably.

'Until one o'clock,' she said, rising to her feet and moving towards the door. 'The address, is it where you live? It's not a friend's house, I hope?'

'No, it's where I live,' Grant replied, standing before her.

'Good.'

'Why do you ask?'

'No reason, Mr Brown,' she smiled, opening the door.

Suddenly realizing that she might send the heavies round, he searched her subconscious and came up trumps. *They'll sort the bastard out when I tell them that he's onto us!*

You'll tell no one about this! You'll go to my house alone, and you'll not remember why you're going to see me!

Go alone. Tell no one.

'Goodbye, Mrs Jenkins!' Grant smiled triumphantly, leaving the office.

'Good day, Mr Brown.'

Walking out into the street, his mind brimming with evil ideas, he hurried home. This was going to be the best yet! he knew. A prudish solicitor, strapped to the table, her buttocks whipped, her cunt shaved, her arse fucked

... I wonder how Melinda's getting on? he mused as he approached his house.

The phone ringing as Grant opened the front door, he dashed into the lounge and grabbed the receiver, wondering where Karen had got to. 'You've pulled another one!' the man chuckled excitedly in Grant's ear.

'Yes, so what?'

'A solicitor, of all people! How do you do it, Grant?'

'Come round and I'll tell you.'

'No, no. I'll come round and watch you screw her. Will it be in your sex den or in the lounge?'

'Neither, as it happens.'

'What time are you seeing her?'

'You'll have to find out, I'm not telling you!'

'Wherever it is, whenever it is, I'll be there, watching you! Enjoy your walk in the park this morning, did you?'

'Yes, thank you. Now, if you don't mind, I'm busy!' Grant bellowed, banging the receiver down and agitatedly running his fingers through his thick black hair.

'Who the hell is he?' he breathed, pacing the lounge floor. 'Who the fucking hell is he?' This was serious! he thought, rubbing his chin, wondering how to discover the man's identity. Trying to piece the facts together, Grant sat in the armchair. *He knows my name, Karen's name, my phone number, my address, what I get up to* . . . Unless he discovered who this pest was, the situation was going to drive Grant round the bend!

'I hope you don't mind me coming round and disturbing your work like this,' Karen said softly, gazing at Chris.

'No, not at all!' he smiled, filling the kettle. 'You're welcome any time, Karen!' he chuckled, recalling the orgy. 'Why are you wearing a polo-neck jumper on a day like this?'

'To hide this,' she confessed, revealing the dog collar.

'Oh, you're still wearing it!'

'Still? Have you seen this on me before?' Karen asked surprisedly.

'Er, no, no. I . . .' Chris began, wondering why she'd not thought he'd seen it during the double fucking session.

'I've been wearing it for some time now, but there's no way you could have seen it, Chris!'

'No, no, I've never seen it before,' he replied, perplexed.

'Grant made me wear it, and I can't get it off. The funny thing is, I don't want to take it off! So much has been happening lately, Chris!'

'What's on your mind? Tell me about it.'

'Oh, I don't know. Grant's changed so much! I've changed! I can't remember half the things I do!'

'You can't remember?'

'Take yesterday, for example. Someone came round, but I can't remember who it was. Anyway, I waited in the bedroom while Grant spoke to the person, and . . . it was early evening, and the next thing I remember was going to bed – very late!'

'Perhaps you fell asleep?'

'No, no, I didn't. Great chunks of time seem to have disappeared! The other evening, Julie, a friend of mine came round. You met her, didn't you?'

'Yes, I remember her.'

'Well, it was early evening and . . . the same thing happened. All I remember is going to bed – and it was very late!'

'How strange!'

'There's something else. I . . . I shouldn't be telling you this but . . . I was never a very sexual person. Grant used to complain that I wasn't adventurous enough in bed. But now, I seem to . . . I seem to want sex all the time! I don't understand what's happened to me!'

'When did all this start?'

'Not long ago. Grant resigned from his job, and I don't know why. He's also been having mysterious phone calls. My friend, Jackie, called in for coffee the other day and we talked about masturbation, of all things! It's just not like Jackie to talk the way she did! Also, Grant's made what he calls his sex dungeon. He's converted the summer house into a sex dungeon, for God's sake! So much has been happening, I can't begin to tell you!'

'Do you remember the other evening when I came round and . . . well, your friend Diana was there and . . .'

'Diana? The name rings a bell, but . . . what happened, Chris?'

'You honestly don't remember?' he asked surprisedly, pouring the coffee.

'No, I don't!'

'Grant rang me, it was quite late in the evening and . . . I came round to join . . . you and Diana were in the lounge.'

'I don't remember that at all! I don't even remember you coming round let alone this Diana, whoever she is!'

'Christ, this is weird!' Chris exclaimed, recalling screwing Karen's tight pussy hole as Grant shafted her anal sheath.

'You can say that again! I don't know what to do, Chris. I mean, great chunks of my life are disappearing! I don't know what to do!'

'As you know, I've not known Grant very long. What's he like? I mean, does he have other women?' Chris asked, passing the girl a cup of coffee as she sat at the kitchen table.

'No, not as far as I know!'

'Have you ever . . . I don't know how to ask you this.'

'Just ask me.'

'Have you ever had sex with two men, Grant and a friend of his, for example?'

'Certainly not! I've never been with another man, not since I met Grant! And I've certainly never been with two men at once!'

'This is incredible!'

'What is?'

'Look, I'll try to discover what's going on, Karen. I don't know how, but I'll try.'

'Do you know something that I don't?' she asked suspiciously, sipping her coffee. 'Are you sure you've never seen me wearing this collar and chain?'

'Of course I'm sure! Where's Grant now?'

'He might be at home. I went out for a while. I haven't been back yet, I came straight here. That's another thing, Grant keeps going out – and I've no idea where to!'

'OK, you stay here and finish your coffee. I'll go round to your place and, if Grant's there, I'll have a chat with him.'

'Thanks, Chris, I'd appreciate that.'

Answering the door to Chris, Grant smiled and invited him in. 'How are you?' he asked, leading him into the lounge.

'Fine! How are things with you?'

'OK, except that I've been having mysterious phone calls!' Grant confessed.

'Yes, so I've . . . mysterious phone calls?'

'Yes, someone's been watching me, following me, and they keep ringing.'

'Why?'

'Because . . . I don't know why! I had another call a short time ago.'

'What does this person say?'

'He tells me where I've been, what I've been doing, that sort of thing.'

'What does he want?'

'I don't know. He followed me this morning. I went for a walk and . . . I ran into an old friend. She's coming round this afternoon and, I don't know how, but he knew all about it! The orgy we had the other evening, he knew about that, too. He'd been spying through the window.'

'Bloody hell! A peeping Tom?'

'It's worse than that, Chris! He knows *everything*, my every move!'

'When this friend of yours comes round, do you reckon he'll . . .'

'Yes, I'm sure he's going to spy on me! She'll be here at one o'clock. I've thought about trying to lay a trap, that's why I went for a walk to the park, to try to bring him out into the open – but it didn't work.'

'Grant, I was . . . I was talking to Karen earlier. She's worried about . . . she told me about the phone calls, the way you've changed recently, the way she's changed.'

'She worries over nothing, that girl!'

'She's genuinely concerned, Grant! She showed me the dog collar.'

'You've seen that before! It's just a bit of fun!'

'Is it? Why don't you tell me what's going on?'

'Nothing's going on, Chris!'

'She mentioned your sex dungeon.'

'That was *her* idea! She's heavily into the kinky stuff!'

'She's losing her memory. She . . . she can't remember our little orgy the other night. Don't you think that odd?'

'I . . . she probably doesn't want to talk about it.'

'She can't talk about it because she can't remember it!'

'Look, I don't know what she's been telling you but, the dog collar was her idea, the orgy was her idea . . . she begged me to convert the summer house into a sex dungeon. She's always been oversexed, the little tart! She's been playing games recently, pretending to forget things. I reckon the daft bitch has fallen out of her tree!'

'She said that she doesn't know who Diana is, and yet . . .'

'She's known Diana for years! They were at school together, for God's sake! She's a funny one, she really is! Oh, that'll be her,' Grant said as the front door closed.

'I'll be going, I've got work to do.'

'OK, Chris,' Grant replied, following his neighbour into the hall. 'Hi, Karen! Chris is just leaving.'

'Oh, er . . . hi, Chris,' she smiled nervously.

'Hi. I'll . . . I'll see you later, perhaps,' Chris stammered, opening the front door.

'Yes, later.'

'See you, Chris!' Grant called as he wandered into the lounge.

Standing by the window, Grant watched Chris walk down the path, wondering how to deal with Karen. She was beginning to cause problems, and he didn't like it! Turning as she entered the room, he glared at her.

'What have you been telling Chris?' he demanded angrily.

'Nothing, I . . .'

'He said that you'd been talking to him!'

'Yes, I . . .'

'You're a bitch, causing me these bloody problems! What did you go and open your mouth for?'

'I'm allowed to speak to my neighbour, Grant!'

'No, you're not! You'll only open your mouth when I want you to suck me off!'

'Why are you . . .'

'I don't want you to leave the house again, Karen!'

'But you can't keep me locked in the house all the time!'

'I can, and I will!'

'I'm not your prisoner, Grant!'

You are, my girl! Take your clothes off!

Sitting on the sofa, Grant watched the girl pull her jumper over her head, revealing her naked, firm breasts, her incredibly long nipples. Perhaps the time had come to be rid of her? he contemplated. The time had definitely come to thrash the bitch! What with Chris now taking an interest in Grant, and the mysterious voyeur . . . He'd put Chris right, he decided. He'd influence Karen to tell the man that she'd made it all up, that she remembered the orgy and that she'd been joking about not knowing Diana. Chris would think the girl was off her head, and end up feeling sorry for Grant!

'Right!' Grant stormed as Karen stood naked before him, her hairless vaginal crack seemingly grinning at him. 'Go to the sex dungeon and get the cane!'

'Grant, I . . .' she stuttered, her expression one of confusion.

Go and get the cane! The key's in the kitchen, on the hook.

'I'll go and get the cane,' she replied softly, leaving the room.

Get the leather belt, the one with the two nipple holes, and some rope!

Where was the voyeur now? Grant wondered, turning

and looking out of the window. He wasn't lurking in the front garden, that was for sure! If he called and said that he'd witnessed Karen's punishment, the thrashing . . . But no, there was no way he'd stand at the window in broad daylight! 'I'll bet that's him again!' he sighed despondently as the phone rang.

'Grant, it's Elizabeth,' the woman said shakily as he pressed the receiver to his ear.

'Hi, how are you?'

'I've . . . I've received a note, a blackmail note, demanding one thousand pounds.'

'What?'

'Whoever it is, they're threatening to tell my husband about . . .'

'OK, don't panic. Look, I'm busy right now, but I'll come and see you later.'

'I don't know what to do, Grant!'

'It'll be all right! Stay calm and do nothing, I'll see you later.'

'All right. I have to deliver the money at five o'clock, so . . .'

'I'll be there long before five, don't worry.'

'OK. Bye, Grant.'

'See you later.'

Replacing the receiver, Grant flopped onto the sofa. 'It's him, I know it!' he breathed, gazing at the window, wondering where the voyeur, the blackmailer, was hiding. This was becoming dangerous, he mused. But it wouldn't stop at Elizabeth, the man would also blackmail Melinda and Wendy, he was sure. *He's ruining everything!* Mulling over the choices, he knew that he'd have to give in and reveal his secret to the man – there was no other way!

'OK!' Grant bellowed as Karen entered the room. 'First of all, I'll strap your tits with the belt! Lift your arms up!' Running the leather belt around her naked body, aligning the holes with her elongated nipples, Grant pulled it tight and fastened the buckle. Gazing at her nipples inflating through the holes, painfully distending, Grant took the rope and bound her wrists behind her back. 'You, my girl, are in for the thrashing of your life! How *dare* you go running to Chris? You'll never leave this house again, I'll tell you that for nothing! And you'll remain naked! Right, bend over the back of the armchair with your feet wide apart!'

'Grant, please, I . . .'

'Do it!'

Dragging the chair to the centre of the room, Grant grabbed another length of rope as Karen obediently bent her naked body over the back of the chair, her taut buttocks projected in readiness for the thrashing. Binding her ankle and running the rope around the base of the chair, he secured her other ankle. 'How dare you go running to Chris?' he stormed again, grabbing the thin bamboo cane. 'How bloody dare you?'

Caressing her rounded buttocks with the cane, running the tip up and down her bottom-crease, teasing her brown anal iris, Grant's lips twisted into an evil grin. 'You've not had the cane before, have you?'

'No, I haven't,' Karen murmured.

'It'll be better than the rope, it'll sting more, bring out weals. Now, before I administer your punishment, I want to know what else you've told Chris.'

'Nothing, I . . .'

Raising the cane above his head, Grant brought it down across the girl's twitching bottom-orbs with a deafening crack, causing her to scream, her young body to jolt. 'I'll ask you again!' he bellowed, watching the thin weal appearing across her tensed flesh. 'What else did you tell Chris?'

'That you keep going out!'

'And?'

'I told him that I can't remember things. I said that you'd made me wear the collar. I said that Jackie had talked about masturbation and that it wasn't like her to do that. I also said that I'd become sexual, that I'd changed.'

'Did he try anything on?'

'No, he didn't. Grant, I don't want the cane! Why are you treating me like this? I thought we were . . .'

'I'm treating you like this because it's what you deserve!'

'Why? All I did was talk to my next-door neighbour!'

'I have secrets, Karen, and I don't want people prying into my private life.'

'What secrets?'

'I can't tell you. Did you tell Chris anything else?'

'No, I swear!'

'Are you sure?'

'Yes! Please, Grant, I . . .'

The cane swished through the air, striking her trembling buttocks. Karen cried out in her fear and arousal. Again, the cane landed across her tensed flesh, leaving a long thin weal in its wake. Gazing at her full cuntal lips swelling between her milk-white thighs, her girl-come oozing between her inner petals, Grant was enjoying the evil, merciless thrashing

'You're lying!' he stormed, flogging her again.

'I'm not! I didn't tell him anything else!'

'You told him about the sex dungeon!'

'Yes, yes! I'd forgotten about that!'

'How convenient! Did you tell him that you'd shaved your cunt?'

'No, I promise!'

Her bottom-globes turning crimson, Grant continued the ruthless thrashing, giving the screaming girl no quarter. He'd thrash the prudish solicitor for her tricks, he decided, and spunk up her tight arsehole! Glancing at the window as he brought the cane down again, Grant smiled. The voyeur wasn't there, he wasn't witnessing Karen's punishment, there was no way he could know about it! But would he be lurking when the solicitor arrived? Yes, undoubtedly! And Grant would catch him!

'Please, no more!' Karen screamed hysterically as the cane landed with a loud crack, stinging her trembling flesh. 'Grant, I'm begging you!'

'Do what you like, I'm not going to stop!' he laughed wickedly, lashing her burning buttocks again. 'You'll not be able to sit down for a week after I've finished with you!'

'I'll leave you! Unless you stop now, I'll leave you!'

'How can you? You're tied up, Karen! You're my prisoner!'

Giving the girl another twenty-odd lashes to the accompaniment of her screams and threats, Grant finally discarded the cane and dropped to his knees, examining her burning buttocks, her dripping vaginal crack.

'You've got nice scarlet bum cheeks now!' he laughed, stroking her fire-red flesh with his fingertips. 'I might thrash you again later!'

'The minute I'm free, I'm leaving you!' she sobbed. 'I mean it, Grant, I'm . . .'

You'll never leave me! You want to stay here as my prisoner, as my sex slave! 'Really? You're going to leave me?'

'No, no, I . . . I want to stay here.'

'Good, that's settled then! Don't mind if I leave you like that, do you?'

'I'm uncomfortable, Grant! My nipples hurt!'

'Good, that's what I like to hear from a slave! Right, there's a solicitor due to arrive soon. I'll get her to lick your cunt out!' he chuckled, rising to his feet.

'No! I don't want . . .'

'I'm going outside to check something, I won't be long.'

Examining the soil beneath the lounge window, Grant frowned. *No sign of footprints*, he mused, wondering how the man had been able to look through the window without standing on the border. Hearing the phone ringing, he dashed back to the lounge and grabbed the receiver.

'You really gave her a good thrashing!' the mysterious man chuckled. 'How long are you going to leave her tied over the chair?'

'Who the hell is this?' Grant demanded angrily, his hands trembling.

'Are you going to tell me how you do it?'

'No, I'm not!'

'I hope you take the solicitor into the lounge because I'll have a far better view of you abusing her.'

'I'm taking her into my sex dungeon, as it happens, and there's no way you'll be able to see anything!'

'I'll give you a ring later and tell you all about it, tell you what you did and . . .'

'Go to hell!'

Banging the phone down, Grant held his hand to his head and gazed at Karen's crimson buttocks. *How the hell could he have seen?* he wondered anxiously. Gazing out of the window at the house opposite, he realized that, even with binoculars, it would be extremely difficult to see through the net curtains – if not impossible!

'Grant, I'm uncomfortable!' Karen complained again. 'My nipples . . . please, take the belt off!'

'No! The solicitor is due any time now, so you'll have to stay like that for a while longer!'

'Who is this solicitor?'

'No one you know – not yet, anyway!' he laughed, patting her burning buttocks.

'My bum is really stinging! I want to . . .'

'Ah, she's here!' Grant breathed as the doorbell rang. 'Right, I'll take her into the kitchen first, and then I'll bring her in here! See you later.'

Opening the door, Grant smiled as the confused woman stepped into the hall and looked about her. 'Come through to the kitchen,' he invited her, walking down the hall. 'I'm glad you could make it.'

'I . . . I don't know why I'm here,' she said hesitantly, following Grant.

'Take a seat, and I'll explain.'

'You came to the office earlier, but I can't remember what it was about, or what I'm doing here,' she breathed, seating herself at the table. 'I'm not usually confused like this! Who are you? What am I . . .'

'OK, you're here because of your embezzlement. The deal is, you give me your body in return for . . .'

'Embezzlement? Oh, yes! I remember now, I was going to . . .'

'You were going to send the heavies round to deal with me! But you've come here alone, haven't you?'

'Yes, I have. Why didn't I . . . I don't understand this! I was going to ring . . .'

'Take your jacket and blouse off and lift your bra up, I want to see your tits.'

'No! I'm not going to . . .'

'Look, Mrs Jenkins, I haven't got all day! Either you strip off, expose your cunt and tits, or *I*'ll expose *you* for the criminal you are!'

'But how do you know about me, about the . . .'

'I know everything, so you'd better do as I say!'

'I'm not taking my clothes off! What do you think I am?'

'You're a criminal! You were pretty cool when I came to your office – calm and collected. Thought you had it all worked out, didn't you? You agreed to the deal, to come here and offer me your body in exchange for my keeping quiet. But things didn't work out the way you'd planned them. Now that you're here, alone, without your muscle men, you don't have a choice, do you?'

'I have every choice! I'm not going to be threatened by you, whoever you are!'

'Twenty thousand pounds is a lot of money, Mrs Jenkins.'

'You can't prove anything!'

'Your partners in crime are Paul Blake and David Hodges. You have a bank account in the name of . . .'

'Look, I'll bring you in on our . . . our sideline.'

'I don't want to become involved in your criminal activities!'

'I could walk out of here and . . .'

'And the police would be at your office, and your house, within minutes!'

'What sort of man are you? Do you really expect me to . . .'

'I'm not expecting, I'm demanding! And I'll tell you what

sort of man I am – I'm desperate to see your tits, your hairy cunt crack!'

'You disgust me!'

'I seem to disgust most women! So, Mrs Wendy Jenkins LL. B. of Partridge Manor stuck-up private estate, I'll ring the police and . . .'

'What do you want me to do?'

'Take your clothes off!'

'And nothing more? I mean, you're not going to . . .'

'Just take your clothes off!'

'How do I know that you won't keep pestering me? How do I know that you won't haunt me?'

'Once is enough for me. You see, when I've degraded and humiliated a woman, that's it, the fun's over. There's no point in doing it again.'

'You won't touch me, will you?'

'It's the degradation and humiliation I enjoy. It's the embarrassment I revel in. Take your clothes off and show me your cunt!'

Standing, the woman slipped her jacket off and hesitantly unbuttoned her white silk blouse. Her face flushing as she gazed into Grant's dark eyes, she parted her full red lips. 'I'm . . . I'm rather enjoying this,' she said softly, unconvincingly. She was shrewd, playing her own game to spoil Grant's. 'I have a good body, even though I say it myself,' she added nervously, slipping her blouse over her shoulders. Eyeing her bra straining to support her ample breasts, Grant decided to play along with her.

'You're not embarrassed, then?' he asked.

'No, not at all!'

'Good! I'm pleaseed that you're enjoying yourself!' he chuckled, gazing at her deep cleavage. 'I'm looking forward to seeing your cunt, Wendy. What colour are your pubes? Having blonde hair, I would imagine they're blonde, too.'

'Yes, blonde,' she said softly, her hands trembling as she forced a smile.

'That'll be a real turn-on for you! Showing me your cunt crack will really turn you on, won't it?'

'Yes, yes, it will. Look, I . . .'

'We'll start with your tits. Take your bra off and let's have a good look at your nipples.'

Reaching behind her back, she paused, obviously trying to think of a way out of her predicament. 'You won't touch me, will you?' she asked shakily.

'Well, if you're really enjoying it . . .'

'Yes, but . . .'

'Let's not rush things, Wendy. Besides, how can I decide whether to touch you or not until I've seen your tits, your cunt? I have to see your wares before I can decide whether I want them or not.'

Unclipping her bra, her cheeks crimson, she peeled the cups away from her heavy mammary globes, revealing her elongated nipples. 'And now your skirt,' Grant coaxed, sitting on a chair, his face beaming. Unzipping her skirt, she tugged it down her naked legs, displaying her red silk panties bulging with her swelling sex. Taking her skirt from the floor and folding it over the back of a chair, she stood upright in her black high heels and tight red panties, her shapely body rigid in her trepidation.

'You look as if you're in the dock!' Grant laughed. 'If you're enjoying it, relax!'

'I . . . I am enjoying it,' she stammered feebly. 'But I . . .'

'But what? Come on, Wendy, pull your knickers down and show me your lovely cunt lips!'

'I thought you got your kicks from humiliating women?'
'I do!'
'But I'm not at all humiliated! If anything, I'm . . .'
'Then show me your cunt!'

'My partners know that I'm here,' she lied, glancing at her gold watch. 'Unless I meet them at one-thirty, they'll come here and . . .'

'In that case, you'd better hurry up! You've only fifteen minutes to go!'

'If they come here and see me like this, they'll . . .'
'They'll probably want to fuck you!'
'Please, don't be so crude!'
'You're wasting time, Wendy! And I'm becoming impatient!'

Slipping her thumbs between the elastic of her panties and her shapely hips, she peeled the garment down, exposing her scant blonde pubes, her gaping vaginal crack. Her embarrassment soaring as Grant slipped off the chair and knelt before her, scrutinizing her womanhood, she clasped her hands in front of her cunt, veiling her pussy slit.

'What's your husband like in bed?' Grant asked the trembling woman as she stepped out of her panties. 'Does he spunk in your mouth?'

'No, he doesn't!' she spat. 'He's a decent man, unlike . . .'
'There's nothing indecent about spunking in your mouth!'
'You're vile!'

'Yes, I know! Now that you're naked, come with me,' Grant smiled, rising to his feet.

'Where are we going?'
'You'll see.'

Hesitantly following him into the lounge, Wendy gasped as she stared in horror at Karen's crimson weal-lined buttocks, her hairless, fleshy cunt lips bulging between her shapely thighs. 'My God!' she cried, turning to Grant. 'What have you . . .'

'Who's that?' Karen bellowed. 'Grant, if you . . .'

'Karen, this is the solicitor I told you about. She's come here to finger your cunt.'

'I have not!' Wendy returned indignantly. 'I've kept my side of the bargain, and now I'm leaving!'

'You're in no position to call the shots!' Grant laughed. 'Finger her cunt, or I'll expose you and your criminal friends!'

'You can't force me to . . .'

'I don't intend to force you! The choice is yours, Wendy – whether you finger her cunt or not, the choice is entirely yours!'

Kneeling behind Karen's tethered body, Wendy parted the girl's cuntal lips and peered at her wet inner flesh. Tentatively slipping her middle finger into her hot duct, she looked up at Grant, her eyes mirroring something – what, Grant couldn't determine. As she slowly moved her hand up and down, driving her finger in and out of Karen's open pussy hole, she peeled the girl's cunny lips wider apart. What was her game now? Grant wondered. Her eyes were still locked to his, her full red lips curling into an impish smile.

She appeared to be deriving immense pleasure from her lesbian act as she slipped a second finger into Karen's tight vaginal sheath. *Perhaps she's a bloody lezzie?* Grant pondered as she turned her head and focused on the girl's crudely opened love hole. No, this was another one of her games, he was sure! The bitch was feigning pleasure to conceal her humiliation!

'Why not give her cunt a good licking out?' Grant

suggested, his penis solid, his heavy balls rolling. 'I can see that you're really enjoying yourself and she's very wet, so why not lick her cunt out?'

'No, I like doing this but I don't want to . . .'

'It's what *I* want that matters, Wendy!' Grant returned angrily. 'Lick her cunt, lap up her fanny juice!'

'The time . . . I have to meet my partners or they'll come here and . . .'

'You've plenty of time!'

'But they'll come here and . . .'

'Let me worry about that, you enjoy Karen's wet cunt.'

Slipping her fingers out of Karen's drenched pussy sheath, Wendy moved her head forward, pushing her tongue out as she came close to the girl's dripping femininity. Coaxing her, Grant waited in anticipation for the tip of her pink tongue to come into contact with Karen's rubicund inner petals, the globules of pearly liquid clinging to her intimate girl-folds. Her eyes squeezed shut, Wendy moved further forward, her tongue meeting Karen's furled pussy lips, tasting her honeydew.

'Push your tongue into her cunt,' Grant breathed. 'Open her lips with your fingers and push your tongue right inside her cunt.' Karen remained silent as Wendy complied, parting the tethered girl's pussy lips and slipping her tongue into her vaginal duct. In her confusion, Karen couldn't think straight, she didn't understand why this was happening, although she was deriving immense pleasure from the female tongue exploring her most private flesh.

'Does she taste nice?' Grant asked. 'Have you ever tasted cunt juice before?'

'No, no, I haven't,' Wendy breathed, licking around the girl's open hole.

'Do you like licking her cunt?'

'I . . . yes, I do.'

'In that case, keep tongue-fucking her!'

Again, Grant couldn't determine whether the woman was feigning her pleasure, or whether she really was delighting in lapping up another woman's vaginal juices. *Time for the real test, the sex dungeon!* he decided, glancing at the window, wondering where the mysterious man was lurking. Untying the ropes as Wendy continued the vaginal licking, Grant took the end of the chain and pulled Karen's head up.

'OK, we're going to the . . . to the summer house,' he grinned.

'The summer house?' Wendy echoed, rising to her feet and gazing in horror at Karen's painfully ballooning nipples. 'But I have to go now!'

'Follow me, you've plenty of time!' he laughed, leading Karen out of the room. 'Besides, I thought you said that you were enjoying yourself?'

'I . . . I am, but the time is . . . I have to go now!'

'You can spare a few minutes, surely? Look at it this way, spare a few minutes now, or spend God knows how many years in prison!'

Silently following Karen and Grant to the sex dungeon, Wendy hung her head, wondering how Grant had discovered her embezzlement – and why she'd not sent her friends to the house to deal with him. But her villainy was nothing compared to the other secrets she harboured – dreadful secrets she prayed that Grant knew nothing about!

Entering the dungeon, Wendy gazed in terror at the table, the leather straps, the whip. 'No!' she screamed as Grant took her arm and ordered her to lie on the table with her legs open. 'No, please!'

'What's the matter?' he asked, grinning as she stood trembling before him.

'This is evil! Please, I'll give you anything, but . . .'

'Yes, I know you will!' Grant laughed, wondering whether to use his power on the horrified woman to defile her naked body.

'Please, I can't . . .'

'Come on, Wendy! All I'm going to do is pleasure you, masturbate your clitty to orgasm with my vibrator! What's so bad about that?'

'I'm a respectable married woman!'

'You might be married, but you're hardly respectable! You're a criminal!'

'Grant, why are you . . .' Karen began, gazing at Wendy's firm breasts, her long milk teats.

'Don't *you* start!' he admonished the girl, tugging on the chain. 'So, Wendy, what's it to be?'

Climbing onto the table, Wendy rested her head on the cushion, gazing up at the pullies and chains as she parted her trembling legs. Whatever she was forced to endure, whatever horrendous sexual acts she was subjected to, she'd eventually be allowed to go home, she was sure, as Grant pulled her arms behind her head and strapped her wrists to the corners of the table. Whether her terrifying ordeal lasted for twenty minutes or two hours, she'd eventually be allowed home – wouldn't she?

Securing the woman's feet in the leather slings, Grant moved to the wall and pulled the chain down, lifting and parting her shapely legs, crudely opening her vaginal crack. Whimpering, her tearful eyes squeezed shut, she was defenceless to protect her vulnerable womanhood. Had embezzlement been worth this? she wondered fearfully as Grant ordered Karen to sit on the chair between her open legs. She'd never dreamed that her criminal actions would lead to this!

'Lick her wet cunt out!' Grant ordered Karen coarsely as he slipped his erect penis from his flies, the bulbous knob wavering ominously before Wendy's wide eyes as she turned her head to face him. 'And you, lick this!' he chuckled, pulling his foreskin further back and pressing his glans to her pursed lips.

'No, please!' she cried, turning her head away as Karen's tongue swept up her yawning cuntal fissure. 'Please, I've never . . .'

'There's always a first time! Suck it or . . .'

Taking his huge knob into her wet mouth, Wendy closed her eyes, her tormented mind swirling with thoughts of the vulgar act she was being forced to commit. Never had she taken a man's penis into her mouth before, never had she tasted a salty, silky-smooth glans – never had she swallowed sperm! As Grant projected his hips, driving his knob to the back of her throat, she tried to turn her head again.

'I'm going to spunk in your mouth so you might as well get it over with!' he laughed.

'I don't want sperm in my mouth!' she sobbed. 'Please!'

'Want it or not, you're having it! Now, suck me off!'

Taking Grant's ballooning plum into her hot mouth again, Wendy resigned herself to the thought that, the sooner she'd endured the crudity, the sooner she'd be released. Like he said, *get it over with!* she thought, running her tongue over his smooth glans as her clitoris responded to Karen's caressing tongue. *Once he's come, that will be the end of it!* But she didn't know Grant, his incredible staying power!

'Use the vibrator on her clitoris!' Grant gasped as his knob twitched within Wendy's hot mouth. 'Fuck her cunt with a candle and bring her off with the vibro!' Trying to block out Grant's crude instructions, Wendy jolted as the buzzing vibrator pressed against her erect clitoris and the candle drove deep into her vaginal duct.

Breathing heavily through her nose as she suckled on Grant's cock-head, her cuntal fluid streaming from her bloated love hole, her clitoris pulsating, she knew she'd be unable to halt her approaching orgasm. Never had she been taken to orgasm with a vibrator, swallowed sperm jetting from a throbbing knob. Was she enjoying the sensations her clitty was bringing her? Grant wondered, watching her stomach rise and fall. Her body becoming alive with new-found sensations of sex, she began trembling, her body shaking violently as her climax rose from her contracting womb and erupted within her swollen clitoris.

Fervently mouthing on Grant's knob as her orgasm gripped her tethered body, Wendy swallowed hard as her mouth filled with sperm. Rocking his hips, fucking her pretty, virginal mouth, Grant gasped, his eyes rolling in his evil act as his spunk trickled over her full lips and ran down her cheek. Her clitoris pulsating, her vagina rhythmically gripping the thrusting candle, the prudish solicitor had been broken, her morals stripped away, her sexuality woken.

The last of his sperm gushing from his throbbing knob, bathing the woman's snaking tongue, Grant's heavy balls finally drained and he slipped his spent organ from her mouth. Still gripped in her vibrator-induced climax, gasping, her body heaving, Grant zipped up his jeans, leaving Wendy to enjoy her lesbian games as he stepped into the garden, hoping to catch the voyeur.

Frowning, he looked around the garden. 'No one!' he breathed as Wendy's orgasmic cries drifted out from the sex dungeon. 'Where the hell is he?' Dashing into the house as the phone rang, his heart racing, his breathing unsteady, he instinctively knew who the caller was.

'Yes?' Grant panted as he grabbed the receiver.

'Nice one, Grant! Do you know, I reckon she quite enjoyed swallowing your spunk!'

'OK, I give in!' Grant breathed. 'I'll tell you all you want to know, but not over the phone.'

'It will have to be over the phone, Grant.'

'No, there's too much to tell, it's too complex. I'll meet you, anywhere you want, on your own terms, OK?'

'I'll have to give it some thought. I'll ring you when I've . . .'

'Are you blackmailing Elizabeth?' Grant asked.

'Now, would I do a thing like that? I'll be in touch, Grant.'

Replacing the receiver, Grant prayed that, at last, he'd get to meet the stranger, discover his identity. He was lying about Elizabeth, he knew, as he returned to the dungeon. Who else would be blackmailing the woman? It had to be him!

'You two seem to be having fun!' Grant chuckled as Karen thrust the candle deep into Wendy's drenched vagina and ran the vibrator around her throbbing clitoris. Ignoring Grant as he padlocked the dog chain to a steel ring set in the table leg, lost in their sexual arousal, the women didn't notice him leave the dungeon and lock the door – imprisoning them.

Driving to Elizabeth's house, Grant wondered whether the voyeur would tail him or, impossible though it seemed, continue to spy on the lesbian session in the sex dungeon. 'How the hell does he do it?' he breathed, parking his car a few doors away from the woman's house. 'How the hell can he see into the dungeon?'

Chapter Eleven

'Here's the note,' Elizabeth said, passing Grant a piece of paper as he reclined on the sofa. 'It's made up of letters cut out of a newspaper.'

'Yes, I can see that. When did you get this?'

'I found it on the mat just before I rang you. I don't know how long it had been there.'

'When I left here the other day, did a man knock on your door and . . .'

'Yes, he said that he thought he'd recognized you and he wanted to get in touch with you. I hope you don't mind, but I gave him your phone number.'

'Describe him.'

'Er . . . about thirty, mousy brownish hair, glasses, a little shorter than you . . .'

'Oh, that blows my theory!'

'Who did you think it was?'

'My neighbour, Chris. It was a long shot, but it could have been him. Were there any distinguishing marks, a scar, a mole, a moustache – anything?'

'No, I don't think so. Wait a minute! Yes, he had a huge nose!'

'That's something to go on, I suppose. At least I have some idea of whom I'm looking for now. This note, it says that he'll tell your husband about you and me, but it also says that he'll tell him about your other man.

How the hell does he know about him?'

'I don't know, you're the private detective, so . . .'

'Am I? Oh, yes, I see what you mean. This boyfriend of yours, Dave, isn't it?'

'Yes.'

'When did he last come here?'

'He turned up shortly after you'd left.'

'Was he here when this man . . .'

'No, he arrived within minutes of the man leaving.'

'So, this blackmailer of ours might have seen Dave go into the house?'

'Yes, he might have done.'

'What happened, did you screw Dave in here?'

'I . . . no, I . . .'

'I have to know, Elizabeth! I know you told me that you didn't want to see your other man any more, but I have to know what happened when he came here. '

'We . . . we made love, in here.'

'He must have looked through the window and seen you, as he did when I was here. It was just luck that Dave happened to arrive while the blackmailer was still lurking in the street. The note says that you're to leave the money next to the litter bin in the car park by Horstead Hill at five o'clock this evening. That figures, I suppose.'

'Why?'

'It doesn't matter. OK, this is what we'll do. Make up a parcel containing folded newspapers and take it to the litter bin at five. I'll be there, hiding in the bushes. When you've gone and he shows himself, I'll nab him.'

'But even when you've caught him and you know who he is, what's to stop him telling my husband about . . .'

'Yes, I see your point. He's also blackmailing me.'

'God, is he?'

'Well, not blackmailing me, exactly, but he's causing me horrendous problems!'

'What made you think that it was your neighbour?'

'Chris knows a few things about me, things I get up to. Living next door, he could have . . . anyway, it's not him. Right, the time's running on so I'll get myself to the car park and into hiding well before he arrives. You know what to do, don't you?'

'Yes, yes, I do.'

'OK, I'll be in touch.'

Following Grant into the hall, Elizabeth grabbed his arm, her hazel eyes betraying her arousal as she provocatively licked her full red lips. 'We have time to . . .'

'No, we haven't. I've got to get to the car park as early as possible. I might be round tomorrow morning to . . .' *To give you a damned good whipping!*

'Yes, please do!'

'Remember, folded newspapers wrapped in brown paper to look like a package containing money,' Grant reiterated, opening the front door.

'All right, Grant. Good luck!'

Parking his car some distance away from the hill, Grant walked to the car park, wondering how Karen and Wendy were getting on. *I think I'll keep Wendy prisoner overnight,* he mused wickedly, deciding to force his massive penis into her tight anal duct when he returned home. *I haven't fucked her wet pussy yet!*

Turning his thoughts to more serious matters, Grant pondered on the voyeur, the blackmailer. He'd know that Elizabeth would tell Grant about the ransom note. He'd also realize that Grant would be lurking somewhere nearby ready to pounce on him. 'Christ!' he breathed, suddenly realizing the man's plan. 'He won't be coming here at all! He'll nab Elizabeth before she gets here!'

Dashing back to his car, he drove to Rochester Street and parked a hundred yards away from Elizabeth's house, praying that he was right, that the man would pounce on the woman as she left the house, probably as she stepped out of the front door. Coming face to face with Elizabeth wouldn't worry the blackmailer, there'd be no way she could discover who he was. *I'd be better off hiding in her front garden*, Grant reflected, leaving his car and walking down the street.

Slipping behind some thick bushes, Grant made himself comfortable and lay in wait. Gazing at the front door through the foliage, he wondered what time the man would arrive. The note had instructed Elizabeth to leave the money by the litter bin at five o'clock, so she'd have to leave the house by quarter to at the latest. *I'll shut the bastard up once and for all!* Grant thought, wondering what to do with the man once he'd pounced on him. *Find out where he lives and use my power on his wife, if the bastard has one!*

Clutching the package, Elizabeth left the house at twenty to five and climbed into her car. *Where the hell is he?* Grant wondered as she backed out of the drive and sped down the road. Leaping from his hide, realizing that the blackmailer was one jump ahead, he raced to his car. *He knew I'd be lying in wait at her house!* he reflected. *Fuck it, he's smarter than I'd thought!*

Reaching his car, Grant kicked the flat tyre and cursed. 'Fucking bastard!' At least Elizabeth was only delivering a package containing old newspapers, he mused, hauling the spare wheel out of the boot. The bastard would expose Elizabeth now, tell her husband of her infidelity, but that wasn't Grant's problem.

He watches me in the lounge, in the dungeon, follows me here, lets my fucking tyre down – and by now he'll be at the car park! And before I know it, he'll be spying on me in the dungeon again! he thought despairingly as he hurriedly changed the wheel.

Driving home, fuming, banging the steering wheel, Grant decided to vent his anger on Wendy's tethered body. 'I'll thrash the fucking bitch!' he swore, pulling up outside the house. 'I'll thrash the bitch and fuck her senseless!' Opening the front door to hear the phone ringing, he checked his watch – ten past five. Dashing into the lounge, he knew it wouldn't be the blackmailer. *Unless he's at the car park with a mobile phone?* he mused, lifting the receiver.

'Hi, Grant! How was Elizabeth?' the man chuckled.

'You let my fucking tyre down!' Grant stormed.

'No, I didn't! I've been watching the lesbian show in your sex den!'

'How did you know I'd been to Elizabeth's place, then?'

'I know everything, your every move!'

'Are you in the car park using a mobile phone?'

'Why would I be in a car park?'

'To collect the money.'

'What money? I don't know what you're talking about!'

'I know what you look like,' Grant enlightened the man. 'I have a damned good description of you, of your big nose!'

'Have you, now? Well, it won't help you.'

'Do you want to discover my secret or not?'

'Yes, of course I do!'

'OK, so where and when do we meet?'

'I haven't decided yet. By the way, Karen needs the loo, so you'd better release her. Bye, Grant!'

Dropping the phone to the floor, Grant raced out of the house to the dungeon and unlocked the door. 'Do you need the loo?' he asked the agitated girl as she stood squirming with her legs crossed.

'Yes, desperately! How did you know?'

'This is crazy!' Grant hissed through gritted teeth as he removed the dog collar from her neck. 'How the fuck did he know?'

'How did who know what?' Karen asked, gazing in awe at her distended nipples poking through the holes in the leather belt.

'Forget it!' Grant returned as the girl dashed to the house. 'So, Wendy, had a good time, have you?' he grinned, gazing at her inflamed vaginal lips, her copious cunt milk flowing from her open love sheath.

'Please, I've been here for hours! I must go home!' she wailed, raising her head and tugging on the leather straps.

'I might keep you here for the night,' Grant smiled, slipping a finger into her drenched vaginal canal.

'You can't do that!'

'I can do what the fucking hell I like! Your cunt's hot, and very wet.'

'That's kidnapping! You can't . . .'

'Kidnapping? How can it be? You came here of your own accord, you stripped off, you lay on the table and allowed me to tie you down – how can you say that I've kidnapped you?'

'You're keeping me here against my will!'

'No, I'm not! You have a choice, you can go home now, if you want to.'

'Yes, I *do* want to!'

'Fine, I'll release you and bring you your clothes, and then I'll call the police.'

'No! Look, I've cooperated, done everything you've asked me to do . . .'

'But I haven't finished with you! I haven't fucked your cunt, yet!'

'You'll pay for this, believe me, you'll . . .'

'So much for your partners in crime turning up and rescuing you!'

'They'll be here!'

'Yes, yes, of course they will! I'll be back after I've had something to eat,' Grant smiled, withdrawing his finger from her tight pussy hole and stepping outside. 'I'll be back to eat your pussy!'

Wandering through the kitchen, Grant grabbed Wendy's clothes. *Better hide these*, he thought walking into the hall as Karen descended the stairs, clutching a bundle of clothes. Her rubicund hairless girl-crack inflamed, wet, he eyed her curvaceous naked body as she tossed her blonde matted hair over her shoulder and asked him to remove the leather belt.

'I'm not taking the belt off, I like seeing your tits like that.'

'My nipples hurt, Grant!' she complained, gazing at her sore breast buds.

'Make me something to eat, slave!' he ordered the girl. 'And don't get dressed!'

'Grant, I'm not going to . . .'

Do as you're bloody well told, bitch! he ordered her telepathically, entering the lounge and dumping Wendy's clothes in the corner of the room. *You want to remain naked!*

'I'll make you something to eat,' Karen smiled amicably. 'I'll take my clothes upstairs first.'

Grabbing the phone receiver from the floor, Grant

dropped it into its cradle, wondering whether he'd been wrong, and the voyeur and the blackmailer were two different people. *They've got to be one and the same!* he reflected. *How the hell did he know that Karen needed the loo? And how the fuck did he know that I'd been to Elizabeth's place if he'd been spying on Karen?*

Shaking his head, he flopped into the armchair, wondering whether to use his power to discover the man's identity. *Eternal impotency!* The frightening words sinking into the mire of perversion swirling in his mind, he rubbed his lined forehead. He'd visit the wood that evening and tell the sect of his problems, he decided. Should the blackmailer follow him, venture into the wood, Veneris might be able to erase all he knew about Grant from his memory.

His incredible power, the perverted sex, money . . . Grant had everything going for him and he wasn't going to allow a stranger to wreck his new life! The man didn't want to meet and discover Grant's secret, and Grant wasn't going to tell him over the phone, so what would happen? *How does he know so much about me, my movements?* he pondered.

'Here's a cheese-and-pickle sandwich,' Karen said as she breezed into the room, the chain hanging between her brown nipples that painfully bulged through the holes in the leather belt. 'Grant, what are you going to do with Wendy? You can't leave her in the summer house, can you?'

'Let me worry about her,' he replied, taking the plate. 'I might leave her strapped to the table overnight – naked!'

'I don't know why, but I don't want to dress. I . . . I like being naked.'

'Good! That's what I like to hear! Girl-slaves should be permanently naked! By the way, when I was out, did you hear anyone moving about outside the dungeon?'

'No, I didn't. I wish you hadn't left us locked in there, Grant! What do you think we are, animals?'

'Yes, that just about sums women up!' he chuckled, munching his sandwich.

'Well, that's nice, I must say!'

'I thought you'd like it!'

'I don't know what's happened to you, or to me, for that matter!'

'Nothing's happened!'

'What about this business of me not leaving the house?'

'What about it?'

'I have to go shopping and . . .'

'Yes, I know. I'll tell you when and where you can go.'

'What about money? We've no income now! I'm so confused! I really don't understand what's going on!'

'I'll go to a bank tomorrow.'

'*A* bank? What do you mean, *a* bank?'

'Nothing, don't worry about it.'

'I *do* worry about it! I worry about all the things that have been happening recently!'

'Well, don't! I'll tell you what, go and release Wendy. Bring her in here and we'll have some fun with her.'

'Don't you think we should let her go home? I mean, she's . . .'

'Just be a good little sex slave and go and release her!'

Finishing his sandwich, Grant switched the light on and drew the curtains, making sure there weren't any cracks for the voyeur to spy through. Slipping his jeans off, he fondled his erect penis, pulling his foreskin back, exposing his knob in readiness to penetrate Wendy's unaccommodating bottom-hole. 'What a magnificent cock!' he laughed. 'There's no way you'll see me fuck her arsehole, whoever you are! No way!'

Frowning as the phone rang, Grant's heart leaped. Surely it wasn't the blackmailer again? *If it's Chris, he can come round and we'll give Karen a double pussy fucking!* he chuckled inwardly, grabbing the receiver. 'Hallo,' he said softly, his penis twitching in anticipation.

'Hi, Grant! Looking forward to having your end away?'

'Who the hell are you? And how the fuck . . .'

'So, you're going to fuck Wendy's arsehole, are you?'

'How do you . . . you've got this place bugged, haven't you?'

'Of course I haven't! I'm going to relax and watch the anal screwing. Bye!'

Stunned, Grant began searching the room for a bugging device. Crazy though it was, the man must have entered the house and planted a bug. There was no way he could have seen into the room, so he must be listening. *He's probably bugged the sex dungeon, too*, Grant reflected, realizing that he could discover what was going on by listening. *There's no need to see, just listen.*

'I must go home now!' Wendy cried as she followed Karen into the room and gazed in horror at Grant's solid penis, his bulbous knob. 'I've been here for hours! Where are my clothes?'

'I haven't fucked you yet!' Grant returned, scrutinizing her pinken girl crack, her distended inner lips. *Is he listening?*

'My husband will wonder . . .'

'Your husband will do more than wonder if I tell him about your sideline! Now, where shall I have you, over the sofa arm? No, I think I'll fuck you over . . .' Wondering again about a bugging device, Grant was about to send out his unspoken instructions when the doorbell rang.

'Shit, I'd better go and see who it is!' he groaned, tugging his jeans on and leaving the room. Opening the door to Chris, Grant invited him in. 'Your timing's perfect!' he grinned. 'I have two naked women in the lounge! Fancy having some fun?'

'*Two* naked women? God, you're sex-mad!'

'Yes, you're right there!'

'Grant, the reason I came round is because I saw a man in your back garden earlier. I happened to be upstairs looking out of the window and I noticed him hanging around outside your summer house. A few minutes ago, he was lurking in your front garden. By the time I'd got out there, he'd gone.'

'This may sound daft, but did you happen to notice whether he had a mobile phone?'

'Yes, he did! But how . . .'

'He's the one I told you about, the one who's been hounding me – the bastard!'

'You still don't know what he's after, then?'

'No, no, I don't.'

'Why would he be nosing around your garden?'

'I don't know. Come through to the lounge, Chris. Come and meet Wendy the wig.'

'Wendy the wig?'

'Yes, she's a solicitor. And I've just solicited the bitch!'

Leading Chris into the room, Grant smiled as Karen clasped her hands together, veiling her shaved pussy lips, her wet girl-crack as Chris scrutinized her naked body. Offering him a slight smile, Karen lowered her head, gazing at her lengthy nipples, the dark discs of her areolae protruding through the holes in the belt, wondering what she was doing, what her neighbour was thinking. Her clitoris swelling, pulsating as she imagined Chris's naked body heaving on top of hers, she sensed her vaginal juices trickling between her distended inner lips.

'Christ, the things you get up to!' Chris gasped, turning his head and focusing on Wendy's elongated nipples.

'I want to go now!' Wendy screeched hysterically.

'Your husband . . .' Grant began.

'I don't care what happens, I'm not going to stay here for another second!'

'I was about to say that your husband, Graham, wouldn't be too pleased to discover your other secret, would he?'

'What . . . what other secret?' she asked, her eyes wide.

'Let's just say that I know what you get up to with a friend of yours.'

'A friend? What do you mean?'

'Carole – need I say more?' Grant replied casually.

'How do you know about . . .' she stammered, wondering how Grant could possibly know of her lesbian lover.

'I know a great deal about you, Wendy! You're often away at the weekends, supposedly on business. The hotel . . . The Swan, room twenty-three . . .'

'Why have you been spying on me, following me? Why me?'

'You're not the only one, I can assure you! I have a string of women I'm . . . well, blackmailing, I suppose.'

'How do you gather so much information? I don't understand how you've discovered so much about me, my private life.'

'I have my ways, Wendy! Let's leave it at that, shall we? I wouldn't want to have to mention that messy business concerning the lesbian prostitute you had to have dealt with! Now, how about getting on the floor, on all fours, so we can have some fun with you, with your cunt?'

Dropping to her knees, the distraught woman took up

her obscene position, her tensed buttocks projected, her vaginal lips swelling invitingly beneath her crudely exposed bottom-hole. Gazing at the opaque liquid trickling between the woman's distended inner lips, Karen became aware of her own juices of arousal flowing down her inner thighs. Her mind racked with confusion, she looked at Grant as Chris whispered in his ear, wondering at his debauchery, at her own rising lust.

'You're blackmailing her?' Chris asked.

'Yes, I am,' Grant replied. 'I've more on her than you could ever imagine! So, she's ready to be fucked! Want to go first?'

'You bet!' Chris replied, gazing at Karen, her nipples painfully ballooning through the holes in the leather belt. Wondering whether she'd recall all that had happened or forget the whole episode, he decided to talk to her later, invite her round for coffee and, hopefully, unravel the mystery.

Karen didn't appear to be too happy, Chris observed, gazing at her pretty face, her fearful expression. As the girl turned, he noticed the thin weals fanning out across her buttocks, realizing that she'd been mercilessly caned. Grant had said that she was heavily into the kinky stuff, but Chris didn't believe that! What with Karen losing her memory, unable to recall the previous orgy, the double fucking, and Grant's strange explanation, Chris was sure that Grant had some kind of hold over the girl.

'Come on, Chris!' Grant chuckled excitedly. 'Are you going to fuck her or not?'

'Yes, damn right I am!'

'You can fuck Karen's arse afterwards!'

'Grant!' Karen cried. 'I don't know whether I want to . . .'

Tell Chris that you'd love him to fuck your arse!
'I'd . . . I'd love you to fuck my arse, Chris.'
Tell him that you want his spunk up your arse!
'I . . . I'd love your spunk up my arse.'
'Anything you say!' Chris laughed, wondering at the girl's sudden change of mind, her crude demand. 'I'll deal with her first!' he added, eyeing Wendy's bloated vaginal lips. 'I'll give her one first!'

Tugging his trousers down, his penis erect, Chris knelt behind Wendy, grinning as she spat her futile protests, threatening Grant with her male friends, her heavies. Ignoring the woman, Chris slipped his purple glans between her bloated pussy lips and drove his penis deep into the welcoming warmth of her wet vaginal canal. Grabbing her hips, his heavy balls swinging, his belly slapping her buttocks, he thrust his solid organ in and out of her spasming pussy hole – using her to gratify his male lust for crude sex.

'Ever had two cocks up your cunt?' Grant asked in his rising thirst for debauched sex, watching Chris's cunny-wet shaft glistening in the light as he repeatedly drove into her quivering body.

'No! Please . . . please!' she gasped, her eyes screwed shut, her head resting on the carpet as her naked body jolted with the enforced cervical pummelling.

'Do you reckon we could manage it, Chris?' Grant chuckled, tweaking Karen's ballooning nipples.

'We could give it a try!'

'Right, if you lie on the floor, Chris, Wendy can straddle you,' he said, tugging his jeans down and kicking them across the room.

'No!' Wendy screamed as Chris withdrew his cunny-wet penis and lay on his back.

'Come on, Wendy!' Grant stormed. 'I wouldn't want to have to tell your husband about Carole! And I certainly wouldn't want to have to mention the prostitute!'

Her face pale, taking her position with her knees either side of Chris, Wendy reached between her thighs and grabbed his solid penis, guiding him into her cunt as she lowered her naked body, completely impaling herself on his solid rod. Resting on her hands, her rounded buttocks jutting out, her vaginal lips taut around Chris's shaft, she waited anxiously as Grant knelt either side of Chris's thighs.

'Karen, open her cunt lips for me,' Grant instructed the girl. 'Stretch her cunt hole wide open!' Following his orders, Karen knelt beside Wendy and parted the woman's fleshy vaginal lips with her slender fingers, exposing her taut inner flesh encompassing Chris's veined shaft. 'Right, here goes!' Grant laughed as he pressed his knob between Chris's organ and the whimpering woman's wet flesh.

'No, please!' Wendy gasped, her pinken hole dilating, allowing Grant's knob to slide alongside Chris's penis and drive into her trembling body.

Gently easing his shaft into Wendy's tight cunt, Grant breathed heavily, his face grimacing as he drove his knob further into her yielding sex sheath. Watching in amazement, Karen couldn't believe what she was seeing as Grant finally buried his knob deep inside the woman's distended sexual cavern. Whimpering, her vaginal walls stretched to the limit, her cunt milk decanting to lubricate the unnatural coupling, Wendy's body jolted as Grant forced a finger into her tight anal sheath.

'Argh! Not there!' she screamed. 'Please, take your finger out!'

'Where's your finger, Grant?' Chris tittered, pinching Wendy's erect nipples.

'Up her arse!' Grant laughed, beginning his vaginal fucking, his huge knob rubbing against Chris's.

'No!' Wendy screamed as Grant slipped another finger into her hot bottom-sheath, stretching the delicate brown tissue. 'Please, I'll tear open!'

'No, you won't!' Grant gasped, increasing his penile thrusting rhythm. 'God, with two cocks up your cunt, you're really tight!'

'Ah, please! Please, I can't . . .'

'Yes, you can!' Grant laughed, slipping his fingers out of the woman's tight rectal sheath. 'Karen, you can finger-fuck her bum while we knob her cunt!'

'Grant, I don't know . . .' the girl began apprehensively, her mind lurching between the delightful act of fingering another woman's anal hole and her uncharacteristic desire to commit the illicit act.

Do it, Karen! Push as many fingers as you can into her arse! Grant willed the tormented girl.

Parting the gasping woman's taut buttocks, Karen slipped a finger past her sphincter muscles and drove it deep into her hot duct. To the accompaniment of Wendy's wailed protests, Karen slipped a second finger into her tight bottom-sheath, stretching her brown anal iris as Grant continued his vaginal fucking.

Pinching her sensitive nipples, Chris drove his tongue into Wendy's hot mouth as she gasped and locked her lips to his. Lost in her frenzied arousal, her animalistic lust, her body quivering with the sensations of the decadent double fucking, her eyes rolled as Karen reached between her legs and massaged her erect clitoris.

'Coming!' she gasped, her lips momentarily leaving

Chris's. His tongue snaking into her mouth again, she projected her taut buttocks, presenting her sexual centre to the two solid penises, offering her anal sheath to Karen's thrusting fingers.

'Ah, ah, coming!' Grant cried as his sperm gushed from his pulsating glans, bathing Chris's throbbing knob, lubricating the forbidden three-way coupling.

'And me!' Chris gasped as Wendy lifted her head, her face flushed, her nostrils flaring, her eyes rolling, as her clitoris erupted in orgasm beneath Karen's caressing fingertips.

Filling the wailing woman's inflamed cunt with their jetting spunk as Karen fervently finger-fucked her spasming anal sheath, their bouncing balls colliding, the men gasped their expletives, their appreciation of the carnal coupling. Their solid shafts pressed together, their knobs pulsating against each other, their sperm amalgamating, they drove their cock-heads in and out of the woman's taut cuntal sheath in unison, revelling in their lewdness to the accompaniment of her gasped protests.

Following Grant's instruction and slipping her fingers out of Wendy's contracting bottom-hole, Karen gazed wide-eyed as he withdrew his orgasming penis from the woman's vagina. His spunk jetting, splattering her taut buttocks, her anal crease, he drove his purple glans deep into her narrow rectal tube, stretching her brown inlet until he'd completely impaled her on his member.

'Argh!' Wendy cried as her bowels filled with Grant's copious flow of spunk. 'God, no!'

'God, *yes!*' Grant returned, withdrawing his penis and driving his spurting glans deep into her bottom-hole again.

'I . . . I can't take it!'

'You *are* taking it!'

Gasping beneath the shaking woman, his balls drained, Chris stilled his penis, resting his glowing knob against her sperm-drenched cervix. Savouring the incredible sensations as Grant continued his anal fucking, causing her vagina to rhythmically contract, her cunt milk to flow, Chris locked his mouth to hers. Their tongues entwining, she let out low moans through her nose as Karen massaged her clitoris, taking her to another shuddering orgasmic peak.

'I can feel her clitty swelling again!' Karen shrieked gleefully, her sensitive nipples swollen through the holes in the belt.

'Good, rub it faster!' Grant breathed, his knob still throbbing, discharging its spunk in his incredible climax. He was thankful that, at last, Karen seemed to be delighting in abusing the woman, revelling in massaging another woman's clitoris to orgasm.

'Shall I try to get my fingers in her cunt, alongside Chris's cock?' Karen asked, much to Grant's astonishment.

'Yes, yes, finger the tart's cunt!' he chuckled, making his last thrusts into their prisoner's sperm-filled anal canal.

Managing to slide two fingers alongside Chris's penis and into Wendy's dripping cunt, Karen grinned triumphantly. Had she changed yet again? Grant wondered, slipping his spent organ from Wendy's inflamed bottom-hole. Sitting back on his heels, he gazed in astonishment as Karen leaned over and lapped up the sperm oozing from Wendy's brown anal aperture. Her fingers thrusting in and out of the woman's cunt, swelling Chris's penis, she mouthed and sucked her anal portal, drinking Grant's sperm, delighting in her obvious debauchery.

'I want my tongue up her cunt with Chris's knob!' Karen gasped, lowering her head and fervently lapping up the heady blend of sexual juices flowing over the man's rolling balls. Yanking Wendy's vaginal lips wide apart, she drove her tongue along Chris's shaft, desperately trying to gain entrance to the quivering woman's hot cuntal sheath. 'God, it tastes nice! I want to tongue-fuck her beautiful cunt!' she declared.

Frowning, Grant watched his frenzied girl-slave licking Chris's wet penis, Wendy's swollen vaginal lips. He'd not willed her to do this! he thought as she slipped a finger into Wendy's sperm-drenched bottom-sheath. She must be possessed by some nymphomaniacal demoness! he concluded as she drove a second finger into the objecting woman's inflamed anal duct.

Beginning his second vaginal fucking, Chris drove his solid penis in and out of Wendy's inflamed cuntal duct, his balls slapping Karen's face as she lapped up the cunny fluid clinging to his pistoning shaft. Was Veneris lurking? Grant wondered, straining his eyes to try to focus on an uncanny green mist swirling between Karen's thighs, her bloated cunt lips.

'God, I love drinking her fanny juice and Chris's spunk!' Karen gasped, her tongue lapping the couple's genitals.

'It's my spunk you're drinking, too!' Grant chuckled.

'Grant, fuck my arse!' Karen wailed. 'Chris, when you're about to come, I'll shove your knob in my mouth and suck out your sperm!'

Moving behind Karen's projected buttocks, Grant pressed his solid glans against her rectal iris, wondering at the girl's debauchery as his knob slipped into her accommodating duct. Her sphincter muscles tightening around his trespassing cock shaft, he grabbed her hips and began his crude anal fucking, gleefully eyeing the weals spreading out across her inflamed buttocks.

The green mist swirling around his penis, bathing Karen's

gaping anal entrance, Grant knew now that Veneris was present. Was the Goddess transforming Karen into an insatiable nymphomaniac? he wondered as the girl murmured her uncharacteristic expletives, breathed her love of licking a woman's pinken folds while her cunt was being fucked. Her lewd coupling, her tongue licking a thrusting penis whilst another cock shafted Karen's arse, was obviously plummeting her into the mire of female perversity.

You are doing well! The words of Veneris echoing in his mind, Grant felt smug, proud – but also fearful. The last thing he wanted was for the Goddess to haunt him, forever plague him! *You are doing very well, but I feel no cruelty, no brutality. Heed my words and treat your women as slaves! Use your women for your own sexual satisfaction! They have three orifices and, by their very nature, were designed to be used and abused by the male species!*

Stilling his thrusting penis, his knob deep within Karen's hot bowels, her brown anal iris gripping the root of his broad shaft, Grant pondered on the words of Veneris. Cruelty, brutality? Hadn't he done enough to prove his allegiance to the Goddess of Carnality? he wondered, eyeing the weals fanning out across Karen's taut buttocks. Wasn't he using the domination he had over women to the full? He'd blackmailed women, chained them, whipped their buttocks, sexually abused them – what more did Veneris want?

'Ah, coming!' Chris cried, his penis swelling within Wendy's gripping vagina.

'Give it to me!' Karen demanded, grabbing his wet shaft and yanking his orgasming knob out of the woman's spasming sex sheath.

Engulfing Chris's ballooning glans in her hungry mouth, Karen drank his sperm, her tongue ardently snaking around his pulsating knob, her wet lips tightly gripping his veined shaft. Resuming his anal fucking, Grant grabbed Karen's hips and shafted her with a vengeance, massaging her inner anal flesh with his pistoning knob, bringing her lewd sensations of debased sex as she mouthed and sucked on Chris's penis.

'Here it comes!' Grant cried as his knob exploded in orgasm, his spunk gushing into the girl's abused rectal sheath.

'God, I can feel you coming!' Karen gasped, licking Chris's purple knob, lapping up the remnants of his sperm. 'Ah, ah! God, how I love having my arse fucked!'

Wendy's vagina, her clitoris, sadly neglected, she crawled away from Chris's trembling body, leaving Karen to intimately attend his wet glans. Spunk dripping from her inflamed sex holes, she looked about her, wondering where her clothes were, desperate to escape the orgy.

Watching the woman as she grabbed her clothes from the corner of the room, Grant smiled as she dressed, concealing her abused body, veiling her inflamed vaginal lips, her sore bottom-hole. Making his last thrusts into Karen's gripping anal sheath, he wondered when Wendy would lose all recollection of her debauchery. In the morning, no doubt, he concluded as she made to leave the room. But he'd not used his power to defile her so perhaps she would remember all she'd been forced to endure?

'Wendy, before you go,' Grant said, slipping his glistening cock out of Karen's brimming anal duct. 'Before you go, there's just one last thing.'

'No, enough's enough!' she spat as he stood before her, his penis pointing skywards, ever erect.

'Bend over and touch your toes!' he ordered her. 'Do it, and then you will be free to leave.'

'But, my husband . . . it's very late and . . .'

'Are you going to ruin your life, your career, your marriage, for the sake of staying a few more minutes longer?'

Bending over and touching her toes, the woman sighed as Grant lifted her skirt and yanked her panties down to her thighs, exposing her buttocks. Raising his arm, he brought his hand down and spanked her quivering bottom-orbs, causing her to cry out as the stinging pain permeated her reddening flesh. Again and again he spanked her, holding her trembling body with his other hand as she struggled to escape the punishment.

Her bottom-globes a fire-red, her sobs echoing around the room, Grant made his last stinging slaps and released the distraught woman, laughing wickedly as she tugged her panties up and fled. *There goes another one for you, Veneris!* he called in his mind, wondering whether the Goddess was still lurking, adjudicating his progress.

'I must be going,' Chris said, climbing to his feet as Karen moved away from his limp penis.

'OK, Chris,' Grant smiled as his neighbour tugged his trousers up. 'We'll be seeing you again, no doubt?'

'You can bet your life on it!' he chuckled, lifting Karen's exhausted body up, helping her to her feet. 'Bye, Karen – and, thanks!'

'Thank *you*!' she trilled as he left the room.

'Well,' Grant breathed as the front door closed. 'You certainly enjoyed yourself!'

'Enjoyed myself? I've never had such a good time!' she giggled, her fingers toying between her hairless cunny lips. 'I'm going to have a bath, Grant – and then I'm going to bed. Take the belt off me, and you can put it on again after my bath.'

'OK,' he replied, unbuckling the belt, freeing the girl's sore nipples. 'I'll see you later,' he smiled, grabbing his jeans and dressing.

Holding his hand to his head as the phone rang, Grant frowned. 'Not again!' he sighed, lifting the receiver.

'Hi, Grant! You really excelled this time! Two cocks up one cunt!' the man chuckled. 'What a show you put on for me!'

'Decided whether to meet me or not yet?' Grant asked indifferently.

'Yes, I've come to a decision.'

'And?'

'I'll tell you tomorrow.'

'No, no deal!' Grant stormed. 'Meet me tonight, by the woods on the hill – or forget it!'

'It's late! I'm not going . . .'

'OK, forget it, then!'

'All right, all right. I'll make my way there now.'

'Right, see you soon!' Grant said, replacing the receiver.

This was it! he mused as he left the room, wondering whether Veneris would help him if he lured the mysterious man into the clearing. The room had to be bugged, he concluded as he climbed into his car and drove down the road. No one could see into the room – he must have been listening to the orgy! Recalling all he'd said about Wendy having two cocks up her cunt, Grant was sure that the room had been bugged.

About to step into the bath, Karen hesitated as the front doorbell rang. 'Who's that at this time of night?' she breathed as the bell rang again. Realizing that Grant wasn't going to open the door, she grabbed her dressing gown and descended the stairs. 'Grant! Grant, where are you?' she called, walking through the hall and opening the door.

'Oh, Chris!' she gasped.

'Hi, Karen. Sorry to disturb you, but I wanted a word with Grant,' he said, stepping into the hall.

'I don't know where he is. Unless he's in the . . . the summer house.'

'Would you mind having a look?'

'No, of course not. Wait in the lounge, I won't be a minute.'

Sitting on the sofa, Chris wondered whether Karen would recall the evening's debauchery. Grant had something on the girl, a mysterious hold over her, and he was determined to discover what it was. *Women don't forget having two cocks up them!* he thought, recalling their first orgy.

'He's not out there!' Karen announced as she breezed into the room. 'He must have gone out, but I can't think where to!'

'Oh, well, not to worry, I'll . . .' His words tailing off as the phone rang, Chris watched Karen lift the receiver, her gown falling open, revealing her shaved pussy lips as she turned to face him.

'No, he's gone out,' she said, her blue eyes frowning. 'To meet *you*? No, he didn't tell me. Well, if you'll only be ten minutes late, I expect he'll wait. Who are you, what's your name?'

Replacing the receiver as the man hung up, she joined Chris on the sofa, brushing her tousled blonde hair away from her pretty face. 'It was that man again!' she sighed.

'What did he want?' Chris asked, eyeing the girl's shapely thighs as her gown fell open.

'Apparently, Grant has gone to meet him. He'll be ten

minutes late and he wanted to know whether Grant had left yet.'

'Karen,' Chris began, taking her hand in his. 'You remember you told me about you forgetting things?'

'Yes.'

'Do you remember what happened this evening?'

'This evening? Yes, of course I do! How could I ever forget . . .'

'I wonder whether you'll remember in the morning?'

'Why shouldn't I?'

'You said yourself that great chunks of time had gone. I'm just wondering whether, after a night's sleep, you'll be able to recall what we did this evening.'

'Yes, I see what you're getting at. Do you reckon that I've been . . . well, the things I did this evening, I wonder whether I've done things like that before, and not remembered?'

'More than likely! This has something to do with Grant, I'm sure of it!'

'How could Grant erase events from my memory? Especially things such as . . . things such as I did this evening.'

'I only wish I knew!'

'And I wish I knew who this man is, why he keeps ringing!'

'Well, if Grant's gone to meet him, no doubt you'll find out. Karen, try and think back to when this all started. You said that you've never been a sexual person, but this evening . . .'

'Yes, I know what you're going to say! I don't understand any of it, I really don't! Perhaps my brain's going round the bend!' she giggled.

'No, no, it's not. Something's affecting you. Whether it's hypnosis or a drug that Grant's been giving you, I don't know, but he's doing something to you. In fact, he seems to have power over several women!'

'Several women?'

'Well, that woman this evening, the solicitor, do you know her?'

'No, I've never seen her before. Who else is there?'

'You wouldn't remember if I told you.'

'Diana! She came here and we . . . you were here! You and Grant – you in front of me, and Grant behind me!'

'You *do* remember?'

'No, I don't remember, I'm getting a picture in my mind! I'm hearing words in my head! God, I must be going crazy!'

'What else can you see or hear?'

'You . . . you're holding a baby! You're in a hospital, standing by a bed. There's a woman in the bed. Anne, her name's Anne!'

'That was my girlfriend!' Chris gasped. 'We had a baby . . . how on earth do you know about that?'

'I don't know! I just heard these words in my head, and I saw pictures!'

'None of this makes sense! How the hell can you read my mind?'

'I can't!'

'Tell me what I'm thinking about now.'

'I can see . . . yes, I can see Anne carrying the baby under her arm, she's opening the door and going out. There's a suitcase in her other hand.'

'That's right! Anne left me. She . . . well, that's not important. How the hell can you read my mind?'

'I've no idea! This is weird! It's nothing to do with Grant, I know that! I reckon that my mind's going funny, that's why I've been forgetting things!'

'That wouldn't explain why you can hear my thoughts!'

'The mind is strange, isn't it? They talk about the power of the mind being formidable, mind over matter and all that. Look, Chris, I'd better have my bath and go to bed. I'll talk to you in the morning. I'm really tired, exhausted, in fact!'

'All right. Karen, don't mention this to Grant.'

'Why not?'

'Because . . . because I don't think you should, not yet, anyway. See how you are in the morning, whether you can recall this evening. Come round for coffee.'

'Yes, OK. I wonder whether I could read Grant's mind? I'll try when he . . .'

'No! No, don't try! It might be dangerous!'

'Dangerous?'

'We'll talk about it tomorrow. Come round for coffee as early as you can, and we'll have a chat. I'll see myself out.'

Rising to his feet, Chris left the room – and Karen confused, bewildered. Ascending the stairs as Chris closed the front door behind him, she entered the bathroom and slipped her gown off, her head dizzy. Sinking beneath the hot soapy water, she pondered on her mind-reading, still unable to believe that she'd heard what Chris was thinking, seen the images in his mind. Who was the man Grant had gone to meet? she wondered, her fingers between her swollen pussy lips, massaging her erect clitoris. Where had he gone to meet him at this time of night?

Caressing her clitoris, fingering her underwater sex cave, she closed her eyes as the sensations permeated her womb, rippled through her tingling flesh. Taking the bar of soap, she slipped it between her swollen cunny lips and pushed it deep into her vagina, shuddering as her clitoris responded to her loving massage.

As her orgasm rose, gripping her shuddering body, she didn't notice the green hue playing between her thighs, her engorged cunt lips. Gasping, her legs thrashing about in the water, her insurmountable climax ripped through her nervous system, gripping her very being – her soul. Taking her higher to her sexual paradise, deeper into the bottomless pool of debased sex, her orgasm peaked, and she screamed in her agonizing pleasure. The green light intensifying, her body rigid, her muscles painfully locked in orgasm, she thought she was going to die from the exquisite pleasure her young body was bringing her.

Her exhausted body finally falling limp, her fingers stilling, she lay semi-conscious in the aftermath of her overwhelming sexual climax. Delirious, her head spinning, her clitoris aching, her cunt lips scarlet, she was blissfully unaware of the uncanny light fading, leaving her sexual epicentre – of the Goddess Veneris slipping away into her unseen world of inconceivable sexual pleasure.

Chapter Twelve

'Oh, Melinda!' Grant gasped, opening the front door to the woman. 'I thought you said we'd never be seeing you again?'

'You bastard!' the infuriated woman shrieked, her green eyes afire with hatred. 'You assured me that . . .'

'Come in, you daft bitch! I can't have hysterical women screeching on the bloody doorstep first thing in the morning! What the fuck are you talking about? I didn't fucking assure you of anything!'

'Yes, you did! I did all you asked of me!' she yelled, her cheeks flushed as she stepped into the house, her long black hair unusually dishevelled, unkempt. 'Why did you send me a blackmail letter? My husband found it, and now he knows everything!'

'I didn't send you a letter!' Grant returned, closing the door and leading her into the lounge. 'Someone's blackmailing *me*, too! And I reckon it's the same man!'

'Don't give me that! The letter said that you'd . . . that you'd got your girlfriend to shave me! No one else knows about that, apart from you and your filthy whore of a girlfriend! Why have you done this to me after all I went through?'

'Someone's been spying on me – I don't know who, but . . . how much did the blackmailer ask for?'

'You know very well that you asked for one thousand

pounds! Well, you won't get the money, not now that my husband knows everything about me! There's nothing to blackmail me over now, is there?'

'What about your boss, Mr Stringer, does he . . .'

'My husband is going to see him to tell him everything!'

'Why?'

'Because he's throwing me out of the house and he wants to see me suffer for all I've done to him!'

'So why come here?'

'I want you to write to my husband and tell him that you made a mistake, that you got the wrong woman!'

'He'd never believe that!'

'He might. I've denied everything, of course.'

'There's no way he'd believe . . .'

'Perhaps you could talk to him. Or if you were to write, telling him that you mixed me up with someone else . . . make out that it was a joke you were playing on a friend and you got the wrong address.'

'No, I don't think I'll bother!' Grant laughed. 'It all sounds pretty boring to me!'

'Please, you *must* try to help me!'

'Why should I? There again, if you were to strip off and allow me to lick your cunt out . . .'

'I'm not having you defile me again!'

'I have an idea, Melinda. This blackmailer, if we . . . come out into the back garden, we can't talk in here.'

'Why not?'

'Come outside and we'll talk. I'll need your phone number, by the way.'

'Why?'

So I can pester you! 'Because I'll need to talk to your husband if I'm to help you.'

Following Grant through the hall to the kitchen, the

distraught woman wiped the tears from her bloodshot eyes, praying that he'd help her – although she knew in her heart that he wouldn't. Knowing Grant as she did, she realized that it was useless pleading with him. All he'd do would be to revel in her plight, delight in her dilemma – and demand that she commit perverted sexual acts with him! But, in her desperation, she had to try to get his help.

Stepping into the garden, the early morning sun hot in the clear blue sky, she wondered why life was treating her so cruelly. Life should have been so good, she reminisced. A comfortable home, a loving husband ... But she was a thief! Was that Grant's fault? Gazing in horror at the sex dungeon, recalling her terrible ordeal, the degrading sexual acts she'd been forced to endure, the stark reality of her predicament hit her.

'I'm not going in there again!' she yelled, her hands trembling, her bottom lip quivering – her clitoris swelling.

'Oh, you remember, then?' Grant asked, wondering whether Karen would recall last night's debauched orgy when she finally woke up.

'How could I ever forget the dreadful things you forced me to endure?' she spat.

'Now, Melinda, this blackmailer ... he was supposed to meet me last night, but he didn't turn up. Anyway, this is my plan. By the way, where are you to leave the money?'

'There's a litter bin in a car park ...'

'Yes, I know where it is.'

'Of course you know, you sent me the letter!'

'Why would I ask you to leave the money there? Think about it. If I'd written the note, I'd have told you to bring the cash here, wouldn't I?'

'I don't know! You might have thought that ...'

'Listen, Melinda! If you want me to help you, then listen!'

Washing and dressing in her miniskirt and tight T-shirt, careful to avoid Grant, Karen slipped out of the house and knocked on Chris's front door. 'Karen, come in!' Chris invited the girl, his suntanned face beaming as he gazed at her nipples pressing alluringly through her T-shirt – brown, long, erect, suckable. 'So, do you remember what happened last night?' he asked as she stepped into the hall. Was she wet? he wondered. Was her cunt wet, drenched with her opaque sex fluid?

'Do I remember last night? What do you mean?'

'Do you remember what happened?'

'Yes, of course I remember! You came round to see Grant, but he'd gone out.'

'Is that all you remember?'

'What else is there, apart from you asking me to come round for coffee this morning? Why are you asking me all this?'

'Don't you remember reading my mind, my thoughts?'

'Reading your thoughts? What *are* you on about, Chris?'

'This is incredible, it really is!'

'What is? You're not making sense! What are you talking about?'

'It doesn't matter.'

'Are you all right, Chris? You're acting very strange!'

'Yes, I'm all right. Anyway, let's have some coffee.'

'Talking of strange, I felt strange this morning,' Karen enlightened him as she followed him to the kitchen.

'Oh?'

'As I was dressing and thinking about coming to see you, I had this strong feeling that I shouldn't leave the house.'

'What do you mean?'

'It was as if I was willing myself not to leave the house. It was as if something was telling me that I wasn't to go out. I can't explain it, but it was weird!'

'Everything's weird, if you ask me!' Chris returned, filling the kettle as Karen sat at the table. 'What has Grant said to you about . . . about anything, I suppose?'

'What do you mean?'

'Well, has he ordered you to do anything against your will?'

'No, he hasn't, but it's funny you should say that. I had a dream . . . it was so real, but it was obviously a dream. I was naked, tied over the back of the armchair in the lounge, and Grant was whipping me with his leather belt! I couldn't stop him, he was incensed, thrashing me and thrashing me!'

'I had a vivid dream. I dreamed that I was with you in your lounge . . . well, we all have strange dreams at times, don't we?'

'Yes, we do – but mine was so lucid! What was yours about?'

'I . . . I can't remember.'

Making the coffee, Chris eyed Karen's shapely thighs, recalling her nymphomaniacal behaviour the previous evening, wondering why she remembered nothing of the perverted acts she'd so eagerly performed. He knew that Grant had some kind of power over her, but he was clueless as to how it worked. *Hypnosis?* he pondered. And as for her dream! Something strange was going on, something evil – but what?

'Karen,' Chris began pensively, passing her a cup of coffee and sitting opposite her. 'I want you to move in with me.'

'*What?*'

'I want you to come and live with me.'

'I can't live with you, Chris! What's come over you? You ask me to come round for coffee, and then you go on about Grant making me do things against my will – and now you're asking me to move in with you!'

'I'm concerned about you, concerned for your safety. Look, stay here for a while, just a day or two, until I can work out what's going on.'

'Nothing's going on! Well, apart from me forgetting things.'

'You're doing far more than simply forgetting things, Karen!'

'I . . . I know that things have been different lately, but . . . I suppose it's just a phase Grant and I are going through. We'll be all right. Once he starts to earn some money, we'll be fine. Grant never wanted me to work, but I might get myself a job.'

'Come with me, I want to show you something,' Chris smiled amicably, rising to his feet.

Following Chris upstairs to the spare room, Karen gazed at the double bed, the ropes tied to the four legs, ominously snaking over the quilt – lying in wait for their victim. Turning as Chris locked the door, her eyes wide with fear, her mouth hanging open, she asked him what he was going to do.

'This is for your own good, Karen!' he replied, scooping her up, lifting her off the floor. Tossing her curvaceous body onto the bed, he pinned her down and tied her wrists and ankles as she desperately fought to free herself. 'I have to do this for your own good!' he reiterated.

'Please, Chris! What are you doing to me?' she screamed hysterically.

'It's all right!' he bellowed, tightening the ropes, securing her struggling body. 'I'm not going to hurt you or do anything to you! As I said, I'm concerned for your safety!'

'Concerned?' she yelled, her limbs thrashing about, pulling on the bonds. 'You're mad! You're tying me down because you're concerned for my safety?'

'Yes!' Chris returned, brushing his dishevelled hair away from his eyes as he perched himself on the edge of the bed and caught his breath. 'Please, allow me to explain!'

'Yes, please do!' Karen spat. 'Please do explain why you've locked the door and tied me down to a double bed! Although it's pretty obvious what you intend to do to me!'

'I'm not going to do anything to you!'

'You could have fooled me!'

'Listen, Grant has some kind of power over you, Karen,' he began calmly. 'As yet, I'm not sure what it is or how he does it, but he's able to influence your thoughts, your actions.'

'Of course he's not!'

'Last night, you performed what I can only describe as a perverted lesbian act with Wendy. I don't know you very well, but I do know that you're not the sort of girl to . . .'

'Perverted lesbian act? Who the hell's this Wendy? I don't know anyone called Wendy! You're off your bloody head!'

'You had oral sex with Wendy on the floor in your lounge, and you . . .'

'Who the hell's Wendy? What *are* you talking about? Have you gone mad?'

'You see, you remember nothing! You sucked me off, you licked her pussy while I was screwing her, you took Grant up your bum, you . . .'

'God, you *have* gone mad!'

'No, far from it! Can you explain the terrible weals I noticed across your buttocks during our orgy?'

'Weals, yes, I . . . no, there are no weals!'

'I'm going to switch the radio on, loud, so that, hopefully, Grant's thoughts won't get to you,' Chris said, rising to his feet and turning the knob on the bedside radio, blasting music into Karen's ears. 'I'll look in every now and then to see if you're OK!' he shouted above the noise. 'This is for your own good, Karen! Hopefully, it won't be too long before you thank me for this! When I've discovered what Grant's up to, I'll release you!' he added, leaving the room and locking the door.

Having waited for five hours for Karen to return, Grant paced the lounge floor, cursing and kicking the furniture. 'Where the fuck has the bitch got to? And why can't I get into her subconscious?' Speculating whether or not she was still alive, he left the house and knocked on Chris's front door, wondering whether she'd called in to see him.

'Hi, Chris!' He forced a smile, his forehead unusually lined in anger as his neighbour opened the door. 'You haven't seen Karen, have you?'

'No, I haven't,' Chris replied, stepping outside. 'Not since last night, anyway.'

'The bitch went out early this morning and I haven't seen her since!'

'She's probably gone shopping, or to see a friend.'

'She knew that she wasn't to leave the house!'

'Not to leave the house? What do you mean?'

'Nothing. I've just had another call from that man. He said . . . come round to my place, Chris,' Grant invited, wandering towards the front gate. 'I need to talk to someone. If you have the time, that is?'

'Yes, yes, of course.'

Entering the lounge, images of Karen sucking his knob and drinking his sperm filling his mind, Chris sat on the sofa. Recalling his penis forced deep into Wendy's cunt alongside Grant's thrusting cock, he frowned. There had been the orgy with Diana that Karen had no recollection of, and now a rampant sex session with Wendy. How could the girl not remember . . .

'He knows everything we did in here last night,' Grant said, breaking Chris's reverie as he paced the floor. 'Wendy, Karen . . . every single thing that went on in this room last night, he told me about in great detail!'

'How could he have seen us?' Chris asked.

'Fuck knows!' Grant returned as the phone rang. 'I'll bet that's him again!' he stormed, grabbing the phone. 'I'll end up in a fucking mental home if this keeps up!'

'I know where Karen is!' the man chuckled as Grant pressed the receiver to his ear.

'Where is she?'

'That's for me to know and you to find out!'

'Unless you tell me, I'll . . .'

'Sorry I couldn't make it last night.'

'I waited for over an hour, you bastard! Where the fuck's Karen?'

'She's safe enough. Now, are you going to tell me your secret, how you have such great power over women, or do I have to strip Karen and . . .'

'Do what you like to Karen, I don't give a toss for the bitch!'

'That's nice, I must say!'

'Unlike you, I can have any woman I want, so I don't need *her*!'

'Well, in that case, I *will* do what I like to her!'

'I'm going to unplug my phone, so don't bother ringing again because I won't answer.'

'Then I won't be able to tell you what I've been doing to Karen, will I? I won't be able to tell you what I've done to your girlfriend's tight cunt!'

'No, you won't!'

'She has a beautiful body, Grant.'

'So do thousands of other tarts! A girl's a girl, they all have cunts! In fact . . .'

Replacing the receiver as the man hung up, Grant turned to Chris, his face reddening with exasperation. 'I can't take much more of this!' he sighed, flopping into the armchair. 'He reckons that he knows where Karen is. It seems that he's got her, kidnapped her, or whatever!'

'I'm sure he hasn't! She's probably gone shopping,' Chris replied. 'Grant, you said that you needed to talk to someone. Why not open up to me, tell me what's going on?'

'Nothing's going on!'

'*Nothing*? Some man rings you, saying that he has Karen, and you say that nothing's going on?'

'He's a crank, a fucking nutter!'

'Karen behaves like a filthy whore, you're blackmailing Wendy . . .'

'No, it's not like that! Wendy likes to play games. It's a turn-on for her, pretending that I'm blackmailing her and forcing her to . . .'

'In that case, she's a bloody good actress! You said the other day that Karen's been playing games recently, pretending to forget things. I haven't known Karen for very long, but I do know she's not pretending to forget things, Grant! And I know that she's not the common slut she makes out she is!'

'You saw for yourself what she's like!' Grant returned, running his fingers through his unruly hair. 'What she did last night proves it – she's a filthy fucking slut of a bitch!'

'She might have behaved like one, but I don't believe that she is!'

'Look, Chris, all this is getting us nowhere! I have to find Karen, she might be in danger!'

'Do you care?'

'Yes! Well, no . . .'

'Why would she be in danger? Come on, Grant, tell me what's going on!'

'You're as bad as that bastard who keeps phoning me! Nothing's fucking well going on, for Christ's sake!'

'Well, if you won't tell me, then I can't help you. I must be going, I have work to do. Keep me posted,' Chris said, rising to his feet and leaving the room.

'Yes, I will. The moment I hear anything, I'll let you know.'

'OK. Don't get up, I'll see myself out.'

Again trying to make contact with Karen's subconscious, Grant closed his eyes, concentrating his thoughts. 'Nothing!' he breathed. 'Where the hell is she?' Did he really care about the girl? he wondered. As he'd told the blackmailer, he could have any woman he wanted, so did it really matter whether Karen returned or not? All girls had wet cunts, so what was so special about hers?

Answering the front door, Grant gasped to find Wendy standing on the step. 'Come back for more?' he chuckled, recalling the crude double fucking as she stepped into the hall.

'No, I have not!' she returned angrily. 'What's the idea of sending me a blackmail note demanding one thousand pounds?'

'Fucking hell, not you as well! I didn't send it! It's from the same man who's blackmailing me!'

'Oh, come on! You don't really expect me to believe that, do you?'

'I don't give a fuck what you believe! I've just about had enough of all this crap!'

'*You've* had enough? What about me?'

'As far as I'm concerned, you can go to hell!'

'You're an evil bastard! You'll not get one penny from me, I can assure you! And if anyone's going to hell, it'll be you!' the distraught woman hissed, slamming the front door shut and storming down the path.

'Stupid fucking bitch! If I ever see you again, I'll shove my fist up your cunt!'

Grant didn't bother answering the phone as he walked into the lounge. Even though he thought it might be Karen, he wasn't going to give the blackmailer any more satisfaction! The afternoon dragging on into the evening, he did nothing other than pace the floor and drink coffee – and ignore the incessantly ringing telephone.

Deciding to go out for a walk as dusk fell, he wandered through the hall and discovered a letter lying on the mat. Ripping the envelope apart, he read the blackmailer's words. 'Meet me by the wood on the hill. I'll tell you all – if *you* tell *me* all.' Slipping the note into his pocket, he closed the front door behind him, praying for the mysterious man to turn up this time. *I'll fucking well get the bastard now!*

'Well, Karen, I've discovered nothing yet!' Chris sighed, entering the spare room and sitting on the edge of the bed.

'So you intend to keep me here tied up until you've . . .'

'I can't allow you to go back to Grant, not until I know what his game is! He's blackmailing women, you seem to be under his control, forgetting the obscene things he forces you to do . . . he's a very dangerous man, Karen! Why aren't you wearing any knickers?' he asked, eyeing the girl's shaved pussy lips, her soft pinken crack beneath her miniskirt.

'I . . . I thought I was!'

'And no bra, by the looks of it!' he added, gazing at her long nipples outlined by her tight T-shirt.

'Yes, I . . .'

'You see, you don't know what you're doing half the time!'

'I forgot to put my panties on, it's as simple as that!'

'No, it's not! Grant told me that the sex dungeon was your idea, and the dog collar and chain.'

'*My* idea? It was his idea to . . .'

'Yes, I know it was his idea. He said that you liked playing games, pretending to forget things and . . .'

'Release me, and we'll talk, Chris. Let's sit in the lounge and talk this over.'

'OK. But don't try to run off because . . .'

'No, I won't. I realize that you're trying to help, and I must admit that I'm very confused by everything that's been going on.'

'Come downstairs, and I'll tell you something you'd never have believed in a million years!' Chris chuckled, releasing the girl.

Helping her off the bed, Chris guided her down the stairs to the lounge. Sitting beside her on the sofa, he pointed to the wall. 'You see that wire sticking out?' he began. 'I drilled a hole in the wall while you and Grant were out. It was quite a job, carefully drilling until I'd reached the plaster on your lounge wall.'

'Why did you do that?' Karen asked, perplexed.

'I scraped the plaster away with a screwdriver until I'd reached your wallpaper. It took ages, it wasn't easy! Then, after making several pin pricks in the paper, I carefully placed a small microphone in the hole, easing it against your wallpaper, and I stuffed the hole full of cotton wool. I can listen to everything that goes on in your lounge.'

'But I don't understand! Why did you do that? Are you the one who's been ringing Grant and . . .'

'No, I'm not. I also drilled a hole in the side of your summer house. First, a very small hole right through the wood, and then a larger one, just halfway through, to take the microphone. No one would be able to see what I'd done because the building's jammed up against the fence dividing our gardens, and it's covered with ivy. All I had to do was run a lead from the microphone into the house and plug it into my hi-fi amp. I can hear everything that's said in your lounge, and in your summer house.'

'I still don't understand why . . .'

'I knew that Grant was up to something. Some time ago, I was walking on the hill, looking for him, and I noticed him wander into the wood. It was a warm evening and I'd gone there to join him, to look for flying saucers and have a chat. Anyway, I was about to follow him into the wood when I heard women screaming.'

'Screaming?'

'Yes, screaming and wailing! I didn't hang around to find out what the hell he was doing! At that time, I didn't want to know! After a while I became mystified so, another evening, I followed Grant, leaving my car well away from the car park. He went into the wood and emerged some time later, completely exhausted, by the look of it! He then drove home and went into his house. I'd parked and was about to get out of my car when Grant came out of the house and walked to the pub.'

'Yes, I remember him saying that he was going to the pub. What happened?'

'Grant did some sort of incredible mind-reading act on the barmaid, telling her all sorts of things about herself, and then he pulled her, went back to her flat. Her name's Diana, the one who . . .'

'You were there, in the pub?'

'No, it wasn't me. By the way, you went into the wood and came out some time later with your clothes all torn and your hair all over the place.'

'*Me*? I've *never* been to the wood!'

'I didn't think you'd remember! Anyway, another time, Grant went to the park. A woman he'd never met before joined him on a seat and she . . . incredible though it is, she sucked his dick!'

'What, a total stranger?'

'Yes, and there's a hell of a lot more! He went to a house in Rochester Street and had a woman strip off and . . . I'll spare you the details! He also went to a solicitor's office in town – that's where he found Wendy. He blackmailed another woman he'd met in the park, somehow got her to go to your house – and he used her for perverted sex!'

'How do you know all this? Who followed Grant?'

'I'll tell you everything, but first, I'll make some coffee.'

Sitting on the moonlit hill by the wood, Grant focused on a man walking towards him. Was this the bastard? he wondered, climbing to his feet. What to do? What to say? he mused as the man approached and stood before him.

He *did* have a big nose! he observed, recalling Elizabeth's description as the stranger grinned at him.

'So, Grant, we meet at last!'

'Yes, we do.'

'Now, your little secret ... I want to learn how to influence women.'

'I've been thinking about that,' Grant said pensively. 'I don't have to tell you anything. With the power I have over women, the money available to me, all I have to do is move away and ...'

'True, you could do that, but there's a hitch. You see, the women believe that you've been blackmailing them. I'm going to send them more notes, demanding thousands of pounds, until they crack up under the strain. Eventually, they'll go to the police and everything will come out. So, you'd better tell me how ...'

'There's no way Wendy can call the police in! After her criminal ...'

'She'll go down for embezzlement anyway, I'll see to that! I'll also see to it that the police discover what you've been up to!'

'You're mad!' Grant bellowed, his eyes widening as an eerie green ball of light gradually materialized behind the man. 'If you think ...'

Stepping back several yards, Grant watched a finger of light weave its way towards the blackmailer and play around his head. Was Veneris going to kill him? he wondered as the man held his head, obviously in pain as he crumpled to the ground. Writhing as the light engulfed him, he rolled about on the grass, gasping, panting for air.

'Christ!' Grant breathed fearfully as the light finally faded. 'What the fuck ...' Rising to his feet, the bewildered man rubbed his eyes and focused on Grant. 'Are you all right?' Grant asked, taking his arm and steadying him.

'I must have passed out!' he gasped. 'Thanks for helping me.'

'Er . . . that's OK. Where were you going?'

'I . . . I don't know. I'd better go home. I think I was going for a walk, I can't quite remember. I'd better go home.'

'Yes, go home and rest,' Grant smiled, realizing that Veneris had erased all thoughts of him from the blackmailer's memory. 'Go home and rest.'

Bounding down the hill as the puzzled man wandered off, Grant wondered about Karen. The poor man wouldn't know who she was when he got home and found the girl imprisoned in his house! he mused. Obviously he'd release her, and she'd return to him, her master – and he'd thrash her until she screamed for mercy! 'Thanks, Veneris!' he called, looking up to the stars before climbing into his car and driving home. 'Thanks!'

'So, what do we do now?' Karen asked Chris, her blue eyes wide as his incredible story sank in. 'I didn't even know that you had a lodger!'

'Brian only moved in a short while ago. It was easy, having him follow Grant, phone him and . . . you see, I had to discover what Grant was up to, how he was able to read people's minds, influence their actions. Not knowing my lodger, Grant would never have suspected him. When Brian sat in the pub, Grant would have thought nothing of it.'

'You've gone to a lot of trouble, Chris!'

'No, not really. I was intrigued and I wanted to discover how Grant did it, but what I didn't realize was that Brian had blackmailed the women! That wasn't part of the plan! It started out as a bit of fun, all we were going to do was discover Grant's secret and try and have some fun with women once we'd learned how to do it. The idea wasn't to blackmail people!'

'Where's your lodger now?'

'He's packed his bags and moved out. When I discovered that he was blackmailing the women, I threw the bastard out!'

'I don't blame you!'

'It worked well, at first. Brian followed Grant, he rang him, trying to discover his secret . . . we spent hours listening to Grant in your lounge and your summer house, and tried to piece the information together – and now, after all this time, I'm none the wiser!'

'So, what next?'

'I don't know. Hang on, I think I heard your front door slam shut. I'll switch the amp on.'

Listening to Grant moving about in the lounge, Chris smiled at Karen, eyeing her shapely thighs, glimpsing her naked pussy crack as she fidgeted excitedly, eager to discover what Grant was up to. She was a very attractive girl, he observed – and Grant didn't deserve her! Would she allow him to pleasure her? he wondered, his penis stiffening at the thought of the girl sucking his solid glans as he snaked his tongue into her hot vaginal sheath. There was no way a bastard like Grant deserved such a beauty!

'Well, that's the fucking blackmailer dealt with!' Grant laughed, moving about in his lounge. 'All I have to do now is get that fucking bitch Karen back, and I'm in business again! When the whore arrives, I'll give her the thrashing of her fucking life!'

Turning to Chris, Karen frowned. 'It's so clear!' she breathed.

'Yes, and it's the same in the summer house, I can hear perfectly. I wonder how he dealt with Brian?'

'God, I hope he hasn't . . .'

'Hang on, he's ringing someone,' Chris interrupted, turning the volume up.

'Hallo, Melinda, it's Grant. Yes, I met him. No, he won't be bothering you again. *Me?* Yes, of course *I'll* be bothering you again! After all, I have enough on you to . . . Well, if your husband doesn't tell your boss, then I will! What? Well, I don't know, I might consider writing to your husband, it all depends on . . . What do I want? You know what I want! Your hot, tight, wet cunt, Melinda, that's what I want – your juicy cunt lips wrapped around my mouth!'

Shaking her head despairingly, Karen looked at Chris. She hated Grant, but she also loved him, she mused. Did love and hate go hand in hand? Whatever her emotions, she couldn't live with him, not now! 'What a faithful, loving bloody boyfriend *he* is!' she sighed despondently.

'He reads people's minds, discovers their dreadful secrets, and then blackmails them to have perverted sex sessions with him!' Chris remarked pensively, his dark eyes catching Karen's. 'I don't know how he does it, I really don't! It's something to do with the wood on the hill, I know that much. There's a clearing and the remains of a fire . . . the occult, that's what I reckon he's into!'

'The occult? God, no!'

'I'm ninety-nine per cent sure of it!'

'Look, I'll go home and suggest that Grant and I go up to the hill.'

'I don't think you should do that, Karen!'

'I must! We have to discover what he's up to!'

'All right, but be careful!'

'I will. Listen to us talking in the lounge and, if Grant gets nasty, you can come round.'

'OK, I'll see you later.'

Gazing in surprise as Karen entered the lounge, Grant looked her in the eye, his expression one of anger. 'And where the fuck do you think you've been?' he hissed.

'I . . . I had to go and see a friend. Grant, I want to go to the hill with you.'

'The hill? What the hell for?'

'I fancy a walk, that's all.'

'A walk, in the dark?'

'Yes, why not? We might even see a UFO!' she giggled, trying to appear happy, relaxed.

'OK!' Grant replied, deciding to take the girl into the wood and have her fucked and spanked by the sect for her insubordinate behaviour. *I'll teach the bitch to defy me!*

The full moon shining above them as they tramped up the hill, Karen wondered what she'd find in the wood. Danger was close, she was sure, sensing something evil lurking, watching. Praying that Chris wasn't far behind, recalling him mentioning screaming women in the wood, the hair on the back of her neck stood on end as she began to have second thoughts. But, after all Chris had told her, the way Grant had lured women to his sex dungeon and had her shave them, abuse them, she knew that she had to go through with it. She knew that she had to discover the truth.

'Let's walk through the trees,' Grant suggested as they neared the wood.

'It looks rather dark in there, Grant!' Karen replied apprehensively, gazing at the trees, imagining the branches reaching out and grabbing her.

'The moon's bright enough, let's go and see what sort of wildlife comes out at night.'

'OK, if you're sure it's safe.'

'Oh, it's safe enough, Karen – don't you worry about that!'

Taking the girl's hand, Grant led her through the undergrowth, wondering whether he'd be in trouble for taking her to meet the sect. He'd been told never to return, but he was sure that Veneris would be only too pleased to have the young men use and defile Karen, a member of the weaker sex!

Entering the clearing, he frowned, gazing at the burnt-out fire. Where were they? he wondered, glancing at the fallen tree, the ropes coiled over the rough bark. 'I don't understand it!' he breathed. 'They're usually here!'

'Who are?' Karen asked, frowning at Grant.

'The . . . it doesn't matter, let's go.'

'What *is* this place?' she asked, looking at the remains of the fire, recalling Chris mentioning the occult.

'I don't know, it's just a clearing.'

'Someone's been here and lit a fire.'

'Yes, kids, more than likely. Come on, let's get out of here!'

Emerging from the wood, they sat on the grass, gazing at the town, the thousands of lights sparkling like stars in the night. Hearing a humming noise, they jumped to their feet and turned to see a silver disc rising from the trees some distance away.

'What the fuck's that?' Grant gasped as the craft rose high above the trees and sped like a bullet into the eastern sky, disappearing from view.

'A . . . a flying saucer!' Karen stammered, clutching Grant's arm.

'Bloody hell! I've actually seen a . . . fucking hell!'

'Let's get out of here!' Karen cried, gazing in terror as a green ball of light rose above the trees.

'Veneris!'

'Who? Grant, what is it?'

'Veneris, don't go!' Grant called as the light hovered ominously above the wood.

'Grant, for God's sake . . .'

Was this a demon? Karen wondered as Grant called to his Goddess, begging her not to leave. A finger of light snaking down from the ball, weaving its way towards Karen, playing around her head, she froze. Her mind swirling with images of the clearing, the naked young men and women, her legs crumpling beneath her, she collapsed to the ground.

What sort of evil entity had Grant called upon? she wondered fearfully, her clitoris painfully swelling, throbbing, her vaginal muscles contracting. Praying for deliverance from whatever evil spirit had her in its grips, she finally regained control over her shaking body as the light faded. Dragging herself up and running down the hill as fast as she could, leaving Grant calling upon whatever evil he'd roused from an unseen world, she finally reached the foot of the hill, her palms wet, her blonde hair in disarray.

Colliding with Chris as she dashed across the car park, she screamed as he grabbed her. 'No, let me go! Let me go!'

'Karen! Karen, it's me, Chris! What's the matter?'

'A . . . a flying saucer! A monster! Take me home! Take me home!'

'All right, all right!' Chris soothed, bundling the hysterical girl into his car. Driving away, trying to make sense of her frenzied words of monsters and flying saucers, he shook his head in disbelief. Flying saucers? Monsters? 'Calm down and tell me exactly what happened!' he bellowed above her screams.

'I . . . I can't remember now. Where have I been? What . . .'

'I don't know where you've been! Come to think of it, where the hell have *I* been? I remember driving to the car park, following you and Grant, and then . . .'

Karen was completely composed by the time Chris led her into his house and seated her in the lounge. Her face serene, smiling, her blue eyes sparkling, she reclined on the sofa and lifted her miniskirt up over her stomach. 'Do you like my shaved cunt?' she asked lasciviously, gazing down at her swollen vaginal lips, her elongated clitoris.

'Yes, very much!' Chris murmured, dropping to his knees and licking the full length of her wet crack. 'God, you taste beautiful!' he gasped, having no recollection of his visit to the hill.

'Let's go to my place and you and Grant can fuck me – fuck my cunt, my arse, my mouth – and then tie me up and whip me!' Karen giggled wickedly in her burning passion for depraved sex.

'Yes, after I've licked your cunt out and sucked an orgasm from your clitty!' Chris chuckled. 'God, you're a dirty little bitch, you really are!'

'I like that! Talk dirty to me, Chris! Talk about my wet cunt!'

'I'll do more than talk dirty, I'll *act* dirty! Kneel on the floor with your head on the sofa and stick your arse out – I'm going to tongue-fuck your arse!'

Finally arriving home, Grant wandered into the lounge and grinned to see Karen and Chris standing in the centre of the room. Karen was naked, her smile salacious, her young body fresh, curvaceous, her cunt lips wet, swollen – fuckable! Removing his clothes, his penis catapulting to attention, Chris stood naked beside Karen, his heavily laden balls rolling. Gazing at Grant, her eyes sparkling with a burning sexual passion, Karen begged him to fuck her, pleaded for both men to use and abuse her young body.

What had happened to Karen now? Grant wondered. Another Jekyll-and-Hyde turn? What had Veneris done to her with her strange green light? Turned her into an insatiable nymphomaniac? Chris wasn't acting suspiciously any more, asking awkward, searching questions. Had Veneris got to him, too?

'I have to make a phone call,' he finally replied, lifting the receiver and punching the buttons. 'I'll be with you in a minute.'

'Hallo,' Melinda replied.

'Melinda, it's Grant.'

'Who?'

'Grant – don't you remember me?'

'No, I'm sorry, I don't.'

'I'm calling about the money you've been taking from your boss, Mr Stringer.'

'What? I . . .'

'We'll have to meet and discus it.'

'No, no, I can't . . .'

'We also need to talk about your son.'

'My son, but . . .'

'I wouldn't want to have to tell your husband that he's not the father!'

'God, no! Please . . . who is this? Please, I . . .'

'Grab a pen and I'll give you my address. I want you to come to my place and we'll discuss the situation.'

'God! Oh, God!'

'*He* won't help you, Melinda!'

'But, how do you know . . .'

'Either you come here, or I'll come to you – what's it to be?'

'All right, what's your address? You'll have to give me some time because my husband's here and he . . .'

'I'll give you an hour, and no more!'

'Yes, an hour, all right!'

Giving the woman his address, Grant replaced the receiver and turned to see Karen on her knees sucking Chris's purple knob. Her eyes closed, she moaned through her nose, savouring his salty glans as she ran her fingers up and down her drenched vaginal slit.

'Chris,' Grant began pensively, slipping his clothes off to reveal his magnificent purple-headed warrior. 'Do you reckon we could both fuck her arse?'

'What, at the same time?' Chris gasped as Karen kneaded his rolling balls and fervently suckled on his pulsating knob.

'Yes, both at the same time.'

'We could try!' he replied, obviously oblivious to Grant's threatening phone call, his immense power.

'Yes, please try!' Karen trilled excitedly, slipping Chris's glistening knob from her wet mouth. 'Chris, lie on the floor and I'll kneel astride you!'

On his back, his penis pointing to the ceiling, Chris grabbed Karen's hips as she straddled him. Taking his penis in her hand, she aligned his bulbous knob with her anal entrance, manoeuvring her hips, bearing down and slipping his plum into her rectal sheath. 'Come on, Grant!' she breathed. 'Stick your cock up my arse!'

Kneeling astride Chris's legs, Grant licked his fingers, wetting his shaft and pressing his glans against the girl's taut anal ring, desperate to enter her, to give her a double arse-fucking. Her anal ring suddenly yielding, the girl screamed as Grant's knob drove into the fiery heat of her rectal sheath, painfully stretching her inner flesh.

'God, it's heavenly!' Karen whimpered as Grant drove his cock-head deep into her quivering body. 'I'd love another big tool fucking my cunt! And one spunking in my mouth! God, I want four cocks!'

'Jesus, Karen, you're a fucking dirty cow!' Grant chuckled, his penile shaft crushed against Chris's cock, their bulbous knobs pressed together.

'I'm enjoying having you two as neighbours!' Chris rejoined as he slipped three fingers into Karen's drenched cunt.

'This is nothing!' Grant returned excitedly. 'I'm going to bring a different tart home every day! There's going to be nothing but fucking and whipping from now on!'

'You'll have a job to get a different girl every day!' Chris breathed, his knob twitching within the dank heat of Karen's bowels as he massaged her inner vaginal flesh.

'No problem!' Grant chuckled. 'No problem at all! Now, shall we give this little bitch the double arse-fucking she deserves?'

'Yes, damned right we will!'

Driving his penis in and out of Karen's hot anal sheath, his knob massaging Chris's pulsating glans, Grant loosed his sperm. Screaming as Chris's spunk also jetted from his swollen glans, mingling with Grant's, lubricating their forbidden coupling, Karen gyrated her hips, her cunt spewing out its girl-come as her orgasm rose from her contracting womb and engulfed her defiled body.

'I can feel your spunk!' she cried, her eyes rolling as her anal duct stretched to accommodate the in-driving cock-heads. 'Oh, God! My arse! God, my arse!' Lifting his head, Chris bit on the girl's nipple, adding to the incredible pleasure her abused body was bringing her. Fingering her wet cunt with a vengeance as his sperm gushed into her tight bottom-sheath, Chris sucked both her nipples harder, causing the elongated brown protrusions to swell, her areolae to darken in her debauchery.

'Don't stop!' Karen cried as a series of orgasmic shockwaves shook her perspiring body. 'Oh, God! Don't stop! Fuck my arse!'

'Christ, your bum-hole's tight!' Grant breathed, eyeing the girl's brown ring, taut around the solid penises. 'I'm going to whip you until you scream when we've finished arse-fucking you!'

'Yes, yes! Whip me! Fuck me . . . whip me and . . .'

The gushing sperm finally ceasing, the men stilled their cocks, absorbing the wet heat of the abused girl's bowels, savouring the post-orgasmic pulsations emanating from their glowing knobs. Slipping his glistening shaft out of her sperm-drenched anal canal, Grant moved to one side, gazing at his gasping girlfriend, her flushed face, as Chris sucked on her huge nipples.

She was a right little tart! he mused. No more split personalities, no more protests, she was completely under his control, his evil domination. When Melinda arrived, he'd tie her naked body to the table in the sex dungeon and watch Karen abuse the woman, lick and finger her cunt to orgasm. Life was good! Life was fucking brilliant! But Veneris had gone, he reflected sadly. Without a trace, the Goddess of Carnality had gone.

Suddenly recalling the photographs he'd taken of the naked group, Grant left the room and grabbed his camera from the hall table. Bounding upstairs to his darkroom, he removed the film and prepared his equipment. *I hope the light from the fire was strong enough to expose the film*, he reflected. *This is the only evidence, I have of the sect!*

As the pictures emerged in the developing tank, he gasped. There had been more then enough light from the fire to photograph the group clearly. The girls' long curly hair glowing violet, their breasts huge, topped with nipples at least two inches long, they were stunning. Their vaginal cracks rising up to their stomachs, their clitorises erect, emerging at least three inches from between their billowing vaginal lips, he knew they weren't of this world. Their feminine curves grossly exaggerated, he noticed that they didn't have navels. Their bodies glistening, their mouths invitingly open, their vaginal entrances glowing with a deep purple hue, they appeared to have been created solely for sex, for nothing other than to serve the male species.

Scrutinizing the photographs, Grant's eyes widened as he realized that the males had a deficit. Their massive erect penises pointing skyward, they had no balls! 'They're fucking aliens!' he cried, placing the prints in the fixing tank. 'Jesus fucking Christ, they're fucking aliens!'

I cannot allow you to keep the photographs! The words filtering into his mind, Grant froze as the pictures faded into the white paper.

Who are you?

The Goddess Veneris. My people are from a world far away from yours. Their craft developed a fault and they were forced to land on your world. We communicate by telepathy, as you are aware.

Yes, I know.

My people's women are slaves . . .

If they are intelligent enough to travel great distances through . . .

Sextro

My people are an ancient race, a race that clings to rituals, to the ways of their ancestors – nothing has changed since my people were living in underground caves. The females are slaves to males, serving them, pleasing them, satisfying their great sexual needs. It is their way, it always has been – and always will be.

Do I still have the power?

Yes, you do. Use it wisely, Grant. Your girl-slave and the male neighbour recall nothing. Those you have come into contact with recall nothing. I have erased from their memories all you have done, all they know about you. You are free to begin again, to use women, to satisfy your hunger for sexual satisfaction. Do not make the same mistakes, but learn from them.

Karen . . . is she still . . .

She craves sex with you, with all males. Use her, Grant, whip her – she is your slave!

Other women, will they still be at my mercy?

All *females are at your mercy* – all *females! You will use them to satisfy your insatiable hunger for sex, real sex – depraved sex. You will whip them, use and abuse them for that is their role in life. I must leave you now, leave you with your power, with your domination over the weaker sex.*

Frowning, leaving the darkroom and wandering downstairs as the doorbell rang, Grant smiled. Melinda? he wondered, opening the door to find the flush-faced woman trembling on the step. *I must contact Emily and give her the arse-fucking of her life!* 'Ah, Melinda!' he greeted the woman. 'Please, come in.'

'Who are you?' she asked, fearfully.

'I'm Grant, and you're going to strip and offer me your body for crude sex!' he chuckled, closing the door.

'I am not!' she returned angrily. 'If you think I'm going to . . .'

'Your cunt's shaved, isn't it?'

'I . . . how do you . . . who are you?'

'Come into the lounge and meet my other guests, Melinda. You have a busy night ahead of you!'

'I am not going to . . .'

'From past experience, I know it will take a while to convince you, it will take a little time before you concede to my disgusting demands – but you *will* concede!'

'Never! How do you know about . . .'

'Come into the lounge and I'll tell you all I know about you, about your systematic thieving from Mr Stringer, your illegitimate son . . . fancy selling your wedding ring and telling your husband that you'd lost it! I'm going to have to fuck your arse by way of punishment, I'm afraid – *and* whip your buttocks until you beg for mercy! Yes, we have a very busy night ahead of us, Melinda! And I have a very busy life ahead of me! Step into my parlour, said the cruel master to the quaking girl-slave!'